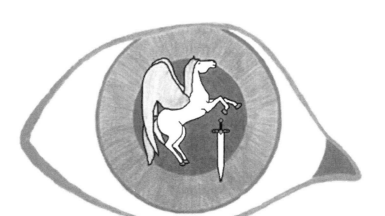

Peace of Evon:

Missing Heir

Dorothy Tinker

ISBN: 978-0-9910839-0-9 (paperback)

To those who would seek peace

against all odds.

To those who would reach

for the dream of their hearts,

even when others claim it impossible

or impractical.

Rachel,
May Peace and
Balance surpass the
chaos in your life.

Contents

Part I
Meetings

Map of Evon

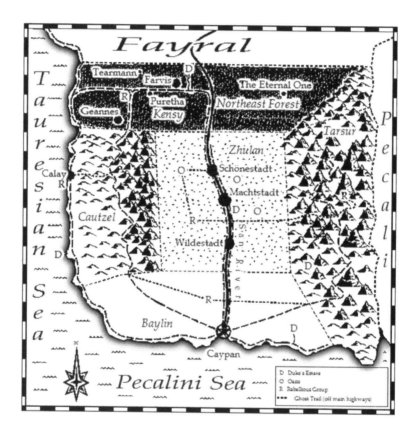

Prologue

Rejoice!
For on the third day of Late Summer in
this, the 208th year of Evon, a baby girl
was born to Lord Jem and Lady Kit
Cosley, Duke and Duchess of Kensy.

Mama Caler released a whoop at the sight of the notice. Ignoring the startled glances and disapproving murmurs from nearby city-dwellers, the 40-year-old Seer danced a little step and clasped her hands together in glee.

Finally, she thought, hurrying down the street of Farvis towards the inn where she'd left her belongings. *Finally, the day has come when the heir is born.*

It had been a simple whim that brought Mama Caler east to Farvis, the largest city in eastern Kensy. Only a sevenday before, she'd been in Puretha, a town closer to the center of the province.

There, she'd participated in a Naming Ceremony for a child who, according to the Fates, would design the new plans for Farvis after its destruction. In a burst of joy and sentimentality, she'd decided to visit.

Yet it wasn't the Sight of the city's destruction that had driven her here. After all, they were in a war with Fayral, the country to the north, whose emperor believed that Kensy should belong to him, not Evon. The war had been going on for longer than Mama Caler had been alive, and she had Seen the destruction of various cities and villages in Kensy and had even witnessed some firsthand.

Nay, it wasn't the destruction of Farvis that had pushed her to travel to the city but rather the Sight of its rebirth. Again and again she had Seen the destruction this war caused, but that child's future had been the first she'd ever Seen that had shone with hope beyond the war.

And now I think I know why, she thought, dancing another step as she entered the inn.

"Wha's got you so happy, Mama Caler?"

The rough voice halted the Seer in her path towards the stairs, and she turned to grin widely at the innkeeper.

"The duke's heir has finally been born!" she proclaimed, practically bouncing over to the bar, where the man sat.

The man frowned and rubbed his chin doubtfully. "You talkin' 'bout those notices they been puttin' up 'bout the duke's new baby girl?" When she nodded emphatically, he gave his head a small shake. "Seems to me, it's just another set up for disappointment."

Mama Caler sighed dramatically, but she understood the innkeeper's doubts. This was the third time this kind of notice had been posted in the

3

decade since Lord Jem became duke, and the first two had been shortly
followed by notices of mourning. Lady Kit Cosley's first two live-birth
children had died within the first sevenday. They hadn't even reached
their Naming Days and had died nameless. Most Kensians had lost hope
that their duke would ever produce an heir.

Shaking her head to rid herself of the depressing thoughts, Mama Caler
reached out and gripped the innkeeper's hands, startling the man.

"Despite past events, I have Seen that this child will be our duke's
heir."

She giggled like a woman half her age and wriggled where she stood.
Then, releasing the innkeeper's hand, Mama Caler clapped her own
together.

"Only three days 'til her Naming Day! Oh, I have so much to do to
prepare."

With that, she turned and strode towards the stairs, the innkeeper
gaping after her.

~~*~*

13 Late Summer, 208
Cosley Estate, Kensy
Northern province of Evon

Lord Jem Cosley leaned against the frame of his bedroom door and
smiled at the scene before him. His lifemate, Kit, was sitting up in bed,
cradling their softly cooing newborn against her chest, her long black hair
tumbling over her shoulders to frame the child. The smile she beamed
down at the baby girl was the happiest Jem had ever seen his lifemate
produce. It was a happiness he hoped would only grow.

"Kit," he whispered, not wanting to startle mother and babe. The
duchess lifted her brown gaze to his, and her smile grew wider.

"Come here, love," she murmured and motioned him towards the bed
with her free hand. His own smile grew wider, and he approached the
bed, taking her hand as he sat on the edge beside her. "Isn't she
beautiful?" Kit whispered, awe echoing through every word as she turned
her gaze back down to their child.

A soft coo answered her, and Jem leaned his forehead against his
lifemate's, so he could stare down at their wriggling baby girl. She had a
full layer of black hair covering her head, hair that perfectly matched her
mother's.

Her eyes, though, were what truly made her stunning. They were
bright and jewel-like, shining a shade of purple Jem would never have
thought possible in a human. Yet, he now stared down at proof that eyes
like amethysts were not only a possibility, but beautifully so.

"She's perfect," he whispered, squeezing Kit's hand and blinking his
own eyes against the sting of tears.

They had been trying for a child ever since their lifebonding, a
desperate 15 years before. After multiple miscarriages and stillbirths and

the deaths of their first two children, Jem knew it was a miracle he finally had his heir. So awed was he by this miracle that he couldn't even bring himself to regret that his heir was female.

A soft knock jarred Jem from his thoughts, and he glanced towards the bedroom's entrance. A young knight stood in the doorway, shifting awkwardly from one foot to the other. Jem felt his lips twitch at the sight. The man had only been knighted a few months previously, yet Jem's current Knight Captain had already recommended the young man as his successor.

"Aye, Sir Paeter," Jem acknowledged, turning to fully face the knight.

"I'm sorry to disturb you, Milord, but the Holy Man and Seer are ready to begin the ceremony."

"Seer?" Jem asked, surprise coloring his tone.

For the last nine days, Jem had sought a Seer who would be willing to See their daughter's future. The two they had managed to locate had doubted the child would survive to see the Naming Day and hadn't thought the possibility worth the risk of traveling to and from Cosley Estate, Jem's home.

Jem had understood since traveling through Kensy always garnered a risk of being attacked by Fayralese or highwaymen. It had saddened him that his province was in such a state that he couldn't even find a Seer for his heir's Naming Day.

"Aye, Milord," Sir Paeter answered, dragging Jem's thoughts back to the present. "The Seer arrived half an hour ago." He chuckled then and added, "She seemed rather frantic that she might have already missed the ceremony, but I assured her she was just in time."

Jem felt his lifemate weakly squeeze his hand, and he turned to meet her smile. "We have a Seer," she whispered, and he nodded, squeezing her hand in return.

"Do you think you can walk, love?" he whispered.

Despite her bright smile, lines of exhaustion still covered her face, and the brightness of her eyes couldn't hide how her eyelids drooped occasionally. After all these years and all the pregnancies, Jem knew it was amazing that Kit was as strong as she was, but she still needed a very long rest to recover. They couldn't even justify having a Mage Healer here to help her because all Mage Healers were dedicated to taking care of the casualties of the war.

"With your help, I think I can," Kit murmured, once again breaking through the duke's thoughts.

Jem nodded and stood. Supporting his small lifemate with one arm wrapped around her back, he folded the other under their cooing daughter and assisted Kit from their bed. Once certain he could support Kit well enough as they walked, Jem nodded to Sir Paeter to lead the way.

The knight led them along the ground floor of the manor towards the main doors. When they were deciding where to hold the Naming Ceremony, Kit had insisted they hold it outside on the grounds of the

Estate, where she could finally get some fresh air after being holed up in their rooms for so long at the insistence of the midwife.

As Sir Paeter pushed open the doors and they walked through, Kit released a long sigh and seemed to relax into Jem's embrace.

"That's better," she murmured, and Jem chuckled, placing a light kiss to the top of his lifemate's head.

The courtyard they had walked out into was rather large. Bordering the front side of the manor, it was framed by the stables on one side and the training grounds on the other. The fourth side opened onto a long dirt road that wandered through fields south to the Evonese Highway.

The courtyard itself was currently occupied by a small group of people. There was the Holy Man of Carith, his bright, multicolored robes making him stand out from the rest. There were also several knights, including Jem's Knight Captain, Second Captain, and a few of those who had just recently been assigned to the Estate. Talking rather animatedly with the Holy Man was a woman Jem didn't recognize.

Remembering what Sir Paeter had said, Jem realized the woman, who looked to be around his own age, must be the Seer. She wore her brown hair loose over her shoulders like a woman half her age, but her clothes were a mixture of styles from different parts of Kensy, representing the experience she must have gained over the years. Jem even thought he recognized one of the bracelets she wore as a style that had been the specialty of a small town destroyed near the beginning of his time as duke.

Jem and Kit had almost reached the group when the Seer caught sight of them and hurried forward. "Oh, Milord, Milady, I am so happy for you," the woman gushed, and Jem suddenly questioned his assessment of her age. She certainly acted like a much younger woman.

The thought disappeared in the next second as the Seer suddenly sobered and held out her arms in the form of a cradle.

"Will you allow me, Mama Caler, to hold your child, Lady Kit Cosley, that I may See what the Fates will show me?"

Jem felt himself relax at the woman's words. He hadn't expected to begin the ceremony so immediately, but he recognized the Seer's name, if not her appearance.

Mama Caler was an old title, and the family that held it was considered to bear the best Seers in Kensy. This Mama Caler was widely known for her lively nature and, like her predecessors, the accuracy of her visions.

"I will," Kit finally murmured, and, with Jem's help, she placed their daughter in the Seer's arms. There was silence then as the Seer stared down at their daughter. Only the babe's cooing and the nickering of the horses in the nearby stable broke the silence as Mama Caler Saw their daughter's future.

~~*~*

Mama Caler had become accustomed to the destruction of the war and how it affected every future she Saw. As she had suspected, though, this child was the very key to life beyond the war. But even she had never considered that the future she Saw for this child would be so…different.

When she could finally pull herself from the future the Fates had woven for the child, she smiled, lifted her gaze from the babe in her arms, and addressed the duke and duchess.

"Lord and Lady Cosley." The couple startled, and Mama Caler offered a soft smile. "This daughter of yours will be no ordinary girl. She will not see distinctions the way most do. To her, there will be no difference between men and women, rich and poor, magical and non-magical. She will help her countrymen to alter their views that they, too, might view the world this way.

"She will bring peace to—nay, she shall be the peace of—this land when it needs her most. At times, she will seem as one person, while, at others, she might seem like another." Turning her gaze solely on the duke, Mama Caler added, "Lord Cosley, I would recommend to you that you raise her both as a son and as a daughter that she might meet her future as your heir well-prepared."

The duke seemed to ponder this for a moment, a small frown marring his features. The Seer knew her recommendation was unusual. Men and women were not considered equals throughout most of Evon. The future she had Seen, however, required that the duke treat his heir, daughter or not, in a rather unorthodox way.

"Very well," the duke finally answered, a small smile pulling at his lips. "What would you have us call her?"

Mama Caler smiled and fell silent then. The question was part of the ceremony. It was customary to ask a Seer for a name for the child. While not everyone used the name the Seer provided, the child's given name often referenced it.

The Seer considered the future she had seen. Name after name came to her as she considered it, but she knew they were not names to be given but rather names to be earned. *No matter how much she is to accomplish in her life, I have no right to recommend those.*

Nodding in answer to that thought, she found a name she thought would suit the child and returned her attention to the duke and duchess.

"From what I have Seen, this child will accomplish much during her life, yet I have learned it is inappropriate to name a child after what she will do. Instead, it is best to name her after what she will be able to do or a personality trait."

She paused then, meeting the couple's gazes. "If I were you, Lord and Lady Cosley, I would name her for her dual personality."

The couple fell silent. Lady Cosley seemed confused by the Seer's recommendation, but Lord Cosley was soon nodding, a small smile playing on his lips once more.

"You would recommend we name her after my own namesakes?"

Mama Caler let her own smile widen, and she nodded emphatically.

"What do you think, Kit?" the duke added, turning his attention to his lifemate. "Shall we name her after the twin moons, Gemini?"

Lady Cosley smiled then and lowered her head as if in agreement. Instead of lifting it again, though, she leaned it against her lifemate's chest, and the Seer felt her heart break.

The lady was beautiful, but she was obviously weak and exhausted. Unfortunately, from what Mama Caler had seen, she didn't think the woman would ever fully recover from her multiple failed pregnancies. Oh, she would love her daughter dearly, but the Seer didn't think she would ever recover her full strength.

"Very well, then," Lord Cosley said, oblivious to the Seer's thoughts. "We shall Name her Gemini Cosley." He nodded then to the Holy Man, who carefully removed the baby girl from Mama Caler's arms and began his part of the ceremony.

As the child was Named, Mama Caler beamed. *Gemini Cosley,* she thought, tasting the name in her thoughts. *This is the beginning of a complicated life for you. There will be many hardships and much pain, but there will be much love and many successes, as well.*

She sighed softly as she heard the words that ended the Naming Ceremony. "By the power granted to me by the great creator, Carith, I bless this child as Gemini Cosley. May the light of Carith be with her always."

There was a murmur of agreement from the crowd, and Mama Caler nodded to herself in satisfaction. *I believe my work here is done for now, but I have a feeling I shall meet Miss Gemini again. Maybe then I'll be able to help her understand her fate.*

With that thought, Mama Caler thanked the duke and duchess for allowing her to See their daughter's future. Politely refusing the couple's offer of a meal and refreshment—the knight who had greeted her had already given her food—Mama Caler left Cosley Estate, bidding a silent farewell to the child, for now.

Chapter 1

Sir Paeter Sartman, Knight Captain of Cosley Estate, caught James' downward swing against his own sword and grimaced. While the power behind the blow couldn't break through his defenses, especially in a light spar like this, the speed, skill, and grace with which it was wielded was enviable.

Especially considering James is only the nine-year-old daughter of my Knight Master, Lord Jem.

The knight snorted as he countered with his own swing. *As much as you can consider James female with such skill.*

The thin girl—a term Paeter always used lightly in reference to James—sidestepped to avoid Paeter's swing. When Paeter moved to raise his sword once more, he was startled to find a blade at his throat and his opponent's body crowding close to his own.

Glaring halfheartedly down at the black-haired girl, he muttered, "I thought we were cooling down, James."

The girl began laughing before he'd even spoken her nickname, her amethyst eyes glittering up at the knight with amusement. She danced back, allowing Paeter room to move, and patted his arm.

"That's all right, Paeter. Maybe you'll win tomorrow."

Paeter grumbled good-naturedly as they sheathed their swords then threw an arm around the girl's shoulders. He and his Second Captain, Sir Leal Highknoll, had been training Gemini Cosley for nearly five years now, and this was not the first time she had beaten either of them.

In fact, I think I've hardly 'won' during the past few days.

"She beat you again, then?" a voice called from the fence surrounding the training circle as they approached.

Paeter cast Leal a slight scowl, but the other knight only laughed and tossed him a towel. Catching the towel and wiping it across his face, he shook his head.

"The brat's been running me through the mill, she has."

Throwing the towel over one shoulder and accepting a canteen of water from his friend, Paeter leaned over and yanked lightly on Gemi's horsetail.

"Hey!" Gemi cried out and gripped the leather strip that held her hair back at the nape.

Paeter snatched his hand back and barked out a laugh. Shaking his head, he took a swig from his canteen and needled, "I'm surprised you're still letting it grow out, James. You know someone could use it against you in a fight."

The girl ducked her head, her cheeks pinking. "I don't care," she muttered.

Leal snorted and handed Gemi a canteen. "Leave her be, Paeter. If the girl wants to keep her hair long, she can. Besides," he added, his grin turning sly, "Lady Kit would thrash all of us for even suggesting she cut it. It's the only thing keeping her looking anything like a girl."

Color spread across Gemi's round cheeks, and she stuck her tongue out at the two knights, who only laughed. However, the words were true enough. Gemi insisted on wearing simple tunics and trousers at all times, even outside of weapons practice. When asked about it, she always complained that she just couldn't move in the skirts her mother wanted her to wear.

Paeter gestured with his canteen towards the girl, who had begun to drink from her own. "You know you're not going to be able to put your mother off for much longer, James, especially with the whippings you've been giving us this past sevenday. I don't know how much more we can teach you."

If Paeter hadn't trained the girl himself, the thought would have appalled the Knight Captain, who had been considered the best swordsman of his age when he was knighted.

Gemi's head shot up then, and water sloshed from her canteen down the front of her tunic. She ignored it as her amethyst eyes locked on Paeter's, her face paling dangerously.

"Don't say that, Paeter!" she cried. "If Mother and Father hear you say that, they'll find me a lady tutor for sure." A shiver rippled through her body, and she shook her head emphatically. "I don't want 'lady-training'."

Paeter sighed and traded a beleaguered look with Leal. Gemini had grown up spoiled, but not in the way the two knights, both of whom had, of course, been born to noble families, were used to seeing nobles spoil their daughters.

Both knights had sisters who had grown up expecting to marry into other noble families and to live lives of leisure. As far as Paeter knew, his lifebonded sisters did nothing more strenuous than dance, play music, and bear their lifemates' children.

Gemini, on the other hand, had been raised as a noble's son was raised, with none of the frivolities associated with ladyship. She had grown up knowing that, as the heir to a duchy, hard work would be expected of her. She would be expected to protect her people and support them to the best of her abilities.

And, despite the doubts of everyone who had attempted to advise Lord Jem not to follow the Seer's advice, Gemi had not only eagerly taken to the work of being her father's heir, she had expressed a definite dislike for the idea of ever learning to be a lady. A dislike which the knights had felt the full brunt of since Gemi didn't wish to break Lady Kit's heart by expressing it to her.

Paeter turned his gaze back to the young girl, knowing from experience that she was preparing to throw a fit on the restrictions placed on ladies. Thankfully, before she could get more than a few words out, a young voice called out "Miss Gemini" from behind Leal.

~~*~*

Gemi stopped midsentence when the boy called her name. Turning her gaze past Sir Leal, she offered the servant a scowl.

"What?"

The boy appeared unbothered by her sharp tone, which didn't really surprise her. Jake Caffers belonged to the family who had cared for the Estate's cattle for generations. He had known Gemi since she was a babe, and, unlike most of the other servants' children, he had never been in awe of her position.

In a way, his insistence on treating her like any other child three years younger than him increased her respect for him, but she would never tell him so.

"Lord Jem's 'requested your immediate presence in his study'."

His words were respectful enough, but the mischievous grin he offered said he knew he had interrupted her.

"But I've still got a lesson with Sir Leal," Gemi whined.

Leal was training her in mounted warfare, and she particularly enjoyed those lessons since it was an easy excuse to spend several hours with her bondmates.

Jake rolled his eyes and shrugged. "Sorry, Gems, but your father said it was important."

Gemi wrinkled her nose at the nickname, which Jake knew she hated. A heavy hand on her shoulder drew her attention up to Paeter, who smiled softly down at her.

"Go on and talk to your father, James. I'm sure Leal will wait for you."

Leal snorted. "I'm not the one you have to worry about making wait."

As though on cue, a large shadow passed over them, and Gemi felt a warm presence nudge her mind questioningly. Looking up, Gemi watched the large, winged shape that had passed overhead circle the stable before disappearing on the other side of it.

"*How was your hunt?*" she questioned the presence that whirled like flying fire against her mind. When the warm presence only hummed contently, a second presence laughed.

"*I think she ate too much, Gemi,*" the second presence nickered, making the girl think of the wild earth and wind in her hair. "*Stuffed herself in the hopes that you won't ride her today.*"

The warm presence grumbled at the wild presence but didn't respond otherwise.

The hand on Gemi's shoulder squeezed lightly, pulling her attention back to the knights, who were both watching her with raised eyebrows. Gemi sighed and grumbled herself. So she was putting off actually going

11

to see her father. They couldn't fault her for it. She could only imagine what her father thought was important enough to interrupt her lessons.

"The lesson's postponed 'til later, you two," she mindspoke to both presences in her mind.

The first presence only hummed again, while the second snorted in amusement. Smiling at the antics of her bondmates, Gemi nodded to the two knights, grabbed her bow and quiver of arrows from where she'd left them before practice, and slipped sideways through the fence.

Gemi made her way through the training grounds, passing training circles and yards of varying sizes. Some stood empty, but, as usual, most were occupied by knights and soldiers training together. Gemi had grown up with the threat of war all around her, and she had learned from an early age that her father's men were always preparing for battle.

She was crossing the large, open courtyard that bordered both the training grounds and the manor when a cry of "Help! Please!" cut through the air. Turning, one hand going to the hilt of her sword, Gemi saw a horse stumble to a halt just inside the courtyard from the road connecting the Estate to the Evonese Highway.

The horse dropped its head, but, even from where she stood, Gemi could see that its eyes were wide and its body was lathered. Its rider looked to be in just as bad a shape as he gasped for air and attempted to speak at the same time.

Gemi took a step towards the horse and rider, but a hand gripping her arm stopped her. She glanced up to find Jake Caffers standing beside her, his eyes firmly on the newcomer. When she attempted to shake his hand off, Jake turned his gaze on her, and she froze.

The twelve-year-old, who usually teased and tormented Gemi, looked more serious than she had ever seen him. The look was one she might expect from Sir Paeter or Sir Leal or even her father, but Jake? Squirming under that odd stare and unwilling to interpret what it might mean, Gemi turned her gaze back to the new arrival.

Sir Paeter and Sir Leal, who had followed Gemi from the training grounds, had already approached the newcomer. She couldn't hear what they were saying, but Leal was stroking the horse's flank, while Paeter seemed to be questioning the rider. Finally, Paeter nodded to Leal, who ran back to the training grounds, and glanced around searchingly, his grim gaze finally landing on her and Jake.

"Caffers, come bring our visitor and his mount to the stable."

Jake hesitated for a second before he released Gemi's arm, but, as he walked away, she heard him mutter, "I don' like this. One was strange enough, but two?" She frowned, not understanding his words, but she lost the thought when Paeter approached her.

"Gemi," Paeter said, and the girl frowned, unused to the knight calling her by her given name. "Since you're going to talk to your father, can you let him know I'm taking some of the men to Farvis? It seems the

Fayralese have attacked the city, and we need to provide as much help as we can."

Gemi swallowed. An attack on Farvis? The large city had only survived as long as it had because the Fayralese had feared the sheer number of soldiers and guards manning the city's defenses. Had the ranks been so thinned over the years that the enemy was now confident of success?

Gemi knew it was possible, of course. Despite her parents' attempts to keep news of the war from Gemi's ears, she wasn't stupid. She knew there were casualties throughout Kensy. She knew those who survived were often sent elsewhere to cover weak points in the province. In fact, many of the people Gemi had known when she was younger no longer lived at Cosley Estate.

"Gemi," Paeter said, forcing the girl to focus back on him. "This is important. Can I trust you to pass this message to your father?"

Gemi hesitated. She wondered if Paeter shouldn't ask her father first before taking the men to Farvis. *But nay,* she thought, *there's no time.* It would take the men at least two hours to get to Farvis, and that was only if they pushed their horses to their fastest speed.

Nay, Sir Paeter's right. They have to leave now.

Gemi nodded and murmured that she would. The Knight Captain patted her shoulder. Turning back to the courtyard, he began shouting orders to those knights and soldiers who had already appeared. Knowing she needed to move—she could already imagine Jake taunting her for being in everyone's way—Gemi turned back to the manor and slipped through the main doors.

~~*~*

As Lord Jem waited for his heir, he slowly wandered around his study, letting his eyes drift over the bookshelves covering most of the walls. The room's other two occupants sat at his desk and chatted about the necessary skills of a lady and what the best forms of instruction were. The duke made a face at the shelves. He really wasn't interested in listening to such things, so, instead, he let his thoughts drift.

He knew Gemi would be upset when she learned why they had called for her. *Especially since we're interrupting her other lessons.*

But he also knew it was safer to give her this information now, in the middle of the day, than it would be to wait until evening. He knew his daughter well, and, despite her training in various forms of warfare, the girl was rather like a deer: easily spooked and prone to running.

Jem glanced over his shoulder at his lifemate and the tutor they'd hired. Honestly, if Jem had his way, they would never have bothered with a tutor. Gemini was Jem's heir and the future duchess. While Seyan Lefas, Duke of Baylin, insisted that his only child, Roselyn, was simply a link to the next duke, Jem believed that Gemi would be able to handle the responsibility of the duchy herself. He saw no reason for her to be trained in the niceties of ladyship.

However, the Seer had insisted that Gemi be raised as both a boy and a girl, and Jem knew it was breaking Kit's heart that her only daughter didn't want to be a lady. So, after putting 'lady-training' off for as long as he could, Jem had finally broken down and sought a tutor for his daughter.

At least Kit and I did manage to agree on one thing.

Jem was pulled from his thoughts by a soft knock on the study door. "Come in," he called, moving back to his desk to stand behind the chair Kit sat in. Briefly, his lifemate smiled up at him, but she turned her gaze to the door as it slowly opened.

As soon as the door was opened wide enough for Jem to see his daughter, he nearly groaned. Her usual worn leather calf-high boots were covered in dust, while her brown trousers and pale linen tunic were sweat-stained and torn in a few places. The tunic even stuck to her chest and stomach in the front, and her training weapons hung from her body, making her true gender even more indistinguishable than usual. Jem suddenly regretted not telling Caffers to send her to clean up before she came to see him.

Unlike Jem, Kit didn't hold back her disappointed sigh. As she shook her head, Jem noted their daughter's face turning red. *At this rate, she'll be gone before we can even finish talking.*

Squeezing his lifemate's shoulder with one hand, Jem motioned for his daughter to enter the room with the other. "Gemi, we have someone here we would like to introduce to you."

The girl had taken a couple steps away from the door—leaving it open, Jem noted with little surprise—but she stopped again with his words. Jem watched as Gemi's eyes landed on the room's only occupant that wasn't family. He watched as the red faded, only to be replaced by obvious confusion.

"Who...?" she whispered, trailing off as she swung her gaze up to meet Jem's.

"Gemini," Kit said, forcing the word to be as strong as she could make it, but Jem could still hear a slight waver in his lifemate's voice. "This is Kale Caphrin. He is going to train you to be a lady."

The man whom they had hired stood from his seat and approached Gemi. Holding his hand out flat, as he would to any lady, he murmured, "It is a pleasure to meet you, Miss Cosley. I hope we will work well together."

The words were followed by a frozen moment as Gemi simply stared up at Caphrin. Jem found himself holding his breath despite his suspicions of how his daughter would react.

All these years, Gemi would have been expecting a female tutor, but Jem and Kit had agreed that a male tutor would suit Gemi better. She had experience with male mentors in every other way of life. Why shouldn't she be trained as a lady by a man, as well?

Finally, Gemi moved, her mouth opening and closing like a landed fish. The shock seemed to move through her system quickly, and she soon shook her head and spat out a fierce "Nay!" before whirling around and disappearing back through the doorway.

Jem released the breath he'd been holding and felt Kit slump against the back of her chair. Ten years ago, Kit wouldn't have dared to do so in front of a stranger, but, these days, her near-constant exhaustion left her with little effort to spare for such pretenses. Patting her shoulder gently, Jem turned his attention to Caphrin, who turned to them with a look of confusion.

"Did I say something wrong?"

Kit sighed, and Jem recognized the exhaustion taking her over once more. *We'll have to make this brief, then.* To Caphrin, he shook his head.

"Nay, you said nothing wrong. It is just that Gemini yet dislikes the idea of being trained as a lady, and she did not expect we would hire a man to do so."

Caphrin nodded and glanced towards the doorway. "I will admit, I was surprised myself that you were searching for a male tutor. I would have thought that, as a future duchess, you would wish her to be trained by a lady."

Jem shook his head and motioned towards the doorway through which his daughter had disappeared. "What you saw was the everyday face of our daughter, Caphrin. Do you really think a lady would be able to handle that?"

Caphrin seemed to consider that before finally smirking. "Nay, I imagine not." He glanced at the doorway once more then asked, "Shall I follow her? Maybe I can convince her that my mentorship will not be as bad as she imagines."

Jem immediately shook his head.

"Nay, leave her be for a while. She just needs time to cool down and think it over. We believe that, once she considers the implications of a male tutor, she will be quite happy with the choice."

Kit sighed again, and Jem nodded, gripping her shoulder once more. "Now, my lifemate is tired, so why don't I send for a servant to show you around. I expect Gemini will be a little more open to you by tomorrow morning."

Caphrin bowed his head.

~~*~*

Kale was pleased when he learned it was Mady who would show him around the manor.

He had first met the maid in Farvis when she had gone shopping for the weakened duchess. It had not been difficult to place her as a servant of Cosley Estate. While she did not wear the coat of arms of the duke, the colors of her livery had still been obvious.

It had been simple enough to charm the young maid while she shopped, and she had willingly spilled the gossip of the Estate. When she mentioned that the duke sought a male tutor to train his daughter to be a lady, he knew he had found his way in. How fortunate it was that he had had the experience of training four ladies already. When he had mentioned this in an offhand manner, the girl had squealed and offered to recommend him to the duke.

"I'm so glad the duke agreed to hire ya, Kale," Mady chattered annoyingly as she led him along the ground floor of the manor. He had already asked about seeing the second level, but she had waved the question away with a simple "Oh, the family only uses the ground floor, I'm 'fraid."

That would be because of the duchess's frailty, Kale thought with a quiet chuckle. It was amazing how easy it was to learn the vulnerabilities of such a noble family.

And the strengths, he amended, thinking of the sheer number of men that protected the Estate and the creature that had guarded the family these past two years.

Kale had not seen the creature himself, but he had heard enough stories from their spies to know what it was and how dangerous it could be. Although the kingdom of Evon had rid itself of such creatures during its founding, they were prevalent throughout Kale's own homeland.

The thought brought a smirk to his lips. He forced it to smooth into a smile as Mady stopped and turned to face him. Leaning in, she offered him a coy smile, which only made him wish to sneer.

Like an Evonese servant could actually interest me, he thought derisively, though he forced his own smile to spread in response.

"How 'bout I show you the kitchen and cellar, Kale," the maid hinted, leaning further into him. "We've got all day, and I can show you the res' o' the ground floor later."

Kale made a show of thinking about the offer, despite already knowing the kitchen was important to his plans. He hummed softly and muttered, "Well, I had hoped to check in on Miss Gemini to be sure she is not too upset."

Mady harrumphed and waved a hand dismissively. "Wi' the way tha' child tore through the halls after meetin' ya, she'll be long gone by now. No doub' she'll be back tonigh', but you'd best forge' 'bout her 'til tomorrow. She'll be too tired to do much more than fall in her bed tonigh', mos' like."

Kale hummed again and rubbed a hand over his mouth to hide the smirk pulling at his lips once more. *Perfect,* he thought. This was further verification of the gossip he had heard from the maid before, but it was just as important as the news that the duke had sought a male tutor.

The heir apparently had a tendency to throw fits and flee the Estate. Kale would not have believed such behavior was accepted during times like these if he had not learned that, where the child went, so too did the creature.

Absolutely perfect.

Certain his plans were running smoothly, Kale gripped the maid's hand and, tamping down his disdain, raised it to his lips. "Then I think it would please me if you showed me the kitchen and cellar."

The maid simpered and pulled open a nearby door, revealing a set of stairs leading down.

Perfect, Kale thought once more as she led him down beneath the manor.

~~*~*

As Gemi raced down the hallways, her main thought was to get away from her father and mother and the *man* they had hired.

How could they do this? A sob worked its way up her throat, and she dashed a hand against her eyes as tears began to blur her vision. *How could they hire a* man?

That was, of course, why she'd run. She'd pretty much been resigned to 'lady-training' despite her protests. She had been sure a new tutor was the only thing her father would consider important enough to interrupt her regular lessons.

But why would he hire a man to teach what only a lady should know?

As she reached her room and slammed the door shut behind her, she became aware of questioning thoughts pressing against her mind. Wanting to drown in the presence of her bondmates, she pressed back against them, letting them see what had happened in her father's study.

"*And they just expect me to accept a* man *as my new lady tutor! Why would they think such a thing was even acceptable?*"

Warmth suddenly filled Gemi's mind, and she groaned and relaxed in her bondmate's comfort. "*I doubt they expect you to accept it so easily,*" the fiery presence murmured, and Gemi felt herself smile despite the situation.

Shaking her head, Gemi forced the smile off her face and herself away from her bondmates' comforting murmurs. When the two presences questioned her, she shook her head again.

"*I'm not accepting this. Never! I don't care what my father and mother think or expect. I won't stick around so some...some...*"

She floundered as she looked for a word to match the disgust she felt but quickly gave up with a scream of frustration.

"*I won't let some* man *teach me what only a woman should know.*"

Throwing open her wardrobe, Gemi grabbed a pack from the bottom of it. Opening the pack, she nodded in satisfaction at the sight of bundled cloth and properly stowed rations. Opening the top drawer of her nightstand, she pulled out a bag of coin, quickly depositing it in the pack.

Turning to her bed, she grabbed the knife she kept beneath her pillow— Paeter and Leal had taught her well that you never know when you'll need a weapon—and slipped its sheath onto her belt, opposite her sword.

She checked the rest of her weapons then: sword on the left side of her belt, daggers in her boots, bow and quiver of arrows across her back. Once satisfied, she secured the pack, slipped it over her left shoulder, and pushed open her window.

Over the years, Gemi had found that one advantage to having a room on the ground floor was the ease with which she could escape the manor without notice. It helped, too, that her window faced the corner of the stable, so she didn't have far to go in order to reach her bondmates.

As she slipped through the window, the fiery presence in her mind muttered, *"It is rather quiet in here. No one should see us leave."*

The words suddenly reminded Gemi of the message Sir Paeter had asked her to pass on to her father. Biting her lip, she paused and glanced back towards her room, wondering if she should go tell her father the news.

Nay! She gave her head a sharp shake. *It doesn't matter,* she thought angrily, stomping towards the stable's northern entrance. *I refuse to run back to Father with my tail between my legs for that.*

Although, I do hope Paeter can forgive me.

The last was more subdued, and she shook her head to dislodge the thoughts. As she came to the middle of the stable, where the hallway leading from north to south entrance intersected with the hallway that ran from east to west, Gemi turned left and paused at the sight that greeted her.

There, in front of one particular stall, lay what looked like a large pile of gleaming rubies and amethysts. When Gemi stopped, the pile seemed to pull apart. Two long sinuous sections pulled from the pile, one swinging back to slide and rustle across the floor of the stable, the second lifting to reveal a long neck and a smooth snakelike head crowned with horns and ridges above two burning eyes the color of deep garnets.

The pile then shifted forward, and two broad, leathery appendages unfolded from the creature's back as it lifted itself onto four strong legs that gleamed the same red and purple as the rest of its body. Even the wings, which it stretched above itself to their fullest extent before folding them back against its body, were patterned in the same colors, duller and darker than the rest of the body.

"Flame," Gemi whispered and continued towards the fire dragon. Even after two years, the girl still found herself awed by the beauty and power of her bondmate, an awe that always amused the young dragon.

"When you are raised with the beauty of dragons and other magical creatures, it is difficult to not be amused by your awe, Gemi," Flame cooed. As a dragon, she couldn't speak human tongues, but, since their dragonbonding, they could easily understand each other's minds.

"Aye, well, since you're the only one here who was raised with magical creatures, could you tone the amusement down?"

Gemi turned to the stall in front of which Flame had been curled. Within it stood a large ebony stallion, his head lowered over the stall's door and tilted slightly to eye them both with one warm brown eye. Approaching the stall, Gemi took the stallion's head in her hands and leaned her forehead against the faint white star that decorated it.

"I'm just as awed by your power and beauty, too, Shadow," she whispered, earning a snort from both horse and dragon.

"*If you start waxing poetic about either of us,*" Shadow nickered, "*I'm going to insist you ride Flame.*"

Gemi giggled. Her bondmates could always cheer her up, no matter the situation. An angular snout nudged her side, and she turned her head to look into Flame's garnet eye.

"*Are you sure you wish to do this, Gemi?*" the dragon murmured. When Gemi nodded insistently, the serpentine creature released a gust of warm air against her body. "*Very well.*"

As Gemi opened Shadow's stall and began to saddle him up, she listened idly to the dragon's thoughts. This certainly wasn't the first time Gemi had insisted on leaving the Estate, and the dragon fully expected to return. Despite Gemi's emphatic denials, the dragon believed it was simply a question of when.

Once Shadow was tacked up, Gemi mounted him, and Flame led them to the stable's eastern entrance. Not far from there was the western border of the Estate's orchard, which separated the manor from the forest on that side. Keeping an eye out for humans, both animals bounded for the nearest row.

They slowed as they reached the forest and slipped through the trees onto their favorite deer path. Once on the familiar route, Gemi urged the stallion into a canter, just to make sure no one followed them.

As Shadow fell into a quick and easy pace, Gemi lifted her head and closed her eyes, sighing as the wind caressed her face. Pulling the leather strip from her hair, she shook her head, laughing as the wind tugged at the now free strands.

They had traveled for perhaps half an hour before Flame and Shadow deemed it safe to slow down. As Flame climbed a tall, thick tree and leapt into the air above the forest, Shadow relaxed to a walk and turned south, away from the main deer path.

"*No point attempting to return to the Northeast Forest,*" he joked, referring to the day two years before when they all first met.

Gemi chuckled. Secure in the knowledge that they wouldn't be found, she sat back in the saddle and reminisced on that day.

Chapter 2

3 Late Summer, 215
Cosley Estate, Kensy, Evon

A seven-year-old Gemi groaned and draped herself, kneeling, over one of the rails of the fence surrounding the training yard Sir Paeter and Sir Leal had chosen for today's lessons. She didn't know why, but her birthday always seemed to inspire the knights to be more merciless than usual. She whimpered, not wanting to even think about the paces through which her mentors had just put her.

"You aren't going to be sick, are you, James?" The tone sounded far too happy for the words, and Gemi turned her head just enough to glare weakly at the Second Captain.

"You shouldn't tease, Leal," Paeter warned, and Gemi turned her gaze gratefully to the Knight Captain. "She might decide to aim for you."

Gemi groaned again and closed her eyes as the two knights chuckled.

Sliding back so she could sit on her heels, Gemi leaned her forehead against the rail and let her arms dangle. They had given her a longer sword today and worked her two-on-one. Her entire body ached, but her arms were feeling particularly jelly-like at the moment.

A warm hand suddenly rubbed her back soothingly, and Gemi sighed as the movement eased some of her tight muscles.

"James?"

Gemi turned her head a little and opened her eyes to pout mutinously at Paeter through some loose strands of hair. Despite the earlier jokes, the knight eyed her worriedly.

"We didn't push you too hard, did we?"

Leal hunkered down beside Paeter. "We must have because you don't look so good."

Gemi made a face, knowing where the two knights were going with this. Sitting up, she forced her arms above her head and stretched her screaming muscles. She must have winced or done something to show how much the move hurt because Paeter sighed.

"Maybe we should return you to the manor rather than the stable. I think your father would understand if you rested before you went to see him."

"But, Paeter..." Gemi whined, dropping her arms. She knew her father had a birthday surprise for her in the stable, and she wasn't about to let cruel mentors and sore muscles keep her from receiving it. "You can't send me to the manor now. Not on my birthday. Please?"

Leal snorted and stood up, slapping Paeter on the back. "Oh, she'll be fine if she can still whine like that. There's no point keeping her from the stable if she doesn't want to be kept."

Paeter rolled his eyes, though he gently helped Gemi to her feet. "All right, then," he acceded.

Bending down to meet the girl's eyes, he added, "But, if your father gets angry with us for letting you into the stable with such sore muscles, there'll be no lessons for the next sevenday. Understood?"

Gemi paused once she could support herself and eyed the Knight Captain warily. She knew that look. He wasn't fooling around about this. Gemi bit her lip and squirmed a bit. She wanted to know what her father had gotten for her, but she knew he might be upset if he saw how tired she was from her lessons. And she hated missing even one day of lessons. An entire sevenday without would be torture.

She squirmed back and forth for a minute more before crossing her arms and sticking out her chin.

"I don't care. I'll risk it."

Leal chuckled and ruffled her hair. "Stubborn, aren't you?"

Gemi scowled, but, when she tried to swat his hand away, he'd already pulled it back.

"Well, shall we?" The Second Captain gestured towards the stable.

The journey to the stable was painful for Gemi. It seemed she could feel every muscle in her back and legs, and they were all complaining—loudly. Crossing the courtyard seemed to ease the tension…or, rather, the pain. Gemi doubted it had as much to do with relaxing muscles as her rising anticipation.

Certainly, the pain might as well have disappeared when she entered the stable. There, in the middle of the stable where the two hallways intersected, stood her father, his stable master, and several stable hands. Yet they weren't what caught her attention.

Between them all, stood a beautiful horse. It stood nearly shoulder-to-withers with her father. The smooth coat shone a pure black, with only a faint star on the forehead disturbing the darkness. The star was framed by a thick forelock, and the mane hung thick and somewhat wavy over the right side of the horse's neck.

As she slowly approached the circle of men, the horse shifted, lowering its head towards her and snorting. As it did so, the men turned, as well.

"Ah, Gemi, there you are!" her father exclaimed.

The horse snorted again, shifting its weight away from the duke. Her father didn't seem to notice as he stepped away from the horse and motioned Gemi closer.

"What do you think?" he asked as he pulled her against his side and turned back towards the horse. "He's a beauty, isn't he?"

"Aye," Gemi whispered, "he is." Tugging on a loose strand of hair and glancing up at her father, she added, unsure, "Whose is he?" She might have expected her father's surprise to be a horse of her own, but this creature was too beautiful to be for her, surely.

Her father chuckled and squatted down beside her. "He's yours, Gemi."

She felt her eyes widen, and she licked her lips. Glancing at the beautiful beast, she breathed, "Really?"

Pressure on her shoulder pulled her attention back to her father, who offered her a soft smile. "Do you think I would lie to you on your birthday?"

She squealed then and leapt into her father's arms. "Oh, Father! Thank you, thank you, thank you, thank you, thank you!"

Her father's chuckles turned to deep laughter as he hugged her close.

Another snort soon caught Gemi's attention once more, and the girl quickly wriggled loose. Once again staring at the horse, she inched closer and began to rattle off questions. "What's his name? How old is he? Where'd he come from?"

"Whoa, Gemi," her father chuckled. He stood back up and squeezed her shoulder, pulling her to a halt. "Slow down there. He's nearly three years old, and his sire was the king's own stallion, Black Lightning."

Gemi gaped up at her father, and the man laughed.

"I thought you might like that."

"Black Lightning?" she whispered. "But..." She glanced back at the black colt, who nickered anxiously and dropped his head closer to her level. "He must have been expensive."

Her father smiled down at her. "Whether or not he was doesn't matter, Gemi. You are my heir. You need a strong companion who will always be there for you." He nodded to the large, solid-looking colt. "He'll do quite well, I expect."

Gemi nodded slowly and took another step closer. This time, her father didn't stop her, and she reached out and laid a hand on the colt's muzzle. The colt nickered softly and nudged his nose against her hand, earning himself a giggle from Gemi.

"What's his name?" she asked again as she lifted her gaze to meet the horse's.

She startled when she realized the colt appeared to be eyeing her in an appraising manner. Lifting her chin, Gemi raised herself to her full height. The colt snorted, and amusement seemed to dance in those dark brown eyes.

"I thought you might like to give him a name yourself," Gemi's father finally said, and she realized he'd hesitated.

Gemi glanced up at her father then, pulling her gaze away from those too-intelligent eyes—though Gemi had never met a horse trained by an Animal Mage as this one must have been if he'd been born in the king's stable.

"But what was his name before?"

This time, her father's hesitation was obvious. He glanced towards the horse, and Gemi found herself snorting along with the beast.

As if the horse will be able to answer for him.

Her father finally sighed. "His name was Nightmare."

Gemi wrinkled her nose and glanced at the ebony colt. He had tilted his head and was eyeing her with one dark brown eye.

"However, Master Ekin," her father continued, and Gemi recognized the name of the Animal Mage who ran the king's stables, "said that he didn't think the name fit him any longer."

Gemi wondered what the horse could have done when he was younger to earn himself such a name, but it didn't really matter. She had already decided to accept her father's gift. The horse was beautiful, he looked powerful, and she thought she could trust a horse with those eyes.

"I want to get to know him before I choose a name for him," she finally said, looking back up at her father. The man smiled widely and nodded.

"Of course. Now, why don't we let Master Coulter get your new horse settled since he only just arrived."

"But, Father..." Gemi whined at the same time the colt whinnied. She glanced at the horse as he nudged her with his nose, and she grinned when she realized he might want the same thing she did. Turning back to her father, she added, "Can I ride him for a little bit, please?"

"You should let him rest, Miss Gemini," Master Coulter finally spoke up. "He's had a long few days traveling north from Caypan."

Knowing it was really the stable master, not her father, whom she had to convince, Gemi turned pleading eyes to the man. "Please, Master Coulter. Can't I just get on him for a little bit? I just want to know how he feels."

"Well..." The stable master glanced at her father, who shrugged.

"It's up to you, Master Coulter. If you think it's acceptable for Gemi to mount the horse for a bit, I don't see why she shouldn't be allowed to."

Master Coulter sighed and shook his head. "It should be all right." He shook a finger at Gemi then. "But you're mounting him for a little while only. I don't want you riding him around and tiring him out."

"Aye, Master Coulter," Gemi answered, even as the horse snorted and swung his head around to eye the stable master.

Since Gemi wouldn't be on the colt for long, they decided to forgo tacking him up. Lord Jem did ask if they shouldn't at least bridle the horse to keep him in place. The question was met with an immediate snort from the colt, who swung his head around to eye the duke. Gemi giggled at the burning gaze the horse aimed at the duke, but she didn't think her father noticed.

"There's no need, Milord," Master Coulter replied, smoothing a calming hand down the colt's neck and earning a soft nicker from the animal. "Master Ekin raised the colt himself. You'll find no horse more intelligent than him." The stable master chuckled. "Master Ekin even assured me the colt knew the importance of his new master."

Lord Jem nodded then and lifted Gemi up so she could swing a leg over the horse's bare back. Once she had her balance, her father let go and stepped away. Shifting herself into a more comfortable and stable position, Gemi wrapped one hand in the horse's thick mane and leaned over to rub his neck.

"So beautiful," she breathed. Sitting back up, she relaxed. Despite her small size and her sore muscles—which probably would have shortened her stay on the horse even if Master Coulter hadn't—Gemi found the colt's back rather comfortable. She was excited to rest up and truly ride him.

Master Coulter was just turning to her father—no doubt to tell him she should come down—when the colt suddenly tossed his head. Tightening both hands in the horse's mane, Gemi barely had time to wonder what was wrong before the horse reared up on his hind legs.

Gemi screamed—she hardly registered the cries of the surrounding men. Next thing she knew, the horse was cantering out of the stable and east through the Estate's orchard, heading straight for the Kensian Forest on the other side.

~~*~*

"So eager to prove yourself, were you not, Shadow?" Flame hissed amusedly, dragging Gemi from her memories. The dragon had dipped close enough to the forest canopy to brush her belly against the tree's highest branches.

Shadow huffed and raised his chin to one side. The pose was such an accurate impression of a haughty human that Gemi broke into giggles.

"I'll have you know I was raised with the belief that first impressions are very important to a new relationship," he nickered.

Gemi snorted. "So you ran away with your new master as soon as you met her."

The stallion gave a sudden shake, his intention to do so appearing so swiftly in his mind that Gemi nearly fell from her saddle before she managed to grab his mane.

"Oy!"

"If I hadn't run off with my 'new master'," Shadow snorted, ignoring Gemi's indignation, *"I wouldn't have had the chance to properly show you my speed, and the gods only know what awful name you would have given me."*

Gemi rolled her eyes. "Maybe I should have stuck with Nightmare. Seems to still fit you sometimes."

Shadow attempted to shake her again, but Gemi already had her fingers clenched in his mane. When she stuck out her tongue at the twitching black ears in front of her, Flame snorted.

"And I thought I was juvenile," she hissed dryly, referring to her relatively young age.

Gemi huffed and closed her eyes, shoving her awareness of Flame and Shadow to the back of her mind as she returned to the memories of her and Shadow's first ride.

~~*~*

24

As the black colt sped through the orchard, Gemi pulled herself as close to his back and neck as she could manage with her hands buried in his thick mane. She didn't know what had spooked him, but she prayed to Carith he wouldn't throw her.

The colt hardly slowed when the dense edge of the forest came into view. Although Gemi tugged at his mane in an attempt to stop him, he plowed straight into the forest, just brushing past the first trees. He avoided colliding with the thick trunks, but the low-hanging branches caught at Gemi's hair and scratched at her face, and she cried out.

At her cry, the colt halted, and that large black head swung around. Gemi swallowed when those all-too-intelligent, brown eyes met her amethyst ones and she realized they were calm, not wide and wild like she had expected. Gemi quickly pulled her hair from the branches as those brown eyes seemed to check her over. Once she had freed herself from the clutches of the surrounding trees, the horse snorted, tossed its head, and—much to Gemi's surprise—trotted further into the forest.

It wasn't long before the colt found a small, barely visible path, along which the trees were easier to navigate. The horse sped up to a canter then, and, despite her earlier fear, Gemi found herself lifting her head in order to feel the wind sweep through her hair, which must have been freed from its leather strip by the tree branches. She laughed as a wild joy filled her.

She didn't know how long they raced before she began to hear a steady rustling sound over the wind rushing past her ears and the steady beat of the colt's hooves. At first, she thought nothing of it, but it quickly grew to a constant roar.

In horror, Gemi realized they had traveled far enough east that they were quickly approaching the San River. She began tugging at the horse's mane, desperate for him to change course. However, like he had in the orchard, the colt seemed to purposefully ignore her commands.

The roar was near deafening when the river finally came into view. Gemi barely had time to notice the waterfall only a hundred or so feet upriver to their left before the horse plunged straight into the flowing water.

She gasped as water lapped at her legs and began to fill her boots. In that moment, she was grateful it was summer and the water wasn't freezing.

The gratitude disappeared when the colt climbed out of the river onto the eastern bank. He trotted a ways into the forest, which appeared thicker than its western counterpart, but he soon slowed and began to swing his head from side to side, his ears tilting back.

Not wanting to know what had the horse so wary, Gemi tugged at his mane once more and muttered, "Come on. Let's go back across the river." When the horse didn't turn, she spoke up louder. "Please!"

A soft trill suddenly sounded then. Gemi gasped and glanced around. Abandoning the colt's mane, she lifted one hand to tug on a strand of her own hair and laid the other on the hilt of her sword, which still hung from her belt.

"Hello?" she called out.

She immediately wished she hadn't. She had no desire to meet any of this forest's residents. After all, they were now in the Northeast Forest, the one 'province' of Evon where humans were not allowed. She could only imagine what the creatures living here might do to any human who dared to cross into their territory.

Another trill sounded, and both horse and girl tensed. Swallowing, Gemi began to unsheathe her sword. She stopped when the muscles in her arms reminded her exactly how sore they were from the morning's lessons.

As she attempted to resheathe the sword, there was a confusing flash of red and purple in front of the horse, and the colt reared and screamed. With no hands on the horse, Gemi quickly found herself in the air before a sharp pain erupted in her head and darkness enveloped her.

~~*~*

A soft hum pulled Gemi from her thoughts this time. Glancing up, she watched for glimpses of red and purple through the high canopy of the forest. Flame, she knew, was now circling lazily above the trees, dipping and soaring idly as she often did when she was forced to keep pace with Shadow.

"What?" Gemi asked.

Flame hummed again, dipping so she almost touched the topmost leaves of the forest canopy. "*I am just musing over the fact that you were unconscious for the entire bonding process.*"

Gemi rolled her eyes. "Not by choice, certainly," she muttered. Lifting a hand to her right shoulder, she rubbed at the fine teeth marks that were the only physical evidence of the dragonbond.

Shadow snorted. "*Aye, well, I was awake for the entire thing. It's not fun having a dragon attack you with her teeth when you don't realize she isn't trying to eat you.*"

Flame burbled. "*Aye, and remind me why I decided to bond with you?*"

Gemi chuckled when Shadow didn't answer immediately. This was an old argument, one she'd listened to again and again trying to piece together exactly what had happened when she'd been unconscious.

"*Because I nearly trampled Gemi in my attempt to protect her,*" he nickered softly.

The sadness in his mental voice spurred Gemi into leaning over and rubbing her hand over the base of his neck, where Flame had bit him in order to initiate the dragonbond.

She felt his mind warm at the reminder of their connection before he added, a bit more blithely, "*And I can't believe you actually mistook us for a centaur.*"

Embarrassment filled the dragon then, and she soared higher into the air. Gemi chuckled and shook her head, smacking Shadow lightly on the shoulder. He tossed his head with a snort, and Gemi turned back to her memories once more.

～～*～*

Gemi awoke slowly. Her head felt muzzy, but it didn't hurt. For some reason, she was certain it should. Unwilling to open her eyes just yet, she shifted and made a face as a soft rustling sound combined with the hardness beneath her made her aware that she was probably on the ground. A nicker and a coo pulled her attention from what she lay on, and she finally blinked open her eyes.

A yelp escaped her lips the moment she did. Sitting up, she scrambled away from the two heads that had been leaning over her. When she hit a tree and couldn't go any further, she stopped and gaped.

One head, large, long, and black with warm, brown eyes, she recognized as the horse her father had given to her only…an hour ago? Two? More? Gemi didn't know how long it had been since the horse had run off with her. She did know that she was beginning to question her decision to keep him.

A strange sadness and disappointment seemed to fill her then. Frowning, she tried to ignore those emotions and turned to the other head to which she had awakened. Like the horse's, this head was long, but the muzzle ended in more of a point, similar to a snake's.

At first, it was difficult for Gemi to grasp the details of the face because it seemed to be all color. Red and purple danced over the head, patterned in ways that obscured the texture.

Finally, the head shifted, tilting to one side, and Gemi found she could suddenly tell what she was looking at. The muzzle was smooth, but there were ridges above the eyes, which shone a deep scarlet. The top of the head was crowned with horns, two long ones that curved backwards and several smaller ones in between and around the larger two.

Once she'd registered all of that, the head shifted again, and Gemi found her eyes being drawn to the rest of the creature's body. Like the head, the body, as well as the long serpentine tail that curled around it, was patterned in red and purple. The body stretched a little longer than the horse's, and Gemi thought this creature's was also thicker.

The legs, on the other hand, seemed to be a bit shorter than the horse's, while the thickness of the hind legs spoke of a power that might make up for that difference in length. The front legs, thick enough where they met the body, tapered to delicate looking hands that were currently folded in front of the creature.

Nay, not just any creature, Gemi realized as she suddenly noticed what looked like large wings folded along its body. *It's a dragon! A real, live dragon!*

"*I am a bit surprised you recognize what I am,*" a female voice that wasn't Gemi's sounded in her head, and she squeaked.

"D-d-did you just speak to me? In my head?" Gemi gasped, staring at the dragon.

27

For a moment, the dragon simply stared at her, and Gemi wriggled under that scarlet gaze. Finally, the head dipped.

"*So you can understand me. Good. I was not sure you would since it has been so long since anyone has attempted a dragonbond with a human.*"

"Dragonbond?"

Gemi didn't like the sound of that. Whatever it was, it sounded dangerous, and she had a feeling her parents were not going to be happy about it.

"*I think your parents are the least of our worries at the moment,*" a second, male voice spoke in her head, and it was only the corresponding snort from the black colt that told her to whom it belonged.

She gaped up at the horse. "You can talk, too?"

The horse lowered its head and eyed her with one brown eye. "*You make it sound like I'm not intelligent enough to do so. Master Ekin and I used to talk all the time.*"

Gemi stared, unable to respond. A warm, amused rumble echoed from the dragon's chest. "*He is quite intelligent for a horse.*"

The colt snorted and turned wary eyes on the dragon. "*I'm still not sure if I should thank you or run.*"

The dragon began to mutter something in return when a loud roar broke through the forest's silence accompanied by a loud "*Trespasser!*" screaming through Gemi's head. All three of them ducked their heads, though the dragon seemed to recover most quickly.

"*Mama Dragon,*" she whined, her head turning to gaze past Gemi further into the forest. Gemi blinked. Fear and anxiety rolled through her mind as the red and purple dragon appeared to shrink in on itself.

Before Gemi could process that, a series of loud crunches echoed through the forest, accompanied by several twitters and screams that seemed to disappear as quickly as they began. Then, with another roar, a large, glittering darkness appeared through the trees.

Suddenly, Gemi felt a hot wind on her face, and a loud snap accompanied the appearance of very large teeth meeting mere inches from Gemi's face. Gemi thought she would have screamed if a large, clawed hand hadn't pressed on her chest then.

"*Who are you?*" a deep voice rumbled dangerously through her mind. The snout that contained those large teeth turned, and one gold eye swept over Gemi. "*Why are you in my forest?*"

"*Mama Dragon, please,*" the red and purple dragon whined as she pressed her body against the leg that held Gemi down. "*She cannot breathe.*"

There was a pause, then the leg lifted, and Gemi gasped for air. That dark, glittering snout turned to the red and purple dragon and growled.

"*I shall deal with you later, Flame Tongue.*"

Flame Tongue? Gemi thought hazily.

The red and purple dragon turned her red eyes to Gemi and nodded shortly. Gemi sensed a thought, not her own, that that was the small dragon's name.

That dark snout snapped again, this time in front of Flame Tongue's, and the smaller dragon reared her head back, quivering.

"Why do you focus so intently on this human, Flame Tongue?" The deep growl made Gemi shiver, and she pushed herself back against the tree as tightly as possible.

With a soft whine, Flame Tongue lifted her neck as high as she could. *"She is my bondmate, Mama Dragon."*

Silence surrounded them. The large, dark head stilled for several beats before pulling back too far for Gemi to see in the darkness of the forest.

The girl closed her eyes. She was going to die; she just knew it. She knew the stories about the Northeast Forest. Any human who attempted to cross the San River and enter the Northeast Forest would die a gruesome death. The little dragon—for Flame Tongue wasn't even half the size of the beast that now threatened them—may have taken pity on Gemi, but the girl didn't think she'd be so lucky with this monster.

She's not a monster. The thought floated through Gemi's mind, but it was soft enough that Gemi was able to ignore it.

"What have you done, Flame Tongue?" That dark voice returned to Gemi's mind, and even Gemi felt shamed by the sad disappointment that filled it. *"You know dragonbonding with humans is forbidden. Why would you threaten the forest with such an act?"*

Flame Tongue's earlier bravado disappeared then, and she lowered her head and curled herself into a smaller ball. *"She was hurt, dying, and I was the reason."* Flame Tongue's voice seemed to match her decreased size. *"I had to help her."*

A warm breeze ruffled Gemi's hair, and a despairing sigh filled her mind. *"I love you like you hatched from one of my own clutches, Flame Tongue, but, sometimes, you are too kind-hearted."*

Gemi frowned. *What's wrong with being kind-hearted?*

When the kindness is directed towards the wrong kind of creature, was the answering thought from Flame Tongue.

Gemi wanted to argue that there couldn't possibly be a creature that you shouldn't be kind to, but a sudden, terrifying image of something dark tearing into the flesh of a large dragon filled her head, and she squeaked.

Some things don't appreciate kindness.

Another deep sigh filled Gemi's head, and she looked up to find the large snout approaching her once more. It nudged and sniffed her, and Flame Tongue growled, surprising Gemi. However, the large snout only snorted, and a sense of amusement filled the girl's head.

"You are protective of her. Good."

"Good?" Gemi whispered, staring up at the large, dark dragon. Only moments ago, this creature was chastising Flame Tongue for…whatever it was that she had done. Now, it—*she*, Flame Tongue's thoughts corrected—was praising her for being protective of Gemi?

"What is going on?" she asked more loudly. She was still terrified, but her sudden indignation was pushing aside her fear.

The dark amusement that filled her mind increased as the snout turned so a gold eye met her amethyst ones. *"You are spirited and young. You and Flame Tongue will make a good match, I think."*

The words only confused the young girl even more. "What are you talking about? Good match for what?"

The snout pulled back slightly before turning to eye Flame Tongue. *"Does she not know?"*

Flame Tongue lifted her head to meet that gold eye and ruffled her wings. *"I did not have much time to explain before you sensed her."*

"Ah." The dark snout turned back to Gemi. *"What is your name, child?"*

Gemi blinked, startled by the large dragon's sudden interest in manners. Even Flame Tongue seemed to relax, those foreign feelings of fear and anxiety easing. Instead, confusion seemed to swamp Gemi from all sides.

"Uh...my name is Gemini Cosley, er, Mama Dragon?"

A deep rumble filled the forest then, and it took a moment for Gemi to realize that the large dragon was laughing. *"Aye, I am called Mama Dragon, youngling. Now, Cosley...that name seems familiar to me."* Silence followed the statement. Gemi wondered if she should tell her who her father was. *"Ah, aye, Cosley was the name of one of the new king's generals, I believe. If I remember correctly, he was named a duke."*

Gemi gaped up at the large snout that still hovered near her. "My father is Duke of Kensy."

That gold eye focused on her once more. *"Kensy,"* the deep voice murmured. *"I am not familiar with that name, but we dragons have never been as interested in dividing the land as humans have."* The dark snout moved from side to side. *"Nay, that name matters little to me. However, Cosley is a good line, if I recall."*

"Now then," Mama Dragon muttered. *"I think a quick explanation of the dragonbond is in order before I execute your punishment."*

"What?" Gemi cried.

The black colt, who had kept himself as still as he could since the large dragon's arrival, snorted then and stepped forward. Flame Tongue hissed and slid between Gemi and that large snout.

"Oh, hush," Mama Dragon said, and she nudged Flame Tongue with her jaw. The smaller dragon only hissed again and hunkered down in front of Gemi. That deep sigh echoed through Gemi's mind once more.

"You know punishment is in order, Flame Tongue. These are the laws of our forest."

"*I will not let you hurt my bondmates, Mama Dragon,*" Flame Tongue hissed. Gemi, awed by the small dragon's determination, reached out and laid a hand on her back. The red and purple dragon flicked a humming thought towards the girl in appreciation.

That deep rumble echoed again. "*Bondmates, Flame Tongue?*" The gold eye turned to the colt. "*You have been busy today.*" The gold gaze shifted back to the smaller dragon. "*But I never said anything about hurting any of you, child.*"

Confusion echoed through Gemi's mind, so thick that she didn't know whose was whose. "*But the punishment for trespassing humans is death, as is the punishment for bonding with them,*" Flame Tongue trilled.

"*Normally, it is,*" Mama Dragon answered. She turned her gold gaze to Gemi, who swallowed under the scrutiny of that heavy gaze. "*But you are both young, and both children and dragonbonds are to be cherished, not destroyed.*"

"So...the punishment?" Gemi asked quietly, not sure she really wanted to know.

"*Exile from the Northeast Forest. None of you are to return to this forest for the remainder of your lives.*"

Gemi stared up into that large gold eye. *Exile? That's it?*

Even as disbelief filled her, so too did sadness, panic, and fear; emotions she knew weren't her own. Turning her gaze to Flame Tongue, Gemi found that the small dragon had laid her head on the ground, and she was quivering.

Leave my home? The thought drifted into Gemi's mind, and the girl felt her heart ache as she realized what exactly exile meant for the small dragon. *Where will I go? How will I survive?* Flame Tongue suddenly whined. *I will be killed by the first human that sees me.*

"Nay, you won't," Gemi said.

She leaned against the dragon's back and tried to hug her, but she couldn't really get her arms around the large creature. Small she might be for her species, but she was definitely much bigger than Gemi.

"I won't let them."

That red and purple head turned, and Gemi met the scarlet gaze. "*You would stand by me when we have only just met?*"

Gemi lifted her chin. "You would stand up against a much larger dragon for me. Why shouldn't I do the same for you?"

Mama Dragon rumbled softly. "*Aye, a good match you two make. Already, the dragonbond is strong and only growing stronger.*"

Gemi looked back up at the gold eye. "You said you'd explain the dragonbond before punishing us."

"*I did. The dragonbond is a permanent connection, mental, spiritual, and emotional, that dragons can form with other creatures if we so desire. We generally stick to sentient creatures,*" the large dragon eyed the colt, "*but, obviously, it is not necessary.*"

The colt snorted and stepped closer to Gemi and Flame Tongue. "*I'm sentient enough, dragon!*"

The horse's indignation only seemed to amuse Mama Dragon, and she turned back to Flame Tongue. Nudging her neck, she murmured, "*This will not be the last time we meet, Flame Tongue.*" When the smaller dragon lifted her head and cooed curiously, the large dragon added, "*Your dragonbond is precious, youngling, and, if it is threatened, I will do everything I can to protect it and you. Do you understand?*"

Flame Tongue nodded slowly, and Gemi felt a wave of awe sweep through her. The girl thought she understood. She didn't know exactly who Mama Dragon was, but to have this large, powerful creature promising to help them as well as she could was comforting.

"*Now,*" Mama Dragon continued, "*the three of you had best leave now before any centaurs come along and start asking questions.*" With that, the large dark head pulled back, and the glittering darkness that had filled the forest disappeared.

Flame Tongue shuddered as Mama Dragon left. When Gemi pressed curiously, the dragon told her that a centaur would most likely require their deaths as the logical solution for their crimes. Agreeing that it was best to leave quickly, Flame Tongue helped Gemi mount the colt, and they returned to the San River.

Chapter 3

Gemi's thoughts returned to the present as she leaned back in her saddle and glanced up at the forest canopy. Flame was still wheeling above the trees, flying higher than before as she nursed the embarrassment Shadow had induced. Gemi sighed. Her bondmates were her best friends, but there were times, like now, when the two acted like they couldn't get along.

Flame blamed herself for dragonbonding with a horse of all creatures, but Gemi knew the two were as close to each other as they were to her. However, even after two years, Shadow still felt the need to prove himself, and he sometimes pushed it too far. It was the very reason he had run off with her on that first day.

Looking for a glimpse of Flame's beautiful gem-tones through the distant canopy, Gemi's thoughts drifted again.

She remembered the dragon's fear about crossing the San when they left the Northeast Forest. According to her, there was a barrier that kept all magical creatures within the borders of the forest. They couldn't even cross the edges of the forest that bordered countries where magical creatures roamed freely.

When the three of them had managed to cross without anything happening, Flame had speculated that their bond canceled out the magic. Gemi herself had never tried to understand the logic of magic, even after two years of being bonded to a dragon.

Their return to Cosley Estate later that day had tested Gemi's determination to protect their bond just as Mama Dragon had tested Flame's. Gemi's father had wanted to get rid of the colt, whom Gemi had named Shadow Racer for his desire to race anything, even his own shadow.

When Lord Jem had told the stable hands to dispose of the horse, Gemi had cried out, and Flame had dropped down from the sky, where she had been circling. The appearance of the dragon had terrified everyone. The knights and soldiers had pulled their swords, while those who were unarmed had run.

In response, Gemi had placed herself in front of her bondmates in order to protect both from her father's men. She'd even pulled her own sword, despite knowing she couldn't defeat one of her father's best kights in a one-on-one fight, let alone stand against the full force of Cosley Estate's defenses.

Her defense of the two had resulted in a yelling match between Gemi and her father that had nearly ended with Gemi leaving the Estate of her own accord for the first time. It had taken the threat of her running away with both creatures, as well as the insistence that both were her bondmates, for Lord Jem to order his men to sheathe their weapons and leave both horse and dragon be.

Her father didn't fully accept either of her bondmates, though, until nearly a month later. Their family had ridden to Farvis to spend a couple days in the city. When they were riding back, their group was attacked by a large Fayralese raiding party.

Gemi smiled as she remembered that fight. It was the first time she'd been able to actually use the skills she had been learning since she was four. She'd been pulled from Shadow's back, but Flame, who had been keeping pace with their party, had dropped on the man, dug her front claws into his shoulders, and lifted him away. Shadow had reared and struck down a second man with his front hooves, and, pulling her sword, Gemi had wounded and disarmed a third who'd approached Shadow from the rear.

They had spared the lives of all three men, much to Lord Jem's surprise. However, the duke had been all too happy to have the three men captured and questioned. According to Gemi's mentors, the questioning had led to a successful battle half a season later. Gemi had grinned for days after being told that, happy to have helped in the war for the first time.

Following that, Lord Jem couldn't deny that Gemi worked well with the horse and dragon. Not only had they saved her life, they had shown that they could control themselves in battle. The duke and duchess had soon accepted the two as part of their lives.

"You would think that, after all these years, they would understand me better," Gemi muttered. "They had to know I would hate being given a *man* as my tutor."

A soft snort echoed against Gemi's mind. "*I told you she would get back to it on her own,*" Flame cooed to Shadow.

Gemi narrowed her eyes. When had they traded that thought?

"*You were distracted, Gemi,*" Shadow answered, flicking his ears back. "*And, aye, Flame, you were correct. She always reconsiders her reasons for leaving eventually. As usual, you have a better memory of such things than I do.*"

The compliment soothed the last of Flame's embarrassment, and she crooned affectionately.

Gemi growled, refusing to let the affection bounding through the bond distract her from the implications of her bondmates' words. "We are not going back." She couldn't believe they still thought they would be.

"*Nay, of course not,*" Shadow nickered, unconcerned. "*But that's a lot of people we're leaving behind. We just thought you might want to be sure your reason is strong enough to justify leaving everyone without saying anything.*"

Gemi grumbled. She knew they were leaving behind a lot. Cosley Estate was her life. Her parents were there. The knights who had trained her were there. Even stupid, stubborn Jake Caffers, who never cared that she was the duke's heir, was there.

"I'm not going back!" she shouted. Rustling filled the air then as a flock of birds took flight from some of the lower branches of the surrounding trees. Shadow snorted. "I'm not," Gemi muttered more quietly.

"*But it cannot hurt to go over the reasons again, can it?*" Flame cooed. She had flown lower and was once again circling close to the forest canopy.

Gemi huffed. "Father wants a *man* to teach me to be a lady. What could a man possibly know about being a lady?"

Flame hummed. "*Well, your society is rather patriarchal.*"

Gemi wrinkled her nose. They'd been bondmates for two years, and Gemi was still thrown by some of the words that the dragon used. "What does that have to do with anything?"

Shadow snorted. "*She means that men are the ones who define a woman's place in human society, right?*" Gemi nodded slowly, pursing her lips. "*Well, so why can't a man know the place of a lady well enough to teach you to be one?*"

Gemi wrinkled her nose again. "Now you're just playing destruction's advocate. You know I hate what it means to be a lady."

"*Aye, we know,*" Flame answered. Her mental voice didn't carry the same harried tone others' would have. "*Ladies do not bear the same rights and liberties as their male counterparts, even if they have the same abilities as said counterparts.*"

Gemi rolled her eyes. "Do you have to make it sound so high and mighty, Flame?" The dragon trilled in response.

"*Well, just for the sake of playing destruction's advocate,*" Shadow nickered, taking on a tone that forcefully reminded Gemi that, despite being the youngest age-wise, the horse was the most mature of their group. "*What would you have done if your parents had hired a lady to tutor you like you thought they would?*"

Gemi sighed, feeling harassed. "I was already resigned to being trained as a lady. I would have accepted it."

Snorts echoed, both in her mind and aloud. "*Hardly,*" Flame responded, and Gemi frowned.

"I would have."

"*We've been with you for two years now, Gemi,*" Shadow replied. "*You can't lie to us. We all know you would have run the moment you met your new tutor, female or male.*"

Gemi's cheeks heated, and she pursed her lips. *The problem with bondmates is their insistence on knowing you better than anyone else.*

"So?" she asked petulantly.

Flame sighed. "*So, how do you think a lady would have responded when you simply ran out of the room in denial of her presence?*" Gemi opened her mouth to answer, but Flame quickly added, "*How do you think she would respond when you did it every time she tried to teach you something you didn't like?*"

Gemi snapped her mouth shut. Her cheeks burned as she considered the dragon's words. A lady—*a true lady,* she thought sharply—would decide that Gemi wasn't worth the trouble. As much as Gemi might like the thought of her tutor giving up on her instead of the other way around, the thought of the disappointed look her mother would give her afterwards hurt too much.

Gemi reached up and tugged at a strand of hair. "She'd give up," she whispered, though she knew her bondmates had heard her thoughts. She could feel pressure beginning to build in her eyes.

Warm comfort filled her mind, even as Shadow nickered, "*And if your tutor was male?*"

Gemi sighed and closed her eyes, leaning into Flame's offered comfort. "He might actually be stubborn enough to deal with me." Amusement filtered into her mind through the dragonbond, and Gemi made a face. "I'm a pain sometimes, aren't I?"

"*You can be,*" Shadow answered. Flame sent him a stinging thought. "*Oy, I was just being honest.*"

Gemi giggled. "That's all right, Flame. He's right, I know." She sighed and scrubbed at her eyes. "Flame, how long have we been gone?" When Flame answered that it had been a few hours, Gemi nodded and tugged lightly at Shadow's reins. "Let's head home, you two. We should be able to make it back by nightfall, right?"

"*Just,*" Flame answered and circled back towards Cosley Estate.

~~*~*

The sun was just lowering towards the western horizon when Flame caught the thick scent of smoke. She had caught whiffs of it before, but she had thought nothing of it. Now, she realized that what she had previously mistaken for storm clouds were dark, billowing clouds of smoke. They hung in the sky to the northwest; in the exact direction they were headed.

Nay! Her thought was sharp enough to rouse her bondmates.

"*Flame, what's wrong?*" Gemi asked, her mental voice sounding more relaxed than it had several hours before.

Once she had made the decision to accept a man as her tutor for 'lady-training', she had begun to consider what Flame and Shadow had already recognized: that he would be just another male mentor from whom she could learn. Shadow had even pointed out that she might learn how to put what he taught her towards being a 'gentleman'. The idea had gained snorts from all of them.

Flashing an image of what she saw through the dragonbond and offering a prayer to the gods in the hope that the fire it represented was not where she feared, Flame winged quickly towards the smoke. Shadow, who had been following the Evonese Highway for the past half hour, broke into a canter.

By the time Flame reached the source of the smoke, she was fighting a scream that clawed through her chest and throat. *Cosley Estate is burning*

36

to the ground! The thought echoed again and again through her mind as she circled above what used to be her home.

The manor was little more than burning rubble and a single stone wall that held the large fireplace that had been the central fixture of the family's large, fancy dining room. The stable, too, had caved in on itself, and flames danced merrily over what remained. Even the fields and the orchard had been set aflame and were sending up thick waves of black smoke.

What made the urge to scream worse was the scent of burnt flesh that filled Flame's nostrils, even at this height. She may be a fire dragon, but, to her, fire was sacred, meant to be used sparingly and with care.

This? This was a desecration of everything Flame had been raised to believe.

Flame was just beginning to identify the different creatures that had been slaughtered—humans, horses, cattle, among others, many of which had been burned in the fires—when Shadow cantered up the road that led north from the highway between burning fields and stumbled to a halt. Shock echoed through the dragonbond as Flame's two bondmates simply stared at the blatant burning destruction of their home that only seemed to become more visible as the sun's light died.

"Flame?" The mental voice was faint, and Flame barely recognized the lost childlike tone as Gemi's. *"Is...?"*

Flame mentally wrapped herself around the girl. This had been home to Flame and Shadow for only the last two years. They both had had homes before this, though neither would have dreamed of willingly and permanently turning their backs on this one.

But Gemi had never known anything else despite the multiple times the three of them had left the Estate. Cosley Estate had always been everything to their human. She had even been raised with the knowledge that, one day, the Estate would be hers to run and protect. And now...

"Flame." That mental voice was Shadow's, much stronger and more confident than their human's. *"Can you tell who all was...?"* Despite the strength of his mental voice, even Shadow could not say what was on all of their minds.

Flame did not answer. Instead, she dove closer to the remains of the manor, circling once before dropping straight down into the still burning ruins. Trying her best to ignore the despair that was beginning to wash through the dragonbond, Flame dug past greedy flames, looking for some sign that what all of her senses were telling her was not true.

Flame began her search in the area of the ruins where the Lord's Chambers had stood. She knew Lady Kit tired easily during the day and often retired to the Chambers in the afternoon. Lord Jem would have sat with her, especially after the confrontation with Gemi earlier that day.

Flame did not bother to search for specific human remains. The stench of burnt flesh was stronger now that she was on the ground, and she knew the fire would have destroyed such evidence beyond recognition. She would not be able to determine if specific servants, like the young Jake Caffers, had died in the fire, but most nobles always carried certain identifying items that would most likely survive.

Unfortunately, her search bore fruit. Lady Kit's favorite jewels, which Flame knew from Gemi's memory had been worn by the lady earlier in the day, glowed amidst the crumbling ruins. Moments later, she uncovered Lord Jem's sword, distinguishable by the remains of the fine design of the hilt. It lay discarded nearby, another, lesser blade buried tip-down in the rubble only a foot away. The scream clawed at her throat again as she considered the implications of her discovery.

Although Flame held her own back, a scream did tear through the silence, and Flame whipped her head around towards it. Gemi knelt on the ground beside Shadow, her body rocking over her knees. The scream that ripped through her was so filled with despair that Flame couldn't fight the whine that began in the back of her own throat in answer.

Why? Why? Why?

The thoughts spilled into Flame's mind through the dragonbond, and the dragon's chest ached from the pain filling her bondmate. She turned to go to Gemi to try to comfort her.

As she turned, something else caught her eye.

The stone wall, which had stood as one side of the manor's great dining hall, was not the same as Flame remembered from Gemi's memories. Burnt into the side that had faced the dining hall were words that filled Flame with dread.

'*May this land be cursed as a no-man's land,*' the words read, '*for those who claim it can never have it and those who have it can never claim it. May Maurus do with it as he wills.*'

Despite the fire surrounding the dragon, cold suddenly flushed through her. It was one thing for the Fayralese—for no one else would have destroyed the Estate so thoroughly—to destroy their home and kill everyone in it. But that they had also invoked Maurus, the immortal they considered to control destruction and who was thought to rule over the Land of the Lost and Damned, was beyond the pale. Those words could only mean that the land would bear no more life—plant, animal, or human—and any life lost this day was damned to Maurus' destructive care.

Unable to contain her own despair any longer, Flame lifted her head and released the scream that clawed at her chest and up her throat. Vaguely, she heard Gemi's scream renew, and Shadow joined his own mournful screams to theirs.

None of them were sure how long they stayed there, spilling their sorrow to the world. Eventually, Gemi's throat gave out, and she collapsed into quiet sobs. Flame let her own screams taper to a soft, steady whine, and she finally pulled herself from the ruins of the only home Gemi had ever known.

When she reached her bondmates, Flame gathered their human against her chest, attempting to give her a comfort she herself did not feel. Shadow sidled up beside them and leaned into Flame, seeking and offering consolation that none of them could truly provide.

They sat like that for only a few minutes before Flame finally lifted her scarlet eyes to the now dark sky. They could not remain here, no matter their despair. This land was no longer safe for them, and they had to find shelter for Gemi, if nothing else.

Forcing her unwilling body to move, Flame helped Gemi to mount Shadow once more, and the three bondmates slowly left the ruins of Cosley Estate behind.

~~*~*

On the eastern bank of the San River, a large glittering darkness rested, gold eyes narrowed against the darkness of the night. Even from this distance, Mama Dragon could feel the despair that filled the dragonbond she had sworn to protect two years previously, and the old dragon mourned. Protection from danger was what she had sworn to provide, but emotional trauma, even of this magnitude, was not something Mama Dragon had the ability to challenge.

"Why do you sit here to watch something that you can only See with magic, Mama Dragon?"

The words were soft and filled with more than a little mourning. The old dragon swung her head to the side to meet the wise gray eyes of the humanoid being that leant her upper body out of a nearby ash tree.

Mama Dragon sighed and closed her gold eyes. "*Because your presence amplifies my ability to See beyond our forest, Gregoria Ash. You know this.*"

Something brushed against the large dragon's nose, and she opened her eyes to meet the tree nymph's knowing gaze.

"The Eternal One does the same thing for you, Mama Dragon." The dragon turned her own gaze away from the nymph. "Why not lie by it in the comfort of your own lair?"

Mama Dragon sighed and laid her large head upon the ground, bare inches from the water of the San. The Eternal One was the oldest, largest tree that stood at the center of the Northeast Forest. Mama Dragon had claimed the tree for herself long ago, centuries before Evon had been formed and the magical creatures had agreed to be restricted to this forest.

Despite the claim, Mama Dragon had been avoiding The Eternal One more and more recently. The longer she stayed near it, the more she Saw things that scared her, things she knew she could not prevent. How could she explain this to a creature who had not yet seen half the number of years that Mama Dragon had?

"What does The Eternal One show you that you do not wish to See, Mama Dragon?"

The old dragon snorted and opened one gold eye to glare at the nymph. Trust the nymph elder to know her well enough to read even her silences.

"You know there are some things I cannot tell you, Gregoria Ash," she muttered. *"That is what The Eternal One would show me."*

The nymph nodded. "You fear for the future of the immortal realms, then."

Mama Dragon eyed the tree nymph. *"Not necessarily,"* she murmured. *"My fear is more for the effect it will have on our own realm."*

The nymph hummed and sank a little further into her ash tree. Mama Dragon recognized the nymph's reaction as fear.

"Soon?" the nymph asked.

A deep, humorless rumble shook the old dragon's chest. *"I have lived for a millennium, Gregoria Ash. What, to me, is soon?"*

The nymph shivered then and disappeared into her tree. The dark dragon sighed and turned her gaze back across the San River. Despair, deep and dark and growing, filled her mind as she focused once more on the dragonbond she had sworn to protect.

One day, she would be required to fulfill that oath.

For now, she could do nothing more than wait.

Chapter 4

7 years later
30 Late Summer, 224
Magger's Line Inn
Just west of Calay, Cautzel
Western province of Evon

Kayley Magger huffed and dropped a tray of dirty dishes onto the kitchen counter, startling Honbrie. The cook eyed her worriedly.

"Tha' bad, Miss Magger?"

Kayley released a quiet scream of frustration and threw her hands in the air. "I hate soldiers!"

Honbrie hummed. Moving to the door that Kayley had come in through, she pushed it open a bit.

"I don' know," she murmured appreciatively as she scanned the inn's common room. "I rather think they look qui' handsome in their uniforms an' all."

Kayley snorted. "Aye, an' you don' 'ave to deal with their attitudes when they're far in their drinks, either."

The cook frowned and let the door fall shut. "Aren' they s'posed to be preparin' for an assault on the docks tomorrow?"

Kayley harrumphed and began to gather dishes of food to take out to her 'customers'. "They say they're 'ere for the pirates, but tha' don' seem to 'fect their vices none. Not a one of 'em 'as had less than three pints, an' I canna say no 'cause it's on the king's gold." Giving another huff, she lifted the new tray and pushed back through the door.

The woman grimaced as she pushed past several men standing near the kitchen door and received no less than two slaps and a pinch to her rump. She did her best to ignore the soldiers' leers and jibes as she deposited the plates in front of their respective diners.

As she deposited the last plate, one particularly drunken fellow—she was pretty sure he was on his eighth pint—sneered, "Where's the real owner, wench?" The jibe was followed by raucous laughter from the man's tablemates.

Stiffening, Kayley straightened and just barely refrained from punching the man. Her right to ownership of the normally quiet Magger's Line Inn was always a sore subject for the widow.

The only reason it was still in her possession was because the deed to both the inn and the land it stood on, a small parcel that lay on the outskirts of the port city of Calay, still bore her dead lifemate's name. Her lifemate had also left her with enough money to support herself and the inn well enough.

It was a small quirk of the laws, but until Kayley was forced to sell the place, or lifebonded again, she could still run it herself. Kayley had decided that she would not desecrate her lifemate's memory by doing either.

Determining to ignore the drunk—normally she would have cut off his drink several pints ago and just thrown him out for the comment—Kayley turned back to the kitchen, but a hand gripped her arm, stopping her progress.

"Oy, wench!" the drunken man jeered. "Don' you get lone'y runnin' this place 'lone? Maybe you can warm my bed t'night, an'—"

The hand disappeared as the words cut off with a yelp. Kayley turned, surprised, to find the man sprawled across his table, one of his arms twisted up behind his back. Holding him down was a rather large man that Kayley knew hadn't been in her inn before; she would have remembered serving such a fine fellow.

"That is not how you speak to a lady, soldier," the drunk's assailant spoke clearly.

"She ain' no lady, you—"

The drunk yelped again as his assailant twisted his arm back further. "Alrigh', alrigh', she's a lady. 'M sorry!"

The large man dropped the drunken soldier back into his chair. The soldier turned to his assailant with an open mouth, but whatever he'd meant to say disappeared, as did the blood from his face.

"M-m-m'lord!" the soldier finally managed to spit out.

Kayley frowned. *Milord?* Only nobles had the right to that address, but this man looked nothing like any of the nobles she had ever seen. His clothes were plain, rather dusty even. Only his boots, as dusty as the rest of him, looked to be of good quality.

Once the soldier fell quiet—in fact, the entire common room seemed to have fallen silent with the large man's arrival—the newcomer turned and offered Kayley a small bow. It was only then that she noticed the fancy sword hanging from his right hip. The hilt was lined with delicate gold and silver filigree, and it took a moment for Kayley to recognize the shape as that of a dancing dolphin.

The innkeeper lifted her gaze back to the man's face as she realized that, not only was this man a noble despite all appearances, he was the duke of Cautzel, Lord Tern Chanser. It was said that the duke had taken a liking to the playful sea animal after a large pod saved the lives of him and his men in the sea battle that was later dubbed the Battle of Dolphin Bay.

"I apologize for my men's behavior, Miss...?" The duke glanced at her questioningly.

"Magger," she answered, lifting her chin. "Kayley Magger."

The large man's eyes registered only a flicker of surprise before he nodded. "Miss Magger. This is a fine establishment you have here. If I had known my men would reward your hospitality with so little respect, I would have left orders with them to ration their drinks to no more than a pint per man."

The duke's eyes never left Kayley's, but his disappointment in his men was still apparent. Even along the edges of the room, she noticed every man set down his drink, pushing it away with a look of unease. The man who had grabbed Kayley was beginning to look gray, and the innkeeper worried he would faint or be ill.

Stepping further from his table just in case, Kayley nodded to the duke. "Thank 'e, M'lord. Shall I close the taps then?"

Lord Chanser smiled and nodded. "Aye, please, if you would be so kind." Kayley turned back to the kitchen, pausing a moment when the duke added, "And, if you are not too busy, maybe you could bring me a plate of food?"

The woman flashed the duke a quick smile. "O' course, M'lord."

As she sauntered back to the kitchen without incident, she knew that, for the first time tonight, she would be quite happy to bring someone their food.

Honbrie was leaning against the wall next to the door, and she jumped when Kayley pushed through. "Wha' was that abou', Miss Magger?" she questioned as she followed the innkeeper further into the kitchen.

As Kayley dished up a plate for Lord Chanser, she told the cook what had happened. When she mentioned the duke, Honbrie bustled back over to the door and pushed it open.

"Tha's the duke?" the cook breathed.

Kayley giggled. "Aye, though you mightn' know it by lookin' at 'im. 'E's got a real fancy sword wit' a dolphin 'ilt, so I doubt it could be anyone else."

Honbrie sighed, though she didn't leave the door. Shaking her head, Kayley replaced the lid on the pot from which she'd been serving. "Honbrie, can you close up the taps? The duke's cut his men off, and I canna imagine anyone else comin' in tonight for anythin'."

Honbrie sighed, somewhat mournfully this time, and pulled back from the door. Before it fully shut, she gasped and pushed it open again. "Miss Magger, c'mere!" The cook hastily beckoned the innkeeper towards the door.

Kayley frowned and carried the plate of food towards the door. "Wha's wrong, Honbrie?"

The cook turned wide eyes to her employer. "Y'migh' wanna get ou' there now, Miss Magger." She lowered her voice to a whisper and hissed, "The Wanderer's jus' arrived."

"Oh, sweet Carith!" Kayley breathed and bustled past the cook.

True, she usually welcomed the Wanderer's arrival at the beginning of the season. However, she had hoped that the boy would have the good sense to avoid her inn with such a heavy presence of the king's men in the city.

Now, she could only imagine the kind of trouble that would arise between the Wanderer and a roomful of the king's men.

~~*~*

Lord Tern Chanser directed the drunken soldier's tablemates to remove the ill-looking man from the inn. As they carried him outside, Tern seated himself at the vacated table and groaned, scrubbing at his face.

When he'd left the king and the other dukes to check on his own soldiers, who had been moved to the inns on the outskirts of the city, he certainly hadn't expected to find them drinking away their wits. His Majesty was expecting to rise with the sun to deal with the commotion at the docks, and, at this rate, Tern doubted his men would be capable of doing so. Rubbing his hand over his face once more, the duke considered the trouble they would face the following morning.

It had been nearly half a season since Tern had learned about the first of the recent pirate attacks on Cautzelian merchant ships. The duke had been surprised by the news at first. Since the peace treaty with Fayral two years before, Tern's province had been fairly peaceful. Despite rumors of a growing threat from rebellious groups since the war's end, there had only been two pirate attacks, and the two ships had been caught or sunk soon after each attack.

Besides the recent rareness of such attacks, Tern's surprise had also stemmed from the unusual survival rate of the first merchant ship's crew. Nearly half the crew had been carried to land by sea creatures with little injury.

That generosity, or oversight, was short-lived as the remains of first one, then another, merchant ship were discovered with no sign of any survivors. It was only the willingness of a couple of dolphins and a whale to provide the name of such a violent vessel to Tern's Animal Mage that assured him they were looking for a single ship: the *Pretty Pauper*.

With the news of the third attack and Tern's own ships no closer to capturing the oddly elusive pirate ship, the duke finally turned to Caypan, and the king, for assistance. While His Majesty had been quite happy to provide whatever help he could, he had hesitated to send too much assistance.

After all, how many ships and men were necessary to take down a single pirate ship?

It had been Lord Seyan Lefas, duke of the southern province of Baylin, who had pointed out that this could be just the beginning. The rumors of the growing threat of the rebellious groups were connected to a rumored leader. Although he was referred to differently in each province, the rumors were insistent that the titles all referred to the same man.

Tern had scoffed when Seyan mentioned the rumored Ghost. The rebel leader was known as the Wanderer here in Cautzel, but, with the relative peace Tern had been seeing, he had found it difficult to believe such a man existed.

That disbelief was only supported by the fact that the rumors mentioned nothing about the rebel leader's true identity. Even the man's title in the eastern province of Tarsur, Nadie, which Tern might have believed was a name, actually meant 'nobody' in Pecalini, according to Lord Peln Sageo.

44

Since learning that, Tern had been prone to believe that the man was just a story made up by those who couldn't deal with peace after so many decades of war.

However, His Majesty had taken heed of Seyan's warning. Ships had been launched from Caypan's port to seek out the *Pretty Pauper* and herd her towards Port Calay, while knights and soldiers had been sent to Cautzel's largest port city in order to bring her crew to justice.

Much to Tern's surprise, His Majesty had also insisted on leading the men himself. "If this is only the beginning," he'd explained, "I want to be where I can provide the most assistance."

And, of course, when the king went to battle, so too did his counsel: Tern and the other three dukes.

Despite Seyan's warning, none of them had expected to arrive in Calay to find not only the *Pretty Pauper* anchored out in the harbor, but the entire port filled with ships flying the red flag known as Maur's Blood. No fewer than thirty ships had occupied Calay when Tern left the docks a few hours earlier, and His Majesty's ships, which numbered no more than half that, were keeping their distance.

Tern snorted. *Understandably so.*

The creak of a door opening broke through the inn's still-quiet common room, jarring Tern from his thoughts. Expecting to see one of his own men, the duke flicked an annoyed glance towards the inn's entrance.

He blinked and stared when, instead of a soldier uniformed in the blue of Cautzel, his gaze landed on a man whose plain, dusty clothes and pack betrayed him as a traveler.

The man stumbled through the doorway a couple steps before halting, his eyes scanning slowly over the common room. Those soldiers who hadn't glanced up before did so as the inn's door swung shut.

Silence fell as several of Tern's men reached for their weapons, but the duke stood and lifted a hand to still them. Even so, his eyes never left the traveler's form. Two swords—one long and straight, the other short and curved—hung from either side of the man's belt. Tern could also see the fletching of several arrows sticking out from behind the man's back on one side and a bow attached to his pack.

What really made Tern pause was the leather band wrapped around the traveler's right thigh. While he had never seen such a thing himself, his eastern counterpart—Lord Peln Sageo, Duke of Tarsur—often spoke of similar bands being worn by the mountain thieves to carry their throwing knives.

If he is a Tarsurian thief, Tern thought warily, laying his hand lightly on the hilt of his sword, *then he is a long way from home.*

"I'm 'fraid I've no more rooms t'nigh', young sir."

The innkeeper's voice cut through the tension in the room, and Tern glanced at Miss Magger as she laid a plate on the table in front of him. Her eyes, like the traveler's, moved around the room, though more quickly.

"I doub' you'll find much o' anythin' further into town, either."

A beat of silence followed the innkeeper's words, and Tern turned his gaze back to the new arrival. Focusing on his face, the duke realized with a start that, despite the ample supply of weapons, the traveler—who actually looked more boy than man—was not a threat. Although his eyes had seemed wary at first glance, Tern realized now that they were half-closed from exhaustion, not suspicion. The boy had even fallen back towards the door and was leaning his right shoulder against the wall.

"Did somethin' 'appen?" the boy asked softly, and Tern felt a pang of sympathy at the tired, scratchy tone.

Tern spotted Miss Magger glancing at him briefly. Nodding to the innkeeper, Tern approached the newcomer, catching the boy's left upper arm when he seemed to waver dangerously. The boy winced at the touch, and Tern frowned and lightened his grip.

"I suspect we can find a spare bed for you, lad."

The boy frowned up at Tern, who startled at the sight of his violet eyes. He had never seen anyone with eyes that color before.

"I wouldn' wanna put anyone ou', sir."

"Nonsense," Tern answered and swung his gaze over his men, many of whom had begun to protest. "After the night my men have had, some of them won't be able to claim a bed anyway."

That quieted the roomful of soldiers, but the boy was already shaking his head.

"There be no need fo' tha', s—"

The boy fell silent as his gaze lowered, and Tern could tell the boy was now eyeing his dolphin sword. After a moment, the boy added a quiet, "M'lord."

He can't be from Tarsur, Tern thought, amending his previous thought, *not if he knows Cautzel well enough to know of my interest in dolphins.*

The longer he spoke with the strange boy, the more intrigued by him Tern became, despite knowing he had larger issues on which to focus. Maybe, if the boy did stay here, Tern would be able to learn more about him once they had dealt with the pirates.

"If there be trouble in the city, M'lord," the boy continued, lifting his gaze back up to Tern's face, "I'm sure I'd rather 'void it. If I could maybe ge' some food and news, though…"

The boy's gaze swung past Tern, who turned to see Miss Magger already nodding and turning back to the kitchen.

"Of course," Tern answered and guided the boy back to the table Tern had occupied before the lad's arrival.

As soon as they'd seated themselves, the innkeeper returned and placed a warm plate in front of the boy. As both Tern and the boy tucked in, the common room once again began to fill with the chatter of the soldiers' conversations.

As they ate, Tern told the boy about the recent events. When the duke mentioned the name of the pirate ship they were after, the boy's shoulders tensed, and he winced and paused mid-chew.

Tern frowned. "Are you all right?"

The boy didn't answer right away. Instead, he ran his right hand over the top of his head, smoothing back a few loose, black hairs, and dragged his long horsetail over his shoulder to hang down into his lap. Only as he began to play with the horsetail did he lift his violet gaze to Tern's.

The duke was struck by just how young the boy looked as he swallowed and muttered, "I think I seen the *Pretty Pauper* once, but I didn' realize 'twas a pirate ship."

Tern eyed the boy and nodded slowly. He wondered when the boy would have seen the ship, but he didn't ask since the lad seemed rather disturbed by the thought. Instead, he continued providing the news for which the boy had asked.

By the time the duke had finished explaining the situation, the boy had already completed his meal. Draining the tankard of water he'd requested, the lad stood.

"Are you leaving already?" Tern asked, surprised. His own plate was still half-full, and he'd hoped to learn more about the odd boy.

The lad offered a tired smile and nodded, reaching for his coinpurse. "If you don't mind, Milord, I would like to find a place to bed down for the night as quickly as possible."

Tern blinked as the boy searched through his coinpurse. His sudden clarity of speech surprised the duke, who was unused to hearing such enunciation from commoners. When the boy dropped a few silvers to the table, Tern shook his head.

"There is no need for that."

The boy, who had bent to retrieve his pack, turned his gaze back to the duke in confusion.

"We have kept you from finding a bed for the night with the trouble here in Calay. The least we can do is pay for your meal."

The boy opened his mouth, but, before he could respond, the innkeeper spoke up from behind him.

"I had my stableman give your moun' a full brushin' 'fore resaddlin' him. 'E's been fed and watered, so 'e's ready when you are."

The boy nodded and turned to the door, but Tern caught his left wrist. With a soft sound, the boy stopped, his right hand going to his left shoulder, and his gaze turned back to Tern.

The duke frowned at the sign of pain, but he wasn't to be deterred. Folding the boy's silvers into his hand, Tern met that violet gaze and murmured, "I insist."

Violet eyes widened slightly before the boy ducked his head and muttered a quick thanks. The boy then turned, and, for the first time, Tern caught a glimpse of what looked like a large piece of stiff leather at the small of the boy's back beneath his pack. Before he could make out what it was, the boy was out the door.

It wasn't until Tern had begun to eat again that it occurred to him that he had never even asked the boy his name.

~~*~*

The black-haired 'boy' left the Magger's Line as quickly as possible. It wasn't until horse and rider were traveling away from the port city that the 'boy' relaxed.

"*Flame?*" Gemi questioned the fiery presence that pressed against her mind.

"*You nearly gave yourself away, James,*" the dragon hissed, unwilling to use her bondmate's true name. Even seemingly alone as they were, the trio was always wary of mages, both Animal and Mindspeaker. "*He might have pressed you about how you knew the* Pretty Pauper. *What would you have done then?*"

"*But he didn't,*" Gemi corrected softly.

She didn't have the energy to argue with the dragon, not after traveling hard from the Rebel Camp in Baylin for three days straight, and certainly not with her still injured left shoulder throbbing in complaint.

"*Flame?*" she asked again, pressing her intentions against the dragon's mind.

Flame huffed. "*There is a small copse of trees a little further down the road on the right.*" She offered the image through the dragonbond, and Shadow snorted tiredly.

"*Just a little further, she says,*" the stallion muttered through the bond. "*Funny.*"

Gemi patted the horse on the shoulder. She knew that, no matter how tired she was, Shadow was even more so.

"*And I was so looking forward to a good bed of straw,*" Shadow complained, following her train of thought.

"*And I, a real bed,*" Gemi offered in sympathy. Shadow tossed his head in agreement.

A few minutes later, he turned off the road and eased through the foliage of a dense, little copse. As soon as they were far enough within the trees that no one would be able to see them from the road, the stallion stopped.

Reaching his muzzle around to one side, Shadow lipped Gemi's knee and nickered, "*Off.*" When Gemi took too long, he added, "*Nearly three days straight with you on my back is about enough for me to collapse. Off!*"

"All right, all right," Gemi muttered and swung out of the saddle.

As soon as she finished removing the saddle and saddlebags, the black stallion lowered himself to the ground, ignoring the blanket that still covered his back and the bridle that still surrounded his head. Gemi chuckled slightly, but her amusement lessened a moment later when his thoughts quieted in sleep.

"*He was not kidding,*" Flame whistled softly.

Gemi nodded, not even bothering to lift her gaze towards the tops of the trees, where she knew the dragon was now circling.

"*Nay, he wasn't.*"

Gemi hesitated then as she settled the saddle and bags near her mount. "Flame?" She whispered the name aloud, despite knowing her bondmate wasn't quite close enough to catch the word.

"*Must I?*" the dragon crooned in answer to Gemi's unspoken question. Without waiting for a response, she sighed and flew back towards Calay. "*Very well.*"

"*Thank you, Flame,*" Gemi murmured against her bondmate's mind, keeping the thought far enough away from Shadow's mind that she wouldn't wake him.

As Flame flew towards the harbor to see if the situation was as the duke had described, Gemi laid out her bedroll next to Shadow. Lying down, she considered the man's words. He had said that there had been three attacks on Cautzelian—and, therefore, Evonese—merchant ships, all supposedly by the same ship, the *Pretty Pauper*.

"It doesn't make sense," Gemi muttered aloud. "We've known the *Pretty Pauper* for four years. There's no way Marlen would attack an Evonese ship."

"*Perhaps he was provoked?*" Flame murmured distractedly. "*There is a provision for that in the Pact.*"

Gemi snorted and closed her eyes. "*Aye, there is, but really, Flame? Three times? And merchant ships, at that.*"

The dragon hummed. "*I do not pretend to know the motivations of men, James. You know that.*" Gemi chuckled quietly in agreement. "*However, the duke was not lying.*" Flame merged her mind with Gemi's so the girl could see through her eyes.

Although no lights shone in the harbor this late at night, through her bondmate's eyes, Gemi could still see every single ship that filled it. As Flame scanned the docks, Gemi could see that thirty-two ships lined them, each one flying the red flag of Maur's Blood.

Even as she learned the count of the pirate ships, she noted the large presence of the king's men on the city's docks, overflow from the inns throughout the city.

"*Lord Chanser claimed that he only knew of one pirate ship when he went to the king. I wonder why they decided to bring so many men for a single ship.*"

"*It hardly matters, does it?*" Flame answered with a snort. "*The number of men he did bring just might be enough to face the full force of the Tauresian Pirates.*"

Gemi sighed. "*Aye, it might. Now,*" she added, "*where's the* Pauper?*"

Flame swung her gaze further out towards sea. There, in the middle of the harbor, an all-too familiar ship was anchored.

Gemi cursed softly. She had hoped that there had been a mistake of some kind, but Flame's eyes were not to be tricked. That was definitely the *Pretty Pauper.*

"*And there are fifteen of the king's navy blockading the harbor,*" Flame added, shifting her gaze towards the open sea.

Just as the dragon said, drifting a ways outside of the harbor were fifteen ships, each flying the flag of Evon—a white pegasus rearing over a sword, pointed downwards, on a purple background.

The sight of the flags made Gemi smile, though not in happiness. Rather, it had always amused the girl that the country that banned magical creatures from its borders bore the magical winged horse on its royal flag.

"*Well?*" Flame asked, pulling Gemi from her drifting thoughts.

Gemi blinked her eyes open, pulling her mind from Flame's in the process. "*Well,*" she answered, "*all thirty-three Tauresian Pirate ships are accounted for.*" Flame hummed idly as she flew another circle over the harbor. "*And I doubt the other ships know what trouble the* Pauper *is in.*"

Flame snorted. "*'And if any ship should break this signed agreement, then it is no longer under its protection, and it is the duty of the other signed ships to punish it.' The Pact is pretty clear on that.*"

Gemi nodded and closed her eyes once more. "*Come on back, Flame,*" she murmured as she let her mind drift once more. "*We should both get some sleep before we have to deal with the situation.*"

Flame growled softly as she winged over Calay. "*You have been putting too much strain on your body recently, James. You need to rest.*"

Gemi slowly rolled her head from side to side. "*I'll get some once we've dealt with the* Pauper *tomorrow.*"

"*Why do I doubt that?*" Flame grumbled softly.

A moment later, she dropped to the ground outside the small group of trees and slid into their makeshift camp. Lying out next to Gemi, she nudged the girl's left shoulder with her snout.

Gemi groaned, opening her eyes to glare at the dragon, and shoved at the snake-like jaw. "Leave it be, Flame. You've healed it as well as you can with the poison slowing the process."

The dragon growled softly. "*If you would let me bite you, I would be able to finish the process.*"

Gemi shook her head. "You've never bitten me outside of the bonding process, Flame. You don't even know if it would work." She sighed and closed her eyes again. "I can't afford to go into battle tomorrow with a slowly healing dragon bite on top of a still healing shoulder."

Grumbling filled her mind briefly before Flame subsided with a sigh, engulfing Gemi's upper body in warm air. The breath was soon replaced by hot, firm scales as the dragon pulled Gemi against her furnace-like chest. Gemi sighed happily and fell into the oblivion of sleep.

Chapter 5

Gemi groaned as warmth pressed heavily against her mind, rousing her from sleep. "Jus' a bi' longer," she muttered. A snort answered her, and the heavy warmth in her mind was suddenly accompanied by a sharp nudge to her ribs.

She yelped. Opening her eyes, she found herself eye-to-nose with two snouts, both of which were just visible in the light of a nearby fire. Groaning again, she shoved at both snouts, hoping to rest a bit longer.

"You must wake up now, James," Flame murmured, pushing back against the hand that shoved at her. *"The sun will be rising soon, and you will not be pleased later if you miss your chance to intervene in the coming conflict."*

The girl huffed but dropped her hands. Flame was right, of course. If Gemi didn't discover the truth of the situation on the *Pretty Pauper* before fighting broke out between the pirates and the king's men, she knew she'd never get another chance. Sighing, she waved her bondmates away and climbed to her feet.

"You could have been a little gentler in waking me, y'know," she muttered.

She stretched her arms above her head, wincing as the move pulled at the still healing muscles in her left shoulder, and began to pack up her bedroll.

"You would have gotten the message across just as well."

Shadow snorted and turned his attention to the grass on which she'd been lying. *"I doubt it,"* he nickered softly. Gemi offered the stallion a glare, but he blithely ignored her and began to eat.

Sighing, Gemi focused on saddling him. She cinched his girth a little tight as revenge for the smart remark. When Shadow turned to her with a glare of his own, she simply offered him a smile and put it right. Once saddle and saddlebags were in place, the girl turned to Flame, who was just putting out the small fire.

"If you two are done...?" the dragon murmured, her amusement obvious. *"You should eat something before we leave, James."* With one clawed hand, she offered Gemi a small leaf-wrapped package, which Gemi accepted with closed eyes and lifted nose.

"It smells wonderful, Flame," she muttered before opening the package and tearing into the enclosed meat.

While this was the trio's usual routine when on the road, Gemi was used to obtaining a little more sleep than she had. Flame, who needed less sleep than Gemi, was always the first to wake and, with her specialized skills in hunting and fire, was always the one to make breakfast.

Once she'd eaten, Gemi turned to Shadow, who lifted his head from his grazing. "If you're ready, Shadow, can you head down to the docks? And try to be as inconspicuous as possible."

Shadow snorted, tossing his head. *"It shouldn't be too hard with so many of the king's horses around."* As he left the trees, he added, *"Maybe I'll even run into somebody I know."*

Gemi rolled her eyes and let a smile curl her lips. It was one of Shadow's running jokes that the stallion might meet a horse with whom he'd grown up at the Royal Stables whenever they were near the king's men and their horses.

As far as Gemi knew, he hadn't yet, which she thought was a good thing. She had learned a long time ago that, even without Animal Mages, horses were major gossipers. If any horse had ever recognized Shadow, it would have been reported straight back to Master Ekin, without a doubt.

"Be careful!" Flame growled forcefully.

Gemi slid a hand across the dragon's neck soothingly. She knew it was during times like these that Shadow's usually flippant attitude grated at Flame the most.

"Don't worry," Shadow soothed, his mental voice becoming more serious as he reached the road. *"I'll be safe."*

Flame grumbled softly and swung her scarlet gaze to Gemi. *"Are you ready then?"*

"Nearly."

Knowing that they'd be flying straight to the pirate ship, Gemi removed her boots and stuffed them in her pack. The two daggers that she usually kept sheathed in them went on the right side of her belt, while the short, curved Cautzelian cutlass that she usually kept there replaced the Fayralese longsword on her left.

The dragon eyed the arrangement as Gemi tied her sheathed longsword to the back of her pack with the bow and arrows.

"Will that not be too much weight on your back?"

Gemi swung the pack up onto her back, settling it over both shoulders and grimacing as the pain in her left shoulder flared once more. Flame crooned, but the girl shook her head.

"It'll be all right, Flame. As long as I can drop it before I have to fight, it won't be a problem."

Flame snorted, but lowered her body to the ground so Gemi could clamber onto her back. *"Then let us pray to the gods that you are given the chance to drop it."*

As Gemi settled onto Flame's back and the dragon left the copse and leapt into the air, the girl considered how depressing it was that they assumed she would be forced to fight a group of people she had spent the last four years getting to know. The trio had even spent an entire two seasons—half a year—on the *Pretty Pauper* before Gemi began her current routine of traveling the entire country every season. That had been three and a half years ago; fourteen seasons of two sevendays each spent on the pirate ship.

"*That is over a year altogether,*" Flame muttered idly.

Gemi nodded and sighed, rubbing a hand over the scales that she could reach. She had spent over a year with them, fighting side by side, manning the ship, unifying the pirates.

She shook her head. Now, Marlen, captain of the *Pretty Pauper*, had gone and done something unforgivable, something she had been sure he would never do. He'd broken the Pact and attacked not one, but three Evonese ships, without provocation.

Flame crooned. "*We will learn the truth when we reach the ship.*"

Gemi smiled slightly at her bondmate's attempt to raise her spirits, but the smile didn't last. She didn't know how this could be a simple misunderstanding. And not even the wind tugging at her horsetail, which normally would have delighted her, could distract her from the depressing thoughts.

As the lights of the city below disappeared, Flame muttered, "*You must be quick about this, James. The king's men are already stirring.*"

Gemi merged her mind with the dragon's. Just as Flame had said, she could hear the sounds of men beginning their day, and Flame glanced back to see large crowds of men moving along the docks.

Glancing around the harbor, Flame and Gemi once again eyed the thirty-two pirate ships that lined the docks. Each one, Gemi knew, was prepared to fight the king and his men, if necessary. Gemi only hoped she could find some way to diffuse the situation before the peace she had helped create between the pirates and Evon was torn to shreds.

"*There she is,*" Flame muttered, drawing Gemi's attention to the lone ship that sat in the middle of the harbor. While it was yet too dark for Gemi to see with her own eyes, through Flame's she could see the *Pretty Pauper* swaying slightly, surrounded by its brethren, yet sadly isolated.

Just as Gemi was beginning to wonder how she should board the ship—Flame could land on deck, but that would draw too much attention, and Flame had never been very successful when it came to fighting aboard a ship—the sound of a sharp "Wanderer!" reached Gemi's ears.

She groaned softly. *Well, there goes the element of surprise.*

"*Perhaps not,*" Flame crooned. "*There is no one on deck.*"

Gemi frowned. There were always at least four or five people on deck, even at night.

"Wanderer," the voice said again, and Gemi blinked. The word had sounded far softer this time, barely intelligible to her ears. She glanced around, confused, despite it still being too dark for her to see much.

"*I believe you first heard it through my ears,*" Flame offered.

The dragon then passed along an image of a small boy standing in the ship's crow's nest, one arm waving wildly, the hand of the other cupped around his mouth. Despite the darkness, the image showed Gemi that the boy had dirty blond hair, and his dark eyes were wide and seemed to be filled with…relief?

"Jique?" Gemi hissed, hoping the boy could hear her. The eleven-year-old, who had joined the crew five seasons ago, had always been rather reserved, so she found his sudden agitation odd.

"Oh, thank gods," the boy breathed, though Gemi had to depend on the dragonbond to hear the words. "Ye've got to stop 'im, Wanderer. 'E's gone mad, 'e 'as."

Gemi frowned. She wasn't sure if the boy's words should fill her with hope or dread. From the sound of it, she wouldn't have to fight the entire crew, but she was still hesitant to fight Captain Marlen. The man had become too good of a friend.

Nevertheless, she was certain of one thing.

"Stand back, Jique," she hissed. "Flame'll drop me in with you." And, before the dragon could protest the thought, Gemi clambered over her bondmate's shoulder.

Flame hissed in annoyance even as she caught Gemi's arms in her front claws. *"You should not be doing this with your shoulder still healing."*

When Gemi responded to neither the admonition nor her screaming shoulder, the dragon huffed, circled away from the ship, and swung around so she could approach the crow's nest directly.

The moment Gemi's feet hit the floor of the crow's nest, small arms wrapped around her waist, and Flame hissed in amusement as she swooped away from the ship. *"I will wait in the clouds if you do not mind."*

Gemi nodded, hardly registering her bondmate's words as she attempted to remove the boy from her midsection.

It wasn't that she disliked hugs; she rather enjoyed them. However, the boy's action had placed his head exactly level with her chest, and, despite the fact that she always bound what breasts she had, she was always conscious of the risk of someone learning her true gender that way.

As soon as she'd managed to pull the boy away from her, she thought she understood the reason for the hug. His eyes, which had been wide earlier, now brimmed with tears, and he sniffled softly.

"Jique," she murmured, framing his face in her hands. "Tell me what happened."

Jique sniffed and muttered, "Borlin's a bilge rat, 'e is."

Gemi blinked. That had certainly not been what she'd expected to hear.

"Borlin?" she asked, confused. She knew the name, of course. Borlin was the *Pretty Pauper*'s first mate, Marlen's second. "What does Borlin have to do with this?"

Jique sniffed again and swiped one hand beneath his nose. "'E's been a right fright e'er since 'e stole the cap'ncy from Marlen, 'e 'as. Been 'avin' us attackin' Evonese ships, an' 'e e'en 'ad poor Pockam whipped an' thrown in the Black 'Old for savin' the crew o' the first ship."

Gemi grimaced. Pockam was the *Pauper*'s most powerful Animal Mage, and he had as much compassion for his fellow man as he did for his animals, barring the cruelty of one towards the other.

That he was being held in the Black Hold, where the dead were usually kept until proper services could be held, was rather callous. The Black Hold was tightly sealed to prevent the spread of whatever disease or infection had caused the deaths, and, while the man might be able to breathe, not even the ship's rats would be able to reach the lonely, injured mage.

"And Marlen?" Gemi asked, afraid that her friend had not survived Borlin's takeover. She knew Marlen would not have given up his captaincy without a fight.

"'E's bein' 'eld in the brig, 'e is," Jique answered, offering a small smile through his tears. "Borlin may be 'sistin' on breakin' the Pact, but mos' the rest o' us still say we're Tauresian Pirates."

Gemi felt a smile pull at her lips then as relief filled her. If that was the case, then there would be very few men that she would have to fight. She opened her mouth to ask for more information, but she stopped short as a nicker filled her mind.

"Hurry it up, James! The inns are nearly empty."

Gemi grimaced and acknowledged Shadow's warning. Bending down so her eyes were level with Jique, she murmured, "Can you stay up here and keep an eye out for approaching vessels? I don't want any more surprises than necessary."

Jique nodded enthusiastically. With a grin, Gemi ruffled the boy's hair then swung herself out of the crow's nest and into the rigging. With practiced ease, Gemi climbed swiftly down the rigging towards the bow of the ship.

As soon as she hit the deck, Gemi worked her pack off her shoulders. Borlin, she knew, could be ruthless, and she was sure he'd attack her the moment he spotted her.

Sure enough, just as her pack touched the deck, Gemi heard the tell-tale *schwing* of a sword being unsheathed, and she immediately turned and dropped into a crouch, already reaching for her cutlass. She froze with her sword half-sheathed when she spotted what the slowly growing light revealed.

Borlin stood in front of her, his own cutlass already at hand, but it was the sight of the four large, armed men surrounding him that made her throat go suddenly dry. Gemi mentally cursed herself for not getting all of the information from Jique.

She had known that Borlin had to have some supporters among the crew, or he wouldn't have been able to hold onto the captaincy. However, she hadn't expected his supporters to consist of the four members of the crew that were both good swordsmen and merciless fighters.

I guess I should have.

"Borlin," she greeted with a nod, allowing her cutlass to slide slowly back into its sheath. She straightened from her crouch despite the instincts that screamed for her not to. "I hear tell that you're the new captain. Congratulations."

"Don' give me that, Caffers," Borlin snarled and brandished his cutlass at her. As she eyed the blade warily, she considered the man's use of her false last name, a formality no one on the *Pauper* had used in over three years. "I know why you're 'ere. I ain' gonna let you steal this from me."

She frowned, pretending ignorance. "I don't know what you mean, Borlin. I'm simply here on my seasonal visit. What reason would I have to steal anything from you?"

The man snarled again and took a step towards Gemi. It took everything in her for the girl not to step backwards. She knew she was a good swordsman, but, even if her shoulder hadn't been wounded, five large men still would have been enough to worry her.

"You canna play me for a fool, Caffers. There ain' no way you coulda miss the king's men gatherin' on the docks." Suddenly, the man grinned, and Gemi stiffened. "Soon, the king's men and the other pirates'll be at each other's throats, an' there ain' nothin' you can do 'bout it."

Gemi suddenly felt nauseous. Had he seriously planned a war between Evon and the pirates as well as stealing the captaincy? Such a thing wouldn't be any easier on the *Pretty Pauper* than on any other ship, but the girl knew that some people thrived on the simple idea of utter chaos. She just hadn't expected one of her supposed allies to be one of them.

"Why, Borlin?"

Gemi knew she couldn't afford the time for such questions—the sky had lightened enough that she knew the sun would be rising soon—but she found it hard to believe that she had misjudged someone so badly.

"*Not so much,*" Shadow nickered. He had hidden himself in an alley not far from the docks. "*We knew he wasn't fond of the Pact.*"

"*Yet we did not expect this,*" Flame added as she circled through the clouds. "*He seemed to accept it well enough.*"

"Why doesn' matter, Caffers," Borlin snapped, dragging Gemi's attention away from her bondmates, who pulled back from her mind then. "Wha' matters is that we're gonna kill yeh."

Gemi dropped back into a crouch and eyed the five men. "Five to one isn't very fair odds, Borlin."

Instead of responding, Borlin simply snarled wordlessly and lunged.

Gemi rolled to the side as soon as Borlin moved. As she reached her feet, unsheathing a dagger with her right hand, she heard the clang of several swords striking each other. An accompanying cry indicated that at least one blade had found an unintended target.

For a split second, the girl let a small smirk pull at her lips. Apparently, the crew of the *Pauper* still had no skill when it came to fighting many people against one, and, for the second time in her life, Gemi found herself quite willing to exploit that weakness.

Even as the thought passed through her head, Gemi turned and shoved her knife into the thigh of the nearest man. He yelled and staggered, even as she removed the blade and jumped away from the swing of someone else's sword. Switching the blade to her left hand, Gemi pulled the second dagger with her right and ducked a second swing.

"Stay still!" snapped the man who had just missed her.

She offered him a quick smile as his sword came down again and lifted both her hands. She saw the flicker of horror in his eyes as he realized exactly what she was doing, but the momentum behind the swing was too much for him to pull it back.

His blade struck her right dagger, while his forearm landed directly on her left. A howl split the air as he dropped his sword, which she ducked to avoid. The sound changed to a scream as Gemi twisted the embedded dagger then ripped it down.

The scream choked off as a blade suddenly slid through the man's midsection, and Gemi yelped, the point slicing along her side as she jumped back to avoid the blade. Cursing softly, Gemi threw her right dagger at the man who was now attempting to remove his blade from his fallen comrade before slapping her right hand over the wound.

A gasp and a gurgle told her the thrown dagger had found its target, but she didn't see it strike as Borlin suddenly appeared in front of her.

"Die!" he growled.

Using both hands on the hilt, he swung his sword up from down at his right side. Gemi knew the man was close enough that she didn't have much chance of avoiding the blow.

Instead, she leapt at him, catching him by surprise and trapping his arms between his body and hers, while unintentionally catching his blade between the sheath of her cutlass and her leg.

She gritted her teeth as she felt the blade cut into her thigh but ignored it as she buried her remaining dagger into Borlin's right shoulder with as much power as she could muster—much to the complaint of her own shoulder.

The blade soon disappeared from her leg as Borlin dropped it in pain. She twisted the dagger just to be sure before the 'captain' dropped to his knees and clutched at the wound.

When he began to cry, Gemi rolled her eyes and pushed him to the ground. "Oy, shush, you big baby!" Pushing aside his hands, she gripped her dagger's hilt and pulled it from the wound, dragging another cry from the man.

"You know," she muttered darkly, dragging her dagger across the crying man's tunic to clean it of his blood, "when I said the odds weren't fair, I didn't mean to me." Her voice, Gemi was glad to hear, sounded more confident than she felt. "That you would think five men could kill me when it took four of you to subdue me four years ago is rather insulting."

She wasn't sure if Borlin heard her or not since he began to cry even harder, and she shook her head. Finally standing up, Gemi was startled by the sight of a small crowd standing around the ship's main hatchway.

Frowning, she shouted, "Well? Anyone else?"

Gemi doubted anyone else would want to fight her, but she was tired and injured and thoroughly displeased with the current situation. When every man visible shook his head, Gemi sighed and rolled her eyes.

"Then someone take care of these bilge rats and release Marlen from the brig." After a brief pause, she added, "Oh, and get poor Pockam out of the Black Hold. His rats have got to be worried sick about him."

No one questioned the orders, or even how she knew where Marlen and Pockam were. Instead, they moved quickly to do as she'd said. Grimacing, both in pain and at the implication of the pirates' obedience, Gemi limped over to a nearby barrel and pulled herself up to sit on it.

"*Careful, James, or they'll start calling you 'Captain',*" Shadow nickered amusedly from his hiding place in town.

Gemi wrinkled her nose. She had no desire to captain a ship, and most of the other pirates knew it. Still, that didn't seem to prevent them from treating her as such.

"*You did just defeat the previous captain, however tenuous his claim may have been,*" Flame added. Gemi didn't bother answering.

"Why in Maur's Fire is tha' shoulder unhealed, Gemini?"

The girl snapped her head up and glared, but the man who had spoken merely narrowed his gray eyes in response.

"Don' look a' me like that. Jus' 'cause you don' wan' anyone else knowin' your real name, don' mean I canna use it when there ain' no one else nearby."

Gemi rolled her eyes. She didn't bother pointing out that there were several men running around mere feet from them. The Mage Healer would only tell her that they couldn't possibly be focusing on their conversation anyway.

"What do you want, Mock?"

The Mage Healer's glare only increased. "I wanna know why you were fightin' with tha' shoulder."

Gemi huffed. It didn't surprise her that Mock knew her shoulder was injured. As a powerful Mage Healer, he would be able to sense her body—and injuries—well enough.

"There ain' no reason that shouldn' be healed."

"*If James would let me bite him, it just might be,*" Flame muttered, though no one but her bondmates could hear her.

Gemi rolled her eyes at both mage and dragon. "I know you've heard of the anti-magic venom the rogues use down in Baylin, aye?" Flame offered a hissed "*anti-human magic perhaps*" that Gemi simply ignored as Mock pursed his lips and nodded warily. "The dagger that was shoved into my shoulder was soaked in the stuff."

Mock huffed and prodded the shoulder in question, earning a hiss from Gemi. "Tha' migh' explain why you of all people still have a wound tha's nearly two sevendays old."

Gemi rolled her eyes at the comment. She had learned over the years that one of the perks of the dragonbond was the magic, specifically of the Healing variety, that leaked through the bond. Every Mage Healer that knew her knew that she usually recovered quickly, so Mock's concern was unsurprising, if a bit unwanted at the moment.

"Shouldn't you be attending the wounded that you can actually do something about?" Gemi muttered. "Like the bilge rats or Pockam?"

Mock snorted. For a moment, he seemed to ignore her question as he began cleaning and wrapping her wounds. He had finished with her left leg and was prodding her left side when he muttered, "Those bilge rats tha' might've died already have."

Gemi grimaced. She hated killing. Ever since the first time she'd taken a life—

"*It is best not to think of it,*" Flame muttered in an attempt to distract her. The girl felt her lips twist humorlessly but pushed the thought away all the same.

"And Pockam?" she muttered to the Mage Healer.

"I'd been workin' on him behind Borlin's back. The Black 'Old migh' be tigh' sealed physic'ly, but it canna keep magic out." Gemi huffed as she realized that left her at the Mage Healer's mercy. "An' it looks like you'll be needin' to replace the bandages on your chest. Seems someone managed to slice through an entire layer."

The girl glanced down to watch Mock finger the frayed and bloodied bandages that framed the long cut along her ribs. She sighed and thought, rather sarcastically, *Great.*

Rebinding her breasts wasn't usually an issue as she had become rather proficient at doing it herself over the years. However, with her shoulder still healing, doing it herself was not an option this time.

At least Mock is a Mage Healer, she thought resignedly. *And he's known me for four years, so his assistance won't be awkward, at least.*

Reluctantly, Gemi opened her mouth to ask for the Mage Healer's help when a shout of "Vessel ahoy!" echoed from high above the deck.

Casting her gaze up to the crow's nest, Gemi saw Jique signaling towards the docks. Cursing herself for forgetting that the situation wasn't fully resolved, she shaded her eyes against the rising sun and looked east towards the docks.

What she found certainly wasn't what she had expected. After a startled moment of staring, Gemi turned to Mock and asked if he had a spyglass on him. Instead of answering, he turned to another nearby pirate and requested his.

With spyglass in hand, Gemi turned back to the approaching, yet still distant, vessel.

It was a small rowboat, just large enough to hold the seven men that filled it. Just as surprising as the size was the white flag that fluttered from the prow of the boat.

"Care's Peace," Gemi muttered as she eyed the flag.

Just as the red flag known as Maur's Blood was considered the universal sign of pirates, Care's Peace was flown by those who wished to talk without violence.

"Do you recognize them?" Mock asked curiously.

Even as he asked, he began to wrap a layer of bandages around her midsection, above her tunic. He had obviously realized that they wouldn't have time to fix her bindings.

"Only one," Gemi muttered, but that one was enough.

Towards the front of the boat sat Lord Chanser, duke of Cautzel. He spoke animatedly with the young man who sat in the boat's prow. If it hadn't been for the duke's presence, or that of the small circlet adorning the young man's head, Gemi knew she wouldn't have realized that the boat held the king of Evon and his four remaining dukes.

Lowering the spyglass, Gemi turned towards the *Pauper*'s crew, most of which were staring out towards the boat. Scowling, Gemi shouted, "If you all are done dawdling..."

The men startled and turned to stare at her, many offering expressions of guilt. The sight briefly amused Gemi; imagine a girl like her eliciting that kind of response from that many large, fully grown pirates. The amusement quickly disappeared as her thoughts turned back to the approaching boat.

"We will be receiving visitors in a very short period of time." After a brief pause, she added, "Well? You all know what to do."

The pirates scattered then, some returning to her previous orders, while the rest set about preparing the ship for visitors.

After a moment of watching the men work, Gemi shouted again, "And where in Maurus' Flame is Marlen?"

Chapter 6

"Guten Morgen, Eure Majestät."

King Ferez Katani sighed and glanced to his right, where Kawn Parshen, one of his advisors, now stood. The duke had spoken in the native tongue of Zhulan, the central desert province of Evon, but the phrase—'Good morning, Your Majesty'—was common enough for the king to recognize.

"And you, Kawn, though I'm not so sure I would consider this morning good."

"Oh?" The duke offered Ferez a small, curious smile. "Why is that?"

Ferez shook his head and glanced back out at the harbor. Unlike the docks where they stood, the harbor was fully dark, not a lamp in sight. Even the twin moons, Gemini, which normally would have lit the water with a faint glow, were hidden behind thick clouds. As far as the king was concerned, the pirates had the advantage until the sun rose.

"I've never considered a morning good when violence is planned for the day." Kawn hummed in response but otherwise remained silent. "To be honest, the only good thing about this morning so far was the warm meal the innkeeper's wife had waiting for me." Ferez chuckled softly. "It was a rather unexpected treat, I must admit."

"Was the food that much better than you thought it would be?" The duke sounded surprised. "If so, then you obviously haven't spent as much time in Gasthäuser as I had thought."

Ferez snorted. He had a feeling he had eaten more meals at 'Gasthäuser', inns, than any of his dukes realized, but that wasn't what he had meant.

"The food was delicious, but the quality of the meal wasn't what surprised me." Kawn chuckled, and the king's lips twitched. "Nay, I simply hadn't expected a warm meal before this battle. I certainly didn't expect the inn's staff to rise so early."

"And why not, Your Majesty?" asked a rather sharp voice to the king's left. Ferez turned to find Lord Seyan Lefas, duke of Baylin, and Lord Peln Sageo, duke of Tarsur, approaching them. "It's only right," Seyan continued, his tone derisive, "that, as king, you be treated to the fullest accommodations."

Ferez frowned but didn't respond. A respected king might expect the fullest accommodations, but he had no illusions that his people truly respected him. They might respect the crown that marked his position, but Ferez was not deaf. He had often heard his nobles deride him when they thought he wasn't listening.

At eighteen, he was the youngest Katani to sit on the throne of Evon. It mattered not that he had peacefully ended the war with Fayral at the age of sixteen, less than two seasons after he was crowned. That had simply led them to call him coward, even if no one had yet dared to say so to his face.

The only people on whose respect Ferez knew he could truly count were his own soldiers and knights. They had fought beside him during the war, even before he had been crowned, and he knew they respected him for himself. They didn't pretend for the sake of his crown like he knew others did.

"Eure Majestät," Kawn murmured, directing Ferez's attention back out to the harbor. The sky had begun to lighten, and the ships in the harbor were just becoming visible. Nodding his thanks, Ferez lifted his spyglass to take stock of their goal.

As the king had noted the day before, the *Pretty Pauper* was, like many of the pirate ships that lined the docks, a three-mast ship. However, what interested him was not the shape of the ship itself, but those who manned it.

Or not.

"It doesn't look like anyone is above deck," Ferez muttered.

"Then they are cobardes," Peln spat, falling into the Pecalini tongue that was often spoken in Tarsur. When Ferez eyed him questioningly, the eastern duke added, "They are cowards to hide behind las armas of others, when they are the ones who committed los crímenes."

Ferez nodded in understanding. He was always intrigued by the way both Peln and Kawn switched between Fayralese and the native tongues of their provinces, but that way of speech sometimes left him with more questions than comprehension. Turning his gaze back to the *Pauper*, the king lifted his spyglass once more.

"It might be more beneficial to observe the enemies that are closer at hand, Your Majesty," Seyan drawled. Ferez shrugged, his gaze not leaving the *Pauper*'s deck.

"The other ships are only our enemy because they protect the *Pauper*, Seyan. If we can—"

Ferez suddenly fell silent as movement aboard the *Pauper* caught his attention. He watched as five large men approached the bow of the ship, where a petite figure seemed to be scrambling out of a pack.

"I apologize for my tardiness, Your Majesty," a new voice spoke then, and Ferez pulled his eye from the spyglass just long enough to acknowledge Lord Tern Chanser, duke of Cautzel. "I'm afraid my men were not behaving as well as I had hoped they would this morning. Nor last night." He muttered the last softly before quickly adding, "Have I missed anything?"

"Nein, you haven't," Kawn answered Tern's question as Ferez returned to the spyglass. "I believe Seine Majestät has just now seen the first sign of movement on the *Pauper*, ja?"

"Aye," Ferez answered. "There are six people. I think I recognize five of them from yesterday, but the sixth is new."

A soft *schick* met Ferez's ears, and he glanced around to see Tern staring at the *Pretty Pauper* through his own spyglass. A moment later, the duke stiffened.

"Tern?" Ferez questioned.

"I believe I recognize him," the duke muttered, a frown marring his features. "But how—Oy!"

Startled, Ferez lifted his spyglass back up to his eye. After a moment, he found what had caught Tern's attention. The six men had begun to fight, and it quickly became obvious that, despite the fact that the five larger men outnumbered the smaller figure, the newcomer had them vastly out-skilled.

The swordfight didn't last long. In moments, the petite figure was the only one left standing, though Ferez noticed that others began to appear above deck. They moved hesitantly, and Ferez was sure that whatever fighting was going to occur amongst them had just happened.

"That was…" Tern breathed, lowering his spyglass.

As Ferez put away his own, the other three dukes began questioning what they had seen. Ferez ignored them and turned his gaze back to Tern.

"You said you recognized him?" When Tern nodded, still looking dazed, Ferez asked, "From where?"

"I met him last night, if he's who I think he is." Tern shook his head then. "But I can't think of how he could have gotten on the ship."

Ferez thought that was the least of their worries. Foremost in his mind was the question of what had just happened. From the movements of the other men on the *Pretty Pauper*, whoever the newcomer was, he was important.

With a sharp nod to himself, Ferez strode across the docks towards the nearest ship, a three-master with the name *Wind Runner* painted along its bow. Before the dukes could even question what he was doing, the king shouted, "Oy, pirate!"

"Your Majesty!" Seyan shouted, but Ferez ignored the Baylinese duke as somebody suddenly leaned out over the ship's railing. The man blinked down at Ferez a couple of times, and Ferez opened his mouth to ask a question.

Before he could say anything, the man disappeared.

Ferez frowned. He had hoped to have a civil conversation with the pirate, despite the protests of the dukes (really it was only Seyan, but he was sometimes loud enough for all four). After the pirate's retreat, Ferez wondered if he should have removed his crown before attempting a conversation. If the pirates didn't realize he was the king, they might be more willing to talk.

Just as Ferez considered retreating back to the area he and the dukes had made their command post, another body leaned out over the *Wind Runner*'s railings, a dark red braid dangling over one shoulder. Unlike the first, this man eyed Ferez shortly before breaking into a wide grin.

"Yer Majesty, to wha' do I owe the pleasure?"

The happy greeting caught Ferez off guard, and he stood there, gaping up at the pirate. Ferez's surprise didn't seem to faze the pirate as the man simply leaned his elbows on the railing and brushed his long, red braid back over his shoulder.

When Ferez finally managed to find his tongue, he shook his head and, feeling rather awkward, asked, "Did you see the fight on the *Pretty Pauper*?"

The red-haired pirate tilted his head. "Fight?" Turning his head over his shoulder, Ferez could hear him shout, "Oy, Sim, was there a fight on the *Pauper*?"

Ferez didn't hear the answer, but, when the red-haired man leaned back over the railings, he looked more thoughtful.

"Sim says Caffers fough' five men. Odd, that. The *Pauper* is Caffers' ship." The red-haired man drifted off thoughtfully, his gaze no longer fixed on Ferez.

"Then you don't know what's happening on the *Pauper*, either?"

That was strange. These ships seemed willing to fight to protect the *Pretty Pauper*. *Why would they do so if they don't understand the situation?*

The red-haired pirate smiled and shrugged. "To be hones', Yer Majesty, you prolly know more abou' wha's goin' on than we do." He plucked at a few loose hairs. "I been wonderin' why you be after the *Pauper* in the first place. Don' really make much sense. Af'er all..."

He fell silent for a moment before perking up. "You could find ou' yerself, mind."

Ferez frowned. "I don't—"

"Actually," the red-haired pirate interrupted, "tha's a grand idea. Wi' Caffers there, you won' face no trouble. Jus' fly Care's Peace. You'll be fine."

Ferez blinked, trying to figure out how the conversation had gotten to this point. Then, something the pirate had said caught his attention.

"Your people honor Care's Peace?" he asked, surprised.

The pirate actually looked affronted. "Course we do. Wha' kind o' sea folk you take us for?" The pirate then disappeared from view, and Ferez was left to mull over the man's words.

As he glanced back out at the *Pretty Pauper*, Ferez realized he didn't have to think over them for too long. The deck of the *Pauper* was milling with people, something that hadn't even happened the day before, when only a handful of pirates had appeared above deck all day.

Now, with the ship returning to a semblance of normality and the red-haired pirate's idea working through Ferez's mind, his curiosity got the better of him.

When he mentioned the idea to the dukes, Seyan's immediate arguments were not unexpected. Ferez was surprised when Peln eyed the protesting duke disgustedly and muttered a sharp "¡Cállate!" that quickly quieted Seyan.

"I would certainly like to end this peacefully, if possible," Tern added, earning a glare from the Baylinese duke that Ferez recognized. Tern was only a few years older than Ferez, and the king knew Seyan believed neither of them was old enough for his respective position.

Before Seyan could add anything, Kawn murmured, "I see no reason why we shouldn't at least try to speak with them, especially if they honor Care's Peace. The experience may be enlightening, at the least."

Seyan glowered at the Zhulanese duke, who, like Seyan and Peln, had been a contemporary of Ferez's father. It hadn't passed the king's notice over the years that Seyan was a little more cautious of questioning his fellows than he was the younger men, and Ferez was thankful when the duke kept silent as they went in search of a boat to take them to the *Pauper*.

They managed to rent a small rowboat from a fisherman, who looked shocked by the number of gold Ferez offered for the boat's use.

"Wouldn' e'en expect this much for its sale," the fisherman had muttered. Then, with a suspicious glance, the fisherman had quickly added, "You are bringin' it back, ain' ya?"

Ferez had quickly assured the man that they would as Tern found two soldiers to row the boat for them. Soon, they were crowded into the boat, the two soldiers—one in the blue of Cautzel, the other in the purple of Ferez's men—at the oars, Ferez and Tern at the boat's prow, and the other three dukes sitting where they could. A white flag fluttered in front of the king.

As they rowed out between two pirate ships, the *Duquesa Risueña* and the *Cresta Surcanda*, they remained quiet in an attempt to pass unnoticed. The tactic was unsuccessful as Ferez saw several pirates peer down at them over the ships' railings, but Care's Peace was honored, and the sailors did little more than watch them pass.

Their small boat was just approaching the open harbor when a melodious voice drifted down to them.

"¡Majestad!"

Glancing up, Ferez spotted a man leaning out over the railing of the *Cresta Surcanda*, his short pale hair forming a kind of halo in the early morning light.

"Aye!" Ferez shouted back, ignoring the soft grumbling from the stern of the boat.

"I don't know why you're after the *Pretty Pauper*, Majestad," the pirate called down.

Ferez was struck first by the clarity of the man's tone, then by the fact that this was the second pirate to claim ignorance of the *Pauper*'s crimes.

"However," the man continued, "la situación seems to have changed."

"How so?" Ferez called back, even as their boat glided steadily away from the *Cresta Surcanda*.

"Caffers won."

The words were faint as they drifted out of earshot, and the pirate waved and stepped back from the rail, disappearing once more from view.

"Caffers?" Peln asked, a frown tugging at his lips.

"It seems to be the name of the man who won the fight on the *Pauper*. That's the second pirate who has mentioned it." The king shook his head. "Whoever he is, the man certainly seems to be well known."

"Boy," muttered Tern, and Ferez turned to the western duke with a frown. Tern shrugged. "The person I met last night was younger than you are, Your Majesty."

"Younger?" Ferez asked, shocked. When Tern nodded, Ferez shook his own head. "How much younger could someone who can fight like that possibly be?"

Tern hummed and rubbed his chin. "I would say a couple years, at most." He glanced at Ferez and the others and chuckled, most likely at what must have been expressions of shock. "And, might I remind you, Your Majesty, your own skill with a sword was not unimpressive when you became king at sixteen."

Ferez frowned. "Aye, but I was trained by some of my father's best knights." The king shook his head once more. "Tell me more about this boy. Is Caffers what he called himself?"

To Ferez's surprise, the Cautzelian duke chuckled and smiled wryly, his cheeks pinking slightly. "Unfortunately, I never actually thought to ask him his name."

Kawn chuckled warmly, drawing the younger men's eyes to him. "Then what can you tell us about him, Tern?"

Tern's smile widened, and he began to describe his first impressions of the boy. When he mentioned the leather band he had noted around the boy's right thigh, Peln spoke up.

"You say he wore it around his right thigh only?"

"Aye," Tern answered, offering the other duke a nod.

"Peln?" Ferez asked, curious why the Tarsurian duke found that important.

"Los ladrones tarsuros wear such bands to carry their puñales, Majestad," Peln replied.

The king frowned. He knew 'ladrones' was what Peln always called the thieves in his province, but he didn't recognize '*poon-yah-lehs*', the word he used to describe what they carried.

"Throwing knives, Your Majesty," Tern added, patting his left thigh. "And I had wondered about that myself when I saw it, honestly. But I don't think he's necessarily from Tarsur." He patted the distinctive dolphin hilt of his sword. "He recognized me by my sword, and I doubt someone who doesn't know Cautzel well would be able to do that."

Peln hummed, eyeing Tern thoughtfully. "And you said he carried a Fayralese-style longsword in addition to a cutlass, ¿sí?"

"Aye, but it looked like he only used daggers in the fight on the *Pauper*. He—"

A sudden strangled sound came from the stern of the boat, and Ferez and the others turned to Seyan, startled. The Baylinese duke was staring at Peln incredulously. It was only when the Tarsurian duke lifted an eyebrow curiously that Seyan seemed to find his voice.

"You can't possibly be thinking that a mere boy like that is the Ghost," he spat.

Ferez frowned, unsure how Seyan had made that connection, while Peln's lips twitched up into a smirk.

"I did not say that, Seyan, though it is una idea interesante. Tern has already confirmed that el chico carries las armas preferred by most of the rebellious groups: los puñales of los ladrones tarsuros, the cutlass of Cautzel's piratas, the longsword of the Kensian highwaymen, and the daggers of los rebeldes in your own provincia."

Seyan snarled softly, but Peln ignored him as he added thoughtfully, "Although I must admit to not recalling which armas Zhulan's nómadas prefer." He glanced questioningly at Kawn, who turned to the Tarsurian duke with an expression of boredom.

"The Nomaden use rather impractical close-range blades that they call Scharfmonde. I have heard them referred to as Twin Moon Blades by those who would...romanticize the Nomaden."

The way he rolled his eyes told Ferez exactly what he thought of such a notion.

"Those are the curved blades, aye?" Tern asked. "The ones that curve up over the knuckles?" He swept one hand from left to right above the curve of the knuckles of the other hand, mimicking the curve that he was describing.

Pursing his lips, Kawn nodded slowly. Ferez didn't think the Zhulanese duke enjoyed speaking about the group of people that freely roamed his province but did not recognize his authority as duke.

"I wonder..." Tern muttered once he had Kawn's confirmation.

He reached one hand behind his lower back, his lips moving silently as he worked out whatever he was considering. After a moment, he turned his gaze back to Kawn.

"Do they carry the Twin Moon Blades in a stiff leather sheath at their lower back?"

If Ferez hadn't glanced at Kawn when Tern had, he thought he might have missed the way Kawn twitched and the way his eyes widened slightly at Tern's question. In the next moment, Kawn frowned at Tern and huffed, and the king wasn't completely certain that the sight hadn't just been his imagination.

"They do. Why?"

Kawn's distaste was palpable, and Ferez actually winced. The Zhulanese duke was usually rather good-humored, and Ferez had never thought he might hear that particular tone from him. Apparently, there were some things of which even Kawn didn't approve.

"Well," Tern replied, sounding suddenly unsure, "I noticed something like that on the boy's lower back just before he left the inn. Of course, I didn't get a very…good…look at it…"

Tern trailed off, Kawn's quelling glare all the more intimidating for its rarity.

"Well, I think that's enough to let us consider the fact that el chico might be Nadie," Peln spoke up, drawing glares from both Kawn and Seyan.

"He may carry the correct weapons, Peln," Seyan sneered, "but how do you account for the boy's age?"

Peln shrugged. "Ladrones begin young, amigo. And considering the age of nuestro rey,"—he glanced at Ferez—"you should not discount the abilities of una persona simply because he is young."

"Nein!" Kawn spat.

Ferez stared at the Zhulanese duke, startled. Out of the three elder dukes, Kawn was the last one Ferez would expect to consider age before skill. He had always been the most supportive of Ferez in his reign, even more so than the old Cautzelian duke, who had supported Ferez almost as much as his son, Tern, did.

When Ferez attempted to catch Kawn's eye, the older man kept his gaze firmly on Peln.

"I find it hard enough to believe," the duke muttered heatedly, "that the Nomaden would accept an Ausländer into their Clans and give him the title of Drache Krieger. But a boy that young could not possibly have earned the Respekt of the Nomaden five Jahre ago at the age of…what? Eleven?"

Ferez blinked. *Five 'yahr-uh'—five years?* Had it really been that long since rumors of the Drache Krieger, Zhulan's name for the Ghost, first surfaced? Ferez had been thirteen then and still sheltered from the war. It wasn't until the war with Fayral had ended that he first heard the rumors of the leader of the rebellious groups.

However, if the Drache Krieger had been around that long, then Ferez had to agree with Kawn. He couldn't see how a boy of eleven could earn the respect necessary for such a title from a people who were renowned for their dislike of outsiders. And the rumors were insistent that all these titles referred to a single man, so if Caffers couldn't be the Drache Krieger, then he couldn't be the Ghost.

"Kawn's right," Ferez said, interrupting the argument that had begun between the three older men.

Kawn shifted his gaze to Ferez then and seemed to relax slightly, offering Ferez a small, relieved smile. The king acknowledged the look. While the duke's reaction surprised him, he promised himself that he would attempt to decipher its meaning later.

Meanwhile, both Peln and Seyan were turning to him with protestations spilling from their lips, and Ferez knew he would have to deal with them quickly before they reached the *Pretty Pauper*.

"Majestad, you can't seriously believe that youth would disqualify una persona from being in such a position, not after la vida you've led."

Ferez raised an eyebrow and stared silently at the Tarsurian duke for a moment. As surprised as he'd been by Kawn's emphatic dismissal of the boy because of his youth, Ferez was even more surprised that Peln would take this stance. Peln might not be as inconsiderate of Ferez's skill as Seyan had always been, but Ferez had heard him make snide remarks to other nobles about Ferez's naivety and youth on more than one occasion.

When Peln glanced away from Ferez and swallowed, Ferez nodded.

"At this point, I'm more inclined to consider the boy a simple pirate, possibly even just a traveler." He glanced at Tern to gauge the Cautzelian duke's opinion on that, and the other young man nodded.

Turning back to Peln, Ferez added, "It seems to me that there is a good chance that the fight we witnessed was a change of authority aboard the *Pretty Pauper*, one which every pirate to whom I've spoken so far claims is in our favor. If that's the case, I don't want to risk provoking any more violence with wild theories on the Ghost, do you understand?"

"Sí, Majestad," Peln murmured. His head was lowered, but what Ferez could still see of his cheeks had darkened to a warm red.

"But, Your Majesty," Seyan spoke up, obviously not convinced. "If the boy truly is the Ghost, then we cannot let this opportunity pass."

Ferez turned to Seyan and frowned. "Opportunity for what, exactly? Even if we had proof that the boy was the Ghost, I'm sure I don't have to remind you of the consequences of attempting to arrest him when we are approaching these people under Care's Peace."

Seyan stilled with those words, and Ferez felt a vicious satisfaction fill him. So his instincts had been right; Seyan had forgotten how they were approaching this situation.

If they violated the peace represented by the white flag they flew, then their own lives would be forfeit. Postulations aside, it didn't matter if the boy was the Ghost or not. They could do nothing with that kind of information until after they'd returned to the docks.

"Yer Majesty," one of the soldiers, who had remained silent as they rowed, suddenly spoke up.

"Aye?" Ferez inquired, turning his attention to the soldier, who wore the purple uniform of Caypan.

The man nodded toward the rowboat's starboard bow. The king turned to find the *Pretty Pauper* looming above them as they began to glide along beside her. A rope ladder dangled down the side of the ship, looking, for all the world, like an invitation to board the much larger vessel.

"Seems they be expectin' us, Yer Majesty."

"So it would seem," Ferez muttered.

The sun had risen less than an hour before, yet the day was already turning out to be more peaceful and more interesting than the king had expected. As they approached the rope ladder, Ferez turned his gaze back to his four dukes.

"I want no trouble from any of you while we are aboard the *Pauper*, do you understand?" Tern and Kawn both nodded, but the other two dukes hesitated. Ferez glared at them. "If the situation with the pirates can be settled peacefully and you ruin those chances, then pirates will be the least of your worries, understood?"

"Sí, Majestad," Peln finally answered, dipping his head once more. Ferez thought the Tarsurian duke must still be thinking of the previous rebuke if the solemnity of his voice was any sign.

Seyan, on the other hand, seemed to have processed few of the king's previous words. His own "Aye, Your Majesty" was more sulky than shamed, and Ferez briefly wondered if the man would actually cause trouble despite Ferez's warnings. The king wasn't able to think on it long as they came level with the rope ladder and began to tie the rowboat to it so the boat wouldn't drift away.

"Well," Ferez said as he tested the ladder, "let's see if our hosts are as friendly as their invitation portrays them to be."

Chapter 7

Once Ferez had both feet on the deck of the *Pretty Pauper*, he turned to face the rest of the ship and the pirates who stood there, waiting. His first impression, upon seeing the men, was that he had just stepped onto one of his own ships.

The waiting pirates stood in ranks, line behind line of men waiting silently for Ferez and his men to climb aboard. Only one man wasn't standing but, instead, sat away from the rest, his body covered in what looked like a fur blanket.

All of these men looked unarmed, though Ferez didn't delude himself into thinking that meant they were harmless. Many of them were large enough that he was certain they could do plenty of damage with their bare fists before a blade could take them down.

In front of the ranks, in the position where Ferez was used to seeing a ship's officers, two men stood. In the foremost position, that usually held by the captain, stood a large, yet gaunt-looking, man. His silvering blond hair and beard were long and unkempt, and his plainclothes looked like they had once seen much better days. Even so, his dark blue eyes were surprisingly sharp and warm, and he offered Ferez a broad smile when their gazes met.

Despite the welcoming look, Ferez found his eyes moving behind the older man. In the position that Ferez had always considered the First Mate's stood the boy who'd defeated five pirates singlehandedly. This close, Ferez could finally get a good look at him.

He really doesn't look Of Age yet.

Not only that, but the boy had a nearly feminine prettiness that belied his skills with a blade. Although he kept his long black hair pulled back at the nape of his neck in a tight horsetail, it couldn't ease the roundness of his cheeks, the smooth hairlessness of his chin, or the petite curve of his nose, despite the sharp look of annoyance that he wore.

More than anything else, it was the boy's eyes that caught Ferez's attention. Even from halfway across the deck, the jewel-tone of the boy's amethyst orbs shone brilliantly, and the king wondered if such a color was possible without magic. Not that Ferez had ever heard of a type of magic that could produce such a pure gem-like color in a person's eyes, but Ferez had been raised to never doubt the breadth of magic.

A soft "Eure Majestät" drew Ferez from his musings, and he tore his gaze from the boy's expression, which seemed to have softened with surprise the longer Ferez had looked at him. Heeding the subtle warning in Kawn's tone, Ferez turned back to the gaunt, older man, whose smile seemed to warm even more.

"Welcome, Your Majesty, to the *Pretty Pauper*." Despite the clarity of his words, the man's voice had a scratchy quality that made the king think of a longing thirst. "I am Marlen Narsus, captain of this fine vessel."

71

Ferez hesitated. Despite his ragged appearance, the way this man spoke and held himself screamed 'captain', and the king suddenly wondered if the fight they had seen was indeed the power play he had thought it was. One could not take on such a bearing so quickly without it appearing affected, and this man definitely seemed sincere.

"I apologize for the intrusion, Captain Narsus," Ferez began slowly, thinking courtesy was the best policy at this point, "but we witnessed a fight from the docks, and I was given the impression that it might be a change of authority?"

To his surprise, Captain Narsus chuckled, a sound that quickly degenerated into a short coughing fit. One man broke from the ranks behind Narsus, stepping quickly to the captain's side, but Narsus simply waved a hand at the man.

"The impression you were given was correct, Your Majesty," Narsus rasped once he could speak again. The man beside him murmured insistently, but the captain seemed intent on ignoring him.

The black-haired boy suddenly huffed and gripped Captain Narsus' elbow, silencing both pirates.

"Marlen, listen to Mock. You aren't going to be able to continue this conversation much longer if he doesn't get something into you."

Ferez's eyebrows rose in surprise, both at the open arguments and the clarity of the boy's words. Certainly, neither had been expected.

The boy's words seemed to convince the captain more than Mock's, which Ferez found odd since he was certain Mock must be a healer by the way the boy spoke of him. As Narsus sighed and nodded, turning to Mock, the black-haired boy turned his gaze back to Ferez.

"Pardon the interruption, Your Majesty, Milords." Ferez didn't miss the way the boy's eyes warily moved over his dukes before returning to him. "However, Marlen has been locked in the brig since the morning after Mid-Summer Day, and he hasn't had time to recover."

Ferez would have thought the boy would blame him and the dukes for the lack of recovery time, but the boy turned an annoyed glare on the captain and healer beside him instead.

His curiosity piqued, Ferez murmured, "And you are?"

Those amethyst eyes swung back to Ferez and eyed him narrowly. For a long moment, the boy remained silent, and Ferez wondered if his question had been too rude. He hadn't meant to offend, but he'd been interested in learning more about the boy since he'd seen him fight.

As Ferez began to wonder if he should retract the question, the healer broke the silence. "Ain' no harm in 'im knowin' yer name, James," the man spoke dryly, his eyes never leaving Captain Narsus. "Bes' to have introductions now so we don' be havin' issues later."

The boy turned his glare back to Mock, but, when the healer refused to acknowledge the look, the boy sighed and rolled his eyes. Swinging his amethyst gaze back to Ferez, the boy offered him a small bow.

"My name is James Caffers, Your Majesty, though I'd have thought you already knew that if it was pirates who told you about the fight's significance."

Ferez shrugged. "Your family name perhaps, but I couldn't be certain." Then, thinking that reciprocation was only fair, Ferez began to introduce his dukes, ignoring Seyan's hissed "Your Majesty!"

Once done, Ferez turned back to find Caffers watching him thoughtfully, his head tilted to one side. Ferez raised an eyebrow questioningly, and the boy shrugged.

"I didn't expect you to be so forthcoming with such information, Your Majesty."

A large hand settled on Caffers' shoulder then, and a warm, smooth chuckle drew the king's attention back to Narsus. Ferez realized, with a start, that Mock must be a Mage Healer as the captain already looked better. His cheekbones didn't look quite as sharp as they had upon first sight, and his skin had already taken on a healthier shade.

"You'll have to forgive James," the man murmured as he absently nodded to Mock. The Mage Healer rolled his eyes but stepped back into the ranks without protest. "He's not usually so prickly, but he gets rather cranky when he's low on sleep and in pain."

The captain offered Caffers a look then that had the boy ducking his head, his cheeks darkening to a nice pink. As he shifted under Captain Narsus' hand and gaze, he grimaced, hissed, and wrapped a hand around his midsection.

It was only then that Ferez noticed that the boy was not in the best of conditions, either. Bandages encircled his midsection, a touch of red just visible on his left side beneath his hand. His left thigh, too, was bandaged, and, now that Ferez was looking for it, he noticed that the boy's weight was visibly shifted to his right leg.

So he didn't win the fight completely unscathed then, Ferez thought, empathizing with the boy. He knew from experience how much those kinds of wounds could hurt.

A moment later, he frowned. *And why is he still injured when a Mage Healer stands only feet behind him?*

"Now that my voice is working again," Captain Narsus said amusedly, halting Ferez's line of thought, "I should be able to answer any questions you might have, Your Majesty."

Ferez nodded and dragged his thoughts back to the earlier part of the conversation. "I believe you were going to explain about the fight and the resulting change of authority…and possibly how this changes matters?"

Ferez would like a peaceful outcome to this day, but he wouldn't allow a guilty party to go unpunished if the situation hadn't changed as much as he might hope.

Narsus nodded. "I was. You said that you saw the fight, aye?" Ferez nodded. "Then you know that young James here won against five others?"

Ferez nodded again and turned his gaze to the boy once more. "Yet, he stands as First Mate, not captain."

Caffers, whose cheeks were still colored from the captain's previous comment, flushed a darker red. Ducking his head, he slid his right hand back over the top of his head before dragging his horsetail over his shoulder. Ferez blinked at the sight of the nervous gesture.

"Fortunately for me," Captain Narsus replied, gaining the king's attention once again, "young James has never been interested in being captain. Once James took care of Borlin, he had me released from the brig so I could reclaim the captaincy. And just in time, by the looks of it."

"Borlin?"

The name was unfamiliar, but, from the captain's words, Ferez suspected him to be one of the men whom Caffers had defeated.

Captain Narsus nodded, still smiling warmly. "Aye, Borlin was my First Mate before he fancied the captaincy for himself. He and his four supporters in the crew grabbed me while I was sleeping off the drink from the Mid-Summer Day celebrations and threw me in the brig with little trouble, I'm ashamed to admit."

He chuckled then, belying the shame he claimed. "Of course, a First Mate has every right to take over the captaincy—there's a provision for that in the Pact—so the crew couldn't rightly complain. But there is no provision for attacking Evonese ships. However, by the first attack, Borlin and his men already had a strong hold on the ship."

"Wait," Tern muttered, sounding as confused as Ferez felt. "What pact are you talking about? What provisions?"

Narsus' grin broadened, but, even as he opened his mouth to speak, Caffers limped forward and interrupted him, offering the captain a quick glare.

"Suffice it to say, Milord, the Pact is an agreement between pirates; a pirates' code, if you will."

Captain Narsus laughed then, pulling the boy back towards him by the shoulder. This caused the already off-balance boy to stumble, and Caffers turned to glare at the older man. The captain shook his head, unconcerned.

"Why are you so worried, James? Don't Lord Chanser and His Majesty have the right to know what rules their people follow?"

The shock those words sent through Ferez was such that he nearly missed the boy's reluctant nod. *Is he actually claiming the pirates as citizens of Cautzel?*

True, even pirates would need to make port occasionally, but it sounded as if Narsus was claiming that the pirates submitted to the authority of both duke and king. That couldn't be right. Pirates, by definition, swore allegiance to no one.

A sudden snort from Ferez's right drew him from his shock, and he turned to find Tern hunched over, one hand over his mouth and his shoulders shaking slightly.

"Tern?" Ferez muttered worriedly.

The duke released a bark of laughter and lifted his gaze to the pirates, a large grin spreading his lips.

"Is that why Cautzel has been so peaceful since the end of the war? Because the so-called pirates are..." He waved one hand in the air searchingly before adding, "Cautzelian pirates?"

~~*~*

Gemi blinked as Lord Chanser dissolved into snickers. She might have expected the Cautzelian duke to be accepting of the Pirates—the man she had met last night had seemed rather kind for a noble—but this amusement was certainly a surprise.

Even the other nobles seemed shocked by Lord Chanser's reaction. Lord Lefas of Baylin and Lord Sageo of Tarsur looked horrified, while the remaining duke and the king simply looked bewildered.

"Technically," Marlen answered, his own grin widening to match the duke's, "we call ourselves Tauresian Pirates, Milord. But you've got the right idea."

While Marlen spoke, Gemi kept her eyes on the five nobles. Lord Chanser sobered with the captain's words, and, while a smile still played on his lips, it was more thoughtful, his eyes staring into the distance. Gemi doubted he had missed the connection between what they called themselves and the Tauresian Sea, into which Cautzel's ports emptied.

Of the others, the king's expression turned thoughtful as well, though disbelief still lingered in his gaze. To his left, Lord Parshen, who had looked bewildered previously, suddenly became unreadable, and Gemi frowned when she saw that. He was hiding something, and that made her wary.

She cast her gaze behind the king and duke when movement caught her attention. While Lord Sageo stared at her and Marlen, one brow raised in obvious disbelief, Lord Lefas shook his head and pushed past Lord Chanser, who simply pursed his lips and stepped aside.

"You can't be serious," the Baylinese duke said. "You're pirates! You don't swear allegiance to any country."

Gemi rolled her eyes. She could hear murmurs break out among the men who stood behind her, and, when she glanced at Marlen, she saw that even his grin had faltered.

She understood the response all too well. She had heard the arguments time and again while Marlen and she worked to unite the Pirates.

Nay, pirates did not, by principle, follow the authority of any one country. In fact, most pirates Gemi knew had become pirates to enjoy the sea life without having to bend to the authority of a country that would force them to fight in the war.

However, the difference between fighting the law and fighting the war had become moot as they discovered that the outcome was often the same.

Eyeing Lord Lefas, she noted that he was glaring at her and Marlen, his gaze lingering on her longer than it did her captain. *Well,* Gemi thought, *I don't like him anymore than he likes me.*

While she had never met the man, he was the noble about whom Gemi had heard the most when she was younger. Aye, her parents had talked about the previous king and her mother's siblings, none of whom had survived the war as far as Gemi knew.

But Gemi remembered well the numerous times her father had spoken of his Baylinese counterpart...and almost never with anything good to say.

Like her father, Lefas had only had one child, a daughter who was rumored to have disappeared two years after the attack on Cosley Estate. But the two men, as far as Gemi recalled, had had contradictory philosophies, and, unlike Jem, Lefas had treated his daughter like a mere stepping stone for his line, not as a true heir.

It was that mindset that had gained Lord Jem's disgust, and Gemi doubted she could think any better of the man.

As the man opened his mouth again, looking ready to continue his protests, the king gripped his shoulder and sharply commanded, "Seyan!" The duke stilled and turned his glare to the king, but it was the anger that filled His Majesty's eyes that surprised Gemi.

"You promised you would not cause trouble, Seyan."

Despite the king's anger, his words were quiet enough that Gemi had to strain to make them out. When the duke's glare turned to a sneer, the king shook his head.

"Must I send you back down to the boat?"

That appeared to make the duke listen. With a glower, Lord Lefas clenched his fists, shook his head, and stepped back, falling in behind the king and Lord Chanser. With a sigh and a shake of his own head, His Majesty turned his pale blue eyes back to Gemi and Marlen.

"I apologize for Seyan's behavior, but I'm sure you can understand how we might be a bit doubtful of your claim."

Gemi shivered as the king's eyes locked with hers. He had spoken just now with a quiet authority that Gemi would not have expected by looking at him.

When he'd first boarded the *Pauper,* she had thought him unremarkable. With short, sandy-brown hair, lightly tanned skin, and a plain, clean-shaven face, Gemi hadn't thought she'd be able to pick him out of a crowd without his crown.

Only his eyes, when they had met hers that first time, had been memorable. An odd, pale shade of blue, they had held a kindness and curiosity that had surprised Gemi.

Now, the plainness of the king's features was overwhelmed by the quiet pride presented in the way he held himself and the strength in his eyes. Power seemed to fill him, the power of leadership that Gemi had learned to recognize over the years as she'd watched the people she'd befriended gather the loyalty of their respective groups.

Gemi was suddenly reminded that this was the man who had negotiated with Fayral for an end to the bloody, decades-long war at the age of sixteen.

This, she thought, suddenly awestruck, *is a man who deserves the loyalty I've promoted all these years.*

~~*~*

Marlen nodded in response to the king's words, though he noticed that the king focused on Gemi, rather than Marlen himself. Not that the captain was surprised. Marlen may be captain of this ship, and even current Head of the Tauresian Council of Ships, but there was simply ¹ something about Gemi that marked her as important, even to those who didn't know her identity, true or public.

What did surprise the *Pretty Pauper*'s captain was the myriad of emotions through which Gemi's expression ranged as she eyed the king. Out of all of them, her surprise, followed by awe, was the most striking. Marlen could imagine the reason for that reaction, but it didn't make sense unless one of the things Gemi had fought for all of these years was something she hadn't truly believed.

Marlen remembered well the day he and his crew had learned that King Eden Katani had died from injuries gained in battle. Nearly two sevendays later, they had heard news that the man's son, Ferez Katani, would take the throne at the mere age of sixteen. The entire crew had mourned for their king and country and thought that both were doomed.

Meanwhile, Gemi had insisted that they trust the young king as they had his father.

That wouldn't have meant anything two years prior when pirates still held no loyalty, but, since Marlen had united the Tauresian Pirates, the men swore allegiance to Evon and its king, whether said king knew it or not.

So Gemi had insisted that they not judge the new king on his youth, and, since it came from the young Wanderer himself, the men had been convinced.

Now, Gemi's reactions made Marlen wonder if some of the girl's insistence had simply been talk. *It doesn't matter,* he told himself as a small smile quirked Gemi's lips. *As long as she believes in the king now, it doesn't matter what she truly believed before.*

Peace of Evon

Dismissing the matter from his mind, Marlen cleared his throat to catch the attention of the king, who was still staring at Gemi. Once those pale blue eyes had settled on Marlen, the captain nodded his head again.

"I can understand how difficult it would be to trust those you thought were against you, Your Majesty. But if you are willing to listen, then I'm sure we can prove our goodwill."

The king eyed him warily. After long moments of tense silence, the king nodded and relaxed, the power of his stance seeming to disappear with a sigh.

"I would appreciate that," the young man murmured.

Marlen blinked, startled by the transition. *Why does he hide his true power and authority when it could lead others to doubt him?*

"Marlen?" Gemi murmured, pulling Marlen's attention to her.

The girl was eyeing him worriedly, and Marlen grimaced as he realized he'd let his thoughts distract him. That could lead to trouble since he'd only just been released from the brig.

His crew might like him, but they were still pirates. Strength and survival were the basis of their lifestyle. If they sensed he was too weak to continue in his captaincy, especially with the nobles here, then they would call for a replacement. And, next time, it wouldn't be a man willing to break the Pact.

Marlen offered Gemi a small nod before turning back to the king and his dukes. "Why don't we take this conversation to a more comfortable and less open setting?" He gestured towards the stern of the ship where the captain's cabin sat.

~~*~*

For a split second, Ferez considered that it might be unwise to follow a pirate further into his ship, even if only to his cabin.

Then again, something about Captain Narsus and Caffers makes me want to trust them. And my instincts are rarely wrong.

Ignoring the soft grumbles behind him, Ferez nodded to the captain and ordered the two soldiers to remain above deck. As he followed Narsus towards the stern, several sets of footsteps joined his own, some more reluctantly than others.

He lost track of them as Caffers began shouting orders to the other pirates, but Ferez refused to glance back to make certain all four dukes accompanied them.

I don't have time to deal with Seyan's prejudices. Not when this conversation could make the difference between peace and another war.

The cabin to which Captain Narsus lead them was spacious. Tall windows occupied the rear wall, providing a view of the outward edge of the harbour. A bed occupied the wall to their left, bookshelves lined the right, and a large, thick desk sat near the shelves. To Ferez's surprise, there was still enough room for all six men to easily file in and find places to sit, which Captain Narsus indicated they should do.

78

As Ferez made himself comfortable on the thick cushions lining the long window seat that ran the length of the wall, Caffers stepped through the cabin's doors and closed them quietly. Stepping away from them, he swung his gaze over the cabin's occupants.

Ferez straightened when that assessing gaze met his. He had the sudden sense that he was about to learn something extremely important.

Finally, Caffers turned to Captain Narsus, who was seated on the bed, and asked, "Shall I explain the Pact then, Marlen?"

Narsus nodded, waving for the boy to continue. "You do know it best, after all," he added.

Ferez raised his brows. *Why would a boy know something of such importance better than a pirate captain?*

The scowl that Caffers offered Captain Narsus showed that he obviously didn't appreciate the acknowledgement.

Whatever the reason, Caffers finally huffed and turned back to Ferez and Tern, who also sat on the long window seat.

Nodding to the duke, the boy said, "The pact that you asked about, Lord Chanser, is known as the Pact of the Tauresian Pirates. Simple, aye," he added when Tern let out a soft snort. A twitch of the boy's lips was the only sign of his possible amusement. "However, we are simple men, so the name works."

Tern nodded.

"The Pact," the boy continued, sweeping his eyes over the other dukes again, "was written four years ago. It lays down guidelines for governance, both of the ships and of the general community of Pirates. It lays down guidelines about what ships cannot be attacked or terrorized without provocation, namely other Tauresian Pirate ships and Evonese ships. It—"

"May I ask…?" Tern spoke up once more, effectively silencing the boy. When Caffers nodded to the Cautzelian duke, Ferez turned his gaze to his friend. "If your pact prevents you from attacking Evonese ships, then how do you explain the two pirate attacks that have occurred since the end of the war?"

Caffers frowned, apparently confused, and he glanced at Captain Narsus, who fingered his beard and glanced toward the ceiling.

"If I remember correctly, those were committed by the *Naked Bones* and the *Black Death*."

Ferez thought he saw Caffers shudder when the captain named the two ships. He couldn't be certain as the boy quickly turned an inquiring gaze on Tern.

"Does that sound right, Milord?"

Tern nodded slowly. "Aye, those sound like the two ships that were punished for the attacks."

Caffers looked startled by that. "They were?"

Captain Narsus threw back his head and laughed loudly. Caffers turned a confused glare on the man, the reddening of his cheeks betraying his embarrassment.

"You are behind on the times, James," Narsus teased once he could speak again. "The *Naked Bones* was sunk nearly a year and a half ago, and the *Black Death* has been out of commission for…" The captain paused, glancing towards Ferez and Tern. "What has it been, Milord; three seasons?"

Tern nodded, more confidently this time. "Aye, just under." He glanced between the two pirates and added curiously, "You do know the ships then?"

Caffers sighed. "Only because they refused to sign the Pact. As the captain of the *Black Death* put it, 'if this be the norm o' pirates, I'd rather be rogue an' the bane o' ye all.'" The boy rolled his eyes. "Rather nasty fellow, that one. I hope he hung, myself."

Tern chuckled dryly. "Well, he was supposed to." Caffers shot the duke an alarmed look before Tern added, "But it seems he impaled himself on one of his guards' swords when he attempted to escape."

Relief washed over the boy's face then, and he chuckled softly. "Good."

"Is it safe to say that the pirate ships that fill the harbor now are all Tauresian?" Ferez asked. Despite his growing curiosity over the reasons behind the boy's reactions, Ferez didn't think they were yet in a position to be trading such stories.

Caffers nodded, focusing on Ferez once more. "Aye, all thirty-three of them."

The wording caught Ferez's attention. "The entire Tauresian Pirate community?" he hazarded.

The boy's expression tightened, but, after a brief pause, he nodded.

"Aye. More than fifty ships signed the Pact, but the war was just as harsh on us as it was on the Royal Navy. We lost nearly twenty ships in the two years we fought in the war against Fayral."

"You fought—" Ferez began, startled, but Tern suddenly gripped his arm, silencing him.

"Hold on one second! Are you saying that pirates were the…the Ghost Ships?" the duke breathed.

Ferez turned to Tern, both eyebrows raised in surprise. While he hadn't made the connection himself, he certainly recognized the reference.

He remembered the stories of nameless ships that flew the purple flag of Evon sailing into battle alongside the Royal Navy. He had only ever seen them once himself, but he remembered hearing speculations that the ships were old Evonese ships that had risen from Maur's Hold to exact revenge on Fayral.

"I'm not certain I follow," Caffers admitted. He glanced back to Captain Narsus, but the older pirate looked just as lost.

"How can you not?" Peln inquired, startling Ferez. The king had nearly forgotten that the three older dukes were still present with how little attention the pirates were paying them. "Even in Tarsur, we heard of los barcos sin nombres that fought beside our navy during la guerra."

Narsus hummed softly before muttering distractedly, "So that's the origin of the name 'The Ghost'."

Ferez nearly groaned when the tension in the room suddenly became stifling. Beside him, Tern stilled, his wary gaze focusing, not on the pirates, but on Seyan and Peln, who had seated themselves near the desk, closest to the door.

Peln was staring at Captain Narsus intensely, yet not nearly as hungrily as Seyan. The Baylinese duke was practically quivering, like a hunting hound that had just caught the scent of its prey.

Closer at hand, Kawn, who had claimed a luxurious armchair in the corner, kept his gaze locked on the floor. Unlike the other dukes, his body looked surprisingly lax, his steadily drumming fingers the only sign that he found the topic uncomfortable.

A soft creak drew Ferez's attention back to the pirates. Caffers had stepped back with his right foot. The position should have been awkward with his left thigh injured, but the boy looked perfectly balanced. He rested his left hand lightly on a dagger and held his right out towards Narsus, who looked startled.

Caffers glanced between the four dukes warily. "Are we all right, Milords?"

The boy's voice was tight and steady, and Ferez mentally applauded the boy for his bravery. He knew Seyan's expression alone was daunting; he'd faced similar from the duke since taking the throne.

"Nay, we are not!" Seyan hissed. Ferez wondered if he could speak now and silence the duke, but he'd already ordered the man down twice today. He didn't think the man would listen a third time. "You know the Ghost!"

Ferez closed his eyes in despair. This was exactly what he had meant when he had ordered the dukes not to cause trouble. Accusations like this were bound to get them killed.

Ferez didn't know who would have moved first if shouting hadn't suddenly sounded from the deck. Eager to break the tension, Ferez leapt from his seat and strode quickly to the door.

He paused with one hand on the handle as the shouting cut off just as suddenly as it began. In its place, a soft, haunting melody filled the air.

Chapter 8

The scene that met Ferez's eyes once he was above deck was chaotic. Coils of rope, in various stages of use, lay about the deck. One portion of the deck was sopping wet, abandoned buckets and brushes lying nearby. Ferez even spotted what looked like a large, overturned Katani game board, the game pieces scattered haphazardly across the deck.

Amidst the various abandoned tasks, several pirates had formed a semicircle in the middle of the deck. In the center, the two soldiers that had accompanied Ferez and the dukes onto the *Pauper* knelt and stared up at the pirates.

The man dressed in the purple of Caypan knelt behind the Cautzelian soldier with his hands wrapped around the other's upper arms. The Cautzelian man had his sword drawn, but it lay on the deck, forgotten.

Above all of this, the mournful tune swelled.

"What happened, Pockam?" Caffers whispered, breaking the spell the scene held on the king.

Ferez turned to find the black-haired boy addressing a man seated on the deck nearby, the same man he had noticed sitting away from the others when he first boarded. With mild disgust, he realized that what he had mistaken earlier for a fur blanket was actually a thick layer of rats.

"Dunno wha' to say, James," the man answered with a shrug, causing the rats lying on his shoulders to scrabble for a hold. "'Twas this or let 'em star' a fight, I think."

"Let who start a fight, exactly?" Ferez asked, keeping his voice low. As much as he wanted an explanation, the haunting melody was distinctly familiar, and Ferez didn't dare interrupt it.

The seated man, Pockam, sighed and nodded towards the semicircle. "The soldiers, Yer Majesty. Seems the Cautzel man 'ad a brother on one o' the ships we attacked. He was pretty upset about it. Brandished his sword an' everythin'. Taersh tried apologizin', but the Cautzel man jus' started yellin'."

Pockam shrugged again. The rats, Ferez noticed with an odd sense of wonder, seemed prepared this time and barely shifted.

"I guess Taersh thought offerin' 'im a Song o' Mournin' might 'elp. Course," he added, a bit more softly, "we ne'er had the chance to mourn 'em ourselves, so it's as much for us as 'im."

Just then, a sob broke through the air, and the slow, haunting tune swelled once more. Ferez could finally make out the words the pirates were singing. He closed his eyes as they filled his ears, reminding him of the many battlefields and countless deaths he'd mourned during the war.

"Send me away from the place I call home...send me away from the one that I love...send me away on the tides of tomorrow...send me away...send me away..."

As the words trailed to an end and the pirates paused before singing the next verse, Ferez felt a soft touch on his elbow. Opening his eyes, he turned and met Tern's watery gaze, knowing that his own wasn't much better. The Song of Mourning had been created decades ago near the beginning of the war with Fayral, and Ferez knew few men who could listen to the song and not recall someone they had lost.

"If they are willing to offer this," Tern muttered lowly, "instead of a fight against two men they could have easily subdued, I say we let them be."

In all honesty, Ferez was willing to agree. He did, however, have one last question.

Turning to Caffers—Narsus might be the *Pretty Pauper*'s captain, but the boy was the one who had won the right to leadership—Ferez murmured, "Can you assure me that all who are responsible for the three attacks will be punished?"

Caffers seemed startled by the question. He glanced questioningly down at Pockam, and, to Ferez's surprise, it was the seated man who answered his question.

"Yer Majesty migh' find it 'ard to believe, bu' Borlin on'y had the four allies in the crew. James killed three of 'em"—Caffers winced—"an' Borlin an' the other are unconscious in the brig, as I understand it."

"But how could five hombres possibly control an entire barco?" Peln murmured.

Ferez glanced at him and the other dukes. All four—even Seyan— looked solemn, no doubt in response to the Song of Mourning, which the pirates were still singing.

"They didn', not a' firs'. Afore the firs' attack, we followed Borlin, e'en if we didn' like it. He hadn' broke the Pact when 'e became cap'n. Bu' when he ordered tha' firs' attack, we did all we could to spare lives. Threw men o'erboard an' all, and I e'en 'ad the sea animals take 'em all to land."

"What happened when the attack was over?" Tern whispered.

Pockam, whom Ferez now realized must be an Animal Mage—which certainly explained the rats—snorted.

"Didn' e'en wait 'til the attack was o'er, did they? I was in the middle o' sendin' the sea animals off when one o' Borlin's brutes grabbed me, strung me up, and began floggin' me silly."

The man paused as a sudden squeaking rose around him. As the Animal Mage turned his attention downwards and began squeaking in turn, Ferez saw that the rats that covered him were now writhing franticly. It was several minutes before Pockam managed to get the rodents to calm down.

"Sorry 'bou' that," the Animal Mage said once the rats were settled again. "On'y I woke up from the floggin' in the Black 'Old, and me rats are still 'fraid I'll disappear again."

"They are your Kräftetier, ja?" Kawn asked softly.

Ferez turned to the Zhulanese duke with a frown, and, by the sudden silence of the group, he didn't think he was the only one who was confused by the word, '*krayf-tuh-teer*'.

"He means 'Power Animal'," Caffers suddenly spoke up.

Ferez turned his frown on the purple-eyed boy. Power Animals were those animals which responded most strongly to an Animal Mage's magic, and Ferez thought it obvious that Pockam had such a relationship with the rats. But he couldn't fathom how Caffers knew the translation for the Zhulanese word when no one else seemed to.

The boy glanced around their group, and a flush crept up his cheeks, but he didn't explain. He simply shrugged and dropped his gaze back down to the Animal Mage.

"Aye, rats are me Power Animal," Pockam answered, seeming to ignore the group's returned tension. "Course, ship rats more than land 'uns. Diff'rent breed, y'know."

Ferez shook his head as the Animal Mage began to talk about the differences between ship rats and land rats. The conversation had once again moved away from topics they needed to discuss, and, for the first time since they'd boarded the *Pretty Pauper*, Ferez found himself becoming impatient.

He was just turning to Caffers with the hopes of asking him about their prisoners' punishments when a loud *squawk* silenced the entire ship. Even the singing pirates fell silent as everyone turned toward the port railing, where a large, colorful bird was neatly perched.

"Caffers," the bird squawked.

Ferez gaped. *It can talk in a human tongue?*

He glanced around the ship and was even more amazed to realize that the pirates didn't find the talking bird unusual. In fact, the boy it had addressed limped forward and crossed his arms.

"What do you want, Tælen?" the boy asked.

Ferez raised an eyebrow. Caffers spoke as though he was addressing a man, not a bird.

"Made a deal with the nobles yet?" the bird squawked in turn. "On'y there looks to be trouble on the—"

The bird interrupted itself with another *squawk* and took off from the rail just as an explosion sounded from the docks.

~~*~*

Gemi cursed, ducking as the *boom* burst against her ears. While it may not have been nearby, her instincts were still sharp from the war, and the sound had been plenty loud.

"What in Maurus' Fire was that?" Marlen shouted. He pulled his spyglass from his belt even as Gemi sought out the connection to her bondmates.

"*Shadow?*"

84

The stallion had already left the alley in which he'd hidden. He nickered a quick, "*I can't tell yet. It came from the other side of the docks.*" Pushing through the crowd, he hurried towards the explosion.

"*Should I chance a look?*" Flame trilled, but Gemi immediately shook her head.

"*If you drop below the clouds, you risk discovery, Flame. It's best if you stay hidden for now.*" The dragon cooed in agreement and continued circling above the clouds.

Pulling back from the bond, Gemi noticed that both the king and Lord Chanser had pulled out their own spyglasses. "Marlen?" she asked, hoping to get an answer from someone.

"It looks like the explosion hit the *Silent Raider* on the starboard bow. Tælen's sure to be—"

A quieter explosion interrupted him, and, to Gemi's surprise, it was the king that cursed next.

"Why are they attacking the ships?" he snapped. He quickly lowered the spyglass and turned to the dukes. "Do we have any Animal Mages on the docks to whom we could send a message?"

Lord Chanser nodded immediately. "My Animal Mage, Calum, should be on the docks." To Gemi's surprise, the duke turned to Pockam. "Could you send a message to him? Tell him to stop the attack? If you use the phrase 'high tide or low, we sail for Evon', he'll know the message is from me."

"Course I can," Pockam answered, even as he cast a questioning glance at Gemi.

She nodded. Pockam may be a mage, but he would need to find an animal by which to send the message, and it would take time for the animal to reach the docks and find the Animal Mage.

"*I'd be quicker,*" Shadow finished the thought. Gemi agreed and passed the information on to him.

~~*~*

Shadow shoved his way through the crowd. The passage was tricky with the docks full of soldiers and horses, and it was made even more difficult by the fact that everyone, men and animals alike, had stopped whatever they'd been doing and were now staring at the far side of the docks, where the explosion had occurred.

As subsequent explosions sounded, mutters broke out through the crowd. "*Have the masters received their orders, then?*" Shadow heard one stallion nicker to another.

Shadow resisted, with difficulty, the urge to snap that they couldn't possibly have received their orders when the nobles were on the *Pretty Pauper*. Instead, he shouldered past the stallion, earning a glare from him.

When Gemi passed the message on to him, Shadow paused and swung his head around, seeking out the closest horses decorated in the blue of

Cautzel. *Hopefully,* he thought as he spotted one such group clustered nearby, *they'll know where I can find the Animal Mage.*

He nudged the neck of the closest stallion, a red beast that turned flat brown eyes on Shadow.

"*What?*" the chestnut snorted sharply, stamping one foot to the ground. Shadow nearly snorted in response but held back. It would only cause more trouble.

"*Do you know where I can find the Animal Mage, Calum?*" Shadow nickered as quickly and politely as he could. The other stallions behind the chestnut turned their gazes to him then, several of them more curious than the first.

"*Why?*" snorted the chestnut once more.

Shadow briefly wondered if the red beast had spent any time at all around Animal Mages. He certainly wasn't much of a conversationalist.

Suddenly, light and sound exploded nearby, and screams reached Shadow's ears, some of them voices he was sure he recognized. Snorting and pushing back his bondmates' sudden questions, Shadow snapped his teeth at the Cautzelian stallions.

"*This attack needs to stop, and Calum's the man I was told to speak to!*"

Unfortunately, he had already lost the attention of the stallions. They scattered quickly, many of them whinnying names that Shadow could only assume were their masters'.

Shadow tossed his head, snorting angrily. He had to find the Animal Mage, but the other animals were not cooperating. He had never had this much trouble passing messages along during the war.

"*If you're looking for Calum, he's the man with the doves.*"

Startled, Shadow swung his head around. A mare with a beautiful, pure white coat stood nearby, her dark eyes trained on him. For a moment, Shadow wondered what a beauty like her was doing on a battlefield and if he could possibly convince her to stick around for some fun after the battle.

Then, he noticed her tack and stiffened. Her black saddle was decorated with a simple purple ribbon and an emblem that bore the sword and pegasus of Evon. With a sinking feeling in his stomach, Shadow thought he must have just been discovered.

"*Well?*" the mare whinnied. "*Are you going to go find him or not?*" Shadow threw his head back, surprised by the mare's question. "*You said you needed to stop the fight. You can't do that by just standing there.*"

Shadow snorted, tossing his head. He was about to ask where the man was—'the man with the doves' didn't seem like much to go on—but, in his movement, he suddenly caught sight of a flock of birds hovering above the docks closer to the original explosion.

Nickering a quick "*Thanks*", Shadow began to shove his way through the crowd once more.

It took him too long to reach the man who stood beneath the cloud of birds, which actually included more seagulls than doves. By the time he shoved past the last horse in his way—ignoring the other stallion's whinnied "*Watch it!*"—Gemi, Marlen, and the nobles had already crowded into a boat and were on their way to the docks.

Upset with himself for taking so long, Shadow's nip to the man's shoulder was probably harder than necessary.

Thankfully, there was no anger in the Animal Mage's eyes when he turned. Instead, he lifted his hands to Shadow's muzzle and nickered, "*What is it, friend?*"

Shadow snorted and pulled his head from the man's hands. There were few people he allowed to touch him like that, and a strange Animal Mage like this was not one of them.

Once free, he snorted, "*High tide or low, we sail for Evon. The fighting has to stop now, by order of Lord Chanser and the king!*"

Shadow had expected the man to hesitate, even just a little. Instead, he immediately turned, grabbed the arm of another man, and shouted, "We've got to stop them, Donogh! The king's orders!"

Donogh, an older man whom Shadow realized must be a knight with the varying colors of his leather armor, glanced at the Animal Mage. He didn't question the man's words and simply began shouting orders to his men, several of whom were crowded around the weapons that had been producing the battlefires.

When another battlefire bloomed against the hull of a nearby ship—the *Silver Girl*, Shadow noted idly—the knight cursed and plunged in amongst his men, pulling them away from the weapons and shouting something about 'an order being an order'.

As the knight went to work ordering down his men, the Animal Mage wasn't idle. He shouted orders at several men, who hesitated before running off through the crowds, shouting as they did so.

So chaotic, Shadow thought with mild disgust. *It's a wonder they ever get anything done.*

"*Shadow,*" Gemi chided against his mind, the rebuke half-hearted. "*Their way is different from ours.*"

"*Aye,*" Flame added. "*It is less productive.*"

Shadow snorted in agreement. Gemi sighed, but Shadow could hear the thought in her mind that agreed with them. She had spent years helping mold groups into well-ordered, peaceful communities, and it hurt her to see hopeful allies fall apart in an area as simple as communication.

"*Well,*" Shadow nickered, "*maybe you can convince the nobles to listen to you after this.*"

Gemi and Flames' answering snorts conveyed their heavy disbelief well enough. Shadow tossed his head.

Nay, I didn't think so, either.

~~*~*

As soon as their boat was close enough to the docks to disembark, Tern leapt from the small boat, shouting for his Knight Captain and Animal Mage. Even from here, he could see that it was mostly his own men who had been involved in accosting the pirate ships with battlefires. He needed to regain control of the situation, especially if he wanted the friendly relationship that the pirates had seemed willing to offer so far. Hopefully, that offer wouldn't be rescinded after this catastrophe.

"Donogh!" the duke shouted again when he couldn't find the man immediately. At least the explosions had stopped. The soldiers seemed to stir violently still, but Tern thought the situation might not be as hopeless as he'd thought it was back on the *Pauper*.

"Milord!"

The duke turned to find Calum striding through the crowds. He wasn't Tern's Knight Captain, but he was pretty much the man's Second, his lack of noble birth the only thing preventing him from actually holding the title.

"Calum, what happened? Where's Donogh?"

"Attempting to keep the men from the battlefires, Milord. I'm afraid things were so chaotic that we didn't know how the attack started or why. Until I got your message by animal, I wasn't sure if I hadn't just missed the orders to attack."

"I can assure you there were no orders to attack," Tern growled.

He glared past the Animal Mage, and several of his soldiers winced as they caught his gaze. To Tern's chagrin, he found that he recognized several of them from the night before at the Magger's Line.

It was several more minutes before the docks had calmed enough for Tern and the others to push their way safely through the crowd. Calum led them towards the battlefires.

They were only about halfway to them when Sir Donogh met them, each hand gripping the arm of a scowling soldier. One fellow was tall and gangly, young enough that Tern thought he must have been a recent addition to the ranks. The other...

"You again!" Tern snarled, recognizing the man who had assaulted Miss Magger the night before. The man paled, his scowl disappearing just as quickly as the color from his cheeks.

"M-m-m'lord," he gulped.

Tern suppressed the urge to roll his eyes at the man's familiar reaction to his presence. He wondered briefly if the man was still drunk.

"Are these the men who started the attack?" Tern asked, turning his gaze to Donogh.

"We didn' start it, M'lord," the gangly fellow interrupted, apparently unconcerned with Tern's anger, or even the presence of the king behind him. "The pirates did. We was jus' respondin'."

A snort drew Tern's attention back to Caffers, who limped forward a step.

"A likely story," the boy sneered, his sarcasm thick enough to cause Tern to stare. "Tell me what they could have possibly done when the captain of the first ship you attacked was consulting the *Pauper* at the time of the first explosion."

Captain? Tern thought, surprised. The only thing he remembered happening during the first explosion was—

"You mean the bird?" the king asked incredulously.

The boy slid his gaze to His Majesty, and Tern was startled by the flat look in his eyes.

"You had best not let Captain Tælen hear you say that, Your Majesty. *Voz*," the boy emphasized the word, "is a lora from the rainforests of Pecali."

A low whistle pierced the air, and Tern glanced at Peln. The Tarsurian duke was eyeing Caffers with raised brows.

"Loros are prized for their inteligencia, and they are notoriously finicky when choosing their amigos." Peln paused before slowly adding, "This capitán, ¿he is un Mago Animal?"

"Aye," Caffers answered lowly, "and he was born mute, so Voz is quite literally his voice."

Peln hummed. "That would explain el nombre of la lora."

The purple-eyed boy turned his gaze to Tern then and his voice nearly dropped to a growl as he muttered, "Can you see why I find it hard to believe that the *Silent Raider* made the first move?"

Tern nodded, but the gangly soldier snapped, "Just because their captain couldn't—"

He gulped suddenly as Caffers glanced at him sharply. There was a darkness in that look that was more than just a silent rebuke. It promised retribution if the soldier dared to continue, and Tern suddenly wondered if he'd misjudged the odd boy.

"Unlike your lot," Caffers sneered, his tone stinging enough to make the soldier flush, "we pirates always follow the orders of our captains in battle. Always!"

The soldier finally glanced down, looking ashamed. Tern considered the boy's words with raised eyebrows. Whether the boy knew it or not, he had just offered the duke the most efficient explanation of how the responsibility for three pirate attacks on Evonese ships could be placed on a single man.

"James," Captain Narsus murmured soothingly, placing a hand on Caffers' shoulder.

The boy angrily snapped his gaze to the older man and opened his mouth to speak. He hesitated then, and his eyes softened, that darkness that Tern had noticed disappearing. Suddenly, the boy simply looked exhausted, and Tern was sharply reminded that the boy was injured and couldn't have snatched more than five hours of sleep the night before.

"If you don't mind, Milords, Your Majesty," Narsus said, swinging his gaze from Caffers to the nobles, "I think we should part ways here.

James and I have business to attend to here in Calay, and we would prefer to finish it quickly so we can return to the *Pauper* and rest."

"Of course," His Majesty answered.

"Your Ma—" Seyan began, but Peln gripped his arm and silenced him with a glare. Even Kawn cast the Baylinese duke a quelling look.

"Majestad," Peln offered once Seyan was quiet, "I believe we'll take our leave and make sure that word has spread amongst los soldados that los piratas are to be left alone. Perhaps we can also clear the docks some so los otros barcos can attend to their own business, ¿sí?" He glanced at Captain Narsus, who nodded and offered a quick thanks.

"¡Ven, Seyan!" Peln commanded as he and Kawn tugged their fellow away. "Before you cause más problemas for Su Majestad."

The Baylinese duke protested being man-handled, but the three older dukes quickly disappeared into the crowds of men surrounding them.

As they left, Tern turned to Donogh and motioned for him to deal with the two soldiers appropriately before returning his attention to His Majesty and the pirates. The king, he noticed, was eyeing the two men with open curiosity now.

"It was a pleasure to meet you both," His Majesty said, offering Captain Narsus his hand.

"And you, Your Majesty," the pirate captain replied as he shook the king's hand. "I wish it had been under better circumstances. My crew and I can be rather hospitable when we're not being threatened with violence."

The king chuckled. "I imagine so. Maybe I can visit the *Pauper* again soon? I confess that I've become curious about your community of Tauresian Pirates."

Narsus laughed loudly and that welcoming smile was back. "If you're ever in Calay when the *Pretty Pauper* is in port, my crew would gladly welcome you, Your Majesty."

"And you, Mister Caffers?" His Majesty added, turning to the purple-eyed youth.

The boy blinked, turning his gaze to the king, and Tern realized with some surprise that the boy seemed to have been scanning the docks for something.

"And I what, Your Majesty?" Caffers' voice sounded distant, as though his thoughts had already left Tern and the king.

His Majesty didn't seem offended by the boy's distraction. "Do you think I might meet you again?"

Tern pursed his lips to keep from chuckling. Obviously, His Majesty had reached the same conclusion that Tern had, that Caffers might be familiar with the *Pretty Pauper* and the other pirates, but he didn't remain with them at all times. Tern was positive the boy had just arrived in Calay the night before, and the fact that the boy had insisted on grabbing his pack before they left the *Pauper* meant that he might not be staying for very long either.

"If you ever catch the *Pauper* in port, Your Majesty," the boy answered, still sounding distracted, "we will see each other again."

Tern caught the king's eye and knew that His Majesty had interpreted the boy's wording the same way he had. Caffers probably only stayed with the *Pauper* while she was at port. Tern would wager that the boy didn't sail on the ship, at least not usually.

Tern and the king bid the two pirates farewell then, His Majesty requesting that Captain Narsus keep him informed on the punishment of the two rogues. Narsus agreed, and the two nobles watched as the two pirates disappeared into the crowd.

~~*~*

"Are you all right, James?" Marlen murmured once he was sure they were far enough away from the king and duke that they wouldn't overhear. "You seem rather distracted."

Distracted was a bit of an understatement, actually. The captain was used to the faraway look Gemi gained when she was speaking to her bondmates and not fully aware of her physical surroundings. But she usually didn't forget herself so fully when strangers were nearby, especially ones as dangerous as the nobles.

Yet she had easily offered up the information that she could only be found on the *Pretty Pauper* whenever the ship was in port. She hadn't said so in those exact words, of course, but Marlen could see that the king and duke were not stupid. He had no doubt that they had interpreted the words in such a manner.

Gemi hummed, still distracted. Marlen wanted to say something else, but a black stallion suddenly pushed past several soldiers and nuzzled the girl's cheek. The girl sighed, closed her eyes, and leaned her head against her mount's.

"Good morning, Shadow," Marlen greeted, wondering if it was simply the girl's bondmates that had her so distracted. However, the stallion turned one eye towards Marlen, and the pirate could read the worry in that brown orb.

Nodding, Marlen gripped Gemi's arm. She dragged her gaze up to Marlen's, and the captain could see that she looked ready to drop.

"Come on. Let's get you to the Golden Bones. You can catch some sleep before the other captains begin arriving for the meeting."

The meeting was the business that Marlen had mentioned to the king. At the beginning of both Spring and Autumn, all thirty-three pirate ships gathered at Port Calay for a meeting of the Tauresian Council of Ships.

Marlen had conveniently forgotten to mention that this was the real reason the entire Tauresian Pirate community was present for this unfortunate incident. He hadn't wanted to complicate things more than they already were.

"I don't know if I should be present for the meeting," Gemi muttered as Marlen and Shadow guided her towards the Golden Bones Inn. "I might start snapping at people like I did with the soldier."

Marlen chuckled at the image his mind produced of the petite James Caffers snapping and snarling at a roomful of pirate captains. If any other child were to try such a thing, Marlen would fear for him. But the Wanderer was well-respected, and possibly even a bit feared, by all of the Tauresian Pirate captains.

"Don't worry about it, James. If that happens, we can always take a break and reconvene tomorrow."

Gemi huffed but didn't argue as they entered the Golden Bones.

Chapter 9

As the king's men began to vacate the docks and prepared to leave Calay, a being stormed angrily through the city's bustling streets, uncaring of where he went. The surrounding humans didn't react as he passed, disgustingly unaware of his presence since few humans could sense him.

The being sneered. If they had been able to see him, they would have cowered from him in fear, despite the futility of such an action.

While he was humanoid in form, his 'skin' was translucent and revealed beneath it the pure black and red substance of his soul. The two colors slid against each other like curls of mist, never combining. His hair, too, portrayed the essence of his soul, the short strands curling in chaotic patterns of red and black.

To complete the image, his eyes held the same colors. However, where a human's eyes would normally be black surrounded by color, his own were red in the center, the black encircling it.

The being, known as a demigod by those who knew of him, suddenly snarled and snapped his head from side to side. Even imagining the humans' reactions to his appearance could not distract him from his anger.

He had *lost*. Again! *She* had won. Again! And, as always, what riled him the most was that *she* did not even realize the significance of what had happened.

A soft *tsk* had him snapping his head to his right, where three females stood, somehow looking both wary and amused.

Like him, they were humanoid in form, and the colors of their souls bled through into their skin, hair, and eyes, though the colors differed. So, too, did the lengths of their hair. The silver one had shoulder-length hair, the pink one waist-length hair, and the white one, older than even he could be sure, had hair down to her knees.

"What do you want?" he growled, wishing the three demigoddesses would leave him be. Even after two hundred years, they still pestered him, despite the fact that the only one who could do anything for him was—

He shook his head again. He would not think about it.

"Really, Belligerence," murmured Love, the pink female, "you can't go on a rampage every time she beats you."

"It's War!" he snarled.

He hated it when the girls referred to him by a lesser name (even if it was more appropriate lately).

The silver female snorted. "It hasn't been War for two years, brother, not since she ended the war with Fayral."

93

War glared at Hope. Did she have to mention such a sore subject? He still didn't even know how *she* had managed to end a decades-long war when *she* hadn't even met the king of Evon yet.

"Frankly," Hope continued with a roll of her silver eyes, "I think you ought to have gotten used to her beating you like that. I mean, it's been six years since you lost control of her."

"I didn't lose control of her," War snarled.

His silver sister's words stung nonetheless.

"Nay, of course not!" Life, the oldest of the siblings, snapped.

To War's surprise, she turned her glare on Hope, who ducked her head and looked ashamed. Once satisfied, the white demigoddess focused her gaze back on War.

"We all know you never actually had control of Peace." War winced and snarled softly, but Life ignored his reaction. "You simply took advantage of her anger."

War sneered half-heartedly. Life was right, of course. She always was.

Seven years ago, Pe-*she* had lost the life she had known to the war that he had gladly fueled between Evon and its neighboring country. That loss had created an anger within her that had allowed him to influence her, an influence he had lost the moment she had taken her revenge.

It still irked him, too, that in the moment she had her revenge, she suddenly gained the mission to ruin everything War had achieved since—

"Nay!" he snarled, shoving the thought away. When he noticed Life staring with raised brows, he shook his head and growled, "Don't you three have other demigods to badger?"

Hope shrugged and offered a sweet smile that had War sneering again. "Of course we do. But, unlike you, dear brother, our twins know when to take a break from the mayhem they cause."

War scowled. More than belittling names, he hated being compared to his three older brothers, the other demigods. He knew he wasn't like them, hadn't been since his own twin 'died'. Now, she was physically incarnated as a human of all things and—

War slammed his eyes closed as anger and despair flooded through him. *Why?* he thought. *Why did she have to leave? Why did she have to forget? Why…?*

"War?" Life whispered.

There was concern in her voice.

Taking a deep breath, War opened his eyes and glared at her. He didn't need her pity. He'd spent two hundred years coping with the loss of…*her*. At least she was in the Mortal Realm again, even if War still felt like the loss was fresh.

Still glaring at his eldest sister, War hissed, "Leave me alone!"

Then, turning away from the demigoddesses, he continued down the street, turning the first corner he encountered.

~~*~*

94

As soon as War had disappeared around the corner—which was only so solid here on the Spiritual Plane because these buildings had stood for so many years—Life released a soft sigh and shook her head.

"I am worried about him."

Hope rolled her eyes. "Of course you are, Life. We've only been worried about him for two hundred years now, ever since Peace gave herself over to Lupus."

Life frowned at the mention of the Hungry Wolf, who ate the memories of souls before they entered the Cycle of Incarnation. He was the one who had informed them that their youngest sister had begged him to take her memories and throw her into the Cycle.

He had never told them why he had not turned her away, despite knowing that her disappearance from the Mortal Realm could be disastrous.

"Maybe," Love replied to Hope, "but Peace returned from the Cycle sixteen years ago. She's even managed to spread peace throughout the region in the last few years."

"Yet War still goes on rampages," Life murmured, her eyes becoming distant as she considered her youngest siblings' situation. "They should balance each other, but it is becoming more and more apparent that if something does not change, only Chaos will result."

All three demigoddesses shuddered.

"Do you think it's because Peace is now human?" Hope whispered.

"Perhaps," Life answered with a shrug. "But it is my hope that it is only because she cannot remember who, or what, she truly is."

Hope groaned. "How is she supposed to remember what she is? There's no way she'll figure it out on her own, and we can't approach her to help."

Giggling suddenly, Love smiled mischievously at the silver demigoddess. "You're losing your touch, Hope, if even you are losing hope."

"Really, Love?" Life groaned, grimacing. "Can you not save the poor puns for Hate? I am sure *he* would appreciate something new to dislike."

The pink sister stuck her tongue out at Life, but her smile did not fade. "You know," she drawled happily, "I wonder why War stormed off that way. I would think he'd still be itching to make trouble with Peace."

Hope snorted. "He hopefully knows better than to attempt anything with the Tauresian Council of Ships. He hasn't been able to influence them since they signed the Pact. Well," she added quickly, "except for Borlin and his lot."

"True," Love replied, still smiling. "But we could head over to the Golden Bones ourselves. Just to make sure nothing untoward happens, of course."

Life traded a glance with Hope, and Love added, "I mean, Peace is awfully tired. I'm sure she would appreciate the extra help."

Life chuckled. "I am sure she would if she knew she was getting it."
She glanced curiously at Hope, who nodded.

"We might as well." The silver demigoddess offered a mischievous
smile of her own. "Besides, I am curious to hear Marlen explain the
situation to the other captains, especially after War managed to get the
soldiers to begin a fight. Rather ingenious, that."

Life sighed. "Even with everything going on, you would appreciate
such a strategy."

Hope shrugged and began to walk towards the Golden Bones. "I have
to find a silver lining somewhere."

~~*~*

War listened as the three demigoddesses ambled down the street back
towards the docks.

When they had begun speaking about him before he was even out of
earshot, he had been angry. When they'd mentioned *her*, he'd forced
himself to stop and listen. It wasn't often he had a chance to hear his
sisters' idle chatter.

He had quickly found his interest dwindling until Life mentioned her
suspicion about the reason War still felt lost. At the mention of Pe-*her*
missing memories, warmth bloomed in his chest. Maybe Life was
right—and she always was—that Pe-*she* only needed to remember who
she was.

Even Hope's quick show of despair hadn't dampened the ideas that
suddenly filled War's head. Maybe they couldn't approach her
themselves, but War thought another way might be possible.

When his sisters began to speak of the pirates, War had wanted to snort.
Nay, he knew the pirates were beyond his influence. It had been pure
luck that Borlin and his men had finally grown tired of submitting to the
will of the more peaceful captain.

Even then, he had known Borlin's time as captain couldn't last. The
beginning of the season always brought *her* to Calay, and, despite the
nature of her soul, her human form had a rather impressive affinity for
battle. The outcome of that little venture had been inevitable.

However, War thought, a smirk forming on his lips, *there is someone
who was rather eager to accept my influence. Perhaps he can…help…me
show her the truth.*

As strategies began to fill his mind, War Transported himself to the
docks. He had a duke to inspire.

~~*~*

Dayphin Strongweather, the young captain of the *Wind Runner*,
whistled as he pushed through the door of the Golden Bones Inn. Despite
two separate encounters with soldiers—one had challenged him to a fight,
while the other had actually grabbed him by his dark red braid and cursed
at him fiercely before his comrades managed to detach him and drag him
away—Dayphin was in a particularly good mood. What had promised to

be a very violent day had only been mildly so, and his own ship had remained unscathed.

His mood quickly wilted when he caught sight of the two captains standing by the Golden Bones' bar. The usually white hair of one looked smokier than usual, his tunic and trousers torn and burnt in places, and soot was smudged across his face and arms.

However, it was the sight of the other that had Dayphin striding quickly towards them.

"What 'appened?" he shouted before he'd even reached them. The two men turned to face him, and Dayphin let his eyes roam over the second man's form.

A bandage was wrapped around the man's right thigh, and another around his right shoulder, showing that, unlike Dayphin's, his ship had been in the midst of the brief battle.

He, too, was covered in soot, so much so that his features were obscured and the usual brown of his hair and beard was darkened to near black. The only reason Dayphin had even recognized him was the bird that perched on his left shoulder, her own feathers darker than normal.

"Hello to you, too," squawked Voz reproachfully, ruffling her feathers.

Bits of soot and small feathers dropped from her wings as she did so, and Tælen reached up to soothe a finger down her chest, his eyes never leaving Dayphin's. The redhead blushed.

"Sorry," he muttered, ducking his head. "G'morning." When he glanced back up, lower lip caught between his teeth, the silent captain was smiling slightly.

A chuckle to Dayphin's left startled him, and he glanced quickly at Orphus, the white-haired captain of the *Silver Girl.*

"Should I leave y'two alone?" Orphus asked, amusement dripping from his words. Dayphin felt his cheeks heat more, but Tælen snorted and rolled his eyes.

"You one to talk, Orphus," squawked Voz once more, always Tælen's loyal voice. Then, turning back to Dayphin, Tælen said, through Voz, "Battlefire hit deck mid-ship. Rather unexpected. Caught me rather close." Voz gave another shake then and muttered, "Demasiado cercano."

Dayphin raised his eyebrows. Voz rarely slipped into Pecalini these days and only when she was voicing her own opinion. The battle must have been rather fierce to shake her so badly.

"Voz wasn't with me when the first battlefire hit," the lora added in Tælen's words.

Dayphin gasped, and he heard Orphus grunt. For Tælen to be so vulnerable at the first moment of the attack...

Dayphin shuddered and leaned closer to Tælen, wrapping a hand firmly around his upper left arm. Voz trilled softly and leaned over, nibbling gently at a strand of red hair that had come loose from Dayphin's braid.

Tælen shook his head and, after a moment, nudged Voz's belly. The lora huffed and offered her captain what Dayphin could only describe as a glare, but Tælen only raised an eyebrow.

Huffing again, Voz squawked, "Not as bad as it looks. Nothing a Mage Healer can't take care of." Switching to Pecalini, the lora nipped Tælen on the ear and added, "Humano tonto."

Dayphin chuckled at Voz's antics and loosened his hold on the other captain's arm. "If so, why no' get yer 'Ealer to patch yeh up?"

Tælen's eyes grew sad. "Not the worst on the ship," Voz trilled and lowered her head.

Dayphin's stomach twisted, and he leaned further into Tælen's side, lifting a hand to rub at Voz's neck in comfort.

"I'll bring my Mage 'Ealer to the *Raider* af'er the meetin' then," he murmured. Tælen met his eyes and nodded, his own gray eyes warming with gratitude.

A *clunk* from the bar drew the two pirate captains from their silent communion. Jemiah, the innkeeper's wife, stood behind the bar, a tray of five plates lying in front of her. "'Ere ye are, boys," she said, laying the plates out. "Tha' should cover the rest o' ye. Drinks?"

"Pint each," squawked Voz before taking the piece of fruit that Tælen offered her from his plate.

As Jemiah began filling tankards with the diluted brew she offered this early in the morning, Dayphin grabbed a plate and eyed the two extras. "Who we still missin'?"

Orphus opened his mouth, but, before he could answer, the door of the inn opened, and the final two captains walked through. Dayphin recognized them immediately as Canor and Bast, the captains of the *Cresta Surcanda* and the *Duquesa Risueña*, the only two Pecalini ships to have signed the Pact. He blinked at the sight of them.

Canor was a tall, willowy man who always kept himself extremely neat. For that reason, Dayphin was startled to see that his pale hair was thoroughly mussed, and he seemed to be nursing a split lip. Bast, on the other hand, looked physically all right, but his expression was rather forbidding.

"An' what 'appened to you two then?" Orphus asked, eyeing the newest arrivals.

"Malditos soldados, tha's what," Bast spat, the Pecalini words sounding odd in his grating voice.

"We encountered un grupo de soldados that was rather…violently inclined," Canor added. His usually musical voice sounded thicker than usual, and he winced as he dabbed at the bleeding lip.

"An' you got away with no more than a bloody lip?" Orphus sounded like he didn't believe it.

Bast growled. "Woulda been worse if some caballero hadn' been around to shout at 'em about an order bein' an order."

Dayphin snorted in amusement. "Sir Donogh?" When the four other captains turned and stared at him, the redhead blinked. "What?"

"'Ow you know that 'is nombre?" Bast growled.

Dayphin shrugged. "I grew up on the Chanser Estate, an' he been the Chansers' Knigh' Cap'n for years." The redhead shrugged again. "An' he always been a stickler for orders. Strictest knigh' you e'er met."

"Tha' may be," Bast grunted, "bu' those malditos soldados were jus' askin' for trouble. If tha' caballero 'adn' come, I'd a given it to 'em, too."

The rough-voiced captain then fell fully into Pecalini, and Dayphin lost track of the man's rant. Despite his association with Tælen and Voz, the redhead had never managed to pick up more than a few words of the eastern language.

A quick jab of Canor's elbow to Bast's side silenced the harsh Pecalini, and Bast turned to Canor with a glare.

"Fayralese, por favor, or nada at all," Canor murmured smoothly, ignoring the glare.

Dayphin snorted. He thought the request a bit hypocritical since Canor had probably been raised speaking only Pecalini himself, being born in Pecali. Bast was only from Tarsur.

Bast muttered something more in Pecalini that had Tælen jerking and glaring at the man. Even Voz squawked and whistled angrily. Canor simply shrugged and stepped up to the bar, where Jemiah was watching them with a faint smile.

"Two more pints, por favor, querida Jemiah."

The woman's smile widened and, with a quick "Of course", she fetched the two drinks.

With a plate of food and a tankard each, the five captains made their way to the back of the Golden Bones' common room, where a door stood open revealing a large private dining room that held one large table, what Dayphin knew would be thirty-four chairs, and a large number of pirate captains milling around.

Greetings were shouted as they entered the room and claimed the table's five remaining places. The noise level, which had been moderate as the pirates traded gossip and advice, only increased as Voz added her own voice to the mix, answering questions when several other captains approached Tælen.

Dayphin himself was quickly pulled into a conversation with a couple of captains whose ships were docked near the *Wind Runner*. He laughed when they asked if he had really spoken to the king that morning and fell into an explanation of his understanding of the situation.

This was, of course, the norm for these meetings. Formally, the meeting was a tool of governance that occurred twice a year, but it also provided a chance for the pirate captains to catch up after two seasons of not seeing each other. True, some ships met out at sea or at other ports, but these meetings provided a secure chance of reunion.

Bast's voice was just starting to rise angrily—*someone must have mentioned the soldiers,* Dayphin thought—when Marlen, captain of the *Pretty Pauper* and current Head of the Tauresian Council of Ships, stood and called for the meeting to start. As everyone sat down, Dayphin got his first look at the head of the table, where the Head of the Council and the Wanderer always sat.

To Dayphin's surprise, the Wanderer, James Caffers, looked to be asleep. His head lay on his arms, which were folded on the tabletop, and he remained still, even as the room became almost silent. Once the pirates were seated and quiet, Marlen reached over and shook the boy's shoulder slightly.

"Come, James. The meeting is about to begin."

All thirty-three pirate captains watched as Caffers lifted his head groggily and blinked around the table. As he lifted his hands to rub at his eyes, Dayphin was struck by how young the boy seemed.

He knew the boy was sixteen, and he had seen the boy in battle, so Dayphin knew how dangerous he could be. But, watching the boy wake up, the redhead thought it rather amazing that someone who could look so young and helpless could have the unwavering respect of so many pirate captains.

"'M 'wake," Caffers murmured finally.

Personally, Dayphin thought he still looked half-asleep, but Marlen seemed satisfied, and he turned back to the table to begin the meeting.

It was quickly decided that the *Pretty Pauper* and the morning's incident were the first order of business. However, as Marlen began to explain the actions and crimes of his ex-First Mate, a commotion broke out in the inn's common room.

"What now?" Orphus growled as shouting filtered into the private dining room. Dayphin, who had claimed the seat closest to the door, rose from the table to see what the trouble was.

As he opened the door a crack to peer through it, a high-pitched voice cut across the shouting. "...the Wand'rer! 'E wan's to speak to the Wand'rer!" Silence followed, both among the pirates and in the common room.

Through the crack in the door, Dayphin saw a young boy, no more than eight or nine years old, standing in front of a group of men that looked like soldiers. Beside the boy stood a man dressed in the finery of a noble.

Dayphin wondered which noble he was then wondered why the boy was trying to help him find Caffers. Those who knew who the Wanderer was knew not to give such information to nobles, knights, or soldiers. They were the ones with the desire and power to arrest Caffers and destroy what he had accomplished for the Evonese people.

"I don' know why you would look 'ere of all places, M'lord," Jemiah said. She had walked around the bar and now stood between the soldiers and the door Dayphin was peering through.

"I know 'e's 'ere. 'E 'as to be," the boy shouted. Panic filled his eyes before he turned to the noble and grabbed the edge of his tunic. "Ye gots to believe me."

The innkeeper's wife shook her head. "'M sorry, laddie, but the Wand'rer ain' here."

"But 'e's al'ays 'ere on the first o' Early Aut'mn." The boy began tugging on the nobleman's tunic, and the noble scowled down at the boy. "The Pirate Council al'ays meets 'ere on the first o' Early Aut'mn, and the Wand'rer is al'ays there."

"What in gods' names is going on 'ere?"

The new voice belonged to a large, wiry fellow that stomped into the room. Dayphin knew the man was the innkeeper, Egan. He didn't often deal with customers because his fiery temper was more often the cause of commotions like this one rather than the solution.

The noble finally looked away from the boy tugging on his tunic, and his features smoothed as he gazed at Egan. "I am simply looking for the Wanderer, good sir, and I had been informed that I could find him here."

The innkeeper growled. "Ye got no business seekin' some'at like that at me inn."

The noble narrowed his eyes, but, to Dayphin's surprise, he continued in a smooth voice, "Very well. Then maybe you can find me James Caffers?"

Dayphin stiffened and pulled his face away from the door to stare back at the still-seated pirates. Each of their expressions held varying degrees of anger and horror, but it was Caffers' expression Dayphin sought.

The boy's eyes were wide, but his jaw was set, and his hands were pressed to the edge of the table in front of him. He looked ready to bolt.

Sudden cursing drew Dayphin back to his position looking through the door. "Git out of me inn afore I throw ye out. Ye got no business 'ere, an' I won' have ye scarin' off me regulars."

The noble smirked then and strode forward. "He is here, then. I assume he is in this council meeting of which the boy spoke. Where might that be?"

Egan cursed again, but Jemiah glanced back towards the door behind which Dayphin stood. *Damn,* Dayphin thought and shut the door as quickly and quietly as he could.

The noble must have noticed the glance because Dayphin heard footsteps quickly approaching the door. Egan shouted, "Wha' do ye think yer—", and was cut short by a sudden pounding on the door.

Dayphin cursed out loud this time. Turning, he frantically waved a hand towards the head of the table. He hoped Caffers saw the signal as the other captains swiftly stood from the table and crowded towards the door.

Chapter 10

The moment he spoke, Gemi recognized the voice of Lord Lefas, duke of Baylin. Panic filled her mind, and suddenly she was fully awake. As no one else spoke up, she had to assume that he was here alone, with neither the king nor the other dukes here to talk him down.

Part of her knew she shouldn't be surprised he had sought her out. The man's words and responses, both on the *Pauper* and on the docks before the other dukes managed to pull him away, should have shown her that he was unwilling to give up a chance at the Wanderer.

Or, rather, the Ghost, as he surely knows me best.

But she had been certain he didn't know she was the Ghost and that he had no chance of learning the information. No one had ever been willing to give her up before.

Yet, here they were now, a voice that sounded like a young boy's spilling information that she would rather a noble not hear.

Then, to make matters worse, Lord Lefas spoke her alias, the name by which most people knew her. That had to mean he knew who she was, that she wouldn't be safe even if she left. He knew what she looked like and the name she used. If he was determined enough, he could hunt her down or, worse, spread the news to the other nobles and have them do same.

Gemi shuddered at the thought.

"*We can't just give up,*" Shadow snorted, pulling Gemi from her panic.

"*Shadow is correct,*" Flame added. "*Allowing them to capture you is not a viable option.*"

Gemi cast a glance towards the door by which she always sat during these meetings. It was at the back of the private dining room and led directly to the alley behind the inn, where Shadow usually waited in case of emergency.

"*I'm here,*" he added, responding to her thoughts, "*but I don't know how good this route will be. I'm surrounded here.*"

He flashed her an image of several soldiers standing in the alley, surrounding the inn. Gemi would have been amused that they didn't seem to pay Shadow any mind if she wasn't worried about possible capture.

"*I even heard a couple talking about who they're looking for. They know what you look like.*"

Gemi didn't have time to respond as someone began pounding on the door to the common room and Dayphin motioned for her to run. Before she could even think of how to respond to that, Marlen was hauling her from her chair and propelling her towards the back door.

"Run, James!"

As her hand settled on the door's handle, Gemi felt the panic suddenly still. She could do this. She'd fought a war for four years and survived. She could find a way out of this.

She pushed the words *"Distract them, Shadow"* into the stallion's mind, then pulled open the door and ran.

~~*~*

Flame hissed as Shadow reared and Gemi flew past the suddenly yelling soldiers.

"What are you doing?" she demanded. *"You cannot possibly outrun them."* Gemi's mind stirred sluggishly in response, and Flame snarled. *"You are too tired. You can barely think."*

"Then think for me, will you?" The girl's thoughts were softer than normal, more distracted than the dragon liked to hear. *"Help me get away from them."*

Flame growled. *She is not thinking!* If she had been, she would have realized what she was asking.

Gemi had always been insistent that as few humans know about Flame as possible, and the dragon could only agree. Too many problems had occurred in the past when the wrong people knew about her.

Then again, if Lefas captures Gemi, then a chance sighting will be the least of our worries.

Flame dropped below the thick clouds that had hidden her all morning. Taking one glance across the city, she easily spotted Gemi and the soldiers that had begun to follow her.

"Left," she commanded, pressing it against Gemi's mind. The girl turned the corner, reaching out a hand to grip at the side of the building so she did not fly into the opposite wall.

As Flame swiftly planned the route Gemi should take, she pressed lightly against Shadow's mind. *"Go to Wægport Market, Shadow. James will meet you there."*

Nickering a soft *"I hope so"*, Shadow trotted out of the alley, still ignored by the surrounding humans.

As long as they continue to ignore him, Flame thought before pressing a quick *"Right"* against Gemi's mind.

As the girl turned the next corner, a hound lying against the opposite wall lifted its head and eyed her warily. Flame hissed thoughtfully. *Perhaps...*

She pushed her Animal Magic through the dragonbond that connected her to Gemi. She had never tried to influence other animals through one of her bondmates, but she had learned over the years that the bond was more powerful than Flame had been raised to believe.

Staring down at the city, Flame watched, amused, as the hound leapt up and snarled just as the first of the soldiers appeared around the corner. The hound jumped on the first soldier, while a second hound, which Flame had not noticed, leapt from the opposite side of the alley and bit into the leg of another soldier.

The yells of the soldiers and snarls of the hounds distracted Gemi, but
both Flame and Shadow pressed on her mind, urging her forward.

"*You have to keep moving, James,*" Flame hissed, then quickly added,
"*Left.*"

Gemi nearly stumbled to a halt when she turned the next corner to find
a group of children kicking a ball around.

"*Keep moving,*" Flame hissed again to make sure her bondmate did not
stop.

Gemi gasped, "Pard'n...me," as she ran between two of the children.
The younglings stopped and stared after her as she sped down the alley.

"*The chil...dren—*" Gemi gasped through the bond, but Flame snapped
her teeth together to interrupt.

"*They will be all right, James. They are not the ones the soldiers seek.*"
And they might even be helpful.

Just as Gemi disappeared around another corner, the soldiers turned
onto the alley, and the first one stumbled to the ground as one of the
children kicked the ball into his stomach. Immediately, the other children
crowded around, effectively stopping the soldiers from continuing their
pursuit.

Flame bared her teeth in a fierce grin.

~~*~*

The next turn put Gemi in an alley that emptied directly into the
Wægport Market. She slowed to a walk, which quickly became a limp as
a sharp pain in her thigh reminded her that she was injured and the wound
had probably reopened.

Her chest heaved, and her sides and lungs burned from the exertion, but
her breath hitched as she touched her bandaged side. It stung more than
her thigh, and she could feel the blood that had soaked through the
bandage.

Not good, she thought as she approached the end of the alley. Just as
she reached the first vendor's stall, Shadow appeared beside her and
nudged her worriedly.

"*Can you mount?*" Shadow questioned. Flame, too, murmured
worriedly, and Gemi could sense her circling just below the cloud cover.

Gemi didn't bother to answer her bondmates' questions, either
mindspoken or silent. Instead, she gripped the front of Shadow's saddle,
lifted one foot to the stirrup—wavering slightly as black stars bloomed
across her vision—and hauled herself onto her mount's back.

"Let's go," she gasped, leaning heavily over the stallion's neck, and,
with a single nicker of worry, Shadow began pushing through the
crowded marketplace.

~~*~*

Seyan growled in frustration as he glared around the private dining
room where the pirates had just reseated themselves.

When he'd first tried to enter the room, all thirty-three pirates—one for
each ship currently in port, apparently—had made a show of greeting him

and welcoming him to the 'Tauresian Council of Ships'. The action had given James Caffers—the Ghost—time to run.

Of course, the soldiers Seyan had brought to the inn, men from Caypan, had chased the boy, but they'd already returned and reported that they had lost him.

The duke snarled. *How can a boy as small and injured as Caffers is outrun a group of grown men trained for war?* It was unfathomable. There was no excuse.

A sudden, indignant squawk drew his attention to the bird they'd seen earlier that morning, now perched upon the shoulder of a nearby pirate. It stared at him with one eye, its expression disturbingly reminiscent of a human glare.

Seyan sneered and watched, satisfied, as it ruffled its feathers and turned its head away. Honestly, the bird unnerved him. *Acting as a voice for a human; it isn't natural.*

Seyan finally turned away and left the dining room. The pirates had actually had the audacity to invite him to stay for the meeting, but he wasn't stupid enough to believe that they really wanted him there. He had recognized the brittleness of their smiles and the darkness of their gazes.

Nay, he knew they didn't want him here. However, they most likely believed themselves safe under the king's protection and thought they could keep Seyan from his true goal: capturing the Ghost and finally ridding Evon of the damn rebel leader.

When Seyan stepped out of the inn, he paused and scanned the docks that the inn faced. Other than the group of soldiers milling around the inn, the docks were surprisingly empty of the king's men.

Instead, pirates and citizens of Calay wandered the docks, mingling in such a way that Seyan knew the presence of the pirate ships was not a surprise to the locals.

How can an entire city welcome the presence of pirates? It's enough to make one's stomach roil.

Seyan's eyes finally landed on the boy who had led him to the inn. He stood further down the docks, squirming beneath the hand of a dark-haired young man.

Seyan narrowed his eyes. It was that young man who had sought Seyan out and confirmed for him that Caffers truly was the Ghost. Now, that man stood watching him, smirking at him like he held secrets he knew Seyan would gladly pay to learn.

Growling softly, Seyan glanced around again to be sure no one was paying him too much attention. Once sure he wasn't being observed—except by the smirking young man who was quickly becoming an annoyance—Seyan approached the two.

Once close enough to get a good look at the man's eyes, the duke felt a shiver run down his spine. Like the bird that spoke for a human, those eyes were not natural. They were red, bright around the center and near black along the edge.

They sharply reminded Seyan that, while the man might be an annoyance, he must also be powerful. And, with eyes like that, it was not a power Seyan dared cross.

"So the Ghost got away, eh?" The red-eyed man laughed even as Seyan scowled at him. "That wasn't exactly the smartest way to handle him, you know. Announcing your presence like that."

"And how, exactly, would you have suggested I…'handle' him?"

The man's smirk widened. "Brute force, obviously. It's the only way you'll catch him. Of course," he paused, his smirk becoming a broad grin, "he's probably already left the city by now."

Seyan had to bite his tongue to keep from swearing at the man. Time and again this morning, he'd had the chance to take down the Ghost, to bring to justice a criminal that was as big a threat to their country as Fayral had been.

Now, he'd lost any other possible chances because he'd spooked the man and forced him to flee the city.

"You are lucky I paid you ahead of time," he bit out. "You would not be paid, otherwise."

The man only chuckled. "Don't be so hasty, *Milord*." He drawled the title, and Seyan's cheeks flushed angrily. "You'll still get your man. All you have to do is follow the Trail."

Seyan growled. "What trail? My men lost track of the boy."

The smirk was back. "Hardly *your* men, were they?" Seyan scowled. "But I'm not talking about any trail the *boy* might have left. I mean the Ghost Trail."

Seyan blinked, now confused. "Ghost Trail? What nonsense are you speaking?"

The red eyes rolled. "That nonsense will help you find your criminal if you bother to listen."

Seyan glared again, but the man simply ignored him.

"You would be surprised how many people know the route the Ghost takes every season. Many people can tell you exactly where you can find the Ghost on any given day. Of course, with his schedule now scrapped…"

The man made a show of thinking it over. Seyan growled impatiently, and the man smirked impishly.

"If you assume he's just going to skip the two sevendays he usually spends here in Calay," and the look in those red eyes made it obvious the man did not doubt he would, "then he'll be heading north next. Just take the West Evonese Highway to Kensy. You'll find him somewhere near the North Evonese Junction, no doubt."

Seyan nearly snarled at the mention of Kensy. Ever since Jem Cosley's death, Kensy had been "wild country". With the war ravaging the forest and the highwaymen robbing people every chance they could, those nobles who hadn't fallen to the war left willingly. As far as Seyan was concerned, the province was simply a lawless territory that Evon could just barely claim as its own.

"And how, pray tell, do you expect me to protect myself in Kensy, let alone capture the Ghost?"

The red-eyed man shrugged, still smirking. "I recommend you don't go alone, certainly. The North Evonese Junction is highwayman territory. Then again," he chuckled, "all of Kensy is highwayman territory."

"And capturing the Ghost?" Seyan bit out. Despite the power the duke suspected this man had, Seyan's patience was running thin.

The man grinned. "I already told you: brute force. It's the only way you'll...conquer the Ghost."

Seyan narrowed his eyes, thrown by the man's word choice. However, he wanted to rid himself of the man's presence as quickly as possible now that he had the information he needed.

Nodding stiffly, he muttered, "Thank you for the information. I'll remember your services." Not that Seyan thought anything would come of the memory. It was simply the polite thing to say.

The duke shuddered when the man's grin suddenly disappeared and his eyes flashed, though he quickly rationalized that the latter must have been a trick of the light.

"If you get the chance, *Milord*," the man drawled darkly, "give my regards to the Ghost. Tell him that Markos sent you."

The red-eyed man then glanced downwards, and Seyan followed his gaze to the boy whose shoulder the man held. To Seyan's surprise, the boy looked like he was close to tears, and his squirming had only gotten worse since the conversation began.

"Come, boy, your mother is probably worried sick about you."

As the man steered the boy past Seyan, the child shot the duke an almost panicked look that he didn't understand. He had thought the two were related since both times he'd spoken with the man, Markos had been holding the boy's shoulder.

Either way, Seyan decided not to question it. He would rather not give the man a reason to subject him to his presence any further.

Turning away from the two, he considered the struggle he had ahead of him. True, he now knew who the Ghost was and where to find him, but he knew the real difficulty would be convincing the king to follow.

His Majesty had shown enough of the wrong kind of interest in the boy to worry Seyan, and the young king had always been more interested in peace than justice. This morning's incident had only proven that.

If only Seyan had brought his own men with him to Cautzel, then he'd be able to travel to Kensy himself and not bother with the king and the other dukes. But he was dependent on the men they'd brought with them, all of which were loyal to either Lord Tern or His Majesty.

And enlisting the king's soldiers for a raid of an inn without the king's knowledge was one thing; ordering them to Kensy without the king's approval was entirely another.

Still, Seyan couldn't let that deter him. The Ghost had been a thorn in his side since the end of the war, and he wouldn't let him slip through his fingers again. The king might find James Caffers interesting, but the boy was still a criminal.

He must be brought to justice.

~~*~*

"Unfair!" Hope cried, staring at their red-and-black brother. She whirled to face the older demigods, pointing a hand back towards War. "He can't possibly be allowed to do that!"

That, Life knew, referred to War taking on physical form. The older siblings, all six of them, had just observed War's new tactic. Despite Hope's protest—which had not come until after War was done—they had watched him take on the form of a young human male and speak to the Baylinese duke, influencing him that way when the demigods had, for so long, only influenced on the Spiritual Plane.

"And why not, dear sister," Hope's twin answered, tugging on one of her silver curls. "He is only doing what Peace has done for the past few years."

Hope narrowed her eyes at the yellow demigod. "Peace doesn't know what she's doing, Fear."

"She doesn't have to, does she?" answered the red demigod who stood near Love. "Her influence seems to be just as powerful without her knowledge as it would be if she stood with us once more."

"Hate's right," Love murmured. She leaned forward to lay a hand on Hope's arm. "And I would even go so far as to say her influence is more dangerous since it's not consciously driven."

Hope pursed her lips and glanced back at War, who had stalked after the Baylinese duke as soon as he'd dropped the physical form. For a silent moment, the six older demigods watched as the warmongering duke began his attempt to persuade the king to follow Peace north.

As the conversation turned heated, Hope sighed. "So...no punishment?"

A dark laugh from Life's left made her twitch and glance at her own black twin.

"Nay, Hope," Death answered, "no punishment."

Life nodded. There had once been a time when they would have demanded War be punished for breaking such a 'rule' of The Game, as the demigods referred to the way they dealt with the lives of mortals.

Peace's 'death' had changed things though. Their purple sister had introduced a new dimension to The Game that the other demigods had never considered, one that made it more personal than any of them had ever wanted. Life knew, as she was sure her siblings did, that the rules were not as rigid as they had once believed them to be.

"It still doesn't seem fair," Hope muttered. "She has no way to defend against such tactics."

Life snorted. "Really, Hope, you need to give Peace more credit." When her sister turned to her with curious silver eyes, Life raised a brow. "Despite her lack of memory, she has managed to bring peace to a land that War ravaged for nearly the entire time she was 'dead'. I do not call that defenseless."

Hope frowned. Before she could reply, Life added, "Besides, I think War is on the right track." Hope gaped at her and even the others looked surprised. "Peace needs to remember who she is, for everyone's sake. She cannot do that without someone forcing her to remember."

The white demigoddess nodded towards their errant brother. "Who better to do that than her own twin?"

After a moment, Hope sighed and nodded, turning back to the nobles. The king had fallen silent and was watching the four dukes argue. Suddenly, he said something—the siblings were too far away from the nobles to hear it without straining—and the dukes fell silent.

The Zhulanese duke then nodded and spoke, which seemed to get the Baylinese duke riled up once again, but the Tarsurian silenced him with a sharp look and quick words. The Zhulanese man nodded, spoke again, and eyed the king questioningly. Nodding thoughtfully, the young man turned to his mount.

"They're going then," Love murmured.

Hate snorted. "Of course they are. Did you really doubt War's ability to make it so?"

Love offered her red twin a knowing smile. "Oh, I don't think it was really War that made it so."

Life frowned. Who else could have influenced the nobles to head north? None of the older siblings were close enough to influence them, not enough for that, at least.

Hate, on the other hand, seemed to understand his twin perfectly well. He rolled his eyes. "He has no reason to understand what he's feeling yet."

Love giggled. "Which is exactly why he'll be insistent on following her."

"What are you two talking about?" Fear asked, looking as confused as Life felt.

"Nothing," Hate muttered and glared at Love, who simply smiled and shrugged.

Life shook her head. She had thought she and Death were bad about keeping secrets from their younger siblings, but Love and Hate might do the same.

Just then, War disappeared, Transporting himself elsewhere, no doubt with the intent to continue pestering Peace. To Life's surprise, he had not looked as happy as she thought he should have. Nor did the Baylinese duke, for that matter.

Curious, Life glanced back at the nobles and blinked when she saw that they were apparently planning to travel alone. They had sought neither soldiers nor knights but, instead, were already riding towards the city's limits. Life worried her lip. She did not know whether the five men traveling alone was a good thing or not.

With War gone, the other siblings began to disperse, as well. Soon, Life and Death, the eldest of the four pairs of twins, stood alone, watching the docks and the ships rocking in the harbor.

They stood, silent, for several long minutes, thinking and simply reveling in each other's presence. Despite the polar nature of their influences, they were equals, and it was only in each other that they could find balance.

Yet, Life thought, reaching out to grip Death's wrist, a grip he quickly reciprocated, *that has never been more apparent than it is now with the situation between Peace and War.*

"What are you pondering, Life?"

The words were quiet, yet insistent enough that Life turned her gaze to her black twin.

"How easily we fall into Chaos." When Death only raised a brow, Life shrugged. "I wonder sometimes if Father and Mother understood just how fragile is the Order we were born to uphold."

Death chuckled dryly. "I think 'futile' might be the word Father would use these days. There are four pairs of us."

Life nodded and turned her gaze back out to sea. "Did you notice?" she murmured after a moment.

Death sighed. "Notice what, Life?"

"Did you notice the way War clung to the human child?" She glanced at Death as he frowned.

"You think he was using the child's physical nature to secure his own?"

Life nodded. Their youngest brother had only been physical when holding onto the boy. "He is more chaotic than we thought if he cannot hold onto a physical form without help."

"Then let us hope he reminds Peace of who she is before that Chaos deals more damage than we can handle."

Life sighed. "I just hope he knows what he is doing."

Death wrapped an arm around her shoulder and pulled her closer, allowing her to lay her head on his shoulder.

"Just minutes ago, you were arguing for his latest tactic. Why the worry?"

"Because The Game is not just about the mortals anymore, Death." The white demigoddess lifted her eyes to her brother's. "If War does not get through to Peace, I am afraid that he is not the only one who will fall to the Chaos."

She held his gaze, trying to convey just how worried she was. With a sigh, Death leaned forward and kissed her forehead.

"I understand," he murmured, "but there is naught we can do now but to encourage or stymie War when necessary, is there?" Life shook her head slowly. "And we have already encouraged War, so we must now watch and wait, aye?"

Life sighed once more. She felt weary but knew that it would only get worse, most likely. "Aye, all we can do now is wait."

After so many millennia of influencing mortals, waiting was the last thing Life wanted to do.

Part II
Kensy

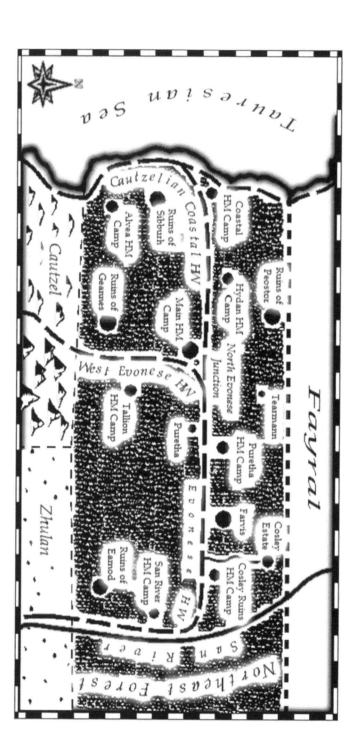

Map of Kensy

Chapter 11

3 Early Autumn, 224
West Evonese Highway near the North Evonese Junction
Kensy, Evon

Kephin Bulderas shifted his weight and sighed as he leaned back against the trunk of the tree in which he stood. It seemed like ages since he had last joined the others on the highway, which was only to be expected.

As leader of the Highwaymen, his days were filled with managing Main Highwayman Camp, maintaining relations with the local villages and farms, and directing manpower, when necessary. He rarely had enough free time to dabble in a bit of scouting.

However, Acker, the man who normally acted as scout at this hour, had been wounded in a rogue attack just yesterday, and Kephin had been pleased enough to take advantage of the opportunity to return to his favorite activity.

Kephin chuckled. One might think that thirty-six was a bit old to be climbing trees, but Kephin was still as nimble now as he had been at twenty-two when he'd first fled Fayral and become a highwayman here in Kensy. And while his opinion of the Evonese people may have changed over the years, Kephin doubted his desire to climb trees ever would.

He was swiftly drawn from his thoughts by a heavy *clop* from below. Still smiling and gripping the branch above his head, Kephin leaned away from the tree's trunk and peered down at the highway beneath his perch.

When he spied the source of the noise, all happy thoughts fled his mind, and his body stilled. The large, black horse that plodded down the highway was both very familiar and highly unexpected.

But it wasn't the horse that made Kephin's heart thunder and his stomach drop. Slumped over the horse's back, unmoving, was Gemini Cosley, a girl whom Kephin had viewed as his little sister for the past six years.

Whistling a sharp warning to his men not to leave the safety of the tree line, Kephin scrambled down through the large tree's branches. As soon as he hit the ground, he ran onto the highway, calling a breathless "James!" as he did so.

When he stopped beside Shadow, the stallion swung his head around and eyed Kephin with dull, brown eyes. Fearing the worst, the highwayman leaned up, placed two fingers against the unresponsive youth's neck, and sought a pulse.

Relief flooded him when he felt the faint flutter beneath his fingertips. Releasing the breath he'd been holding, he dropped his hand to the stallion's shoulder and observed the girl. As he did, the worry quickly returned.

Gemi might be alive, but she was unconscious. Rope covered her thighs and the saddle, preventing her from falling from Shadow's back, and she lay limp across his neck. Bloody bandages surrounded one thigh and her midsection, and a faint odor indicated that the wounds not been properly cleaned.

On top of that, a fine shiver shook her body and her clothes were damp, no doubt a result of one of the late summer rainstorms that plagued western Cautzel's mountains and foothills at this time of year. Shadow, too, was still damp, and mud was spattered across his lower legs.

Loud rustling suddenly drew Kephin's gaze up to the forest's canopy. He watched, unsurprised, as a large, red-and-purple winged creature dropped to the highway. Giving herself a single shake, Flame slid forward and nudged Kephin's side, crooning softly.

"What happened, Flame?" the highwayman demanded, even as he knew he wouldn't be able to understand her response; he wasn't a mage.

However, he did understand her when she shook her head and ambled slowly towards the northern tree line. *Not now,* she seemed to say, *camp first.* Nodding, Kephin gripped the side of Shadow's bridle and led him off the highway.

They had only gone a few steps before Kephin realized that Shadow must be exhausted. His movements were slow, and, despite Kephin's desire to get his friends back to Main Highwayman Camp as quickly as possible, the horse refused to be hurried.

Thankfully, Kephin's station on the highway wasn't far from the camp. They broke out of the tree line soon enough and were greeted by murmurs as men, women, and children alike turned to them, no doubt already alerted to their arrival by Flame sweeping through the camp. Already, the dragon had disappeared from view, and Kephin suspected that the large serpent had gone in search of Lakina, the camp's Mage Healer.

"What 'appened, Kephin?" shouted one man, and soon other questions assaulted his ears as people began to crowd around him.

"I don't know yet," Kephin said forcefully, shaking his head and pushing a man out of Shadow's path. While the horse refused to be hurried, he didn't seem inclined to stop, either, and Kephin didn't wish to see any of his comrades trampled by his old friend.

A sharp hiss startled the people surrounding Kephin, and they backed away enough for Kephin to see Flame baring her teeth at the other highwaymen. Her tail whipped back and forth behind her, and Kephin recognized the look in her red eyes. It wouldn't take much for her to start snapping and snarling.

"Move away and let them through!" snapped a female voice.

Kephin watched as the men and women who had surrounded him returned quickly to their previous tasks, though they continued to glance curiously at the small group.

"James better have a good explanation for this!" the female voice snapped again.

Pursing his lips so he wouldn't smile at the annoyance in the woman's tone, Kephin turned to face the voice's owner.

The old woman was small, but her silver hair was pulled back into a tight bun, her expression fierce. Kephin had learned long ago that the woman was not to be trifled with, and he pitied anyone with injuries that were earned from either sheer stupidity or neglect.

"Lakina," he murmured, laying a hand on her shoulder as she fell into step with him and Shadow. Flame took up Shadow's other side, nudging his side and neck with her snout. "Why don't we get James settled and healed before you start questioning how foolish he is."

The Mage Healer huffed and nodded. "We'll have to settle him in your tent."

Kephin frowned. "Why?"

Not that Kephin would mind. Gemi always stayed in his tent while in Kensy anyway, but Lakina usually preferred to have her patients close at hand.

The Mage Healer released a heavy sigh. "I have no room in my tent at the moment." She paused, offering Kephin a significant look. "Frick was attacked by rogues on his way from the Lily Grove."

Kephin hissed. "Another attack?"

That was the second in two days, fourth in the last sevenday. The rogues were becoming bolder, more organized, and Kephin couldn't help but wonder if their numbers had increased, as well.

Lakina nodded. "We're going to have to do something about them soon, Kephin." She glanced up at the girl who lay slumped across Shadow's back. "Although, as much as I hate the thought of it, we might have to wait until James is fully healed."

Kephin nodded grimly. Gemi would want to help bring down the rogues, if only because she believed even the presence of one person could make a difference. Since Gemi fought like several men and her two bondmates were just as dangerous, Kephin was inclined to agree with the sentiment.

When they reached the center of camp, where both Kephin's and Lakina's tents sat, Shadow finally stopped, his head drooping to lip at the grass, though Kephin doubted he was actually eating. Enlisting the help of a nearby man, Kephin untied the ropes securing Gemi to her saddle and gently pulled the injured girl from the stallion's back.

Once free of his burden, Shadow plodded to the side of Kephin's tent and rolled to the ground. Flame nudged him once before sticking her head into Kephin's tent as they settled her human bondmate onto Kephin's spare cot.

As Lakina began to remove the bandages that encircled Gemi's body above her clothes, Flame trilled. Confident that Lakina was quite capable of caring for the girl's wounds, Kephin stepped away from the cot and smoothed a hand along the dragon's snout.

"She'll be fine, Flame," he murmured. In his own tent, with only Lakina and Gemi's bondmate present, Kephin knew it was safe to speak of Gemi truthfully. "Lakina will Heal her. Don't worry."

Flame trilled again, more sharply, and whipped her head back through the tent's entrance. Frowning curiously, Kephin followed her out and watched as she lifted her head and whistled loudly.

It wasn't until Kephin heard an answering chitter that he realized the whistle had been a call. Seconds later, a young boy came dashing through the camp, a large grin pulling at his lips.

The ten-year-old trilled happily as he ran in between Flame's forelegs and attempted to wrap his arms around her neck. Cooing softly, the dragon embraced him in return, one clawed hand resting gently on his back.

Kephin smiled as boy and dragon fell into conversation. The boy, Maxwell, was an Animal Mage, one that Flame had discovered when he was only four. Despite the misgivings of the boy's father, Flame had become close with Maxwell and insisted on training the boy's magic.

After a couple minutes of various noises being traded back and forth, Kephin cleared his throat, drawing the attention of the two friends to him.

"Maxwell, does Flame need me for anything?" He thought she must. She'd sounded frustrated that he couldn't understand her.

Maxwell turned back to Flame, but she whistled before he could say anything. The whistles turned to trills, then hisses, and Maxwell finally nodded.

"Flame says Lakina will not be able to do anything, not with the poison still in James' system."

Kephin felt his lips twitch at the boy's formal tone. One side effect of Maxwell's friendship with Flame was clear, high speech, something that had stupefied the boy's father the first time he'd heard it.

Maxwell trilled then, looking curious. When Flame answered, he turned wide eyes up to Kephin.

"She says James has anti-magic poison in his veins."

Kephin groaned. It was bad enough that Gemi was injured as much as she was, but if Lakina couldn't help her...

"How?" he asked, needing to give Lakina as much information as possible.

The pair traded trills and whistles once more before Maxwell replied, "A knife to the shoulder, two sevendays ago."

Nodding, Kephin ducked back into his tent. "Any luck?" he asked. Perhaps two sevendays was enough time for the poison to work its way out of her system.

Lakina huffed. "Nay, I'm not having any luck at all." She shook her silver head. "Something is denying my magic entry into her wounds."

Kephin sighed. "Then Flame's right. The poison is still in effect."

118

Lakina stilled, her hands pausing in the middle of pulling off the girl's damp clothing. She turned narrowed eyes on Kephin. "What are you talking about, Kephin? I haven't sensed any poison."

"Can you sense anti-magic poison?" he asked, curious.

He'd never had to deal with the poison himself as its use was restricted to the southern province for some reason, but Lakina had traveled for the war when she was younger. She probably knew more about it than he did.

To Kephin's surprise, the Mage Healer growled. "Those damn Baylinese!" she spat. She turned back to Gemi and gently, yet swiftly, removed the girl's tunic.

Kephin cleared his throat and glanced away, suddenly uncomfortable. Bandages might cover Gemi's most private parts, but he had been born the son of a Fayralese noble. It just wasn't proper for a man to see a mostly naked young woman, no matter that he saw her as family.

Just then, another trill drew the man's attention back to the entrance of his tent, where Flame had stuck her head back through. When she jerked her snout to the side, he slipped back outside, grateful for the distraction.

"Flame believes she can remove the poison if she is allowed to bite him," Maxwell proclaimed before the tent's flap even fell shut.

"And why haven't you done so before now?" Kephin asked curiously. The dragon narrowed her eyes and trilled sharply.

Maxwell giggled. "She says James has been too stubborn to listen to her."

"Flame," said a sharp voice behind Kephin. He turned to find Lakina standing in the tent entrance. She was frowning at the dragon. "Do you really think your magic is plentiful enough for that after attempting to Heal him for the last two sevendays?"

Kephin turned back to the dragon and watched as she shook her wings slightly and tilted her head. After a moment, she crooned.

Maxwell stared at her. "Would that work?" he asked, surprised enough to slip out of the animal tongue.

Flame hesitated before nodding and crooning again.

Maxwell turned to Lakina. "She thinks if you use your magic on her, it will allow her to heal him."

Lakina hummed softly. "That might work," she muttered. She considered it for another moment before nodding and waving Flame towards the tent and added, "Come, child, let's see if we can't get your bondmate back on his feet."

~~*~*

Gemi groaned as pain made itself known to her once more. She kept moving in and out of consciousness. Each time she woke, she had to work past the pain to remember what had happened and where she was.

This time, the pain seemed smaller, less threatening and more just a simple annoyance. Groaning again, she rolled her head and immediately stilled when she realized that there was something insistent

119

Peace of Evon

and…comfortable pressing against the back of her head. Panic rolled
through her as she realized she was no longer mounted on Shadow's
back.

"*Calm yourself,*" a familiar warmth murmured against her mind, and
Gemi instantly relaxed. If Flame felt they were safe, then Gemi knew
they had to be.

"Wha'…happ'ned?" she muttered slowly, too tired to trust herself to
form the words in her mind alone. She thought herself likely to drift off
into other thoughts if she tried to keep the conversation mental.

"Shush, child," replied a second voice, this one cool and sweet, like
water against her ears. Like Flame's, this voice was familiar, but Gemi
couldn't place it immediately. "You need to rest. Flame says you've
been pushing yourself hard this past sevenday."

Gemi wanted to roll her eyes but knew it would take too much effort.
Even so, the words had reminded her whose voice she was hearing.

"Lakina?" she whispered.

"Aye, child, you're safe. Now sleep. Carith knows you need the rest."

Gemi rolled her head from side to side, with no little difficulty. Before
she could say anything, a deep, rumbling laugh filled her ears.

"It's no use, Lakina. You know she won't sleep until she knows what's
happening."

Frowning slightly, Gemi groggily open her eyes.

At first, all she saw were light browns, silver, and black. Blinking, she
managed to focus on the black, which turned out to be black, curly hair
just brushing broad shoulders and framing a very familiar face that stared
down at her with bright, green eyes.

"Keph'n," she murmured as her lips attempted to twitch into a smile.
"Wha' happ'ned?"

The black-haired leader of the Highwaymen chuckled and nudged
Lakina, who sat next to the cot on which Gemi lay. "What did I say?"

Lakina only rolled her soft blue eyes and leaned forward to sweep a
hand across Gemi's face. "How are you feeling, dear?"

Gemi sighed and closed her eyes once more. She was among friends,
one of the safest places she could be at the moment. "Bettah," she
muttered. "I still ache, but feels li' the cu's are mos'ly gone."

A frown tugged at her lips then, and she opened her eyes to gaze up at
Lakina once more. "'Ow'd you Heal me, Lakina? I though' I still had
pois'n in m' syst'm."

Lakina shook her head. "Oh, you did, all right, but Flame insisted that
her bite would help remove it." The Mage Healer's lips twitched up into
a smirk. "As it turns out, she was right."

Her smirk turned to a frown then, and the look she gave Gemi was
stern. "I want to know why you didn't let her do that sooner, Gemi. It
would have been easier on all three of you."

Gemi let her eyes slip closed again, unwilling to meet the Healer's
gaze. How could she explain, knowing now that her previous arguments

120

had been wrong, that she had feared the bite itself? It seemed silly when she dealt with pain almost daily, but she had never felt physical pain intentionally caused by her bondmates, and it wasn't something she ever wanted to experience.

A warm sigh brushed her mind. *"I wish you had shared that worry the first time I mentioned biting you, James. Shadow could have told you that there is little pain in the bite when my magic is involved."*

"And if it hadn't worked?" Gemi asked mentally. She could already sense Flame's thoughts that Lakina had been forced to use her own magic to bolster Flame's.

Flame was silent for so long that the churning of her thoughts against Gemi's mind and Lakina's exasperated sighs nearly lulled Gemi back to sleep. When the dragon finally addressed Gemi again, her firm words caused Gemi to twitch.

"My magic was not yet depleted when I first mentioned this solution, James. If you had listened to me instead of fighting help when it is offered to you, like you so often do, you could have been well enough to leave Baylin when we were supposed to instead of waiting three days and pushing Shadow harder than you usually do."

Gemi winced and reached for Shadow, but the stallion was already deep in slumber.

"'M sorry," she whispered aloud, offering the apology as much to Lakina as to her bondmates. "I didn'..."

Her words choked off as the corners of her eyes prickled dangerously. *"I didn't realize..."*

Flame sighed and wrapped her mind around Gemi's, offering warm comfort even as she curled her body around Shadow's. *"Just do not hide from us. We only want what is best for you, James. After all these years, I would think you knew that."*

Gemi sniffed and nodded. Flame murmured soothingly and let her mind still.

A soft sigh touched Gemi's ears then, pulling her back to her physical surroundings. Lakina was tucking the blanket that covered Gemi more tightly around her shoulders.

"Everything is fine now, child, but you need to learn from your mistakes, aye?" Gemi jerked her chin towards her chest, and Lakina sighed again. "Now, sleep. I won't be able to finish Healing the rest of your wounds for several more hours, and I want you to get as much rest as you can before then."

Gemi nodded and slid her eyes shut. She had every intention of following the Mage Healer's command to join Shadow and Flame in sleep, but, just as she began to ease into unawareness, a sudden thought had her jolting awake.

"Kephin!" she gasped, panting as adrenaline suddenly rushed through her.

Hands smoothed across her shoulders and face, and she could hear Lakina murmuring that she was safe and that she needed rest, but Gemi needed Kephin to know what she had just remembered. She felt Flame stir slightly, but even that was secondary.

"What is it, Gemi?" Kephin's voice rumbled over Lakina's assurances.

The girl reached out and grabbed his forearm, pulling him closer. "The highway…" she breathed urgently, "you gotta…keep safe…"

The sudden awareness and exhaustion were at war within her, and her tongue just wouldn't cooperate.

"What do you mean?" Kephin murmured.

His green eyes were so kind, and Gemi was tempted to just relax and let her friends take care of her, but this was too important. She needed them to know, so she swallowed and tried to make her mind slow down and organize her words.

"I was…run out o' Cautzel…" She swallowed again and forced her eyes back open when she realized they had slipped closed. "The…duke o' Baylin…he knows who I am…tha' I'm the Ghos'."

The hands on Gemi's face and shoulders finally stilled then, and it wasn't until Lakina fell silent that Gemi realized the Mage Healer had still been murmuring assurances. Kephin's green orbs grew worried as he leaned closer.

"'M 'fraid…" Gemi added quickly before Kephin could interrupt, "that 'e'll follow me. Don'…let th' others…start anythin'…I don' wan'…anyone hurt."

Kephin was nodding before she finished, and he laid his free hand along her cheek. "Don't worry, Gemi. I won't let anything happen. I promise."

Gemi nodded slowly, her eyes already slipping shut. "Thank…you," she breathed.

Already, darkness pressed in on her, and she let her mind slip into the unawareness of sleep.

~~*~*

Kephin sighed as Gemi's grip on his wrist loosened and she slipped back into sleep. Lakina immediately leaned over the girl and tucked the blankets more tightly around her.

As Kephin watched her, Gemi's words continued to echo in his head. She claimed the duke of Baylin knew that she was the Ghost—the Traveler, as she was known here in Kensy. He wasn't sure if that was better or worse than his first thought when she'd claimed the man knew who she was.

Would it be better for the duke to know she was heir to the duchy of Kensy?

He shook his head before he could follow that line of thought for too long. Gemi had spent six years hiding her true identity as the daughter of Lord Cosley from most of Evon. He could still remember her original claims when he'd first learned the truth: as an orphaned girl, she would have been restricted to a single location and most likely not allowed the use of her weapons, but she had wanted to learn about her people and to help in the war.

However, even then, he had understood that there were other reasons, ones that weren't quite so rational.

Kephin sighed again and rubbed his chin. More than her claims, he could still remember the way he'd found her all those years ago. He'd thought she was a boy then, and she'd been covered in blood and in shock from a battle in which, he'd later learned, she'd taken revenge on the men who killed her parents and destroyed her home.

That fight, Kephin knew, had nearly destroyed her. It had been the first time she'd killed a man—several men, even—and, despite her training, it had nearly broken her peaceful spirit. It had taken nearly the full two seasons she'd spent with Kephin to lose the broken look that had filled her eyes then.

And when Kephin let himself think about it, he knew she had never fully recovered from that fight. She'd simply become better at hiding the pain and fear.

Now, she was sixteen, less than a year from her Coming Of Age Day. Once that day came, Gemi would be able to claim her title without being restricted as a child. Yet, the closer that day came, the more Gemi seemed to fear discovery.

"Are you worried?"

"Hmm?" Kephin replied distractedly and glanced up at Lakina. She had finally pulled away from Gemi's cot and was eyeing him with a frown.

"The duke, Kephin," she answered with a small huff. "Are you worried about him following Gemi?"

Kephin shrugged and rubbed at his eyes. The sun hadn't even set yet, but worry over Gemi seemed to have sapped his energy.

"If Gemi thinks he'll follow her, then there's a good chance he will," he said and snorted.

Gemi might be terrified of being discovered, but he would never call her paranoid. She had good instincts when it came to predicting someone's next move. Kephin believed it was one of the reasons she was so talented in battle.

"It's really just a matter of how many he brings with him," he continued. He let his gaze drift to the small contained fire he had lit in the center of the tent. "And if the rogues decide to pick a fight."

Lakina sighed. "With the rate they've been attacking, I wouldn't be surprised." She pursed her lips. "You know, I am curious why they didn't attack Gemi before you found her. She was vulnerable enough that they shouldn't have thought twice about it."

Kephin shook his head. "You're assuming they saw her. From Frick's description of the attack on his wagon, I'd say they'd been planning it for a while, and they probably didn't bother with any other posts in the area today." He chuckled and added, "If we're lucky, the rogues won't even know she's in Kensy yet.

"However, you're right that the rogues are more likely to attack the duke than not, no matter how many he brings with him." He shook his head again. *Bolder and bolder.*

He climbed to his feet then and stretched. "I'll increase the number of men on the highway for tonight and tomorrow, see if we can't prevent a second war from breaking out here in Kensy. The gods know we wouldn't be able to handle another one."

Turning, he pushed past the tent's flap, leaving Lakina to watch over Gemi and make sure she stayed asleep.

Chapter 12

4 Early Autumn, 224
Kensy, Evon

Ferez and the dukes didn't reach Kensy until the evening of the third day of Autumn.

After waiting out the midmorning rainstorm, which seemed to amuse Tern as much as it annoyed Seyan, they set up camp on the outskirts of the forest. Even Seyan agreed that traveling at night through known highwayman territory would only invite unnecessary danger.

However, Seyan insisted on breaking camp not long after sunrise, and they had been riding towards the North Evonese Junction ever since. The Junction, where the West Evonese Highway merged with the Cautzelian Coastal Highway to form the Evonese Highway, was where Seyan had insisted that a man named Markos had said they would find the Ghost; where they would find James Caffers.

Ferez sighed and shifted in his saddle, earning a quick glance and a soft, questioning nicker from his mare, Last Chance. He patted her shoulder, distracted by his thoughts.

He still didn't quite believe that Caffers was actually the Ghost. Even if he ignored how young the boy was—and Ferez was certain the boy was no older now than Ferez had been when he was crowned—there was still the matter of the events of three days ago.

He just couldn't reconcile the image of a violent rebel leader, whose main goal was to pull Evon into chaos again, with the boy he had met. And if the Ghost really was so heavily involved with the pirates—which Caffers must be since everyone seemed to know who he was—why, then, was Cautzel the most peaceful of Evon's five provinces?

After all, if the Ghost had thirty-three ships under his command, he could easily terrorize not only Cautzel's entire coastline, but Baylin's as well.

It was that question, actually, that had led Ferez to agree to travel to Kensy with Seyan. More than anything right now, he wanted to talk to Caffers. He wanted to ask the boy if he really was the Ghost, and how. He wanted to learn if the rumors were true, and how someone who was rumored to do such terrible things could turn around and claim an allegiance to the throne.

For that matter, Ferez thought with a snort, *I'd like to know if he really is loyal to Evon.*

"Majestad," Peln murmured, drawing Ferez suddenly from his thoughts. The king turned a questioning gaze on the Tarsurian duke. "I believe we are being watched."

Ferez glanced at the surrounding foliage, unsurprised. They were deep in highwayman territory and should soon be approaching the North

Evonese Junction. If James Caffers was camped nearby with a group of highwaymen, then there would most likely be several men posted along the road.

Especially, Ferez thought, a bit sadly, *if he expected us to follow him.*

"Can you be sure?" Ferez asked Peln in order to keep his mind off Caffers' possible thoughts on him and his men.

Peln was glancing at the tree line on either side of the highway. "I feel now as I do when there are ladrones nearby." He shrugged and glanced briefly at Ferez. "And I thought I saw movement among the trees to our right."

"Shall we engage them, then?" Seyan asked, forcing his mount to slow. "If we can capture one, we can force him to lead us to Caffers." His voice practically quivered in his eagerness, and he looked ready to lead his horse off into the tree line.

Ferez sighed and closed his eyes in frustration. No matter how many times Ferez said it, the Baylinese duke couldn't seem to understand that he simply wished to speak with Caffers, not engage in violence with any groups they might encounter here in Kensy.

"Stay yourself, Seyan," Kawn murmured.

There was a steel in his voice that forced Ferez to open his eyes once more. Kawn had leaned over and grasped Seyan's elbow in a firm grip, which the Baylinese duke didn't seem to appreciate.

"This is not the plains of your beloved Baylin. You cannot chase senselessly after possible Feinde with no Angst of losing your way."

"Sí, Kawn is correcto," Peln muttered in turn. His eyes were still scanning the tree line, and he seemed to have grown warier. "The highwaymen would no doubt lead you on a merry chase if you attempted to engage them amongst the trees."

He spared Seyan a fierce glare. "Surely you remember los problemas of fighting within Kensy from la guerra. Becoming lost was just as much a worry then as being killed by los enemigos."

Seyan's lips thinned as Peln spoke, and the Tarsurian duke's words seemed only to harden his resolve to chase the highwaymen who possibly watched them.

"We are not engaging them, Seyan," Ferez bit out as commandingly as he could. "There will be no violence unless—"

A long, low whistle forced Ferez silent. He didn't know its source, but, instantly, he ducked, dropping his body along the neck of his mare. Last Chance dropped her own head in response, allowing his body to drop lower. As she did, Ferez felt something fly above his back, close and fast enough that its passing stirred his tunic.

A soft thud drew his eyes to the ground to his left, where an arrow had buried its head into the road. Ferez felt his lips firm at the sight. He did not wish for violence, but such a proclamation of intention could not be ignored.

"Your Majesty!" Tern shouted.

The king looked to his right just as men began to boil out of the forest on that side.

~~*~*

Gemi stood in one of the tall trees whose branches arched over the West Evonese Highway. When she spotted the noblemen, she whistled a warning to the Highwaymen for whom she scouted to stay amongst the trees.

At the same time, shock had her tightening her grip on the tree as she realized the nobles had come alone. There were no soldiers, nor even knights; only five men riding carelessly through Kensy.

They are inviting trouble, she thought incredulously.

"*Not the Baylinese duke's idea, surely,*" Shadow muttered from his point just within the forest's tree line. "*If he had his way, they would have brought the entire force of the king's men down on Kensy.*"

Gemi nodded idly, her eyes narrowing as she watched the noblemen slow to a stop almost directly beneath her. The Baylinese duke seemed ready to dive into the forest on the opposite side of the highway from her men. The other nobles seemed more reasonable, thank the gods.

The quiet argument between the men seemed to hold their attention fully, which worried Gemi. She had learned early in life that the enemy always attacked when you were most distracted.

Sure enough, as the king began to speak, movement in the branches across from Gemi caught her attention. Standing in a tree nearly opposite her was an archer in the process of nocking an arrow.

Hissing softly, Gemi took a quick second to decide what to do, but the decision was simple. As much as Gemi did not want to be discovered, she would not leave the king at risk.

As the archer pulled his arm back, Gemi released a long, low whistle, the signal that was understood among the Highwaymen as a warning of attack. She had hoped to at least catch the king's attention, but the way he immediately dropped along his mount's neck was startling. He had taken the warning as seriously as any Highwayman.

When rogues began to spill out of the tree line opposite her position, Gemi simply watched, her awe increasing as the nobles pulled their swords and fell easily into battle. Their mounts fought just as fiercely, too, lending aid to their masters as easily as any soldier.

As she watched, Gemi was sharply reminded that these men had been through training similar to her own. Each would have been trained from a young age by knights and would qualify as a knight in his own stead.

Movement from the trees across from her once again caught Gemi's eye, and she snarled silently when she saw the archer reach for another arrow. Pulling her own bow, she was able to sink an arrow into the rogue's neck just as he released his, and his shot went wide as he screamed and fell from the branch.

Gemi hadn't expected the man's descent to end so close to the king, though. The body landed just in front of his beautiful white horse—*why*

127

does she look so familiar? Shadow wondered—and the horse reared with a sharp whinny.

The mare's movement threw His Majesty off-balance. When she came down, the rogues surrounding her rear surged forward, some grabbing her bridle, some the king's leg and body, pulling him from her back.

Gemi cursed and signaled for her men to attack before scrambling down her tree's thick trunk. When she finally made it out onto the highway, all five nobles were dismounted. His Majesty's sword had been removed from his hand, but that didn't seem to hinder him.

Gemi paused briefly and watched him dodge a rogue's sword, only to come up under the man's defenses to stab him in the stomach with a dagger Gemi hadn't noticed beforehand.

After that, Gemi's attention was caught by attacking rogues, and she set about fighting off the latest rogue attack.

~~*~*

When Ferez was pulled from Last Chance's back and disarmed, fear twisted his gut, but the war had taught him that even the most hopeless situations could turn in his favor. Even the sight of more men pouring out of the forest couldn't dampen his determination to fight.

To his relief, the new arrivals turned their weapons, not on him and his dukes, but on their attackers. When he finally spotted James Caffers, he was unsurprised to see him cut down one of Ferez's own opponents.

Wherever his loyalties lie, he thought, ducking the swing of another sword, *he does not wish me dead, at least.* From what he had seen of the boy's abilities, Ferez found that comforting.

For such a large number of men, the fight ended surprisingly swiftly. Sooner than Ferez might have expected, many of the most recently arrived men were hauling injured and unconscious men from the ground, some gently, others rather unkindly, and hauling them towards the left tree line.

Seyan, who had been momentarily distracted as he nursed a cut on his thigh, surged forward towards the retreating men. Kawn and Peln easily caught him, Kawn cuffing the man across the ear as Peln snapped something sharply into the other.

Ferez, however, didn't wish to allow the retreating men the chance to disappear again either, even if not for the same reason as Seyan.

"Caffers!" he called, striding forwards several steps.

The black-haired boy, who was the last person to head for the tree line, paused but didn't turn.

"I only wish to talk."

~~*~*

Gemi frowned at the king's words, though she was momentarily distracted by Shadow's snort of disbelief.

"Surely a man wouldn't risk riding through such dangerous territory nearly alone just to talk," Shadow muttered. Gemi nodded slightly in agreement and turned her head to glance at the king over her shoulder.

"I find that hard to believe, Your Majesty," she called back to him.

"Yet it is true." The king's voice sounded so sincere that Gemi turned around just to see the man's face. He stared at her with such earnestness that Gemi thought she could do nothing but believe him. "I only wish to speak with you."

"We spoke only three days ago, Your Majesty," Gemi responded, hoping to downplay the importance of the king's words.

His Majesty's stare didn't lose its intensity. "And I didn't know then that I was speaking with the Ghost."

Gemi stiffened. She had expected the king to know. Of course she had. The duke of Baylin had known it before she left Calay.

But to hear him say it...

Gemi shivered. She had hoped that her secret could still remain just that: a secret. It seemed the Fates were against her in this.

"I only wish to know," the king continued, his voice dropping lower, "how someone so young managed to gain such a...reputation as you have."

"*And arrest you once you've confessed,*" muttered Shadow, but Gemi mentally shoved the stallion away.

Even if the king did wish to arrest her, he would have a hard time of it here in Kensy with only four other men accompanying him. Whether Gemi wished them to or not, the Highwaymen would defend her viciously before the nobles could even touch her.

"And what would you do once you had that information, Your Majesty?"

Whether or not he attempted to arrest her here in Kensy, he and the other nobles could still pursue her in the other provinces. Gemi didn't know if she could bear to be hunted so personally.

The king shook his head. "I admit that you intrigue me, Caffers. If you truly are the Ghost..."

He shook his head again before turning his attention back to Gemi. Her breath hitched as the king's gaze seemed to pierce her.

"I would appreciate the chance to hear your words before I decide what I want to do about any of this. If I promise to consider your words without the threat of violence or arrest, would you agree to speak with me?"

"Your Majesty!" Lord Lefas cried out, shocked.

The king didn't even bother to glance his way, and Gemi was rather amused when the Zhulanese and Tarsurian dukes quickly silenced him.

"*Consider his offer, James,*" Flame trilled softly. "*If you can convince him to support you in what you do instead of hunt you, our lives could only be easier.*"

"*Do you really think that's a possibility, Flame?*" Shadow nickered disbelievingly. "*The nobles have never taken kindly to what James does.*"

"*Does the king seem like a typical noble, Shadow?*" Flame asked, amused.

Shadow grumbled softly before nickering a reluctant "*Nay.*"

"If you agree to actually consider my words," Gemi finally answered, interrupting her friends' bickering, "then I will tell you what you wish to know."

Within reason, she added mentally, earning snorts from both of her bondmates.

~~*~*

Ferez grinned when Caffers agreed to speak with them. *Now I just need to decide what I want to ask him.*

Before he could continue the thought, the boy turned back to the forest.

Worried that he would disappear despite his verbal agreement to talk, Ferez hurried forwards, only to stumble to a halt when the boy made no other moves. Instead, Caffers waved to someone in the forest as though urging them to leave the trees.

When nothing happened, the boy shook his head.

"Well, come on," he said, exasperated. "You can't expect us to just stand around on the road to talk. We'll go to the Lily Grove, and you can get some oats there."

Ferez was confused by the boy's final words until a riderless black horse hesitantly stepped out of the tree line. It paused with its body half out of the foliage and swung its head around to eye their group.

A sudden, heavy presence distracted Ferez from the latest arrival. Turning, he found his own mount, Last Chance, quivering at his side and eyeing the black horse warily.

Murmuring soothingly, Ferez stroked a hand across her white coat. She had always had a distinct dislike of unknown stallions, and Ferez suspected that was the reason for her sudden tension.

A warm chuckle drew the king's attention back to Caffers, who had managed to coax his horse fully out of the surrounding forest. The boy offered Ferez a small smile.

"It seems your mare recognizes Shadow better than Shadow recognizes her."

The snort the black stallion offered in turn sounded indignant, and he turned a scornful eye on his master.

"I'm sorry?" Ferez responded, confused, when the boy's smile only seemed to widen at the stallion's look. "But why would either of them recognize each other? Neither of us had our mounts with us when we last met."

He hadn't missed the stiffening of his mare's muscles beneath his hand, however, and he reached up to massage the crest of her neck, threading his fingers through her mane.

Caffers stepped closer, leading the stallion with a gentle touch under the horse's chin. "I believe she gave Shadow directions when he sought out your Animal Mage on the docks. The mage with the doves, I believe?"

Ferez blinked. He couldn't fathom how the boy could know that when they had both been on the *Pretty Pauper* at the time. Although…

"Are you an Animal Mage?" he asked tentatively.

He'd heard many rumors about the Ghost, but none of them had hinted that the man—*boy*, he corrected himself—was a mage of any kind.

Caffers laughed, a full-throated sound that belied the wariness the boy had shown previously. "Hardly! I—"

He hesitated for a moment before shaking his head. "I think it would be best if we made our way to the Lily Grove Inn before we get further into this discussion."

"Is it close?" Ferez asked.

He found he was suddenly anxious to learn more about this boy. How was it that he knew what their horses could possibly be thinking? And why did he seem so much more relaxed now than he had in Calay?

Although, Ferez thought with a quick glance over the boy's body, *that last might have to do with the fact that his injuries seem to have been fully healed.*

That surprised the king. It meant there were most likely Mage Healers here in Kensy about which he and his men hadn't known. He wondered idly if those Healers had helped during the war, just as the pirates had.

"As close as you can get here in Kensy," Caffers answered, drawing Ferez from his thoughts. "It's in Puretha." Ferez frowned, recognizing the name, and the boy nodded. "The village is at least an hour's walk from here."

"Can we not just talk here then?" When Caffers raised his eyebrows, Ferez amended, "Or off the highway a bit?"

The boy chuckled and shook his head. "As anxious as you seem to be to have this conversation, Your Majesty, even I don't feel completely comfortable out here on the open road. As you've witnessed, our Highwaymen aren't the only ones who watch the roads.

"As to speaking in the forest…" Caffers lips twitched. "I would think you would feel more secure at an inn than in the middle of a forest, of which I doubt you have fond memories."

"And you would not feel less secure?" Tern asked curiously, speaking up for the first time since the fight ended. "Surely being alone with five possibly hostile men would make you no more comfortable than being out in the open here on the highway."

Caffers shrugged and offered Tern a soft smile. "Not really. Not when His Majesty has already promised to consider my words before deciding anything as drastic as violence or arrest."

He turned his gaze back to Ferez and smiled wryly. "And if you do decide to arrest me…" The boy shrugged and held his hands out to the sides. "By all means, try. It may not be as easy as you think."

Despite the subject matter, Ferez chuckled. He was certainly not under the impression that arresting James Caffers would be easy, and he thought it might even be impossible, here in Kensy if nowhere else. But he had the feeling that arrest was not going to be the fate he would want for James Caffers.

"Very well," he answered with a nod.

Turning to Last Chance, Ferez swung himself up onto her back. Settling himself in, he watched as Caffers and the dukes followed his lead. Seyan, he noticed, was more reluctant than any of the others.

"Let's be off then. The sooner we reach this inn, the sooner we can have this discussion."

Caffers chuckled and directed his mount down the highway towards the North Evonese Junction and farther into Kensy.

~~*~*

Puretha turned out to be a large village northeast of the North Evonese Junction. While Ferez was sure he had been there before—its proximity to the highway alone meant that it would have seen a lot of traffic during the war—the village itself didn't seem at all familiar to him.

As they rode into the village, people turned to watch them. Looks of curiosity quickly turned to surprise, puzzlement, and even, to Ferez's dismay, anger. Although no one moved to attack them, Ferez could easily sense that he and the dukes were not welcome here.

"I feel like we're about to be tarred and feathered," muttered Tern, glancing around at the unfriendly faces.

Caffers shook his head. "Nothing so drastic, Milord."

Tern stared wide-eyed at the boy's back.

Caffers didn't seem to notice and added, "You have to remember that Kensy has been without nobles for the past two years. These days, men like yourselves simply don't travel through Kensy."

"And that gives them reason to watch us with such hatred?" Seyan sneered.

Just then, Ferez caught sight of one villager spitting on the ground towards their group before turning back to the small shop out of which he'd stepped. Another grabbed her young son, who had stood staring as they passed, and ushered the boy back between two buildings.

When another man, younger than the first, spat on the ground and glared openly at them, Ferez felt sadness fill him. He had the sudden sense that he'd neglected his people horribly, something he had sworn never to do when he was younger.

You weren't fighting a war back then, he told himself, but the excuse sounded hollow in the face of such unwelcoming gestures. *Perhaps,* he answered the thought, *but I'm not fighting one now, either.*

Caffers didn't answer Seyan's question, and they all remained silent as he led them to a large building that sprawled along the road about halfway through the village. The sign above the front door declared it the Lily Grove Inn.

Despite the open hostility, a nearby group of boys eagerly offered to groom and lodge their horses in the stable across the road. Unwilling to turn down such friendliness, Ferez quickly accepted the offers and paid the boys before Caffers could intervene.

The boys stared at the coins with wide eyes before they each grabbed the reins of a horse and led the mounts across the road. Ferez chuckled as the boy who had taken Last Chance's reins slowly reached up and stroked her cheek, earning a stiff nudge from the mare in response.

As far as Ferez knew, Last Chance had never spent much time around children. He was the only child with whom she had interacted in the palace stable, and he was already twelve when his father had bought the mare off a Pecalini ship.

"That was rather kind of you, Your Majesty," Caffers said, pulling the king's attention back to him. When Ferez frowned at the boy in puzzlement, he added, "A silver each is more than anyone would have expected you to provide."

The sadness that had filled Ferez earlier twisted in his chest now as he glanced back across the street to where the boys had disappeared into the stable. A silver was what he always paid the boys who offered to stable Last Chance during his travels.

Is Kensy so bad off that such a price is considered too high?

That will have to change, he determined, his sadness morphing into resolve. *No matter how this conversation with Caffers turns out, I need to do something for the people of Kensy. I cannot continue neglecting them.*

The resolve firming within him, Ferez turned back to the inn. Seyan was glaring around the village with an expression of annoyance, but Caffers and the other dukes watched Ferez curiously.

"The care of our horses is worth at least a silver."

Caffers' gaze turned thoughtful. "I did not say I disagreed, Your Majesty," he murmured.

Jerking his head towards the inn's door, he added, "Now, shall we head inside? I believe I promised you a discussion, and I don't think food would be amiss, either."

Ferez agreed and followed Caffers inside.

Chapter 13

By the time Gemi and the nobles were seated in the Lily Grove's small dining room, Gemi was beginning to regret bringing the nobles here.

With the distinct lack of noble presence in Kensy, she had never realized just how fiercely the innkeeper, Mikyl, disliked noblemen or, as he called them, 'them rich types'. The man had nearly refused them a place to eat, even with Gemi vouching for them.

Of course, Lord Lefas hadn't helped matters. With the first denial out of Mikyl's mouth, the Baylinese duke had drawled that the man could hardly afford to turn away their coin. The conversation had nearly degenerated to an exchange of insults that was only avoided because the older dukes managed to quickly silence Lord Lefas.

After that, the only reason Mikyl allowed them to stay was Frick's interference. Frick worked as a jack-of-all-trades here in Puretha, and he was in charge of transporting supplies from the Lily Grove to Main Highwayman Camp each sevenday. Although he'd been attacked just the day before by rogue highwaymen, he had been allowed to return to Puretha on the condition that he rest.

When Mikyl continued to deny them food and seats, Frick had yelled, from his seat against the common room's far wall, that the Traveler wouldn't bring a threat into the Lily Grove. Gemi had sighed at the formal address but hadn't complained. She was used to men like Frick insisting on the use of her title even when they knew her name perfectly well.

After Frick's statement, Mikyl grumbled angrily and reluctantly offered them the small dining room. The atmosphere was tense as Mikyl accepted their orders of food, and Gemi winced as he slammed the door closed behind him as he left.

"I'm sorry," she said in the silence that followed the innkeeper's departure. "I hadn't realized he would be quite so angry about your presence."

Lord Lefas opened his mouth, no doubt ready to snap something in response, but Lord Sageo elbowed him in the ribs, and the Baylinese duke released nothing more than a strained breath. Gemi pressed her lips together tightly in order to restrain her laughter.

"His reaction is only understandable," Lord Parshen answered, startling Gemi. She had only heard the man speak twice since she'd met the nobles, and his words surprised her.

"You mentioned that there are no nobles here in Kensy, ja?" Gemi jerked her chin down in agreement. "Then, perhaps the innkeeper believes we are of similar stock as those who left and that we wish only to take advantage of his hospitality without taking responsibility for those who would need our assistance?"

Gemi stared at the Zhulanese duke. His words echoed what she stood for so closely that she wondered why there were as many issues in the central province as there were everywhere else.

"*Because he only considers the river-dwellers his people,*" Flame reminded Gemi sharply. "*It is the Nomads for which he does not take responsibility.*"

Gemi pursed her lips at her bondmate's reminder and nodded to the Zhulanese duke. "That is a rather accurate description, Milord, both of Mikyl's stance and of my own."

Lord Parshen raised his brows in surprise before his expression became rather distant, and he glanced away from her. Gemi narrowed her eyes. She was reminded of her assessment on the *Pretty Pauper* that the duke was hiding something, but she couldn't think what he would possibly have to hide among his peers.

"How is that?" the king asked, distracting Gemi from the Zhulanese duke.

She leaned back in her chair, resigned to beginning the discussion before Mikyl returned with food. She had hoped for a few fortifying bites before she was forced to attempt to convince the king of her views. She doubted she'd have much of a chance to eat once she began to talk.

"You know me as a rebel leader, aye?" The nobles all nodded, some more eagerly than others. "Do you know anything concrete about me?"

"You have led vicious attacks on nobles and merchants alike," Lord Lefas growled before either Lord Parshen or Lord Sageo had a chance to quiet him.

Gemi chuckled. "That's hardly concrete, Milord." The Baylinese duke narrowed his eyes. "I've never led any attacks, at least not on nobles or merchants."

All five men looked dumbfounded at her words, and Gemi felt a grin threaten to split her face. After several moments of silence, Lord Lefas spluttered and spat, "I don't believe it!"

Gemi shrugged. "Believe it or not, Milord, but I have never led an actual attack on anyone who was not considered a rogue."

After a brief pause, she added, "Or an enemy of Evon."

~~*~*

Ferez considered the boy's words carefully. The addition had not passed his notice, and he understood quickly that the boy was most likely referring to Fayralese soldiers. The term 'rogue', however, piqued his curiosity.

"Who, exactly, do you consider rogue?"

The boy's grin renewed, and Ferez was caught by the way his eyes seemed to dance with sudden amusement.

"I'm sure you've heard me use the term before, Your Majesty; in Calay, if not here in Kensy."

Although Ferez couldn't recall hearing it, he simply replied, "That does not mean I understand your use of it."

Caffers nodded. "We consider a rogue any man who considers himself rebellious and violent against the people and throne of Evon."

Ferez blinked, unsure how to reconcile that with what he knew of the Ghost. It was Peln who muttered, "And your rebellious groups are what, exactly?"

Caffers shook his head. "First of all, the rebellious groups are hardly mine, Milord. Despite the rumors, I don't actually lead any of the groups with which you associate me."

Ferez nodded slowly. "Captain Narsus had mentioned that you had no interest in captaining a ship. That applies to you among the other groups, as well, then?"

The boy raised an eyebrow. "You could say that, Your Majesty, but my lack of interest in captaining a ship is a bit more personal than that." He shrugged. "As much as I love the *Pauper*, constant life at sea is not for me."

"Then what is it that you do?" Tern asked, sounding impatient. Ferez glanced at the Cautzelian duke, who looked a bit frustrated.

"If you're looking for a name for what I do, Milord, then think of me more as…an advisor to each group. I travel around the country every season. I don't have time for much else."

"Every season?" Ferez asked, shocked.

Evon was a large country, even if it was nowhere near the proportions of the empire of Fayral to the north or the rainforests of Pecali to the east. It had taken Ferez's army nearly eight days just to march from Caypan, which sat at the mouth of the San River in the middle of the Baylinese coastline, to Calay, which sat about halfway up the coast of Cautzel. That distance was, perhaps, the breadth of the country, yet Ferez thought it had to be less.

If Caffers traveled the entire country in a single season, he couldn't possibly spend very long in one place.

"Aye, every season," the boy assured. "Surely whoever told you to seek me here in Kensy mentioned the Ghost Trail."

Ferez turned his gaze questioningly to Seyan, who shifted in his chair. When the duke insisted on ignoring Ferez, the king sighed.

"Seyan?" he pressed.

The duke sneered, still refusing to meet Ferez's eyes. "He might have mentioned something called the Ghost Trail, aye. I don't see what difference it makes."

The king shook his head. He wouldn't get any more out of the duke; he was sure of that. Just as much as Seyan disdained youth, he could also be very stubborn, and Ferez didn't have the patience to deal with him right now.

Caffers seemed to understand the situation well enough as he offered, "The Ghost Trail is my usual seasonal route through Evon. I spend two sevendays with each group and travel hard on the days in between in order to reach the next province in time.

"As you might have guessed, I always begin the season with two sevendays in Calay, then two here in Kensy, two with my Clan in Zhulan, two with my familia in Tarsur, and two with the Rebels in Baylin."

Seyan hissed at those last words, but he didn't seem inclined to respond.

"By then, the season is coming to a close, and I travel to Calay to begin it all over again."

"Sounds lonely," murmured Ferez. *To spend only two sevendays each with the only people he knows sounds terrifying, actually.*

"I don't exactly travel alone, Your Majesty," the boy answered with an easy shrug.

"I find that hard to believe with how quickly you left Calay," Seyan sneered, surprising Ferez. The king had thought the man would remain stubbornly silent for a while longer yet.

Caffers frowned thoughtfully at the duke. "My companions are not as difficult to contact as you might think, Milord."

Ferez was suddenly reminded of his earlier question about whether the boy was a mage. "You said earlier that you weren't an Animal Mage. Are you another type of mage then?"

The boy was shaking his head before Ferez had even finished the question. "Not a mage, Your Majesty, just…"

~~*~*

Flame suddenly pressed heavily against her mind. *"Do you think it prudent to tell them* that?" the dragon asked.

Gemi blinked, startled. She had been about to tell the nobles about Flame and Shadow, which was something she never would have considered before now.

"I…" she began to mindspeak, but she didn't know how to answer Flame's question.

They'd maintained a fine balance between hiding the dragon from those who had the power to threaten her work and allowing their allies the knowledge of the dragon's presence in Evon and of her relationship with Gemi. That she had suddenly been willing to offer the king and his dukes that information with little prompting worried her.

"Does it really matter?" Shadow nickered. *"You're telling them everything else about James Caffers. If you don't tell them about Flame now, I'm sure they'll learn about her soon enough if they attempt to arrest you."*

"There are only five of them, Shadow," Flame chided. *"Surely they are not stupid enough to attempt to arrest James when they are surrounded by so many people who dislike them."*

"You don't know that for sure, Flame," Shadow nickered. *"The Baylinese duke seems eager enough to cause trouble of some kind."*

"Whether or not," Gemi broke in before horse and dragon could dissolve into a bickering match, *"they attempt to arrest me might very*

well depend on this conversation. If I can convince them to trust my words, perhaps we can even make things better for the people of Evon."
Silence reigned in her head for several long seconds. Gemi was just about to return her attention to the nobles—surely they were wondering why she had stopped talking—when Flame regained her attention.

"Do you truly believe that they will not use my presence against you?"
The worry in the dragon's tone surprised Gemi. Flame was, she realized, more worried about the men attacking her because of Flame than about Gemi giving away her presence.

"Perhaps the dukes would," Gemi answered gently, knowing her bondmates would already recognize the sentiment within her own mind. *"But the king...I don't think that he would panic as others might, and I don't think he would let the others, either. I'm not sure why, but..."*
She mentally shrugged. While her sudden willingness to share had worried her when Flame pointed it out, she couldn't fight the part of her that argued that the king was trustworthy, even if his dukes were not.

Flame sighed gustily but didn't answer. Her silence, and the sudden lightness of her touch on Gemi's mind, was enough of an acceptance for Gemi.

Turning her attention back to her surroundings, Gemi was startled to see Mikyl laying a tray of food on the table. He looked unhappy, but, thankfully, he held his tongue. He did glance sharply at Lord Lefas, though, who looked quite willing to start a fight.

Gemi thanked Mikyl for the food as the king pulled out several coins and pressed them into the innkeeper's hand. When Mikyl glanced at the payment, he blinked, opened his mouth, then quickly snapped it shut with a shake of his head and left the room. Gemi raised an eyebrow, curious about how much His Majesty had actually paid.

They ate quietly for several minutes before the king asked Gemi if she had decided if she could tell them what she had been considering. She flushed and glanced away but quickly nodded.

"You have to understand, Your Majesty, that this is not information I would normally offer a noble freely. However," she quickly added before any of the men could express indignation, "I think it might help you understand me a bit better."

The king nodded. "And what information would that be?"
Gemi swallowed, suddenly nervous. "You see, I have..."
She frowned, unsure how best to tell these men the truth. It was one thing to introduce people to Flame because she had inadvertently given herself away. It was entirely another to tell someone about her and hope they believed her.

Although, there are some things the nobles might already believe about me.
"Have you ever heard the rumor that connects the Ghost to flame and shadow?"

138

The king seemed confused by the question. Surprisingly, it was Lord Parshen that answered her.

"'He travels by shadow and fights with flame,' is the version I have heard." The Zhulanese duke immediately shook his head. "But I never put much stock in it. I have always considered the Nomaden ein bisschen too willing to believe in the mystical."

Gemi stared at the duke in surprise. While the words he had spoken had been disdainful, his tone and expression were rather neutral. The girl was once again struck by the impression that he was hiding something but still couldn't think what it might be.

"Actually, Milord," she answered once she had found her voice, "that one is based in truth."

"What?" Well, that had gotten all of their attention.

"Not a mage?" the king asked, and his voice twisted with a touch of amusement, even as he offered her a curious smile.

Gemi shrugged. "Well, you have already met my stallion, Shadow Racer. Everyone calls him Shadow."

That had all five men blinking at her, and she didn't bother to fight the grin that formed on her lips once more.

"And flame?" Lord Chanser asked, his voice both curious and cautious.

She shrugged again. "Flame Tongue, or Flame as she is better known, is a fire dragon."

Silence and stillness filled the room so thoroughly that Gemi wondered if she should worry about one of the men dying from shock at her proclamation.

"*That would be interesting,*" Flame murmured, but Gemi didn't acknowledge the words.

"A dragon," the king finally murmured, his gaze lowered to the table. He shook his head before glancing back up at Gemi. She was thankful to note that his gaze was fairly curious, with no sign of the panic she often feared when people first met Flame. "How?"

"*How?*" Lord Lefas repeated incredulously before Gemi could answer. "Your Majesty! You can't honestly think the boy is speaking the truth! Evon has been safe from magical creatures for years. There's no reason to think a single one made it into Evon when we have been safe from such attacks from the Fayralese for decades."

Gemi frowned at the duke. Against her mind, Flame bristled at the duke's implication that magical creatures, and therefore dragons, were something against which Evon required protection. Thankfully, Shadow was attempting to calm the young dragon, so Gemi could focus on answering the duke's disbelief.

~~*~*

Ferez was unsurprised by Seyan's outspoken disbelief, though he did mentally wince at the thought of Caffers' possible reaction. Ferez had promised to consider everything the boy said, and, as far as he was concerned, that included the odd claim that the boy knew a dragon.

However, considering everything else I've learned about him, a dragon does not seem too farfetched.

When Caffers finally worked past his anger—at least, Ferez thought it had to be anger that had stilled his tongue for so long—his words were low and cutting.

"Despite what you might have learned growing up, Milord, not all magical creatures are beings to be feared. I'll have you know that Flame has been my faithful friend, and almost my only family, since I was seven."

Ferez blinked at what sounded like an admission to being an orphan. It probably made the most sense since the boy traveled so much, but it still took Ferez by surprise. He pushed the information to the back of his mind for later.

"You have a...Dracheband...with her?"

That inquiry was Kawn's, and Ferez eyed the Zhulanese duke curiously. The word was one Ferez had never heard before, and Kawn had sounded reluctant in asking it.

Caffers looked surprised by Kawn's question. "A dragonbond, aye, but I hadn't thought any of you would know what that was."

Peln nodded. "Many nobles are raised learning our country's *historia*, even about the magical creatures." He glanced at Seyan, who, once again, looked ready to protest. "Some of us, it seems, learned *una historia* that is a bit more skewed."

Seyan snapped his jaw shut and glared at Peln.

Caffers frowned, and Ferez offered his own thought. "A dragonbond is a magical connection with a dragon, aye?" Caffers nodded slowly, looking a bit distant. "I assume you're connected to your stallion the same way, as well?"

The boy started and stared at Ferez. After a moment, he blinked and nodded.

"Aye, both Shadow and I are bonded to Flame. We always assumed that was the reason she was able to cross the boundary around the Northeast Forest."

Ferez nodded. He appreciated the amount of trust it took for Caffers to share such information about his...friends with them. Even so...

"As curious as I am about a dragon in Evon, I do still have questions about your life as the Ghost." Caffers' cheeks reddened, but he nodded. "Could you explain why, or even how, someone as young as you managed to gain such a reputation?"

~~*~*

Gemi grimaced. Explaining the why was the part of the conversation that she most dreaded because she was sure the nobles would not appreciate what she had to say. However, since the king had already addressed it directly, she didn't have much choice but to explain.

"The how and why are rather connected, Your Majesty," she began slowly. "I'd like to say the how is mostly a result of happenstance since I was only ten during the first unification, but that would be a lie. I became close with the eventual leader of each group, and I was thoroughly involved in their unifications, so I did play an active, if reluctant, role in the forming of my reputation.

"The why…"

Gemi hesitated. She wasn't sure how best to explain her reasons since nobles and merchants were the very people upon whom the rebellious groups preyed.

Weighing her words carefully, Gemi asked, "Have any of you ever wondered why there are so many who claim a part in the rebellious groups?"

When all five men stared at her in confusion, Gemi sighed. *Aye, this is going to be difficult.*

"The rebellious groups, as they are known today, provide protection and support for the poorer peoples of Evon." Taking a deep breath, she added, "A protection and support that should be provided by the throne and nobility."

The reaction was immediate.

Lord Lefas jumped to his feet, his chair falling back against the wall, and he shouted, "How dare you accuse—"

"What would you know of how we should treat nuestra gente?" Lord Sageo interrupted, his anger directed at Gemi for the first time since she'd met him.

Lord Parshen muttered something under his breath that Gemi couldn't hear, but his expression was no longer neutral. Instead, he was glaring at the table in front of him.

"It's not that bad, is it?"

That was Lord Chanser. He looked suddenly lost. For the first time, Gemi wondered what it was like for him and the young king. The three older dukes had spent years in their positions and had surely known the state of their provinces and country for years before now.

Lord Chanser and the king, on the other hand, had been dropped into their fathers' positions only a few years before, and, while they should know the state of their responsibilities, they only had others who had been living these same mistakes to guide them in learning their positions.

Attempting to soften the blow of her words, Gemi turned her gaze to Lord Chanser and asked, "Have you ever visited the parts of your cities that don't line the main streets, Milord? Have you ever gone off the main roads and visited the villages that don't have direct access to them?"

Lord Chanser swallowed and shook his head. Gemi sighed. "Then how can you know if it is that bad or not, Milord?"

"I have."

The words were quiet and firm, cutting through the continued protests of the other dukes and silencing them. Gemi blinked and turned to the king.

"Excuse me?" She wasn't sure she had actually heard the man correctly.

The king met her gaze, and she was startled by the sadness and weariness that hung in them.

"When I was younger," he said. His voice remained quiet, but it was firm enough that none of the dukes seemed willing to interrupt. "I used to leave the palace and wander around Caypan and the countryside under the guise of someone else."

Gemi opened her mouth, then closed it and blinked. That was…unexpected.

"I talked to people back then, tried to learn what I could about them." The king had closed his eyes, and he shook his head now. "So many people who could barely support themselves because the war had taken so much from them: men, supplies, food."

"So the damned rebellious groups took care of them?" Lord Lefas sneered. Gemi didn't miss the way the king winced. "We've been fighting a war. Some of us don't have time to go out and explore. If our people have issues, they can bring them to us."

Gemi ground her teeth. It was obvious that Lord Lefas refused to listen, but he was frustrating her. It was no wonder her father had never had anything good to say about the man.

"I suppose then," she bit out once she was sure she wouldn't scream, "that the men that guard your estates so well aren't ordered to keep out the rabble?"

Lord Lefas sneered and opened his mouth, but Gemi's remark seemed to have gotten through Lord Sageo's stubbornness. The Tarsurian duke grabbed Lord Lefas' arm and hissed something in his ear that had the Baylinese duke stilling suddenly.

"If you're so concerned about the rebellious groups," Gemi said, taking advantage of the duke's stillness, "then go out and learn about your people and their problems. True, they might be suspicious of you at first," she added, thinking of the reactions of Mikyl and the other villagers, "but the only way you'll be able to regain their trust and support is to go out amongst them."

Silence filled the room then, and Gemi took advantage of the nobles' consideration to take a couple bites of her food. When the king finally broke the silence with a murmured "Caffers", she eyed the food sadly before nodding to the king.

"As king, I owe responsibility to all of Evon, aye?" Gemi frowned and nodded. She wasn't sure where the king expected to go with this, and, by the confusion in the dukes' faces, neither did they. "Then I would need to travel all of Evon to learn what I need to of my people."

"I…"

That was what she had said, but her words had been more for the dukes than the king. His Majesty already seemed more inclined towards his people's wellbeing than any of the other men.

"I wonder if you might be willing to allow me to travel with you," the king added, and Gemi felt her jaw drop. Even the dukes seemed too surprised to say anything, so the king continued without interruption.

"I would have a hard time traveling the entire length and breadth of Evon on my own without knowing where to go or for what to look. You seem to know our people better than we do. You could help me see my people the way you say I should."

Gemi worked her jaw for a moment, floundering for words. She'd been attempting to get the nobles to understand their people and now...

Well, this certainly wasn't what I was expecting.

"Majestad, are you seriously considering traveling with Nadie?" That was Lord Sageo, who had managed to quiet the Baylinese duke once more.

"I am," His Majesty answered. "Caffers is right. We don't care for our people the way we should. I knew this before I became king, but I let the war take priority after I was crowned." He shook his head. "I won't let that neglect continue, not when I can stop it."

"Your Majesty," Gemi finally managed to say, and the king turned his attention back to her. "I'll tell you now that I'm not accustomed to traveling with other humans. As I told you earlier, my only traveling companions are Shadow and Flame, and I ride hard—harder than you can possibly be accustomed to yourself.

"If I let you travel with me, I won't slow my pace for you, and there will be many times when we won't be able to find a bed indoors for the night."

To Gemi's surprise, the king shrugged—*and why he still surprises me after everything else, I can't imagine*, she thought wryly.

"I may be king, but that does not mean I cannot survive the rough life. If I am to learn about my people, shouldn't I attempt to live as they do?"

"'Live as they do', Majestad?" Lord Sageo asked. "What do you mean?"

The king smiled. "I mean it would be difficult for me to learn anything about my people if they knew I was their king and they didn't feel they could trust me with their ways of life."

Suddenly, Lord Chanser chuckled and grinned. "But you think the people might be more accepting of Frenz Kanti."

Gemi blinked, confused, but Lord Lefas, who apparently couldn't stay silent any longer, groaned.

"But, Your Majesty, you promised your father you would leave behind this Kanti business when you became king."

"Nay," the king corrected sharply, "I promised him that I would accept the responsibilities of the throne willingly, and, if that required me giving up my other self, then I would."

Gemi snorted softly as she considered the similarities to her own life. *He said he used to wander under the guise of someone else, but I didn't realize that meant he already had another self.*

"Is something amusing?" the king asked. Gemi bit her lip and shook her head.

"I simply hadn't expected the king of Evon to have need of a second identity, is all."

The man shrugged. "As I said before, I used to wander Caypan and the countryside when I was younger. I often preferred it to learning my studies."

"Indeed," Gemi muttered. "Reminds me of—"

She bit her lip, hard, then to keep from saying 'myself'. *Too close,* she chided herself.

"If you're willing to travel under this alias without anyone knowing who you really are," she continued once she felt she had control of her tongue, "then I'll accept your companionship until we reach Baylin. I do ask that you consider everything I tell you while we travel. The rebellious groups might be unified, but there are still rogues in each province. I can't promise you safety if you don't listen to me."

"Of course," Ferez answered.

Gemi glanced around the table and realized with a start that, despite the arguments and protests, the four dukes had managed to eat all the food that had been brought for them. Smiling grimly, she nodded to the men.

"For the sake of your anonymity, Your Majesty, it would be best if the five of you were seen leaving the village together. I recommend all of you ride a bit to the east before Your Majesty changes and turns around."

Pausing, Gemi considered briefly before inquiring, "Do you have a set of plainclothes with you, Your Majesty, or do you need to borrow one?"

"I have some, thank you. And, please, call me Ferez. There's no need for formality if we're going to be traveling together."

The offer wasn't one Gemi expected, but she nodded and added, "Then call me James, Ferez." She shook her head slightly; the name felt odd on her tongue. "If you insist on a lack of formality, there's no reason for you to continue referring to me by my family name, either."

The king—*I guess I should start thinking of him as Ferez, as well*—smiled. "I would like that."

Nodding, Gemi turned her attention back to the dukes. "Once His Majesty has left your company, the four of you should continue east along the Evonese Highway. I'll have Flame spread the message along the Animal and Plant channels that the four of you are to travel safely through Kensy. Hopefully, the change in your group's number will go unnoticed between here and the eastern groups."

The dukes, even Lord Lefas, seemed to accept that Ferez's mind would not be changed, and the five men were soon leaving the small room. As Gemi waved Mikyl into the room to have him remove the remaining food and fetch her a fresh plate, she wondered just how this disaster in the making would play itself out.

Chapter 14

Gemi had finished eating by the time someone knocked at the door of the small dining room. Assuming it was the king, she stood and called for him to enter.

To her surprise, Mikyl peered around the door and eyed her with one brow raised. "Seems yer rather pop'lar t'day, James. There be some'un else here to see ye."

Gemi nodded. Perhaps the king was serious then about traveling with her anonymously. "Send him in, will you?"

Mikyl nodded and disappeared behind the door. "Well, lad, he'll see ye." And the man to whom he spoke stepped through the door and closed it softly behind him.

Gemi blinked and stared when the man turned around to face her. If it hadn't been for the odd color of his eyes—she'd noticed earlier that it was more of a silver-blue than a pale blue—Gemi knew she wouldn't have recognized him as the king.

Gone was the small crown that had sat on his head previously. Instead, his hair was damp, even a little muddy, as if he had had dust in it from traveling and stopped by the stable troughs to quickly run some water through it.

His clothes, too, had been changed, and, while she had expected that, the effect was startling.

His previous clothing hadn't been as rich as Lord Lefas' or even Lord Sageo's, but it had been nice enough for a noble or possibly a knight. The dusty clothes he wore now—a plain tunic, simple brown trousers, and a pair of well-worn leather boots—were better suited to a farmer or villager, and the king wore them with an ease and air of contentment that struck Gemi as ironic.

The only thing that might have detracted from the image he made was the sword slung over his back in a worn leather sheath. However, with Kensy's history of violence, it was only expected that a man know how to use a weapon, and, even after the war ended, many people still owned the weapons they'd used in battle.

Gemi must have been staring for longer than she thought because the man cleared his throat, stepped forward, and offered his hand.

"Frenz Kanti," he introduced himself, and merriment danced in his silver-blue gaze.

Still at a loss for words, Gemi shook her head and clasped his hand. Even his words sounded different, more energetic than before, and Gemi realized that the king felt able to relax in this role in a way he couldn't as the leader of Evon.

"Surely I don't look that strange?" Ferez mused, a smile spreading his lips as Gemi ducked her head.

"Not strange, nay," Gemi answered, offering the king a small smile of her own, "just better fit to the role than I expected. I nearly didn't recognize you."

Ferez hummed. "But you did recognize me?" There was worry in his tone now, and Gemi shook her head, hoping to dispel it. She found she enjoyed seeing this side of the king.

"Only because of the color of your eyes, Fer-Frenz." Gemi grimaced at the slip. *That's going to take some getting used to.*

"*That should not be difficult for you, James,*" Flame crooned. "*You, more than anyone, are accustomed to multiple names, even ones that are similar to each other.*"

Gemi snorted, and Ferez raised an eyebrow curiously.

"Sorry." Gemi offered him a grin even as she waved for him to have a seat. "Flame's simply making comments on the irony of our situation, that's all."

"Flame?" Ferez asked, taking the seat he had before. "So you can communicate with your two companions at all times?"

Gemi snorted again and waved a hand about her head. "The good and bad thing about the dragonbond is that they're always in my head."

"*Oy!*" Shadow snorted. The amusement thrumming through the bond belied his apparent indignation.

Flame made a small comment about her being the good and Shadow being the bad, and Shadow's amusement quickly disappeared. Gemi rolled her eyes as they began to bicker.

"The arguments are what make it difficult sometimes," she added, and the two quieted, shame rolling through the bond. When Ferez simply looked curious, Gemi said, "Flame and Shadow sometimes pretend that they can't get along."

The king nodded thoughtfully. "And you hear everything between them." When Gemi nodded, Ferez whistled lowly. "You weren't joking when you said you don't actually travel alone."

Gemi shook her head and frowned. "That's true, but my bondmates are the only ones with whom I ever travel. People will wonder why I'm suddenly allowing someone to travel with me after all these years."

"Have you had people ask to travel with you before?"

"Aye," she answered with a grimace. "Sometimes with a request for the king, sometimes just for the chance to travel with me."

And I've never been willing to risk my secret by letting them accompany me, she thought, earning a croon and nicker from her bondmates.

"Perhaps," Ferez responded with a chuckle, "now that you have met the king, you would actually be willing to take a request to, er, Caypan?"

Gemi stared at the man for a moment before laughing. *That would actually be believable,* she thought, amazed.

"*By most people, perhaps,*" Flamed crooned. "*What about Kephin, Lakina, and the others who know you best?*"

"*They'll understand that I no longer have a believable excuse once I tell them that I've met the king and he believes in what I stand for,*" Gemi answered the dragon.

To the king, she said, "Then all we need is a request that I would actually be willing to help you take to Caypan."

~~*~*

Ferez considered Caffers'—*James'*, he corrected himself—words. The request needed to be reasonable then, one that most people would believe and something that he himself would actually consider granting. He considered the ways he had neglected his people these past two years and what he could possibly do to right the situation.

He considered a request for assistance against attacks but immediately disregarded it. He had seen enough to know that his people relied on the rebellious groups, the highwaymen in particular here in Kensy, to protect them from threats of violence. They would be unwilling, most likely down to a man, to turn to the crown for that.

However, there was something that Ferez had been considering ever since he'd realized just how thoroughly he'd ignored his duty to the people of Kensy especially. He thought that even a real citizen of Kensy might be willing to travel to Caypan in order to demand his attention for it.

"Would a request for a new duke here in Kensy seem reasonable?"

James stilled. Thinking the boy was debating the plausibility of the story, Ferez hastened to add, "Since I came from the east of here, I can say that I'm a farmer from…" He paused, considering what he knew of Kensy's eastern cities and towns. "The area near the old duke's estate, perhaps?"

James had opened his mouth when Ferez was attempting to think of an appropriate location, but he snapped it shut again and offered Ferez an odd look when he continued speaking. When the boy frowned and glanced away, Ferez asked, "Did I say something wrong?"

James remained silent for several moments, and Ferez began to wonder if he had already offended the boy. When he finally turned back to Ferez, he shook his head slowly.

"You didn't say anything wrong per se, it's just…"

James bit his lip. The king raised an eyebrow. The longer the boy hesitated, the more Ferez's curiosity grew.

He never had a chance to learn what the boy was agonizing over as a loud cry suddenly rent the air.

~~*~*

Gemi stiffened when she heard the scream, the internal debate over the king's story already shoved to the back of her mind. Another cry soon followed the first, and Ferez was out of his seat and turning to the door. Gemi reached out and snagged his wrist to keep him from leaving the room just yet.

"Flame, Shadow, what's going on?" she asked, even as Ferez turned back to her. His expression was an odd mixture of curiosity and anxiety.

"Can't see," Shadow answered quickly as he lipped open the latch on his stall door and pushed it open. Thankfully, Flame's answer was more satisfying.

"Puretha is under attack. They look to be rogues."

Gemi groaned. "Another one?" she asked, exasperated. These recent rogue attacks were becoming ridiculous in their frequency.

"Another what?" Ferez asked.

Gemi blinked up at the king, faltering in the middle of requesting Flame to send a message to the Highwaymen through the Animal and Plant channels. Despite the interruption, the dragon understood and fell silent as she dropped into the forest to extend her magic.

"Another rogue attack," Gemi answered with a shake of her head. "They've been attacking more frequently of late. If you count the attack on you and the others earlier today, then this will make four in the last three days."

Ferez tugged at his wrist where she held him. "If there's an attack, then why are we just sitting here? We need to go out there and help fight them off."

"In a second," Gemi answered, though she stood up as well. "I need—"

A loud hiss echoed through her mind then, and Flame suddenly snapped, *"The channels are blocked!"* Frustration dripped through the bond. *"The rogues must have both an Animal Mage and a Plant Mage."*

Grimacing, Gemi quickly asked, *"Can you stop them, Flame?"* Flame hissed angrily in agreement. *"And capture them alive, if you can."* The dragon grumbled but agreed, and she began darting through the forest in search of the two mages.

"Shadow, can you release the other horses? We're going to need as much help in this fight as we can get until Flame can send a message to the Highwaymen."

"Of course," Shadow answered and began lipping open the latches on the stalls of the other horses.

Once she was sure that the others were doing what they could and that she could do no more from where she stood, Gemi tugged the king towards the dining room's door.

"Now we can fight," she tossed over her shoulder as she pulled open the door.

~~*~*

Despite his eagerness to help protect the village, Ferez was intrigued by the expressions passing over James' face. His eyes had taken on a faraway look as though he was listening to some distant sound that only he could hear, and he grimaced and winced with little indication of the reasons.

Ferez knew the boy must be communicating with his companions, and he found it both disconcerting and fascinating to watch. However, thoughts of the boy's expression were chased from his mind as they left the dining room.

Ferez might have expected chaos within the inn's common room, but, to his surprise, the room was nearly empty. The few remaining men were in line at the bar, where the innkeeper was apparently handing out weapons. Two women steered another man, the one Ferez remembered intervening with the innkeeper on their behalf, up the stairs that most likely led to the inn's rented rooms.

"Traveler!" shouted the man being led up the stairs. "We're under attack!"

James didn't pause as he led Ferez towards the bar, but he did nod towards the other man. "I know, Frick, and we won't let them destroy the village."

When he reached the bar, he rapped his knuckles against the counter. "Do you have enough weapons, Mikyl?"

Even as he asked, the innkeeper handed a weapon to the last man and waved him towards the inn's entrance.

"Course I do," the innkeeper growled. "'Tain' like we had an increase in able-bodied men in th' village, y'know." James grimaced. "Y'know how many there be?"

Silence followed the words, and Ferez watched James' eyes grow distant before he focused on the innkeeper once more.

"Flame says she counted twenty-five before she dropped into the forest, but she thinks there were still more beyond the tree line."

The innkeeper released a string of curses that had both Ferez and James cringing. "We ain' got th' men to hold off those kind o' numbers here. Are the Highwaymen comin' at least?"

James shook his head. "Not yet. The rogues have mages blocking the channels, but Flame's chasing them down now. We do have the horses."

"And ye already taken care o' that, aye?" the innkeeper questioned as he grabbed a staff from the doorway to the kitchen.

"Aye, Shadow's already let them out. We should at least have a chance of holding the rogues back with their help."

That surprised Ferez. He knew Last Chance, his own mare, could fight well, but she had been trained for war. He would never have expected a simple village horse to know, or even need to know, how to hold its own in a fight.

Is that a result of the war with Fayral, or has my kingdom fallen so far that even the village animals must be trained for warfare?

"Well, come on then," the innkeeper snapped, tapping his staff against the floor as he headed for the inn's door. "Le's go teach these rogues no' to mess wi' Puretha."

Ferez drew his own sword and saw James lay a hand on the hilt of his longsword. They followed the innkeeper out of the inn.

~~*~*

Gemi had a brief moment, as she crossed the threshold of the Lily Grove, to observe the chaotic battle that had broken out across the village. Men filled the street, interspersed with the horses that had spread out from the stable across the road. The animals, including Shadow, bit and kicked and filled the air with their angry screams.

Closer at hand, she observed several groups of fighters and noticed, with alarm, that the enemy was more distinguishable than she had imagined.

When did the rogues become organized enough to have uniforms?

Her dismay was cut short as one uniformed man swung his blade at her head.

She ducked the blow easily and drew her longsword but was bewildered when the man stepped back and fell into a dueling stance. He grinned at her, waving with his free hand as if inviting her to attack.

Instead, she took a moment to look him over as she, too, fell into a dueling stance. The man was short and wiry, but it was his outfit she wanted to inspect. He wore a sleeveless, worn forest green tunic, and his gray trousers were tucked into worn brown boots.

She realized, with a start, that it wasn't the first time she'd seen the outfit either. The rogues she had fought earlier in the day had worn the same thing, but she'd been too preoccupied with worry for the nobles to notice.

Suddenly, the man she was observing growled impatiently. Gemi lifted her gaze back to the man's face just as he lunged.

~~*~*

Ferez quickly lost track of both the innkeeper and the boy. Unlike James, he sought out his first opponent, attacking a man who had cornered one of the villagers. With the man distracted with the villager, a quick jab to the back of the head with the hilt of his sword was all Ferez needed to knock the attacker to the ground, unmoving.

The villager, a man who carried an ax rather than the longswords the rogues seemed to prefer, nodded to Ferez before running off to help someone else.

Ferez turned around to find the closest rogue and ducked just in time to avoid a blade that had been aimed for his head. As it was, it grazed his shoulder, and he ground his teeth to keep from crying out.

He had a familiar impression of dark green and gray as he ducked another blow, and he grabbed the dagger from his boot before coming up and catching the next. As Ferez continued to trade blows with the man, he realized that his fighting style was familiar. He couldn't place from where he knew it, but he was grateful to find that his body remembered how to face it.

When he found an opening in the man's defenses, he quickly took it, and the man was soon down on one knee, cupping his hands over his bleeding stomach, pain and confusion chasing all other emotions from his eyes. Ferez winced with pity as he delivered a heavy blow to the man's head.

Two opponents later, that pity had only increased. Ferez still couldn't remember why he recognized the style of fighting, but he was sure it didn't come naturally to these men. The style was composed of quick, light blows that should have strengthened their defense while allowing them to wear down their opponents.

However, these men seemed too eager to make killing blows, which made finding cracks in their defense that much easier.

If only fighting the Fayralese during the war had been this easy, Ferez mourned. The next moment he stiffened. *That's why I recognize the style.*

He winced as a blade suddenly caught his thigh, and he was forced to shove the realization to the back of his mind.

~~*~*

Gemi's dismay over the rogues' acquisition of uniforms only increased when she realized that someone had trained them in swordplay. They still couldn't match her for skill, but they were much better fighters than any rogues she had fought even a season ago.

Still, she wouldn't have had difficulty defeating them if a number of them hadn't decided to attack her all at once.

When she found herself isolated from the other villagers and surrounded by five men, Gemi silently cursed the purple eyes and long black hair that made her easily recognizable, even to her enemies. She may have defeated five pirates at once just days earlier, but those men had been notoriously unable to work together to defeat a single opponent. The men she fought now had apparently been trained in coordination as well as swordplay.

The increased number of opponents forced her to draw her cutlass with her left hand as she attempted to block the incoming blows. Even using both blades, several of the light blows struck their targets, and she choked back cries more than once as pain blossomed beneath the steel.

One particularly well-placed jab struck her shoulder joint, right where the knife had slid through just two sevendays before. She cried out, unable to ignore the pain any longer, as the cutlass slipped from her loosened grip. Another cut caught the front of her right thigh, and Gemi hissed.

Shouts of "James!" and "Caffers!" distracted two of her attackers then, and a third suddenly dropped to the ground. Behind him, the king was already turning to engage one of her distracted opponents, while Mikyl landed a blow with his staff against the ribs of the other.

Reminding herself to thank the king for his intervention later, Gemi turned to her two remaining opponents. Even with her left arm hanging awkwardly, both men hesitated to attack, and their eyes darted uncertainly between her and each other.

Unwilling to give them a chance to decide their next move, Gemi lunged at the man on the left, her blade sliding past his hesitant block and between his ribs.

Even as the man collapsed to his knees, his fellow turned and fled for the tree line. Gemi considered pursuing him, but even pulling her blade from her fallen opponent jostled her shoulder enough to make her hiss.

"*Do not worry, James,*" Flame murmured distractedly. "*The Highwaymen are already approaching. He will not escape.*"

Nodding in acknowledgement of Flame's words, Gemi turned back towards the village, only to nearly stumble into the king.

"Will you be all right?" he asked, gripping her right arm and eyeing her injured shoulder worriedly. "It looks like they mangled your shoulder."

"I've had worse," she bit out, thinking of the shoulder wound Lakina and Flame had just healed. Thankfully, she could already feel Flame's magic working on the torn muscles, though she knew Lakina would give her a stern scolding for getting herself injured again so soon.

"*Especially since it's the same shoulder as before,*" Shadow added absently.

Gemi grimaced. "I'll just be glad when this fight is over."

As soon as the words were out of her mouth, shouting rose from the tree line, and a new group of men ran into the village.

~~*~*~*

Ferez nearly groaned when more men appeared out of the tree line. Only the way James relaxed under his hand kept him from releasing the sound. He quickly realized that they wore plainclothes, not the uniform of the rogues, so they were most likely friends rather than the enemies that Ferez had nearly expected.

The appearance of the new men—Highwaymen, as James answered when Ferez asked—heralded the end of the battle. Any rogues who were still fighting were quickly overwhelmed and subdued, with few injuries incurred in the process.

With the fight winding down, Ferez led James back towards the inn, hoping someone there could care for the boy's wounds. By the time they reached the inn's entrance, the door was already being propped open by one of the women who had remained upstairs, and she offered them a strained smile.

"Th' attacks been gettin' worse, Traveler," she said then waved them inside. "Le's see if we canna fix ye up a bit afore ye go back off to Lakina."

When Ferez tried to help James inside, the boy held back and shook his head.

"Can you bring a couple of chairs out here, Fonda? I'd like to be outside when Flame returns."

The woman frowned slightly, but eventually nodded and called inside for two chairs to be brought out. From the sounds Ferez could hear through the doorway, the women were turning the inn's common room into a makeshift infirmary.

Once they were settled in front of the inn, James seated in one chair, Ferez the other, Fonda and another woman began to tend to their wounds. Ferez attempted to wave off the woman tending to his leg, insisting that there must be others with more serious injuries, but she favored him with a sharp look before returning to his wounds.

"Aren' you suppose to be in Cautzel righ' now?"

Ferez glanced up as a man who looked to be near his thirties stopped in front of them. His questioning gaze had settled on James.

"Or am I mistaken 'bou' what day it is?"

James shook his head, offering the man a smile. It suddenly turned to a grimace, and he jerked his head to one side with a hiss. Fonda murmured an apology.

"Well?" the older man asked. "You've ne'er broken yer schedule afore now."

James sighed. "Does it matter, Geoff? I'm here now, and a good thing too. It seems the rogues are getting more aggressive...and organized."

Geoff scowled. "You got tha' right. We had a village to the eas' o' here attacked a sevenday ago, and another to the sout' only two days ago." He shook his head. "And more an' more of 'em been wearin' that odd green and gray uniform."

Ferez remembered the realization he'd had during the fight. "I think the colors may be importan'," he said, softening his words the way he thought a farmer might.

Geoff turned a frown on Ferez and muttered, "An' who's this?"

Ferez stood and offered his hand. "Frenz Kanti." Geoff blinked at him, and Ferez added, "I've a farm further east, closer to the ol' duke's estate."

The man clasped Ferez's hand and answered, "Geoff Kariff, leader o' the Puretha branch o' Highwaymen." Tilting his head curiously, he added, "Wha's a farmer from tha' far eas' doin' 'ere in Puretha?"

Ferez glanced down at James, wondering if the boy had anything to say on the matter. He knew the boy had been going to say something when the village was attacked, but James simply watched him now with a look of mingled curiosity and wariness. Ferez knew then that the rest of the details of his story were up to him.

Deciding that he'd stick with the story he'd mentioned to James already—the boy hadn't appeared to think it too unbelievable—he answered, "I was hopin' to find someone willin' to travel wit' me to Caypan."

The man's eyebrows shot upwards, and he glanced curiously at James. "Did you hear afore we did tha' James was already in Kensy?"

Ferez shook his head. That wouldn't be plausible, he knew. He thought it best to depend on pure coincidence to support his story.

"Heard it from one o' the villagers when I stopped into town for a quick meal, actually."

The man frowned and scratched his head. "Seems a bit out o' the way to come wes' jus' to find some'un to travel sout' wit'."

Ferez shrugged. "M'neighbors all thought I was mad for wantin' to travel at all, let alone to see the king. But I'm not mad enough to travel through another province wit'out some'un to watch m'back."

The man eyed him curiously for a moment before chuckling. "Nay, jus' mad enough to travel half o' Kensy by yerself."

Ferez simply grinned.

~~*~*

As disconcerted as Gemi had been by the story the king had decided to use, she was almost glad that the decision had been taken out of her hands.

You're just amused that he's claim—" Shadow suddenly paused, his attention diverted.

Gemi glanced across the road to where he and a gray horse stood alone by the stable. The other horses had already returned to their stalls, a couple of women following them to tend to any injuries incurred.

Gemi blinked when she realized that the gray mare standing stiffly beside Shadow was practically glaring at the stallion. She snorted and tossed her head, and Gemi raised an eyebrow when she heard the mixed thoughts pressing against her mind through her link with Shadow.

I know we need to protect his identity as tightly as we do Gemi's, was almost immediately followed by, *Hmm...feisty.*

Gemi frowned at the second thought. Shadow had a bad habit of flirting with any mare he came across, and this one didn't seem to be an exception.

Careful, she thought back, but the stallion gave no indication of having heard her.

Just then, there was a pause in the conversation between Ferez and Geoff, and she turned back to the two men to take advantage of it. The longer she could put off someone asking Ferez about his 'request', the greater chance they had of working out the details together.

"What did you mean about the color of the rogues' uniforms being important, Frenz?"

She wasn't sure if the king realized what she was doing, but he nodded and offered her a smile.

"I recognized the fightin' style from the war."

Gemi blinked. That certainly hadn't been what she had expected to hear.

"I don't remember any particular style like that," she muttered.

She thought she would have, too. She had first fought in the war at the age of ten, though she'd left Kensy soon after and hadn't returned until she was twelve, when she began to travel the Ghost Trail. Between then

154

and the end of the war, she had fought against Fayral here in Kensy for two sevendays out of every season.

"'Twasn' widespread or long-lastin'," Ferez answered. Gemi blinked, shoving her memories away, and frowned. "'Twas used by a small group o' well-trained fighters close to the end o' the war. Heard they were trained by a Fayralese master swordsman."

Gemi grimaced then hissed as Fonda pressed something against the back of her shoulder that made the wound sting horribly. Gritting her teeth against the increased pain, she turned her head and waved her good hand insistently at the woman.

"Let up, will you?" she bit out.

"It needs t' be cared for, Traveler," Fonda answered with a frown, even as she removed the soaked cloth from the wound.

"Bandage it up then, and I'll have Lakina take a look."

She nearly regretted the harsh words when the woman glared at her, looking offended. Even so, Gemi wasn't going to just sit there under her ministrations while it felt like she was making the wound worse.

"*I doubt she was,*" Flame commented, sounding satisfied. When Gemi nudged the dragon curiously, Flame simply added that the emotion was for her prey, not Gemi's childishness. The girl winced.

"Couldn' the similarity in fightin' style jus' be a coincidence?" she heard Geoff ask then, and she turned her mind back to her conversation with the two men.

"Nay, it couldn't," she answered. "The colors of Fayral are gray and green. Together with the familiar fighting style…"

She sighed and shook her head. "It seems someone from Fayral is training and organizing the rogues."

Chapter 15

Ferez wanted to reassure James that he knew how to fight against people using that style, but he was distracted by a sudden, loud screech from the tree line.

Looking towards the sound, he saw the foliage rustling before something stepped out from among the trees. At first, Ferez wasn't sure what he was seeing as his mind only registered bright reds and dark purples. Then, as more of the body appeared from the tree line, he realized that it was a large, red-and-purple reptilian creature.

Its snake-like head was raised high as it snapped idly at a hawk that flapped angrily around it. As the long body continued to slide from the tree line, half-folded wings appeared, raised against its sides and hovering over its back. When it finally left the tree line completely, its long tail rasped across the ground and curled around its hind legs.

"There you are!" James shouted as Ferez began to comprehend that this was the dragon the boy had spoken about earlier. He whistled lowly.

Beautiful, he thought. *Dangerous, maybe, but beautiful.*

"Where are the mages?" James called out again as the dragon came closer.

The dragon trilled then lowered its wings, revealing two men draped across its back. Both were dressed in the green and gray of the rogues. One, a small fellow, was bound with what looked like vines, while the other, a burly chap, actually had a large snake wrapped around his chest. The two men looked to be unconscious.

Geoff guffawed at the sight. As his laughter dwindled to chuckles, he called for several of his men to relieve Flame of her burden. When the hawk, which had swooped down on the snake-bound man the moment he'd been revealed, began to attack the Highwaymen, Geoff quickly sobered and called for someone to fetch an Animal Mage.

As soon as the dragon was free of her burden, she wandered over to them and lay down on the other side of James. The dragon trilled, and James chuckled. "Indeed," the boy muttered before turning to Ferez.

"Frenz, this is one of my bondmates, Flame Tongue. I'd recommend calling her Flame, as it's her preferred name." Turning his gaze back to the dragon, James add, "Flame, Frenz Kanti."

The dragon tilted her head to one side before cooing and dipping her nose to the ground, swinging her tail forward to brush his leg. Smiling, Ferez bowed his head in return.

"A pleasure to meet you, too, Flame."

Before anyone could say anything else, movement across the street caught Ferez's attention, and he glanced up to see his mare, Last Chance, standing by the stable, the black stallion he recognized as James' nearby. The mare had stiffly tossed her head, and now she was baring her teeth at the stallion, one hoof scraping at the ground anxiously.

156

Recognizing the warning, Ferez leapt from his chair and strode across the street, ignoring both the pain in his thigh and the questions that followed him. Unfortunately, the stallion didn't show signs of understanding the danger he faced.

~~*~*

Gemi had been confused when Ferez suddenly strode towards the stable until she saw Shadow nudge the gray mare's neck.

Immediately, the mare screamed and struck out, first with her teeth before rearing up to strike at Shadow with her front hooves. Shadow whinnied in surprise as the teeth cut into his neck, but he managed to dance away from her hooves before they could connect.

Then the king was beside the mare, dodging her flying hooves to lay his hands on her side. Before Gemi could do more than gasp in fear for the man, he was stroking the mare's side, easing his way up her neck until he could grasp her head. By then, the mare had visibly calmed, and she met his eyes with one of her own.

"What did you do?" Gemi asked Shadow as he skirted around the mare and trotted over to her. She didn't bother to keep the question, nor the exasperation she felt, silent.

"*Nothing,*" he nickered defensively, but a touch of shame flowed through the bond. "*I was just...*"

He trailed off as he searched for the right word.

"*Flirting,*" Flame finished for him. The dragon shook her head and offered Shadow her own look of annoyance.

Gemi sighed. "What have I told you about flirting, Shadow?" Even after six years, she still couldn't fathom why the stallion couldn't just leave the mares alone.

Shadow shifted his weight. "*Hmm...never in battle?*" he tried innocently.

Flame snorted and nudged his leg. "*Wrong one. Try 'make sure the mare is interested first'.*"

Shadow tossed his head. "*How was I supposed to know she wasn't?*"

Flame's glare turned to a look of disbelief. "*I could have told you she was not interested, and I am a dragon.*"

Shadow snorted. "*Aye, but you're also female.*"

Disgust filtered through the bond from Flame, but she shook her head slowly. "*Either way, you do realize that we have to travel with her for the next season, do you not?*"

Horror slowly seeped through the bond then, and Shadow swung his head around to glance back toward the stable.

Gemi had been following the argument, but, when Flame mentioned that the mare would be traveling with them, she also glanced back across the road. The king had calmed the mare and now seemed to be trying to coax her to cross the road. Gemi wasn't sure if that was such a good idea so soon after she had attacked Shadow—even with the emotions roiling through Shadow's mind, Gemi wouldn't put it past him to try again.

However, Flame was right, and, if the mare really was Ferez's, she would be traveling with them for the next season. No matter how Shadow usually treated other mares, he couldn't do the same to her.

"*All right, all right,*" Shadow nickered sullenly, the shame once again rolling through bond. Gemi nodded but continued to watch as Ferez finally convinced his mare to cross over to the inn.

Like the king as Frenz Kanti, Gemi wouldn't have been able to place the gray mare Ferez led over as the white beauty she had seen the king riding earlier. He must have spent some time rubbing dirt into her coat after he changed, but Gemi couldn't see any clumps in the mare's hair. However he'd managed it, the disguise showed Gemi just how serious Ferez was about learning about his people anonymously.

"I'm sorry about that," were the first words out of Ferez's mouth once he was close.

Gemi blinked. "Hardly necessary, I should think. Shadow's needed a good lesson on not flirting with mares for a while."

She turned a hard look on the stallion, but he glanced away from her, his head pulled high. She could already feel him attempting to bury the shame he'd felt.

The king huffed softly. "And Last Chance has always been a bit...unfriendly towards stallions."

Gemi hummed. "Well, I'd offer to finish introductions, but it might be a bit late for that."

"*Some of us have certainly lost any chance of starting off on good terms,*" Flame trilled.

Shadow swung his head back around, the bond thrumming with his desire to protest. The look Flame met him with quelled that desire. The mare, on the other hand, glanced between the two animals warily before nickering and nudging Ferez's arm.

"I don't think introductions would hurt," Ferez answered with a smile, lifting one hand to scratch at the mare's ear.

At the same time, both Flame and Shadow turned to the mare, shock echoing through the bond from them both. "*You are resilient, are you not?*" Flame trilled.

"This is my mare," Ferez continued, oblivious to the dragon's comment, "Last Chance for Hope and Freedom. I call her Last Chance," he added with a crooked smile.

"I should hope so," Gemi answered as both Flame and Shadow murmured their greetings to the mare. "It sounds like there's a story behind that."

The king shrugged. "Seemed like we were bot' each other's las' chance."

He glanced to the side then, and Gemi remembered with a start that they were not alone. Geoff was watching them curiously.

"I'm sorry, Geoff. We've been wasting your time."

The Highwayman waved her words away. "Nay, o' course not. It's been entertainin' enough." He offered Ferez a quick smile. "Mus' admit to wonderin' wha' reason you go' for travelin' to Caypan tha's got James' interest."

Gemi stared at the man. Out of all the people she had thought she'd have to worry about pressing the issue of Ferez's 'request', Geoff Kariff had not been one of them. Ferez, however, answered readily enough.

"From what I hear, it's pure luck o' timin' on my part. James says he jus' met the king recently, an' I jus' happen to be the firs' fellow he's met since wit' a reques' the king might actually respond to."

"Wha' request?" Geoff asked curiously.

Gemi held her breath as Ferez answered, "New duke."

"Good," Geoff said to Gemi's utter shock. "Gods know we need a new duke. Or at least some'un to keep order. Carith bless the heir, where'er she be, but Kensy needs some'un now. We can' be waitin' for the ol' duke's heir to finally decide to come out o' hidin'."

For a moment, silence settled over them before Ferez asked, "Heir?" He hesitated before adding, "You've heard news o' the ol' duke's daughter?"

Geoff frowned. "Rumors, o' course. Haven' you? Af'er all, you live closer to Cosley Ruins."

Ferez shrugged. "I try no' to pay much min' to rumors."

Geoff snorted. "Maybe we should, too. People been 'sistin' that the girl's alive an' well, but we ain' seen no sign o' her."

"Then we'll just have to make sure the king realizes that," Gemi replied, hoping to get past the subject. She felt as though her stomach was trying to climb up her throat, and even Flame and Shadow's soothing wasn't doing any good.

"Good," Geoff said again and nodded. He glanced down the road, where several of his men were waving to him. "Well," he said, "looks like my men are done cleanin' up. We got all of the rogues, and they'll be dealt with accordin'ly."

Gemi shot the man a sharp glance. "You will consult Kephin, won't you?"

Geoff rolled his eyes. "James, tha' incident was over two years ago. Have a little faith." Gemi felt her frown deepen, and Geoff raised his hands in surrender. "Alrigh', alrigh'. O' course I'll contact Kephin. No' like I can make a decision this big wit'out 'im, anyway."

Gemi nodded then offered the man her hand. Geoff frowned and eyed her curiously. "You don' wanna come with us to the Puretha camp?"

Gemi shook her head. "I need to get myself to Lakina."

The Highwayman raised a brow and whistled lowly. "You actually want Ol' Iron to heal you?" He shook his head. "Well, it's your head that'll be rollin', not mine. Good luck to you."

He grasped her hand and pumped it once before waving farewell and leaving with the other Highwaymen.

"Old Iron?" Ferez asked once they were alone with the animals.

Gemi barked out a laugh and winced as it jostled her shoulder. "All that information," she said as Flame leaned around her back to nudge her wounded shoulder, "and that's what you want to know?"

Ferez shrugged. "I'm certainly curious about all of it, but...seriously, Old Iron?"

Gemi laughed again, more subdued this time. "It's a nickname for Lakina, Main Highwayman Camp's Mage Healer. There are a few reasons for it, but if you try to use it to her face, you'll learn one of them real quick."

She shuddered, thinking of Lakina's sharp tongue. She knew Lakina would be giving her a harsh talking-to before the day was over.

"Then you do have a Mage Healer among the Highwaymen?" Ferez asked.

Gemi nodded. "Multiple, actually. Lakina is just the first one I met and the one I trust the most."

"Multiple?" The king sounded surprised. Gemi couldn't fathom why.

"Of course. Surely you have several Mage Healers at the—where you're from," she quickly corrected herself. They might think they were alone, but she and her bondmates had decided over the years that you could never be too careful. "Kensy's a large province, with the Highwaymen spread throughout it. Each camp has at least one Mage Healer."

Ferez shook his head slowly. "During the war, Mage Healers were always so difficult to come by. And since the war..." He continued to shake his head. "I have heard of few that didn't remain at the palace."

Gemi snorted and stood. They should leave soon, and she knew they could continue the conversation as they rode. "You simply don't know where to look, Frenz. I have met plenty of Mage Healers, let alone other mages, during the years I've traveled this country."

As she spoke, she led their group to the stable. A brief contemplation of how she would saddle Shadow with only one arm ended when she spied one of the boys who had stabled their horses earlier in the day. Calling the boy over, she pressed two silver into his hand and requested that he prepare Shadow for the journey to Main Highwayman Camp.

They remained silent as they prepared for the journey, and it wasn't until Gemi was preparing to mount that Ferez gripped her good shoulder and forced her to face him.

"Are you sure you're well enough to ride?" Gemi blinked up into the king's face. He looked worried; more than she thought was warranted.

"*You only think that because you are injured too often,*" Flame crooned. "*And, if not for the dragonbond, you would not tolerate the wounds so easily, either.*"

Gemi shook her head. She knew she had a high tolerance for pain, but that could only be for the good when she fought so much.

"*I do not consider desensitization to violence a good thing,*" Flame answered. Gemi winced and pushed the dragon away.

"I've ridden with worse," she answered Ferez's question. When she turned back to Shadow, he didn't relinquish his hold on her shoulder.

"Like the ride between Calay and here?"

Gemi sighed and glanced back over her shoulder. There was a sympathetic light in the king's eyes that Gemi once never would have expected to see in a noble's eyes—barring her parents, but thoughts of them still made her heart ache. Pushing down the memories that threatened to rise with the thought of her parents, Gemi nodded.

"I am sorry," the king murmured.

Gemi huffed. She could feel her cheeks heating, despite telling herself it was stupid. "No reason for you to be. You weren't the one who flushed me out at the Golden Bones."

"Maybe not," he replied sadly, "but I knew he thought you were the Ghost. I should have realized he would press the issue and seek you out."

Gemi sighed and turned back around. Lifting her good hand to squeeze the hand on her shoulder, she met the king's silver-blue eyes. "What's done is done, Frenz. I don't hold you responsible, and…" She glanced around the stable. Thankfully, only horses surrounded them as the boy who had saddled Shadow had already left. "We'd best leave the rest of this conversation for the solitude of the highway."

Ferez startled and glanced around, his cheeks reddening as he quickly nodded. He did insist on helping Gemi mount, and she sighed as she settled into the saddle. She was in much better shape than she had been when she'd left Calay, but she knew the ride was not going to be comfortable on her shoulder.

They rode out of Puretha in silence, Flame taking to the air as Shadow and Last Chance navigated the small road that led from Puretha to the Evonese Highway. They were halfway to the highway when she glanced behind her and asked if Ferez had any questions she could answer.

He was silent for long enough that Gemi nearly stopped Shadow to see if something was wrong. When he finally spoke up, it was to ask about the reprimand she'd given Geoff.

"Reprimand?" she asked, frowning.

"Aye, your reminder to 'consult Kephin' sounded like a reprimand to me."

"Ah," she said, nodding. "I guess you could say that."

"Can I ask what it was about then?"

Gemi chuckled. "You can, but you'll have to learn more about the structure of the Highwaymen to understand."

"So teach me about it," he answered. "We have a while, don't we?"

Gemi nodded. They had about an hour, since the post she had met them at had been one of the closest to Main Highwayman Camp.

"First of all, the Kephin I spoke of is Kephin Bulderas, leader of the Highwaymen. And, just so it doesn't come as a surprise later on, he's originally from Fayral."

A strange sound from behind her had Gemi glancing back at the king, who wore an odd expression. "How did he end up in Kensy, as a proponent of the people, of all things?"

Gemi chuckled. "As I understand it, he was the son of a Fayralese noble. The emperor chose him for a task that he couldn't stomach, so he fled Fayral." She shrugged. "After he became a highwayman, he found he really couldn't stomach what some of the crueler highwaymen did to the people of Kensy, either. When one particularly cruel highwayman threatened to unite Kensy under himself, well, I guess you could say I convinced Kephin that he was a better candidate for the job."

Silence lay over them for several minutes, and Gemi let the memories fill her mind. Those days had seemed like simpler times, especially before Gaffen Sabares killed Kephin's original group of highwaymen and threatened to unite the highwaymen of Kensy under his cruel reign.

But then, in those days, Lakina had been the only human who knew Gemi's true identity. Despite the fact that Kephin had felt like an older brother to her, it had been so lonely hiding who she really was from him.

"*It still is,*" Flame added, but Gemi tried to push the thought away. Ever since her sixteenth birthday last month, Flame had been pressing her to think about coming forward as the Cosley heir. "*You will be traveling with the king,*" Flame added. "*You will have the perfect opportunity for it.*"

But Gemi didn't want to think about it. She'd hidden herself away as James Caffers for so long that she feared the response of the people when they learned that she had deceived them for years. But, more than their response to her, she feared their response to the groups she had helped build. If the people felt they could no longer trust the Traveler, or whatever else they saw her as, then what would keep them from losing faith in the groups to which she was connected?

"How old were you?" The soft question seemed to come from nowhere, and Gemi jerked her head around and jolted her shoulder.

Reaching up to rub gently at the wounded joint, she stared at Ferez. "What?"

"How old were you when you convinced Kephin to unite the highwaymen?"

Gemi blinked. It wasn't a question she had expected, and she wasn't sure if she should answer it. She was so used to hiding everything about herself from people that didn't need to know. She feared that even something as small as that would lead someone with the right knowledge to discover her identity.

"*He should not need to discover it on his own,*" Flame crooned. "*You should tell him.*"

Gemi sighed. She may not like what Flame was insisting she do, but the dragon was right about one thing: Gemi was so tired of hiding.

"Ten," she answered, turning to face forward so she wouldn't see the man's reaction to her words. "I'd just turned ten almost two months before."

That silence filled the air again before the king murmured, "So young." A couple more beats of silence followed before he added softly, "You were a war orphan, weren't you?"

Gemi stilled and swallowed. That hadn't been a reaction she'd expected. Most would praise her abilities or call her a liar when she told them how young she'd been when she began to help unite the rebellious groups. The king had seen past that to what she'd really been back then: just a lost child trying to find peace during the war that had stolen her parents from her.

"Aye," she answered, just as softly. She lowered her head as she suddenly found her appetite for conversation deserting her.

The silence grew around them, though there was a hesitant quality to it. Gemi could almost feel the king debating whether to say anything more, and she kept her head bowed, hoping he would remain silent.

~~*~*

Ferez knew he probably shouldn't have asked the question, but James Caffers raised a curiosity within him that he hadn't felt since before he'd fought in the war and still wanted nothing more than to learn more about the people he'd one day rule. Then, he'd donned plainclothes and ridden from the palace on Last Chance to explore both the city of Caypan and the surrounding countryside.

Now, he found himself watching James as the boy hunched in on himself, the lines of his back tense. And he found himself wishing to learn more about this boy, not just about the people he represented. He wanted to learn what the boy was like and why he did things. He wanted to get to know *James*.

Despite the shortness of the boy's answers about himself, Ferez had already learned a lot from them. Like Ferez, the boy had lost his father to the war with Fayral. Since James was ten, or younger, when he joined a band of highwaymen, he had lost his mother, too, about the same time or earlier. And, Ferez suspected, James was originally from Kensy.

Ferez had met many war orphans since he'd joined the war. For every man who died under his command, he had gone to their family, consoled their wives or mothers, and met the lost looks in the eyes of their siblings or children. Those children who had survived both mother and father were often taken in by others in their village or neighboring farmers and townspeople. Those that weren't were usually older, and Ferez had met many young soldiers who joined the war to follow in their father's footsteps or seek revenge for their deaths. Ferez suspected, too, that others joined the rebellious groups for similar reasons.

That James had lost both parents to the war and had joined the rebellious groups at such a young age meant to Ferez that James had had nowhere else to go; that he had lost his home, his village or wherever he lived with his family, at the same time. Since the war had never extended south of the Kensian forest, that meant that James was from one of the many Kensian towns and villages that the Fayralese had destroyed throughout the war.

Ferez sighed softly. He couldn't help the curiosity within him that urged him to ask the boy how he had managed to survive such an attack. He didn't ask; couldn't really, not with the tension holding the boy stiff in his saddle.

However, he thought he might understand how. A dragon like Flame Tongue would not let her bondmate be killed without a fight.

Suddenly, Ferez recalled James' words about how long Flame Tongue had been with him. He'd even mentioned that she was from the Northeast Forest. *He's from east Kensy, then,* Ferez realized with some surprise. *Not only that,* he thought, his mind conjuring up the memory of James' odd reaction to Ferez's mention of the old duke's estate, *he's from Cosley Ruins.*

The realization was striking, and Ferez wondered what the boy would say if he knew Ferez had figured out that much. But James was just beginning to relax from the scare Ferez had given him before—and Ferez was sure it had been fear that had made him tense, though of discovery or of letting someone close, Ferez couldn't be certain.

He did know that he didn't want to make their association more strained, so Ferez pushed down his curiosity for now and contented himself with the silence of the ride back to James' highwayman camp.

Chapter 16

The light spilling through the forest's canopy was growing weak when James led his mount off of the highway and into the surrounding trees. Off the highway, it was nearly impossible for Ferez to see past the few trees just in front of him, let alone the horse and rider he and Last Chance were following.

So it was to his great surprise that light began to seep through the trees ahead of them, leading them easily to their destination. When the horses stepped out of the tree line, Ferez pulled Last Chance to a halt and simply stared.

A multitude of lamps and fires lit what looked like hundreds of tents and small buildings that spread away from them, interspersed with giant trees that dominated the area and spread their reaching branches over the camp like protective beings.

Then again, he thought idly as he considered the sheer number of people that must live in a camp this size, *if they have powerful enough Plant Mages, those trees could very well be a form of defense.*

A chuckle drew his gaze from the camp sprawled out before him to the boy who sat atop his stallion nearby. The boy was grinning at him, which was such a thankful change to nearly an hour before that Ferez felt his own lips spreading to match.

Stretching his uninjured arm out to encompass the entire camp, he proclaimed, "Welcome to Main Highwayman Camp, the center of Highwayman activity here in Kensy."

Ferez shook his head as his eyes turned back to the large camp. "It looks more like a town than a camp." James chuckled again. "How long has this been here?"

James waved for Ferez to follow him and directed his stallion down one of the paths between tents. Ferez urged Last Chance into a trot until she was walking side-by-side with the boy's mount.

"We first created the camp during the winter of the 218th year of Evon." Ferez frowned. That was nearly six years ago.

"How did you manage to hide a camp this large from either m—the king's men or the Fayralese for four years?"

James shrugged and offered him a sly grin. "You'd be surprised how useful plants and animals are to warding off intruders. Well-placed animal dens and impenetrable thickets around parts of the camp have played a large part in its protection."

"You have enough mages here for that?" Ferez asked, shocked. Plant and Animal Mages were more common than Mage Healers—at least, that's what Ferez had grown up learning—but he still couldn't imagine a single camp, even one this size, housing that many mages.

The boy nodded, though his gaze had grown distracted, and he'd begun rubbing gently at his injured shoulder. Curious, Ferez had opened his mouth to ask if something was wrong when a sharp female voice cut through the camp.

"James Caffers!"

The tone was that of a mother calling out her child for bad behavior, and Ferez winced in sympathy as James grimaced.

"That's Lakina," James muttered, and he urged his stallion into a quicker pace.

Ferez pursed his lips in amusement as he and Last Chance followed James. *'Old Iron' indeed,* he mused.

James pulled his mount to a halt in what looked like a central area of the camp. Several tents circled around a large open area, at the middle of which sat a cooking fire. A few people milled around the area, but it was the matronly woman standing in front of one particular tent that James was watching warily.

She was a stout woman with silver hair tied back in a tight bun, and her brown eyes glared up at James with a mixture of determination and disappointment, her arms akimbo and her fists on her hips.

"James Caffers, I could sense your wounds halfway across camp. I want you off that horse and in my tent in the next five minutes or else..."

The threat was left hanging, but it was effective enough. Before she'd even finished speaking, James had thrown a leg over the front of his saddle and was sliding off the stallion's back. A grimace crossed his face as he landed, but he waved a hand carelessly at Ferez when he offered to help.

As the boy disappeared into the tent behind her, the woman, Lakina, harrumphed and turned her piercing gaze onto Ferez. He shifted uncomfortably as he got the impression that she was summing up all of him and not just his wounds.

With a short nod, she told him, "I'll take care of your injuries when I'm done with his."

Then, she turned and disappeared into the tent, leaving Ferez alone in the middle of a camp he didn't know with Last Chance and James' two animal companions.

~~*~*

Kephin had peered out of his tent when he heard Lakina's voice ring through the camp. He would have liked to speak with Gemi, but he knew better than to try to get a word in edgewise when Old Iron Lakina was accosting one of her patients, especially one she felt as strongly for as Gemi.

Once Lakina had disappeared into her tent, he found himself observing the still-mounted man who had arrived with Gemi. Curious about the newcomer, Kephin left his tent and approached him.

"I take it this is your first visit to Main Highwayman Camp." The mounted man startled and stared down at Kephin, blinking uncertainly. Kephin chuckled. "Most people are used to Lakina's sharp tongue. However, her hands and magic are gentle. You'll be safe with her."

"Er…" the man began. He seemed lost, and, understanding the feeling, Kephin waved him down off his horse.

"I'm Kephin Bulderas," he said once the man had dismounted. The man looked surprised but offered his hand to Kephin.

"Frenz Kanti."

Kephin nodded. Instead of taking the offered hand, he threw an arm around the man's shoulders and steered him towards the cooking fire in the middle of the camp's center. "Let's get you something to eat while we wait for Lakina to finish with James."

Thankfully, Flame and Shadow appeared willing to take care of Kanti's horse. Already, Flame was crooning to the mare and herding her towards the area between Lakina and Kephin's tents where Gemi's bondmates usually slept. Kephin reminded himself to have Cassidi put out extra oats for the mare.

Once he had Kanti settled on one of the logs surrounding the cooking fire and a bowl from Cassidi in his hands, Kephin finally asked the man the reason for his visit.

"Actually," he began hesitantly, "I'm here wit' James."

Kephin frowned. That was rather obvious since the man had arrived with Gemi. But that didn't explain why the man was visiting Main Highwayman Camp.

A trill caught Kephin's attention, and he glanced behind himself to find Flame staring at him rather intently. After a moment of meeting her red gaze, he sighed. Why was it that she always had something important to tell him when Gemi wasn't around to translate?

"Well, call Maxwell if you think it's that important, Flame."

The dragon continued to stare at him for a moment longer before lifting her head and giving the loud whistling call she had used the day before to bring Maxwell running.

Sure enough, Kephin heard Maxwell's answering chitter before the boy appeared between two tents. He paused when he noticed the newcomer and tilted his head like a bird warily observing a snake. When Flame trilled at the boy, Maxwell's eyebrows shot up, and he whistled back, walking closer as he did so.

Dragon and Animal Mage traded sounds back and forth before Maxwell turned his gaze back to Kanti. His eyes were more serious than Kephin honestly thought any ten-year-old's had a right to be, but he had known Maxwell for six years and knew the boy could be more serious than some grown men Kephin knew.

"You are special," were the first words out of Maxwell's mouth, startling both men. Before Kephin could ask what he meant, the boy added, "James never travels with anyone, ever."

Confused, Kephin turned to the man who sat beside him. For a moment, Kanti looked uncertain. Nodding, he slowly replied, "Aye, maybe. Bu' James hadn' met the king afore today."

"King?" Kephin asked, surprised.

167

The only reason Gemi hadn't remained in bed all day today was because she had insisted on being on the highway when the duke arrived in case there was trouble. There had been no mention of the king being involved in any of this.

Kanti nodded, looking more certain of his words. "Rather lucky for me, I think. Apparen'ly, 'e an' his men had left Puretha jus' an hour or so afore I arrived. E'en think I passed 'em on the highway, though I coudna told you tha' was who they was."

Flame whistled, and Kephin turned to her and Maxwell, hoping the young Animal Mage could shine some light on what the other man was talking about.

Maxwell nodded thoughtfully, his eyes still locked on Kanti curiously. "Flame says the king came north with his dukes." The dragon trilled, and Maxwell finally turned back to her, his lips spreading wide. "Are you serious, Flame?" The dragon whistled, sounding indignant. Maxwell only nodded. "If the king believes James, then that is a good thing, is it not?"

Kephin turned to stare at Flame, shocked. He couldn't believe his ears. Six years, the Highwaymen had been united and serving Evon despite the throne's ignorance. Now, Flame was insisting the king actually believed in…what, exactly?

He said so and Flame huffed and seemed to glance almost apologetically towards Kanti before trilling again.

"She says he believes he has been neglecting his people; that he will work towards a better life for them."

Kephin knew the words were straight from Flame, and that they had to be true, but he still couldn't believe it. The Highwaymen had fought for Evon for four years during the war and kept themselves hidden at the same time because they had feared the actions the king and his men would take against them if they showed themselves. Now, Flame was saying that their hiding had been for naught?

Not the same king, though, he realized the next moment and shook his head.

That was the reason. Kephin could still remember his surprise when the news arrived that the war had officially been ended. It had taken two sevendays of no fighting—not even the rogues had dared to start any fights right after the war—for Kephin to understand that the news had not been idle.

With that understanding had bloomed a respect for the new king that Kephin had never had for his father. The young king was the kind of man Kephin enjoyed serving, whether the king knew of his service or not.

A soft coo pulled Kephin from his memories, and he met Flame's red gaze steadily and nodded. "Very well. So James believes the king is finally willing to help his people." Kephin turned his gaze back to Kanti. "That doesn't tell me why James would go against a decision he'd made years ago not to travel with anyone but his bondmates."

~~*~*

Ferez shifted under Bulderas' gaze, feeling very uncomfortable and, once again, uncertain of his story. It had made sense while talking with the leader of the Puretha Highwaymen, and that man had even agreed that Kensy needed a new duke.

However, there was something about this man that screamed that he would not be so easy to impress.

When Ferez glanced at Flame, hoping the dragon might be able to offer some help, the reptilian creature just met his eyes steadily, a slight movement rippling down her body, almost like a shrug.

Great, he thought, turning his gaze back to Bulderas. *No help there.*

Before he could think of a way to appease the man, the young boy, whom he assumed was Maxwell, frowned up at Bulderas.

"It is not fair of you to ask him, Kephin. How is he supposed to know why James would do something like that?"

Bulderas' frown became more pronounced before he suddenly sighed and shook his head. "Of course he can't know that," he muttered. He smiled apologetically at Ferez then. "I'm sorry. If you hadn't noticed, I'm rather protective of James. It just seems odd to me that he's suddenly taken a human companion after all these years."

Ferez smiled back as relief overwhelmed him. He'd feared attempting to explain the boy's motivations when he doubted the boy had told him all of them himself.

"No problem," the king replied. "I'd prolly be jus' as protective if I though' my own family was bein' threatened."

Bulderas startled and waved a hand dismissively in front of himself. "James is not—"

"Maybe no' by blood," Ferez interrupted. He understood the man's concern, but he hadn't thought the two related.

They might both have black hair, but Bulderas kept his shoulder-length, and it sprung into curls that Ferez thought were more appropriate for Bulderas' birthright as a noble in the Fayralese emperor's court than for a highwayman in the forest of Kensy. His eyes, a bright jewel-tone similar to James', were the color of emeralds, not amethysts.

"Bu' James said 'e was ten when the two o' you began to unite the highwaymen. I imagine you think o' him as family, aye?"

Bulderas stared at him with wide eyes even as Maxwell giggled. "Kephin and James have been like brothers since I can remember."

Bulderas shook his head slightly, still staring at Ferez. "James never gives away information like that freely." He finally closed his eyes. "And he only just met you."

Ferez frowned at that. He wasn't sure what the Highwayman was trying to say. He hadn't coerced James to answer him. The boy could have easily refused, and Ferez had thought the boy might at one point during their ride. But Ferez had simply asked questions. There wasn't anything suspicious about that; was there?

"I told you, Kephin," Maxwell chirped. "Frenz Kanti is special." The boy paused and met Ferez's gaze.

Ferez felt the sudden urge to shift under that gaze. Like Lakina, he suddenly felt that the boy could see more of him than just the outer guise of Frenz Kanti. It seemed ridiculous since the boy was so young, but he had such a serious demeanor and he spoke so clearly that Ferez felt the ridiculousness of the thought didn't matter.

"James trusts you," the boy finally said, addressing Ferez for the first time since he'd arrived. "I do not know why, and I do not think Flame does either, but, for some reason, James trusts you more than he does most people."

That startled Ferez, and not just because he hadn't thought James trusted him that considerably or realized that the boy was that distrusting by nature. On the ride here, he had been considering similar thoughts about himself.

While he had learned to follow his instincts since before he joined the war, Ferez had been just as surprised as anyone by his willingness to trust James Caffers. After all, the boy had claimed to be the Ghost, a man who was considered to be the most dangerous criminal in Evon.

Yet Ferez had been willing to look past all of his supposed crimes because the boy's words had made sense to him. Ferez wasn't completely sure he understood why.

Now, this young Animal Mage was claiming that James trusted Ferez to a greater extent than he trusted most other people, as well. Ferez didn't know what to say to that.

A croon and a nudge drew his attention to Flame Tongue. She stared intently at him with one dark red eye, and Ferez could imagine James listening to what Flame Tongue heard—at least, he thought dragonbonds must work like that—and he nodded to the dragon.

"Thank him for me, will you, Flame?"

He kept the words soft. He would have preferred to thank James himself or at least pass the words through Flame with no one else to hear, but he gave up such privileges when he took on the guise of Frenz Kanti.

The dragon crooned again and nodded, pulling her head up and back to eye their group before lying down and wrapping her neck around the side of her body. Ferez nearly chuckled.

She might appear relaxed, but he doubted she wouldn't be listening to the remainder of their conversation. If she'd just wanted to sleep, she could have joined her bondmate next to Lakina's tent instead of staying close enough to speak up, if necessary.

They remained silent for a while, and Ferez took the opportunity to eat the food he'd been given. It was a spiced stew, with chunks of meat he thought must be venison. The flavor was worthy of the palace kitchens, but he was more reminded of the many times he had sat around a fire with his men during the war, trading stories of home and family.

He felt an old pain in his heart as he remembered that he had had to visit many of those families and homes following the deaths of those men in battle. He rubbed idly at his chest where a physical reminder of those deaths lay; a daily reminder of the pain the war had caused his country.

It was that reminder that had forced him to seek an end to the war as soon as he was crowned king, despite the actions of his forefathers. He had never understood how the Katanis before him, even his father, could focus so much effort on the war with Fayral and so completely ignore how their country was being destroyed in the process.

Ferez had become so lost in the old thoughts that he didn't realize he'd stopped eating until a hand on his arm jerked him back to the present. Bulderas was watching him carefully, an appraising light in his eyes that made Ferez twitch.

"Are you all right?" the Highwayman asked.

Ferez nodded and glanced away from him but quickly found that Maxwell was watching with just as much curiosity.

"You looked like you were awfully far away, Mister Kanti," Maxwell said.

Ferez felt his lips twitch at the formal address. "I'd rather you call me Frenz, if you don' mind." Maxwell flashed him a bright smile, though his expression just as quickly became serious again.

"Well?" he asked.

Flame snorted from beside him, and Ferez felt his lips finally widen into a smile. Apparently, whatever reason was behind the general formality of his words had not quelled the curiosity of his youth one bit.

"To tell you the truth, I was thinking about the war."

He didn't think it would hurt to use part of the truth as his story. Plenty of farmers and villagers throughout Evon, and not just in Kensy, had fought in the war as soldiers. It wouldn't seem odd that he had as well.

As if to prove his point, Bulderas nodded. "It dominated our lives so much, it's hard not to think about it at times."

The dull pain in his eyes was familiar to Ferez, and the king suddenly felt a kinship with this man he'd just met. Ferez had no doubt that Kephin Bulderas knew what it was like to lead men into battle and watch as they died under his command for a cause that might not have been their own.

"Perhaps, but we survived," Maxwell suddenly spoke up. Flame Tongue lifted her own head and crooned, and Maxwell nodded. "We cannot let it continue to dominate our lives."

Ferez stared down at the boy. "How old are you?" he asked incredulously. The boy spoke like a wise man, not a child.

"Ten," answered the boy, a wide smile splitting his face.

Kephin chuckled, and Ferez had no doubt that he wore a dumbfounded expression. "If you're wondering where he gets it, we blame it on his friendship with Flame. Conversing with a dragon from the age of four apparently has its consequences."

Ferez frowned, thinking of the way James spoke. The boy had said that he had been bonded to the dragon from the age of seven, which Ferez thought must have been nine years ago. Although James spoke clearly enough, he didn't speak with the same formality that young Maxwell did.

Just then Flame Tongue nudged Ferez and trilled softly. Maxwell glanced between the two before saying, "It sounds like Lakina is ready to tend to you." He pointed to Ferez's bowl. "But I would finish eating first if I were you."

Ferez nodded, ate the last few bites of the now cold stew, and left the comforting light of the fire. He hesitated at the entrance to the tent into which James and Lakina had disappeared before pushing it aside and ducking into the tent.

The inside of the tent was dimly lit with a lamp hanging in the center of the tent. Lakina seemed to be leaning over a cot; Ferez was behind her, so he couldn't see what she was doing.

At first, the king couldn't see James at all. Then, Lakina stepped away from the cot, swept a hand up over the top of her head, and turned towards Ferez, revealing James as the occupant of the cot.

"Ah, Mister Kanti," Lakina greeted him.

Behind her, James pulled his tunic down over bandages that seemed to cover his entire upper body. *Was he hurt that badly?* Ferez wondered.

He didn't have time to contemplate the question as Lakina bustled forward, gripped his arm strongly, and directed him to the cot beside James'. As Ferez seated himself, he met James' eyes, which quickly skittered away from his own.

He blinked. The boy had never acted shy before now.

"Now, I've already Healed James' injuries as much as I can for now, though," and she turned to James and shook a finger at the boy, "I don't want you putting anymore strain on that shoulder for the next several days. After two sevendays of it being injured, another injury so soon after healing could very well have destroyed your use of it. Even magic has its limitations, James."

"I know, Lakina," the boy practically whined, and Ferez had the feeling this was not the first time the Mage Healer had said this.

Lakina huffed. "I just want you healthy and whole, James." When James rolled his eyes, the Healer pursed her lips. "Don't think I won't tell Kephin to keep you off the highway, because you know I will."

The boy actually groaned then, and Ferez covered his mouth the keep from laughing at the put-out expression on James' face. "But, Lakina…" the boy whined.

"You can always spend the next few days showin' me aroun' the camp, can'cha, James?" Ferez spoke up before Lakina could find a reason to cut into the boy some more. Both boy and Healer turned to him, James with surprise, Lakina with confusion.

"Are you staying for a while, Mister Kanti?" the Mage Healer asked.

Ferez glanced at James with one brow raised. He had already had to begin the explanation to Kephin, so he was surprised that James hadn't done the same for the Mage Healer. James offered him a small smile and shrug before touching Lakina's arm with his good hand.

"Frenz is going to be traveling with me until we reach Baylin, Lakina. I'm taking him to see the king."

That had the Healer staring at the boy with such shock that Ferez wondered if she would faint. He need not have worried as she quickly recovered and snapped her gaze to Ferez, her eyes narrowing suspiciously.

Ferez sighed. Was he really going to face this kind of suspicion from every person close to the boy?

"Don't look like that, Lakina," James commanded, his voice taking on a sharp tone that could rival Lakina's. "I just met the king earlier today, before Frenz arrived in Puretha, and he seems amenable to the plight of his people. I believe he'd be willing to listen to the requests of his people."

The Healer had turned her sharp look on James while he spoke. Once he finished, she pursed her lips and nodded, but Ferez doubted the issue would be forgotten. He suspected that she, and quite possibly Kephin, would question James thoroughly about the abrupt change to his routine when they were alone. Ferez silently wished the boy luck.

"Well," Lakina finally said as she turned back to Ferez. Thankfully, her eyes had softened. "If you are going to travel with James, then you will most likely be under my care more than most."

Ferez raised an eyebrow but didn't respond to the comment that seemed as much a warning as a jibe at James. James caught Ferez's gaze and playfully rolled his eyes.

"That being the case," Lakina continued, oblivious to James' antics, "I'll take a more thorough look at your overall health now than I would if you were just a visitor."

The Mage Healer began to hum softly as her eyes moved slowly over his form. Ferez swallowed nervously at the intent look in her eyes. However, it wasn't so much her magic that worried him as what she might find.

When her eyes appeared to be level with his torso, she frowned. She didn't say anything, but the frown deepened as she continued her perusal. When her gaze finally returned to Ferez's face, she gestured towards his tunic.

"Off with the tunic, Mister Kanti. Your wounds are pretty mild compared to what I'm used to, and whatever you do for a living seems to keep you in good shape,"—Ferez nearly snorted; *Aye, knight training will do that*—"but there is something at which I would like to take a closer look."

Ferez swallowed again and laid a hand over his chest. He knew what it was that she had sensed. The scar that he now considered a physical reminder of the pain the war inflicted on his people lay there, and he had absolutely no desire to remove the tunic and show it off, especially with James Caffers sitting directly in front of him.

He stared into the Mage Healer's eyes pleadingly, but, while her gaze softened, she didn't relent. With a resigned sigh, Ferez dropped his hands to the hem of his tunic and lifted it over his head, dropping it to the cot beside him.

Chapter 17

Gemi gasped when Ferez removed his tunic. She briefly considered that the king's chest was well-built—an idle thought that she would later deny if her bondmates ever asked about it.

The observation was quickly overrun by the sight of the scar that crossed the chest diagonally. An angry, ragged thing, it stretched from his left shoulder towards his right hip, disappearing below his trousers.

As she watched, Lakina reached out and smoothed her fingers along the scar. Ferez twitched under her hand, his head jerking to one side.

Gemi blinked and finally lifted her gaze to the king's face. To her surprise, the muscles in his jaw stood out as he clenched his jaw, red bloomed across his cheekbones, and his eyes grew distant.

"How did you get this?" Lakina murmured softly.

Gemi jerked her gaze from Ferez up to Lakina. There was anger simmering in Lakina's voice, but, from what Gemi could see of the Healer's face, Lakina was simply intent on the wound.

Ferez's jaw worked silently for a moment before he finally whispered, "The Battle of Shanala."

The words burned with shame, and, before she could think about it, Gemi reached over and placed her hand on the man's knee. He tensed beneath her hand, but, as she held it there, he began to relax and finally nodded to her.

Lakina hummed, but Gemi ignored her as she considered Ferez's words. The Battle of Shanala had been one of the worst battles of the war. She hadn't been there herself—she had been on the road to Baylin at the time—but she had heard enough about it from Kephin and Lakina to know that it had been bloody.

Many had died in that battle, but the most significant death had been the old king's. King Eden Katani hadn't actually died in battle, but his wounds had been such that even the large number of skilled healers, both magical and otherwise, that had attempted to heal him hadn't made a difference.

"As y'know," Ferez added slowly, drawing Gemi's gaze back to him, "healers were scarce af'er the battle."

Gemi nodded. The king's men had recruited every healer they could find in the attempt to heal the king.

"I don' remember much from those days followin' the battle. I do remember some'un takin' me in, but the res' is los' in the haze of fever dreams."

Gemi swallowed. She remembered now the news she'd learned while in Baylin that season. Rumors had spread that not only was the king dead, but his son would soon follow. She had feared the chaos that would overwhelm the country without a king. She had been so happy to learn that Ferez Katani survived that she hadn't even worried then that the king was young.

Lakina sighed suddenly, a gusty sound that had Gemi staring at the woman in surprise. "If I could do something to the Heal the scar, I would offer to, but I'm afraid that even I am not that powerful."

For some reason, Ferez relaxed fully with those words, and he shook his head. "I've lived wit' it for two years now, and I've learned to work wit' it."

Gemi blinked. Only then did she realize what a scar like that could mean. Not only would Ferez's life have been in danger, from infection if not from blood loss or something worse, but the wound would have destroyed many of the muscles in his chest.

"It certainly doesn't seem to have hindered your fighting ability," she put in with a small smile.

Ferez ducked his head, the red returning to his cheeks, and he shrugged. "'Twas several sevendays afore I was even allowed to touch my sword, let alone able to fight in battle again."

Lakina huffed. "I'm amazed you managed to train yourself enough to fight again before the war was over."

Gemi glanced at the Healer curiously. There was such an odd tone to Lakina's voice that she couldn't imagine what the older woman was thinking.

"Well," Lakina continued, "I better take a look at your actual wounds." She waved at Ferez again. "Off with the trousers please so I can take a look at your thigh."

Gemi felt her face burn with those words, and the heat in her cheeks only increased when Ferez reached for his boots. It had been bad enough that she hadn't been fully covered when Ferez entered the tent earlier—Flame had laughed at Gemi's embarrassment at the near discovery. Now, Lakina was just pushing her.

Jumping to her feet and startling Ferez, Gemi muttered some excuse to leave—food might have been involved—before dashing for the tent's entrance. As she pushed through, she heard Lakina chuckle and say, "I swear that boy can be shier than a newborn fawn sometimes."

Gemi's cheeks burned hotter with those words. Lakina might be a Healer, but Gemi thought the woman could sometimes be merciless enough to rival Sir Paeter and Sir Leal on her birthdays.

Gemi stumbled to a halt, the blood rushing from her face so quickly that she wavered. Why, now, would she think about her old mentors when she hadn't thought about them for years?

She had never learned what had actually happened to them, but she had always assumed that they had either died at Cosley Estate that day or in the attack that had destroyed Farvis around the same time. Yet, now, her mind had raised thoughts of them casually, as though they hadn't most likely died several years before.

"*James?*" Flame crooned.

Gemi blinked her eyes a few times before she realized that she was surrounded. Flame had her neck wrapped around Gemi's back, Shadow's nose was nudging at and snorting into her hair, and Kephin stood in front of her, his hands wrapped tightly around her upper arms.

"James, are you all right?" Kephin was asking as Gemi finally focused her mind back on reality. She nodded slowly.

"I am," she muttered. Kephin didn't look like he believed her, so she lifted a hand and patted his chest lightly. "I'm fine, Kephin; just a bad memory, is all."

"I haven't seen you look like that in years, James," Kephin said with such an intense look that Gemi glanced away, unable to meet it.

"I'm fine," she repeated.

Pushing past the man, she settled on one of the logs circling the central cooking fire and accepted a bowl of stew from Cassidi, determined to ignore the memories that plagued the edge of her mind.

~~*~*

In the tent that the Mage Healer occupied, the demigoddess Life watched the Healer examine the young king. She, like the humans, remembered the Battle of Shanala well. She had lost so many souls during that battle, but the scar that marred the king's chest haunted her more than she had once thought possible.

A hand on her shoulder pulled Life back against a firm chest, and she relaxed against her black twin. "You are reminiscing, Sister," Death's dark voice whispered against her ear.

Life rolled her eyes and glanced up at her brother. "Aye, perhaps, but can you blame me?" She turned her gaze back to the young king, whose chest was still visible. "I remember that scar too well, Death."

The black demigod hummed softly, his lips against her ear. "He still lives."

Life shook her head. "Aye, but at what cost?" She felt Death's lips twitch and shook her head before he could speak. "You were not there, Death. You cannot possibly understand."

She felt his lips twitch again and suspected that he might be smiling, but his next words were solemn.

"Nay, I was not there. We both know that if I had been anywhere near the boy, then he would not have survived, no matter what you did."

Life shivered at the reference to her transgression and lowered her head. "What have I done?" she whispered.

"What you had to do," Death answered, wrapping his arms around her midsection and pulling her further into him. "Why do you think I never questioned why you risked saving young Ferez Katani when you could have easily saved his father instead?"

Life blinked up at him and found that a small smile did quirk his lips. "I can feel it, too, Life. I cannot understand why, but I can feel that Ferez Katani is important."

Life nodded, her own lips twitching upwards. *That is the crux of the issue, is it not? We can feel that this human is important to us, but we do not know the reason.*

With a sigh, Life turned her gaze back to the young king, and her small smile turned sad as she eyed that long, gruesome scar once more.

~~*~*

When Gemi finally felt in control of her emotions again, she asked Kephin about sleeping arrangements. She usually stayed in Kephin's tent, but she knew the man only kept the one spare bed, and Gemi wasn't about to leave the king alone in a strange place, even if she did trust everyone involved.

Kephin attempted to turn the conversation onto her reasons for taking on a traveling companion, but Gemi firmly moved the conversation forward onto where she and Ferez could sleep. She didn't want to have to explain her reasons to Kephin and Lakina separately. It was the reason she hadn't broached the subject with Lakina before Ferez had entered the tent, and she wasn't about to break now.

Once he realized she was going to be stubborn about it, he relented. He narrowed his eyes at her when she told him she would stay wherever Ferez stayed, but he didn't argue.

"The only person that I know has two extra beds is Lanzure."

Gemi grimaced. Lanzure was Main Highwayman Camp's weapons smith, but the man's feelings towards Gemi were...ambivalent. Actually, it wasn't so much Gemi that Lanzure had issues with as Flame.

Lanzure was young Maxwell's father, but the weapons smith had been terrified and suspicious of Flame from the first time he'd met her. Yet, despite that fear and suspicion, Lanzure had recognized that Maxwell and Flame had taken a liking to each other immediately and that Flame would be able to train his son in a way he could not.

After all, it had been Lanzure's lifemate who had been an Animal Mage, not he. After she was killed by Fayralese raiders, he had been at a loss as to how to raise a young mage, especially one that was already attracting the attention of large predators without the willingness to actually control them.

For that reason, he'd tried to remain understanding when it came to his son's friendship with a dragon, but he had never become comfortable with it.

"If he's the only one with two empty beds," Gemi finally replied with a sigh, "then I'll have to ask him. I just hope he says aye."

"*If he does not at first,*" Flame trilled, "*you know Maxwell will convince him to.*"

Gemi chuckled at that. Despite Lanzure's mixed feelings over his son's friendship with a dragon, his son was his world, and he was often willing to do anything the boy asked.

When Ferez and Lakina exited the Healer's tent, Lakina propelled Ferez toward Kephin and shot the Highwayman a look that made Gemi

178

frown. To her surprise, Kephin nodded and asked Ferez to accompany him to Lanzure's tent.

"Perhaps he'll be more willing to take the two of you in if he sees the man who needs a bed, rather than the one who wants one."

Ferez looked confused by the remark but agreed anyway, and the two wandered off down one of the paths that led off the central area.

Once the two had disappeared, Gemi turned her gaze to Lakina, who was accepting a bowl of stew from Cassidi with a grateful smile. For a moment, she blew on the warm stew, her gaze distant.

Gemi continued to watch her, not fooled by her silence. Lakina wanted to speak with her about something; Gemi just had to wait for the woman to decide how to broach the subject.

Finally, the Mage Healer lowered her gaze to Gemi. With a sharp nod, she seemed to reach some kind of decision and murmured, "Can I have a word with you, James?"

Gemi felt her lips twitch, but she nodded and indicated the open space on the log next to her. Lakina quickly shook her head and added, "In my tent?"

That worried Gemi. It meant that whatever she had to talk about was a topic that she wanted no one else hearing. Gemi couldn't imagine anything good falling into that category of conversation at the moment.

Gemi followed the Healer back into her tent and sat on the cot she'd occupied previously. Once inside, Lakina placed her bowl of stew on a table and began to pace the length of the tent. The longer the woman paced, the more worried Gemi became until she nearly spoke up in order to beg the woman to tell her what was wrong.

Finally, Lakina stopped and turned to face her. Her face was set in a determined frown, and Gemi swallowed, suddenly unsure she actually wanted to hear what she had to say.

"Never once," Lakina began, "in all of my years, have I betrayed a secret placed in my trust, Gemi, but I fear this is something I simply cannot ignore."

Gemi felt her heart start to race. Lakina was known as Old Iron, not just because of the sharpness of her tongue, but also because her lips were like iron doors. As a powerful Mage Healer, she learned the secrets of hundreds of people, but, as she'd said, she had never broken any of those confidences. If Lakina was considering breaking her silence on someone's secret, it had to be serious.

Knowing now that this was not a conversation she wanted to have, Gemi gestured towards Lakina's bowl and muttered weakly, "You really should eat, Lakina. You've got to be exhausted after Healing both Frenz and me."

Lakina glared at the girl briefly, obviously recognizing the words for the attempted distraction that they were. However, she really must have been hungry because she picked up the bowl and began to eat. As soon as she was finished, she set the bowl back down and continued speaking.

"Do you even realize with whom you've agreed to travel? Or has he truly disguised himself well enough to fool even you?"

Gemi's heart was racing harder now, and she fought not to drop her gaze. "What do you mean, Lakina?" she asked, hoping to throw the woman off. "He's Frenz Kanti, a farmer from near Cosley Ruins."

Lakina sighed, relaxing as she did so, but the look she offered Gemi was one of exasperation. "Child, you should know better than to lie to me like that. You know I can sense your heartbeat racing."

Gemi flushed and dropped her gaze. One of the things Gemi hated about Lakina being so powerful was her ability to detect lies. Then again, Gemi hadn't been hiding her reactions very well.

"How do you know who he is?" Gemi asked warily.

Lakina hadn't said who she actually thought Ferez was, just that she thought he was not who he said he was. When Lakina didn't answer right away, Gemi glanced up and caught a sad look in the Healer's eyes.

"I recognize the scar," she whispered.

She closed her eyes, and Gemi bit her lip as she realized that the woman must be picturing the wound the king's scar had once been. "Like most other healers, I was locked away with King Eden when he was dying." She shook her head.

"His wounds weren't that bad. We should have been able to save him, but it was almost like something wanted him dead, and there was no turning that force away. Every complication that could happen did." She sighed and quieted for a moment.

"When the old king died, we were finally allowed to do sweeps of the injured to see who could be saved. I remember hearing people murmur that no one had seen the old king's son since the battle, but I didn't think anything of it until an elderly man approached me and requested that I take a look at a young man who had fallen into his care after the battle."

Lakina shook her head again. "I wouldn't have recognized the boy even then if I hadn't just spent a sevenday attempting to save his father." She paused, then, more softly, she added, "He had lost so much blood, and the infection was so deeply rooted by the time I saw him…"

She sighed. "He should have been dead. But it was as though, whatever force was intent on his father dying, an equally powerful force was intent on him living."

She fell silent then, and Gemi contemplated her words. Gemi had never known that Lakina was the one who had found young Ferez Katani after the Battle of Shanala. Then again, Lakina never told the secrets she learned, so it didn't surprise Gemi that the Healer had kept silent on this, as well.

"Now," Lakina finally spoke up, her voice heavy with exasperation, "you've brought the young king amongst the Highwaymen, pretending he's a farmer of all things. Why?"

Gemi squirmed, but Lakina's gaze only became sharper at Gemi's restlessness. The girl sighed.

"I might have told him that he needed to travel among his people to learn about the problems they faced."

As disbelief unfolded across the Healer's face, Gemi hurried to add, "I meant it more for the dukes since they were the ones who seemed to need convincing. I didn't mean for the king to ask me to let him travel with me." As she spoke, Gemi's voice inched into a whine, and her face reddened at the sound.

Lakina sighed and shook her head. "You implied he was taking a request to Caypan. What request is he claiming to take?"

Gemi squirmed again and glanced away from Lakina. "New duke," she muttered.

Lakina gasped. "Oh, Gemi," she breathed, sadness settling into her words.

"What was I supposed to do?" Gemi half-cried, half-sobbed. She shook her head and swallowed back the sudden threat of tears.

"I tried to say something, but then Puretha was attacked, and Geoff asked him what his request was before we could talk more about it, and…"

Gemi groaned and dropped her head into her hands. "I don't know what to do, Lakina," she muttered through her hands.

A hand rubbed across her back then, and Gemi sighed as tension eased out of her muscles. "You'll travel with him," Lakina answered. "You'll teach him about his people."

Gemi blinked and lifted her gaze up to Lakina's. To her surprise, the Mage Healer was smiling fondly at her. "You'll help him build a relationship with his people that he won't be able to forget."

Gemi nodded. She could do that, had been planning on it, actually. But it seemed more possible when Lakina said it.

The Healer suddenly smirked, and Gemi blinked, surprised. "You do realize that this means you're going to have to tell him who you are, don't you?" Gemi stiffened. "Unless, of course, you don't think he'll follow through with 'granting' the request."

Gemi groaned. Nay, she didn't doubt the king would follow through. Which meant Lakina was right, but—

Gemi shook her head as panic clawed up her throat. "Not yet," she muttered.

"Gemi," Lakina sighed.

"Nay!" Gemi said, shaking her head harder. "I can't. Not yet."

Another sigh, and Gemi felt Lakina squeeze her shoulder. "Very well," the woman murmured. "But you will have to tell him before the season is over."

Gemi nodded emphatically, grateful that the Healer had dropped the subject for now.

"I assume that you want me to keep his secret then?" Lakina asked. Gemi nodded and stared up her gratefully. The Healer huffed and nodded. "I will bring this up with him, though."

Gemi nodded again. It was Ferez's secret. He deserved to know that Lakina knew the truth.

Just then, Gemi yawned widely, suddenly tired. Lakina huffed again and shook her head, waving Gemi towards the tent's entrance.

"Go," she said. "You need rest."

Gemi nodded and left the Healer's tent in search of Ferez, Kephin, and a bed.

~~*~*

Two hours ride north of the North Evonese Junction
Kensy, Evon

The clearing was dimly lit, only a single lit torch futilely battling against the darkness of the night. He knew the other men, the five who watched warily as he paced, would have preferred the blaze of several fires, but he would not let them risk the forest and his animals by lighting more than the single torch. Even that was irritating to the eyes that surrounded them.

His strides became faster the more he paced, his own irritation growing to anger, before he suddenly snarled and stopped, spinning to face the five men standing to one side of the clearing.

"Thirty-two men, lost," he growled lowly, causing a shiver to run through his five subordinates. "Two mages, lost." Slashing a hand through the air, he suddenly snarled, "Unacceptable!"

"I am sorry, Charlen," answered the man who had trained the men who'd been captured. Anger ruled his voice, and his false apology simply grated against Charlen's ears. Charlen growled lowly, and the other man dipped his head. "I am afraid the men were simply not disciplined enough for the techniques I taught them."

A snort sounded from one of the other men. "More like yeh couldna been botha'd to train 'em proper-like, Sloan."

Sloan sneered. "And what would you know about it, Moss? You have never even lifted a sword."

The man he'd addressed, a Plant Mage whose name was actually Mosan, glared at him and reached for his club. A snarl from the edge of the clearing made him still, and all five men glanced, scared, towards the sound. Charlen smirked as he followed their gazes.

At the edge of the clearing stood a large wildcat the size of a full-grown man, its dark brown fur glinting softly in the torchlight. Its large, pale eyes shone through the darkness, a trait that Charlen knew would have occurred even without the torchlight present.

At the sight of the wildcat, the five men bowed their heads and began muttering apologies. Charlen's smirk grew. They often seemed to forget that they had agreed to make him their pack leader, and Charlen was not above using his animals, even his precious cats, to remind them why.

"I won' have you fightin' among yerselves," he growled, satisfied when they shivered and nodded in agreement. "If we wanna destroy the Traveler's highwaymen, we mus' work together."

No matter how distasteful it may be.

"Charlen," murmured Sloan, his voice holding the respect it hadn't before. Charlen eyed the swordsman approvingly. "There is something else I was told by the men who managed to escape Puretha."

The Animal Mage felt the smirk slide from his lips, and he glared at the man. "What?" he snapped.

Sloan flinched, but, instead of dropping his gaze, he straightened his spine and met Charlen's gaze. Charlen growled. The swordsman's pride would be his downfall if he was not careful.

"My men mentioned that the Traveler was in Puretha. They—"

Charlen interrupted with a wordless snarl. *The Traveler? How is that possible? He's not even supposed to be in Kensy.*

Another snarl dragged Charlen from his thoughts, and he turned to meet the calm, pale gaze of his wildcat. Once she had his attention, she growled, *"What is so important about a single human?"*

The cat's tone was dismissive, and, if it had come from a human, Charlen would have snapped an immediate rebuttal. But he had always considered wildcats saner than his more erratic human brethren, so, instead, he tilted his head and held her gaze, considering her words.

"This particular human is the pack leader of our prey," he finally answered, hoping the words were sufficient; he held the wildcats' opinions in high regard.

She growled thoughtfully. *"Our prey might disperse or fight amongst themselves then if this human were killed?"*

Even as Charlen grumbled an agreement, a strange voice suddenly filled the clearing. "But it seems that killing that particular human proves troublesome to you."

Charlen whirled around, a snarl ripping past his lips. Behind him, he knew his subordinates had pulled their weapons, but it was his animals to which he was reaching out with his magic.

To his horror, the circle of animals that had previously surrounded the clearing had disappeared, and even the wildcat with whom he'd been conversing was crouched low to the ground and slowly creeping towards the edge of the clearing.

"Who's there?" he growled.

As he peered into the darkness of the forest, he could see no sign of the strange speaker until, suddenly, two points of glowing red appeared through the darkness.

A growling chuckle sounded then, and the voice growled, "You can call me Markos." The sound sent a shiver down Charlen's spine, and his wildcat yowled and ran into the trees.

Feeling oddly bare without the presence of his wildcat, Charlen snapped, "Wha' do y' wan'?"

That animalistic chuckle spilled through the darkness once more, and those red points seemed to creep closer. "I have a proposition for you, if you are interested."

Charlen twitched. His instincts were screaming for him to run, that this was a creature more powerful than he, but his mind had already latched onto the mentioned offer.

"What?" he growled back.

For a moment, those red points disappeared, and, when they reappeared, they were closer and seemed to dance amusedly. "You seem to be having difficulty killing one particular man, and I have another that I would prefer to see dead but that I cannot touch myself."

Charlen took a step back before he could stop himself, and he tucked his chin against his chest. "An' y' propose to trade?"

Again the voice growled out a chuckle, and again those eyes came a bit closer. "I do. I believe my man would be easier for you to kill, and I can access the Traveler in a way you cannot."

Charlen shivered. He didn't know if he trusted this creature that called himself Markos, but he wasn't sure he would survive saying nay, either. Although he questioned how the creature expected them to kill a man he couldn't when he claimed easy access to the Traveler, Charlen found himself nodding.

"Who would you have us kill in exchange for the Traveler's death?"

An amused rumble filled Charlen's bones. "The Traveler has a new human companion. He is the man I wish you to kill."

Charlen frowned then. Everyone knew the Traveler never traveled with other humans. Like Charlen, the Traveler preferred the companionship of animals only, something that had formed a reluctant respect for the boy in Charlen's mind.

As though he had access to Charlen's thoughts as easily as his words, the voice growled, "He has broken his conviction to travel only with his animals. For this, the human must die."

A shiver shook Charlen again, and he nodded, despite the doubt he felt. His instincts were screaming at him not to antagonize the voice, and Charlen had always prided himself on listening to his instincts. He could do no less now.

"Good," the voice growled. "It shouldn't be difficult for you to separate the man from the Traveler. Once you kill him, I will rid you of the Traveler easily enough."

Suddenly those eyes lunged closer. Charlen dropped, ducking out of the path of those eyes. When he came up and turned around, a wildcat, different from the one with whom he'd been conferring before, stood facing him, its pale eyes filled with confusion.

Chapter 18

7 Early Autumn, 224
Main Highwayman Camp, Kensy

Three days of exploring Main Highwayman Camp, and Ferez was bored. It wasn't even that he had nothing to do. In fact, despite the Mage Healer's insistence that Caffers rest, the boy had spent the majority of the three days showing him around the camp and introducing him to every person they met.

Ferez huffed as they left one such family. They were a widowed mother and her three sons, the eldest of which had been acting as a fighter on the highway since two years before. Already, Ferez had forgotten all but the youngest boy's name, and he doubted he would remember that for much longer.

His mind had been filled to the brim with so many names, faces, and tidbits of information that he was sure he had forgotten most of them, and the rest were so jumbled that he didn't think he'd be able to keep them straight.

He rubbed at his temple and slowly shook his head. Even his studies as a boy had been easier and, sadly, more interesting than this. At least then, his tutors had provided him with connections so the information he'd been learning would interest him and actually stick.

Now, Caffers simply threw everything at him. Ferez wasn't even sure what the boy hoped to accomplish by it all.

They'd been silent for several minutes before Ferez recognized the route they were taking. Caffers was leading him back towards the center of camp, where Cassidi, one of the few people for whom Ferez was sure he could put face to name, tended the central cooking fire.

Good, Ferez thought with a soft groan. *Maybe food will prevent the throbbing in my head from becoming a full-blown ache.*

"Oy, James!" shouted a voice Ferez didn't recognize.

The king groaned again and shut his eyes as the throbbing in his head increased. *It doesn't seem I'll be getting that food soon enough,* he thought regretfully. Opening his eyes again, he turned to follow Caffers' gaze.

"Whatcha doin' here in Kensy?" the voice asked, and Ferez found himself looking up at a tall, lean man with pale brown hair and dancing eyes. "Arn'cha s'posed to be in Cautzel righ' now?"

Caffers grinned. "Haven't you heard? I decided to come up early this season. I came into camp on the third."

The tall man released a low whistle and shook his head. "Huh, guess I been outta camp longer 'an I thought." Ferez noticed Caffers' brow furrowing, but the tall man continued before the boy could say anything. "I lef' for Tearmann on the firs'. You e'er heard of it?"

185

Frowning, Caffers nodded. "You mean that little village that was right in the middle of all the fighting, right? The one that had sentries keeping watch at all times?"

"Tha's righ'."

Caffers hummed. "Tearmann survived the war pretty well for being in the midst of it all, if I remember correctly."

The tall man snorted. "If you c'n call rebuildin' the village several times o'er survivin' well, aye."

Ferez blinked through the pain that had manifested itself behind his eyes. "Enough o' the villagers survived to rebuild the village tha' many times?"

The tall man—and Caffers, to Ferez's consternation—glanced at him, surprised. The king had the unsettling feeling that neither man had even realized he was there, which irked him since Caffers had just been showing him around. He pursed his lips and wrapped an arm around his chest, while the other hand lifted back up to rub at his temple.

Thankfully, the surprise quickly disappeared from Caffers' face, only to be replaced with the quick flash of an apologetic smile before the boy nodded firmly.

"No one's sure how, but there were few war-related deaths in Tearmann, despite the village being razed at least half a dozen times. People-wise, the village weathered the war rather well."

"True 'nough," the tall man added, glancing between Caffers and Ferez. "Who's your friend, James?"

Caffers' smile widened then, and he turned to make introductions. The process had become so monotonous to the king that he nearly tuned out the boy's words in favor of nursing his growing headache. Only his sudden curiosity about the village they'd mentioned helped him focus past the pain.

The tall man, whom Caffers introduced as a scout named Wellen, offered Ferez a strange look when he learned he was traveling with the boy. Ferez sighed. He had become accustomed to that look too since nearly every person he met couldn't fathom why the Traveler would suddenly take on a human companion.

Not that I really blame them, he considered, the thought nearly lost amongst the insistent pain behind his eyes. *The boy's traveled alone since he was ten. His suddenly taking on a traveling companion would seem a bit strange.*

It just irked Ferez since he had taken on the role of a farmer in order to avoid suspicion, and now it seemed that the position of human companion to the Traveler bore some form of suspicion no matter who occupied it.

"Well," Wellen said, rubbing his chin lightly. "Y' migh' jus' get a chance to learn Tearmann's secrets, James."

Ferez blinked at the man, positive he must have missed part of the conversation. Caffers was watching the other man curiously and seemed to understand his meaning.

"We wen' there in response t' rumors of a rogue attack." Caffers made a curious sound, and Wellen nodded. "The village was razed ag'n, no doubt o' that, but they'd a'ready rebuil' mos' o' the stable and laid down the outlines for many o' the other buildin's by th' time we arrived."

Ferez blinked rapidly, and he noticed James gaping at Wellen out of the corner of his eye. "When were they attacked?" Ferez asked, unable to hold back his curiosity.

Again, the tall man eyed Ferez with that odd look, but Ferez was able to ignore it more easily now that he had something of interest on which to focus. Even the pain behind his eyes became less noticeable.

"Early on the thirtieth, if y' hear it from them." James looked dumbfounded, and Ferez was sure he did, too. Wellen shook his head. "We arrived in the ev'nin' o' the first, so e'en I'm 'avin' trouble believin' it."

James shook his head slowly. "Less than two days," he muttered. Frowning up at Wellen, he added, "Any casualties?"

Wellen shrugged. "Three dead, two wit' light inj'ries. 'Bou' th' same as th' war, mos'ly."

James huffed. "And you said I might be able to learn their secrets?"

"Oh, aye," Wellen said suddenly, as though he'd just remembered. "We asked 'em 'ow they managed t' survive the 'ttack, an' they said they wouldn' tell no'un bu' Kephin or you."

James groaned. "They were just looking for a reason for me to visit, weren't they?"

Wellen shrugged. "Per'aps. Course, every'un knows Kephin don' leave camp or highway for long 'less 'e absolutely need to, so I wouldn' be surprised."

James nodded again. "Have you reported to him yet?"

Wellen shook his head. "Was 'opin' for food firs', actu'lly."

"We were just heading towards Cassidi's fire ourselves."

The three of them continued towards the central cooking fire. As the silence grew between them, so did the pain in Ferez's head, and he returned to nursing the headache. It wasn't until he felt something press against his free hand that he realized that the pain had distracted him from his surroundings.

Blinking open his eyes, he found a bowl being pressed into his hand. Accepting it, he lifted his gaze and found James staring at him with concern in his purple eyes.

"Are you all right?" the boy asked, the concern leaking into his voice.

Ferez nodded and quickly grimaced. "Jus' a headache, is all."

That only seemed to increase James' concern. "Should I fetch Lakina?"

Ferez grimaced for an entirely different reason this time. The Mage Healer had confronted him the morning after they arrived at the camp and had told him how she knew who he was. He was mortified by the realization that she had seen him at his worst, at his weakest. It was one thing to know a Mage Healer could read what had happened through his wounds, and entirely another to know she had seen it with her own eyes.

"Nay," he choked out. He didn't think he could bear to meet Lakina's eyes after learning that, and he'd avoided her since. "I think food'll help."

James didn't look convinced but nodded reluctantly and turned to the others seated around the fire. Finding a seat for himself, Ferez began to eat, but he quickly found that the pain in his head had chased away his appetite.

He was staring into the bowl longingly—Cassidi's food was always delicious—when something brushed the back of his neck. Jerking away from the touch, Ferez spun around to find Lakina frowning down at him.

"You shouldn't let such pain grow, Frenz."

Her voice held a note of disappointment that had Ferez ducking his head before he thought about it. As he glanced back up, he realized that the pain had already begun to subside.

"Thanks," he muttered, dropping his gaze again. His cheeks had already begun to burn as his earlier thoughts returned to him.

There goes trying to avoid her.

Lakina sighed softly, but her feet turned to the side. "And you," she added, "should ease up on the poor man. You're overwhelming him."

~~*~*

Gemi blinked up at the Mage Healer. She had hoped Lakina would ease Ferez's headache, but she hadn't expected the reprimand.

"What do you mean?"

Several people around the fire snorted. "You been runnin' 'round camp introducin' 'im to ever'one like a chil' wit' a new toy, James," someone on the other side of Wellen muttered.

Laughing agreement echoed around the fire, and Gemi frowned. The king had wanted to get to know his people, so she had been showing him around, aye. As the days had worn on, it had seemed that he was losing interest, and she had begun to panic. If the king lost interest now, how would the remainder of the season play out?

"Well, tha' explains the odd introduction y' gave me," Wellen added. Gemi eyed the man curiously, and he grinned. "Y' were awf'ly enthusiastic, bu' I don' think the poor fella'll e'en 'member m' name."

Ferez chuckled then. "Oh, I remember yer name, Wellen, but I think tha's got more to do wi' the news you brought o' Tearmann than anythin' else."

"Tha's right. You been to Tearmann," someone else said, and, as quickly as the conversation had turned to Gemi and Ferez, it moved onto Tearmann.

Gemi took the opportunity to turn to Ferez. He had begun to eat with vigor now, and he glanced curiously at her when he noticed her watching him.

"Are you all right?" she repeated.

Ferez paused, lowering his bowl a bit. "Aye," he answered, sounding a bit confused. "Thanks t' Lakina, the pain's gone now."

"That's not…" Gemi began then sighed. She wasn't sure how to ask what she was thinking.

Maybe she had been a bit…overzealous in her quest to introduce the king around, but she hadn't known what else to do to help ensure that he learned how his people lived. Now that she thought about it, she realized she'd been shoving so much information at him that he couldn't possibly remember most of it

"I have been pushing kind of hard, haven't I?" she murmured.

Ferez chuckled. "Maybe a bit. I'm 'fraid a lot o' what you told me disappeared no' long afterwards."

Gemi grimaced. "Sorry." Glancing around the fire, she added, "Do you remember who anyone here is?"

Ferez groaned. "A test?"

Gemi bit her lip to keep from laughing and waved a hand at him. "Nay, nay, I'm just curious."

Ferez glanced around and shook his head. "Wellen's th' only one, I'm 'fraid. Though," he added with a grin, "I do remember li'l Sproul's name." Gemi blinked. Sproul was the youngest of the three boys they'd met before running into Wellen. "Maybe I'll take 'im up on 'is offer to kick a ball round sometime."

"You would want to?"

Ferez shrugged. "Why not?"

"'Ey, Kanti," one of the other men called then, and they both turned back to the fire. "You play Katani?"

Gemi stilled when the man mentioned the country's board game and glanced quickly at Ferez. The man didn't seem to have even twitched at the sound of his real name.

"Course, but it's been a while."

"Care for a game? We'll let'cha play Kensy or Baylin if y' like."

Ferez wrinkled his nose. "Why would I wan' those? I've lived in Kensy my whole life, an' the only int'restin' thin' in Baylin's the king."

Gemi snorted. "Me, I'd rather climb a mountain. 'As any'un claimed Tarsur?"

The others laughed and let him claim the gray pieces that represented Evon's mountainous province. Then, Ferez and three other men settled around a Katani board that had been set up, and Gemi watched, amused, as the four began to play.

~~*~*

10 Early Autumn, 224

Despite Gemi's desire to travel to Tearmann, Lakina insisted that she wait three more days before she left camp. On the morning of the tenth of Early Autumn, Lakina finally gave Gemi her blessing to leave.

"But that doesn't mean you can just go and get yourself into another fight, you hear?"

Gemi rolled her eyes and assured the Healer that, aye, she would be careful, and, nay, she wouldn't get into another fight. She meant it, too. After the trouble in Calay and the battle in Puretha, she was ready for some restful times.

As good as she was with her multitude of weapons, Gemi had always preferred peace. It was the reason she recommended and fought for unification amongst the rebellious groups in the first place.

Still, the fighting seemed endless. There was always one more conflict, one more battle, one more person who wanted to hurt others for his own personal gain.

At least we're only going to Tearmann, Gemi thought as she urged Shadow onto a deer path that led north towards the village. Ferez and Last Chance followed not far behind. *Little chance of a fight when the rogues just attacked a few days ago.*

It was nearing sunset when Flame mentioned they were approaching the village. *"Finally,"* Shadow huffed. *"I'm ready for some oats and a bed of straw."*

"You are always ready for a bed of straw," Flame teased, sweeping low across the treetops.

"That's because we tra—"

Something dropped in front of Shadow, and he stopped short with a snort of annoyance.

"Trav'ler! You came!"

Ignoring Shadow's comments about rude men meeting the wrong end of his hooves, Gemi peered around the stallion's head. Standing in the middle of the path was a man she vaguely recognized from the last time she'd visited Tearmann, back during the war.

"And a good evening to you…Wallitz, isn't it?"

Not for the first time, she was glad Flame had an excellent memory. She knew she wouldn't have recalled the name if Flame hadn't been able to supply it.

"You were head of the village council during the war, aye?"

The man bobbed his head, grinning. "Aye, you 'member righ', Traveler. 'Fraid I'm no longer head o' council though. I'm a fighter; no' much good fo' leadin' in peace."

Gemi frowned. "I find that hard to believe, Wallitz. You did well by the village in the war. I don't see why that can't carry over."

The man shrugged, lifting a hand towards Shadow's bridle. When the stallion snorted, Wallitz stepped back and nodded, turning away to wander down the deer path towards the village.

"Doesn' matter anymore, one way o' the other. Pallen's head o' council now, an' 'e's done well by us since the war ended."

Gemi hesitated, trying to place the name. When Flame pushed an image through the bond, Gemi blinked then chuckled. Pallen's temperament, last she had met the man, was quite the opposite of Wallitz's.

While Wallitz was impulsive and assertive, Pallen had always thought things through and insisted on listening to what others had to say. Both were good men, but Gemi could see how the village might consider Pallen more fitting for these more peaceful times.

She was distracted from thoughts of the two men as the trees thinned out and the village of Tearmann came into sight. Her jaw dropped slightly. Wellen had told her the villagers had already begun to rebuild, but she hadn't expected them to have rebuilt so much of the village already.

In the center of what should have been the village, two large buildings stood almost fully completed. Around them, spreading out towards the forest, many other buildings had already been started, while those closest to the tree line were merely cleared land marked and waiting to be built on.

As Gemi nudged Shadow back into motion, she contemplated the two central buildings. She knew, from previous visits, that one would be the stable. Wellen had mentioned it was the first building they'd rebuilt, and Gemi understood why.

With as many animals as a single village kept, between mounts, companions, and food animals, the stable was an important part of the village. And, while most might think it pointless after an attack that completely destroyed the village, Gemi had long ago learned that the animals of Tearmann survived the attacks just as well as the people.

The second building, which Gemi knew stood across a road from the stable, was known as the village council house. Not only was it the center of the village's social activity, it was also the spiritual center, where villagers brought their prayers to Carith.

Wallitz led them towards those two buildings. On the way, they passed multiple tents and families. Women were cooking dinners, men setting up lamps as the sun's light began to fade, and a couple children were running around between the temporary homes. If Gemi hadn't known the village had recently been under attack, she would have thought she'd entered a highwayman camp with how normal everything seemed.

"After so many attacks, this probably is normal for them," Shadow snorted with a toss of his head.

Gemi could only agree.

~~*~*

As Wallitz reached the stable, he was greeted by his lifemate, who kissed his cheek before turning her attention to their guest, who had dismounted.

"'Tis good to see ye ag'in, Trav'ler. We wondered if th' rumors o' your early 'rival in Kensy were untrue af'er all."

Confusion clouded the boy's face before he shook his head and chuckled. Wallitz thought one of his bondmates must have reminded him that Tearmann had an Animal Mage. Starbuck was the only mage in the village, but his magic had been invaluable during the war and even in the village's day-to-day life.

"Unfortunately, I was confined to Main Highwayman Camp for several days to recuperate from battle wounds. Lakina was insistent."

Wallitz nodded. He'd never met the Mage Healer himself, but he had heard plenty of stories about the woman to know that even the Traveler would not wish to cross her.

"Trav'ler, y' remember my lifemate, Amena?"

The boy nodded to Amena and, after a brief pause, added, "You were with child when I last saw you. Did your babe survive?"

Amena beamed, and Wallitz felt an answering smile of pride pull at his lips. "Aye, Trav'ler, he did. Born th' day we learnt o' th' peace. 'E's a stong 'un, jus' like 'is pa."

She turned a fond look on Wallitz. Unable to resist, the man leaned down and kissed her cheek.

"If 'e was born on a day o' peace, then maybe he won' e'er have to fight."

Wallitz turned to stare at the man who had spoken. Somehow, he had overlooked a second man following him into town, and even Amena and the Traveler looked startled by the man's presence.

"Er…a friend o' yours, Traveler?"

The stranger's expression tightened briefly before he glanced at the Traveler. To Wallitz's surprise, the boy offered the stranger an apologetic smile then turned back to Wallitz.

"Aye, he is. His name's Frenz Kanti. He's traveling with me for a while."

Wallitz raised his eyebrows. He'd always heard that the Traveler never allowed anyone to accompany him around Evon. Then again, he was the Traveler. He could do whatever he wanted to.

Shrugging, Wallitz greeted the man before turning back to the Traveler.

"We didn' know you'd bring any'un else wit' you, Traveler. I don' think Pallen'll wan' to share Tearmann's secrets wit' a stranger, e'en if 'e is wit' you. Per'aps he can stay wit' Amena while we speak wit' Pallen."

Amena nodded and offered Kanti a smile.

~~*~*

Gemi sighed and bit her lip. She knew it was unreasonable to expect the villagers to share their secrets with someone they considered a stranger, but she was uncomfortable with leaving the king with people he didn't know.

It wasn't even that she feared for his safety, either. She did remember Amena from her previous visits, and Gemi was sure the woman would watch over Ferez as fiercely as she did her own children.

Do not worry, James, Flame crooned, landing nearby.

She approached their group and nudged Ferez. The man smiled and lifted a hand to the base of Flame's horns, where he had already learned she preferred attention the most.

"*I will stay with him,*" she added, her voice dropping to a coo as the king found a particularly pleasurable spot.

"Don' worry, James," Ferez added, unintentionally repeating Flame's words. He flashed her a smile. "I'll be fine."

Gemi chuckled then. She was being silly, fearing that something would happen when there was almost no chance it would. She shook her head and turned back to Wallitz.

"Very well, shall I settle Shadow into a stall so we can go find Pallen?"

"No need, Trav'ler," Amena answered. She stepped forward and held a hand in front of Shadow's nose. He snorted softly before nudging her palm. "I c'n settle Shadow, while you boys go speak wit' Pallen."

Gemi agreed and allowed the woman to lead Shadow into the stable. When Ferez began to follow with Last Chance, Gemi gripped his arm.

Her expression still must have shown some worry because, when the king looked at her, he smiled, gripped her arm in return, and repeated, "We'll be fine, James." He shoved at her arm lightly and added, "Go learn what you came here to learn."

Gemi nodded and, with a wave, she followed Wallitz across the road towards the council house.

Chapter 19

They were met at the entrance to the council house by Pallen and two other men that Gemi supposed were members of the council. The two greeted her enthusiastically before saying their farewells to Pallen and disappearing back out into the village.

"I'm glad you could come, Traveler," Pallen said as he shook Gemi's hands. "It has been a couple of years since you last visited."

Gemi nodded. She had forgotten how well-spoken the man was.

"Aye, well, Kephin and I have been curious for years about how your village survived the war so well. When you offer the information freely, it's difficult to turn down that kind of invitation."

Pallen nodded and motioned for Gemi and Wallitz to follow him into the council house. Once she'd crossed the threshold, Gemi paused and glanced around.

Although it had just been rebuilt, it looked the same as the last time she'd visited, before the war had ended. It seemed to be a single large, long room with a high ceiling supported by rafters. Gemi had thought the roof yet incomplete, but she couldn't see any holes as she stared up at it.

Then again, with the sun setting, perhaps there's not enough light to leak through.

"What do you think?" Pallen asked, drawing her gaze back down from the high ceiling. She grinned and shook her head.

"Amazing, really. I can't fathom how you managed to rebuild this building and the stable in the…what, ten days since the attack?"

Pallen shrugged. "Let's just say that the village has enough experience to do the work quickly." Gemi chuckled in agreement. "Do you want to take a look at some of the artwork while we're here?"

"Artwork?" Gemi asked, surprised.

She had never spent much time in this building during any of her previous visits, but she couldn't recall seeing any artwork. And she did have to wonder how that artwork had survived the attack.

The same way the people did, perhaps?

Pallen gestured towards the wall to their right. Stepping closer, Gemi realized that the wall was hung with tapestries. Here was Carith, the creator, swathed in the colors of the rainbow, souls of various colors spilling from his hands like gems. There was Maurus, the destroyer, dressed in drab grays, surrounded by destruction and fire.

Gemi grimaced as her thoughts turned to that day so many years ago when she found the words that damned her childhood home to Maurus. Shadow nickered softly and pushed against her mind. Pushing back, Gemi shook her head and turned her attention to a different tapestry.

The next bore three females, all of different ages. The youngest sat with a spindle and spun colorful threads. Those threads flowed from the spindle to the middle-aged female, who worked them into a loom that

194

dominated the tapestry. The eldest, who looked to be a wrinkled hag, held a wicked-looking blade in one hand and loose threads in the other.

"Who…?" Gemi began, even as she thought she might know the answer.

"Those are the Fates: the Maid, the Matron, and the Crone. They shape the Tapestry of Life using the Spindle, the Loom, and the Double-Edged Dagger."

Gemi hummed. She had heard Seers mention the Fates before, often referring to them as the Ladies. Mama Caler, in particular, always spoke about the Ladies showing her the futures they had weaved.

Stepping past the tapestry portraying the Fates, Gemi glanced at one that bore four animals. "The Cycle of Incarnation," Pallen said before she could even ask, "and its guardians."

The tapestry displayed what looked like a pool of multi-colored water in the center, surrounded by the four animals she had noticed. An eagle and a fire bird—"*A phoenix*," Flame corrected idly—hung in the top corners, while a wolf and snake crouched in the bottom two.

Something seemed familiar about the images, yet Gemi couldn't think why. As a child she had never learned about any gods other than Carith and Maurus, and, since then, she hadn't had much interest in religion.

Moving on, she stopped in front of the final tapestry on the wall and stared. The main figure in the tapestry was a woman, but she seemed to glow darkly. Gemi was reminded of the endless night sky when the Gemini moons were not in sight, and only the stars could be seen.

Around this woman stood eight figures. Each was a different color, and Gemi had the impression that those on the woman's right were female, those on her left male. Hesitantly, Gemi lifted her hand and let it hover over the tapestry's edge.

"Who are these?" she whispered.

"The Lost Goddess and her children, the demigods."

Gemi frowned at the tapestry. "Lost Goddess?" She'd at least heard of all of the others, if only in passing, but the Lost Goddess and the demigods were completely unknown to her.

Gemi jumped when something landed on her shoulder, and she glanced back to see Pallen smiling at her. He nodded to the tapestry.

"I doubt many acknowledge the Lost Goddess. As it is, the only reason we here in Tearmann know of her existence is because of these tapestries."

Gemi turned her gaze back to the image of the dark lady and her colorful children. "But who is she?"

"The old stories say that she was Carith's lifemate and that the demigods are their children."

"Was?" Most people referred to the gods in the present tense since they were eternal.

"Aye, well, we call her the *Lost* Goddess for a reason, you understand."

Gemi hummed and traced a finger lightly down the line of colorful figures on the Lost Goddess's right. "And the demigods?"

Pallen hummed and drew her away from the tapestry. "They're said to represent the polar opposites of human life. Now, why don't I show you what you're really here to see?"

Gemi nodded distractedly. The sense of familiarity she'd had upon seeing the tapestry representing the Cycle of Incarnation had only increased at the sight of the dark lady and her colorful children. It didn't make sense since she had never heard of any of them before, and she knew she had never seen anything like that tapestry before.

"You have never been this curious when it comes to the gods, either," Flame crooned softly.

Gemi shrugged. After what had happened during the war, she had never felt the gods important enough to be curious about them.

She was brought out of those thoughts as Pallen stopped in front of a rug that was laid out across the middle of the council house's floor. He motioned to Wallitz, who had been following them quietly, to assist him. Crouching down, they gripped one corner each and flung back the rug, revealing a trapdoor underneath.

As the two men turned to her, Pallen patiently, Wallitz grinning, Gemi frowned down at the door. "What's down there?"

Wallitz laughed. "Y' wanted to know how th' people o' Tearmann 'ave survived fer so long."

With a nod, Pallen leaned over, hooked a finger in the trapdoor's handle, and tugged it open.

As he straightened and stepped back, Gemi stared down into darkness. She could see the beginning of a set of stairs leading down, but there was no light at the bottom, no way to tell how far down it went.

Then, there was light at her shoulder, stretching down the stairs to dimly light a large room that opened out around the stairs. Slack-jawed, she glanced up to find Wallitz still grinning at her and holding an open lantern.

"Af'er you," he said, motioning towards the stairs.

The underground room that Gemi climbed down into looked to be almost as large as the hall of the council house, though not nearly as tall. As Wallitz followed her with the lantern, Gemi saw that the walls weren't flat. Instead, they were riddled with little alcoves and a bench had been carved out of the earth at the base of each wall. Several of the alcoves also contained various items like jars, blankets, and drying meat.

"What is this place?" Gemi asked. She was having difficulty comprehending that this room was underneath the village of Tearmann.

"This is one of five underground rooms that we use to hide during attacks." Pallen's voice was low and steady, just as it had been as he explained the tapestries upstairs.

Gemi swung her gaze back to the council leader. "The entire village?" At his nod, she returned her stare to the large earthen room. "How is this even possible? I mean, you've built buildings on top of these rooms. How have they not caved in?"

Pallen hummed. "I'm sure you understand, Traveler, just how powerful the remnants of the old Earth Mages can be."

Gemi sucked in a breath and gaped at the man once more. "These rooms were formed by Earth Mages? They've been around for that long?"

Earth Magic had disappeared nearly a millennium ago, at the same time as six other magics. Despite its disappearance, Gemi knew several old cities that had been formed by Earth Mages and still stood, apparently just as strong and beautiful as they had been when they were formed.

When Pallen simply nodded in answer, Gemi shook her head. "But why?"

"If you consider our village's origin, you'll find your answer, Traveler. The village was created as a sanctuary for those who openly practiced the old religion when Fayral's half-elf emperor created the Religion of Carith."

Gemi blinked. She had heard the stories of Fayral's first emperor that claimed he'd been born to a human and an elf, but she hadn't realized he had had anything to do with religion.

"What's the difference between the two?"

"Y' saw th' diff'rence in th' tapestries, Traveler," Wallitz responded, waving his free hand towards the room above them.

Pallen sighed and nodded. "The Religion of Carith focuses solely on the conflict between Carith and Maurus, creator and destroyer. It claims that Carith is the highest good and Maurus the greatest evil."

Gemi swallowed at the mention of Maurus. "And the old religion?" she asked hesitantly.

Pallen offered her a comforting smile. "Those who practice the old religion believe that every god is important, that the only evil is Chaos and imbalance. We celebrate all of the gods: Carith, his Lost Goddess, and their children; Maurus, the Fates, and the Guardians of the Cycle."

Gemi nodded and shifted awkwardly. As much as she thought she could believe that Chaos was the only real evil, Maurus was not a name of which she could easily end her fear.

In an attempt to move away from the uncomfortable topic, she asked about the village being a sanctuary.

"The village's name, Tearmann, is actually Fae for 'sanctuary'. When their beliefs were threatened, our ancestors came south to the edges of the forest, far enough to be out of the emperor's sight, but not far enough that they would completely place themselves in possible enemy territory. When the village was created, the Earth Mages formed the underground rooms so the people could hide from magical creatures and other threats that roamed the forest."

"A tradition that your people still hold to today," Gemi finished, glancing around the room once more. "Do you always keep it furnished?"

Pallen nodded. "Food, blankets, lamps. Anything we might need to survive down here for several days."

"Days?" Gemi asked, startled. "How can you stay down here for that long without suffocating?" For that matter, Gemi wondered how the villagers could survive the heat from fires burning above the ground.

Pallen shrugged. "I've always assumed the Earth Mages provided for that sort of thing."

Shadow snorted. *"It's so much a part of their everyday lives, they don't even—"*

Pain suddenly ripped through the bond. A roar filled Gemi's mind, but she had been pulled so far into the bond she couldn't be sure if she was hearing it through her ears or someone else's.

A steadying hand on her shoulder brought her back to the earthen room. Blinking, she focused with difficulty on the two men peering down at her.

"Flame," she gasped, shoving at the hand gripping her shoulder. Pushing past the two men, she stumbled towards the stairs.

~~*~*

When Gemi and Wallitz crossed the street, Flame followed Amena and Ferez into the stable. As the two humans settled the horses, Flame curled up next to Shadow's designated stall and observed the activity of the other humans spread throughout the building.

Several men were tending to a herd of food animals that had raised a racket at the sight of Flame. Another man, whom Flame recognized as Starbuck, Tearmann's Animal Mage, was quickly hurrying towards the group, no doubt to calm down the poor creatures.

Closer to the center of the stable, a large group of children played. They had turned as one when Flame slid into the stable. Even now, they cast her curious stares and whispered amongst themselves. To Flame's amusement, it was also that group which Ferez approached once Last Chance was settled.

Flame listened with half an ear as Ferez introduced himself and asked them what they were playing. Thankfully, the younger children were easily distracted and immediately began explaining the rules of their game. The older younglings soon followed suit, and the king was quickly incorporated in their play.

As Ferez's enthusiasm became apparent, Amena approached the group. "If yer willin' to keep an eye on 'em, Frenz, the lot o' you c'n move outside."

Everyone must be busy enough that these children are kept here in the stable for easy supervision, Flame thought as Ferez agreed to loud cheers from the children.

"*Good luck,*" Shadow nickered as Flame heaved her body up and ambled after the king and the children. She flicked her tail once in acknowledgement.

She followed as the children tugged Ferez away from the stable and towards the forest, where little more than outlines of houses lay and the children would have more room to run around.

Once the children appeared satisfied with their chosen location, they pulled Ferez into another game, which he joined with a laugh. Hissing her own amusement, Flame settled herself near a partial foundation to keep an eye on the man and his charges. At the same time, she focused part of her attention on the conversation Gemi was holding with Pallen and Wallitz.

Flame sighed happily as she laid her head across the ground and closed her eyes to mere slits. It was a beautiful evening, and the dragon crooned as she extended her magic and senses to enjoy her surroundings to the maximum.

Despite the coming darkness, the village was alive with the scents of meals and the sounds of conversation. The forest, too, was alive, the activity quieter, calmer. Flame reveled in the contrast.

Her magic stirred lazily as it reached out towards the trees. As an adolescent dragon, Flame's magic did not flow quite as freely or powerfully as it would when she was older, but it was still extremely useful for sensing animals, plants, and mages. The presence of the animals in the stable had already caused her magic to flare, but that sensation only increased as it touched the trees and the animals that made them their home.

The dragon lost herself in the sensations of the forest, the words of Gemi's conversation, and the games of Ferez and the children. At one point, she noted the correlation between the number of earthen rooms beneath the village and the number of casualties the village had suffered in the latest attack—three dead, two injured. She also wondered idly if there was a room beneath the stable large enough for the animals and how anyone, even an Animal Mage like Starbuck, could convince such a large number of animals into such a space.

As one of the little girls that Ferez was playing with tumbled to the ground, Flame felt a change in the forest stir her magic. The king was just kneeling to help the girl to her feet when the sensation of change became disturbing, and someone stumbled out of the tree line.

"Rogues!" the man gasped before he collapsed forward, two arrows sticking out of his back.

Immediately, Flame was on her feet as the children began running back towards the center of the village, yells of warning spilling from their lips. Only one child, the little girl who had fallen, seemed paralyzed with fear, her small arms clasped tightly around the king's neck.

Ferez had attempted to stand, but the child must have been heavier than he had expected as he stumbled back down to his knees. More arrows were breaking through the tree line, and, with a hiss, Flame leapt forward and curled her body around the king. Swinging her head around, she snarled at the man to move.

That snarl quickly became a hiss as pain ripped through her wing. Dropping her wings around her body, she swung her head back towards the forest and reared. She instantly regretted the move as a fiery pain engulfed her stomach.

The roar she released in response was just as fiery as the wound, and the fire filling her mouth and burning past her teeth reached for the forest and engulfed the closest trees. As she rolled to her side, she was vaguely aware of screams emitting from beyond—or within?—the fire, but the pain was drawing her senses inward, and she could not find the energy to care.

~~*~*

Ferez winced as an arrow passed through the thin membrane of Flame's wing. When she turned and roared, he gripped the little girl still clinging to his neck and dropped to the ground, covering her body with his. Heat poured over his back, but it was the pain behind Flame's roar that worried him.

As Flame fell to the ground, the king glanced towards the tree line. Once he was certain the rogues would no longer be a problem—the flames had quickly spread across the tree line like a shield of fire—he turned his attention to the dragon's injuries. While he doubted the hole in the wing was life-threatening, he assumed that, for a dragon, like any animal, an arrow in the gut was dangerous.

A screamed "Flame!" split the air then, and Ferez glanced over his shoulder as James ran towards them. Despite knowing the boy could probably sense it through his dragonbond, Ferez began detailing the injuries as soon as he was beside him.

When James reacted with nothing more than a distracted nod, Ferez wondered how much of the dragon's pain the boy could feel. He knew from experience how painful a gut wound could be. Squeezing the boy's shoulder, he turned to find someone who might be able to help.

When he found his movement restricted, Ferez glanced down and realized with some surprise that the little girl he had protected was still clinging to his neck. Murmuring softly to her, he reached up and gently detached her arms from his neck.

With a final murmur about the village being safe now and a soft nudge, he sent her hurrying back towards the stable. Then, he quickly returned to his mission to find help.

He spotted the council leader directing the efforts to douse the fire, which seemed to be resisting most of the water they were throwing on it. Calling to the man, Ferez asked if the village had a healer of any kind. Grimly, Pallen nodded and jogged back towards the village's center.

The man with whom he returned lugged a large bag with him, and Ferez knew immediately that he wasn't a Mage Healer. When Pallen

200

motioned him towards Flame, the healer paled and turned back to the council leader, but Pallen had already returned to the efforts to quell the flames.

"Please tell me 'm not s'pose to heal a dragon of all things," the healer muttered as he lowered his bag to the ground.

"Is there nothin' you can do?" Ferez inquired softly.

He knew gut wounds were dangerous, but even non-magical healers had herbs and potions they could use to attempt to stem the damage.

"'m sure there be somethin' I c'n do," the healer mumbled as he began to dig through his bag, "but I know not'in' abou' dragon 'natomy."

"Do something!" James suddenly demanded.

Ferez blinked at the boy. He had thought him lost amid the dragonbond, and he hadn't even glanced at the healer when he spoke. A sudden nudge to his shoulder caught his attention then, and he turned to find Shadow staring down at him.

"Mis'er Shadow Racer seems to think I c'n be o' some assistance?" a voice questioned calmly. Ferez glanced to the stallion's side and realized that he had brought another man with him.

The healer grunted as he continued to dig through the bag. "Only if y' know anyt'in' abou' dragon 'natomy, Starbuck." He suddenly sat up, a cloth in one hand, several bottles in the other, and turned to the wounded dragon.

"This migh' sting a bit," he added softly before drizzling something from one of the bottles over the scales that the arrow had slid between. Flame's only answer was an audible whine, and James shivered.

"Well, Burdock," Starbuck answered thoughtfully, as though there wasn't a wounded dragon lying out in front of him. "I c'n sense animal's anatomies, you know."

Ferez stared at the man in surprise. He hadn't expected an Animal Mage in a village so far from the highway. He realized, in the next moment, that the man's previous words should have alerted him to the man's magic.

The healer, Burdock, looked even more surprised than Ferez felt. He recovered quickly, and waved the mage down beside him.

"C'n y' tell me if there be any cuts to her insides? I need to know how bad the wound is afore I try to move the arrow."

Starbuck hummed and stroked the dragon's belly. "There be some bleedin' but no bile that I c'n sense. Tha's good, in't?"

Burdock huffed. "Better 'an it could be, but, if I canna stop the bleedin', it c'n cause all type o' problem."

"Do y' have any dragon's blood?" Ferez asked, remembering one of the old stories he'd learned as a child.

When both mage and healer looked at him with confusion in their eyes, he searched his memory for the words by which the substance was better known.

Snapping his fingers as the memory surfaced, he added, "Sangre de Drago."

Starbuck still looked confused, but Burdock sucked in a sharp breath. "Actually…" he muttered before diving back into his bag. A minute later, he sat up with a shout of triumph, a small vial held between two fingers.

"Sangre de Drago," he proclaimed.

The substance within the glass vial was a rusty brown, the color of old blood, and it moved sluggishly as the healer tilted the vial from side to side.

"Do y' think y' c'n guide the arrow out o' her wit'out nickin' anyt'in' else?" Burdock asked Starbuck.

The mage immediately nodded, gripped the shaft of the arrow, and began to slowly work it out of the wound.

"Y' really think that'll help?" Starbuck asked as he worked. His voice, while still calm, held a skepticism that Ferez couldn't fault.

"Migh' no' be o' much use to us humans for a wound this big," Ferez answered, "bu' th' ol' stories say it's like a healin' potion for dragons. Why it's called dragon's blood, I'm sure."

"Well, don't know if it's true, but it's more 'an I got to offer."

The arrow slipped smoothly out of the wound then, and Burdock leaned over to pour the sluggish substance onto the wound.

~~*~*

Gemi gasped when a new kind of warmth suddenly filled the bond and fought the pain for her attention. The battle was so harsh that she wasn't sure if the warmth was another kind of pain or something else entirely. As aware as she was of her physical surroundings, she knew she could have been on fire and not realized.

However, the pain had been particularly intense, probably because Flame was rarely injured so badly. The dragon had only been badly injured once before, and Gemi had been out of it for sevendays as no one had sought a Mage Healer for her. As odd as it might seem, Gemi thought she dealt better with her own wounds than with her bondmates'.

The warmth finally managed to overwhelm the pain, and Gemi groaned as it filled her entire body. It was only then that she recognized the feeling as pure Healing Magic, much more intense than she was accustomed to.

As the pain eased, Flame pushed Gemi out of her mind, and the girl once again became aware of her surroundings. There was a hand gripping her shoulder. When she turned towards it, she found Ferez eyeing her worriedly.

"Are you a'right?" he asked once she'd met his eyes.

Gemi nodded slowly, even as she glanced at Flame. The dragon was breathing heavily, and something thick and red clung to part of her belly.

"What happened?" she whispered, feeling ashamed. All she had known was the pain. She hadn't even recognized where her bondmate had been injured.

"*Hardly your fault, James,*" Shadow nickered, snuffling the hair at the nape of her neck. "*You aren't used to feeling us in so much pain.*"

She frowned up at the horse. "*Yet you seemed to have handled it rather well.*"

The stallion snorted. "*Aye, but I'm accustomed to your injuries. That wasn't much compared to some of the wounds you've received over the years.*"

Gemi grimaced and returned her gaze to Ferez, who squeezed her shoulder. When she indicated she was listening, he told her how the attack had happened and how it had been handled.

When he mentioned the Sangre de Drago, Gemi frowned down at the red still clinging to Flame's stomach. She had heard the name before, but she hadn't known what properties it bore.

"That's what helped with the pain?"

"Seems like it," Ferez answered with a nod.

"Certainly did somet'in', a'right," the man Ferez had introduced as Burdock replied. He cast the king a curious glance as he finished sewing up a hole in Flame's wing. "An' 'ow you know so much abou' dragons anyway? Seems to me you jus' me' the Traveler."

Gemi blinked. She wasn't sure what the last had to do with anything since she hadn't even known Sangre de Drago could be useful. To Gemi's bewilderment, the king simply shrugged.

"M' farm's close to the San. Ou' there, we still pass down stories o' the creatures across the way."

And, whether that was true or not, the mage and healer accepted it easily with nods and hums. Gemi knew she was gaping, but she couldn't convince her mind to gain control of her jaw again.

Deeming that they had done what they could, both men left them alone, already calling to Pallen to ask what more needed doing. As soon as they were out of earshot, Gemi gripped Ferez's arm and hissed, "How do you do that?"

The man blinked at her, confusion filling his eyes. "Do what?"

Gemi huffed, though she loosened her grip. "Make up reasons like that without knowing they're actually true and have people believe you."

Ferez hesitated then shrugged. "I just go with what seems most believable, honestly. It worked when I was younger, so I figured it would work just as well here."

Gemi stared at him for a little longer before huffing and glancing away. Her eyes landed on Flame's wound, and she reached out to trace a finger around the Sangre de Drago lightly.

"*How are you doing, Flame?*" she pressed against the dragon's mind.

"*Still hurts,*" Flame muttered. "*But it is more bearable, and I think I will be able to move to the stable soon.*"

203

Gemi looked around and realized that most of fire that had lit up the tree line had been extinguished, with only a couple of tongues still being doused into submission. Most of the villagers were now drifting back towards the village center and their temporary homes. Soon, the four of them would be the only ones left near the forest.

"When you can," she murmured.

She didn't feel comfortable staying near the forest alone with Flame wounded, but she wouldn't risk Flame causing herself more damage. The dragon agreed, and she soon levered herself up to her feet. The four of them slowly ambled back towards the stable.

Chapter 20

13 Early Autumn, 224

Flame's injuries restricted them to Tearmann for the next three days since Gemi was unwilling to travel with her bondmate injured.

"Funny," Shadow had snorted when she told the others they would be staying. *"You never have that qualm when you're the one who's injured."* Gemi had just rolled her eyes. *"Aye, because I'm not doing the actual traveling."* Shadow had snorted again but, otherwise, remained silent.

The stay turned out to be rather productive, as far as Ferez's purpose was concerned. The tale of Ferez saving little Luvina had spread quickly, and the villagers had easily accepted the man as trustworthy. Pallen even agreed to let Ferez see the earthen room beneath the stable when Gemi did—which irked Gemi a bit, even if it did allow the king to get to know his people better.

They spent much of their time in the village helping out with the construction. When they weren't doing actual work on the buildings, Ferez split his time between conversing with the villagers and playing with the children, who had quickly grown attached to him. And, no matter what he was doing, Luvina trailed after him, much to the amusement of the entire village.

When Flame finally felt well enough to travel back to Main Highwayman Camp, the children complained loudly about their new friend leaving. They crowded around Ferez, tugging at his tunic and trousers and begging him not to go. Gemi had to bite her lip hard to keep from breaking into giggles at the sight.

Even so, Ferez was amazingly patient with them. Gemi had noticed in the last three days that the king seemed most relaxed around the children, and Amena and the other mothers had often asked him to supervise them so they could play outside without worry.

At one point, Gemi had even overheard a couple of young women speculating that the man would make a wonderful mate and father, which had amused Gemi to no end. No matter how friendly the king was with his people, he would never consider taking a woman who wasn't a noble as his lifemate. It simply was not allowed.

Finally, even the parents were becoming exasperated with their children's antics, and Amena stepped forward in an attempt to wave the young ones away from Ferez.

"C'mon, children. Th' Traveler an' 'is friends need t' return t' camp."

"Bu' why canna Frenz stay?" Luvina begged, turning a wide-eyed pout up to Ferez. "'E don' 'ave t' 'turn, do 'e?"

Gemi bit her lip harder, but Ferez knelt down in front of the little girl and stared seriously into her face. "Would it 'elp if I promise to come back and play wit' you soon?"

Peace of Evon

Luvina blinked a few times before breaking into a grin. "Will ya?" she asked excitedly. Ferez nodded, and the girl squealed and threw her arms around his neck, clinging to him the way Gemi had heard she clung to him during the attack.

Gemi frowned thoughtfully as the children finally pulled away and let Ferez finish saddling Last Chance. She knew he wanted to learn about his people, but she would never have expected him to make such a promise, even to a child.

Gemi considered his words as they mounted up, said their farewells, and left down the deer path they had arrived on, Flame following behind the horses on the ground to avoid aggravating her healed injuries. Once Flame had assured her that they were out of earshot of Tearmann's lookouts, Gemi turned around in the saddle.

"Did you mean that?"

"Mean what?" Ferez's voice was calm, relaxed, and Gemi could feel her lips tilting up into a smile to see the king so comfortable.

"The promise you made to Luvina. You know she won't forget it."

Ferez chuckled, his smile widening. "Oh, I meant it, all right. I would love to come back sometime after this season and play with her and the other children."

Gemi hesitated, trying to think how best to ask her next question. "*Just ask, James,*" Shadow snorted. "*He doesn't seem the type to be easily offended.*" Last Chance nickered, and Shadow added, "*Even she agrees.*"

"Do you want to form a relationship with your people then?" Before the king could answer, she quickly added, "I mean a close, long-lasting relationship."

Ferez snapped his mouth shut and met her gaze. His eyes were so steady and intense that Gemi bit her lip to fight the sudden urge to squirm in the saddle.

"I do. When I was a boy, before I was pulled into the war with Fayral, I wanted to get closer to the people my father ruled, to make friends. By the time I was fourteen, I knew so many people who would greet me on sight and talk with me about their everyday problems."

He sighed and shook his head. "I doubt any of them would recognize me now or even believe I was still alive after I stopped visiting to join the war."

Gemi nodded slowly. "I guess I hadn't realized just how serious you were about knowing your people."

She turned back around so she was looking past Shadow's ears and began to play with her horsetail.

"I think that's the reason I insisted on introducing you to so many people at first. I was afraid you'd lose interest."

A soft chuckle reached her ears, and she glanced over her shoulder once more. "Let me meet people as they come, and I doubt very much that I'll lose interest." That chuckle came again, and he added, "I had

206

enough of people attempting to cram information into my head when I was younger, if you know what I mean."

Gemi nodded and opened her mouth, but she hesitated when she realized just how she was about to agree with that statement. The urge to compare the king's life to her own childhood had welled up within her, and the suddenness of that desire startled Gemi.

"*You will have to tell him eventually,*" Flame answered her thoughts, but, as before, Gemi shoved the dragon's presence away from her mind. She wasn't ready to consider telling the king her secret, even if her deadline for doing so had been moved forward by the king's proposed request.

"You had tutors when you were young?" she asked instead of the words that had risen in her throat.

Ferez hummed in agreement. "A few incidents of skipping my lessons to travel around Caypan taught them to slow down and find ways to actually interest me in the information."

Gemi laughed, even as that urge to share similar stories from her own childhood grew stronger. "I suppose the panic of losing the king's heir would do that."

"Apparently," Ferez agreed dryly. When Gemi glanced back at him again, the king was smirking. "However, it took them nearly a sevenday to find the courage to tell my father. When they did, my father simply asked them if they had learned their lesson and made me promise that my wanderings wouldn't interfere with my studies."

"Like the promise Lord Lefas mentioned?"

Ferez nodded. "My father seemed amused by my desire to wander, and he thought it harmless as long as I didn't shirk my duties as knight or king."

Gemi snorted. "What he thought was harmless was something *he* should have been doing."

When the king didn't respond, Gemi frowned back at him. The man was staring thoughtfully at his mount's neck. Wondering if she'd misspoken, Gemi opened her mouth, hesitated, then turned back around.

Maybe it was best to leave him to his thoughts. He had done the same for her before. It was only right to return the favor.

~~*~*

By the time they wandered into Main Highwayman Camp, Kephin and Lakina stood waiting for them in front of Kephin's tent. As the horses slowed to a halt, Flame slunk around them and nudged Lakina's hand with a questioning croon.

The Mage Healer sighed. "When it's not one of you, it's the other, isn't it?" She shook her head. "At least you don't hide your wounds for as long as possible."

Gemi opened her mouth to protest, but Flame hissed a soft "*Leave it be*" before following the Mage Healer towards her tent. The weariness in the dragon's tone stalled Gemi's complaints.

"Is she still injured?" Ferez asked.

Gemi glanced at him and blinked when their eyes locked. Despite his enduring silence for the remainder of their trip, his gaze now was clear and worried, not distracted like she had expected.

"She was well enough for the trip from Tearmann," Gemi murmured, "but she's still tender and exhausted from the sap on her magic. Nothing Lakina can't handle, certainly."

"*I still wish it had not happened,*" Flame muttered, and Gemi acknowledged the complaint before dismounting and turning her attention to Kephin.

"We need to deal with these rogues as soon as possible. They're getting out of hand."

"I agree," Kephin responded. Without saying anything else, he turned to his tent, lifted the flap, and waved the two of them inside.

Gemi frowned. Kephin sounded serious, which didn't bode well for the state of current affairs. She glanced at Ferez and found the man looking worriedly at his mare.

"Don't worry about the horses," Kephin added. "The others can remove their saddles and tack while we discuss plans."

Even as he spoke, two men approached Shadow and Last Chance, and young Maxwell was stepping up in front of the mare and reaching for her muzzle with both hands. The frown on the boy's face as he nickered softly to the mare made Gemi even warier.

Gemi gripped Ferez's elbow and led him into the Highwayman's tent. To her surprise, nine other men stood around the inside of the tent, and a table stood in the middle, a lamp above it clearly illuminating the map that was spread out on its surface.

Gemi stiffened at the sight. "What happened?" she asked, scanning the faces of the other men already present. She recognized each of them; seven were the leaders of the seven other Highwaymen camps, the seven men who answered directly to Kephin. Geoff, who stood towards the back of the tent, offered a small wave when her eyes landed on him.

The remaining two were mages: Bracken, the most powerful Plant Mage in Main Highwayman Camp, and Histion, the most powerful adult Animal Mage.

"There have been three more rogue attacks since you left, not including the one Flame prevented in Tearmann."

"*I did not prevent it,*" Flame snorted. "*There were two casualties among us and our allies, and several of the attackers died in my flames.*"

Grimacing, Gemi relayed Flame's words, which only caused the ten other men to look grimmer.

"Whether o' not we consider it an actu'l attack," spoke the leader of the Cosley Ruins branch of Highwaymen, "there's been too many attacks to simply let 'em pass by unnoticed. We mus' respond an' bring the figh' to them."

Gemi nodded, all too willing to agree. She had been amazed when Kephin had told her just how many times the rogues had attacked recently, but this was beyond ridiculous.

"What do we know?" she asked as she looked over the map laid out over the table. The eight Highwayman camps were labeled, along with a general estimate of each camp's manpower. There were other points marked, and, when she noticed one was the village of Puretha, she realized that they were the locations of the recent rogue attacks.

"Fo' one thin'," Histion hissed softly, "th' animal channels are blocked near constant now."

Gemi jerked her head up to stare at the Animal Mage. "They are?"

The man nodded. "We didn' 'ear abou' th' 'tack on Tearmann 'til it 'ad passed along the plant channels."

"How's that even possible?" she asked, nudging Flame curiously at the same time.

"*It would take a very powerful Animal Mage leading a number of other mages spread throughout Kensy to accomplish such a thing,*" the dragon growled. "*I have not noticed such widespread power, but I have been restricted to a barn for several days now.*"

Frowning, Gemi passed her bondmate's words on to the others. Histion bowed his head. "Tha's what I believe 'as 'appened. Bu' now we mus' depen' on the plants only." He indicated Burdock.

The Plant Mage nodded. "A sevenday ago, I spread a burst o' seekin' magic 'long the plant channels. I asked 'em to look for large groups of 'umans that were not supported by buildin's. I jus' got the repor' back yes'erday."

"And?" Ferez asked curiously.

Unfortunately, that drew the attention of those who didn't know Ferez, and the leader of the Coastal branch frowned at him.

"Who's this?" he barked.

"Easy, Gara," Kephin soothed. "Frenz is a friend of James."

"Tha' don' mean we need 'im 'ere," spoke the leader of the Tallion branch, which usually focused their efforts on the West Evonese Highway close to Cautzel.

"Well, don' know abou' that, Shaw," Geoff put in. "'E's the one who recognized the fightin' style they used in the Puretha attack."

Shaw scowled. "I still say tha' was simple coincidence. We ain' seen not'in' like wha' y' described since it."

"Prolly 'cause we captured so many of 'em," Geoff answered with a roll of his eyes.

"Should I leave?" Ferez whispered to Gemi as the other men continued arguing amongst themselves.

Gemi shook her head. "You should see how we operate when we're planning a large attack. Besides," she added with a shrug, "like Geoff mentioned, you have experience we don't have. You might be able to see something we don't."

The others had quieted by the time Gemi finished speaking, and most of them stared at her like she was mad. "What?" she snapped.

"Wha' d' you mean, experience we don' 'ave?" Gara asked.

Gemi huffed. "Unlike the rest of you," she said, thinking quickly, "Frenz fought in the king's army towards the end of the war." She knew each of the men in the tent, even the mages, had been highwaymen before Kephin unified them. "He might have a fresh view on the situation with the rogues that'll help."

For a moment, the others stared at Ferez, and Gemi could feel the king shifting beside her. A couple of men looked like they wanted to ask something, but Kephin spoke before they could say anything.

"There's no reason Frenz can't stay and listen, but why don't we let Burdock finish what he was saying?"

The seven leaders nodded and felt silent. "Thank you," Burdock sighed, "but I'm afraid tha' I don' 'ave much to offer. The plants returned wit' only the eight sites used by us Highwaymen."

~~*~*

Ferez frowned at the map in the center of the tent. The plants hadn't found any sites that weren't used by the Highwaymen? Then where were the rogues gathering?

He vaguely heard the others fall into disappointed mutters as he continued to stare. He wasn't sure for what he was looking, but he had fought in and planned battles for several months toward the end of the war. Surely there was some way to discover the rogues' locations if neither the animals nor the plants could pinpoint them.

Ferez blinked as he began to notice a pattern in the points on the map. There were clusters; loose, perhaps, but there. He stepped forward, hoping a closer look would help him interpret what he was seeing.

"Frenz?" James asked, surprise coloring his tone.

"You see somet'in'?" Geoff asked.

Ferez raised a hand in a request for silence and was faintly surprised when everyone else fell quiet. "Wha' requirements did you give the plants for seekin' out other groups?" His words were for the Plant Mage, but his eyes never left the map.

"Groups o' twenty o' more 'umans stayin' in one place wi' no sign o' permanent buildin's. Why?" The man sounded confused.

Ferez hesitated. He compared what he knew about Main Highwayman Camp with that description, as well as the villages that he had visited over the years.

"How do the plants define permanent buildings?"

The mage hummed. "I s'pose structures built o' wood an' stone. Perhaps more stone than wood since it comes from trees an' the plants would be less willin' to consider it permanent."

Ferez nodded before turning his gaze to Kephin. "Do you have a quill an' ink?"

The Highwayman's brows rose, but he nodded and turned, picking up a set of writing tools from a side table. Ferez took them with a murmured "Thanks" and began marking several points on the map.

As he marked the last point, he felt James stiffen behind him. The king wondered if the boy recognized what Ferez had. Once done, Ferez laid the quill and ink aside. He looked around at the other men before meeting the mage's eyes.

"I think the reason the plants couldn' give you locations migh' be 'cause your specifications didn' match the rogues' camps." He tapped the first point he'd made. "Here in the eas', surrounded by three attack locations, are the ruins o' the city o' Farvis."

"Farvis?" one of the men Ferez didn't know snapped. "Wha's the ol' easter' city got to do wit' anyt'in'?"

Despite the other man's protest, the Plant Mage nodded. "E'en af'er the city was destroyed, there'd be enough stone structures to convince the plants tha' it was still a human city rather than a ruins used by the rogues."

"Sounds a'righ'," Histion added, "bu' c'n we verify tha'? Th' animals won' respond an' c'n we depen' on th' plants to ge' th' information right this time?"

"I don't think we have much choice," James answered. "The only other choices are Flame or spy. Flame is too conspicuous; they would see her as soon as she sees them. And I don't think we can wait for people to ride to each of the ruins for reconnaissance and return. There's a reason we've depended on mages for so long."

"Do we not 'ave any Animal Mages wit' bird Power Animals?" Ferez asked. *It's a shame that Captain Tælen is not here,* he thought, remembering the silent pirate captain with the lora. *We could use him right now.*

The others turned to stare at him, confusion in the eyes of most of them. "There be several wit' bird Power Animals, aye," Geoff answered. "Wha' good coul' tha' be, though?"

Ferez shook his head. Apparently, the Highwaymen had become dependent on open channels. "If they have a particularly trusted bird, it could fly high enough to avoid the influence o' the powerful Animal Mage and still be able t' see what we need 'em to."

~~*~*

Gemi felt like an idiot. Even Flame was slowly shaking her head, wondering how she had not considered such an idea. The most annoying thing was that they both knew who would be best to send.

"Flame, are you healed enough to find Beka and Falco for us?"

"I am," the dragon hissed, *"but I will send Maxwell for them. The boy needs something to do now that the animal channels are blocked."*

Gemi nodded her agreement.

Around her, the men had begun arguing if Ferez's idea could possibly work. To Gemi's amusement, the king was watching the exchange with an expression of exasperation. The girl didn't blame him. By the way he'd said the words, Gemi was sure the theory had been tested during the war, when the Fayralese would have focused their attention on the main portion of the Evonese army with little care for the highwaymen that pestered bystanders of the war.

Clearing her throat, Gemi called for the attention of the other men, gaining it quickly. "The idea certainly has merit," she answered the questioning looks they gave her. "An Animal Mage who focuses their magic on one Power Animal in particular should have a relationship with that animal similar to my relationships with Flame and Shadow. Isn't that right, Histion?" She met the Animal Mage's steady gaze.

'Tis," he hissed and patted a long bump under his tunic. Gemi knew that bump would be Histion's python, his own Power Animal.

As the leaders of the other camps began to murmur to each other, the flap at the tent's entrance was pulled back, and a small woman stepped through. "Some'un sent fo' us?" she asked.

"Ah, Beka," Kephin answered and waved her forward, easily accepting Gemi's choice. As the small woman stepped away from the entrance, a man only slightly taller than her passed through the tent's entrance as well.

As the two approached the table in the center, the light from the lamp illuminated a small brown and gray ball of a bird on Beka's shoulder and a larger falcon on Falco's. When they stopped, the ball of a bird, which was actually a small owl, shifted, turned its head, and released a piercing whistle as its large, yellow eyes scanned the room.

"How c'n we help, Kephin?" Falco asked, his eyes as sharp as the birds'.

"We were hoping your birds could gather some information for us since the animal channels are currently being blocked."

The siblings glanced at each other for a moment before nodding to Kephin. "Wha' do they need t' look fo'?" Beka asked.

Kephin turned their attention to the map, pointing out the five city ruins that Ferez had marked. He explained what they hoped to find and, by the time he finished, both birds were bobbing anxiously, whistling and shrieking in their excitement.

"We're 'appy t' do wha' we c'n," Beka answered. She lifted a hand to stroke the head of the tiny owl on her shoulder. "Gnomewise'll fly fo' th' southern an' wes'er' ruins."

Falco bobbed his head. "And Elfinbrac'll take the ot'er three. They shoul' be back no later than two mornin's from now."

Gemi nodded as Kephin thanked them and dismissed them to go send off their birds. If Ferez was right, and the rogues had holed themselves up in the ruins of the old cities, then the Highwaymen would soon be able to bring the rogues' cruel ways to an end. Kensy might finally get the peace it deserved after decades of fighting just to survive.

Chapter 21

Once the birds had been sent for reconnaissance, Gemi spent the rest of the evening—and the next day—listening amusedly as Ferez questioned the camp leaders about everything to do with their people. The men questioned why he would want to know, but Gemi and Kephin both insisted that there was no harm in him learning the information, especially since they wouldn't be able to plan until they knew their enemies' locations and numbers.

What amused Gemi most was the amount of notes Ferez took as he questioned the others. At first, he simply made notes on the map, but he quickly asked Kephin for parchment as he came up with more questions.

He asked about the numbers and types of mages each camp had, how powerful they were, the specialties of their men, the tactics each group preferred, and so on. As he continued to ask, Gemi found herself becoming more interested and listening intently to the answers as much as the questions.

By the second morning after their return to Main Highwayman Camp, the birds returned, weary but bearing news. Beka and Falco confirmed that, aye, the rogues were occupying the five cities Ferez had suspected. The birds also assured that none of the other, smaller city ruins they had passed showed signs of humans.

After the siblings had marked down the numbers of their enemies, they all stared down at the map grimly. The five city ruins, each occupied by a larger number of men than any of them had imagined, were spread out across Kensy as much as the eight Highwayman camps were.

"This is not promising," Kephin muttered, tracing his fingers over the marked camps.

"I wouldn' say that," Ferez answered, startling everyone. He was already bending closer to the map and, as they watched, he began to prove that the interrogation of the past couple days had not been idle.

The plan that Ferez outlined for the rest of them proved that the man was a tactician with the experience of war. While the others whispered questions about his role in the war, Gemi was sharply reminded that, not only was Ferez king, but he had also been on the front lines of the war with Fayral, not scurrying about in an attempt to help like the Highwaymen had towards the end.

Five days later, in the predawn darkness of the twentieth of Early Autumn, Gemi and Ferez lay flat on their stomachs beneath a low cover of creeping vines. They crawled steadily towards the crumbled walls of Geannes, the southern city ruins currently occupied by rogues.

Around them, hidden by darkness, trees, and the moving foliage, the bulk of the Highwaymen from Main Highwayman Camp crawled towards the old city's walls. Spread evenly throughout the group were the camp's Plant Mages, their magic willing the vines to grow and creep forward.

Everyone else formed pockets around them, ready to guard them during the battle so they could focus their attention solely on the plants.

Gemi knew, as she moved forward, that the men from the other Highwayman camps were acting out similar tactics at the other four ruins at this same moment. It had been one point on which Ferez had been insistent. If the rogues had control of the animal channels, then it wouldn't take long for news of each attack to travel to the other groups of rogues. Therefore, to prevent any of the rogues from gaining the advantage of a warning, the Highwaymen had to attack all five city ruins at the same time.

"Keep your attention on the rogues you are about to attack, James," Flame hissed through the bond. *"You can praise Frenz for his tactical genius later."*

Gemi rolled her eyes. *"Stop worrying, Flame. You're only a flight away from the battle."*

"Several minutes too long," the dragon growled.

Gemi shrugged and kept crawling. Despite Flame's complaints, everyone had agreed it wasn't worth the risk to bring Flame or the camp's Animal Mages to the initial attack. With the rogues controlling the animal channels, mages and dragon would give away the attack before the Highwaymen came within bowshot of the ruins. Even the horses had been left far enough away to prevent mages from turning them against their masters.

A sharp rattle and hiss jerked Gemi back to the present. Around her, the others paused and turned back towards their Plant Mage, who alternated between cursing in Fayralese and hissing and rustling at the vines covering them.

"Acker?" she whispered.

The mage made a sharp snapping sound and shook his head. "They have—"

A horn blew then, loud enough to roust the birds from their branches and send the surrounding forest into an angry chatter.

Gemi didn't know who reacted first, but both she and Ferez were up and running before the blast ended. Behind and around them, shouts and cries broke out, so convoluted that she nearly missed the questioning tone behind them.

"We can't allow them the advantage! Press forward!"

~~*~*

The confused shouting dwindled quickly as James' words passed from mouth to mouth until only one phrase echoed around them: "Press forward!" Just as quickly, the men fell silent, only the thud of heavy footsteps audible above the commotion of the animals.

The contrast to the actions of his own men on the docks of Calay was so striking that Ferez hesitated between one step and the next and nearly stumbled into a tree. But James' hand was on his elbow, tugging on and

214

steadying him, and Ferez cast the boy a grateful smile, uncaring that it would be nearly invisible in the early morning darkness.

Then a stirring of the air near his ear and a soft *thunk* behind him brought him sharply back to the battle.

"Bowmen," he hissed.

"Sentries," James hissed back.

And, suddenly, the trees fell away behind them, and the harsh, crouching ruins of the old city of Geannes spread out in front of them. Dark and heavy, its jagged edges shone softly in the orange glow of hidden fires.

Ferez could easily recall the last battle he'd fought within these ruins, but a gasp and gurgle from behind reminded him that now was a time for battle, not reminiscences.

Lowering his upper body, he sprinted for the crumbling remains of the city's outer wall and clambered up what was now a long ridge of rubble. At the peak, he found a sentry, arrow nocked and mouth agape.

Perhaps we yet have the advantage.

A slide of Ferez's blade was enough to snap the rogue's bowstring, earning him a scream as the man dropped the weapon in favor of clutching his now bleeding face. A knock to the head sent him to ground, where he whimpered and fell still.

"Neat trick," James muttered before clamping one hand on Ferez's shoulder and steering them both down the other side of the ridge.

Oddly enough, the rogues who met them were no more difficult to face than the sentry. Most had obviously just stumbled from their bedrolls, half-dressed and unfocused.

If only the Fayralese had been so easily caught unawares.

He let the thought drift as he dropped his mind into the fighting instincts his knight mentors had trained into him from a young age. He dodged wild swings, deflected more precise ones, and incapacitated his enemies as quickly as he could.

A brief respite brought the realization that the sky was turning pink and orange with the rising sun. The morning light lent the ruins a beauty that Ferez might have appreciated if it hadn't illuminated just how violent the battle was.

While the Highwaymen had managed to catch the rogues off guard, the sight of the rising sun seemed to rally them. Or perhaps that was caused by the sight of a large willow amidst the city ruins lashing out at and beating back anyone who came near it.

"Tha's 'im!" someone snapped.

Ferez turned and found Acker, the Plant Mage he and James had been guarding originally, pointing towards the willow. Trailing vines encircled his wrists, but he didn't appear to notice them.

"Who...?"

But Ferez's gaze returned to the large tree, and he quickly realized he could answer the question himself. Amongst the tree's branches, higher up than Ferez would have thought the willow could support, stood a large, solid-looking man with a wooden club in one hand and a cruel grin spreading his lips.

"Plant Mage?" Ferez muttered.

Acker made a loud snapping sound that Ferez thought might be a curse and nodded. "He's powerful, too. Sensed us comin' afore any of us coulda sensed 'im."

Ferez nodded and indicated Acker's trailing vines, which seemed to writhe against his wrists. "Y' migh' wanna keep those away from 'im then, aye?"

Acker glanced down at his wrists and made that snapping sound once more before trotting back towards the edge of the ruins.

Ferez glanced around for James, but the boy had apparently been recognized and was once again surrounded by several men. Thankfully, he appeared to be faring better than he had in Puretha, but that meant Ferez would have to deal with the tree and its Plant Mage himself.

And it needed to be dealt with. From what he could see, the tree had already managed to snap the necks of three Highwaymen, and more were being chased towards it by other rogues.

He briefly considered fighting his way to James' side and asking him if Flame could simply burn the tree. He dropped the thought quickly though. He had yet to see the flash of red and purple that would indicated the dragon's arrival, and he couldn't allow the rogues to continue utilizing such a deadly weapon.

Well, if we can't remove the weapon, we can at least remove its wielder.

Nodding his head sharply, Ferez sprinted towards the tree.

As soon as he was within range, the tree creaked, and several branches whipped towards him. Ducking, he avoided the first, but two more followed him down and wrapped around his left arm and torso.

Rolling, Ferez drew the branches taut and sliced his sword across them like he had the sentry's bowstring. An angry *shush* reverberated around him as the detached switches dropped from his body like headless snakes.

More branches swayed closer as he rolled back to his feet and bounded towards the trunk. He ducked and dodged them, swinging his blade when he couldn't avoid them completely. Once close enough, he sheathed his sword, leapt up, grabbed the base of a branch, and hooked his feet into the trunk's crevasses.

"Impressive!" called a voice from above.

Ferez hesitated and glanced up. The Plant Mage was smirking down at him, his grip on both the tree and his club still relaxed. Ferez frowned.

He's not even worried that I made it past the willow's branches.

A sudden burning sensation in his hands distracted him from the mage then. Hissing, he jumped back off the tree, certain the pain was connected to the stickiness he'd felt when he first touched the bark

Or, rather, he tried to jump off the tree. Instead, branches crowded close, some wrapping around his torso, others simply pressing him closer to the trunk.

"Leavin' so soon? I thought yeh were 'ere to fight me."

Ferez scowled, not bothering to answer. He kicked at the trunk and attempted to wriggle out of the tree's grasp, but that only encouraged it to wrap more branches around him. He pulled at the ones creeping around his neck before several slid around his wrists and pulled his now red and blistered hands around the trunk.

"Painful, ain' it?" the mage called down just as the skin on Ferez's neck and wrists began to burn. "'Er sap is poisonous." He patted the trunk. "Tha's the beauty o' fire willows. No matter how yeh 'proach 'em, they c'n kill yeh."

He peered down at Ferez, who was trying to keep his face away from the bark, with little success.

"Course, I've a certain…skill wit' 'er kin'. Pleasan' surprise, that. Mos' o' my men were a bit wary o' me plantin' 'er 'ere, but..." He chuckled, and Ferez grit his teeth as his cheek and jaw began to burn. "I don' think they have any complain's now."

The willow chose that moment to brush its leaves against Ferez's uninjured cheek. He gasped and closed his eyes, only to scream as tears spilled down his cheeks and the pain multiplied.

Suddenly, an answering roar filled his ears, and a different kind of heat surrounded him. Another scream, not his own, pierced him, and the branches holding him whipped away, throwing him to the ground.

Ferez had a brief impression through watery eyes of orange dancing behind roiling black before something else wrapped around his chest. He panicked as he was dragged up against something large and firm, and the sudden restraint on his eyes, forcing them closed, increased the feeling.

Only the familiar croon in his ear informed him that the slick, delicate hand over his eyes belonged to Flame.

Taking a deep breath and attempting to relax despite the pain, he focused on the movement of her muscles against his back, the brush of wind tugging at his hair and clothes, and the screams and yells filling his ears. He could just make out someone shouting that the smoke was dangerous and poisonous and that Flame was crazy for setting the damn thing on fire.

Any answers were lost in the roar of the wind, and, before he could wonder too much about it, a rushing cold engulfed his face, and he gasped.

Immediately, he began coughing and spluttering as water filled his mouth. Throwing his hands out in front of himself, he scrabbled painfully at the stones he felt there and pushed himself up.

Whatever body of water he'd been thrown into couldn't be very deep, he realized, as his head emerged with little effort. Gasping for air, he tried to turn his head and quickly found that Flame still held his face gently in one of her clawed hands.

"Wha' in Maur's' Fire was tha' abou', Flame?" he spat once he had enough breath to speak.

The dragon only snarled and growled before tugging Ferez's head to one side and dunking half of his burning face back into the water. Ferez tried to curse, but all that accomplished was water invading his mouth and nose, and he was once again spluttering and snorting in an attempt to breathe.

"Flame!" James shouted, and suddenly Ferez was above the water again, coughing and groaning at the ache in his lungs. "What are you doing?"

~~*~*

Gemi couldn't believe her eyes when she ran to the small stream where Flame had taken Ferez. The dragon had told her that his wounds needed tending, but she hadn't expected to find her nearly drowning the poor king.

Wading into the water, she grabbed the man by one shoulder and lifted a hand to help him wipe the water from his face. Before she could even touch his blistered cheek, Flame growled and grabbed her wrist with the hand not holding Ferez's upper face.

"*Do not touch his face until the sap has been washed from it.*"

"Sap?" Gemi frowned down at Ferez's face. "From the tree?"

Flame hissed. "*That tree was a fire willow. One drop of its sap, even slightly diluted, can burn flesh like fire would. We have to remove all of the sap before he can be healed.*"

Gemi nodded and reached for the pouch on her belt, removing a pair of leather gloves. Pulling them on, she returned her attention to Ferez, who seemed to be breathing easier now.

"Frenz, how are you doing?"

The king snorted then coughed and jerked his head within Flame's grasp. The dragon trilled impatiently. "I'd be bette' if your dragon wasn' tryin' to drown me."

Gemi grimaced and explained what Flame had told her. After a moment of silence, Ferez's shoulders dropped, and he huffed.

"She coulda been a bit gentler about it."

Gemi silently agreed, making Flame aware of her disapproval. The dragon growled and reminded Gemi that she may disapprove of her methods, but the sap was still causing damage.

Nodding, Gemi slid her left hand beneath Ferez's burnt cheek, pulling a hiss from the man's lips. "Sorry," she murmured.

"Doesn' matter," the king answered, his words strained. "Jus' get rid o' the stuff."

Gemi nodded again. At Flame's insistence, she slid her other hand beneath Flame's, replacing the dragon's grip over Ferez's eyes with her own.

"You have to make sure he does not open his eyes," Flame crooned in explanation. *"If the sap gets in his eyes, he will be blinded."*

Pursing her lips, Gemi slowly lowered Ferez's head towards the stream's surface, making sure to keep his lips and nose above water-level this time. Gently, she ran her gloved hand over his cheeks and jaw, working the water over the blistered flesh. Even through the glove, she could feel the warmth of the sap, and Gemi was suddenly very aware that her gloves were made of animal flesh.

"Clean the wounds quickly, and we will not have to learn if the sap can burn through leather," Flame crooned urgently.

Gemi continued gently cleaning off the sap, lifting the man's face occasionally to check for remaining stickiness. Once she was sure she'd removed all of the sap from his face, Flame bade her to check his hands. Both had remained on the streambed since Gemi had arrived, and the constant flow of water over them had apparently removed the sap well enough.

"Anywhere else?" Gemi asked.

"M-m-my n-n-neck," Ferez chattered, grimacing. Although Gemi had removed her hand from his eyes, he still kept them tightly closed, and his body was trembling slightly.

Gemi pulled at the neck of his tunic, revealing bands of blisters around his neck, the sap still covering them shining softly. She was contemplating how best to clean the wounds when a familiar voice caught her attention.

"There you three are."

Gemi glanced up to find Lakina striding towards them from the direction of the city ruins. Worry filled her eyes, and she kicked off her shoes and waded into the stream without hesitating.

"Kephin said that Frenz had been injured, but then no one was sure where Flame had taken him."

As she talked, she gently replaced Gemi at Ferez's side, wet a small cloth she'd pulled from her bag, and, without asking what still needed to be done, began to smooth it lightly over the king's neck. Still anxious over the man's wounds and unsure what else to do, Gemi let her hands linger over his shoulders and back and watched silently as Lakina did her work.

~~*~*~*

Ferez huffed and twitched where he sat in his saddle. Lakina had Healed his burns enough for there to be no lingering damage, but parts of his skin beneath the bandages were still slightly raw. And they itched, terribly so.

He shifted again, wishing he could relieve the annoyance. Snorting, Last Chance curved her head around to stare at him, and Ferez stilled, his cheeks heating. However, that only seemed to make the itching on his face worse.

"How are you doing?" James asked, not for the first time. He had stayed close to Ferez from the moment he'd found him with Flame at the stream. Even Kephin hadn't been able to tempt the boy from his side with a discussion of the battle.

Now, Kephin, James, Ferez, and most of the uninjured Highwaymen were riding back to Main Highwayman Camp, those of the enemy who still lived and could travel coming with them. James had expressed his concern about Ferez riding with the still healing burns, but Ferez had simply gazed steadily at the boy with one eyebrow raised until the boy blushed and glanced away.

Honestly, if James can ride from Puretha to Main Highwayman Camp with a wounded shoulder and leg, then he can't complain about me riding with mostly healed burns.

Then again, Ferez hadn't realized he'd be spending the entire trip attempting not to scratch. "Itching," he muttered in answer to James' question.

The boy nodded. "We're nearly to Main Highwayman Camp. We can find something to ease the itching there."

Sure enough, they soon arrived at the camp. Near the central fire, Kephin, James, and Ferez were greeted by Histion, the Animal Mage with the python Power Animal; young Maxwell; and a young woman, who turned out to be a healer. Ferez knew Flame must have passed a message along because, as soon as the horses had halted, the healer approached Last Chance and waved for Ferez to dismount.

"Le' me have a look a' those burns, Mister Kanti. I shoul' be able to help finish wha' Lakina started."

Ferez dismounted and allowed the woman to lead him over to Cassidi's fire. She removed his bandages and began to gently apply a cool, crisp-scented gel to his reddened skin as Histion began to speak.

"The animal channels're open ag'in," the man hissed. "We've heard news from th' other camps tha' th' other four battles were jus' as successful as the one in Geannes. Two o' the five camp leaders were captured alive. Th' other three were killed."

"Was the Animal Mage behind the channel blocks killed or captured?" Kephin asked. James frowned, and both Animal Mages shook their head.

"Neither," Maxwell answered with wide eyes full of frustration. "He was not present at any of the battles."

"Are you sure?" Kephin asked.

James nodded. "Flame says the animals still won't say who or where he is, but they are insistent about that point."

"We 'ave learned 'is name from one o' the captured camp leaders though," Histion added. "He said he's known as Charlen."

"Not that it helps if we know nothing else about him," James muttered.

"At least he shouldn' be able to cause any more trouble, aye?" Ferez asked.

Kephin nodded, but Histion hesitated. Maxwell bounced in place and cried, "But the message said he was the leader of the rogues."

"The rogues had a central leader?" Ferez asked, surprised.

James huffed. "Well, even if they did, we've destroyed any structure they had. If he wanted to reform the rogues, it would take him years to find enough men to cause the Highwaymen significant problems."

"And we have no way of finding him, aye?" Kephin asked the Animal Mages. Both Histion and Maxwell shook their heads. "Then there's no reason to worry about him for now. We'll keep an eye out for him, but we don't need to devote manpower to it."

There were murmurs of agreement from the others, and Ferez found his attention was soon claimed by the healer once more.

~~*~*

Two hours ride north of the North Evonese Junction
Kensy, Evon

He was awakened by snarls and snapping. Lifting his head, he glared at the two wildcats standing nearby. A mangled corpse lay between them. Assuming that was the reason for their argument, he snarled wordlessly at them.

The two cats fell silent, their heads swiveling until their pale eyes met his. The one on the right, a female, growled lowly.

"*Your human packs have fallen.*"

Charlen stilled. He considered denying the statement, swearing that it could not be true, but his cats would never lie to him. If they said that the highwaymen he had gathered beneath him had fallen, then they had.

"*Our enemies?*"

"*They had few deaths,*" the cat snarled. He knew that, had she been human, she would have sneered. "*They remain strong, as always.*" After a small pause, she added, "*And the Traveler's companion survived.*"

Charlen growled. When he fell silent, the sound did not, and the two wildcats turned tail and disappeared through the trees. Stiffening, he turned towards the sound and nearly whined when he saw the red orbs staring at him through the darkness between the trees.

"You have failed me, Charlen."

He shivered at the sound of the familiar growling voice and shook his head, hoping to stave off whatever punishment it had in mind for his failure.

"I c'n still kill 'im, Markos."

Silence followed his words, and those red eyes narrowed to thin slits. "You have lost all of the men under your command. How do you propose to kill him?"

Charlen swallowed and shook his head again. "I don' need men t' do me killin'. Me cats c'n rip a man t' shreds faste' th'n five swordsmen."

A growling chuckle met his words as those red eyes widened once more. "Really? Then why have you depended on other humans so far?"

221

He growled. The mere suggestion that he would put his cats in unnecessary danger was enough to raise his hackles. "I woul' rather tes' a man's strength wit' a 'undred useless men than e'en jus' one o' me cats."

The growl that Markos answered with was soft, almost a hum. "But you will use them now?" When Charlen hesitated, the growling voice added, "If you will not, I can simply kill you now and seek out someone else willing to kill the Traveler's companion."

Charlen closed his eyes. This was no longer a matter of bargaining the life of the Traveler for that of his companion. Nay, it had become a matter of the Traveler's companion or Charlen.

Swallowing once more, he muttered, "Why's this death so important t' ye?"

More silence followed, and Charlen wondered if he should have held his curiosity in check. The silence grew longer, and Charlen lowered himself into a crouch, desperately wishing he could follow his wildcats through the trees and away from this creature.

"The real name of the man I want you to kill is Ferez Katani."

Charlen wasn't sure which startled him more, the sudden break in the silence or the name that Markos spoke. Charlen may not care about human affairs, but even he knew the name of Evon's current king.

"You wish me t' kill th' king."

He was too shocked to make the words a question. When those red eyes simply turned amused and Markos offered another growling chuckle, cold filled his chest and stomach.

Kill the king? Can I really do such a thing? The answer came immediately and fiercely. *I will to save my life and those of my cats.*

"I thought so," Markos growled as though in answer to Charlen's thoughts. "See that you do, and I will make sure you and your cats live through the ensuing Chaos."

Charlen couldn't answer except to swallow and nod. A final growling chuckle reached his ears before those red eyes faded and changed to the pale orbs of a wildcat. Like before, the cat seemed confused and butted its head against Charlen's leg, asking if he was well.

"*I don't know,*" he growled back. "*I truly don't know.*"

~~*~*

War growled once he let go of the wildcat. It was tiring to take physical form, even with the help of the physical creatures he grabbed to assist him. Worse yet was the near certainty that Charlen would fail in the task War had assigned him. *She* had become so very protective of the king, despite the fact that *she* had only known him for a few sevendays.

War snarled and kicked at the ground, but the action was useless. The Spiritual Plane was not formed in such a way that the immortals that roamed it could take out their frustration without harming each other. Then again, War didn't think immortals were supposed to get this frustrated.

Taking a deep breath to stem the emotions whirring through him, War closed his eyes and Transported himself away from Kensy and *her*. He would let Charlen attempt to finish his task. If the mage failed, he would not live for long, even if War was not the one who offered the killing blow.

If *she* managed to leave Kensy before the king was killed, War needed to make sure Zhulan was prepared for her arrival. Opening his eyes, the demigod smiled at the sight that greeted him.

Aye, this will do.

Chapter 22

27 Early Autumn, 224
Highwayman post along the Cautzelian Coastal Highway

Gemi shifted in the saddle and scanned the road.

The sevenday since the attack on the rogues had been almost boringly routine compared to the sevendays before it. She and Ferez had traveled to two more villages before she insisted on introducing him to the duties of the highway.

As she shifted again, Ferez paused in his conversation with the other Highwaymen and glanced at her curiously. She offered him a quick smile, which he returned before turning back to the others.

As soon as his attention was elsewhere, Gemi dropped the smile and sighed.

It wasn't boredom that filled Gemi's mind now, but worry. Despite the routineness of the last sevenday and the destruction of the rogues, the animals had become increasingly restless.

At first, the Animal Mages thought it was simply the lingering effects of Charlen's control over the channels, but it didn't quite make sense. After all, according to Maxwell, the restlessness only occurred around Gemi and her companions.

Then, three days ago, Flame confided in Gemi her suspicion that the animals were reacting to Ferez and no one else. The realization had both her and Shadow watching the king more closely, and Last Chance, who had apparently overheard their conversation, never left her master's side now.

Thankfully, Ferez hadn't shown any sign of noticing their animals' increased caution, and Gemi preferred to keep it that way. They would be leaving for Zhulan in a few days, and she hoped that whatever trouble the animals sensed could be avoided until then.

Gemi jerked and startled from her thoughts as a sudden burst of growls and yips sounded to the southwest. Silently chastising herself for being so jumpy, she grabbed Ferez's arm as he reached for Last Chance's reins. When he glanced at her questioningly, she shook her head.

"It's just a pack of wolves," she muttered, conscious that the words were just as much for herself as for the king. "They should—"

"Help! Please!"

Gemi cursed and spun towards the sound. The words, and the cry that followed them, were weak and so full of fear that she knew she couldn't ignore it.

"Stay here!" she snapped at the other Highwaymen even as she reached for Flame and urged a reluctant Shadow onto the highway. She nearly demanded that Ferez stay behind as well, but the need to keep him close so she could protect him overwhelmed that instinct.

"*Flame?*" she pressed when the dragon didn't answer her immediately.

"*Down the highway towards Cautzel,*" Flame growled. "*The pack is attacking a single human.*"

Gemi frowned. "*Can you tell why?*"

Flame's growl deepened. "*Only that they are being controlled by powerful Animal Magic.*" She snapped her teeth together. "*And I cannot sense the source.*"

"*Charlen?*"

The dragon hesitated. "*Perhaps.*"

The pack turned out to be larger and farther away than Gemi had expected. Nearly twenty wolves lunged in a frenzy of snapping and snarling, attacking each other as often as their prey, whose only defense appeared to be a tree branch.

"*Any ideas?*" Gemi asked as she led Shadow into a wide circle around the pack. "*We can't just kill them; not when they're being controlled like this.*"

Flame hissed. "*If this is a trap—*"

Gemi yelped as Shadow suddenly screamed and leapt away from the snapping jaw of a wolf. Immediately, the entire pack shifted its focus towards them, and Gemi scrabbled for Shadow's mane as the stallion broke into a canter.

"*Now what?*" he whinnied, tossing his head angrily. When both Gemi and Flame hesitated, he snorted, "*Don't tell me you expect me to lead them on a merry chase.*"

Flame huffed. "*I still cannot sense the source of the magic.*" She hesitated then added, "*Perhaps you can lead them out of Charlen's range?*"

"*When you don't even know how long that will take?*" Shadow tossed his head again. "*I may be faster than them, but I don't know if I've got the endurance for that.*"

Gemi soothed a hand across Shadow's neck. "You're stronger than a pack of wolves, Shadow; I know you are."

The stallion snorted. "*So says the human on my back.*"

But Gemi felt the warmth that flushed through the bond as he lowered his head and lengthened his stride. Hoping to help as much as she could, she leaned further over his neck and matched the rhythm of her body to his pace.

They ran in silence for several more minutes, only the sounds of the pursuing wolves filling the air, before Flame released a roar of triumph.

"*They are beginning to falter! He is losing control!*"

Gemi glanced over her shoulder and saw that, aye, half the wolves had fallen behind and several were already bounding for the tree line. Pressing herself more tightly against the stallion's neck, she murmured, "Just a little further, Shadow; just a little further."

When Flame finally told Shadow he could stop, his sides heaved, and his flanks were damp with sweat. Rubbing his shoulder and murmuring soothingly, Gemi nudged him in a circle so she could stare back down the highway in the direction from which they'd come.

"I don't understand. Why would Charlen bother to send wolves after us?" she muttered idly. "Surely he could have guessed that we'd outrun them?"

A sudden growling through the bond jerked Gemi's gaze upward, even as she felt Flame wing back towards their post.

"Flame?"

"*I do not believe the mage was after* you."

Gemi caught her breath at the image Flame pressed through the bond before kicking Shadow into a run. The horror she felt echoed threefold through the bond.

We left Ferez behind!

~~*~*

When the wolves turned and chased after James and Shadow, Ferez nearly followed. He hadn't spent much time apart from the boy since they'd begun traveling together, and he wasn't inclined to start now.

Only the pitiful cry of the wolves' original prey had Ferez pulling back on Last Chance's reins. She jerked against the hold and gave a sharp whinny but halted when he tugged again.

"Easy," he murmured, only to receive a one-eyed glare from the mare in response. "Wha's wrong wit' you? You canna wanna fight wolves that badly."

Last Chance snorted and bounded forward, stumbling to a halt when he pulled on the reins again. Before she could attempt another start, he swung off her back and patted her neck.

"Hones'ly, I haven' seen you this jittery in years."

She snorted and hooked her muzzle around his chest.

Ferez froze. The gesture was a protective one she hadn't used since the war, and it had almost always predicted an attack. It was a warning to which he'd learned to listen.

But I don't see how it could possibly apply now. With a shake of his head, he gently nudged hers out of the way.

"The wolves are gone, Last Chance," he murmured. "The only thin' left is their victim, an' I need to make sure he's alright."

Last Chance swung her head to stare at the wounded man but, thankfully, did nothing else as Ferez approached him.

"Ever'thin's gonna be alrigh' now," he soothed as he knelt beside the whimpering stranger. Keeping his hands gentle, he pulled carefully at the man's shredded clothes, hoping to find the sources of the blood that stained them.

When the man grabbed his wrists in a tight grip, Ferez stamped down his sudden panic and murmured a soft "You're safe". After all, it wouldn't be the first time he'd tended to a wounded man whose adrenaline caused him to lash out at friend and foe alike.

However, the grip only tightened, squeezing tendon to bone, and Ferez yelped as he jerked his gaze up to the man's face.

His mouth went dry at the sight of burning eyes and sneering lips, and he began tugging at his wrists.

"Thank y' so much fer yer 'elp," the stranger snarled, completely ignoring Ferez's fruitless efforts. "Yer Majesty."

Ferez froze, feeling like he'd just been kicked in the stomach.

How...?

"Markos'll be please to 'ear 'ow easily I ensnare an' kill ye."

Ferez cursed and tugged harder at his wrists. How this man knew who he was didn't matter, not if he planned to kill him.

"Pity abou' the mare though. Such a beauty she is."

Last Chance!

Ferez spun his head around and swallowed when he spotted his mount. She was standing only a foot away, her eyes wide enough he could see the whites encircling her large brown pupils. As he watched, she tossed her head and stamped her hooves, but she didn't move from that spot.

He's an Animal Mage? But—?

"Canna see why she's so loyal to ye, though. Ye 'umans are so stupid. Y' couldn' e'en be bothe' t' listen t' her warnin' abou' me." He bared his teeth when Ferez turned back to him. "Now, she'll be too full o' grief t' be useful t' any'un once she kills ye."

Fear froze Ferez's insides. *He can't do that! He...*

He glanced back at Last Chance as she stepped closer and shifted her weight towards her hind legs. Her eyes were still wild, and Ferez felt his throat close up.

Even Master Ekin couldn't control her. He always said she'd been trained to resist Animal Magic.

However, that didn't prevent Last Chance from rearing up like the mage demanded.

The scream that tore from her throat, on the other hand, was defiant and definitely all her. The Animal Mage's gaping proved that.

Taking advantage of the mage's suddenly loose grip, Ferez twisted his wrists free and rolled backwards. As he came to his feet, Last Chance fell to all fours, and the mage screamed.

As she reared again, another scream, more feral than the mage's, split the air. A dark brown blur broke from the tree line and struck her, sending both creatures sprawling.

"Last Chance!" Ferez cried, reaching for his sword.

He froze when he realized the creature struggling with her was not alone. More stalked from the trees, at least two dozen large wildcats in all. Two more pounced on Last Chance, finally pinning her, while the rest encircled Ferez and snarled at him.

"Stupid, clever mare!"

Ferez spun around, finally drawing his sword. The mage, whom Ferez was beginning to think might be the missing Charlen, had climbed to his feet. His face dripped blood, his right arm clung to his torso, and his left dangled from the shoulder.

"Ne'er," he spat, "'ave I met 'n animal so…stubborn in m' life." He glared at the pinned mare.

"Leave her be!" Ferez snapped.

The mage turned his narrowed gaze back to Ferez and eyed him quietly. "Leave 'er be, Yer Majesty? Wha' do y' care if I kill 'er or not? All she is t' ye is a mount, not'in' more."

Ferez shook his head and tightened his grip on his sword. "I don't know why you hate me so much or why you want to kill me, but Last Chance is one of my best friends, and I won't let you destroy her just because you couldn't use her to kill me."

Charlen tilted his head. "Ye actu'lly consider yerself friends wit' 'er?"

The words held a growl of surprise and curiosity. Even as Ferez answered in the affirmative, the mage turned back towards Last Chance and the three wildcats pinning her and growled wordlessly.

When Last Chance jerked and screamed, Ferez stepped forward, lifted his sword, and shouted, "Leave her alone!"

Two cats pounced into the space between Ferez and Charlen, halting Ferez's progress, even as Last Chance fell silent. As the two cats snarled, the mage turned back around and eyed Ferez more thoughtfully.

"She calls y' friend, too. How odd. Mos' 'umans are too self-absorbed t' value animals properly."

Remembering a similar comment the mage had made earlier, Ferez asked, "If you hate humans so much, why do you involve yourself in their affairs?"

Charlen snarled. "Th' Trav'ler's 'ighwaymen spread themselves across th' entire forest, into places they're no' welcome. I on'y organized the other 'ighwaymen so I wouldn' 'ave to risk th' animals."

"And the reason you want me dead?"

Charlen gave a barking laugh, reminiscent of a hound's. "Ye assume me task t' kill ye is an 'uman affair."

Ferez hesitated. "Isn't it?"

Charlen gave that barking laugh again and focused darkly dancing eyes on Ferez's. "Me task was set t' me by one who's more than man, more powe'ful than any mage. 'E calls 'imself Markos, an' 'e 'as promise me a place among th' chaos o' yer death."

"And death if you don't, I imagine," Ferez muttered, wondering why someone so powerful wanted him dead and why he couldn't be bothered to do it himself.

He briefly considered Fayral's emperor, who was unable to cross Evon's borders for the same reason Fayral's magical creatures couldn't— his part-elf heritage prevented it. But he discarded the thought quickly. That advantage had been one of the reasons Ferez was able to gain peace with Fayral—and the name Markos was vaguely familiar, but it did not belong to the elf emperor.

Ferez was deep enough into his thoughts that he didn't notice the effect his words had on the mage. A snarled "How dare you!" was his only warning before something heavy hit his back.

Pain burned through his hands and knees, then chest and face as he collapsed completely to the ground. However, none of that compared to the piercing agony that erupted across his neck, back, and thighs.

Screams filled his ears, so varied and all-encompassing that Ferez couldn't place any of them. Only the burning in his throat, nearly overwhelmed by the wet, crushing pressure on his neck, told him that one of them was his own.

Stars burst behind his eyelids, and he lost sense of everything but the sheer weight on his neck and skull. Even the pain eased, and Ferez scrabbled to think and to fight.

But not only could he no longer feel the pain, he could no longer feel his body. And the one thought he managed to grasp terrified him as much as the oblivion that followed it.

Is this how I'm to leave my kingdom?
~~*~*

As soon as Flame was far enough down the highway to see the site of the wolf attack through the forest's canopy, she cursed herself vigorously for not recognizing the danger before it was too late.

Now, wildcats filled the highway, almost thirty of them, and the man she had thought was the wolves' victim stood confidently among them.

Briefly, she panicked as she could see neither Ferez nor Last Chance. The panic turned to ice in her veins when she realized that both were hidden under the large felines.

Swallowing the roar that rose in her throat—and the wave of gas that would ignite upon hitting the air—she dove through the arching canopy and dropped to the ground.

She fell so quickly that the cats on top of Ferez received no warning before her claws dug into several of them and her jaw snapped the neck of the most dangerously placed one. Thrashing her tail and unfurling her wings to keep back the rest, Flame carefully worked her front claws between the dead cat's jaws and Ferez's neck, tossing aside the corpse once it was safe.

A hiss broke past her teeth as she finally observed Ferez's back. Bloody, shredded flesh covered his back and thighs, and the white of bone appeared frequently enough that Flame turned her head to keep from screaming. She did not even let herself consider just how deeply the cat's teeth might have punctured the king's neck.

"James, Shadow, get here now! Ferez will not survive much longer without a Mage Healer, and I cannot leave with these cats endangering us."

"We're coming!" Gemi answered.

"I'm...pushing...as hard...as I can," Shadow returned. Through the bond, Flame could feel his sides heaving and his lungs burning, but she could also feel his determination not to fail their newfound friends.

Flame gave a sharp nod and lashed out at the nearest wildcat, catching its shoulder and raking her claws along its side. It snarled and leapt back, and Flame was forced to turn her attention to several others as they leapt at her sides.

"As soon as you are in range, James," Flame added as she flared her wings once more, catching two of the cats in the throats, *"you have to shoot Charlen. It feels like the wildcats are his Power Animal, and distracting him will only increase their attacks. You must kill him."*

"Understood," Gemi replied grimly.

Flame felt Gemi grip Shadow with her knees as she reached for the bow slung over her back and the quiver of arrows strapped to Shadow's saddlebags. Flame was just aware of a wave of gratitude for the training the girl had received in her multitude of weapons when pain in her flank drew the dragon's attention fully back to the fight.

With a sharp hiss, Flame swung her head back towards the offending cat, which had sunk its teeth into the scales above one hind leg. Sliding her tail around behind it, she forced its body towards her head, both of them snarling as she did so. The cat released its hold on her flank just as she had forced it into a position close enough for her to grab it, and it leapt at her neck.

The angle the cat started at was not the best for it, and Flame sank her teeth into the middle of its back even as it scrabbled for purchase in the scales of her neck with teeth and claws.

Unfortunately for the cat, the scales that covered all but the underside of her neck were much thicker than the scales along her flank. She shook the cat and squeezed her jaw tightly around it, growling softly as a sharp *crack* let her know she had done it enough damage.

Something small suddenly whistled past Flame, quiet enough that the dragon knew no human would have been able to hear it.

Dropping the now quiescent cat from her jaws, Flame swung her head towards Charlen. The Animal Mage was staring slack-jawed down at his chest, his working hand pressed just below the entry point of the arrow that stuck out of the center.

As Flame watched, another whistle touched her ears, and a second arrow found its target in the mage's forehead, almost directly between the eyes. As the man dropped to the ground, Flame took a moment to appreciate her bondmate's accuracy. Flame knew few humans could shoot a target like that from the back of a cantering horse.

"Thanks, Flame," Gemi muttered, her voice twisted with an emotion that the dragon recognized but had never truly understood. It was the same emotion that had filled the girl years ago when they had finally found the men who had killed Lord Jem and Lady Kit and they had killed them in turn.

The reaction of the wildcats to Charlen's death was instantaneous. The cats hesitated in their attacks, stared at Flame for a confused moment, then bounded away into the trees, leaving their fallen brethren behind without a single glance of interest.

Just like cats, she thought with a snort as she quickly and gently cradled Ferez against her chest. *They do not care for anyone but themselves.*

"Flame?"

The dragon hesitated at the tremble in Gemi's voice and swung her head around to stare at her. Tears were already pooling in her eyes, something Flame had not seen in years.

"Will he be all right?"

Flame wished she could confirm that he would be. By the gods, she herself was fighting a thick pain that rose in her chest, pain she had never expected to feel for anyone but Gemi or Shadow. Only the small, reedy breaths rattling through the king's lungs prevented her from releasing the scream that had been building since she saw his back.

"*I do not know,*" she finally crooned.

Before either of her bondmates could say anything more, Flame made certain her grip on the king was secure before she leapt into the air, pumped her wings, and broke through the high canopy once more.

~~*~*

Gemi stared blankly at the hole in the forest canopy for what felt like hours after Flame disappeared, though Shadow assured her it hadn't been that long. The tightness in her chest and the dampness in her eyes was an old familiar feeling, but it had never been one she enjoyed. She had been helpless in her parents' deaths, and she'd lost so many people then. Afterwards, she had promised she would never feel this way again.

Yet, here she sat, tears carving tracks down her face, and that pain heavy and tight within her chest. How had she managed to become so close to the king that this fear for his life was reminiscent of a grief she felt for people that were long gone?

A nudge to her leg finally drew her attention back down to the present. To her surprise, it wasn't Shadow who had nudged her but Last Chance. The mare gazed up at her with a look so familiar that Gemi swallowed and leaned over in the saddle to cup her ear.

"He'll be fine, Last Chance," she murmured, trying to convince herself as much as the pale mare. "Flame and Lakina will make sure of it."

The mare nudged her again and snorted. Despite not knowing exactly what Last Chance was saying, Gemi nodded.

"I know," she murmured. "We've all been there." She buried one hand deeply in Shadow's mane as she buried the other in Last Chance's.

By there, Gemi meant the helplessness of not being able to do anything to prevent the pain of those you loved most. Gemi had felt it when she discovered the death of her parents and everyone she knew. Flame and Shadow had felt it when Gemi was severely injured at the age of ten by the first cruel highwayman they'd met, and both animals had been tied up. Gemi had felt it for the two of them when they had been stolen from her by thieves in Tarsur, and she had been left with no way to find them except through the bond.

"And we still feel it for you when you dwell on things like this," Shadow nickered, nudging Gemi's opposite leg. *"There are some things horses and dragons just can't understand."*

Gemi snorted, a small smile quirking her lips. That was true enough.

But Shadow's words had had their intended effect. Feeling a tad lighter—as much as she could when Ferez's life still wavered—Gemi wiped the tears from her face, pushed down the pain in her chest, and asked Shadow to stop by the Highwayman post on the way back to camp. They would send the men from the post to fetch Charlen's body—as well as those of the dead wildcats—off the highway. It wouldn't do to leave any of them where travelers could easily come across them.

Chapter 23

It seemed to Flame that Charlen's death enhanced the speed of the animal channels. Although it did not take her long to reach Main Highwayman Camp at her fastest speed, Kephin and Lakina were already waiting for her by Lakina's tent. Young Maxwell stood nearby, wringing his hands as he watched the sky, and Flame wondered if the urgency of her message had rushed the words from animal to animal faster than she had thought possible.

Flame landed as quickly and gently as she could over the stretcher that had been laid out. Carefully, she lowered Ferez onto his stomach, lowing mournfully as she once again caught sight of the blood and torn flesh that covered his back side. Stepping out of the way, she watched as two young men carried the stretcher into Lakina's tent, the Mage Healer already leaning over the king's body.

Flame's intense stare was interrupted as Kephin laid a hand on her nose. Shifting her gaze to the black-haired man, the dragon released a soft whine. He nodded.

"I know, Flame."

His voice was solemn, and his eyes shone damply, which startled Flame. Kephin had not known Ferez for very long.

But then, neither have we, she realized with a jolt.

Yet Flame could feel the emotional pain welling up within her human bondmate, and even Shadow was feeling weighed down with grief for the dying king. Flame's own emotions had run the gamut since she first sensed the Animal Magic controlling the wolves.

Now, all she could feel was despair that Ferez was on the verge of death, and she knew it had little to do with his title or his mission.

~~*~*

When the young king was first attacked by the Animal Mage, Life simply stepped closer to him, hoping—and praying to the Fates—that her presence alone would be enough to save the man's life.

Thankfully, Death had decided not to come when the Fates told them whose soul was at risk. They both knew his presence could have made this impossible for Life. If Life succeeded in keeping the young king alive, then she would thank her twin endlessly.

As it was, the white demigoddess feared she would not be able to save the man. When the wildcats attacked, Life silently begged for Peace and her bondmates to hurry. When the dragon did arrive and pulled the wildcat from the young king's back, the dragon just sat there, refusing to carry the man to safety or even attempt to Heal the man herself.

Even as the dragon hissed at the surrounding wildcats, so did Life wish to hiss at the dragon. How could the creature not see that the king was dying right there beneath her vaunted protection? How could the creature fight while a man she was currently thinking of as a friend slipped away towards death?

As it became apparent that the dragon refused to help the young king just yet, Life focused her full attention on the man. She watched blood ooze from the torn flesh of his back, flank, and neck. She watched his face pale nearly to white. She listened to the rattling in his lungs and the slowing beat of his heart.

Most importantly, she watched the silver-blue of his soul flutter against the constraints of his physical body, eager for death. Nothing but these mattered to Life, not even the ghost of Aquila's wings against her back as the Royal Eagle waited to transport souls to the next part of the Cycle.

Just as those lungs took one last, laborious breath and that heartbeat slowed dangerously, Life understood that she had no choice about what to do. Just like two years ago, when men were too stupid to realize that the future of their kingdom was dying, Life would have to take matters into her own hands.

Just like two years ago, the demigoddess shoved her hands into the king's back, gripped his soul just as it began to slip from the physical form that held it, and forced it back into place, keeping it from death and the Royal Eagle's claws.

Immediately, Life felt her energy begin to drain, but the white demigoddess did not care. The king was more important than any of the silent rules that ran the Game. In fact, for reasons Life could not fathom, she knew the death of this one man would be more disastrous than the breaking of all the Game's rules.

"Oh, child, not again."

The words reached Life's ears as if from a distance as the demigoddess felt the strain on her power suddenly ease.

Blinking, she lifted her head to find that she no longer knelt on the dirt road on which the young king had nearly died. Instead, she now knelt next to a cot in a familiar tent, a very familiar Mage Healer leaning over the king's back.

"You have the oddest luck, don't you, Your Majesty?" the old woman sighed.

She soothed her hands over the man's back, seeping her magic into the torn flesh there and, whether she realized it or not, down into his very soul.

Life groaned as the soul stopped fighting her grip and settled where it belonged. Releasing her grasp on the soul was nearly painful, and she tiredly wondered how long she had held on, waiting for the Mage Healer to come along and work her magic.

"Life?" a small voice asked as the oldest demigoddess slipped her hands from the king's back.

Startled, Life jerked her hands up to her chest and stared at Love, who stood at the edge of the tent, a barrier that was hardly visible here on the Spiritual Plane. Life swallowed at the realization that any of her siblings could have witnessed her transgression—it was bad enough that Aquila had witnessed both this and the previous one.

Hoping her pink sister had not noticed what she had done, Life lowered her hands to her lap and nodded to the other demigoddess. "Aye, Love?"

"Will he be all right?" Love stepped closer then hesitated. "You can't let him die, Life," she finally added. "No matter what, you can't let Ferez die!"

Life blinked at the vehemence in her younger sister's voice, startled. The pink demigoddess had always been a passionate spirit, but Life thought it was a little odd that Love would be so insistent that the king survive.

"He is going to be fine, Love," Life murmured, glancing at the king and Mage Healer just to be sure.

The old woman had managed to stop the bleeding. Currently, she was using her magic to fix the damage to his neck and encourage the man's body to reform his skin and regenerate blood more quickly than was natural.

Turning back to her younger sister, Life added, "But why do you care? This is my influence, not yours."

Love bit her lip before nodding sharply, releasing the lip, and standing taller. Life smiled. She would always consider Love her baby sister, but the pink female was the second eldest of the four sisters. She had tens of millennia more experience than even Hope and Fear could boast.

"In this case, Sister, I believe our influences overlap."

Life raised an eyebrow, but the pink demigoddess did not elaborate. However, as the oldest sister considered the last month, she thought she understood what Love meant.

Life and Hope had followed Peace for most of her human life, helping their youngest sister whenever they could. Love had never accompanied them, had never had a reason to, but after Cautzel, she had become a constant companion for Life and Hope in their self-appointed task to assist Peace.

Life eyed her younger sister curiously. "Is such a pairing a good idea? I mean," she added quickly when Love crossed her arms and frowned. "Peace is immortal, and the king..."

Love shook her head as Life trailed off. "You should know we don't always have control over such things, Life." The pink demigoddess leveled a piercing gaze at her sister. "Even you felt the need to save Ferez's life, no matter the cost."

Life was certain her face would have paled if she had been mortal. It seemed none of her hopes and prayers would be answered today.

"You saw?"

Love sighed, came forward, and knelt beside Life. "You can't be ashamed of it, Life. He's important. I know you can feel that, but you can't imagine just how important he is."

Life narrowed her eyes. "What do you mean?"

Love simply shook her head and turned her gaze back to the young king. They remained there for the next few hours as the Mage Healer worked on the king, Life attempting to decipher her sister's words and Love refusing to explain.

~~*~*

That evening, Gemi sat near Cassidi's fire, a bowl of cold stew clenched between her fingers. No one had spoken to her since she'd arrived at the camp, only gripping her shoulders and nodding whenever she met their gazes. She had been thankful for the silence, her mind and body too full of grief to even contemplate the words of others.

As she stared into the fire, her mind kept spinning around the question of whether she could have prevented what had happened to Ferez. She kept going over the events of that morning and of the previous sevenday. Even Flame was snapping and snarling softly, berating herself for not sensing Charlen's presence sooner.

A warmth on her shoulder drew Gemi partially from the downward spiral into which her mind had fallen. She shifted her gaze to the hand on her shoulder and nodded in acknowledgement of the offered comfort.

Instead of pulling away, the hand settled more heavily and squeezed.

Blinking, Gemi lifted her gaze past the hand to the face of its owner. She scrambled to her feet, dropping the bowl in her hands, when she realized Lakina stood behind her, a warm smile spreading her lips.

"How is he?" Gemi gasped, digging her hands into the Healer's arms. "Is he—?"

"He's *fine*, child," Lakina assured, her smile widening as she smoothed her hands down the girl's arms. The panic and grief that had filled Gemi's mind for the last few hours suddenly calmed, and she blinked up at Lakina, surprised.

"You didn't exhaust your magic?"

Lakina chuckled and pulled away from Gemi to accept a bowl from Cassidi, who glanced curiously between the two of them. The Healer waved the woman away and guided Gemi towards her tent.

"Nay, not completely. It helps that I didn't need to depend solely on my magic. Once his life was no longer in danger, I was able to slow down the healing process and use more potions and poultices than magic."

Gemi shook her head, slightly dazed from the magic-induced calm. "But he's truly all right?"

Lakina chuckled again and pulled open the flap of her tent. "Why don't you see for yourself?"

Gemi quickly ducked through the opening then paused to let her eyes adjust to the dimmer lamps within. A murmured "James?" reached her ears just as her eyes focused on the tent's only occupied cot. Ferez was lifting himself up onto his elbows, a grimace crossing his features as he did so.

Gemi rushed forward with a hurried "Don't get up" even as a roar and a whinny broke through the deafening silence that Gemi hadn't even realized had filled the camp. Trying not to press on any of the bandages, Gemi eased Ferez back down onto his stomach and attempted to quiet Shadow and Flame, who were now spreading the word of Ferez's health to any who could understand them.

"You shouldn't strain yourself," she insisted, kneeling near his head and smoothing a hand over his arm. "You're going to need your rest since Lakina's insisted on healing some of your wounds non-magically for now."

Ferez huffed, the corners of his lips tugging upwards. "Is that why my back is still so sore?"

Gemi smiled, glad for the king's attempt at humor. However, the smile felt weak, and she could feel her emotions churning beneath the calm Lakina's magic had induced. "I'm just glad you're all right, Ferez. We were afraid you wouldn't survive."

~~*~*

Ferez frowned. He hadn't thought he would survive either, but there was a remoteness in James' voice that seemed odd. He had thought they had become closer than would warrant such a tone.

"And the other Highwaymen are glad you're well, too. You can hear some of them cheering if you listen."

Ferez nodded. He could hear the cheers coming from outside the Healer's tent, and he could still hear the roars and whinnies that he recognized from Flame, Shadow, and Last Chance. The warmth that filled his chest at the confirmation of his new friendships was tempered by the doubt that the distant tone in James' voice had formed.

"I should let you rest, I guess," James suddenly said. Ferez glanced up, surprised, to find the boy already turning back to the tent's entrance. "I'll check on you later and…"

James paused at the tent's entrance, glanced back at Ferez, then nodded and turned away again.

"I'm glad you're all right." Then the boy was gone, and Ferez stared at the rustling flap, confused.

Lakina hummed, drawing his gaze up to her. She smiled down at him and patted his arm. "You can truly count yourself among James' closest friends, young man."

Ferez frowned. Had she seen something he hadn't?

"Are you certain? He seemed a bit…distant." Ferez shifted where he lay and bit his lip. There had been a whine in his tone that he hadn't expected.

Lakina's gaze softened, and she squeezed his arm. "That would be my fault, I'm afraid. James was a bit…overwhelmed when I went to fetch him, so I calmed him down so he wouldn't overexcite you. I can assure you that James cares a great deal for you." Ferez opened his mouth, but

237

Lakina shook her head and added, "And I don't think it has as much to do with your title as you might fear."

Ferez snapped his mouth shut and buried his face into the pillow beneath him. Was he that easy to read? But then, he had always been afraid of people only befriending him because of his title. It was the reason he'd created his Kanti persona when he was younger. Perhaps Lakina understood that.

He felt Lakina pat his arm again before she pulled away. "However, James is correct about the rest. If you stick to his normal schedule, you two will be leaving in four days. I would like you to remain in here until then. Now, sleep."

Ferez nodded and shifted again in an attempt to get comfortable. He didn't bother arguing with the Healer. That steely, no-nonsense tone that he had begun to associate with her had crept into her voice on those last few words, and he didn't wish to incur Old Iron's wrath.

~~*~*

30 Early Autumn, 224

"Where is this young man I See capturing the hearts of everyone he meets?"

The question drifted through the thick fabric of Lakina's tent and drew Ferez from a midday doze. Three days after the attack, Lakina had stayed true to her word. He was still restricted to her tent and had little more to do than sleep.

Laughter drew his thoughts back to the sounds coming through the tent's walls. His lips quirked as he recognized the laughter as James'.

"And good day to you, too, Mama Caler."

"Don't try to change the subject, James," scolded a woman's voice, laughter easing the harsh words. As Ferez sat up and rubbed the sleep from his eyes, he realized it was her voice that had awakened him in the first place. "I want to see him. It's important."

Ferez blinked at the amount of emphasis the woman placed on the final word.

James chuckled. "I wasn't trying to change the subject, Mama Caler. If you'd let me continue, I'd answer your question."

"Well?" the woman asked, her voice rippling with amusement. "Are you going to take me to him, or shall I look for him myself?" As she spoke, her voice grew louder, and Ferez realized she was coming closer to Lakina's tent.

"Oh, I'm taking you to him," James answered, still chuckling. "He's in Lakina's tent." As he spoke, the flap of the tent opened. Ferez watched as James motioned for someone to enter the tent before him.

The woman who ducked through the entrance looked to be nearly as old as Lakina, though she left her silvering brown hair loose over her shoulders. Her brown eyes blinked a few times once James let the flap close before she peered at Ferez and smiled.

"Ah! There's the king that claims a place among his people."

Ferez startled at the words and gaped at the woman. He was thankful to note that she had lowered her voice; it wasn't as wont to carry as it had been.

"I-I'm sorry, Ma'am," Ferez stuttered once he found his voice. "I think you must have me confused wit' some'un else."

To the king's surprise, James chuckled and shook his head. "Don't worry, Ferez. This here is Mama Caler, the most well-known Seer in all Kensy."

The Seer's smile softened, and she gave a small curtsey before seating herself neatly on the cot in front of Ferez. "I've Seen through many the young king who would travel his country as one of his people, but only one future has ever shown me that you and the king are one."

Ferez shifted on his cot, uncomfortable with even one more person recognizing who he was. "And whose future is that?"

The soft smile lighting her face with a wisdom that only Seers held quickly grew to a grin.

"Young James', of course," she exclaimed with an excitement Ferez thought was better suited to a woman much younger than she appeared to be. "Only he knows your secret and guides you on your journey."

Ferez frowned. "Lakina knows as well."

James laughed as he sat down beside Ferez. "Aye, but Lakina has never allowed Mama Caler to See her future. She insists that there's no need for such things since she has seen more than Mama Caler has."

The Seer giggled and nodded. "Aye, and I defer to her seniority, however little of it there may be."

Ferez blinked and glanced between his two visitors. They spoke as though their words were an old joke. "Er…did you wish to see me for any particular reason, Mama Caler?"

The old woman nodded and turned back to Ferez with that small, soft smile. Holding her hands out in front of her, she murmured, "I wish to See your future, if you will let me, Ferez Katani, King of Evon."

Taken aback by the woman's sudden formality, Ferez glanced at James, but the boy seemed to have expected the request and simply nodded to Ferez when their gazes locked.

Swallowing, Ferez murmured, "I give you my permission to See my future," and laid his hands in hers.

Immediately, Mama Caler's eyes lost focus, and Ferez had the sudden, strange feeling that she was staring through him now. She remained like that for several minutes, blinking slowly, and Ferez shifted under that odd gaze.

Just as Ferez was contemplating looking away from the woman—Seers had always made him uncomfortable—Mama Caler released his hands and blinked rapidly. After frowning at Ferez for a moment, she held one hand out to James and whispered, "May I, James?"

Ferez swallowed. What had she Seen in his future that she needed to see the other boy's, as well?

~~*~*

Gemi hesitated. She didn't know why Mama Caler wanted to See her future as well when she had seen it so many times before, but she didn't think the reason could be good.

"Please," Mama Caler murmured, meeting Gemi's eyes with a solemnity that the girl was unaccustomed to seeing in the older woman. Nodding slowly, Gemi reached out and grasped the Seer's hand.

Mama Caler's eyes fluttered shut, and she tightly gripped Gemi's hand. That in itself was unusual since the Seer always kept her grip gentle. Gemi glanced at Ferez and found the man staring wide-eyed at Mama Caler.

"Oh, dear," the Seer sighed, dragging Gemi's attention away from the king.

"Mama Caler?" she whispered. "What's wrong?"

The Seer blinked open her eyes. "The Fates seem...unsure of how to weave the future."

"Is that bad?" Ferez asked. There was a hope in his words that made Gemi's lips twitch.

"Well," Mama Caler replied slowly, "I'd say nay if the alternate futures they showed me were both...positive."

"But...?" Gemi added when the Seer didn't seem inclined to continue.

Mama Caler sighed. "But the Fates have never shown me two such disparate futures." She glanced between Gemi and Ferez then added, "One depicting the very peace you've been seeking, James, and one depicting utter chaos."

Gemi stilled. Ever since she'd first met Mama Caler at the age of ten— the Seer had told her that she was at her Naming Ceremony, but Gemi didn't think that actually counted—the Seer had been predicting the peace for which Gemi had been hoping, had in fact told her that she was the key to it. But now she said that future was uncertain?

"How is that possible?"

Mama Caler sighed. "As my mother told me—and her mother told her—the Fates can predict the decisions of all mortals. If there is indecision, it doesn't come from the Mortal Realm."

"What does that mean?" Ferez asked, his brows drawing down over his eyes.

"I assume," Gemi interrupted before Mama Caler could, "it means that something immortal has decided to interfere?"

"Not necessarily something immortal as much as something not restricted to our physical world."

"Something not restricted..." muttered Ferez. "Oh!"

Gemi glanced at the king sharply. "What?"

Ferez met her gaze evenly, no longer as wide-eyed as he'd been. "I don't know if it means anything, but, before Charlen had his wildcats attack me, he mentioned that someone had ordered him to kill me."

Gemi frowned. "What makes you think that has anything to do with this?"

"Because he said that the person was more than human and more powerful than any mage." He hesitated a moment before adding, "And because the name he mentioned then is one I had heard before."

"What name?" Gemi asked warily, thinking of the tapestries she had seen in Tearmann.

"Markos." Gemi blinked and stared at Ferez curiously. The king shrugged. "Before Charlen mentioned it, I heard it from Seyan. Apparently, the young man who sent Seyan after you had claimed that same name."

Gemi shook her head. "I don't recognize the name, but that is a strange coincidence." Turning to the Seer, she asked, "What do you think, Mama Caler?"

The older woman shook her head. "I can't See who it is that threatens the peace of your futures, but I can tell you that Autumn will decide which future will come to be. Of that, the Fates are certain."

Gemi bowed her head and took a deep breath. Through the bond, Flame and Shadow nudged her and reminded her that they would always be there for her. Nothing could destroy their bond.

"*It's still daunting,*" Gemi answered.

A pressure on her back pulled her thoughts back to her surroundings. Lifting her head, she met Ferez's calm gaze.

"Just because there is something threatening the peace we want for Evon, it doesn't mean we can't face it and still succeed."

Gemi stared. "We…?"

"*He agreed to travel with us for the full season,*" Flame interrupted. "*Perhaps he considers us as much friends as we consider him, and he will not leave us to this fate.*"

As if in answer to Flame's words, Ferez said, "I won't leave you to face whatever threatens our future alone. Besides," he added, a grin tugging at his lips, "Charlen proved that it's after me as much as it's after you."

"I believe that is true enough," Mama Caler said, startling Gemi. The Seer stood and straightened her skirt. "Now, I think I'll get going and leave the two of you to discuss how you'll handle what I've Seen."

"You won't stay for dinner, Mama Caler?" Gemi asked.

"I'll grab a bowl from Cassidi on my way out." The Seer then said her farewells and left the tent.

Silence followed her exit before Gemi finally turned back to Ferez and whispered, "Are you sure you still want to travel with me? You could travel back to Caypan through Cautzel. You don't have to risk your life for me."

Ferez shook his head. "I already pointed out that this Markos, whoever he is, is apparently after me as much as he is you. And I won't let a friend face this challenge alone."

Gemi lowered her gaze again, but this time it was not because she was overwhelmed by the challenge of the months ahead, but because she wanted to hide her suddenly burning cheeks.

"Thank you," she murmured. A squeeze on her shoulder was Ferez's only answer.

Chapter 24

Last Chance for Hope and Freedom nickered wearily as her master finally guided her off the highway. The soft light of the forest day had long faded to the darkness of night, and the mare could barely make out the deer path she was following. Even the stallion in front of her was invisible in the darkness, only his quiet nickers and the rustle of his passage assuring the mare he was still there.

Last Chance kept her head low, her exhaustion and the darkness threatening to make her stumble and lose her way. Long days hadn't been rare during the war, but even then she had never been forced to travel from dawn to beyond dusk with only a single meal halfway through the day.

A light pressure on her nose alerted her that they had reached their destination for the night, despite the darkness that hid the differences in their surroundings as she staggered to a halt. Only the sudden lack of plants pressing in on her from all directions made her aware that they had stumbled upon a clearing.

A crackling above her, followed by a heavy *whumpf* and a slight shaking of the ground beneath her hooves, alerted Last Chance to the sudden presence of the dragon, and she stepped warily away from the sounds. Above her, her master shifted in the saddle and laid a hand lightly against her shoulder, murmuring soft words in a tone that sounded as tired as she felt.

Suddenly, light overwhelmed the mare's eyes, and she blinked against the glare that seemed to fill the clearing.

Once she could see through the brightness, she found that the dragon was tending a small fire. The stallion—whom Last Chance had been trying to avoid as much as she could when she had to travel with him daily—was easing his way through the trees on the other side of the clearing. Their human companion was approaching Last Chance with a smile and eyes for her master only.

Last Chance snorted softly and lowered her head in search of grass. She didn't understand Ferez's newest friends.

Oh, she understood the reason he traveled with them. It had always hurt him to see his people suffer during the years they'd traveled around Baylin.

But Last Chance couldn't fathom the reason for the human female's deception.

Or how she's managed to convince the entire country she's male. She glanced at the girl, who was now leading Ferez towards the fire. *Her gender seems obvious to me.*

Last Chance didn't even think her old friend of eight years would be too upset if he learned the truth. She thought he liked the girl too much to care.

She snorted again. *He might actually be relieved to learn she's a girl. Then some of those new emotions he's feeling wouldn't seem quite so forbidden.*

Not that the humans cared if males mated with other males. The humans had odd customs like that. It was only her friend's title that would restrict him to finding a lifemate among certain human females.

Last Chance huffed. *Humans are strange creatures indeed.*

"You seem to be keeping yourself entertained."

Startled—she had thought the stallion on the other side of the clearing—the mare tossed her head. She immediately regretted it as exhaustion dragged at her, and she staggered to one side.

"Easy," a soothing voice cooed, and Last Chance felt something solid press along her right side. *"I believe water, food, and sleep would be best, aye?"*

The mare swung her head to the right and found red eyes there, staring at her. She considered refusing the offered assistance, but the fact that she was already using the dragon to keep herself on her hooves had her nickering in reluctant agreement.

When warmth pressed along her left side as well, Last Chance whinnied sharply, jerked her head around, and bit at the stallion's neck. He jerked away from her—which meant she staggered in that direction, but she would rather fall than have him so close to her. His whinnied response was half-pained, half-indignant.

"Quiet, Shadow!" the dragon hissed, reaching her head around in front of Last Chance to address the stallion. *"Leave her be. She is not accustomed to traveling for so long. You cannot expect her deal with your flirting just now."*

"I wasn't—" the stallion began, but something—Last Chance could never be sure what passed between Ferez's new friends—interrupted him. He snorted, tossed his head, and wandered over to an open portion of the clearing to lie down.

"There," the dragon cooed, her voice once again soothing. *"I will help you to the river, and then you can hopefully graze some before sleep claims you."*

Last Chance eyed the stallion warily one last time before turning her attention back to the dragon. The dragon led her to the other side of the clearing and through the trees to a large river that Last Chance had been able to hear but hadn't realized was there.

Last Chance drank her fill and ate as much as she could before sleep came too close. Half leaning on the dragon, she wandered back into the clearing. Under the dragon's persuasion, she settled herself on the ground with her rump towards the fire and let herself slip into a heavy sleep.

~~*~*

Gemi watched curiously as Flame coaxed Last Chance into settling down to sleep. The mare's reaction to Shadow's attempt to help had surprised her, but she knew the stallion loved to press his attentions on every mare he met. Despite Shadow's continued insistence that he hadn't been flirting, Gemi suspected the black stallion had simply pushed Last Chance too far.

"She must be more exhausted than I thought," Ferez murmured from her right, where he leaned against his saddle and bags.

Startled, Gemi turned back to him. She had thought him already asleep after eating the travel rations she had provided.

"Oh?" she asked. She didn't want to press the question since his eyes were closed and his head was nodding towards his chest, but she was curious about what he meant.

Ferez hummed for a moment before jerking his head up and meeting her eyes with his half-closed. "She doesn't usually let others get so close to her."

Gemi frowned and considered the mare's different reaction to her two bondmates. "I thought her reaction was just a result of Shadow's flirting."

Ferez blinked at her slowly before shaking his head. "I don't know about flirting, but I was talking about how close she let Flame get to her." He chuckled tiredly. "Stallions are another story altogether. She holds a special…wariness for them."

Gemi frowned, while Flame crooned softly. A twitch of Shadow's ears was the only sign he gave that he was still listening and that the king had caught his attention.

"How so?" Gemi asked, speaking the question on all three of their minds.

Ferez waved a hand lazily in the air. "When I brought her to the Royal Stables, the stallions there weren't exactly…welcoming." He paused a moment then added, "There were several attacks during the first few months I worked with her. It reached the point where she could never relax around any of the other horses at the stable for fear they would attack her."

By the time Ferez finished speaking, Shadow had his head raised and his ears forward. "*I don't remember that,*" he nickered softly.

"*You did not recognize her, either, did you?*" Flame responded, snorting softly enough not to wake the mare she had curled around.

"Was she not born at the Royal Stables?" Gemi asked Ferez, considering her bondmates' words.

The king offered her a small smile and a shake of his head. "You might have noticed that Last Chance has a very distinctive coat."

"Aye, I'd worried about you traveling anonymously with such a noticeable mount. Clever, rubbing dirt into her coat to darken it."

Ferez nodded, his eyes closing as he did. "The white coat is specific to Pecali. As far as I know, she's the only one of her breed here in Evon."

He paused, a frown tugging at his lips. "Well, perhaps there are some in Tarsur, but I wouldn't know.

"Anyway, I found Last Chance when I was ten on a Pecalini trade ship that had docked in Caypan's harbor for the sevenday." He sighed. "She was gray then, but I couldn't tell her color from the dirt. But the dirt couldn't hide the sores on her legs or the fact that her ribs stood out against her skin, and I begged my father to buy her off the ship, if only so we could save her from such a life."

"Was she raised on that ship?" Flame whined. She nudged the white mare's neck gently with her snout, her desire to comfort the mare pulsing through the bond.

Ferez shrugged when Gemi repeated the question. "Master Ekin—he's the Animal Mage who runs the Royal Stables—he was never able to learn all of Last Chance's history. The one thing he was certain about was that she must have been raised by a powerful Animal Mage for her to resist Animal Magic as well as she does."

Gemi nodded. Ferez had already told her how he'd survived as long as he had on the highway that day because of Last Chance's ability to deceive Charlen.

"Finding her like that," she murmured, "it must have taken a lot of work to get her to trust you."

"Aye, but it was worth it." The king opened his eyes and focused his gaze on the mare. "I wouldn't trade her for any other mount in Evon."

Gemi felt her lips twitch into a smile. That was a feeling she understood well, no matter that her own companions were connected to her more permanently than Last Chance was to Ferez.

"So sentimental," Shadow nickered softly, but his thoughts churned against Gemi's mind, and she knew he was considering everything Ferez had said.

Suddenly, Ferez jerked upright, and Gemi stifled a chuckle as he blinked and looked around. "I think it's time for sleep," Gemi said in order to keep from laughing. She helped Ferez unroll his bedroll, and the king was asleep in minutes.

~~*~*

Ferez woke suddenly to something wet dripping onto his face. Wrinkling his nose, he batted at the air above him in the hopes of knocking away whatever was dripping on him. When his hand slid into and caught on something fibrous, a gasp reached his ears, and he opened his eyes.

He blinked when he realized that James was leaning over him, his long, wet hair caught around Ferez's fingers. The boy grimaced as he touched Ferez's hand and helped him untangle from the black strands.

"I didn't mean to startle you," James said once he could lean back on his heels and run a hand through his hair. "I only meant to wake you."

"By dripping water on me?" Ferez asked, sitting up.

James ducked his head and wrung the long strands of his hair, squeezing excess water onto the ground beside the king's bedroll.

"Sorry, I hadn't thought about that."

Ferez watched as James continued to comb his fingers through his hair and squeeze out excess water. "Why do you keep your hair so long?" he suddenly asked, thinking of the boy's expression when Ferez had only accidentally caught it. "Surely, in all of the battles you've fought, someone has used it as leverage in combat."

James rolled his eyes, and the king was certain he wasn't the first to ask the question. "Rarely, actually. Most people don't think to use it in the middle of a fight, probably because they aren't trained to."

"But it has happened?" Ferez pressed.

James sighed and nodded. "A couple times, aye."

When the boy didn't elaborate, Ferez added, "So, why do you keep it long?"

James glanced at him, surprise widening his eyes. "I—"

He frowned, his eyes darting to the side, where Ferez could see Flame tending the fire. The dragon crooned softly, and the boy's cheeks reddened.

Ferez raised his brows, wondering what reason the boy had to be embarrassed. James briefly met Ferez's eyes again before shrugging and ducking his head.

"My mother had long, black hair."

The boy didn't elaborate, and his hands began to toy with the loose strands of his hair as he waited for Ferez to say something. The king didn't know if James was expecting to be teased, but he didn't find the words humorous or absurd. His own mother, Queen Falen Katani, had died giving birth to him, so he understood the desire to hold onto any connection he could find. At the same time, Ferez had never had the chance to know his mother, so he could only imagine what pain James felt from losing his mother after being raised by her.

"Nothing to be ashamed of," Ferez muttered, patting the boy on the shoulder.

As he climbed to his feet, James lifted his gaze to stare at Ferez, his mouth slightly agape. Ferez ignored the look as he stretched and began to put away his bedroll.

By the time he'd finished gathering his things, James had recovered. Ferez was preparing to saddle Last Chance when the boy pressed something into his hands and propelled him towards one side of the clearing.

"You'd best bathe and change before we head out for the day. We'll be entering Zhulan today, and this could be our last chance to bathe for the next two sevendays. We certainly won't be able to bathe in private."

Ferez blinked down at the pile of cloth James had handed him. Glancing back over his shoulder, he realized the boy was wearing a different set of clothing than he'd become accustomed to seeing on him.

"Why can't I wear my plainclothes?"

James paused, leaning over his saddlebags. Turning his eyes back to Ferez, he straightened and nodded to the cloth in the king's hands. "These are better suited to Zhulan's desert climate. More than that, they'll mark you as a nomad."

Ferez frowned. "Wouldn't it be better to wear plainclothes and blend in?"

The boy smiled and shook his head. "Unlike the other rebellious groups, the ways of the nomads are millennia old. They're proud of their lineage in a way most people don't understand. Most would rather risk persecution than forsake what they are, and one of the reasons I relished becoming a nomad was that absolute refusal to bend to fear."

Ferez stared at James, then huffed and shook his head. "So…the clothes are a necessary part of learning how they live." It was the only justification Ferez could find for why the boy seemed insistent on risking his life again.

James chuckled. "The treatment of nomads in the cities isn't all that bad, Ferez." The king simply raised an eyebrow, unimpressed. "Most people don't attack nomads on sight, and the guards no longer arrest them without some provocation."

"No longer?" Ferez asked, alarmed.

The boy shrugged. "There was a time when guards would arrest a nomad the moment he entered the city, but that was years ago. Now…"

The boy frowned and waved Ferez towards the sound of rushing water. "Go bathe and change. We've already dawdled longer than we should."

That was when Ferez realized that the clearing was no longer depending solely on the fire for light. Instead, a soft light had begun to pierce the high canopy, declaring the sun already risen. Ferez hurried out of the clearing to finish preparing for the day.

He kept the bath short. Despite James' threat that this was most likely the last time they'd be able to bathe for the next two sevendays, the king just couldn't stand the vulnerability of bathing within sight of the Northeast Forest. As soon as he spotted the thick fog that crept over the San River's eastern bank, he hurried his movements and pulled himself from the water as quickly as possible.

However, that speed meant he was faced with the new pile of clothing that much sooner. His worry that they wouldn't fit—James was a bit smaller than him—was apparently baseless. Both the trousers and the tunic—which was softer and lighter-weight than Ferez's own tunic—were loose-fitting. The trousers brushed the tops of Ferez's shoes, and the tunic's sleeves reached just past his wrists. He frowned as he considered how hot he would feel in the long sleeves under the desert sun.

When he realized those thoughts were occupying too much time—here by the river, he could actually see the sun creeping above the Northeast

Forest—Ferez finally turned his attention to the remaining articles of cloth.

Immediately, he was puzzled by their purpose.

There were three pieces remaining: a large square of cloth; a long, thin piece of fabric; and a circlet of cordage. The square was simple and unmarked, but the long, thin piece was dyed a deep purple at both ends, several shades darker than James' eyes. Both seemed to be made of the same material as the tunic—a shiny, billowy fabric.

Shaking his head, Ferez decided to question James about the remaining pieces and ambled back towards the clearing.

As he approached the clearing's edge, he called out, "James, I can't..."

A sudden flash of light caught his attention, and he jerked his gaze up and stared.

Within the clearing, James—at least, Ferez assumed it was James since his hair was now hidden from sight—seemed to dance from side to side. His hands moved as quickly as his feet, and Ferez thought the boy was shadowboxing until he noticed the curved blades hovering over James' knuckles.

The king was suddenly reminded of the conversation he'd had with his dukes on the boat ride to the *Pretty Pauper*. Tern had suspected James carried a pair of the blades Kawn had called Scharfmonde—Twin Moon Blades. Since then, Ferez himself had noticed the sheaths James wore at his lower back, but he had never seen the actual blades before now.

He gaped as he watched James practice. The boy's movements were fluid, which didn't surprise him, but he was accustomed to seeing that fluidity with a sword, not with...boxing blades. It was the only comparison Ferez could find, the memory of the one boxing match he and his father had attended several years ago standing out sharply in his mind.

When the boy pivoted on one foot and brought up one hand as though to block while the other sliced low—Ferez winced at the thought of the wound such a blow might cause—James paused as he caught sight of Ferez. Grinning, he swung his hands down and behind his back, quickly sheathing both blades.

"Need help?" he asked even as he wiped his forehead with a corner of the large cloth that now covered his head. The cloth seemed to be held in place by a ring of cordage similar to the one Ferez held. The king also noted the long, thin fabric tied around the boy's waist, the ends dangling in front of one thigh.

"Here," James said and held out one hand.

Ferez jerked his gaze back up to the boy's face and flushed as he handed him his extra pieces. The warmth in his face confused him, but he ignored it in favor of James' explanation.

"This," the boy said, holding up the large square of shimmering cloth, "is a Kopfabdeckung."

"*Kohp-fahb-deh-koong*," Ferez muttered.

James blinked then grinned. "Something like that."

He tugged on his own square cloth. "It's pretty self-explanatory, I think. For nomads, it's a necessity since it protects the head and neck from the constant sunlight. Believe me; you'll be glad to have it."

He tossed the cloth over Ferez's head then and quickly secured it with the circlet of cordage.

"And the belt?" Ferez asked curiously, eyeing James' as the boy finished affixing the Kopfabdeckung to his head.

"It's called a Statusgürtel."

"*Stah-toos-ghewr-tehl.*"

James chuckled and nodded. He wrapped the belt around the king's waist and knotted it above one leg. "It declares a nomad's clan as well as the status of…certain individuals." He chuckled. "And we'll have to get you your own once we reach camp so people don't start getting the wrong idea about who you are."

Ferez frowned. "Why's that?"

The boy grinned. "Most Statusgürtel are only dyed at one end. Double-dyed represents members of the Häuptlinge's family."

"*Hoypt-ling-uh?*"

"Aye, the leader of each clan is called Häuptling. My Vater—my father—is Häuptling Hausef Kanten of the Katze Clan. Hence, my double-dyed Statusgürtel."

Ferez chuckled. "So I'm not the only one in this group who's royal?"

James rolled his eyes and turned to his stallion, who ambled over for the boy to begin saddling. "It's really only a technicality. I sort of saved his eldest son's life, so he adopted me in return."

Ferez blinked. "How did that happen?"

James glanced back at him and waved him towards Last Chance and his own saddle and tack. Once Ferez had begun preparing his mare for travel, the boy answered.

"It's actually how I met the Katze Clan. On my first night in Schönestadt, I overheard a woman begging the innkeeper to help her injured son. He refused, so I offered my own assistance."

The boy tugged on his saddle to make sure it was secure before swinging himself up onto Shadow's back. "It wasn't until we'd arrived at their camp that we learned the two had been the wife and eldest son of their clan's Häuptling. Hausef offered us a place to stay for a while, then adopted me once he'd decided the debt wouldn't be satisfied by anything less."

"But they are your family." Ferez didn't doubt it. Despite the objectivity of his words, there was a tenderness in the boy's voice that the king couldn't mistake.

"Aye," James murmured. After a moment, the boy motioned to Ferez to hurry. "Up with you now," he insisted. "We're already late enough."

Ferez chuckled. He mounted soon enough, and they quickly left the clearing for the Evonese Highway once more.

Part III

Zhulan

Map of Zhulan

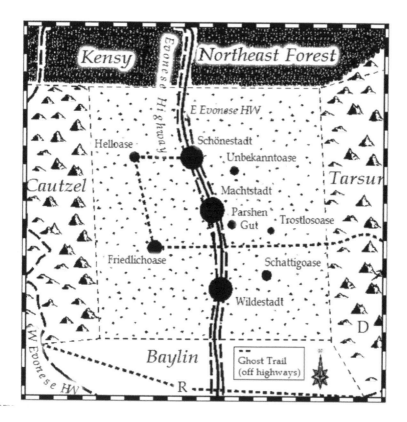

Chapter 25

4 Mid Autumn, 224
Zhulan, Evon

The sun was just brushing the western horizon when Schönestadt came into sight. The city, Zhulan's northernmost, was large and brightly colored. To Ferez, it looked like a giant dragon sprawled across the San River.

Ferez chuckled softly. Before this season, he never would have considered comparing anything to a magical creature, except perhaps the winged horse depicted on Evon's flag.

It seems James has done more for me than simply reawaken my concern for my people.

The king turned to comment on the city's beauty but hesitated when he caught sight of the city's gate.

"Seems a bit crowded for sunset."

James shrugged. "Few people travel between Zhulan and Kensy these days, so most people that actually use the northern gates are farmers and villagers that live along the San River north of the city. They usually travel at night to avoid the heat of the desert sun."

Ferez frowned and asked why they had traveled during the hot day then. James shook his head.

"I always travel by day for the journey to Schönestadt. Once there, we can explore the city for as long as you're willing to remain awake before we claim our beds for the day. We'll leave for Helloase tomorrow night."

Helloase, Ferez knew from James' stories, was the oasis where the boy's clan stayed during this time of the season.

"And you do that every season," Ferez remarked with a shake of his head. It amazed him how strict James was with his routine. After so many years, it was only Ferez and his men who had forced the boy to change anything.

As they came closer to the city, they began to pass other travelers, many of whom cast them odd looks before hurrying past. One man spat on the ground and raised a fist towards them before his companion grabbed his arm, hissing something in his ear as he pulled him away.

Ferez turned in his saddle to watch that particular pair.

"Just ignore them," James muttered. "Things have gotten better in the last few years, but there are still those who hate nomads."

Ferez nodded slowly as he turned back around. After the friendliness he'd seen the Kensians offer the Highwaymen, it was disconcerting to be faced with hatred from Zhulan's citizens when they considered him a nomad.

I once thought the rebellious groups were all the same, but even the provinces' peoples treat each group differently.

Ferez was distracted from such thoughts once they reached Schönestadt's north gate. The horses snorted as they pushed through the crowd, tossing their heads and nudging people aside when they wouldn't move.

They were just coming level with the city walls when a shout on the other side of the gate drew the king's attention. Someone yelled something that Ferez couldn't understand—he thought the harsh words must be Zhulanese—before swinging a fist at a uniformed man. The scuffle that broke out drew the presence of several other uniformed men—the city guards set to watch the gate.

As the crowd around the horses churned and pushed back from the conflict, Ferez tugged on Last Chance's reigns, already planning to help break up the fight. A hand on his arm made him hesitate, and he glanced at James, who shook his head.

"Don't," the boy muttered. "No one will thank you for interfering."

Ferez grimaced, recognizing the truth of James' words. He had become accustomed to helping in any fight he witnessed while in Kensy, but, as long as others thought he was a nomad here in Zhulan, such help would be spurned. Instead, he allowed Last Chance to push through the crush of bodies alongside Shadow until both horses could walk freely through the city streets.

"How do you do it?" Ferez asked once they were free of the crowd. James frowned at him curiously, and he clarified, "Shift your attitude. In Kensy, the fighting's open. You're always involved when there's conflict. But here…"

He gestured back towards the gate, from which shouts could still be heard. He suspected more people had become involved in the fight.

James shrugged. "It's a necessity, is all. I—"

"Verdammte Nomaden!"

The coarse words were accompanied by grasping hands, and Ferez yelped as he was suddenly dragged from the saddle.

~~*~*

"Frenz!" Gemi gasped when her friend disappeared from Last Chance's back. At the same time, the mare swung her head around and, from the following cries, bit at least one of the attackers.

"*James!*" Flame growled as Gemi swung off Shadow's back. "*Be careful! There are two dead nomads hanging from the gallows!*"

An image flashed through the bond, so vivid through the dragon's eyes that Gemi paused to control the sudden urge to gag.

"*Flame!*" Shadow chastised, even as he swung his head around to nip at several people crowding too close. "*Not all of us have stomachs built of iron.*"

Flame's protest sped through the bond, but Gemi shoved the mental awareness of her bondmates to the back of her mind just as she shoved through the crowd to reach Ferez. Several people tried to grab her by the arms or shoulders, but these river-dwellers were obviously neither guards nor boxers, and she easily slipped through their weak grips.

By the time Gemi reached Last Chance's other side, Ferez had regained his feet and was evading the wild swings of a particularly large man. By the stranger's stance, Gemi would have thought him a boxer, but he didn't use the economical jabs that she was accustomed to seeing from a master boxer or a nomad.

She was just reaching for the man's arm in the hopes of pulling his attention away from Ferez when a shrill voice cut through the noise of the crowd.

"Oi, Herren!"

Gemi stilled, as did most of the people surrounding her. The voice had sounded like a child's, and a quick glance around revealed a young boy standing on a stack of crates to one side of the road. The boy raised his hands, from which several small pouches dangled.

Cries exploded from the crowd. When two more children clambered up behind the first, several pouches clutched in each of their hands, the crowd surged forward. Even Ferez's attacker stomped towards the children, one hand clapped to his belt.

As the children disappeared on the other side of the crates—and into an alley on the other side—a tug on Gemi's Statusgürtel had her jerking around and down into a crouch.

She blinked when the move brought her eye-level with a young girl.

"Kommt!" the girl commanded. "Afore they realize they ain' gonna catch th'others an' come back for yeh."

"*Follow her, James!*" Flame growled as the girl disappeared back into the crowd. "*There are guards converging on your position from both the gate and further into the city.*"

Gemi nodded and grabbed Ferez by the wrist. As she pulled him after the girl, Shadow nickered, "*We'll rejoin you later,*" and shoved Last Chance in the opposite direction.

Gemi had already lost sight of the girl, but Flame directed them to an alley across the street. Several turns down the alley, Gemi and Ferez found the girl leaning up against the wall, her gaze sharp.

"Took yeh long 'nough," the girl hissed. She bounced on the balls of her feet and glanced back and forth down the alley. "Thought yeh'd been nabbed by the Wachen."

Vah-kin? Gemi wondered then shook her head. *Guards, of course.*

Normally, by the time she reached Schönestadt, she would have already shifted her thoughts to the mixed language most often spoken here in Zhulan, but traveling with Ferez seemed to be affecting her schedule more than she'd thought.

Forcing her thoughts into Zhulanese, she asked, "If the Nomaden are in so much trouble, why are the Schlingel willing to help us?" The Schlingel, Gemi knew, cared for nichts but gold and their Gangs.

The girl snorted and rolled her eyes. "Wille's got nichts to do wit' it, Violettauge Nomade."

Gemi frowned. It wasn't often she heard that nickname, despite her unmistakable purple eyes.

"Was a request from Dame Clarimonde. The Gang to find yeh on this Tag and send yeh to her has their debts paid in full." The girl's gaze sharpened before she added, "Yeh will tell her Ratte sent yeh?"

Gemi nodded. Dame Clarimonde was a powerful moneylender here in Schönestadt, and Gemi knew the Frau often accepted repayment in tenders other than coin.

"Danke," Gemi replied, but Ratte had already stepped past her and Ferez and was sprinting back towards the highway. Gemi shook her head.

"James?" Ferez spoke then, and Gemi turned to face him. "Eh...*shling-ehl*?"

The word held such confusion that Gemi laughed. She answered the König's question as she led him further away from the highway.

~~*~*

Ferez shook his head as James compared the Schlingel to Caypan's street runners: children who lived on the streets and more often than not became thieves in order to survive. It took some work to understand the boy's words and not just because he was now interjecting Zhulanese into his description. Ferez had known Kawn his entire life, so the mixed language wasn't completely new.

What the king was having difficulty with was actually the boy's current accent. From the moment he'd begun speaking with the girl, Ratte, James' voice had changed, becoming deeper and brisker. The sudden change from the Fayralese accent to which Ferez was accustomed was astonishing.

There's still so much I don't know about him, Ferez realized as they stepped around lazing animals and piles of refuse and ducked under clotheslines. *I wonder if he changes so much for every province.*

A hand on his chest halted his steps, and he glanced at James curiously. The boy nodded further down the alley. Peering through the growing darkness, Ferez made out a door guarded by two hounds and a small pack of rats. It was such an unlikely combination that Ferez knew there had to be an Animal Mage within.

"Do you think it's safe to pass them?" he whispered.

"That's Dame Clarimonde's Haus."

Ferez frowned, attempting to place the name. He blinked when he realized that was the name Ratte had mentioned.

"You mean that's the door we want?" When James nodded, Ferez shook his head. "Isn't that dangerous?"

James chuckled. "Hardly. You see the Falken?"

He pointed up, and Ferez lifted his gaze to the edge of the roof above the door to Dame Clarimonde's home. A flock of large birds, their hooked beaks and long talons looking sharp, crowded along the ledge and circled the alley.

Entranced, Ferez nodded.

"Most Tieremagier wouldn't attract such a large number of Falken unless that was their Kräftetier. And the only Tieremagier I know with such a Kräftetier is mein Familie."

Ferez jerked his gaze back down to James. Before he could ask what he meant, James stepped toward the animals. They focused their eyes on him, but none of them moved to attack when he passed them and reached for the door.

With one hand on the handle, James glanced back at Ferez and beckoned.

"Komme, Frenz. They won't—"

He cut off with a grunt as the door was suddenly wrenched open, and he stumbled through the opening. Ferez thought he saw a hand grab James by the neck before the door slammed shut, leaving the king alone in an unknown alley in the dark of night.

~~*~*

Raymond growled as he slammed the stranger back against the closed door. It was bad enough that the Stadt was filled with Feinde at every turn with the Wachen hunting down Nomaden and the river-dwellers openly attacking them. Now it seemed that even Dame Clarimonde's Haus, a Nomade safe haven about which only the Kreis should know, was at risk of being discovered.

Knowing he had to remove the threat before it could harm his charge, Raymond braced a forearm against the stranger's chest and reached for his Scharfmond with the other hand.

"Raymond Schmidt! If you pull your Scharfmond, I swear I'll tell Ulla, don't think I won't!"

The words stilled both Raymond's thoughts and his motions. The voice was familiar, and he pulled back enough to get a look at the person's face in the lamplight.

"James?"

Raymond took a step back to let the boy breathe. "How—"

He was interrupted by a rattling of the door's handle and a hissed "James!" Immediately, James turned and pulled open the door, dragging in another Mann dressed in the clothes of a Nomade. When Raymond caught sight of the double purple of his Statusgürtel, he growled.

"James, who's this?" He knew every Kanten, the Familie that wore the double purple, and this was not one of them.

"A Freund," the boy answered with a frown. For a moment, he peered up at Raymond with narrowed eyes. "What's wrong?" he finally murmured. Glancing around, he added, "And where's Zuk?"

Raymond slammed his eyes shut. He had temporarily forgotten his failure with James' arrival, but now the ache in his chest returned with full force. Tossing his head back towards one corner of the room, he muttered, "The bed."

He kept his eyes closed as James brushed past him, but a gasp had him turning around before he thought about it.

The boy had pulled back the sheet to reveal Zuk, Raymond's best Freund and charge. His hair was sweaty, his face was pale, and the bandages that covered his chest were stained brown. Only the soft rattle of his breath and the slight rise and fall of his chest reassured Raymond that his Freund still lived.

"Oh, Bruder," James whispered and dropped to his knees. For a moment, his hands hovered above the bandaged chest before he pulled them back and raised his gaze to Raymond. "What happened?"

Raymond grimaced and dropped his eyes to the floor. "He insisted on trying to save the two Falken."

"Falken?" James asked. Raymond glanced at the boy and saw him blanch. "You mean the two Nomaden hanging from the gallows?"

Raymond grunted and nodded. "I tried to tell Zuk it was suicide to try to stop the hanging, but..."

He closed his eyes again and swallowed back the bitterness climbing up his throat.

A hand squeezed his, and he opened his eyes to see James staring up at him with wide eyes.

"It's not your fault, Raymond. You can't expect to protect him from his own stubbornness."

The man snorted and felt his lips twitch. He bit them then, afraid he would start laughing and not be able to stop.

Once he felt more in control, he grunted, "Maybe not." He shook his head. "And I don't blame myself. I blame those verdammte Schlangen."

James stilled and narrowed his eyes. "What have the Schlangen done now?"

"They killed Volker and Wilhelm," Raymond spat, aware that James wouldn't know what had occurred in the last few Tage. "They killed them and left Statusgürtel on their bodies. Now, Othman's on a rampage, hunting down all Nomaden in retaliation."

As James groaned and dropped his head into his hands, his companion glanced between them. "Volker an' Wilhelm? You mean the governors o' Machstadt an' Wildestadt?"

Raymond turned and frowned at the stranger. With his accent, the Mann was obviously not even a Zhulanbürger, let alone a Nomade. However, James had vouched for him and even dressed the man in his own Statusgürtel, which meant Raymond should be able to trust him...even if Raymond didn't like placing such trust in an Ausländer.

"Ja, I mean the Gouveneure. Volker and Wilhelm were freundlich towards us Nomaden, and they accepted the renewal of the old alliance when the Erstehäuptling approached them. With them dead..."

"The likelihood that we'll be able to renew the alliance again is almost nonexistent," James sighed. Shaking his head, he added, "I assume that's what the Schlangen were after, too. Anything to hurt the Vereinte Clans, even if the increased hatred includes them as well."

Raymond snorted. "Not that the Gift Clans have ever cared what the river-dwellers think of them."

"Gift Clans?" James' Freund asked.

James shook his head. "He means the Schlange and Skorpion Clans. When they refused to accept mein Vater as Erstehäuptling, they became known collectively as the Gift Clans." Wrinkling his nose, the boy added, "Although, in this case, I prefer to use the Fayralese translation of Poison Clans."

Raymond snickered and began to tease James about mistaking Zhulanese words for Fayralese. He was interrupted by the soft scraping of the room's second door opening.

~~*~*

Ferez turned towards a door he hadn't noticed before and nearly flinched as he met the hard gaze of the woman standing on the threshold. She was tall and thin, with an equally thin face and severe features that made him want to duck his head, though he was sure he hadn't done anything of which he should be ashamed.

"Herr Caffers," she spoke, her voice sharp. "I see you received my message."

James stood and offered the woman a small bow, greater formality than Ferez could remember the boy offering anyone since they had first met.

"Ja, Dame, danke. A Schlingel known as Ratte was insistent that her help would repay her Gang's debt to you."

The woman inclined her head slightly. "She spoke true. I believe the Leben of the Erstehäuptling's Sohn is worth such a payment." More softly, she added, "And I feared you would be arrested if you attempted to take refuge with Arvin as you usually do."

James straightened and frowned at the woman. "What's happened to Arvin?"

"He and the rest of the public Kreis were arrested for conspiring against the Gouverneur." Her nostrils flared. "This Katastrophe has only increased Othman's belief that he is the finest Gouverneur Schönestadt has ever had."

"Is 'e a bad governor?" Ferez asked, concerned.

The tall woman turned her sharp gaze on Ferez, who swallowed. The urge to hide returned as she inspected him.

"And who might you be?"

"Dame," James replied, stepping closer to Ferez. "This is Frenz Kanti, mein Freund." The boy turned to Ferez and added, "Frenz, this is Dame Clarimonde, one of the most powerful moneylenders in Schönestadt."

Ferez nodded and bowed to the severe woman. "Pleasure, Madam."

A sharp nudge to his ribs startled Ferez into straightening. Turning, he found Raymond frowning at him.

"It's Dame," the other man grunted.

"That is quite all right, Herr Schmidt. Herr Kanti is obviously not a Zhulanbürger. We have forgiven Ausländer for worse."

"Dame—" James began, but Dame Clarimonde shook her head before he could continue.

"Now, Herr Caffers, I do not know what Herr Schmidt has told you, but your Bruder needs the attention of an Arztmagier as soon as possible. I would have had mine attend to the young Mann, but Othman commandeered all available Arztmagier when he first learned of the murders of the other Gouverneure."

James nodded and glanced at Raymond. "Your Pferde?" The man shook his head.

"Gone, of course," Raymond grunted. "Zuk insisted on riding them when we tried to stop the hanging. They ran when Zuk was injured and we were nearly captured."

"They ran?" Ferez asked, surprised. He'd understood from James' stories that the nomads were exceptional warriors. He would have expected their horses to rival those of the crown, not run at the first sign of trouble.

Raymond nodded. "They're trained to avoid capture. If they can't remove their masters from trouble, they'll go for help. By now, they should have made it to the Oase and alerted the Erstehäuptling to the situation."

James nodded. "I figured as much. We'll have to travel two Männer to a Pferd then." He glanced to Ferez then. "Do you mind, Frenz? I know I told you that we would explore the Stadt this Nacht."

The king shook his head. He wouldn't be the one to prevent James' brother from reaching a Mage Healer. He just hoped Last Chance agreed.

"I've already greeted your Pferde in the stable, Herr Caffers, if you wish to leave now. I believe mein Tieremagier is having them fed and cleaned as we speak."

"Danke, Dame. Do you have anything we can use to carry Zuk to the stable?"

Dame Clarimonde stepped back from the doorway and spoke sharply to someone who stood beyond it. Whoever it was murmured a response before the sound of hurried footsteps echoed down a hallway.

Several minutes later, two men entered the room carrying a stretcher between them. They were accompanied by a small, harried-looking man, who stepped up beside Dame Clarimonde and began to whisper hurriedly.

They were just getting Zuk settled on the stretcher when Dame Clarimonde suddenly snapped, "How dare they!"

Ferez snapped his head around. The Dame was glaring down at the short man, who dipped his head in a quick nod. "I convinced them to wait at the front doors for you, Dame, but they don't appear to be very patient."

"Dame?" James whispered. "What's wrong?"

The Dame shook her head and motioned towards the small man with one hand. "Tell them, Cort," she demanded.

Cort nodded again. "There are Wachen at the front doors demanding entry. They claim someone informed them of Nomaden taking refuge here."

"So it seems your window for leaving is quickly closing," Dame Clarimonde added. "Hurry to the stables now and hope that they haven't considered surrounding the Haus."

Gripping Cort by the upper arm, she dragged the man from the room. As she left, Ferez heard her hiss, "I will give them a proper tongue-lashing for taking such liberties. Then, I will discover which pathetic, little Wurm is handing out secrets of the Kreis, and I will have his head for this."

"*Kryse?*" Ferez asked James as they followed the two men carrying Zuk out of the room. He had heard the word earlier, but it seemed to carry more significance than he had attributed it.

The boy nodded, his eyes never leaving his brother's body. "The Kreis is made up of those river-dwellers who are freundlich to Nomaden. Some, like Arvin, who I usually stay with, are part of the public Kreis. They don't hide their involvement with the Clans from the rest of the Stadt."

James finally turned his gaze to Ferez, his expression grim. "But Dame Clarimonde is part of the private Kreis, those who provide their aid in secret. If the Wachen know she's hiding Nomaden, then there's a traitor among the Kreis."

"And they'll regret their betrayal once Dame Clarimonde learns who they are," Raymond growled.

Remembering the urge to hide that Dame Clarimonde's gaze had evoked in him, Ferez nodded. He didn't doubt the Dame's abilities in that regard.

~~*~*

Gemi was impressed by the efficient commotion that filled the Dame's stable when they arrived. Shadow and Last Chance waited in the open area between stalls, two stable hands checking the straps on their saddles and bridles. Several other Männer were putting away grooming supplies and feed buckets, while another, whom Shadow identified as the Tieremagier, stood in front of the Pferde and quietly gave orders.

As the Männer carrying Zuk set the stretcher down, Shadow nudged the Tieremagier and tossed his head. "*We need to leave,*" he nickered.

The Tieremagier nickered in reply then turned and offered Gemi and the others a small bow.

"Herr Caffers, Herr Shadow has informed me of the urgency of the situation. Both Pferde have received food, water, and grooming. They should be prepared for the Nacht's journey."

"Danke," Gemi answered. Turning to the Männer who had carried the stretcher, she indicated the Pferde. "Get him up on Shadow's back. And be careful!" she added as they bent to the task.

"Don't worry, Drache Krieger," one of the Männer soothed. "He's not the first injured Nomade we've dealt with."

Gemi nodded and watched as Zuk was lifted onto Shadow's back and tied into place.

Once her Bruder was secured, she turned to his protector. "Raymond—"

"*I'll take him,*" Shadow interrupted.

Gemi turned and stared at the stallion. Shadow had never before volunteered to carry someone without Gemi being able to ride with him.

He dipped his head. "*I'm sure Raymond would prefer to keep Zuk close. And...*"

He hesitated, one ear flicking towards the mare. When he continued, his tone was softer.

"*Last Chance doesn't know Raymond. I doubt she'd be comfortable with a stranger riding behind her master for several hours.*"

Gemi felt her jaw slacken. "*Are you being considerate of a mare?*"

"*James!*" Flame growled, her presence suddenly heavy against Gemi's Geist. "*You must leave now!*"

An image of Dame Clarimonde's front door passed through the Dracheband. Two Wachen restrained the struggling Dame, while several others shoved past Cort and into the Haus.

"*The stable doors?*" Gemi asked, blinking away the image.

"*The guards are entering only through the front doors, but you know it will not take them long to reach the stable through the house.*"

Nodding, Gemi turned back to Raymond, who was watching her with raised brows.

"Take Shadow. He can follow Flame's direction out of the Stadt. I'll ride with Frenz just in case we become separated."

"*Convenient,*" Shadow snorted as the three humans mounted. "*Did I even need to volunteer?*"

"*Now is not the time, Shadow!*" Flame snapped. "*You must leave—before the guards just down the street come into view of the stable.*"

"*All right, all right,*" the stallion nickered before trotting through the now open stable doors.

Chapter 26

Flame Tongue drifted closer to the ground as Shadow and Last Chance galloped west, away from the city walls. It had been tricky navigating the two horses through the city streets without incident. The city guards were out in full force, no doubt seeking nomads, and the setting of the sun had not lessened their determination.

Neither had it significantly reduced the city's crowds. With the desert climate, a Zhulanbürger, either river-dweller or nomad, was as likely to be active during the night as he was during the day.

So it was that, despite the horses' initial speed to avoid the guards, the trek out of the city had been slow. It had taken nearly an hour for Flame to guide them to a hole in the city's western wall that remained unguarded.

Flame growled as she circled lazily. That lost hour would cost them dearly come sunrise. With two riders each, the horses would not travel quickly enough to arrive at Helloase before the sun became too hot.

"*James,*" Flame mindspoke as the horses began to slow. When Gemi indicated she was listening, the dragon explained her worry. "*I can fly ahead with you and Zuk instead, and we can return later to finish the journey with the others, if you wish.*"

Gemi shared the idea with the others, who quickly agreed to Flame's suggestion. When Gemi asked for Flame to land, the dragon crooned and descended.

Once she had landed, Zuk was carefully transferred from Shadow's back to hers. As soon as he was secured with rope, Gemi swung up into place behind him.

"*Let's go,*" Gemi mindspoke.

The dragon launched herself into the dark sky and propelled herself west. Helloase was due west of Schönestadt, nearly a full night's journey for a horse.

However, Flame no longer had to worry about keeping pace with a horse. Trilling, she stretched her wings to their fullest and flew hard.

She had traveled about the distance a horse would have covered in an hour when reluctant pleasure began to seep through the dragonbond.

Pressing part of her attention through the bond, the dragon crooned when she realized that Gemi had her head lifted high, one hand pressed against her Kopfabdeckung to prevent it from flying off. The smile that played on the girl's lips was reminiscent of less stressful times, and Flame pushed herself harder, unwilling to deny her bondmate, or herself, the joy of the flight.

Flame's wings were just beginning to burn from the extra strain when the light of several campfires caught her eye. Drawing Gemi's attention towards the ground, Flame reached out with her magic, seeking the familiar mind of one of the clan's Mindspeakers.

"*Isa!*" she called down as her magic brushed the woman's.

There was a brief pause, confusion stirring against Flame's mind before the Mindspeaker's familiar magic pressed back.

"*Flame? What's wrong?*"

Flame restrained a snort. Of course Isa would realize something was wrong without the dragon having to say anything. They were a day early.

"*Fetch Mandel, Isa! Zuk is injured!*"

A huff echoed through the mental magic. "*Again?*" But Flame could feel the woman's determination and knew she was already running to find the Mage Healer.

The moment Flame's talons dug into the ground in the middle of the camp, Gemi was swinging off her back, calling for anyone nearby to help. Several men had already begun to pull Zuk down by the time Mandel, Isa, and the rest of Gemi's family appeared.

A hand on Flame's snout distracted the dragon from the activity on her back. Snorting, she nudged the man and offered a greeting.

"*Gute Nacht to you too, Flame,*" the Animal Mage replied. "*It seems I once again owe you Dankpflicht for saving mein Sohn.*"

Flame turned her head to view the man through one eye. "*Do not say such things, Hausef. You are family. There are no debts among family. You taught us that.*"

The man shook his head, but the smile he offered was wide and familiar. "*Perhaps not, but this seems to be a habit I must speak about with Zuk.*"

Flame snorted in agreement as Hausef turned his attention to Gemi.

~~*~*

Gemi was hovering around the Männer pulling Zuk from Flame's back when a hand on her shoulder startled her. Jerking around, she was halfway into a crouch when she realized the hand belonged to Hausef Kanten, her Vater.

"James," he murmured, his smile gentle.

"Vater," she answered, straightening. When the Mann spread his arms, Gemi stepped closer, accepting the hug and burying her face against his shoulder. "Es tut mir leid," she apologized softly.

"Nonsense," Hausef answered, and a hand pressed against the back of her head. "These are stressful times. All of us are a bit jumpy, I think."

Gemi nodded. Despite the pleasure she'd felt during the flight, worry for her Bruder twisted her gut, and her instincts were still sharp from the attack in Schönestadt and everything that had happened in Kensy.

"I—"

"Bruder!"

Suddenly, small hands tugged at her tunic and Statusgürtel. Pulling back from the embrace, Gemi glanced down to find her younger Bruder and Schwester crowding close.

"Are you all right?" her Bruder asked.

Gemi smiled and dropped to her knees, laying a hand against young Lorenz's cheek. "I'm well, Lorenz. I'm just worried about Zuk. That's all."

"Zuk will be all right, Bruder," Ava replied, the hand tightly clutching Gemi's tunic belying her apparent certainty. "Mandel'll take care of him."

"Of course he will," snapped an older voice.

Recognizing her Tante Isa's scratchy tones, Gemi stood to greet her Tante, Mutter, and older Schwester.

"Mandel would be offended to hear we might doubt his Magie."

"*Worry does not necessarily constitute doubt, Isana,*" Flame chastised. With Zuk finally removed from her back, the Drache stretched her wings and hissed as the muscles twinged.

"Flame?" Gemi asked worriedly.

The Drache shook her head. "*Nothing a little rest cannot cure.*"

"Surely Zuk's injuries didn't necessitate you straining yourself, Flame," Hausef added.

The thoughts bounding through the Dracheband from Flame in response to Hausef's worry surprised Gemi into giggling. When her Familie eyed her curiously, she shrugged.

"Flame and I haven't had the chance to enjoy a proper flight in a while. We decided to take advantage of the long journey."

Gemi's older Schwester, Ulla, snorted. "Then you strained yourself for the fun of it?"

"*Like I said—*"

Panik suddenly flooded the Dracheband.

Gasping, Gemi closed her eyes and reached for the source. Angst washed over her like a torrent of cold water when she touched Shadow's Geist, and she reached for Flame's neck without thinking.

"James?"

Gemi paused just long enough to glance back at her Familie, who watched her in confusion.

"We have to go. Shadow—"

"Go," her Vater interrupted, nodding. "Do what you must."

Gemi nodded, swung herself up onto Flame's back, and clung to the Drache's neck as she launched herself up into the sky.

~~*~*

Shadow sighed as Flame took off for Helloase. *Well, this journey's going to be long and tedious.*

Of course, he'd be able to speak with his bondmates at any time during the trip if he wanted. They'd long ago discovered that distance had no effect on the bond.

But it didn't seem right to talk to them when another horse was traveling with him.

And I don't want to risk offending her by talking to her.

Shadow snorted softly. He had never felt this torn concerning a creature other than his bondmates, let alone a mare.

Then again, I've never met a mare quite like her.

Shadow snorted again and tossed his head. *Why did Ferez have to complicate things by telling us her history?*

"Are you all right?"

Shadow nearly stumbled when the soft nicker reached his ears. Ignoring the question from the human on his back, Shadow swung his head to stare at the pale mare through the dim light of the Gemini moons and the stars.

Almost a minute of silence passed before Last Chance huffed.

"It seemed like you might need to talk. Sorry." She shook her head. *"Wait—but—"*

Shadow didn't know what to say. He had expected total silence from her, but now—

A sudden tug on the reins at his nose jerked his attention up to the human on his back. "What's wrong with you, Shadow?" Raymond was saying.

Snorting, the stallion swung his head around and nipped the man's leg, too annoyed to keep the bite gentle.

As his rider yelped, Shadow turned back to Last Chance, surprised to see that she had stopped. When he vaguely heard Ferez ask Raymond if he was all right, he realized it was more the king's idea than the mare's.

Taking advantage of the pause in their journey, Shadow nickered, *"I didn't think you'd want me to talk to you."* When Last Chance turned her head to watch him with one eye, he added, *"You seem to take offense at everything else I do."*

The mare continued to watch him silently before swinging her head around to eye her master. Shadow heard the king chuckle then before he raised his hands and murmured, "Jus' don' take too long, Last Chance. We've a long night ahead of us."

She dipped her head before turning back to Shadow.

"Did you mean it then?"

Shadow tilted his head, unsure what she meant. The mare huffed again.

"When you offered to take both nomads, you mentioned that one of your reasons was that I would not be comfortable with a stranger riding behind my master for hours. Did you really mean that, or were you just saying it?"

Shadow flicked his ears in surprise. *"Of course I meant it. I know what it's like to travel between Schönestadt and Helloase with strangers on my back. At least when I did it, the Animal Mage was semi-conscious, and his companion was female."*

Last Chance snorted and pawed at the ground. *"You say that as though females cannot be a threat."*

Shadow whinnied in surprised amusement. *"Hardly. With bondmates like mine, I'm the last stallion to claim that females cannot fight.*

"But Mina Kanten is neither large nor a warrior. She wouldn't hurt a beetle, and her concern for her son endeared her to James immediately.

"On the other hand, her lifemate's sister, Isa, is a fierce warrior." Shadow tossed his head and nickered. *"She alone could deter an attack on their family."*

Silence followed his assessment of the Kanten females. Shadow shifted his weight, suddenly aware that he could scare the mare away again if he wasn't careful with his words.

Think before you speak, Shadow. It was something he'd never had to worry about before, especially since his bondmates could hear his thoughts as easily as his words.

"You are not like any other stallion I've ever met," Last Chance finally said, interrupting Shadow's thoughts. *"Most think I can't be a warhorse because I'm a mare."*

Shadow swung his head from side to side. *"They're fools for thinking so. I saw you fight in Puretha and on the highway. You can take down a human as easily as any stallion."* After a brief pause, he added more softly, *"And probably better than many of the warhorses I knew when I was younger."*

Last Chance eyed him silently for a little longer before tossing her head and turning west once more. When Shadow nickered questioningly, she replied, *"We might as well continue this conversation while we travel. We do have a long journey ahead, aye?"*

Warily, Shadow agreed and trotted to catch up with her, ignoring the muttered complaints from his rider. Once he was level with her, they settled into a steady clip that they'd be able to continue for several hours and would hopefully let them reach Helloase before sunrise.

"You were raised as a warhorse, aye?" Last Chance asked after they'd traveled for several minutes in silence.

Shadow tossed his head, startled. *"What do you mean?"*

"You fight like a warhorse. I noticed it in Puretha, but I didn't think much of it then. However, you don't act like most warhorses I know."

Shadow snorted. *"Considering some of the horses I met in Calay, I'll take that as a compliment."*

Last Chance nickered amusedly. *"So who trained you?"*

"What makes you think I didn't pick up my training along the way? My bondmates and I have been traveling for years."

The mare snorted. *"The way you fight and react speaks of formal training. Besides,"* she added, *"you mentioned that you knew other warhorses when you were younger."*

Shadow lowered his head and cursed silently. Seven years of hiding his upbringing as a warhorse to protect Gemi's true identity and he'd thrown it all away on a compliment.

"*You can trust me, you know,*" Last Chance nickered softly as Shadow continued to silently berate himself. "*I would no sooner give away the secrets of you and your bondmates than I would give away Frenz's.*"

Shadow hesitated. "*I...do trust you.*"

Shadow wondered if the mare could hear the surprise behind his words.

"*We've only been traveling together for less than a month, but I...we can tell how close you are to Frenz. And we've come to consider him a friend.*"

Shadow swung his head away from the mare and muttered, "*That's why I've tried to stay away from you mostly. I was afraid everyone would think I was just flirting like I usually do. And with your history—*"

The stallion stopped his words short. *Why can't I just keep my mouth shut?*

"*Frenz shared how we met then?*"

The nicker was quiet, but, to Shadow's surprise, he could hear no anger.

"*Aye,*" he answered, turning to eye her warily, "*that first night by the San River.*"

Last Chance bobbed her head but didn't respond for several minutes. When she finally did, it was with a low, nickered "*Thank you.*"

Shadow tossed his head. "*For what?*"

"*For being considerate.*" She turned one eye towards him. "*I'm not used to that from stallions.*"

Shadow snorted. "*Aye, well, to be honest, I'm not used to being considerate of anyone but my bondmates and those we consider family, so I think we're both running new paths here.*"

Last Chance released a sharp whinny of laughter that seemed to startle both their riders. "*I think we'll get along all right now that we know this is new for both of us.*"

Shadow nickered his own amusement.

The two horses continued on in silence until Last Chance asked, "*So...you never did tell me who trained you.*"

Shadow eyed the mare. "*You're not going to let that go, are you?*"

"*Nay, not when your style reminds me of—*"

A sudden yowl split the air then, silencing whatever thoughts she had about his fighting style.

Shadow halted—and not just because Raymond had pulled tightly at his reins. He knew that yowl. He'd heard it several times before, but he had always been in a large group with multiple Animal Mages.

Never had he heard it when the cry actually meant true danger.

~~*~*

A second yowl broke over Last Chance just after the first. Immediately, Shadow nudged her shoulder and whinnied, "*Run! Now!*"

As she tried to move forward, her reins pulled tight and Ferez whispered, "What was that?"

The words brimmed with terror, and Last Chance knew her master was thinking of the attack on the highway.

"Katzen," was the nomad's reply.

"*Desert cats,*" Shadow supplied shortly. "*And it's a mated pair, so we have to run!*"

The stallion then lifted his head behind Last Chance's. She couldn't see what he was doing, but the yelp from her master and the suddenly loosened reins made her think he'd nipped Ferez.

"*Come on!*" he whinnied and nudged her again.

With her head free to move again, Last Chance quickly broke into a gallop. Shadow was instantly beside her, his nose at her shoulder urging her into a canter.

"*No matter what you hear, just keep running!*"

"*Why are we running?*" she snorted as she sped up. "*If there are only two of them, surely we can take them.*"

The fingers tightly gripping her mane and the knees squeezing her sides told her that Ferez would not be willing, or able, to fight, but Last Chance remembered the wildcats from Kensy. Surely two cats would not be too difficult to defeat.

"*Maybe if this were any other province,*" Shadow answered. "*But these cats make the ones in Kensy look like street cats.*" Last Chance twitched her head and stared at the stallion in horror. "*We wouldn't stand a chance against one desert cat, let alone a pair.*"

Last Chance grimly faced forward once more. If they couldn't fight the cats, they would have to outrun them. Bowing her head, she focused on covering as much ground as quickly as possible.

The mare wasn't sure how long they'd been running before another yowl sounded, louder than the first two. Last Chance tossed her head, hoping to glimpse the source, but Shadow nipped her shoulder.

"*Don't look! Just keep running!*"

Last Chance snorted but kept her eyes forward. From the movement on her back, Ferez hadn't been given the same advice.

"They're gaining on us!" Ferez shouted, and the near hysteria in his voice made Last Chance's heart ache. "How are they gaining on us?"

"Because they're Katzen," the nomad shouted back, "and we don't have nomadisch Pferde."

"*What does he mean...?*" Last Chance gasped. "*Because they don't...have nomad horses? What difference...would that make?*"

"*Nomads...train their horses...for speed...and endurance,*" Shadow answered. "*A nomad horse...might be able...to outrun a desert cat...but that...is not a bet...I would make.*"

"*We can't outrun them?*" Last Chanced snorted. "*Then why...are we bothering?*"

"*Because...the longer we put off...a confrontation...the more time...Flame has to get here.*"

Last Chance tossed her head. She didn't reply, but she doubted the dragon would be able to reach them in time. She had left them about an hour before with the desire to return the injured nomad to his camp as quickly as possible. That she might cover that same distance quickly enough to save them seemed impossible.

Still, Last Chance was unwilling to deny the stallion his hope, so she attempted to stretch her legs farther and move them faster, but her muscles already burned. Her sides heaved and her chest hurt, but those thoughts quickly disappeared as she became aware of the soft, steady *whumpf* that was now audible above her heavy breathing.

"*Just keep running!*" Shadow whinnied once more.

In the next instant, he was no longer level with Last Chance.

Fearing the worst, the mare swung her head around to see what had happened. She stumbled to a halt when she saw that Shadow now stood toe-to-toe with a monster.

~~*~*

Shadow's sides heaved as he found himself nearly eye-to-eye with the giant cat.

Giant dead *cat*, he amended, but the thought didn't make him feel much better. He'd never been this close to a desert cat, and, even dead, the creature terrified him.

Trying to tamp down that terror, Shadow examined the cat. It looked to be larger than him, though Shadow didn't know if that was true or just a trick of the way it had landed. It's eyes, still open, stared emptily at Shadow, and the Scharfmond buried deep in its skull was proof that it truly was dead.

When Raymond had given Shadow the signal for the about turn maneuver, the stallion had thought the nomad was crazy. Yet, training overrode instinct, and Shadow had told the mare to keep running before he stopped and used his momentum to turn himself towards the cat.

For a split second, Shadow had been sure he was going to die as he watched the desert cat hurtle towards him. The sudden flash of metal in the moons-light had been little comfort until the cat skidded through the dirt right into Shadow's front legs.

Unwilling to be so close to the beast, Shadow had danced back from the cat's corpse.

"*Shadow?*"

The stallion snorted when he heard the nicker. Swinging his head around, he was startled to realize that Last Chance had stopped and was staring at him. He couldn't tell from this distance and in this light, but he thought horror might fill her eyes.

Suddenly, relief flooded through him, relief that it was him, not her, who carried Raymond. Although she might know the about turn maneuver, she would not have recognized the signal when the nomad gave it.

Shadow had taken a single step towards the mare when a sudden, desperate yowl pierced the air.

Cursing, Shadow swung his head back around, seeking the yellow eyes of the remaining cat. He'd nearly forgotten about the second cat, and fear filled him once more as he realized that the remaining cat was the female mate.

There was a reason that mated pairs were much more dangerous than single cats that had nothing to do with numbers. When one of a mated pair was killed, the surviving mate usually became more desperate, willing to do anything for food and revenge.

That this cat was female only meant that it was larger and, therefore, that much more dangerous.

"Shadow," Last Chance nickered tiredly. *"I don't...think I can...run anymore."*

Shadow huffed and silently agreed. His own head drooped even as he sought the live cat, and his body already felt too heavy now that he stood still. Reaching through the bond, he questioned Flame about her whereabouts, but silence was his only answer, her attention solely devoted to the flight.

Sudden movement on his back—accompanied by Ferez's shouted "What are you doing?"—quickly drew Shadow's attention back to the present. Swinging his head around, he snorted when he realized Raymond was dismounting.

"Idiot! What do you think you're doing?"

He reached for the nomad's shoulder with his teeth, but the man deftly avoided the bite and reached for the dead cat.

"If we have to fight the other Katze, I won't face it with only one Scharfmond."

As Raymond wrapped his hand around the handle of his blade, a yowl cut through the desert night, and Shadow finally spotted the remaining desert cat. It broke into a run and headed straight for the vulnerable nomad.

Whinnying sharply, Shadow threw himself in front of Raymond. Praying that his death wouldn't hurt his bondmates too badly, he turned towards the cat and screamed.

Chapter 27

"Shadow!" Last Chance screamed when the stupid stallion moved to protect the nomad.

Idiot, idiot, idiot!

Suddenly, her voice was drowned out by a sound so deafening she closed her eyes, dropped her head, and flattened her ears back. In the next instant, the ground rocked beneath her hooves, and she was nearly knocked to the ground. Dust filled her nostrils, and she snorted and shook her head in an attempt to dislodge it. Coughing from above informed her that Ferez was in a similar predicament.

Once she could breathe, she opened her eyes and peered through the dust cloud that now surrounded them. She was startled to see that the dragon now crouched in front of Shadow, her wings thrown back and her teeth sunk into what remained of the second cat. A low snarl, which Last Chance had attributed to the cat, actually seemed to come from the dragon.

"Flame! James!" Ferez shouted, and Last Chance finally noticed the girl scrambling down from the dragon's back. As soon as her feet touched the ground, the girl turned and threw her arms around Shadow's neck.

"Don't you ever do that again!" Last Chance heard her gasp before Shadow staggered and dropped to the ground.

~~*~*

When Gemi found herself on the ground, she nearly laughed.

"*Hardly funny,*" Shadow nickered tiredly, but the affection pressing through the Dracheband was enough to make her grin.

"*Maybe not,*" she pressed back through the Band, "*but we're alive.*"

She quickly sobered as she remembered Shadow's last thought before Flame landed on the attacking Katze. Slapping the stallion lightly on the neck, she added, "*And no Dank to you.*"

"Dummkopf."

The insult made Gemi blink, and she tilted her head up to find Raymond and Ferez leaning over her.

"You should know better than to suddenly put so much weight on a Pferd that has just finished running for his Leben."

Gemi sighed as the two Männer helped her up. To her surprise, Last Chance nudged Shadow and helped him climb to his feet. Gemi brushed the stallion's Geist questioningly, but he nudged back with a muttered "*Later*".

"Are they both dead then?" Ferez asked, indicating the Katzen.

His voice held a wariness that worried Gemi. Glancing at his face, she saw that his eyes were wide and his face pale, and she stepped closer to him and laid a hand on his arm.

"Are you all right?"

272

He dipped his head more quickly than she liked and indicated the Katzen once more. "They are dead, right?"

"Ja," she answered, even as Flame crooned an affirmative.

"Can Flame tell if they had cubs?" Raymond added.

Ferez turned his wide-eyed gaze to the Nomade. "Would we have to worry about cubs if they had them?"

Last Chance nickered and nudged Ferez, but the König didn't appear to notice.

"Ja, of course," Raymond answered with a frown. "They are our Clan's Heiligetier. Our sacred animal," he added, most likely mistaking Ferez's sudden stiffening for confusion. "We cannot just leave them to die."

"Flame says they didn't have cubs," Gemi interjected before Ferez could finally react. She wasn't sure what he would say, but she didn't want to risk him insulting her Clan in his Angst.

"And even if they did, none of us are in any condition to go searching for their den."

"Flame—"

"Is just as exhausted as the Pferde," Gemi interrupted the Nomade. "She pushed her wings and her Luftmagie to their limits to travel as quickly as she did."

"*Looft-mah-ghee?*"

Gemi turned and smiled at Ferez. Apparently, she'd managed to pique his curiosity enough for him to ignore his Angst.

"Air magic," she clarified. "One Aspekt of being a Drache is the ability to use Magie to which humans have long lost access."

The König nodded slowly, and Gemi was dankbar to note that his face was returning to its natürlich color.

Squeezing his shoulder, she added, "We should start moving again."

Ferez glanced back towards Last Chance, who was leaning her head against his back. "But the horses are exhausted."

Gemi sighed. "And Flame says we won't be able to reach Helloase before sunrise as it is. The sooner we leave, the sooner we can all have water and rest."

"What about the Katzen?" Raymond asked.

"What abou—?" Ferez began, but Gemi squeezed his shoulder again and shook her head.

"Flame'll take care of them. Kommt!"

She steered Ferez west, waving to Raymond to follow. Shadow huffed and nudged Last Chance, and the two Pferde followed as well.

When they were far enough away from the Katzen, Flame released a breath of Feuer, setting the two creatures ablaze instead of leaving them for the scavengers. Once done, she joined their group as they slowly journeyed west.

~~*~*

The desert sun had long since risen when the six companions finally
arrived at Helloase. Several Nomaden shouted greetings as they passed
through the Lager, but none of them had the energy to respond. Their
sole focus was the spring in the center of the Oase.

As soon as they reached the water's edge, Drache and Pferde collapsed
to the ground and lowered their muzzles into the water. The three
humans were quick to follow, and soon all six had drunk their fill and
were quite ready to fall asleep where they lay.

"James," a voice called out, pulling Gemi from the edge of sleep.
"Bruder."

The voice was accompanied by twittering and the feeling of many little
weights suddenly landing across Gemi's body. Opening her eyes, Gemi
smiled at the little desert sparrows that now covered her, signaling the
arrival of her little Schwester, Ava.

Rolling over and forcing the sparrows to take off and resume their
roosting on her back, Gemi lifted her head to smile weakly at the young
girl.

"Hallo, Ava," she greeted.

Ava giggled and greeted Gemi. "Guten Morgen, James." She quickly
peered around at the six companions, most of who had not responded to
her arrival. Shaking her head, she added, "Although I guess the Morgen
is not that gut for any of you."

Gemi simply shrugged in response as she attempted to suppress a yawn
and failed. "Where's Vater?" she asked once she could focus on her
Schwester once more.

Ava nodded her head in the direction of Mandel's Zelt. "I think he's
sitting with Zuk. I can fetch him if you'd like."

"Ja, bitte. I'll try no' to fall asleep 'til 'e gets 'ere."

Ava giggled again and turned around, running for Mandel's Zelt. On
her way, she passed an older Nomade, who walked towards them at a
leisurely pace. Gemi groaned and dropped her head as she recognized the
Nomade as her older Schwester, Ulla.

I don't think I can handle any of Ulla's taunts right now.

"Guten Morgen, James," Ulla greeted.

Gemi grunted. "Wha's gut about it, exac'ly?"

The young Fräulein sniffed softly. "Well! You're grumpy this
Morgen."

A snort from Gemi's right alerted them that Raymond was still awake.

"James's al'ays grumpy 'round you, Ulla," he grumbled. "No' that I
blame 'im," he added more softly.

A brief pause followed the Mann's assessment before Ulla asked, "Is
that true, James?"

Gemi sighed softly. She loved her Schwester dearly, but the older girl
could be condescending sometimes. She often took advantage of the fact
that she was a Jahr older than Gemi, something that Gemi had lost
patience with after the first Jahreszeit.

Ulla huffed suddenly. "Well," she said, her voice strained. "If you really feel that way…"

The Fräulein trailed off and sniffed.

Gemi jerked her head up at the sound of tears. "Ulla?" she queried.

Her older Schwester hung her head and turned around.

"Aw, Ulla," Gemi repeated, wishing she wasn't so exhausted. Ulla, however, was already walking away, and Gemi knew she would have to talk to the Fräulein as soon as she woke later that Tag.

As she contemplated what she could say to Ulla to assure her Schwester that she didn't hate her, Gemi felt the sparrows on her back suddenly shift. When their twitters rose in volume, she lifted her head once again and watched as Ava and their Vater approached. Both looked worried, and she knew they had passed Ulla.

"Es tut mir leid for upsetting Ulla, Vater," Gemi apologized before either could speak.

Hausef frowned. "What happened?"

"Is my faul', 'm 'fraid," Raymond muttered before Gemi could answer. "Didn' realize she'd take m' words so hard." When Hausef continued to frown at the Mann, he added, "I told her tha' James is al'ays grumpy 'round her."

"An' I said nichts against it, so it's both our faults," Gemi amended.

"I see," Hausef replied slowly. "The two of you will speak with her later to clear up any misunderstandings, ja?"

Gemi nodded, and, since her Vater didn't stare at Raymond overly long, she assumed the other Mann did as well.

"Before then, you two need sleep, as do the rest of your companions."

Gemi watched as her Vater looked over their small group and saw his surprise when his gaze hesitated. Assuming he'd spotted Ferez, she muttered, "Tha's Frenz Kanti."

"A Freund of yours, James?" He continued to stare at the Mann as Gemi gave an affirmative answer. "It seems he's a heavy sleeper."

Blinking, Gemi pushed herself up and looked over Shadow and Raymond, who lay between her and Ferez. Sure enough, the König lay on his back, his head lolling to one side and his face relaxed.

Gemi chuckled tiredly. "He's still not used to our traveling schedule."

Shadow snorted then, lifting his head to join the conversation. *"Not that he's experienced much of our normal traveling schedule."*

Hausef chuckled and finally returned his gaze to Gemi. "Let's get you three into beds before the rest of you fall asleep, shall we? I'll have Mina make up another bed in our Zelt for your Freund here."

Gemi offered her Vater a tired smile. "Danke, Vater. I'd 'oped you'd say that."

"Of course," Hausef answered with a nod. "He is a guest of the Familie."

He then turned and called several others to come help the three humans to their respective Zelte.

~~*~*

Ferez woke slowly, opening his eyes to reveal light-colored fabric hanging high above his head. He didn't remember falling asleep, but he felt much more comfortable than he would have expected for the desert, which was the last thing he remembered clearly.

Maybe arriving at the oasis wasn't a dream then.

A gentle tugging on his tunic finally pulled Ferez's attention away from the drifting fabric that seemed to glow softly. Tucking his chin down, the king was surprised to find a small boy seated on his chest. He'd been so comfortable that he hadn't even noticed the weight of the child, whose hands plucked gently at Ferez's tunic. Despite the gentleness of the boy's touch, his brow was furrowed and his small lips tightly pursed.

"Hello," Ferez murmured curiously. The child lifted his gaze to Ferez's face, but the small hands didn't still their persistent tugging.

"'Allo," the child answered shortly before turning back to his work. Ferez blinked, suddenly unsure of himself. He was accustomed to children who were more excitable.

"Lorenz," a new voice suddenly hissed softly. "Are you in here?"

Turning his head, Ferez spotted another small figure ducking through what appeared to be the tent's entrance.

"Ja, I'm 'ere," the boy on Ferez's chest answered softly. His fingers continued tugging as the new arrival drew closer.

"Herr Kanti," the second child, a girl by the sound of it, chirruped as she knelt by Ferez's head. "You're awake."

As Ferez nodded, the girl turned to Lorenz and tugged on his sleeve. "How many does he have left, Lori?"

The boy wrinkled his nose and stuck his tongue out at the girl, his hands finally stilling.

"Ava," he whined. "You know I 'ate tha' name."

Ava giggled. "True, but I also know that you tend to grow the seeds instead of just removing them if you're left on your own."

"I do not," Lorenz denied, even as his face reddened. He caught Ferez's gaze then and ducked his head, muttering, "Not on people, I don'."

Ferez smiled and gently patted the boy's leg. "I'm sure you don'. Although," he added with a soft chuckle, "I am curious what it is you're talkin' about."

Lorenz nodded quickly and tugged once more on Ferez's tunic before holding one hand out in front of Ferez's face. Blinking, Ferez focused on the hand and realized the boy held a sprouted seed in between two fingers.

"They're Senf seeds," the boy explained. "They get blown 'bou' by the deser' wind, and they grow on anythin' they land on."

"Including Tier and humans," Ava added, plucking the seed from the boy's fingers and burying it in a pot of dirt Ferez hadn't noticed before then. "I've heard it's really painful if they manage to start burrowing into the skin." She plucked the sleeve of her own tunic. "It's one of the reasons we wear long sleeves and Kopfabdeckungen."

"But ever'one needs deseedin' ever' once in a while," Lorenz added as his fingers began tugging at Ferez's tunic once more. "'Specially af'er a long journey."

He twisted and tugged on the fabric for another minute before releasing a cry of triumph and holding his hand out for Ferez to see. This time, the sprouted seed seemed to writhe within the boy's grasp.

"Tha's the las' one. I'd 'ave pulled it sooner, bu' they tend to grow fas'er when I'm around." The boy dropped his gaze and buried the seed in the pot of dirt.

"Because you're a Plant Mage, aye?" Ferez confirmed, remembering what James had told him about his youngest brother. "The only one in your family?"

Lorenz blinked before nodding and smiling shyly. "James told you about me?"

The king chuckled. "About all of you actually." He turned his gaze to the girl at his head. "You're his sister, Ava, then? An Animal Mage?"

The girl dipped her head before tapping Lorenz's leg and motioning him off of Ferez's chest.

"You can meet the others, too, now that Lorenz has finished deseeding you. James and Vati'll want to know you're awake, but introductions will probably have to wait until after James finishes apologizing to Ulla."

"Apologizing?" Ferez asked as he stood and stretched. "What for?" He did note that Ulla was the name of James' older sister, the only Mindspeaker among the siblings.

"For things said and unsaid this Morgen," Lorenz answered. Gripping the man's hand, he pulled him towards the tent's entrance with an unnecessary "Komm."

Ferez chuckled as he stumbled after the two children, one hand reaching up to straighten his Kopfabdeckung. As they left the tent, he nearly halted, startled to see that the sun was already dropping towards the horizon. However, the children didn't give him the chance to pause and, instead, dragged him away from the tent.

They passed several other nomads, all of who were dressed in the same type of outfit that Ferez and James had been wearing since they'd left Kensy. Even the boy's younger siblings, Ferez realized, wore similar outfits.

Lorenz tugged him along until they reached a group of nomads seated near a cold fire pit. As they approached, Ferez recognized James kneeling in front of a young woman about their age.

That must be Ulla, he thought as he watched his friend plead with her.

~~*~*

"Bitte, believe me, Ulla," Gemi begged, all too conscious of the other Nomaden surrounding them. "I didn't mean to hurt your feelings. I was just tired. You know how I get when I'm tired."

277

Ulla sniffled and swiped a hand under her eyes. "Slow to react," she mumbled. "Quick to anger."

Gemi grimaced but nodded. Most who knew her knew that her temper was closer to the surface when she was exhausted, though anger really wasn't what had gotten her into this mess.

"You're mein Schwester, Ulla. I love you. You know that, don't you?"

Ulla sniffled again and lifted her head to meet Gemi's eyes. After a moment, she nodded.

"Ja."

Gemi smiled reassuringly. "Gut."

However, Ulla sniffled again and frowned. "But I still don't get why." Gemi must have looked puzzled because Ulla added, "Raymond's right. You usually are grumpy around me. I want to know why."

Gemi's cheeks heated. She really wished she didn't have to have this conversation in front of so many people, even if they had all known her since she was ten. But the Clan was the Familie, according to Nomade tradition. It was the one thing about Leben as a Nomade that she still found disconcerting.

"Well..." Gemi whispered. She wasn't sure how to explain to Ulla without upsetting her Schwester more than she already was. "You remember the first time we met?"

Ulla sniffed and wiped at one eye. "Of course I do." Her voice still sounded choked up.

Gemi felt her lips twitch as she remembered her first meeting with the Katze Clan. "Do you remember that first conversation we had?"

To Gemi's surprise, Ulla actually blushed. Shifting her gaze from Gemi's, Ulla muttered, "I guess I deserve that."

Gemi blinked at the unexpected reaction. "What?"

Ulla sighed and sat up straighter. "I guess I can be a bit of a Gör, sometimes."

Gemi gaped at her Schwester, as those around them chuckled. "I would never call you that," she finally said.

Ulla's smile was soft. "I know." The smile widened into a grin. "You'd probably prefer 'brat', or something else from your native tongue."

Gemi groaned and dropped her forehead onto Ulla's knees. "And this is why I'm often grumpy around you." When Gemi felt Ulla's hand gently touch the top of her head, she sighed.

"I take it I'm forgiven, then?"

Ulla's chuckle was answer enough, and the Fräulein slid her hand under Gemi's chin to lift it.

"Of course, Bruder," the young Geistmagier whispered. "I forgave you a while ago."

Gemi raised an eyebrow. "And the tears?" She found it hard to believe that Ulla would continue crying after forgiving Gemi.

Ulla grinned. "I just wanted to see if you could actually explain it."
She shrugged. "You got your point across, at least."

Gemi sighed and rolled her head back. She might have responded, but
she caught sight of a double purple Statusgürtel to her side and quickly
swung her head around to the wearer.

She was surprised to find Ferez standing there, frowning as his gaze
moved back and forth between Gemi and Ulla.

Gemi's cheeks burned then. She didn't know which was worse: the
possibility that Ferez had heard her pleading with her Schwester, the
teasing that followed, or the position that Ferez had found her in, with her
head practically in Ulla's lap.

Why should that bother me? she wondered, even as she pulled back
from Ulla. *We're Schwestern. It's not like we're interested in each other
in more than a familial way.*

Despite her self-assurances, the heat in her cheeks didn't abate.

Hoping to distract herself, Gemi scrambled to her feet and grabbed
Ferez's hand. "Let me introduce you to mein Familie."

~~*~*

As Ferez watched James lay his head in Ulla's lap and listened as they
referred to the first time they met, a growl swelled in his chest.

Biting his lip to keep the sound from escaping, Ferez frowned at them.
This level of intimacy hardly seemed appropriate for such a public place,
even if he still had a lot to learn about the nomads and such might be
normal within the clan.

Not to mention, they're siblings, Ferez thought, chastising himself for
the sudden anger.

Even so, the anger didn't ease until James jumped up and grabbed
Ferez by the hand. The king didn't have time to wonder over the odd
emotion as the boy began introducing the small group that surrounded
them.

"Frenz, this is mein Schwester, Ulla."

The young woman to whom James had been apologizing stood and
nodded before brushing off her trousers, though Ferez couldn't see how
they needed that much cleaning.

"Mein Mutter, Mina," James continued, turning to a woman seated to
Ulla's left. While Ferez had been distracted by the conversation, the
boy's younger siblings had joined her, Lorenz in her lap and Ava
kneeling by her feet.

"A pleasure, madam," Ferez greeted, offering her a small bow.

"Hardly necessary, young Mann," Mina dismissed with a wave of one
hand. "A Freund of James is a Freund of the Familie."

"You are too trusting, Mina," someone accused in a rough voice.

Ferez turned towards the speaker and swallowed as he took in the
melted appearance of the left side of the woman's face.

"He is a stranger."

Mina shook her head. "I trust mein Sohn not to bring with him someone who might mean harm to the Clan. Surely you cannot fault James' judgment, Isa?"

The scarred woman must be James' aunt, then, Ferez thought idly as he watched the exchange.

Isa scowled. "It is not his judgment I'm questioning."

"Tante," James interrupted sharply. "Frenz has been traveling with me almost since the beginning of the Jahreszeit. He's a Freund."

"He doesn't mean any harm, Tante," Ava twittered. "He's just curious."

She flashed Ferez a smile that he couldn't help returning.

"Bitte, Freund, forgive mein Schwester."

Ferez glanced to the man who'd spoken and nearly bowed a second time. He didn't need to see the double purple of his Statusgürtel to recognize that he must be the Clan's leader. The way he held himself was too reminiscent of Ferez's own father for the man to be anyone else.

"Frenz," James spoke with a quick squeeze of his hand. "This is mein Vater, Häuptling Hausef Kanten, Erstehäuptling of the Vereinte Clans."

Chapter 28

Once introductions were complete, Hausef led the Familie back to their Zelt. Now that everyone was awake, there was no reason not to finish the conversation there.

As Hausef let the entrance flap drop behind the last of his Kinder, he took a moment to observe his Familie and their guest. Mina settled atop their bedding, Ava and Lorenz leaning against her. Isa took up position beside one of the Zelt's support poles, her crossed arms and sharp frown signs that she still wasn't comfortable with their easy acceptance of the Mann who accompanied his wandering Tochter.

As Gemi and her companion settled near the girl's bedding, Ulla stopped in front of them and planted her fists on her hips.

"What I don't understand," she demanded, "is why, after six Jahre of traveling alone, you suddenly have a human companion that you insist is trustworthy."

"Ulla!"

Hausef frowned at his oldest Tochter. She tended to take after his Schwester in many ways, but he hadn't expected her to be so suspicious of the newcomer.

"But, Vater," Ulla complained with a glance over her shoulder. "Flame says the Mann's Geist is off-limits. I want to know why."

Hausef sighed and rubbed his forehead. *Well, that explains both Ulla and Isa's dislike of the Mann.*

Both were Geistmagier. To be told not to touch the Geist of a stranger with their Magie, even if they had not planned to do so, would only increase their curiosity.

"This is not how we treat guests, Ulla." He shook his head. "Especially ones accompanying Familie."

"But—"

"Nein, Ulla!"

His oldest Tochter pursed her lips and crossed her arms, looking much like the Gör she'd called herself earlier. When Hausef didn't relent, she huffed but nodded and turned to her own bedding.

"Ulla might have approached the subject in the wrong way," Isa's mental voice suddenly drifted through Hausef's Geist, *"but it is curious that Flame would insist the Mann's Geist remain untouched when the circumstances are so unusual. We've never even heard James mention this Mann before this Jahreszeit."*

Hausef turned his frown on his older Schwester.

"Tante," Gemi sighed before Hausef could chastise Isa. "Would you let me explain before you start conjectures throughout the Geisternetz?"

To Hausef's amusement, Isa's cheeks darkened, and she huffed softly. *She must have mindspoken loud enough for Flame to hear.*

He couldn't prevent a smile from spreading his lips.

"Ja, bitte, James," he replied when it became apparent that Isa would not. "I believe all of us—"

He stopped and turned as a rustling indicated that someone else was at the Zelt's entrance. When Zuk stepped through, the entire Familie called out greetings, while the youngest two quickly scrambled over and latched onto their Bruder's Statusgürtel.

"You feelin' bettah, Bruder?" Lorenz asked. Ava twittered the same in the language of the Tiere.

"Ja, much better," Zuk answered with a soft chuckle as he tweaked his youngest siblings' Kopfabdeckungen. He looked to Gemi and added, "I hear I have you to thank for that. Again."

Gemi only shrugged. Hausef knew she believed that the gratitude was unnecessary since Zuk was her Bruder. Then again, she hadn't expected anything in return the first time she'd saved his Leben either. It was simply the girl's nature.

A chuckle drew Hausef's gaze to Gemi's new Freund. The Mann was smiling at Zuk, who stared at the Mann in turn.

It seems we still have introductions to perform.

"I understan' the circumstances were similar as well."

Hausef glanced at Gemi with one brow raised. She was blinking at her Freund, but the smile that soon followed told Hausef that the unexpected words were not actually unwelcome.

She's told him about that?

"I suppose," Zuk muttered. He turned to Hausef and asked, "Who...?"

"Zuk," Gemi answered. "This is Frenz Kanti. He's a Freund of mine."

Herr Kanti snorted and shook his head. "So you keep sayin', James, but I don' think you're family's acceptin' that as your only answer." Gemi frowned at the Mann, and he added, "Don' know why you can' jus' tell 'em I'm a farmer from Kensy. Wha's so wrong wi' that?"

Gemi rolled her eyes. "It's not so much your identity they have questions about but rather the breaking of my habits."

"And it's no' like everyone in Kensy didn' have the same questions. I've learned tha' tha's just one o' the hazards o' travelin' wit' you."

"And just why exactly are you traveling with James, Herr Kanti?" Isa asked.

Hausef rolled his eyes. His Schwester had finally found her opening.

"Please, call me Frenz," the Mann replied with a smile. "I'm travelin' with James to Caypan with a request for the king, so I'll—"

"A request?" Ulla interrupted. "James doesn't..."

She trailed off. Hausef wasn't sure if it was only because of the glares now aimed her way, or if someone had mentally chastised her.

Frenz nudged Gemi. "I think now migh' be a good time for an explanation."

To Hausef's surprise, his wandering Tochter actually chuckled.

"You do realize they'll require a much longer explanation than most of the people you met in Kensy, ja?"

Frenz shrugged. "Better to have it all out now, aye?"

Gemi shook her head before turning her gaze to Hausef. "I met the König earlier this Jahreszeit."

~~*~*

Gasps filled the tent after James' declaration, but they were quickly followed by a barrage of questions.

"How did you manage that?"

"Does he know you're the Drache Krieger?"

"Does he know we support him as König?"

"He didn't hurt you, did he?"

"Is he handsome?"

"What's he like?"

"He's kind, ja?"

The last came from young Lorenz, who now knelt in front of Ferez and James. The boy had his lower lip caught between his teeth, and his eyes were so wide, Ferez feared the child would start crying in a moment.

James reached out and tugged on Lorenz's Kopfabdeckung, offering him a small smile.

"Ja, Lorenz, kinder than you might imagine for a noble." The small boy grinned. "He's also courageous."

James lowered his voice and whispered conspiratorially, "He rowed a small boat past a line of known pirate ships to investigate a scuffle aboard one that was considered extremely dangerous."

Several whistles greeted James' words, and Ferez felt his cheeks heat. Thankfully, no one seemed to notice.

"This sounds like a story you should tell from the beginning, James," Hausef added.

James nodded and began to tell his family how he'd arrived in Calay to find the Tauresian Pirates and the king's men threatening war upon each other. Although Ferez knew most of the story, he found that he was just as enthralled as the rest of the boy's audience.

When James mentioned Mock being upset with him for fighting with a wounded shoulder, Ferez straightened. He never had learned why the boy had still been wounded then but healed when they'd next met. Apparently, he wasn't the only one who was curious as both of the boy's parents questioned him about it.

James ducked his head, his cheeks turning a dull red. "The injury was from a fight in Baylin. One of the rogues caught me in the shoulder with a poisoned blade."

Ferez winced. He didn't have to be told what kind of poison had been on the blade. One of the things Baylin's rebels were known for was their use of anti-magic poison, even if the poison wasn't restricted to that group in particular. The thieves in Caypan also used that specific poison, though more sparingly.

"Flame let you fight with the Gift still in your blood?" Isa asked.

James' cheeks turned darker, and he dropped his chin to his chest.

"I wouldn't let her bite me," he muttered.

Ferez blinked. *How would that have helped?*

Isa sighed. "James—"

"Don't, bitte," the boy pleaded. The shame in his voice startled Ferez, and the king gripped James' shoulder tightly. "I already received a scolding from both Flame and Lakina. I don't need one from you, too. Bitte?"

Isa sighed again, and Hausef asked James to continue his story.

When the boy began to describe Ferez during their first meeting, the king was overwhelmed with the sudden desire to hide. The boy thankfully avoided an actual physical description, but the detail he provided about the power Ferez had exuded when he rebuked Seyan brought heat to his cheeks once more.

To hear James praise him as a worthy king to his family in the next moment only made it worse.

"And what did he do when he learned you were the Drache Krieger?" Hausef asked.

James shook his head. "He didn't find that out until later, and I didn't learn about his reaction until Kensy." More questions broke out then, but James raised his hands.

"Are you going to let me tell this story or not?"

The family fell silent once more, their anticipation palpable. Ferez suddenly wondered if James often told his family stories of his adventures.

He realized that the boy must have as they began asking after specific pirates when he mentioned the attack on the *Silent Raider*. James shook his head.

"Tælen and Voz are all right, though I believe there were several in their crew with major injuries. I understand Dayphin was planning to send his Arztmagier over to the *Raider* to help out."

Isa snorted. "More than likely, he took the Magier over himself."

James shrugged. "Knowing Dayphin and Tælen, that's probably true, but I couldn't tell you either way. I had to leave the port not long after the battle."

He described the Countil meeting then, which Ferez found interesting since it was information he hadn't heard before. When he then mentioned how Seyan had called him out and forced him to run and leave Calay, Ferez grimaced.

I'll have to do something about him once I return to Caypan. I can't risk him threatening our peace after everything we've done.

"And after all that," James said with a finality that made Ferez suspect he had missed a portion of the conversation, "the König simply wanted to talk."

"An' 'e wen' into Kensy wit' only four ot'er nobles?" Lorenz gasped.

When James nodded, the small boy whispered, "Bu' tha's even braver than rowin' to a dangerous pirate ship." His face shone with an awed look that made Ferez shift uncomfortably.

"Or even more foolish," Isa added, but Lorenz didn't seem to hear her. Shaking her head, James' aunt turned to eye Ferez.

"I still don't see how any of that would lead to you gaining a human companion, James."

"Mos'ly circumstances o' chance, actually," Ferez answered, suddenly tired of the woman's suspicion.

He knew they were only worried for James' safety, but surely the boy had long ago proven himself capable of judging whether or not someone meant him harm. And if James wasn't a good enough judge of character, surely Flame was.

"And what circumstances would those be?" Isa asked, her eyes sharp. The look was disconcerting in the half-melted face, but Ferez had faced scarier things—like the knowledge that Lakina had been the Mage Healer to find him after his father's death.

"I'd been lookin' for some'un to travel wit' to Caypan, an' I jus' 'appened to stop in Puretha on the same day James spoke wit' the king an' his nobles. I caught him…"

Ferez glanced at James. "How long did you say it was? An hour or so after they'd left?"

James nodded. "Seine Majestät had expressed an interest in his people and his concern that he had neglected his duty to them. I felt that, since I had met him and discovered that he supported my work, I had no reason not to help someone bring their concerns to the König.

"Granted, of course, that they could keep up with me on the road and in battle."

Ferez glanced at the boy in surprise. Ferez actually remembered the traveling requirement. James had been rather firm about not slowing his pace for Ferez.

However, following him into battle had never been mentioned.

Then again, he probably didn't expect as much fighting as we've seen this Season, and he had already seen me fight.

A low whistle from the tent's entrance drew Ferez's gaze to James' older brother.

"You're a fighter then?" Zuk's tone alerted Ferez that James' words had increased the other man's respect for Ferez.

The king dipped his chin. "My farm's in Kensy. My father and I both fough' to protec' our livelihood durin' the war."

"And he's rather talented with his blade," James added.

A snicker came from James' older sister, earning a glare from the boy before he added, "He's a talented swordsman and tactician. His skills were invaluable in bringing down the rogues once and for all."

That had all of the adults straightening. "Completely?" Isa queried.

James grinned then and nodded. "The rogues won't be causing any more trouble in Kensy."

The woman hummed softly before turning her piercing gaze on Ferez once more. He didn't know what she sought, but, after a moment, she nodded and turned to an empty set of bedding and sat down.

"Well, that is gut news," Hausef finally said. "Hopeful, even." He shook his head then turned to Ferez with a wide smile.

"And I find myself curious what concerns you're taking to the König, if you don't mind me asking. It must be important if James is willing to let you travel with him, even if you are a talented swordsman."

Ferez chuckled, having expected the question some time ago. *Curiosity is something everyone has in common, I think.*

"I'm bringin' 'im a reques' for a new duke for Kensy."

~~*~*

Gemi winced when she saw concern fill the eyes of all her Familie. Even young Lorenz seemed to understand the significance of Ferez's chosen request. He gripped her tunic in one hand.

"But isn't—?"

Gemi quieted her younger Bruder with a quick tug on his Kopfabdeckung and a small shake of her head.

"I had thought there were rumors that the old Herzog's heir still lived," Hausef quickly added, no doubt to cover the boy's slip. "Is that not true?"

For a moment, Ferez eyed Hausef curiously before he shrugged and answered.

"Per'aps, bu' no one knows where she is. An' I'm no' the only one who thinks it's abou' time Kensy had another duke." He offered a rueful smile. "The Highwaymen take care o' people, bu' they canna provide the order a duke could."

Gemi grimaced. The words were reminiscent of Geoff's in Puretha, and Gemi couldn't decide if she would rather curse or thank the Mann for providing Ferez with such rhetoric.

Magie pressed against her Geist then, just hard enough for Gemi to hear a soft, worried "*James?*" from her Tante.

I don't want to discuss it, she projected before shoving her Tante away like she would Flame and Shadow.

At least they know when to not press something.

"Enough!" she snapped when it looked like Isa would say something aloud. The Frau pursed her lips and eyed her narrowly but, thankfully, remained silent.

"James?"

Gemi closed her eyes and sighed. She focused on the pressure of Ferez's hand on her shoulder and imagined its warmth soaking into her muscles until she relaxed under his palm.

"Es tut mir leid," she murmured, opening her eyes to meet his worried gaze. "I guess I'm still ein bisschen tired."

He didn't look convinced, but he nodded and leaned back.

Gemi turned to her Vater. "I want to know more about what's been happening here in Zhulan that has the Städte in such Chaos."

Hausef nodded and motioned to Isa. "Why don't you explain, Isa? You're connected to the Geisternetz, after all."

Her Tante sighed. "It's been almost nine Tage since we learned of Wilhelm's Tod. Volker was found the next Morgen, and those Nomaden still in the Städte have been in hiding ever since."

"Then there are Geistmagier still in the Städte?"

"Ja, in all three. Several were arrested when their safe Häuser were raided by the Wachen, but they are still connected to the Geisternetz."

Ferez leaned forward. "Are there any still free in Schönestadt?" Isa frowned but nodded. "You migh' wanna warn 'em tha' the guards'll probably come lookin' for 'em."

Isa shook her head. "Those that are still free are hiding with the private Kreis. I doubt they have anything to fear."

Gemi glanced at the König as he shook his head. Before he could reply, she gripped his shoulder and gave him a quick warning glance. This wasn't news her Familie should hear from a stranger.

"That's not completely true, Tante. It seems there's a traitor among the Kreis. I believe Dame Clarimonde was arrested just as we left her Haus."

Mina gasped, while Hausef and Isa simply shared a glance.

"Very well," Isa answered, her lips tightening. "I'll share the news over the Geisternetz, whatever Gutes that might do."

Her eyes lost focus then, a sure sign that she was communicating with the other Geistmagier that belonged to the Vereinte Clans.

"The situation is worse than we thought, then," Hausef murmured. "Volker and Wilhelm will surely be replaced with river-dwellers unwilling to speak with Nomaden, let alone renew the alliance. And if Othman is hunting down the private Kreis as well as the public, then it will not be long before the Wachen find all of the Nomaden and our allies in Schönestadt."

He shook his head and sighed. "I do not know how the Vereinte Clans can survive this Katastrophe intact."

Gemi bowed her head. She hated hearing her Vater lose Hoffnung, but the situation was dire, and even she couldn't see a way to fix what the Schlangen had wrought.

Here, Ferez and I just attained victory with the Highwaymen in Kensy, and we arrive in Zhulan to find that the Nomaden face much worse.

Gemi had a brief thought of Mama Caler's words and the speculation Ferez had made about the identity of whatever force threatened the Frieden they both sought. She sighed softly. She didn't think it mattered if it was behind the Katastrophe. They would have to think of a solution either way.

The sound of a throat being cleared broke the silence that had followed Hausef's lamentation. Gemi blinked and looked to Ferez, who watched her expectantly.

"There is somethin' we can do, aye, James?"

Gemi stared at the König. She had the impression she wasn't the only one, but most of her attention was for the Mann.

"What do you mean?" she asked once it became apparent Ferez wouldn't elaborate on his own.

Ferez glanced around the Zelt before turning back to her. "Well, you told me tha' the king wasn' the only one among the nobles you met who seemed amenable to your work."

Gemi frowned. Ja, only Lord Lefas had actually spoken vehemently against Ferez's decision to accept her work, but she wouldn't have said any of the Herzöge, except perhaps Lord Chanser, had been amenable to what she did.

"*He might be referring to Lord Parshen's odd reactions, James,*" Flame muttered lowly. Several memories flashed through the Dracheband, all of them instances in which the Herzog had seemed strangely unreadable.

"*You think...?*"

Gemi had believed the Mann was hiding something at the time. *Could he have been hiding an interest in his people? But then, why didn't he say anything when the König spoke of his desire to help his people?*

A squeeze to her shoulder brought her back to the present. Blinking, she looked around to find everyone watching her. When her gaze met Ferez's, he nodded.

Well, even if Lord Parshen wasn't completely amenable, he seemed much more willing to listen to his König than Lord Lefas did. Surely, we could convince him to help, at the very least.

Satisfied, she turned back to her Vater with a nod.

"Frenz is right. Many of the Herzöge seemed just as willing to accept my work as the König did. We might be able to convince Herzog Parshen to help us find a way out of this Katastrophe."

"You want to request an audience with the Herzog?" Isa asked. "With the trouble we're having, his Soldaten would most likely kill a Nomade on sight. You wouldn't get past the front gate."

Gemi offered her Tante a grin. "You're assuming we'd let the Soldaten see us."

Isa stared at her for a moment before throwing her head back and laughing. "Ach, the benefits of having a Dieb in the Familie."

"James?" Ferez asked, catching Gemi's attention once more. "I'm no' sure I follow."

Gemi's grin softened. "Isa's right that attempting to enter Parshen Gut through the front gate would only get us killed before the Herzog ever realizes we're there. We'll need a way to gain an audience with Lord Parshen without meeting any of his Soldaten first."

"Alrigh', tha' makes sense, but, uh, wha's a '*deeb*'?"

Gemi chuckled. "A Dieb is a thief. We'll need my training from Tarsur in order to avoid the front gate and the Soldaten."

Ferez nodded, frowning slightly. "It won' be too difficult to get in, will it?"

Gemi shook her head. What she had in mind was easy enough, but before she could say so, she was distracted by sounds of protest from Isa and Zuk.

"You talk like you assume you'll be going with James," Zuk growled, speaking over his Tante.

Gemi glanced between Ferez, who looked uncertain how to respond—they both knew he had to go to Parshen Gut with her—and her Bruder. She frowned when her gaze landed on Zuk. He had one hand pressed against his chest, and the pale lines around his mouth worried her.

"Maybe you should sit down, Bruder," she said, ignoring his previous protest for the moment. "You look ready to collapse."

Zuk glared at her. *Pride*, Gemi thought with a roll of her eyes.

Before he could protest against Gemi's worry, Mina stood and stepped forward. Shooing away Ava, who still clung to Zuk's Statusgürtel, she pulled her eldest towards his bedding.

"Mutter," the twenty-one year old complained as she pushed him down into his bedding. The fact that she could, Gemi knew, was sign enough that he wasn't at his strongest.

"James is right, Zuk," Mina said. Her voice was quiet yet firm. "Mandel may have allowed you to leave his Zelt, but you obviously still need rest. Now, lie down, or I will force you to."

The glare she leveled at him was proof that the threat was not an idle one.

Zuk grumbled but swung his legs onto his bedding and lay down. Ava sat down next to him, and Lorenz scrambled to follow. Once he was seated by his Bruder's head, Lorenz's fingers began plucking at the fabric of Zuk's Kopfabdeckung.

Gemi frowned at her little Bruder's busy fingers. Zuk's deseeding would have been taken care of last Nacht after the Healing, or this Morgen at the latest, which meant Lorenz's plucking was more a sign of the seven-year-old's worry than any real need.

With her Kinder settled, Mina turned back to the others, her hands on her hips and her face set in a frown. Gemi swallowed. Many underestimated the Häuptling's Lebensfrau, thinking she was too emotional, but Gemi had had firsthand experience of her Mutter's emotional strength when it came to the welfare of her Familie.

"As for Frenz accompanying James to Parshen Gut," she said, her quiet voice steely, "he's really the only one who should."

When everyone continued to stare at her in surprise, she huffed.

"Honestly. If this is going to be a stealth operation, James should only take one person; someone whom he can trust to guard his back. And we don't know for sure how the Herzog will respond to Nomaden. It would be best if only James and Frenz went."

She shrugged then. "It might even be best if they dress in plainclothes; less likely to get them killed, at the very least."

Hausef hooked his arm around her waist. "When did you become such a tactician, Liebling?" The term of endearment rolled off his tongue with ease.

Mina huffed again, though she relaxed into her Lebenmann's embrace. "I have attended your Kriegrat, Lebenmann," she murmured, naming the council the Nomaden held to discuss battle tactics. "Even a Pazifistin like me can learn something from that."

"Ja, of course, Liebling." Hausef pressed a kiss to Mina's temple, and Mina smiled contentedly. Gemi looked away from them. Even after all these Jahre, such casual displays of affection made her feel as if she were intruding.

As she turned away, her gaze met Ferez's. The König was watching her, rather than her Familie, and her cheeks warm at the realization.

She didn't look away until she heard someone ask for clarification on her plans for accessing Parshen Gut. As she turned back to her Familie, her Geist already moving on to the necessary techniques and information, she didn't miss the private smile Ferez sent her, or the warmth that filled her when she saw it.

Chapter 29

6 Mid Autumn, 224
Parshen Gut
Zhulan, Evon

Kawn Parshen, Herzog of Zhulan, sighed and dropped the reports onto his desk. With a groan, he leaned back in his chair and rolled his head back.

The reports from the Städte had been coming more frequently for the past Siebentag, and with more urgency. The Hauptmänner of Machtstadt and Wildestadt insisted on sending lists of captured Nomaden and their conspirators, possible candidates for the new Gouverneur positions, and questions and suggestions for how to deal with the current situation.

Gouverneur Othman was sending similar reports, though his mentioned the hangings of two Nomaden (for which Kawn very much wanted to yell at Othman) and hinted at an informant who had led his guards to several Nomaden safe Häuser.

Kawn rubbed his hands over his face and groaned again. He was in desperate need of someone with whom he could talk over the situation. He was unwilling to trouble his Familie with this matter, and the two Männer outside of his household who knew of his true views on the Nomaden were now dead.

Kawn sighed mournfully as he thought of the two Gouverneure. The two had shared his interest in the Nomaden and, equally, his fears of the reactions of others should that interest be discovered by the wrong people.

Unlike Kawn, they had been able to do something gut with their desires to help the Nomaden. He had encouraged, albeit quietly, the alliances that his two Freunde had entered into with the Clans.

Still, Kawn knew he had to do something about the reports. It had already been ten Tage since Wilhelm was found in a pool of his own blood in his study, his hands tied with a Statusgürtel, the color of which Kawn had insisted on learning: black.

The next Tag, the people of Machtstadt had awakened to find Volker hanging from the window of his study, a Statusgürtel tied around his neck. The color was, once again, black.

Kawn knew the color of the belts were significant. They signified which Clan claimed the wearer. Kawn also knew, from his talks with Wilhelm and Volker, that the Clan of the black Statusgürtel was not part of the alliance.

It was for that reason alone that Kawn had done nothing yet. He hoped, with dwindling expectations, to be approached by two particular Männer. After Jahre of hiding his true feelings concerning his people, he feared to do what he wanted without some support.

A sound from the corridor outside his study drew Kawn from his thoughts. It was nearly Mitternacht, he knew, but the sound did not worry him. Wachen, servants, and often his errant Kinder roamed the corridors at Nacht, and, most Nächte, someone would come to speak with him before he retired.

He was halfway out of his chair, curious as to who wished to speak with him this Nacht, when the door opened. He froze when it revealed, not a member of his household, but two Männer that he nevertheless recognized very well. As they entered and closed the door, he dropped back down into his chair.

When the two turned to him, one watching him warily, the other smiling warmly, Kawn tilted his head back and laughed.

~~*~*

Gemi frowned at the Herzog and glanced at Ferez. Thankfully, the König looked just as puzzled as she felt. While she had not known how the Herzog would greet them, she had certainly not been expecting laughter.

"Mylord?" Gemi asked. She was uncertain how to proceed as their plan had not accounted for the Herzog's amusement.

Thankfully, the Herzog quieted his laughter and waved them further into the room, which Ferez had insisted was Lord Parshen's study. "I may no' come 'ere of'en, but I do remember tha' Kawn prefers to spend his time in there," the König had whispered as he'd led the way through the manse's corridors.

"Just the two Männer I was hoping to see," the Herzog stated, pulling Gemi abruptly from her thoughts. She blinked at the Mann.

"You were expecting us?"

Gemi wondered if they'd been seen and how they could have been so careless. She dismissed the thought when the Herzog shook his head.

"Nein, nein, I had simply hoped to speak with you two at some point soon. Although," he added with a wry smile, "I must admit I hadn't expected that you would simply walk into my study."

There was a curious light in the Mann's eyes that made Gemi chuckle. While she was hoping to find a new ally in the Herzog, she wasn't about to give away all of her secrets. A glance at Ferez's grinning face let her know that, while the König was remembering their journey into the Haus favorably, he wouldn't give away her secrets either.

"What did you wish to speak with us about?" she asked, ignoring the implied question. The Herzog's responding chuckle and shrug let her know he didn't resent her avoidance.

"Most likely the very situation you are here to discuss, I imagine." He waved them closer, indicating the two chairs in front of his desk. "Kommt, sit. I do not bite."

That drew a chuckle from Ferez, who immediately took one of the seats. Gemi, while still wary, took the other. She wouldn't be here if she didn't trust Ferez's judgment.

"You wished to speak with us about the situation between the Städte and the Nomaden?"

"Ja," the Herzog said with a nod. "Normally, I would speak with Wilhelm or Volker concerning anything related to the Nomaden, but…." He shrugged and sighed. "You can understand my predicament, ja?"

Gemi stared at the Herzog. After a moment, she snapped her jaw shut and shook her head. "Mylord, you—"

"Honestly, it's Kawn," the man interrupted with a frown. "And, ja, I have always considered the Nomaden to be an important part of my people." He turned an apologetic smile to Ferez. "I am afraid I have simply never had the courage to share my views."

Gemi turned to look at Ferez and watched him blink. "I would've listened, you know," Ferez replied. "I listened to each of you equally."

There was a pained undertone to Ferez's words. Gemi reached over and squeezed his forearm in comfort.

Lord Kawn shook his head. "I'm afraid it was never that easy, Eure—" He paused and glanced at the study door with a small frown. "Frenz," he amended, at which Gemi nodded. "Your Vater was never one to show interest in the fringe groups of his people."

~~*~*

Ferez felt his throat tighten at the reminder of his father's reign.

His father had been a good man, a kind man. Ferez would argue with anyone who said otherwise.

But Eden Katani's entire reign had been overshadowed by the war with Fayral. Ferez knew his father had felt that winning the war and securing peace and stability for his kingdom outweighed any thoughts for the "rights" of his people.

Ferez remembered the arguments he'd often had with his father. Some had concerned Ferez's lack of interest in parts of his studies, aye, but the majority actually involved Ferez attempting to change Eden's focus to his people rather than the war.

Ferez grimaced as he realized that his own interest in the welfare of all his peoples had been pushed aside with his father's death and his own crowning. He was dismayed to realize that, even with a peace treaty between Evon and Fayral, it had taken almost two years for him to rediscover that interest.

"I'm no' my father," he whispered even as he reached up to rub his palm against his aching chest, an ache that had nothing to do with his scar.

"Nein, you are not," Kawn answered just as quietly. Ferez glanced up at the man whom he considered to be one of his closest advisors. The duke was watching him with a small, sad smile.

"But, after so many Jahre of holding my tongue around your Vater and the others, I couldn't bring myself to mention my true views on the Nomaden. I feared yours, and the others', reactions."

Ferez sighed. He could understand how Kawn would have found it easier to simply continue holding his tongue, even with a new king.

"Can you tell me now?" he asked, hoping to alleviate the regret dulling Kawn's eyes and filling his own heart.

Kawn smiled. "Ja, I can do that."

He waved a hand around the study, and Ferez's eyes followed its path, taking in the shelves that filled the study's walls. Honestly, Ferez had always considered the room more library than study. The shelves lined the entire length of the walls, running from floor to ceiling, and were filled with so many books and scrolls that Ferez couldn't imagine how one man could ever read them all.

"Mein Familie has always been proud of Zhulan's history. Nearly two thousand Jahre fill these shelves."

James gave a low whistle, and Ferez silently agreed with the assessment. He often forgot that, while Evon was only two and a quarter centuries old, the Zhulanese culture had been around for nearly ten times that, older, even, than Fayral.

James stood and wandered to the shelves, drawing his hand along the wood as he eyed the writings. "How can they be so well preserved if they're so old?"

Kawn chuckled. "The same way the Städte and my own Gut have been preserved: Magie."

James turned from the shelves, a small frown forming on his lips. Ferez bit his lip to keep to himself the comments rising in his mind about how young and endearing the boy's obvious confusion made him look. Now was certainly not the time.

"What kinds of Magier could possibly preserve Tier hide and Pflanze material for so long? I didn't think Tieremagier and Pflanzenmagier were capable of that."

Kawn shrugged and leaned further back in his chair. "Perhaps not by themselves, but, as I understand it, Schutzmagier—Protection Mages," he added when Ferez made a questioning sound, "were instrumental in the preservation of both these writings and the buildings along the river."

James nodded absently, a thoughtful expression chasing away the frown. "That would mean that most of these writings are over a thousand Jahre old. That's when much of the old Magie disappeared."

Kawn nodded. "That's also about the time that the Nomaden began to lose their power."

Ferez stared at the duke. "The nomads?" This was history he didn't know.

Kawn smiled as James returned to his seat. "The Nomaden were the original political power here in Zhulan. Almost two thousand Jahre ago, the different Clans were united under one Mann, Walfred Kanten, the first Erstehäuplting." He glanced at James. "He was also known as the Drache Krieger, as he was bonded to a Wasserdrache, or water drake."

Ferez turned to James and noticed the boy's face had reddened, and he was squirming in his seat.

"Flame's no' the only reason they call you the Drache Krieger, is she?" He could understand why the boy hadn't told him the history behind the name. He already knew that James always downplayed his importance to the rebellious groups. That the nomads had named him after their first Erstehäuptling, the very man who united them in the beginning of their near-millennium-long reign of power, had most likely horrified James.

James gave a small shake of his head, but it was Kawn who answered the question.

"Nein, the Nomaden would not hand out that title to just any Mann bonded to a Drache. After all, there are records of many Nomaden bonded to Drachen since Walfred Kanten, but James is the only Mann besides the first Erstehäuptling to ever be named Drache Krieger.

"As it is, when I first heard there was a new Drache Krieger, I thought it must be a Witz. But then I heard it more and more, and Wilhelm and Volker began to hint that they had spoken with Nomaden. Eventually, I realized that not only was there a new Drache Krieger, but the Clans were once again uniting and rebuilding the old alliances."

Kawn chuckled. "Of course, I had expected the Drache Krieger to be the Erstehäuptling, or, at least, someone from the original Kanten line. I never expected the name to be given to an outsider."

~~*~*

Gemi felt her cheeks burn. She had thought she'd been embarrassed when she was apologizing to Ulla, but that was nothing compared to how she felt at hearing the Herzog's words.

She knew he meant them as praise—his smile and shining eyes made that clear—but she had always questioned Hausef's decision to name her Drache Krieger, especially once she had learned the full history behind the name.

"He's close enough to both," Ferez interjected fiercely. Gemi blinked at her Freund, unsure what warranted such a vehement response. Even she could tell the Herzog was only teasing. "The man who adopted him is Hausef Kanten, the current Erstehäuptling."

Gemi reached out and squeezed Ferez's wrist. When he frowned at her, she patted his arm.

"I don't think he was disdaining the decision."

"Nein, of course not," Lord Kawn replied with a shake of his head. "It is all the more impressive, really, that the Nomaden would respect you enough to give you such a title when you were so young. And it is gut to hear that the Kanten line is still so strong."

Gemi smiled at that, even as Flame nudged her to remind her just why they were here.

"I assume, from something you said earlier, that you know about the alliances Hausef built with Wilhelm and Volker?"

When Lord Kawn nodded, she added, "Unfortunately, those alliances fell apart with their Tode. We only have the Kreis now, and even that is threatened by a traitor."

Lord Kawn seemed to sit up straighter at those words. "A traitor? What is this Kreis?"

Gemi sighed. "The Kreis is made up of those river-dwellers willing to deal with the Nomaden. In Schönestadt, someone has been leading the Wachen to members of the Kreis, even those that are only known to the Kreis and the Nomaden."

Lord Kawn nodded and frowned. "It seems I need to have a word with Othman then."

Gemi glanced at him sharply, and he added, "Othman has been hinting about such an informant. If I can learn from whom he's been receiving his information, I can pass that information on to you."

Gemi blinked, surprised. "You would do that?"

The Herzog nodded. "As I said, the Nomaden are an important part of my people. Besides," he added, baring his teeth as the skin around his eyes tightened, "I also need to have words with Othman concerning the hangings. If the Mann is not careful, I will have to find three new Gouverneure instead of only two."

Gemi traded a look with Ferez, who smiled and nodded slowly. Gemi smiled back as warmth filled her chest. She had come here with the hope of convincing the Herzog to help the Nomaden restore relations with the Städte with whom they'd had alliances before. However, the Mann's words had sounded like a threat towards Othman.

Perhaps Lord Kawn will help us build relations with Schönestadt, as well.

"So you will attempt to find new Gouverneure who are not hostile towards Nomaden?" she asked, attempting to ease the Mann from his obvious anger and back towards their current goal.

The Herzog nodded, relaxing. "It might take a little while. I need to speak with Othman, have the Wachen called off the Nomaden, and have those who have already been captured released. Only then will I be able to worry about new Gouverneure."

Gemi sighed and felt herself relax back into her chair. "Danke." She suddenly wondered if there was anything she'd have to worry about for the next couple of Siebentage if Lord Kawn was already willing to do so much for the Nomaden.

Lord Kawn chuckled. "Don't thank me yet, Drache Krieger." Gemi made a face, and the Mann laughed again. "I still have to try to find people who are freundlich to Nomaden. That is not going to be easy when such opinions are shunned."

"Actually," Ferez spoke up, "couldn' you jus' look to the Kreis?" When both Gemi and Kawn stared at Ferez, the König frowned right back. "Earlier, you implied tha' the Kreis was located in all three cities. Is tha' no' right?"

Gemi nodded slowly, realizing where Ferez was going with this. "The Kreis does span the entire river in Zhulan."

"If I knew who was part of the Kreis…" Kawn trailed off thoughtfully. Suddenly, a grin formed on his lips. "Ah, that might work."

Gemi opened her mouth to ask after his thoughts, but she was interrupted by a sound from the corridor. Turning around and tensing, she watched as the study door creaked open.

~~*~*

Ferez had seen James tense, but the sudden surprise that appeared on his face when the door swung fully open drew a chuckle from the young king. For there, standing in the doorway, one small fist rubbing at her eye, was a girl younger than Lorenz.

"Vati?" the little girl mumbled, one hand still on the door.

Kawn was already on his feet and around the desk. As soon as he reached the door, he scooped up the child, tucked her in against his chest, and closed the door. As he returned to the desk, he ran a large hand against the back of her head.

"What is it, Gretchen?" he murmured. Ferez startled as he realized that the last time he had seen this little girl, she had still been a baby.

"Der Geist won' leave me 'lone, Vati."

The small voice sounded tired and plaintive, and Ferez winced in sympathy for the girl. *And Kawn,* he thought when he saw how stricken the man looked.

"Geist?" James asked, surprise coloring his voice. Ferez glanced at the boy questioningly, but James was intent on the father and daughter.

"Ja," Kawn replied, and the duke suddenly sounded as tired as his daughter. "Last Nacht, Gretchen came to me, unable to sleep. At first, she seemed unable to tell me why."

"Der Geist said I couldn' tell any'un ye'," the little girl murmured. She looked half-asleep already, but her head was tilted like she was listening to someone, and, every once in a while, she would wince.

Kawn swallowed and nodded, patting his youngest softly on the back. "It wasn't until Morgen that she finally told us it was a Geist. It—"

A tiny shake of the girl's head interrupted him, and he glanced down at her. "*Der* Geist, Vati." The girl looked as if she wanted to cry but couldn't. "'E said *Der* Geist."

Kawn sighed and nodded. "Very well, *Der* Geist. It—he," he corrected himself when Gretchen gave another small shake of her head, "hasn't left her alone since last Nacht, and she's been unable to sleep because of it."

He began stroking the girl's hair again. Ferez glanced at James, wondering if there was something they could do, and realized that James had already stood up.

~~*~*

Gemi rounded the desk and knelt beside Kawn. She waited for the Herzog's nod before brushing a hand against Gretchen's cheek.

"Can you see Der Geist, Gretchen?" She kept her voice soft, but the small twitch that the Kind gave showed that she had heard the question. "Or can you only hear him?"

Gretchen whimpered softly and shook her head. She raised a hand slightly then dropped it. It was obvious the girl was exhausted.

"I canna see 'im," she whispered. "But 'is wor's…"

She bit her lip then cried out, burying her head against Kawn's chest. Gemi felt her chest tighten as Kawn stared down at his Tochter, Angst and helplessness evident in his eyes.

"*Flame?*" Gemi reached for her bondmate hopefully. "*Is there anything you can do?*"

Flame rumbled thoughtfully for a moment before answering in the negative.

"*She is not a Mindspeaker with whom I can communicate. Even if she was, I would not be able to protect her. Whatever is afflicting her, I cannot sense it from here.*"

Gemi frowned. "*What could be causing this, then?*"

Flame seemed uncertain. "*I cannot be certain, but I have learned over the years that young humans are more sensitive to powerful magic and spirits than older ones.*"

Gemi nodded. She could remember many times when Kinder seemed to know or understand something that their elders could not. Turning her attention back to the Herzog and his Tochter, she realized with a start that Gretchen was staring at her.

"Gretchen?" she whispered.

The little girl's mouth worked silently for a moment before she blurted out, "Can 'ou 'ear 'im, too?"

The next instant, she winced and pulled herself back into her Vater's chest, though she still faced Gemi. Her eyes gained a faraway look that Gemi recognized from her Tante and Ulla.

Placing a hand on the girl's knee, Gemi said calmly, "Nein, I can't hear him, Gretchen. What is he saying?"

For a moment, Gretchen simply shook her head. After a long stretch of silence, the girl whimpered, "'E says 'e won' leave me 'lone 'til I say 'allo."

Gemi felt a chill run through her. "Say hallo?" she whispered. "To him?" When Gretchen shook her head, Gemi added, "Then who does he want you to say hallo to?"

Gretchen blinked and stared at Gemi once more. Her eyes took on that faraway quality once more, and Gemi wondered if the girl would be able to answer her question. Suddenly, the girl's eyes focused and widened.

"You," she whispered. "'E—" She squirmed in her Vater's arms, and Kawn's grip on her tightened. The Herzog looked terrified, and Gemi couldn't blame him. "'E…'e…"

She whined then said in a rush, "Markos says 'allo, Eirene."

~~*~*

298

War smirked as Peace stiffened. Satisfied, he pulled back from the girl, releasing the hold he'd had on her mind since the night before. Almost immediately, she collapsed in her father's arms.

War chuckled as the duke began to panic. Peace was soon able to assure the man that his daughter was simply sleeping, but it didn't matter. War had accomplished his goal.

"I'm not sure I see the point of that little exercise."

The smirk dropped from his face, and War snarled as he turned on the sudden intruder. *Or not so sudden,* he snapped to himself. The words and the way the pink spirit lounged in the middle of the room was proof enough that she had seen more than he liked.

"Venita!" he spat then paused as he realized that he'd spoken the intruder's ancient name. Shaking his head, he growled "Love" in correction. "What are you doing here?"

It hadn't passed his notice that his pink-haired sister often trailed after Peace these days, even when Life and Hope were absent, but he had hoped she would stay away from her for this, at least.

Unfortunately, Hope wasn't on his side, either.

"Don't you have your own twin to pester?"

The demigoddess waved a hand dismissively, causing him to scowl.

"Hate could use a little free reign for a season or so." She smiled. "What I want to know is why you would bother to influence a five-year-old human for more than a day, only to drop her the moment she…what?"

Her expression twisted thoughtfully. "Gave your message to Peace? And using the ancient names, no less."

War's scowl deepened. "I don't have to explain myself to you, Love."

The demigoddess shrugged gracefully. "Nay, you don't, but I have to wonder: if you want Peace to be able to decipher your meaning, then why don't you just use your common names? Markos and Eirene haven't been used for millennia, dear brother."

After a beat of silence, she added softly, "Neither has Venita, for that matter."

War frowned before forcing himself to relax and shrug. "She wouldn't make the connection if I used our common names. Besides," he added, and his smirk returned. "I've always thought 'Markos' sounded much more intimidating than 'War'."

Love sighed and rolled her eyes, but she did chuckle at the joke.

"Very well, brother. I just hope you know what you are doing."

The demigoddess turned her gaze back to their physically incarnated sister. War was thankful for that as he found himself suddenly staring at Love in surprise. Her voice had sounded so tired on those last words, and her eyes had seemed so old.

Love was always so carefree and loving that he often forgot she was part of the second-oldest pair of demigods. She had seen so much, and he now wondered if she knew something important, something that he had felt he should know, but could never quite recognize.

Scowling, he turned back to his twin, but the thought just wouldn't go away completely.

~~*~*

Even as they said farewell to the Herzog, with promises to keep each other updated, Gemi couldn't put those four words out of her Geist. The message seemed to confirm Ferez's theory that Markos was the name of the powerful force about which Mama Caler had warned them, but Gemi didn't understand the use of the name 'Eirene'.

When Gemi and Ferez reached the San, they were joined by the Pferde and Flame. The companions traveled north along the river toward Machtstadt, each keeping to their own thoughts. As the lights of the Stadt became visible in the distance, the silence was finally broken.

"Wha' do you suppose he meant?" Ferez asked.

"What do you mean?" Gemi asked, surprised by the calmness of the König's voice.

Ferez shrugged. "Tha' name, Eirene; I don' recognize it. But you were obviously the intended recipient of the message."

"Obviously?" Gemi asked, wondering if the König remembered something she had missed.

"Aye, obviously. Even I can recognize tha' 'Der Geist' mus' be a Zhulanese translation of your Baylinese title, The Ghost." Gemi blinked. She hadn't considered that. "But, still, why Eirene?"

Gemi shook her head and sighed. "I don't know. That's what I've been trying to understand. It must be important. Otherwise, why would he bother saying hallo?"

Ferez snorted. "Jus' to scare us, maybe?"

Gemi raised an eyebrow, amused. "You don't sound very scared."

Ferez shrugged. "No more than I already was." When Gemi made a questioning sound, he added, "We already knew somet'in' powerful was threatenin' the peace we wan' for Evon. This just confirms tha' tha' somet'in' does go by the name o' Markos."

Gemi nodded.

"An' givin' us a message in an attempt to scare us seems plausible for…him."

This time, Gemi chuckled. "Ja, but the name seems out of place." She sighed. "It doesn't seem like we have enough information."

"Maybe we can mention it to Hausef." Gemi glanced at her Freund in surprise. The Mann shrugged. "It couldn' hurt, and he migh' be able to help us understand."

Gemi blinked then nodded slowly. "Ja, he might. I hadn't thought of that."

Ferez smiled kindly. "You know, for a boy wit' two bondmates, you seem to spend a lot of time thinkin' like a loner."

Gemi stared at the König. She was further surprised by her bondmates' murmured agreements.

"*He's right,*" nickered Shadow. "*Outside of Flame and me, you never really consider asking others for help.*"

"*And even asking us for help is difficult,*" Flame added softly.

A hand on Gemi's shoulder drew her attention back to Ferez. "You know you're not alone, right?" His silver blue eyes were solemn, and his smile kind. "You have so many people who are willing to help you that it's rather amazing."

With a small shake of his head, he added, "You don't have to depend solely on yourself, especially during this season with the threat Markos poses."

Gemi felt her eyes sting. Blinking, she glanced away, only to meet Flame's warm red gaze.

"*He is right,*" the Drache murmured, echoing Shadow's earlier words. "*There are so many of us on whom you can depend.*" Flame tilted her head thoughtfully, and her glance flicked past Gemi. "*Maybe Frenz can finally help you realize that.*"

For some reason, Gemi felt her cheeks burn. The squeeze of the hand on her shoulder had her glancing back up at the König. He didn't say anything else; he simply smiled. Gemi slowly returned the smile.

Maybe they're right.

She had spent so long thinking she alone had to take care of herself, as well as everyone else. Maybe she could start looking to others for help.

Reaching up, she laid a hand on Ferez's wrist and squeezed in return. His smile broadened.

Chapter 30

As they approached Machtstadt, Ferez remembered a thought he'd had after riding all night from Helloase to the San. Turning to face his relaxed companion, he whispered the boy's name, not eager to break the easy silence.

"Hmm?"

James glanced at him, a small smile playing on his lips. Ferez felt his own smile grow at the boy's happy look.

"I was wonderin' if we migh' be able to spend the night...er, day in one o' the cities."

He almost wished he hadn't brought it up as James' smile disappeared, a small frown replacing it.

"I mean," he added before James could protest, "we're dressed in plainclothes, an' no one would be able to recognize us as nomads, right?"

James seemed surprised by this and glanced down at his own body, blinking. Then he chuckled, relaxing once more.

"Ja, that is true, isn't it? Honestly," he added, still chuckling, "I'm so used to wearing the clothes of the Nomaden while in Zhulan that I forgot."

Ferez grinned. "So we can spend a day in the city afore returnin' to Helloase?"

James smiled at Ferez. "You really want to explore one of the Städte, don't you?"

Ferez felt his cheeks heat as he realized how eager he must have sounded.

"Aye, I do. When I was younger, one o' my favorite thin's was bein' able to explore Caypan under the guise o' Frenz Kanti. No one gave me a second glance; I was jus' another boy."

He shrugged. "It's been so long since I las' wandered the streets of Caypan, and I've never had the chance to explore one o' Zhulan's cities."

James chuckled. "We'll just have to remedy that, then. We'll spend the Tag in Schönestadt."

Ferez frowned. He had assumed that they would spend the day in Machtstadt since James hadn't led them from the road in order to circle the central city like they had on the way to Parshen Gut.

Before he could ask, James added, "But first..." and nodded towards the city.

Ferez turned and realized that they were quickly approaching the city gate. James' nod had most likely been for the pair of guards that stood beside the gate, eyeing their group as they approached. Ferez glanced past James and saw that Flame was nowhere in sight. When the dragon had disappeared, he couldn't say.

As they came level with the guards, the two men stepped forwards, each holding out an arm to stop the horses. Shadow snorted and pawed the ground, and Last Chance nickered unhappily, but both halted.

"Gute Nacht, Reisenden." The guard who spoke smiled and nodded at James.

"Gute Nacht to you, as well, Wachen," James replied. "Is there a problem?"

The second guard grunted and frowned up at the boy. "Little late for travelin', don' you think?"

Ferez frowned. From what James had told him, traveling at night was common enough in Zhulan not to be suspicious. James simply shrugged.

"My companion wanted to visit Schönestadt, and we thought that we'd take advantage of the cool Nacht to travel there."

The first guard hummed softly. "Ein bisschen of bad timin', then?"

Now James frowned, as well. "What do you mean, 'bad timing'?"

The second guard grunted again. "Don' tell me you haven' heard abou' the Tode o' the Gouverneure. Gouverneur Wilhelm died firs', after all."

Ferez wondered if the man thought they were from Wildestadt.

James nodded slowly. "Ja, we've heard, but what does that have to do with us?"

"Ah, don' mind Eward," the first guard replied, stepping aside to let them pass. "He's gained ein bisschen o' paranoia since the Gouverneur died."

Eward scowled and didn't move. "Is not paranoia, Ottokar. I doub' the Nomaden who killed the Gouverneur entered the Stadt dressed as Nomaden. Or durin' the Tag, for that matter," he added and turned his scowl on James.

"Excuse me," Ferez interrupted, keeping his words clear. When the guards turned to him, both looked surprised. "I fear the night travel is my fault."

James glanced at him questioningly, but he ignored the look.

"Oh? How so?" Ottokar asked, his lips twisting in a small smile.

"I'm from Caypan, and I had enough of the desert heat when entering the province. I didn't really want to risk traveling the length of Zhulan in it."

Ferez wasn't sure if it was the lack of Zhulanese words in his speech or simply his accent, but Eward stepped back and nodded.

"Mos' likely not used to the odd hours, either, are you?" he added gruffly.

Ferez chuckled and shook his head. "Nay, not yet."

Ottokar smiled more fully. "You can pass through the Stadt." He glanced at James. "When you leave, jus' let the Wachen at the nort'eas' gate, Irmigard an' Harvey, know that you've already spoken wit' Eward and Ottokar. They'll let you through."

"Ach, and if Wache Irmigard gives you trouble," Eward added, "tell her that her Lebenmann will explain in the Morgen."

303

"Danke," James replied. Ferez echoed him with a quick, "Thank you." They rode into the city. Ferez was surprised to see that the streets still thrummed with activity, despite the late hour. When he mentioned it to James, the boy chuckled.

"Remember how I'd said that we would explore Schönestadt that first Nacht?" Ferez nodded. "There's always something to do in the Städte, and the same is true for the Clans." James offered a smile. "You'll come to understand that once we can stay with the Clan for more than a few hours."

Ferez hummed softly then asked, "Do you s'pose they're questionin' all travelers?"

James shook his head. "Nein, only during the Nacht, most likely. There's too much traffic in and out during the Tag to stop everyone. But there are most likely Wachen on the gates at all times now."

He shook his head. "It's certainly enough to caution any Nomaden still in the Stadt against leaving."

Ferez nodded, remembering Isa Kanten's words. "Is tha' why we're here?"

"Nein," James answered with another shake of his head. He directed Ferez's attention further down the road. One building was particularly well-lit, while voices from within reached their ears, even at this distance.

"I thought we might take care of a little business while we're in the area."

As they approached the inn, Ferez spotted a sign hung above the door. In the lamplight that spilled through the inn's windows and from streetlamps on either side of the building, the words 'Rotvogel Gasthaus' were visible below a red bird with wings spread.

"The Kreis?" Ferez whispered as the horses stopped in front of the inn's door.

"Ja," James confirmed as he swung down from Shadow's back and patted the stallion's neck. "Go ahead and get some water, Shadow," the boy added. "I don't know how long this will take."

Shadow dipped his head, and he nudged Last Chance once Ferez had dismounted, leading her down the street.

The purple-eyed youth led the king into the well-lit inn. As soon as they pushed open the door, their ears were assaulted with loud laughter and music, and yelling seemed common as people attempted to be heard above it all.

James stepped easily into the crowd, and Ferez stayed close, glancing around wide-eyed. It had been years, it seemed, since he was last in such a crowded place without being the center of attention. He grimaced at the thought.

A cry of "James!" pulled Ferez's attention to the inn's bar, where a mountain of a man stood. As soon as James was close enough, the man pulled the boy into a bear hug, and the king wondered briefly if he should worry for his friend's well-being.

As he released James, the mountainous man held the boy out and looked him over.

"Is been a while, James." The man's voice boomed easily over the sounds of the crowd, yet no one nearby seemed to pay heed to his words. "Mus' admit I'm surprised to see you. I wouldn' 'ave thought you'd be stoppin' in now."

James, whose head was tilted far back in order to stare up at the other man, grinned and yelled, "Believe me, I'm just as surprised as you, but I have business to discuss."

The large man nodded. "Well, komm, then. This is no place to be talkin' business."

He waved a hand at a rather petite woman behind the bar, yelling that he would be in a meeting. Then, he gripped James' shoulder and steered him towards the back of the room. Ferez followed, winding his way through the crowd and wondering that others seemed to overlook him so easily these days.

Well, you wanted to blend in, he told himself as he caught the door the large man was beginning to close behind himself.

Ferez was glad to see that James was twisting in the man's grip, hopefully protesting that he wasn't alone, but Ferez couldn't hear him over the din. The large man turned and frowned at Ferez as he seemed to notice the door's sudden resistance.

"Ach," the mountainous man practically growled. "Who're you? Why're you followin' us?"

~~*~*

Gemi huffed, finally managing to remove her shoulder from the large innkeeper's grasp. "*That's* what I've been trying to tell you, Berg. I didn't come alone."

Berg turned to frown at Gemi. "You didn'?" He peered back down at Ferez, his eyes narrowing as he took in the König's features. "'E's not anybody I recognize."

Gemi heard Ferez sigh, despite the noise from the crowded common room, and she offered him a sympathetic smile. It was gut that no one had recognized the König yet, but even she had caught the dismissive tone of Berg's last words.

"You wouldn't," she answered. "He's not exactly a local."

Berg's frown only seemed to intensify at that, but the large Mann held the door open for Ferez. He didn't speak as he led them down the hallway and through another door. As soon as the second door closed, he returned his stare to Gemi.

"Does 'e have anythin' to do wi' the business you wanna discuss, James?" His voice, which had easily been loud enough to be heard above the din of the inn's common room, was thankfully soft in the new room's near-silence. "I doubt I'd 'ave room for 'im if you were 'opin' to stash 'im away for ein bisschen."

Gemi frowned, sidetracked by that piece of information. "How many Nomaden are you currently hiding?"

Berg scratched his beard thoughtfully. "Eight, at the momen'." Gemi gaped. "From what I've 'eard, the others're all filled, as well."

Gemi's jaw worked for a moment before she finally managed to speak. "There's that many Nomaden in the Stadt?"

Tante Isa had said that several Nomaden had been caught in the Stadt, but she hadn't hinted at such a large number. Berg nodded, and Gemi cursed, earning stares from both Ferez and Berg.

"This is worse than I thought."

"E'en worse, actually," Berg replied. Gemi pursed her lips and saw Ferez frown.

"How so?" she asked tightly.

"From las' repor', seven Nomaden've been imprisoned, as have Hariman, Millicent, an' Peppi."

"Peppi?" Gemi asked, shocked. "I can understand Hariman and Millicent. They're part of the public Kreis. But how did Peppi manage to get arrested?"

Berg grunted. "'Ow d'you think? 'E tried to petition 'Auptmann 'Errick for the release o' the Nomaden."

Gemi groaned. "And with everything going on, he would have been arrested on the spot." She rubbed her temples and shook her head. "Well, at least Herrick won't do anything without the Herzog's permission."

Berg growled. "Like tha' means anythin'. Ever'one knows 'Erzog Parshen don' care one wit abou' the Nomaden."

Gemi saw Ferez wince, and she grimaced in turn. Lord Kawn's reputation, which he had cultivated to protect himself against those who shunned the Nomaden, was only going to work against him now.

"Actually," Gemi replied, "that's the business I wish to discuss."

Berg frowned. "What?"

"I've spoken with the Herzog. It turns out that he is of the same mindset as Wilhelm and Volker."

~~*~*

For a moment, Berg simply stared at the Drache Krieger. He had first met the boy five Jahre ago, and he had never heard anything so preposterous come from the boy's mouth. He shook his head.

"Nein, I don' believe it. There's no way the 'Erzog could care for the Nomaden, not after all these Jahre."

The Drache Krieger's companion winced, and Berg frowned at the Mann. He didn't know this Mann, and, for that, he didn't trust him. James' sigh pulled Berg's attention back to him.

"I understand how you feel, Berg, but Kawn Parshen spent his entire Leben as Herzog dealing with the König and the other Herzöge. Surely you remember what König Eden was like?"

306

Berg frowned. He did remember how the old König had been. The Mann had been so intent on winning the Krieg mit Fayral that he had given not a single thought to the rest of his people. In fact, Berg thought the Mann had often taken advantage of his people in that sense. He nodded to James.

"Then you have to see that if Kawn Parshen ever attempted to stand up for the Nomaden under König Eden, he would have been laughed at, at best."

And imprisoned or killed, at worst, Berg finished the Drache Krieger's statement silently.

He growled. Ja, he did understand that. It was true that the Herzöge were said to be the König's advisors, but that was the new König, Ferez. Under Eden's rule, the Herzöge were more like the König's Generäle, leading his Männer into battle and executing his orders.

However...

"König Eden died two Jahre ago. What's the 'Erzog's excuse since König Ferez was crowned?"

Again, James' companion flinched, and, again, Berg frowned at the Mann. Before he could question the stranger, James shrugged, regaining Berg's attention.

"Until recently, no one knew the König's true views on the fringe groups of his people."

"True views?" Berg asked, suspicious.

James smiled. "It turns out that he cares very much for all of his people and is very interested in the united rebellious groups."

Berg silently mulled that news over. "Does 'e know that you're the Drache Krieger?"

James' smile widened, and he nodded. "Ja, he and the four Herzöge do."

Berg blinked. "All of 'em?" When James nodded, Berg sighed. "All right, now I'm curious."

James laughed, and his companion chuckled softly. James proceeded to explain how he had met the König and his Herzöge in Port Calay, Cautzel. "When I spoke with them, only the Herzog of Baylin seemed adverse to the König's interest in his peoples."

Berg shook his head. "And you've spoken wit' 'Erzog Parshen since then?"

He found James' story difficult to believe, but Berg trusted the Drache Krieger. If the boy said it was true...

"Ja," James answered with a nod. "He was quite eager to take up the alliance."

Berg nodded. "So what's this mean for the Städte, exactly?"

"It means that Herzog Parshen is going to look to the Kreis for the new Gouverneure, possibly all three."

For a moment, Berg simply stared at the boy. "Is this a Witz?"

James shook his head, his smile softening. "Nein, it's not. That's the real reason for my visit. I wanted to let the Kreis know that the Herzog would be looking for the new Gouverneure among their number."

Berg grunted but didn't answer. If what James said was true, then the ultimate goals of the Kreis could finally reach fruition. It would no longer be dangerous to accept and help the Nomaden. He and the others who were private members of the Kreis could publicly show their support for the Nomaden without fear of losing their businesses or the Respekt of the other citizens.

Berg suddenly chuckled as another thought crossed his Geist. "You do know who the best Kandidat for Gouverneur is 'ere in Machtstadt, don't you?"

James chuckled. "Ja, Peppi." He sighed and shook his head. "He's the most politically minded Mann I have ever met. What possible reason could he have had for attempting to petition Hauptmann Herrick for the release of the Nomaden? He should have known he would be arrested immediately."

Berg grinned. "You're assumin' the Mann was thinkin' straight." James raised an eyebrow, and Berg chuckled again. "One o' the first Nomaden to be arrested was Alys Reiter."

James groaned and dropped his head in his hands. His companion, on the other hand, looked puzzled. "Who's Alys Reiter?"

Berg frowned at the Mann. He didn't think the stranger had a right to be nosy about the Nomaden if he was an outsider. However, James simply turned his head and answered the question.

"Alys is the eldest Tochter of the Häuptling of the Pferd Clan, and," he added with a soft chuckle, "Peppi has been verliebt with her for the past two Jahre."

The Mann frowned. "*Vehr-leebt*?"

Berg watched as James lifted his head and gave the Mann an apologetic look. "Es tut mir leid. He's been in love with her for the past two Jahre, er, years."

James' companion nodded. Berg growled and leaned forward, slamming his hands on the table between them, and causing James and his companion to jump.

"Why do you bothah to teach Zhulanese to this…Ausländer?" He spat the last word in contempt.

James went still, and Berg suddenly wished he could retract the question as unease settled over him. When James spoke next, his gaze was cool, and his voice was slow and fierce.

"Frenz is a very close friend of mine, Berg. If I wish to help him understand those I consider my people, I will. Is that understood?"

Berg nodded frantically, pulling himself back off the table. He had never realized exactly how much of a Zhulanese accent James had managed to gain over the Jahre, or how scary it would be to hear it suddenly dropped. The boy had sounded completely foreign when he'd spoken those words.

The Mann, Frenz, placed a hand on the Drache Krieger's shoulder. James shifted and glanced back at his companion, and Berg saw him relax as he met Frenz's eyes. That, more than the Drache Krieger's words, made Berg realize how much he'd misjudged the stranger. It was apparent that James trusted Frenz more than Berg had thought the boy could possibly trust anyone who wasn't Familie.

Berg cleared his throat, catching the attention of the two companions. James opened his mouth to speak, but Berg kept his eyes on Frenz and spoke quickly and softly.

"Es tut mir leid. I didn' realize 'ow important you were to the Drache Krieger. Bitte, accep' my apologies."

The Mann's cheeks reddened, but he smiled and nodded. "Not a problem. I understan' 'ow hard it can be to accep' someone you jus' met an' 'ave no reason to trust."

James looked ready to protest, but Frenz squeezed the boy's shoulder and smiled at him. "And, nay, he has no real reason to trust me." Frenz glanced back up at Berg. "Aye?"

Berg shrugged his massive shoulders. He was rather unwilling to upset James further, even if the stranger was providing a ready excuse. Instead, he cleared his throat rather uncomfortably and asked the Drache Krieger if the boy wanted him to spread the news among the Kreis.

James frowned but nodded. When he spoke, Berg was thankful that his Zhulanese accent had returned.

"Ja, I was hoping you would." He paused a moment then smiled hesitantly. "If you would send a messenger to Wildestadt as well, I would appreciate it."

Berg sighed softly and nodded. "Ja, I will." After a moment's pause, he added, "Should I send someone to Schönestadt, as well?"

James shook his head immediately. "Nein, don't bother. The messenger would only be risking his Leben since most of the Kreis is probably already imprisoned in Schönestadt."

"The rumors're true, then? Othman's been arrestin' the private Kreis, as well as the public?"

James' eyes tightened in anger, and Berg was glad the look wasn't directed at him this time. "Ja, there is a traitor in Schönestadt. The Herzog has agreed to help us discover that information, as well."

Berg wondered about trusting so many important tasks to their newest ally, but, if James believed the Herzog capable and willing to fulfill his role, then Berg would trust the boy's judgment. No one had ever accused him of making the same mistake twice.

"Well," James sighed, rubbing a hand over his face, "we should probably get going if we want to reach Schönestadt by Morgen."

"James."

Frenz laid a hand on the Drache Krieger's shoulder as the boy turned to the door. When James had turned his attention to his companion, the Mann added, "What abou' the Nomaden still in hidin'?"

Both Berg and James stared blankly at the Mann. "What about them?" James asked, and Berg silently agreed.

Those Nomaden whom he was hiding had already settled in to wait until the situation calmed down. True, that would take a while as far as they knew, but the Nomaden had long accepted their position in the Städte.

Frenz huffed. "Canna we help some of 'em out o' the city tonight?"

Berg shook his head. "Wit' all the Wachen at the gates, I wouldn' recommend it. You'd all be arrested when they stop an' question you."

James' companion shook his head. "But the guards at the southeast gate gave us an easy way past the northeast gate."

James frowned at his companion, but, after a moment, he nodded slowly. "Ja, they did." He seemed to ponder that for a moment before turning to Berg. "Who are you hiding?"

Berg listed the Nomaden he was currently hiding then added, "Their Pferde are in the stable." With the distances between Machtstadt and the Oasen where the Nomaden set up Lager, the Nomaden's Pferde were especially important.

James nodded. "They might all be willing to don plainclothes and leave the Stadt with us. Then you might be able to take on some of those hiding with the public members of the Kreis."

Berg shrugged. "If you wish to try this, I won't argue."

He led them out of the meeting room and towards one of the large rooms in the back of the Gasthaus.

As it turned out, all eight Nomaden were quite willing to attempt to leave the Stadt. Several cited the possible worry of their Clans and Familien. Berg found plainclothes for them, and, once they were changed, he led the ten to the stable, where Shadow waited with a pale colored mare.

Berg watched silently as the ten mounted their respective Pferde. As they said their quiet farewells, Berg hoped James' trust in his companion was not misplaced. He knew he wouldn't be able to sleep until he could confirm that the Drache Krieger had managed to leave the Stadt safely.

~~*~*

Even as they approached the northeast gate, Gemi worried that Ferez's idea wouldn't work.

However, while Gemi knew Zhulan better than Ferez did, she knew the König was a better tactician. She'd had proof of that during the last few months of the Krieg mit Fayral and during the planning in Kensy for the coordinated attacks on the rogue highwaymen. Despite her worry, she trusted Ferez to make this work, even if she wouldn't trust herself to.

"Halt!" called a Frau as they came upon the gate.

Pulling Shadow to a halt, Gemi watched as two Wachen approached, eyeing their group with narrowed eyes. She hoped none of the Nomaden did anything to jeopardize their story.

"What reason d'you have for leavin' the Stadt at this hour?" the Frau, whom Gemi assumed was Wache Irmigard, questioned.

Ferez huffed, and Gemi glanced at her Freund in surprise. The König wore a put-upon look. He glanced at Gemi, who was amused to realize her Freund was playing a part she hadn't expected.

"Is it customary for travelers to be stopped at every opportunity?"

Gemi pursed her lips to keep from smiling. Ferez had taken on a clear, haughty tone that reminded her strongly of Lord Lefas.

The second Wachen, the Mann, looked puzzled. "You've already been stopped?"

Ferez nodded. "I apologize."

Gemi restrained a snort. He didn't sound at all apologetic.

"I left Caypan with the aim of traveling to Schönestadt. However, my friends in Wildestadt," he motioned to Gemi and the surrounding Nomaden, "would not let me continue my journey at first because of everything that has happened with the nomads and the governors."

Ferez's voice held just enough carelessness that Gemi winced for fear of the Wachen's reactions. Wache Irmigard bristled, but before she could say anything, Ferez continued.

"Even so, I was not about to let that stand in my way. I insisted on going to Schönestadt, and they insisted on coming with me. They say it is to protect me in case of nomads."

Gemi was a bit shocked to see Ferez roll his eyes.

"Honestly, I do not know why. And now," exasperation crept into his voice, "we have been stopped both entering and leaving Machtstadt." He turned to Gemi and made a beckoning motion with his hand. "What did those guards that stopped us earlier say?"

Gemi sighed, though she cut it short. She hoped Ferez knew what he was doing. All she could do now was play along.

"I apologize for my Freund's attitude." Ferez frowned at her, but, from a twitch of his hand, she knew it was for the part, not actual disapproval. "Wachen Ottokar and Eward told us to tell Wachen Harvey and Irmigard that we could pass through the Stadt this Nacht."

Wache Irmigard pursed her lips and glared at Ferez. "I don' see why you were e'en allowed into the Stadt."

Gemi grimaced. "Es tut mir leid, but Wache Eward said that your Lebenmann would explain in the Morgen?"

Wache Harvey chuckled, while Wache Irmigard grimaced. "Very well," she reluctantly replied. She stepped to the side and frowned at her fellow Wache. "You may go."

"Danke," Gemi murmured, but Ferez's pretentious "Thank you," drowned her out. She sighed and threw him an exasperated look, but her Freund didn't respond until the Wachen were no longer visible.

311

"Thanks for followin' along," he whispered, smiling apologetically. Gemi sighed and shook her head. "You're just lucky that didn't get us arrested."

"James's right. Why act like that?" asked one of the Nomaden, a Frau Gemi recognized from the Spinne Clan.

Ferez shrugged and smiled back at the Frau. "I though' they migh' still be suspicious of our number if I used the same story we used to enter the city. I figure an arrogant outsider is more likely to have such a large entourage, so they wouldn' question the story too much.

"Besides, I though' they'd be more willin' to jus' kick me out o' the city than arrest me for my arrogance."

This earned chuckles from several of the Nomaden. "Well, it certainly worked," answered a Mann from the Falke Clan. "Where did you find this Mann, James? Has he been traveling with you since Baylin?"

Gemi chuckled and shook her head. "Kensy, actually. Although," she added and smirked at the König, "he does play an arrogant Caypanbürger rather well, doesn't he?"

Ferez shrugged. "Who d'you think directed the battles durin' the war?"

Gemi laughed, suddenly certain Ferez had based his attitude on the Baylinese duke.

With enough distance now between them and the Stadt, the Nomaden thanked Gemi and Ferez, said their farewells, and rode off in the direction of their respective Clans. Not long after, Flame rejoined them, and the five companions continued on towards Schönestadt.

312

Chapter 31

Ilse Parshen, Herzogin of Zhulan and Lebenfrau of Kawn Parshen, had been born to nobility, despite the relatively low rank of her Familie of birth.

However, unlike most lady nobles, Ilse had never been one for sitting idly by and depending solely on her Lebenmann. Even before their life-bonding, Ilse had been interested in helping Kawn with any issues he had to deal with as Herzog.

Therefore, it had been a shock for Ilse when Kawn had insisted on dealing with the recent Katastrophe in the Städte alone. It wasn't even that Ilse didn't know Kawn's true views on the Nomaden. She had supported his views and his public silence for Jahre.

But now, he pushed her away, insisting he not bother her with the mess with which she knew he must be dealing.

Ilse sighed sharply and shook her head. Her Zofe paused in her attempts to tame the Herzogin's curls and glanced questioningly at Ilse in the mirror. Ilse smiled and shook her head again to indicate her previous actions weren't for the Frau's work, and the Zofe continued, leaving Ilse to her thoughts.

Her Geist continued along the same line as she finished her Morgen routine. It wasn't until she was checking her Kinder's bedrooms, as she did every Morgen before breakfast, that her thoughts moved on.

She paused outside of her youngest Kind's room, remembering what had occurred the Nacht before last. Wondering if Gretchen had been able to sleep at all, she pushed the door open quietly.

Ilse smiled and sighed in relief when she saw the small lump under the covers on the bed. Stepping further into the room, she noted the sound of steady breathing as her Tochter slept peacefully. Grateful that her youngest had finally found sleep, she kissed the girl's forehead and opted to let her sleep longer instead of waking her for breakfast like she normally would.

When Ilse entered the dining room several minutes later, she was startled by the sound of her Lebenmann laughing heartily. Her other three Kinder, her older two Tochtër and her only Sohn, were grinning at their Vater, though they seemed as surprised as Ilse.

"And what is all this about?" she asked, approaching her Lebenmann's side.

Kawn quieted to a soft chuckle and turned his gaze to her. She felt her breath hitch. There was a confidence in his gaze that she realized had been missing since they had learned of Wilhelm's Tod.

"I was simply telling the Kinder that I was planning to go into Machtstadt this Morgen, and they insisted rather emphatically that we make it a daytrip for the entire Familie."

Ilse paused, surprised, before laying a light kiss on Kawn's lips. "You've made your decision then."

It wasn't a question. Her Lebenmann's steady gaze and voice were enough to answer any doubts. Somehow, Kawn had found the courage he needed to do what they both had always known was right

His grin softened, and he nodded. "Ja, I have." He turned back to the Kinder and rubbed his hands together. "And I believe a Familie trip is in order. I don't think any of us have been to the Stadt this Jahreszeit; not since I returned from Cautzel, at any rate."

All three Kinder cheered and began talking amongst themselves about their plans for their daytrip. Ilse chuckled, kissed Kawn's temple, and took her seat at his side.

"So what brought about this sudden change?" Ilse asked once she had filled her plate. Taking a bite of a sweet roll, she hummed softly. The Koch, Weizen, always made the best breads.

Before Kawn could answer her question, the door to the dining room opened, and a tall Mann entered. He strode quickly towards Kawn, his movements seemingly unhindered by the large, dark Falke that perched calmly on his shoulder.

"A message, Mylord." The Tieremagier stopped next to Kawn and offered him a scroll.

Kawn hummed and took the scroll, offering the man a quick "Danke, Fohlen" as he opened it. A moment later, he chuckled. "Well, that was fast."

Ilse frowned, but Fohlen beat her to the next question.

"Fast, Mylord? I don't recall you sending a message yesterday or this Morgen."

Kawn chuckled again as he laid the scroll open on the table and patted his pockets. "Nein, I didn't. This is from a Freund I spoke with last Nacht."

He huffed as the search of his pockets turned up nothing and turned to Fohlen. "Do you have any writing materials on you?"

"Of course, Mylord."

Fohlen reached into a bag at his belt and removed a piece of parchment, a quill, and a bottle of ink. As he arranged them on the table for Kawn, Ilse turned the scroll towards her and read it over.

A frown formed on her lips as she realized it was simply a list of names. Each one had something written beside it, and, while the style seemed familiar, she didn't recognize any meaning in it. At the bottom of the page, the writer had simply signed 'J.C.', which did little to inform her of the writer's identity.

Turning her gaze to her Lebenmann's parchment, she watched him write. At first, she was confused as her Lebenmann wrote in the same shorthand as the sender, but, as she watched, she began to realize why it looked familiar. It was the same used during the Krieg in notices between the König and his Herzöge.

Scanning what Kawn had written so far, she realized he was thanking the sender for the list and promising to consider his recommendations.

With that understanding, Ilse turned her attention back to the original scroll. *What could possibly be so important that Kawn has returned to using the Kriegschrift?*

A few scans of the scroll gave her a possible answer. Each name had the shorthand for a Stadt, either Machtstadt or Schönestadt, written next to it, as well as at least two other identifiers. She thought one shorthand might refer to Nomaden. It was the shorthand for 'imprisoned', 'hiding', 'free', and 'unknown' that made her realize what this list might be.

"Who wrote this?" Ilse asked as Kawn finished his own letter.

He glanced at her then the scroll where she was tapping the sender's initials. Instead of answering, he turned to the Kinder.

"If you're done eating, why don't you three go get ready for our daytrip?" There was a flurry of movement as the three stood from the table, young Adal stuffing one last biscuit in his mouth before leaving. "Oh, and Didrika?"

Their eldest, a girl of fifteen, paused and glanced over her shoulder, even as she pushed Kuonrada, who had paused with her, towards the door.

"Ja, Vater?"

"Will you wake Gretchen so she can eat before we leave?"

Didrika nodded, replied with another "Ja, Vater", and left, steering Adal and Kuonrada away from the dining room as she went.

"Well?" Ilse asked once she was sure the Kinder were out of earshot.

The fact that her Lebenmann didn't want the Kinder to hear inflamed her curiosity. There wasn't much that would interest Kuonrada or Adal when it came to the political state of Zhulan. Kuonrada was only thirteen, and Adal wasn't even ten yet.

And, while Didrika had begun to show interest in her Vater's work, Ilse wouldn't have thought that would be an issue for Kawn.

Even so, Kawn still wouldn't answer her question. Instead, he rolled the letter he'd written and handed it to Fohlen.

"Have the Falke take this back to the person who sent it."

The Tieremagier took the scroll but frowned. "How can I be sure I'm sending the Falke to the right person? I don't know who he came from."

Kawn chuckled. "I would think it would be difficult for the Falke to forget who sent him."

Ilse sighed and shook her head, laying a hand on Kawn's forearm.

"Honestly, Liebling, stop being so secretive. You know as well as I do that everyone in the Gut is trustworthy." She raised an eyebrow. "We've had to be sure of that with our opinions."

Kawn laid his hand on Ilse's and smiled at her. "You are right, I know." His voice dropped to a whisper as he added, as if to himself, "We do trust them with our secrets."

Ilse could imagine the question he wanted to add. *Can we trust them with another's?* She smiled and nodded. With a sigh, her Lebenmann turned back to Fohlen.

"Let the Falke know that he's to return that letter to the Drache."

Ilse gasped, and Fohlen's eyes widened. *The Drache?* Her hand tightened slightly on Kawn's forearm. *No wonder Kawn was hesitant to give a name.*

She watched as Fohlen nodded shakily and left, the Falke on his shoulder ruffling its feathers in agitation. Once the Magier had left, she glanced back down at the scroll in her hands and traced the initials.

"J.C.," she whispered. "James Caffers?"

Kawn had told her about the boy after his return from Cautzel, but she'd nearly forgotten about him. She looked up and met her Lebenmann's gaze. There was a calmness in his eyes that hadn't been there yesterday and had been missing for days now, if not longer. In fact, a weight seemed to have lifted from her Lebenmann, making him seem freer and lighter than ever.

A sudden thought distracted her from her Lebenmann's new demeanor, and she frowned as she remembered something he'd said earlier.

"He was here last Nacht, and you did not wake me?"

Kawn threw his head back and laughed. Ilse felt her lips twitch in response, and she pursed them to keep from smiling in return. Instead, she simply raised an eyebrow and waited for her Lebenmann to calm down.

~~*~*

Kawn was content.

It seemed like an eternity since he'd last felt this way. Even before Wilhelm and Volker had died, even before the Krieg mit Fayral had ended, Kawn didn't think he had felt truly content. Since he could remember, he had watched as his people, the Nomaden, suffered, unable to do anything for them for Angst of the reactions of his peers.

Now, Kawn knew he had the support of his König. He could finally stand up for what he truly believed without fearing consequences that could not be reasonably resolved.

And to think I have James Caffers, the Drache Krieger, to thank for this.

Kawn finally calmed his laughter and smiled back down at his Lebenfrau. Ilse was trying hard not to smile, but that only made Kawn's smile widen. Even after almost two decades, he didn't know how he had been lucky enough to find such a jewel of a Lebenfrau among the noble Familien.

"I am afraid I didn't think to wake you, Liebling."

316

That wasn't completely true, of course. He had known, then, that she would have wanted him to wake her, but, at the time, he had thought Ferez's secret was more important than Ilse's desire to help him.

Ilse eyed him for a moment then turned her gaze to the scroll in her hands. Kawn chuckled softly, knowing that it might not matter that he hadn't wakened her. She was intelligent enough to figure out the truth eventually. It was one of the things that had drawn him to her when they first met.

Finally, she sighed and shook her head. "You are keeping something from me, Lebenmann." Her voice was soft, but her gaze was steady as it met his. "However, I cannot fault you for protecting another, especially if it is who I believe it is."

Kawn pressed a light kiss to her temple. "Danke, Liebling."

Ilse finally let her lips spread in a smile, and Kawn was unsurprised when she once again tapped the parchment in her hands. However, before she could ask her next question, the dining room door opened again, and a small, tired voice caught their attention.

"Gut Morgen, Vati, Mami."

~~*~*

Ilse quickly left the table and pulled Gretchen into her arms. As she returned to the table, her Tochter wrapped one hand in Ilse's curls and smothered a yawn with the other. The girl's obvious tiredness would have worried the Herzogin if not for the bright smile that appeared after the yawn.

"And Guten Morgen to you, little Perle," Kawn replied. Gretchen's smile widened at the use of her nickname, but she burrowed her face against her Mutter's neck. "How are you feeling?"

"Ti—"

As if on cue, a yawn stretched her jaw once more. Afterwards, she rubbed at her eye and smiled a little. "Tired."

"And Der Geist?" Ilse asked worriedly. She glanced at her Lebenmann, but he shrugged and shook his head.

"Oh, he lef'," Gretchen murmured, burying her head against Ilse's neck once more. "'E jus' wan'ed to say 'allo to Eirene."

Ilse blinked. "Eirene?"

Kawn chuckled. "His name is James, Liebling, not Eirene."

Gretchen lifted her head and frowned. "Bu' Markos insisted that 'is name was Eirene."

Markos and Eirene? The names seemed familiar to Ilse, but she couldn't place them. She told Kawn as much.

Her Lebenmann shrugged. "I think James recognized them, but he didn't tell me their significance. Otherwise, I've never heard of them myself."

Ilse nodded and promised herself that she would try to remember why they sounded familiar. Watching another yawn plague her Tochter, she lifted a sweet roll from her plate and offered it to Gretchen.

"Eat, Perle. We're going to the Stadt later this Tag, and you'll need your strength."

Gretchen gasped happily and took the roll, eating it quickly before grabbing another. As their Tochter ate, Ilse and Kawn turned their attention back to the scroll.

~~*~*

Their Pferde were approaching Machtstadt's southeast gate when a Wache hailed them. Kawn pulled his Pferd to a stop and frowned as he realized who stood at the gate.

"Hauptmann Herrick?" The current military leader of Machtstadt smiled up at Kawn. "Why are you watching the gate?"

Herrick's smile turned slightly bitter. "I'm attempting to prevent a repeat of last Nacht, unfortunately."

Kawn felt his frown deepen, but, before he could reply, he felt a hand on his arm and looked up to find Ilse glancing between him and the Hauptmann.

"If you don't mind, I believe the Kinder and I should continue on into the Stadt."

Kawn nodded, even as he glanced at Herrick to make sure the Hauptmann was not worried for their safety.

Herrick shrugged. "No reason you can't, Mylady. You have your knights with you, and this might take a while."

Ilse nodded. "Danke, Hauptmann."

Herrick gave her a small bow. "Mit Vergnügen, Mylady. Guten Tag!"

"And you," she replied before leading the Kinder and five of the knights who had accompanied them through the gates. Sir Leal, the knight captain of Parshen Gut, stayed behind, relaxing in his saddle.

Knowing Herrick was right, Kawn slid out of his saddle and handed the reins to a page, who had hurried forward to accept them.

"What happened last Nacht?" he questioned, crossing his arms over his chest.

Herrick grimaced. "Two Männer entered the Stadt through this gate late last Nacht. Awhile later, they left through the northeast gate, but they were accompanied by eight others."

Kawn raised his brows in surprise. Thinking about his late Nacht visitors, Kawn asked, "And how did they manage to leave the Stadt if you know that this happened?"

Herrick sighed. "Unfortunately, the two Männer managed to convince the two Wachen at this gate that they were simply taking advantage of the cool Nacht air to travel from Wildestadt to Schönestadt. So convinced, my Männer gave them the names of the Wachen at the northeast gate and a statement that would convince them that they were freundlich so they wouldn't be too bothered."

Kawn nearly snickered. If the two Männer of whom Herrick spoke were the Drache Krieger and the König like Kawn suspected, then this stunt was certainly laughable.

318

He knew he should be worried that the two, who were currently residing with the Nomaden, might have managed to come and go without raising suspicions during a time like this and, at the same time, managed to sneak several Nomaden out with them. It didn't bode well for the security of the Stadt, especially since the Wachen were supposed to have been on high alert.

However, Kawn couldn't bring himself to care.

"Do you have descriptions of these two Männer?" he asked to keep himself from laughing.

Herrick, who didn't seem to notice Kawn's struggle, nodded. "Both were young, just barely Of Age. One spoke like an Ausländer and had light-brown hair and pale blue eyes. The other spoke like a Zhulanbürger, had long dark hair, and…"

Herrick hesitated. When Kawn encouraged him to continue, he added reluctantly, "All four Wachen swear the second Mann had purple eyes. I'm not quite sure if I believe such a report. It could have simply been a trick of the light."

Kawn chuckled, unable to help himself. "Believe me, the reports are correct."

"Mylord?" Herrick asked, shocked.

Kawn grinned at the Hauptmann. "There's no need to worry about them, Herrick. I doubt they would risk returning to Machtstadt for a while after pulling such a trick."

For a moment, Herrick simply stared at the Herzog, seemingly unable to speak. Finally, his eyes narrowed.

"Do you know of these Männer, Mylord?"

Kawn nodded and patted Herrick's shoulder.

"The two are acquaintances of mine. While it might seem troublesome that they managed to pull such a Trick, I wouldn't worry myself if I were you. There's no reason to believe that they caused more harm than simply helping a few Nomaden out of the Stadt, and you can be sure that none of the Nomaden that they helped to escape were connected to Volker's Tod."

Instead of asking more questions or arguing, which is what Kawn expected, Herrick searched Kawn's eyes. Kawn met the Hauptmann's searching gaze evenly, knowing he needed his cooperation if he wanted to change the way things were.

Eventually, Herrick nodded, and Kawn released a small breath before glancing around.

"So, what exactly are you doing to prevent another such incident?" He turned a dubious look on the Hauptmann. "I doubt increasing the number of Wachen on the gates would help."

"Nein, increased numbers wouldn't help."

Herrick glanced across the heads of several travelers to the other side of the gate. One of the Wachen on the other side noticed his gaze and nodded before turning his attention back to the incoming people. Herrick sighed and glanced back at Kawn.

"We're using Geistmagier."

Kawn straightened at the mention of the Magier. "Geistmagier? Surely you aren't having them read everyone?"

Herrick was shaking his head before Kawn had even finished speaking. "Nein, of course not, Mylord. But several Wachen have agreed to allow the Geistmagier access."

"Ah," Kawn replied, realizing what Herrick was implying. "The Geistmagier are reading those Männer on the gates, then? Is that why you are here?"

When Herrick nodded, Kawn grinned. "Gut, gut. You've always been unwilling to ask your Männer to do things you wouldn't do yourself. That's gut."

Herrick lowered his head, his cheeks flushing lightly and a small smile curling his lips.

They fell into silence then. Kawn turned his attention to those entering the Stadt. The flow wasn't as steady or as heavy as it normally would have been, but even the Tode of the Gouverneure could not keep people from traveling to the Städte when they needed to.

"Did you come to Machtstadt for business or pleasure, Mylord?" Herrick asked finally, having recovered from Kawn's praise.

Kawn sighed and turned back to Herrick. "Business, I fear," he answered, knowing he'd been putting off what he'd decided to do. "The Kinder decided that we needed to make a Familie trip of it, though."

Herrick nodded. "Ja, Kinder have a way of taking over your decisions, don't they?" Kawn chuckled, knowing Herrick was speaking from experience. "I take it that you came to discuss Volker's Tod and the Nomaden, Mylord?"

"Ja." For a moment, Kawn contemplated how to begin revealing his decision to the Hauptmann. As Herrick made a questioning sound, he sighed. "Could you take me to see those you've arrested in connection to this Katastrophe?"

Herrick stiffened slightly. Before Kawn could question his reaction, the Hauptmann beckoned a page forward and requested that the boy bring their Pferde to them. Once mounted, Herrick led Kawn through the streets to the Stadt's Gefängnis.

Inside, the Hauptmann led Kawn down a hallway that, while well-lit, seemed dusty and unused. Cobwebs hung from the corners of the ceiling, and the echoes of their footsteps preceded them.

"Because of the circumstances, I had the set of cells in this corridor opened. I thought it'd be best to keep the Nomaden and their…conspirators separated from other prisoners."

As he finished saying this, they stepped up to a barred door. Although Kawn was surprised to find no Wache on this door, once through it, he was pleased to find that the prisoners seemed no worse for wear.

As Herrick closed the door behind them, Kawn took a moment to examine the prisoners. Eight wore the Kopfabdeckungen and Statusgürtel of Nomaden. That was one more than James had claimed, which meant one had been captured sometime during the Nacht or early Morgen.

Several bore the green Statusgürtel of the Pferd Clan, including one who bore the double green of the Pferd's ruling Familie. Two bore the pale yellow of the Spinne Clan, while the rest bore the red of the Wolf Clan.

Turning his gaze to the river-dwellers, he noted that the short, stocky Frau must be Millicent Wäschemann, while the broad-shouldered Mann must be Hariman Biermann.

The tall, slender Mann, however, was someone Kawn recognized quite well: Peppi Kluger. Kawn had often seen the Mann in Volker's court, petitioning the Gouverneur for one consideration or another. Kawn also knew that Volker often spoke fondly of the political Mann.

To be honest, when James had labeled Peppi in his list as the best Kandidat for Gouverneur of Machtstadt, Kawn couldn't have agreed more. When Kawn read James' list, he realized that he had been considering Peppi from the beginning. That he was a part of the Kreis was a pleasant affirmation.

Finally stepping away from the door, Kawn addressed Peppi first.

"I am surprised to see you here, Herr Kluger."

The Mann, who hadn't reacted to his and Herrick's arrival like the others had, jerked his head up.

"M-mylord?" He shook his head then peered back up at Kawn. "What are you doing here?"

Kawn sighed. "I am here on business, I fear." He raised an eyebrow and eyed the Mann, despite his sudden desire to laugh. "You, though, Herr Kluger? I would have thought you of all people would have been clever enough to avoid detection as a member of the Kreis."

Suddenly, all eleven prisoners stiffened as they turned to stare at Kawn, horror dawning on each of their faces. Herrick made an odd sound, but Kawn ignored the Hauptmann for the moment.

"Well?"

Peppi shook his head again and stood, the horror on his face slowly fading. By the time he spoke again, his voice was steady and smooth.

"I am afraid I forgot myself, Mylord. I was not considering consequences when I made my petition to Hauptmann Herrick." He glanced past Kawn, but Kawn didn't bother to look at Herrick.

"That doesn't seem like you, Herr Kluger," Kawn rejoined, tilting his head thoughtfully. "Volker always claimed that you never did anything that would jeopardize your cause." The Herzog glanced at their surroundings and shook his head. "I wouldn't think you could do much good for the Kreis while in Gefängnis."

Peppi's cheeks reddened, but, before he could reply, the Nomade with the double green Statusgürtel stood and spoke sharply.

"Peppi was brave to stand up to Hauptmann Herrick when others simply hid themselves away." The strong voice was obviously female, and her features were set in determination.

Kawn turned and bowed to the Nomade Frau, which seemed to startle everyone.

"Of course, Adlige." He used an old formal title in deference to her Nomade nobility. "I never meant to impugn his honor or disdain his courage. I simply wondered why a politically minded Mann like him would risk everything as he did." He turned his gaze back to Peppi.

He hesitated when he caught sight of the small smile that Peppi now wore. Glancing back to the Adlige, the Herzog grinned at the sight of the Frau's reddening cheeks.

"Well, then. I think I might know the answer to that."

Peppi's eyes widened as he jerked his gaze back to Kawn, and he spluttered, "Mylord, I can—"

Kawn simply shook his head and waved his hand to dismiss the Mann's protests.

"Hardly necessary, Peppi. A passionate Mann is exactly what we need in a Gouverneur."

Silence followed, and Kawn chuckled at the shocked expressions on everyone's faces. He knew he could have gone about revealing his 'change of heart' in a different manner, but, really, he hadn't had this much fun in a while, and he doubted they would believe him otherwise.

The Frau with the double green Statusgürtel was the first to recover. "You want Peppi," she began doubtfully, "to become the next Gouverneur, Mylord?"

Kawn smiled at her and nodded. "Ja, Adlige, I do. Especially in times like these, we need Gouverneure who will stand for all of their people, not just the river-dwellers."

The Frau eyed him thoughtfully, the distance in her eyes portraying her distrust. Finally, she glanced around at her fellow prisoners. Most of the Nomaden seemed to share her distrust, only the two Spinne and one of the Wölfe, an older Frau by the looks of it, offering smiles of encouragement. Frau Wäschemann and Herr Biermann weren't watching her but, instead, continued to eye the Herzog. When she looked to Peppi, the politician shrugged but nodded encouragingly.

The small smile that formed on the Pferd's lips then encouraged Kawn's belief that this Nomade Frau was the reason Peppi had thrown caution to the wind as he had. The smile still in place, she turned back to Kawn and gave a small bow.

"I do not believe we have been properly introduced, Mylord. I am Alys Reiter, eldest Tochter of Roswalt Reiter, Häuptling of the Pferd Clan."

"Angenehm, Adlige!" Kawn replied with a nod.

The greeting, like the title, was old and formal, but he thought it appropriate. Adlige Reiter's eyes widened slightly. The next moment, her lips twitched, and the sudden crinkling around her eyes let him know she appreciated the greeting's significance as well.

"I don't wish to interrupt, Mylord," Herrick suddenly spoke, finally succeeding in catching Kawn's attention. "But may I presume that you wish to continue the alliance that Gouverneur Volker held with the Nomaden?"

"You know about it?" Kawn asked, surprised.

The incredulous looks on most of the prisoners' faces showed that the others were having a hard time believing this.

Herrick had the grace to look ashamed. "I've known for several Jahre, ja. I was the one who executed the Gouverneur's orders with regard to the alliance."

"But you had us arrested!" accused a young Mann who wore the red Statusgürtel of the Wolf Clan.

Herrick scowled. "Would you prefer that I had left you to those river-dwellers who'd rather see you dead for a crime that wasn't yours?"

The Wolf gaped at him.

"Believe me," the Hauptmann sighed and shook his head, "I'm not proud to have gone against the alliance, but I'd rather see you in Gefängnis and alive than free and dead."

Kawn stared at Herrick, considering his words. The ease with which he'd dropped the issue of James and Ferez sneaking in and out of the Stadt suddenly rose to the surface of his Geist, as did his desire to separate the Nomaden and their Freunde from other prisoners. The latter could be interpreted as a desire to protect the falsely accused Nomaden rather than to isolate them. Then, there was the strange sound he'd made when Kawn had mentioned the Kreis.

Kawn shook his head and chuckled. "You even knew of the Kreis, didn't you?"

Herrick nodded sheepishly. "I hadn't realized you did, though. Volker implied several times that you wouldn't jeopardize the alliance, but that you didn't wish to know the details, either."

"Nein," Kawn sighed. "At the time, I did not. I thought that if I knew the details, then I might become a risk that the alliance could not afford. I was simply glad that Volker and Wilhelm were willing to do what I believed I could not."

"But that opinion has changed, Mylord?" Adlige Reiter asked. When Kawn answered in the affirmative, she narrowed her eyes and asked, "Why?"

Kawn chuckled. "James Caffers."

Herrick gasped. When Kawn turned to him with a questioning look, the Hauptmann was gaping at him.

"You know the Drache Krieger?" Herrick asked.

Kawn raised an eyebrow. "Do you?"

The Hauptmann snapped his jaw shut and shook his head. "Nein, not personally, but Volker spoke well of the boy. I've heard he's the one who instigated the old alliance's renewal."

"In a way," Adlige Reiter said with a sniff. "However, I am surprised that you would speak kindly of James, Mylord. I had thought that the König, his Herzöge, and the other nobles considered him a fiend." The final word was spoken with disdain.

Kawn grinned, half at the Pferd's attitude. "We did, right up until he sat us down and gave us a basic understanding of his history."

Herr Biermann snorted and leaned back against the wall behind him. "Tha' soun's like James."

Adlige Reiter rolled her eyes. "If anyone can find a way to deal with a situation peacefully, James can. But I do not see how simply knowing his history would change how you deal with the Nomaden, Mylord." She leveled her gaze at him, the doubt once again rising in her eyes. "I fear it is not very believable."

"Perhaps not," Kawn answered with a shrug, "but the König was very interested in James and the groups he represented. That gave me the courage to tell the König my own beliefs, beliefs he is very willing to support."

"So now you have decided to openly support and protect the Nomaden?" Peppi questioned. Kawn nodded. "And you wish to make me the new Gouverneur?" Kawn nodded again and opened his mouth to reply when a Wache pushed open the door.

"Lord Kawn, komm, quickly. Your Lebenfrau—"

Kawn turned sharply to the newcomer. "What?"

The Wache blinked and glanced around before continuing. "Your Lebenfrau, M'lord! Several Nomaden grabbed her an' are threatenin' harm to her if you don' come at once."

Several of the prisoners groaned, but Kawn was more focused on the messenger. "Where are they? And what of my Kinder?"

"Your Kinder're safe, M'lord. They're wit' their knights. But the Nomaden have barricaded themselves wit'in the Tempel o' Carith."

Kawn nodded and turned back to Herrick.

"I want you to release these prisoners as quickly as possible. Then, spread the word that no one is to harm the Nomaden or any who act to protect them. I want this situation dealt with as quickly as possible."

After a quick pause, he added reluctantly, "Use the Geistmagier to spread the word among the Wachen, if you think it necessary. But join me when you can."

Kawn turned back to the messenger then and nodded. "Take me there!"

Chapter 32

Ilse walked with her Kinder and their knights along Marktplatz, admiring the wares they found there. She had always enjoyed the road. The variety of colors found in the buildings and stalls was only matched by the variety of wares and people buying and selling them.

Some might think the road was too loud, but the sounds of the merchants hawking their wares and haggling with would-be customers for the best prices combined with the common sounds of the Stadt to bring a smile to the Herzogin's face.

The thing she enjoyed most about Marktplatz was the freedom she felt when she haggled with the merchants herself. Many might think that she could get an unfairly good deal as a noblewoman, but, as far as Ilse had been able to overhear over the Jahre, the merchants of Zhulan were just as ruthless, and ingratiating, with her as they were with any other person. They had to be, or they risked being criticized for such unfairness.

Ilse was admiring a beautifully made silver and Katzenauge necklace when Kuonrada tugged at her skirt. Smiling down at her second Tochter, she asked, "Ja, Liebling?"

Kuonrada simply pointed to a nearby building and, pouting, said, "Bitte, Mutter?"

Ilse glanced at the building and chuckled. She hadn't realized they had already reached the Tempel of Carith, which stood about halfway down Marktplatz. The Tempel fit into Marktplatz rather well, its multicolored façade blending with the colorful buildings and stalls of the Markt. As was usual, the Tempel's doors stood open to accommodate any people that wished to enter, as well as any breeze that was willing to blow through.

Glancing back down at her Tochter, Ilse smiled fondly and murmured her assent. As Kuonrada cheered happily and ran off to tell her siblings, her Mutter chuckled. Ilse's second Tochter had shown an interest in the old religion from a young age, and the girl never missed an opportunity to stop in at the Tempel.

Turning back to the necklace she'd been admiring, Ilse sighed softly. Now that she had given her assent, Kuonrada would want to be going into the Tempel immediately. Thanking the merchant for allowing her to look at the piece, she turned away and looked for her Kinder.

Kuonrada was nearby, chattering happily, while her older Schwester and younger Bruder simply listened and nodded idly, their Geister more than likely still on the surrounding wares. Neither had ever been as interested in the Tempel as Kuonrada had, but both knew, by now, not to protest.

Gretchen, tired as she was, didn't say a word as she slept peacefully in the arms of her knight protector, Sir Ritter. The other knights stood around, their postures relaxed but their eyes still scanning the crowd.

Catching Didrika's eye, Ilse nodded towards the Tempel. Didrika nodded back even as her lips parted slightly, no doubt emitting a soft sigh. Ilse simply smiled as her eldest then rolled her eyes and turned to Kuonrada rather deliberately.

Didrika might try to portray reluctance in her duties as the oldest sibling, but she was old enough to understand how important this was. Such an extended interest in the old religion needed to be encouraged as it meant that Kuonrada might, one day, become a Handmaiden of Carith. Such an occupation was one of the few considered worthy of a noble-born Frau.

As Ilse turned to the Tempel, her Kinder continued to tarry over the selection of wares. Even Kuonrada, who was always eager to enter the Tempel, seemed to have had her attention caught by something in particular. Knowing they would soon follow, Ilse approached the Tempel alone.

~~*~*

"Go on, Kinder," Hoffnung urged, waving a silver hand towards the distracting wares, despite knowing they couldn't actually see or hear her. "It's beautiful, ja? The Tempel can wait a few Minuten. It'll still be there. You just need to admire this for ein bisschen longer, ja?"

Even as Hoffnung said the words, she felt disgusted with herself. She was interfering more than she was comfortable doing.

True, it was not as bad as Krieg taking on physical form to speak directly with the mortals or Leben touching a Geist directly to keep it from leaving its physical body. (Hoffnung doubted she was supposed to know about Leben's little indiscretions, but walls weren't always solid in the Spiritual Plane, and Leben was never very subtle in her desperation to save the Geister under her protection.)

It wasn't even that Hoffnung had never influenced a mortal before. She often did since it was part of The Game.

It was the situation that made her so disgusted with her actions. Normally, she'd have no reason to make an item in a Markt stall seem more tempting than it actually was, especially to three Kinder who lived rather happy Leben. Hoffnung's specialty usually ran to the more subtle, like offering a small light to an otherwise dreary perspective. She provided silver linings, as the Fayralese liked to say.

"That's it," the silver Halbgott encouraged once the Kinder were thoroughly engrossed. Looking up from her current targets, Hoffnung gave an irritated huff as she watched Zhulan's Herzogin approach the Tempel.

Of course, the Herzogin wasn't the one with whom Hoffnung was irritated. It was this verdammt situation or, rather, her Bruder, Krieg.

He was the one who had set these events into motion. He, the one conscious Halbgott not currently in Machtstadt, was the reason the Schicksale had gathered Hoffnung and her siblings to discuss things that could and needed to be changed without affecting the situation between Frieden and Krieg too much.

Apparently, though Hoffnung couldn't see how, the mess between Frieda and Krieg had to be settled between the two of them. That was something in which none of the older immortals could interfere.

Hoffnung was brought back to the present when the unwitting Herzogin was only a few steps from the Tempel's open doors. Four Nomaden suddenly appeared from within the Tempel, one grabbing the Herzogin and putting a Scharfmond to her throat.

The others stepped around the Frau, brandishing their own blades at the surrounding crowds. Hoffnung winced as people began screaming and pulling back from the small group.

Remembering her mission, Hoffnung focused her influence onto the Geister of the Herzogin's two older Töchter, making sure they didn't try to do something stupid.

Unfortunately, she should have been more worried about the boy.

~~*~*

Ilse hardly had time to blink at the sight of the Nomaden before she was pulled tight against a Mann's body and a Scharfmond was laid against her throat. She swallowed her gasp and attempted to stay still, but the screams of the people around her had her craning her neck in an attempt to make sure her Kinder were safe.

"Mutter!" she heard Adal cry.

His older Schwestern promptly followed suit. Through the crowd, which seemed to ebb away from her, Ilse managed to spy her two older Töchter. Sir Waren and Sir Tabbert had grabbed the two, though both seemed too shocked to put up much of a fight. Sir Ritter seemed to tighten his hold on Gretchen, who was beginning to stir, while he grabbed for Adal with his free hand.

However, to her horror, Adal had already darted further into the crowd.

Adal was just pushing past the edge of the crowd when Sir Neff, his knight protector, finally grabbed him around the waist and picked him up.

"Nein!" Adal yelled, gripping Sir Neff's arm with one hand while he beat at it with the other. "Le' me go!" Then, reaching out one hand towards Ilse, he screamed, "Mutter!"

Meanwhile, Sir Bren, Ilse's own knight protector, pushed past those people trying to get away from the Nomaden. As he approached, the Nomade who held Ilse tightened his hold and raised his blade higher. She winced at the press of the blade on her skin.

"Stay back!" the Nomade who held her growled. As he shifted her, Ilse spotted the Statusgürtel of the Mann in front of her; a purple Statusgürtel.

Katze? she thought, shocked. *But why?*

"Let her go, and we won't hurt you," Sir Bren commanded, his own sword drawn but lowered to the side.

The Nomade to her left, who, to her dismay, wore the red of a Wolf, struck out wildly with one Scharfmond.

327

"N-nein. W-we won't." The trembling voice was decidedly young, and Ilse realized the Nomade might actually be a girl. "N-not until…"

Ilse caught a glance of the girl's face as she looked to Ilse's captor. Her eyes.were wide and wild, her chin trembling violently. The Nomade looked like she was about to cry.

"Send for her Lebenmann," the Nomade to Ilse's right, another Katze, finished. His voice was dark, but even it bore a slight tremble. "If you don't, we will harm her."

Suddenly, Ilse was wrenched backwards towards the Tempel's doors. She thought she heard Adal scream "Mutter!" one last time before the doors were pushed shut and barred from within.

Now, Ilse was seated on some cushions in front of the Altar, seemingly forgotten. A steaming mug had been pushed into her hands by the trembling girl before the Nomaden had gathered in another area of the Tempel. Ilse noted idly that the area was usually occupied by those in need of healing.

"Es tut mir leid for this, Mylady."

The words pulled Ilse from her thoughts, and she glanced up at the Fräulein who had addressed her. The Fräulein was clothed in the simple dress of a Handmaiden of Carith.

"Do I know you?" she asked, realizing the Fräulein looked familiar. The Fräulein giggled and sat down beside the Herzogin.

"My name is Lise, Mylady. Mein Bruder is Sir Ritter, young Gretchen's knight protector."

Ilse blinked. "I had thought his Schwester was life-bonded to Lord Howe."

Lise bobbed her head. "Ja, Mylady. That would be our eldest Schwester, Lind. I, on the other hand, did not wish to simply be a Lebenfrau to some nobleman, and, as you know, there are few other choices for those Frau of our birth."

"Ach, ja! I understand how you feel. I am lucky that Kawn is willing to share his burdens with me, or simply being a Lebenfrau is all I would have." Lise giggled, and Ilse nodded towards the Nomaden. "Tell me, Fräulein Lise, what is happening?"

Lise's smile slipped as she, too, glanced towards the Nomaden.

"We received news last Nacht that room had opened up at one of the more private Nomaden sanctuaries. As soon as we heard, the Nomaden staying here decided to risk moving there."

The Handmaiden hesitated. "You see, everyone knows that the Tempel is always open to the Nomaden, so they were worried that the Wachen would soon come to search the Tempel and arrest them."

She paused as a loud whimper reached them from the group of Nomaden. "They didn't leave in time?" Ilse whispered in sudden comprehension.

Lise bit her lip and shook her head.

"Nein, they did leave. It's just—"

She paused and glanced again towards the Nomaden. "Heilig Oswald tried to tell them that he would never allow the Wachen to break the sanctity of the Tempel, but they wouldn't listen." She shook her head. "Even I hadn't realized that the Wachen were so strict about respecting the Tempel as the Haus of Creation. They must have known there were Nomaden here, but, as long as they stayed inside, they were safe."

Ilse gripped the Handmaiden's hand. "What happened exactly?"

Another pained whimper drew a wince from the two Frauen. "The Wachen captured one Nomade, a young Wolf, almost as soon as he left the Tempel. But, while the others began to come back, the Wolf's Bruder attacked the Wachen."

A sudden cry had Ilse climbing to her feet. "Is there no Arztmagier here to heal his wounds?"

Surely an Arztmagier could at least help with the pain.

Lise gripped Ilse's arm and tugged her gently back down onto the cushions.

"Nein, Mylady. The Arztmagier connected to the Tempel had been called away on emergencies before this, and none have yet returned. The non-magical Ärztin has done all she can, but the Wolf's pain is too immense for the remedies we have available."

Ilse shook her head, worry for the young Mann she didn't know filling her heart. "Is this why they abducted me? Did they think that kidnapping me would help them get an Arztmagier?"

"Honestly, I don't know, Mylady." Lise glanced at the Nomaden and lowered her voice. "I think they've simply become too desperate. When we saw you in the Marktplatz, Jakob—he's the one who grabbed you— simply seemed to snap. The others followed his lead."

Lise turned imploring eyes to Ilse. "You see, the same messenger that brought news of open space also brought another message. He said that the Herzog would look to the K—er, the more Nomade-freundlich river-dwellers—"

"The Kreis," Ilse offered, understanding that the Fräulein did not realize exactly how much Ilse knew. The widening of the Fräulein's eyes confirmed Ilse's thought, and the Handmaiden nodded.

"Ja, the Kreis." After a quick pause, she added, "Then it is true? The Herzog is looking to the Kreis for the new Gouverneure?"

Ilse smiled and nodded. "Ja, he is. He already knows who he wants here in Machtstadt." She glanced over at the Nomaden and chuckled. "Assuming this incident didn't interrupt him too quickly, he should have already offered the position to the Mann."

"Who?" Lise breathed.

Ilse turned back to the Handmaiden and was surprised at the desperate Hoffnung that had suddenly filled her face. Ilse felt a pang in her chest.

Is this what our people have come to, that, when Hoffnung comes, it hurts too much for them to even believe in it?

Ilse gripped Lise's hand once more. "He wants Peppi Kluger for Gouverneur."

She watched as the painful desperation on Lise's face morphed to surprise before her lips spread in a wide smile and she gave a soft laugh tinged with desperation.

"Oh, bitte, tell me this is no Witz."

"What Witz?"

The rough voice spoke before Ilse could answer, and she looked up to find one of the Nomaden standing in front of them. Unlike the others', his Statusgürtel was blue, marking him as a Falke. The Herzogin remembered that he had been the one to grab her outside the Tempel.

"Oh!" Lise gasped, jerking her head up. "Jakob! You startled me."

The Mann glowered at the Handmaiden, and her cheeks reddened. "Uh, well, the Herzogin was just telling me that...her, er—"

Ilse squeezed the Fräulein's hand as she trailed off, too flustered to continue. Glaring up at the intimidating Mann, she said, "I was simply assuring Fräulein Lise that mein Lebenmann is now looking to the Kreis for the next Gouverneur, as well as any other assistance they might be able to provide."

The Mann, Jakob, snorted and shook his head.

"I find that hard to believe, Mylady." The last word left his lips with such disdain that Ilse raised her brows in surprise. "The Herzog has never shown any concern for us Nomaden before now. Why should that change?"

Ilse pursed her lips, but Lise, who seemed to have recovered her tongue, spoke first. "But the Herzogin has already said that Peppi Kluger is to be the next Gouverneur. Surely, you can believe that!"

Jakob laughed sharply, startling the other Nomaden. "Can't you see it is a Trick, Handmaiden? Surely, you are not naïve enough to believe her lies!"

"Ruhe, young Mann!"

Ilse jumped at the strong-voiced command, while Jakob only lifted his gaze past her head. Turning around, Ilse saw an older Mann walking towards them from a doorway behind the Altar. His bright, multicolored tunic marked him as a Holy Man of Carith, a Heilig as they were known here in Zhulan. His weathered face was set in a frown.

"Why should I?" Jakob sneered. "Do you, who have always been open to the Nomaden, now stand behind this...Lügnerin, as well?"

Ilse stiffened. It wasn't so much that he called her a liar. Certainly, he was right that their decision seemed rather sudden. But the way he sneered it made the word seem so much...worse than it should.

"Ruhe!" the Heilig commanded again. While Jakob simply sneered, Ilse knew that if the command had been directed at her, she would have gone quiet immediately. "I will not have such dreadful things spoken within these walls."

"Or what, old Mann?" Jakob mocked. "You think you can silence me?"

~~*~*

As a Geistmagier, Heilig Oswald had long ago learned to keep himself from unconsciously touching the Geister of humans around him. However, he had also learned from a young age that humans were not the only ones whom he could hear, nor were other Geister so easy to ignore. These Geister could not be seen. Some, of course, were the Geister of the dead whom Adler, the Royal Eagle, had yet to claim. This was most common in times when there were many dead, such as after a battle or plague.

But it was the immortals that Oswald most appreciated, and sometimes most dreaded, hearing. When he was young, his Mutter used to call Oswald's gift prophetic and a gift of the Götter. Oswald would always laugh at her for such things.

Ja, he had learned many things from them over the Jahre, especially when he could get them to speak the truths of the old religion that most people had forgotten. He also had a healthy Respekt for them and the tasks with which each was charged.

However, the immortals, especially the Halbgötter, whom most people had forgotten, often spoke of mundane and repetitive things. Oswald had found that, because the immortals lived forever, so, too, did their arguments, interests, and sorrows.

This Tag was one in which he dreaded hearing the immortals. Early this Morgen, when the Nomaden had attempted to leave and had been driven back with one injured, the Halbgötter seemed to have settled themselves within the Tempel.

It was the first time Oswald had heard so many of the siblings at one time. He was used to only hearing one pair at a time, usually Leben and Tod as the Tempel was often used as a place of healing and not all who came for healing survived. The sudden presence of nearly all the Halbgötter of which he knew was draining.

When he'd realized that none of them would be leaving anytime soon, he had left the Altar room to meditate. The activity had helped him relax and simply let the Halbgötter's words drift over him.

Even so, he knew the moment the Nomaden had abducted the Herzogin. The Halbgötter persisted in conversing about the Nomaden's activities, as well as teasing one of their own about the part she'd played in protecting the Herzogin's Kinder. They didn't manage to drive him from his meditation, though, until a dark voice spoke from right next to him.

"You should not ignore us for too long, Heilig."

Oswald sighed as he opened his eyes. He couldn't see the Halbgott, but he had spent so much of his life listening to the siblings that he recognized Tod's dark amusement easily.

"And why shouldn't I?" Oswald whispered.

He knew he didn't have to speak out loud for any of the immortals to hear him as they would respond just as easily to his projected thoughts as they would to his words. It was simply his preference to use words as well as thoughts.

Tod hummed darkly. *"Because you know I do not relinquish Geister easily, Heilig."*

Oswald straightened. He'd heard those words once before as a preface to a warning. Then, he'd been able to stop a massacre from occurring within the Tempel of Carith that would have allowed Tod to claim twelve Geister. If Oswald had learned anything over the Jahre, it was that, even if Carith himself never set foot in those Tempel claimed for him by his creations, the Halbgötter, his Kinder, did not take kindly to mortals destroying anything within a Tempel of Creation.

"Who would dare?" He mindspoke the question, not wishing to be overheard.

"A Mann who has not yet arrived is in danger."

Oswald frowned at the evasive answer. He knew the Halbgötter, especially Tod, had good reason to be cryptic when speaking with mortals, but warning him before the would-be victim had even arrived was a bit odd.

Tod's dark huff quickly destroyed that thought.

"There will be little time between his arrival and his Tod, Heilig, so I suggest you remove yourself to the Altar room. Besides, I know you are not fond of liars, and one of the Nomaden is currently acting as such."

The Halbgott fell silent then. Knowing better than to ignore such a warning, Oswald picked himself up and left his small sanctuary.

That was how he found himself being insulted by an impertinent Falke. He scowled at the young Nomade even as the Halbgötter made several comments about the Mann that made Oswald want to laugh. That was one thing about the Halbgötter that Oswald enjoyed. They spent enough time around humans to not be completely indifferent to their personalities and attitudes.

"I do not hide my abilities, Falke," Oswald spoke once he felt they'd glared at each other enough. "I do not wish to incapacitate you, but I will, if necessary."

For a moment, Jakob continued to glare at Oswald. Soon enough, he huffed and turned away, grumbling under his breath. The other Nomaden eyed him warily and didn't speak to him as he rejoined them.

Oswald nodded, his lips lifting slightly in acknowledgement of the chuckles he'd earned from the Halbgötter. Turning to the Herzogin, he gave a small bow.

"Es tut mir leid, Mylady. I'm afraid you haven't had the best reception this Tempel can offer."

Lady Ilse shook her head and stood, offering a small curtsy. "No need to worry, Heilig Oswald. I understand these are stressful times, and the

Nomaden still have little reason to trust my word or that of mein Lebenmann."

Handmaiden Lise scrambled to her feet. "But, Mylady—"

Oswald laid a hand on her arm to quiet her and shook his head. "The Herzogin understands the situation quite well, Lise." The Fräulein opened her mouth to protest, but Oswald gave her a quelling look. "No matter how much we may not like it."

Lise flushed then and nodded. "For what it's worth, Mylady," she mumbled softly, "I believe what you said about your Lebenmann, the Kreis, and Herr Kluger." Before Lady Ilse could thank her, she quickly added, "I should continue with my duties," and hurried off to another room of the Tempel.

Oswald chuckled at his Schützling's antics. "Do not worry, Mylady," he said when he saw the suddenly lost look on Lady Ilse's face. "She will be fine."

The Herzogin nodded, though the lost look didn't disappear completely. In order to distract the Frau from her distressful musings, Oswald turned his attention to something Lise had said.

"So, Herr Kluger is to be the next Gouverneur, then?" Lady Ilse stared at him in surprise, and he smiled. "That is gut to hear."

Lady Ilse looked confused as she replied. "I didn't realize you had heard that part of the conversation, Heilig."

Oswald shook his head. "Nein, I didn't. But," he glanced towards the murmuring Halbgötter with a wry chuckle, "there are Geister who are more than willing to share such news."

Giggles and some deeper chuckles were the Halbgötter's response.

"Oh!" Lady Ilse blushed and smiled. "I'd forgotten you were a Geistmagier."

Oswald nodded and glanced towards the Nomaden. "It seems many—"

His words were interrupted by a sudden pounding on the doors and a voice shouting from the other side.

"This is Kawn Parshen, Herzog of Zhulan." There was what sounded like a momentary scuffle before the Herzog spoke clearly once more. "Nein, I go in alone. I will not risk unnecessary violence."

Oswald stiffened. *Surely Tod didn't mean…*

He didn't have a chance to finish the thought as several Nomaden moved towards the doors, and he was nearly overwhelmed by the Angst and nervousness that suddenly filled the room. Even so, as the two Katze lifted the plank from the doors, the Heilig moved forward. He couldn't knowingly let anything be destroyed, especially not in the Tempel of Carith.

The moment one of the doors was opened, a Nomade reached out, grabbed the Herzog, and pulled him through the door. The barest glint of a blade in the light coming through the closing door was the only warning Oswald had.

The next moment, just as the plank was dropped back into place across the doors, the sharp clang of metal against stone echoed through the Tempel, quickly followed by a solid *whumpf.*

Chapter 33

Oswald collapsed to his knees and gasped for breath, one hand on the back of the Falke's neck, the other braced against the stone of the Tempel's floor. The sprint forward to grab the rogue Nomade hadn't taken much effort, but the deep, focused, and instant penetration he'd made into the Mann's Geist had.

Soft, slow clapping caught his wavering attention. Casting his eyes in the direction of the sound, he realized that he couldn't see the clapper, and he frowned.

"*Gratuliere, Heilig,*" a voice seemed to whisper. It was barely audible, and it took a moment for Oswald to realize that the Halbgott wasn't whispering but that his own Magie was weakened. "*You protected the sanctity of our Vater's Tempel. You have our Dank.*"

Those words seemed to drag Oswald back into awareness of the Physical Plane. The Heilig groaned as his ears were assaulted by noise and his vision went starry. He could feel his Geist attempting to shut down as it screamed for rest, but he forced himself to focus on the physical. There was one more thing he had to do, a message he had to pass on. Someone had to know what he had seen in the Nomade's Geist.

Oswald suddenly became aware of a hand squeezing his shoulder, and he focused on that to keep from blacking out. Raising half-closed eyes, he found the Herzog kneeling beside him and watching him with concern.

"M-mylord." Oswald winced at the breathiness of his voice.

"What happened, Heilig? Are you all right?" Lord Parshen asked.

The Heilig suddenly felt laughter bubble up in his chest, though all that emerged from his lips were weak groans as his vision swam. He closed his eyes and tried to take steadying breaths. His breathing wouldn't slow, and Oswald began to worry that he wouldn't be able to pass on his message.

"*You shouldn't...self. You...rest.*"

The voice was barely there, and Oswald realized that, if he was awake much longer, he would stop hearing the Halbgötter altogether. Gathering what strength he could, the Heilig opened his eyes to look at the Herzog, who was still watching him worriedly.

"He tried to kill you, M'lord." Oswald's voice was still breathy, but he pushed on. "Would've—"

Suddenly, the noise level was nearly unbearable, and Oswald lowered his head with a groan. The voices of those surrounding him overlapped and tangled together, but he was able to decipher some of what was said.

"How could..."

"...he's a Falke..."

"...allegiance to the Herzog..."

The Heilig shook his head without lifting it. That would take too much effort, effort he couldn't afford to waste.

"Not...Falke."

Once again, the noise level soared, and Oswald swayed on all fours. He knew that the only thing keeping him steady was the Herzog's hand on his shoulder, and he was dankbar for that.

"If he is not a Falke, then what is he?"

The words pierced through the nonsensical noise that filled Oswald's ears. The Heilig found himself dankbar for the Herzogin's clear voice as well.

"Skor...pion."

He barely managed to whisper the final syllable before his starry vision went dark and the roaring in his ears melted into blessed silence.

~~*~*

Kawn caught the Heilig as he collapsed and slowly lowered him to the ground with the help of his Lebenfrau and a familiar-looking Fräulein in the plain dress of a Handmaiden. At the same time, an older Frau bustled over, the large half-open bag in her hand marking her as an Ärztin.

Once the Heilig was settled enough for the Frauen to fuss over him, the Herzog stood and turned his attention to the unconscious Nomade.

Everything had moved too quickly for Kawn to be sure of what had happened. In one moment, he was being pulled through the Tempel door, yet, in the next, the Mann who had pulled him in was on the ground, the Heilig kneeling above him. There had been a few moments of shocked silence before everyone had reacted.

"What did he say?" one of the Nomaden asked, pulling Kawn's attention back to the present.

Turning his gaze from the unconscious Nomade, Kawn eyed the two male Nomaden who were still standing. The two looked similar, and both wore the purple Statusgürtel of the Katze Clan.

James' Clan, Kawn thought idly.

"He said, 'Skorpion'," Kawn replied, wondering if the unconscious Nomade was the only one wearing a Statusgürtel of the wrong color.

Both Katzen went still, and even the third Nomade, who had been crying in another part of the Tempel, lifted her head and went quiet. Then, one Katze, the older of the two, shook his head violently and cursed.

"Nein!" he exclaimed. "It can't be. It can't...."

He quieted as the second Katze laid a hand on his arm and gave him a quelling look.

"It makes sense, Bruder," the second Nomade replied. "It makes more sense than a Falke attempting to kill the Herzog."

The first shook his head again. "But to lie with one's Statusgürtel? That's against Nomade law. Surely even the Skorpione would not condone such a thing. It would only cause Chaos."

"Isn't that what they want?" a young voice sniffed.

Kawn and the two Katzen turned to the young Nomade girl, who now stood nearby. The Wolf glanced earnestly between the three Männer, and

Kawn had the impression that speaking up like she had had taken all of her courage.

"What do you mean?" Kawn asked softly.

The two Katzen simply stared at the girl in surprise, neither seeming to know what to say. The Wolf's eyes continued to dart back and forth, and, for a moment, the Herzog was sure she was going to bolt. Finally, she took a deep breath, settled her gaze on Kawn, and steadied her trembling chin.

"Well…it's just that the Gift Clans aren't exactly fond of Ordnung. They refused the call of the Erstehäuptling and continue to do so. They killed the Gouverneure. What's to keep them from turning their backs on Nomade law, especially if doing so helps them bring down an ally of the Clans and make Leben harder for the rest of us?"

Kawn just stared at the girl as she finished. He realized, with surprise, that she was not as young as he had originally thought. Without meaning to, he said as much, and the Wolf promptly blushed.

The younger Katze chuckled softly. "Ja, Viveka's Of Age, despite how young she looks." The Wolf's blush deepened. "And her tears only make her sound younger."

Suddenly, the Fräulein's face paled, and her eyes welled with tears. "Aw, Viveka," the Mann sighed and reached out to pat her shoulder. She flinched under his touch, and he sighed again. "Harti will live. You'll see."

Instead of being comforted, the Wolf began to wail and hurried back over to the cot by which Kawn realized she'd been kneeling before. She was soon joined by the Ärztin.

"Harti?" Kawn asked.

He kept his eyes on the cot. There was a figure lying rather still there, and, as soon as she knelt next to it, Viveka's keening grew louder. When the Ärztin arrived, she leaned over the cot, touching the figure in a few places. She then reached back and patted Viveka on the shoulder, murmuring something that caused the Fräulein to quiet.

Next to Kawn, the older Katze nodded solemnly.

"Harti is Viveka's older Bruder. He was badly wounded last Nacht when we attempted to move to another safe Haus and the Wachen captured their younger Bruder, Hewitt."

Kawn frowned. "Is there no Arztmagier here to heal such terrible wounds?"

"Nein," the younger Katze answered. "They've been gone since yesterday Morgen, at the latest, and none are expected to return until this Nacht."

Kawn finally turned his focus to the two Katzen. Both Brüder were young, but the shadows around their eyes and the lines of their faces proclaimed just how tired and strained they were.

It had been ten Tage since Volker had been found hanging from his study window. Ten Tage that Kawn had spent mourning for his Freunde and trying to decide what to do. Ten Tage that the Nomaden had spent running and hiding, fearing that they would be imprisoned or, worse, killed.

Kawn suddenly wished that it hadn't taken him ten Tage to make his decision.

Reaching out, Kawn laid a hand on the older Katze's shoulder. The Mann blinked then narrowed his eyes warily, but Kawn just smiled.

"We can get him help now instead of waiting for this Nacht. Ilse," he glanced towards his Lebenfrau, who stood nearby listening to their words, "can fetch an Arztmagier. The Wachen should have some if the Gouverneur's is not available."

Both Katzen gasped even as Ilse nodded and stepped forward. The younger Bruder glanced between the Herzog and his Lebenfrau, eyes wide.

"You would do that? Even though…"

He flushed as he trailed off, but Ilse nodded.

"From what Lise says, it seems you were simply following Jakob's lead, ja?"

Both Katzen nodded, the younger more emphatically than his Bruder. Kawn frowned. "Jakob?"

"The Skorpion," Ilse answered.

"Ah," her Lebenmann murmured and nodded in understanding.

"But why would an Arztmagier with the Wachen be willing to Heal a Nomade?" The older Katze sounded more skeptical than his Bruder. "They have been hunting us for Tage. What's to keep them from killing us the moment we open the Tempel doors?"

Kawn began to shake his head before the question was even finished. "I won't allow any harm to come to my allies; not if I can help it."

The Brüder traded a glance. They seemed to come to a decision together as they nodded to each other and turned towards the barred doors.

~~*~*

"They're all too trusting," Hope muttered as the two nomads unbarred the temple doors. A sudden hand on her shoulder startled her, and she glanced over her shoulder to find her twin frowning at her.

"Too trusting, Hope? That doesn't sound like you."

The silver demigoddess offered her brother a humorless smile. Honestly, she hadn't felt like herself for a while. She had only noticed it in the past few days, but she was sure the effects had been there for years, maybe even the past two centuries.

"Would it be wrong of me to blame Peace?"

"Nay, it would not," Love said, surprising her silver sister. "We've all become more susceptible to each other's influence because of Peace's 'death'."

Hope blinked. That hadn't exactly been her reasoning, but…

"What do you mean, Love?"

338

Love raised an eyebrow. "Haven't you noticed how War always has more influence on Peace whenever she's tired?"

Hope rolled her eyes. "Aye, I have. But that's understandable. War and Peace haven't been able to balance each other for the past two centuries. Of course they'd be more susceptible to each other, even if Peace seems to be affected more than War."

She shook her head. "I don't see what that has to do with the rest of us. We're still balanced." She glanced quickly at Fear, who nodded.

Hate chuckled even as his pink twin sighed. "Our pairs are not as independent as you seem to think. Surely, after several millennia, you'd have realized that."

Hope frowned. Aye, she had wondered about that over the years, especially more recently, but it was not something she and her siblings often discussed. In fact, the discussion in Cautzel at the beginning of the season was possibly the only other time Hope could remember her siblings actually discussing the more serious aspects of their relationships.

"If one of our pairs is unbalanced," Love continued, dragging Hope's attention back to her, "then the rest of us become unbalanced. That's why you've become more pragmatic."

Hope made a face. Honestly, before Peace's 'death', Hope was sure pragmatism hadn't been a possibility for her.

"That's also why I've become more serious," Love added, and Hope chuckled, "and why Hate has become more willing to accept Soul Bonds."

Hope blinked. She didn't understand from where that topic had come, or why Love was now eyeing her twin with a small smirk.

Hate rolled his eyes. "I've always accepted Soul Bonds, Sister. There's nothing I can do against them. I've just become more willing not to interfere with potential ones."

Love laughed, and, while she might have become more serious because of Peace's 'death', her laughter was still light-hearted and joyous.

"Oh, I know, dear Brother."

"It is also the reason," Death added, surprising the four middle siblings, "that Leben has been having more difficulty keeping Geister in their bodies." His voice was quiet and held a note of awe, like he had just realized something important.

Hope turned her gaze to her oldest siblings. Life knelt next to the wounded nomad, her concentration evident in her steady gaze and lined face. Death stood about a foot away, his arms casually crossed in front of his chest, his face utterly relaxed. Hope suddenly realized that before Peace's 'death', the stance would have meant that Death was giving up on claiming the soul.

Now, it simply meant he was giving his twin a fighting chance.

Frowning, Hope asked, "Is that why…?"

She trailed off when she realized what she'd been about to say. Discussing War taking physical form to interact with the humans was one thing. He was expected to go against the rules of The Game since he had been imbalanced for so long.

But should she really mention Life's indiscretions?

Then again, Life was part of the oldest pair of Demigods. She and Death had been alive for several millennia before even Love and Hate were born. As far as Hope knew, they had actually invented The Game themselves. If one of them did something 'improper', could it really be considered against the mostly unspoken rules of The Game?

Death seemed to understand her sudden indecision and shook his head.

"Nein, that is not the reason. Ja, Leben has been having difficulties with the Geister, but that is not the main reason she has been so…'physical' in how she deals with certain ones."

A small smile formed on his lips then. "Unless, of course, you are thinking of something other than how Leben handles the König's Geist?"

Before Hope, or any of her other siblings could reply, a soft sigh drew their attention to Life.

"You know," she murmured, "just because I am concentrating on a Geist does not mean I am not listening to your conversation."

Then, to Hope's surprise, she lifted her pale gaze from the wounded nomad.

Wondering if the nomad had died when she wasn't looking, Hope focused on the Physical Plane. She blinked when she saw that another human knelt next to the injured man's cot. One glance at the newcomer's soul was all Hope needed to confirm that Life had relaxed because the nomad was now in the hands of a Mage Healer.

"Already?" Hope muttered.

She honestly hadn't expected a Mage Healer to arrive so quickly. A soft, tired chuckle drew her attention back to her oldest sister.

"You need to learn to keep an awareness of the Physical Plane if you plan to have these kinds of discussions, Hoffnung." Her white eyes blinked slowly, and she tiredly lifted a hand to point towards the temple doors.

Hope turned to find the duke standing in the doorway. In front of him, along Marktplatz, crowds of river-dwellers and guards murmured amongst themselves, their eyes mostly on the duke.

Behind him, inside the temple, stood his family and several nomads, including the young Wolf who had been captured in the early morning. He was holding his sister, who sobbed against his shoulder. He, too, was watching the duke, as were the other nomads, their gazes holding more awe than those of the river-dwellers outside.

Confused, Hope turned back to Life, who chuckled again before she could ask what had happened.

"The Herzog just publicly accepted the Nomaden as Zhulanbürger. He also said that all Nomaden cannot be held accountable for the actions of a few, and that, while he and the Wachen will continue to search for the Gouverneure's Mörder, the Nomaden have just as much Recht as any river-dweller to move freely around Zhulan."

Life sighed breathlessly as she finished, and Hope blinked. She wasn't really surprised by the duke's words. His lifemate had been insistent to the nomads that he had decided just this and more.

She was surprised by Life's continued use of Zhulanese when she was no longer influencing a Zhulanbürger. When she said so, Life just gave her a blank look.

Death laid a careful hand on his twin's shoulder then, pulling her attention to him. As soon as their eyes met, Life leaned into the touch and sighed. Her face, which had relaxed some once she released her influence on the injured nomad, smoothed. Her shoulders dropped, and she settled her head against Death's arm.

"She is right, Sister. The influence of the nomad's soul should no longer be affecting you. You need to rest."

Life shook her head slightly, her eyes already half-closed. "Nein, noch nicht, Tod. The Schicksale warned us—"

"That War was causing more trouble than we could allow him, aye," Death interrupted.

He pulled Life to her feet, pulling a soft groan from her at the same time. Hugging her to his chest, he tipped her head back so he could look her in the eyes.

"But the others can take care of War's fallout as well as we can now that the Mage Healer is here. I won't let you push yourself like this, especially with the season less than half over."

Hope shivered. She watched as Life laid her head on Death's shoulder, and the oldest Demigods disappeared, no doubt Realm-jumping to a Realm where they wouldn't be bothered by mortal affairs. A hand on her shoulder pulled her attention back to her own twin, who was frowning thoughtfully.

"Do you think Death's right?"

Hope didn't need to ask what he meant. The way Death had spoken those final words had sounded like a promise of worse to come.

Remembering Peace's last visit from Mama Caler, the Kensian Seer, Hope knew that this trouble between Peace and War might actually be settled by the end of the season. But none of them, not even Life and Death, or even War himself, could imagine how that would happen, or what the results might be.

The realization that Death was certain the season could only get worse made Hope feel heavy. Even if it did get better afterwards, could that trouble really be worth it?

The hand on her shoulder squeezed, once again dragging her back to the present. Glancing up into Fear's face and seeing his earnest yellow gaze, Hope realized he wasn't just trying to get her attention. She placed her hand on his and squeezed it in return.

Immediately, she felt herself relax and saw him do the same.

It was the same for each of their pairs. None of them could truly rest unless they were consensually touching their respective twin. Alone, each of them was constantly fighting the Chaos that the Demigods had been born to balance.

Before Peace's 'death', that had never seemed to be a problem for any of them. Now, with each of them more susceptible to the influences of the others, they seemed to be putting up twice the effort for the same situations.

"I don't know," Hope murmured, answering Fear's original question. "But I fear he might be."

"I hope not," Fear sighed.

Hope turned her attention back to the temple at large, keeping her hand entwined with Fear's. Catching sight of Love and Hate, she smiled when she realized that they, too, had decided to rest. As per usual with Love, their form of touching was a little more intimate; Love had her arms wrapped around Hate's neck, her ear pressed against his chest as she watched the mortals interact.

"However he does it, I hope War fixes this mess with Peace soon," Hope sighed. She saw Fear nod out of the corner of her eye. "I am tired of feeling so pessimistic."

Fear chuckled. "I agree, Sister. I'm supposed be the pessimistic one, not you. I find it's a bit tiring being so hopeful all the time."

Hope snorted and slapped her yellow brother lightly on the chest. Silently, she acknowledged that he was right.

They were each born to handle a specific emotion, range of emotions, or situation. It wasn't that they couldn't feel the other emotions or handle the other situations in their own lives, but they weren't meant to deal with them for long periods of time.

And, even for immortals, two centuries was a long time.

~~*~*

Kawn was relieved by how easily the Wachen seemed to trust his declaration of acceptance towards the Nomaden. While they were trained to put aside personal feelings for the Wohl of the Stadt, Kawn had feared their reaction to such a drastic reform. Their obedience was gratifying.

To his surprise, Hauptmann Herrick and several of his higher ranking Offiziere even took it further and offered the Nomaden a public apology. Adlige Reiter, as the highest ranking Nomade currently available, accepted the apology.

She did make one snide remark about the way the Wachen had treated the Nomaden, but Herrick simply bowed his head in acknowledgement. Behind him, a couple of his Offiziere began to protest but were quickly hushed by their fellows with elbows to the ribs and sharp looks.

Unfortunately, the reaction of the onlookers wasn't as subdued. The crowd surged forward, their sudden shouts mingling unintelligibly, and the Wachen scrambled to hold them back from the Tempel and the group that stood before it.

Kawn laid a hand on his sword when fighting broke out, but he hesitated to draw. These were his people as much as the Nomaden, and he wished them no ill. Nearby, Adlige Reiter had one hand behind her back, no doubt reaching for a Scharfmond, but her eyes were on Kawn, not on the unruly crowd.

Before Kawn could decide how to handle the sudden riot, a loud "Ruhe!" cut through the commotion.

Silence fell over the Marktplatz with astounding speed, and Kawn turned to find a large Mann towering over the crowd on the other side of the street. The people surrounding him cringed away, making his bulky presence appear even more conspicuous.

"The Nomaden 'ave every Recht to take the Wachen to task for their trea'ment," the giant Mann growled. In the deathly silence, Kawn was certain everyone in the Marktplatz could hear him. "Their customs may differ from ours, but they're jus' like you an' me." He glared around at the crowd. "They 'ave Familie an' Freunde, they feel Liebe an' pain, jus' like anyone 'ere in this Stadt."

The large Mann glanced towards the Tempel. "Even Gouverneur Volker believed tha' the Nomaden were Zhulanbürger, tha' they had the Recht to live in Frieden wit' us river-dwellers."

"Ja, an' look where it got 'im!"

The shout came from a single Mann in the crowd. It wasn't difficult to spot him because, suddenly, no one was standing near him. The challenger looked wholly surprised to find himself so suddenly alone.

"Dummkopf! Didn' the 'Erzog jus' finish sayin' that all Nomaden shouldn' be held accountable for the actions of a few?"

Kawn recognized the stocky figure of Millicent Wäschemann stepping towards the separated Mann from the crowd surrounding him.

"Tha's not…" he muttered. His confidence seemed to have disappeared with his anonymity. Murmurs filled the Marktplatz as his silence lengthened.

"There's no need for name-calling, Millicent," Peppi Kluger soothed. He stepped up beside the large Mann and laid a hand on his forearm, securing his attention. "And I think you are scaring people, Berg."

Berg frowned and glanced around. To Kawn's surprise, a smile widened his lips, and he laughed loudly. "Es tut mir leid. I forget 'ow easily intimidated you lot can be."

"Don' know 'ow," shouted a Mann nearby. "Your size's 'alf the reason you're so well-respected."

"The other 'alf bein' the Rotvogel," added another Mann, naming a Gasthaus that Kawn knew was rather popular here in Machtstadt. The words were quickly followed by laughter from most of the crowd.

"Didn' know you were Nomade-freundlich, Berg," a middle-aged Frau spoke up as the crowd quieted.

"You weren' s'pose to," Berg answered with a snort. "I find tha' the volume o' my Gäste cover the presence of any Nomaden I hide quite well. 'Sides," he added with a grin, "I couldna found a better use for the Köter who fill my Gasthaus."

The insult raised protests from several in the crowd, which prompted others to reprimand the protesters, but they all sounded good-natured. Kawn had never met Berg before, but he was infinitely grateful for the way the Mann had turned the attitude of the crowd. If he was the owner of the Rotvogel Gasthaus, then Kawn had no doubt that he had a lot of experience with rowdy groups.

Soon after, the crowd began to break up. From the way the people talked, the news of Kawn's announcement would reach the rest of the Stadt by Nacht and, quite possibly, the other Städte by Morgen.

Kawn frowned. He had decided how he might approach Othman in order to find the traitor in Schönestadt but, if Othman heard about this before Kawn wanted him to, it could ruin his tentative Plan.

"What is wrong, Lebenmann?" Kawn turned to his Lebenfrau and gave a small, tight smile.

"I don't know if I'll be able to reach Schönestadt before the news of what has happened here does."

Ilse frowned thoughtfully. "I don't see why not. If you leave soon, you should have most of the Nacht to speak to Othman without interference."

She seemed to think about it ein bisschen more before nodding sharply. "Ja, that would be best." She gave Kawn a significant look. "Just in case Othman decides he needs to make an Exempel of more Nomaden."

"But what about you and the Kinder?" Said Kinder were standing around Ilse, the younger three holding onto her skirts while Didrika stood just to the side, one hand fingering her Mutter's sleeve. "And the situation here in Machtstadt isn't completely settled."

Ilse shook her head and smiled fondly at her Lebenmann. "The Kinder and I will be fine, Kawn. We have our knight protectors with us. There is no reason we can't return to the Gut safely."

She paused and glanced to the side, where Kawn suddenly realized Peppi was waiting to speak with him. "I am certain, too, that Herr Kluger would be willing to help you settle the situation here in Machtstadt."

Obviously taking that as his cue, Peppi stepped forward. "Ja, Mylord, I would. Assuming, of course, that your offer is still open?"

Kawn felt his lips spread wide. "Ja, it is." He offered his hand, which Peppi shook firmly. "I'm glad you've decided to accept, Peppi."

Peppi smiled. "Honestly, I would have accepted in the Gefängnis, but you left too quickly."

Kawn chuckled. "Indeed."

"Mylord," someone spoke from farther into the Tempel, and Kawn turned to find the older Katze Bruder standing nearby. He was watching those river-dwellers who still lingered near the Tempel doors. "My

Bruder and I were wondering if we could speak with you about the Skorpion."

"Skorpion?" Peppi asked with a frown.

Kawn just nodded and led Peppi and his Familie into the Tempel. Both the Heilig and the Skorpion were still unconscious, but they had been moved to cots near the wounded Wolf. Two Pferde now stood guard over the Nomade along with the younger Katze.

"What about him did you wish to discuss?" Kawn asked.

Peppi made a noise of disgust then, no doubt realizing what was going on. It was the younger Katze who answered Kawn's question.

"I know he tried to kill you, Mylord—"

"He tried to kill you?" Peppi asked, shocked.

Kawn nodded and sighed. "He did, but after the announcement I just made, I would rather not punish him publicly. It might give some people the wrong idea, especially since he's not wearing the correct Statusgürtel."

"But to not punish an attempted Mörder would give people worse ideas," Peppi rejoined.

Kawn nodded but was interrupted before he could reply.

"Excuse me, Mylord, but that's why we were hoping you'd let us take him."

The Herzog turned to the elder Katze in surprise. The Mann looked frustrated, and Kawn smile apologetically when he realized why.

"Es tut mir leid," he said, nodding his head to the younger Katze. "We didn't let you finish." Glancing between the two, he added, "Why do you think that would be best?"

The younger Katze looked like he was trying to keep his cheeks from turning too red. "If we took him to the Erstehäuptling, he'd be punished for all of his crimes, not just those that the river-dwellers consider crimes."

He lost the fight with the red in his cheeks as he quickly added, "No offense intended, of course."

"Of course not," Kawn returned with a smile. He glanced at Peppi. "What do you think, Gouverneur?" Peppi looked at him in surprise. "Does that sound acceptable?"

Peppi thought for a moment before nodding. "I, too, would like to see him punished for wearing the wrong Statusgürtel, though perhaps not quite for the same reasons as the Nomaden. We river-dwellers, those that can recognize the meanings anyway, rely on those Statusgürtel to know who is Freund and who is Feind."

He shook his head. "I never once thought that anyone would wear the wrong color, let alone for these reasons." He smiled at Kawn. "I am certain that Hausef will provide a fitting punishment.

"Not to mention," he added in a lower tone, "that the Nomaden will most likely find him ein bisschen useful before they punish him."

"Ach, we would." Adlige Reiter walked up and gave a small bow to the Herzog. "Now, if you do not mind, Mylord, my Männer and I would like to return home. I am sure my Vater is worried about me."

Kawn nodded. "I'm sure he is. The Wachen shouldn't give you any trouble. At the very least, the Geistmagier will have informed the Wachen on the gates of the current situation."

"Danke, Mylord."

She made to turn away, but Kawn stopped her as he realized something.

"Do you need Pferde, Adlige?"

She gave a small smile and shook her head. "Nein, Mylord. We know the location of several others of our Clan. They should have access to their own Pferde."

Kawn nodded. "Very well. Guten Tag, then, Adlige Reiter."

"And you, Mylord."

She left then, her fellow Pferde following her and leaving the Skorpion to the Katzen.

"I believe Hauptling Herrick and I can take care of anything else that comes up if you wish to leave for Schönestadt now, Mylord," Peppi offered once the Pferde had left.

"Danke, Peppi." Noticing the stares he was getting from the Katzen, Kawn asked, "Is something wrong?"

They both shook their heads, even as the older replied. "Nein, Mylord. It's just that we, too, will be traveling towards Schönestadt, and we must leave soon if we hope to reach the Oase before sunrise."

Kawn chuckled. "Then we can travel together, ja? Do you have Pferde?"

Both nodded. "We stabled them with the Marktplatz stable master," the younger Katze answered. "He's always willing to care for any Tier, no matter who the owner is."

"Gut," Kawn said with a nod. "Why don't you fetch your Pferde, then, and we'll prepare to leave."

The two Katzen left quickly, talking excitedly together. A hand on his arm drew the Herzog's attention to his Lebenfrau, though it was quickly drawn down to his Kinder as his legs and waist were suddenly enveloped.

"Do you have to go, Vati?" Gretchen whined.

Kawn was relieved to realize she was sounding more like herself than she had that Morgen at breakfast. With a chuckle, he lowered himself onto one knee so he could see her better.

"Ja, Liebling, I do. I know it seems like I haven't been home that long, but there's something I need to take care of in Schönestadt as soon as possible."

"Bitte, can we come with you, Vater?" Adal begged.

A hand squeezed the boy's shoulder, and he turned his face towards his Mutter, a pout already pulling at his lips. The look had no effect on his Mutter's stern expression.

346

"Schönestadt is too dangerous right now!"

Adal looked like he wanted to press the issue, but Kawn laid a hand on his other shoulder, pulling the boy's attention back to him. He gave Adal a warm smile.

"Your Mutter is right, Sohn. Besides, I have a task for you and your Schwestern." Kawn glanced around at all of his Kinder. "I want you to cooperate with your Mutter for the next few Tage. She's going to need you to move quickly and stay out of trouble," he emphasized those last four words with a stern look for all four Kinder, "while she completes her own tasks."

Adal bowed his head, his cheeks turning pink. Kawn hooked a finger under his Sohn's chin and raised it so he could look into the boy's eyes. "Can you do that for me, Adal?"

Adal nodded solemnly. "Ja, Vati."

Kawn looked around at his three Töchter. "Girls?"

They all nodded and murmured their agreement, though Gretchen's was quickly followed by, "But I still wish you didn' 'ave to go, Vati."

Kawn chuckled and kissed her forehead. "I know, Perle. But it should only take a couple of Tage. Before you know it, we'll all be back at the Gut, ja?"

Gretchen sighed but nodded reluctantly.

"Kawn?"

The Herzog looked up. Ilse looked just as confused as she sounded. Climbing to his feet, he pulled her into his arms and kissed her cheek.

"What tasks of mine do you mean?"

Kawn smiled at Ilse. "Well, I realize that, while Schönestadt is a higher priority for me, a Gouverneur still needs to be chosen for Wildestadt."

Ilse blinked and narrowed her eyes, but Kawn rushed on before she could speak.

"I know it might sound like a bit much since James didn't give us any recommendations, and you'll still have to find out who is in the Kreis, but I am sure it is a task you can handle."

They stood for a moment in silence as Ilse studied Kawn's face. He simply smiled. He knew he had been pushing her away during this Katastrophe, something that had been upsetting her. He wanted to make it up to her, and, knowing how much she wanted to help him with his political burdens, he thought she might enjoy this.

Besides, he hadn't been lying. Wildestadt needed a new Gouverneur just as badly as Machtstadt had.

"You would trust me to make such a decision, Kawn?"

Ilse sounded so unsure that Kawn kissed her lightly before nodding.

"Of course I do, Liebling. You know our people just as well as I do, if not better. I trust your judgment more than I do James', to be honest."

Ilse frowned and shook her head. "There is no need to demean young James, Kawn. I'm certain that, in these matters concerning the Kreis and the Nomaden, James knows better than anyone."

Kawn chuckled. "Perhaps, but he is only sixteen, Liebling. He cannot possibly understand all of the political matters that need considering, not like you and I do."

Ilse smiled warmly then, and her cheeks tinted pink.

"Very well, Lebenmann. I will travel to Wildestadt and see if I can't find a proper Gouverneur."

"Gut!"

Kawn noticed the two Katzen returning then, both smiling widely. He leaned forward and kissed Ilse's cheek.

"Could you stop by the Gut and send some of the knights to Schönestadt, just in case?"

Ilse chuckled and agreed.

~~*~*

Once Ilse and her Lebenmann said their farewells, the Herzogin took a moment to observe her Familie.

While Kawn went to help the Katzen and Sir Leal with the Skorpion, Kuonrada wandered over to speak with Handmaiden Lise and Sir Ritter. Gretchen followed after and immediately began babbling happily to her knight protector.

Meanwhile, Didrika and Adal approached the Nomaden. The older struck up a conversation with the two Wölfe not mourning the wounded Mann, while her Bruder began talking with the Spinne Männer.

Ilse smiled as she watched her Kinder. They had grown up with their Vater's Liebe for the Nomaden, and it showed in Didrika's lively expression and Adal's excited banter.

Knowing they would be safe in the Tempel, Ilse returned to the doors. She had seen some river-dwellers loitering around the entrance that she thought might be part of the Kreis. Perhaps they could give her an idea of who to approach in Zhulan's southern Stadt.

Chapter 34

"Shadow, where are you?"

The inquiry woke Flame from her light doze just as the sun sank below the horizon. Despite her nap, she knew exactly where Shadow was, even before he told Gemi that he and Last Chance had been at the river and were now heading back to the inn.

Flame uncurled her sinuous body, stretching out her wings and tail as she did so. Her jaw parted in a wide, toothy yawn, which ended with a loud snap, startling a flock of desert sparrows out of a nearby, barren-looking bush. The dragon hissed softly in amusement as the sparrows fluttered about before landing along the ground farther away.

Flicking out her long, snake-like tongue, Flame tested the evening air. She crooned softly.

Although the western sky was still painted with the warm colors of the desert sunset, the heat of the day had already begun to dissipate. In a couple of hours, she knew the air would be quite chill. That mattered little to her, but her bondmates always appreciated the cool night air after the long day of desert heat.

Knowing her bondmates and their companions were preparing to leave Schönestadt, Flame coiled her body and launched herself into the air. Taking advantage of the remaining heat, she quickly gained altitude with only a few flaps of her wings. Once high enough that no humans would notice her, Flame turned towards Schönestadt and sped towards the city.

Flame had purposefully hidden herself about an hour's trot west of Schönestadt. Not only did it assure that she would not be seen, but it also gave her the opportunity to really stretch her wings and fly at a speed she could not properly achieve while following a horse's steady pace.

However, an hour's trot was not even a ten minute flight, so she quickly found herself circling above Schönestadt, searching the streets for the two horses and their riders.

From this height, Flame had the perfect view of the entire city, as well as much of the desert that surrounded it. Even so, as a dragon, she could still see every detail of the city streets, which were quite lively at this hour.

In the Marktplatz, children darted after each other, dodging browsing customers and vendors who were beginning to pack up or put out their wares. This was the time of day when the day vendors gave way to the night vendors.

In other parts of the city, things were not so much quieting down as shifting tone. The owners of daytime-only businesses were closing down shop and heading home. At the same time, the night life for which the Zhulanese cities were famous was waking up. Inn- and tavern-owners lit torches outside their establishments, inviting in those who wanted a bed and food, or perhaps something a little stronger.

And amongst all of the usual life of the city, the guards were out in full force, as they had been since Schönestadt had learned of the death of the two governors. Flame would have felt sorry for the guards if it had not been her friends they were hunting. Even for a dragon, ten days of constant awareness was exhausting.

Idly following the path of one particular set of guards with her gaze, Flame bared her teeth and growled when she realized where they were going.

"*James,*" she hissed, ever wary of Animal Mages and Mindspeakers, even when she was so high above the city. "*Guards are en route to arrest Heiss Schmied.*"

Gemi groaned slightly, interrupting her conversation with Ferez. The dragon did not have a chance to hear the girl's response, though, as Flame's attention was suddenly drawn away from the city.

Traveling north along the Evonese Highway at a quick, yet steady, pace were four horses. Flame recognized two of those horses as nomad-trained. The other two held themselves like river-dweller horses, and they wore the saddles and tack of such.

Flame broke the circle she had been flying and drifted towards the four horses, idly wondering if some river-dwellers had managed to capture a couple of nomad horses. It was highly improbable with their training, but Flame could not think why a river-dweller other than Gemi and Ferez would be traveling amicably with nomads.

In her mind, Gemi's and Shadow's curiosity echoed her own.

Once she was closer, she realized that the riders of the two nomad horses did wear the Kopfabdeckung and Statusgürtel of nomads. Their Statusgürtel were even purple.

"*Katzen,*" she muttered to her bondmates.

Circling lower to get a better look at the river-dwellers, Flame was surprised to discover that she recognized one. "*Lord Kawn is approaching Schönestadt.*"

"*Already?*" Shadow nickered in surprise, even as he turned south at Gemi's prodding.

Flame understood his reaction. None of them had expected the duke to deal with Zhulan's northernmost city so soon. With her bondmates' questions echoing in her mind, Flame pulled her wings close to her sides and dropped into a dive.

Flame landed as silently as she could and padded up to the road. She stepped up onto it just as the four horses approached, and all four slowed to a stop and nickered at her curiously, though the river-dweller horse not belonging to Kawn took a step back and whinnied uncertainly.

However, the horses' riders caught Flame's attention more as all four shouted her name.

Flame recognized the two nomads as a pair of Katze brothers who often traveled between the oases and the cities to trade goods with the Clans' allies. They greeted her with friendly shouts of her nickname, the younger brother raising a hand to wave at her.

The duke greeted her similarly with her full name, and his tone was tinged with surprise. He obviously had not expected the Drache Krieger to still be in Schönestadt.

The fourth voice, however, was unexpected. The river-dweller, whom Flame had not recognized on first glance, wore the armor of a knight, the colors of which proclaimed his own house and that of this Knight Master, Lord Kawn. Despite this, he addressed Flame with the same familiarity that the Nomads had, but his voice was filled with a shocked recognition that caught the attention of the other humans as much as hers.

Flame narrowed her eyes and looked at the knight more closely. As far as she was concerned, there was no reason for a knight of Zhulan to recognize her as she had always made certain that none saw her. As she looked him over, she realized his face seemed familiar, yet different, as if it had been a long time since she had last seen him.

Suddenly, the wind shifted, and Flame found herself downwind of the horses and their riders. Inhaling the scent of both horses and humans, she sifted through them, hoping that the knight's scent would trigger her memory.

When she found the scent for which she was looking, she jerked her head back.

At the same time, the knight bowed his head. As he gave it a small shake, she heard him mutter, "James Caffers. I should have known."

Baring her teeth, Flame hissed.

~~*~*

Sir Leal Highknoll hadn't felt this shocked since he, Paeter, and the other survivors from Cosley Estate had returned from the battle of Farvis only to find that the Estate had been attacked in their absence. Leal remembered wandering through the ashes of the manor, hoping to find some sign that someone had survived.

But there had been no sign of life. The massacre had been complete and utterly devastating. Even the horses and livestock had been butchered, the crops burned, and, as they later discovered, the fields strewn with salt. That convinced them, more than the words burned into the manor's lone brick wall, that the land had been damned.

The manor fire had burned so hotly that no identifiable human remains were distinguishable among the ashes. Only some items had been recovered, including Lord Jem's sword and Lady Kit's favorite jewels, neither of which would be left behind willingly. Both had been found among the remains of the Lord's Chambers, and Leal and the others knew this could only mean that both had been caught and killed during Lady Kit's afternoon rest.

The one hope that had sustained them all was that there had been no sign of young Gemini and her bondmates. Gemini's sword, a strong blade of simple design, had not been among the ashes, Shadow's corpse

351

had not been among the dead animals, and, as a fire dragon, Flame would not have burned in the fires.

It was a small hope, of course, but they had held onto it fiercely.

As the years passed, that hope had faded. The longer they went without news of Lord Jem's only child, the more they wondered if she still lived. None of them doubted that she had survived the attack, but Leal wasn't the only one who had wondered if something else had claimed her life since.

Now, he had proof that she still lived. As a dragon, Flame had no reason to interact with humans on her own. Leal knew that from personal experience as he had trained the three to cooperate in fighting, with James both on the ground and on the back of one of her bondmates. While Leal had learned to interpret many of the dragon's sounds and expressions, he had also learned that she would not seek out humans unless Gemi needed her to.

"James Caffers," he whispered with a shake of his head and a soft laugh. "I should have known."

When Lord Kawn had mentioned that the Drache Krieger was a boy named James Caffers, Leal had recognized the family name certainly. He remembered young Jake Caffers' constant teasing of the duke's daughter. Despite his certainty that the boy's family had been killed in the attack, he had wondered if this James was a surviving relation about which he hadn't known.

He hadn't made the connection that the Drache Krieger might have an actual dragon. Now, he wondered if that shouldn't have been his first thought.

Leal was suddenly pulled from his thoughts by a hand on his arm. Lifting his head to look at his knight master, Leal took in the man's concerned frown and gave a slight smile.

"Are you all right, Leal?"

Lord Kawn was studying him. Lifting a hand to his face, Leal was surprised to find wetness on his cheeks. Scrubbing both cheeks dry with his hands, Leal sighed and nodded.

"Just memories, is all."

"Memories?" Lord Kawn asked, but a sharp growl drew their attention to Flame, who was baring her teeth and glaring at Leal.

The knight sighed again. Even after all these years, he could still interpret that. It was a warning, most likely to keep James' secret.

But the warning was unnecessary. Lord Kawn may be his current knight master, but Kensy was where Leal had been born, and the Duke, or Duchess, of Kensy deserved his loyalty first and foremost.

Leal nodded, both in acceptance of Flame's warning and in answer to Lord Kawn's question. "Aye, memories. I haven't seen Flame in seven years."

The dragon's growl pitched higher, but Leal ignored her. He wasn't planning on giving anything away. Nothing important, anyway.

The significance of the number of years was apparently not lost on Lord Kawn, who raised his eyebrows and glanced at Flame.

"You knew Flame Tongue in Kensy?" Leal nodded. "Why didn't you ever mention her?"

Leal chuckled, even as Flame's growl rose in volume. "She was a bit of a regional secret, you could say."

The growl suddenly dropped to a more threatening octave, and Leal grimaced. He'd have to assure the dragon quickly that her bondmate's secret was safe with him, or he was at risk of being attacked.

"By the gods, Flame, I know you're protective of young James, but no one here wants to harm him, do they?"

The growling suddenly ended, and Leal almost chuckled at the confused whine that replaced it. With a soft sigh of relief—Leal hadn't fancied being attacked by a dragon, especially one he'd known several years ago—he turned back to Lord Kawn.

In the dim light of the stars and moons, he could see that the duke looked decidedly bemused as he glanced between Leal and Flame. On his other side, the two Katzen snickered softly.

"I take it you know James, then," Lord Kawn finally said, his gaze settling on Leal.

The knight nodded. "I used to, at least. Like I said before, it's been seven years." His voice dropped to a whisper as he added, "I wasn't even certain the boy had survived the attack."

He remained silent for a moment before shaking his head and speaking more loudly. "That he has become the Drache Krieger, let alone everything else, is not something I would have imagined." He chuckled. "When you told us who the Drache Krieger was, I didn't even make the connection."

A soft croon eased through the air, and Leal glanced back at Flame. Smiling at the red and purple creature, Leal swung off his horse, who shifted nervously. Leal wasn't surprised. The animal was his second mount since Kensy, so it had never met the dragon.

Leal rubbed his mount's nose soothingly before approaching Flame. Once close enough, he lifted a hand to the dragon's snout but stopped just shy of touching her. He knew better than to presume such familiarity after all these years.

They stood like that for a full minute, Flame watching him warily. Leal simply waited patiently. He wouldn't rush this, not when the trust of his old knight master's heir would be his reward.

Finally, with a soft snort, Flame pushed her face against his hand. Leal smiled and smoothed his palm up the dragon's nose, between her eyes, and back to the base of her horns, where he remembered she enjoyed the attention. She closed her eyes, and a deep rumble started in her chest, reminiscent of the purr of a large cat.

Chuckling softly, Leal whispered, "How are you, Flame?"

There was a slight pause in the dragon's rumble before it continued smoothly. Flame's blood-red eyes opened to a thin slit and seemed to pierce him in their intensity.

Leal sighed. He still recognized that look, too. Something was going on, something that Gemi needed help with but would most likely be unwilling to admit.

The knight would have responded to the look, but a steady beating sound that was quickly gaining volume suddenly became recognizable as hoof beats. Looking towards Schönestadt, Leal saw two horses galloping towards him and Flame.

"Sir Leal!" one of the riders cried as the two horses slowed to a halt.

Suddenly, a pair of arms wrapped around his neck, and his arms were filled with the slim body of a child he had feared he would never see again.

~~*~*

James hadn't explained to Ferez why they were traveling south out of Schönestadt when they had originally planned to leave through the same hole in the wall they'd used several days before.

Therefore, Ferez was surprised to find four horses and their riders standing in the middle of the Evonese Highway with Flame. He certainly wasn't prepared for the sight of James throwing himself into the arms of the man standing next to Flame. Nor was he prepared for the fire that seemed to ignite in his gut at the sight.

Ferez pursed his lips and glanced away. For the first time since the season began, he found himself wishing he hadn't asked to travel with James. If he hadn't, he wouldn't be afflicted with this churning pain or the confusion that seemed to have grown within him as the day wore on.

Today, he and James had simply been commoners. They hadn't had to worry about fighting or planning attacks. They hadn't had to worry about the political consequences of their actions. They had simply relaxed and explored the city, and Ferez had seen a new, relaxed side of James, one he found he liked just as much as he did any of the others. One he wished James could show more often. And that liking and wishing had grown and, with it, the confusion.

"You survived."

The words were whispered, but the voice was so choked with sorrow and relief that Ferez was jerked from his thoughts. Those words had been James', and Ferez suddenly realized that he had recognized the name he'd called out.

Sir Leal?

He peered through the soft light of the desert night at the man who hugged James. Sure enough, the man was none other than Sir Leal Highknoll, current Knight Captain of Parshen Gut and previous Second Captain of Cosley Estate.

Suddenly, Ferez remembered his assumption that James was from Cosley Ruins. *If he lived on Cosley Estate before the massacre...if he didn't think anyone else had survived...*

Ferez grimaced. If that was true, he couldn't fault the boy's reaction.

"Aye, I did, James," the knight replied, pulling back enough to look the boy in the face.

Ferez couldn't see the knight's expression very well in the dim light. Instead, his own mind provided him with an image of hunger-filled eyes that Ferez quickly banished, alarmed.

"We were certain you had survived the attack, but, when we received no news of you, many of us feared you had fallen to something else."

Ferez couldn't see James' expression, but the choked teasing tone of his response hinted at a small smile on the boy's face. "I don't know why when you and Paeter trained me personally."

Ferez blinked, surprised. Apparently, a smile wasn't the only thing James' response implied.

The next moment, James startled and glanced around. Ferez suspected that Flame or Shadow had just reminded James that they weren't alone. The king felt his stomach clench. No matter how close he felt to James, it seemed there were still some things about himself that the boy was unwilling to share. He supposed he shouldn't blame the boy. They'd only known each other for little more than a month.

And what does that say about me then?

The harsh sound of a throat being cleared dragged Ferez from his thoughts and his attention to one of the other riders who had been waiting for them. The Kopfabdeckungen declared him, and the rider next to him, a nomad. The third mounted man, Ferez realized with little surprise, was none other than Kawn.

"I do not mean to interrupt your reunion, Drache Krieger," spoke one of the nomads, "but we should leave for the Oase as soon as we can." He patted something large that lay across the saddle in front of him. "We won't be traveling as quickly as we normally would."

Ferez still couldn't see James' face as Last Chance stood behind the boy, but Ferez couldn't miss the sudden tensing of his shoulders and the way he shifted slightly from side to side. Ferez thought he could even guess the conflicting sides of the boy's sudden internal struggle.

On the one hand, they had intended to return to Helloase tonight, and the nomad's words would have piqued James' curiosity, if nothing else. On the other, James had suddenly been presented with a chance to catch up with an old friend and mentor, someone he had once thought dead.

Ferez didn't like to see James so distressed, especially since he had been so relaxed not that long ago. The sight only added an ache in his chest to the other emotional pains he'd been feeling.

"James," he spoke softly, catching the boy's attention.

Dark eyes turned to him, and, for a second, Ferez was struck by how lost James looked. It was something the king had never fancied seeing before, and he realized he would do anything to dispel that look.

"One more day in Schönestadt wouldn' hurt, would it? I'm sure the duke an' 'is knight 'ave news to share, an' they could prolly use any help they can get, aye?"

James relaxed as Ferez finished, and his face softened into a small smile, his eyes shining in a way that made Ferez shift in his saddle. Then Flame crooned softly, and James huffed softly, his smile widening.

"Ja, and I don't relish introducing you to an Unwetter while traveling."

Ferez blinked. Before he could ask what an '*oon-veh-tehr*' was, the nomad who had spoken before groaned and guided his horse off the road.

"Komme, Bruder. Let's water the Pferde and be off. If a storm is coming and James insists on not riding with us, then we must leave immediately."

The second nomad quickly followed the first off the road. The others remained quiet as the nomads led their horses to the river to drink then returned.

"Is there any message you wish us to take to your Vater, Drache Krieger?"

The nomad's voice was tight, his disappointment obvious. It seemed, like so many others Ferez had met, the nomad had looked forward to traveling with the Drache Krieger, if only briefly.

James reached up and patted the man's leg. "Just let him know that we should return on the next Nacht. He'll understand." The nomad nodded stiffly, and, with several wishes of "Gute Nacht"—and a quick "Danke" to Kawn—the two nomads rode west for Helloase.

~~*~*

Once the Nomaden were out of sight, Gemi turned to introduce Sir Leal to Ferez. No sooner was the König's pseudonym out of her mouth than the knight turned to stare up at her companion.

"Frenz?"

The word was sharp with recognition, and Gemi frowned as she peered between her old mentor and her newer Freund.

"You know him?"

She wouldn't have been surprised to learn that Ferez knew the knight, but she had been sure Ferez's alter ego had been more of a secret than that.

"Aye, he knows who I am," Ferez answered. While Gemi frowned, he leaned over Last Chance's neck and offered his hand to Sir Leal. "Good to see you 'gain, Sir Leal."

"And you, Frenz." The old knight took the Mann's hand and shook his head slowly. "I must admit, I never expected to run into you here in Zhulan."

A chuckle came from behind them, reminding Gemi that Lord Kawn was still with them. "He has been riding with young James almost since

356

the beginning of the Jahreszeit, Leal." The knight nodded, and Lord Kawn turned his attention to Gemi. "And Leal knows Frenz so well because he also trained him for several Jahre."

He glanced between Gemi and her old mentor. "Maybe longer than he trained you?"

Gemi sighed. She didn't know how she was going to explain her previous slip. She had never been able to think of a probable explanation for her young sword training that wouldn't give away her true identity. Thankfully, she'd never had to explain her childhood to any who didn't already know who she was—before now.

"Nay," Sir Leal spoke, startling her from her considerations. "I trained them both for about the same amount of time."

Gemi stared at her old mentor in the ensuing silence. *Is he mad?* He had seemed more than willing to help her keep her secret, but now he was edging dangerously close to giving her away.

"You were four when you began to train?"

Gemi grimaced at the disbelief that was heavy in Ferez's voice. She suddenly worried for her Freundschaft with the König. The more time she spent with him, the closer she felt they were getting and the fewer secrets she wished to keep from him.

Even so, she was still scared to give up her biggest secret to someone so powerful. She didn't know how he would receive it.

"Aye, he was," Sir Leal answered for her. Gemi swallowed nervously and glared half-heartedly at the knight. He simply ignored her. "Being the best friend of the very stubborn daughter of a duke will do that."

"Sir Leal!"

"What?" the knight asked, amusement clear in his words. "Was that supposed to be a secret?"

Gemi gaped at her old mentor, speechless. It wasn't necessarily his words that shocked her into silence as much as the fact that he had managed in a few Minuten to do what she had been unable to do in six Jahre. With one sentence, he had provided a plausible explanation for her entire childhood that still hid her true identity.

When Gemi finally found her voice, she scowled at the knight, despite the fact that none of her companions would notice in the darkness that had settled over the desert.

"It wasn't exactly something I wanted to advertise."

Sir Leal sighed. "Gemini can't stay hidden forever, James."

Gemi felt her scowl deepen. "I know that." After a moment's thought, she quickly added, "We both know that."

She shook her head. It felt odd to refer to herself as two different people. "But you know what's likely to happen the moment she comes forward as heir to the duchy. You can't blame her for being a little wary."

"You might be surprised, James," the knight responded. "I'm sure her political pull as future duchess combined with your own influence would lessen any negative reactions her return might cause."

For a moment, Gemi simply stared at her old mentor as she processed his words. With a huff, she tossed up her hands in frustration.

"And what influence could I possibly have that would affect the way her future peers treat her?" After a beat, she added, "No offense, Mylord," with a quick glance at the Herzog.

Lord Kawn chuckled lowly. "None taken, mein Freund. However, as interesting as I am finding this conversation, we really must head into Schönestadt. I have a Gouverneur to speak with before anyone else from Machtstadt can come and spread rumors of what has happened. I am sure you can finish this while we travel or even once we reach the Stadt."

Gemi's interest was piqued by the Herzog's words, but they also made her wary. "Surely you aren't suggesting that Frenz and I travel with you to the Regierhaus," she cautioned, naming the home of the Gouverneur and the political center of the Stadt.

"Ach, nein, nein," the Herzog assured with a quick shake of his head. "That would hardly help my Pläne. Nein, I simply meant that Sir Leal should travel with the two of you. It would give you a chance to catch up. After all, a few Minuten of reunion can hardly make up for the last seven Jahre."

"But, Lord Kawn," Sir Leal quickly protested, "I'm here as your knight protector. I should—"

The Herzog cut him off with a raised hand. "I'll only be going to the Regierhaus, Sir Leal. I doubt there will be anything there that you need to protect me from that I cannot handle myself."

Although Sir Leal remained silent, Gemi sensed that he still wanted to protest. After a quick thought to her bondmates and an affirmative response from Shadow, Gemi broke the growing silence.

"In that case, Mylord, may I send Shadow with you?"

"Why?" Lord Kawn asked curiously, while the other two Männer made sounds of surprise.

Gemi shrugged. "I would feel more comfortable if you had someone to watch your back, Mylord. Also," she added quickly before anyone could question that, "if Shadow goes with you, we can keep in contact. Shadow will let us know if you need any help."

There was a moment of silence while the Herzog seemed to consider her offer. Hesitantly, he asked, "Do you wish to switch mounts?"

Immediately, Shadow and, to Gemi's surprise, Last Chance both snorted loudly and tossed their heads. Flame hissed in amusement, letting Gemi know that both Pferde had expressed the same thought. With a chuckle of her own and a shake of her head, Gemi answered the Herzog.

"Nein, that would not be a gut idea. Shadow does not take kindly to anyone but myself riding him unless absolutely necessary. And it seems that both he and Last Chance are in agreement that I should ride no Pferd but them."

Glancing at Ferez, she added, "If you don't mind, that is."

The König chuckled. "Course not. I didn' mind it the las' time, why should I mind now?"

Gemi considered mentioning that last time was a necessity born of the approaching threat of Wachen, but the touch of relief in the Mann's voice gave her pause. Before she could think too long on it, Lord Kawn spoke up.

"Very well. I don't see any harm in having Shadow follow me to the Regierhaus. But we should head into Schönestadt now."

Nodding in agreement, Gemi and Sir Leal mounted their respective Pferde. As Flame took wing once more, the small group turned their mounts north and continued riding towards the Stadt.

Chapter 35

Kawn arrived at the Regierhaus with little incident. The Wachen on the gate had recognized him, and, after James had changed mounts, they had escorted Kawn further into the Stadt. They had eyed his Pferd shadow curiously, but they seemed to know better than to ask about the stallion.

As they entered the Hauptplatz, which the Regierhaus bordered on one edge, the stench of Tod nearly overwhelmed Kawn's senses. Taking in the horrible sight of two corpses hanging from the gallows, he covered his nose and mouth with one hand in an attempt to block out the putrid scent of rotting flesh, with little success.

A tap on his arm drew his attention to the Wache next to him, who offered him a bundle of cloth. Taking it from the Mann, Kawn noticed that he and the other Wachen had pulled scarves up over the lower portions of their faces.

"Es tut mir leid about the smell, Mylord," the Wache said as Kawn wrapped the cloth around his head in imitation of the other Männer. "Gouverneur Othman insists that the bodies be left up as an Exempel to any Nomaden who might still be free in the Stadt."

Kawn paused in tucking the cloth in place. The Wache's voice had grown bitter towards the end. Looking around, the Herzog noticed that the other Wachen watched him with weary eyes. He hoped that boded well for the transition he had planned for Schönestadt.

"Then we shall simply have to endeavor to end this quickly," Kawn replied, but the Wachen didn't look impressed.

The Wachen led Kawn past the gallows, which thankfully stood at the end of the Hauptplatz opposite from the Regierhaus. The distance seemed to lessen the stench somewhat, but Kawn still found himself dankbar that he had seen worse during the Krieg. His stomach would most likely have rebelled otherwise.

Word of his arrival must have preceded him as Gouverneur Othman was standing by the doors to the Regierhaus when Kawn pulled his Pferd to a halt. Swinging off his mount, Kawn greeted the portly Mann with a stiff handshake and small nod.

"Mylord, I am glad you were finally able to come deal with our situation."

The words would have made Kawn suspicious about the Mann's attitude, but his smile seemed sincere. That Kawn could see his smile startled the Herzog. The Gouverneur did not seem to be bothered by the stench.

Othman gave the Herzog little time to respond as he gestured across the Hauptplatz in the direction from which Kawn had arrived.

"You had a chance to take a look at our precautions, ja, Mylord?"

Kawn frowned and glanced back across the Hauptplatz. As before, all he could see were the gallows and the two rotting corpses that hung from them.

"You mean the dead Nomaden."

He tried his best to keep his voice neutral. He had hoped to be able to cajole the Gouverneur with an agreeable attitude of his own, but the sight of the executed Männer, as well as Othman's seemingly cavalier attitude, left him scrambling for his wits.

The stout Mann nodded rather energetically. "Ach, ja. An Exempel had to be made, Mylord. Two Nomaden for two Gouverneure, and those were the first two young Männer that were captured. 'Course, we captured several Nomaden before them, but I couldn't very well execute a Mutter and her Kinder or any elderly. The people would have rebelled."

Kawn felt his gut twist in a way that it hadn't at the stench of Tod. Why had he never before noticed Othman was capable of this…this…horrifying disdain for human Leben?

Hoping the horror didn't yet show in his eyes, Kawn asked, "And how long have they been hanging there?"

Othman paused and seemed to consider. "Almost a full Siebentag, I think." He shrugged and smiled once more. "A fine warning it is, too, since I am still alive and well."

Kawn doubted the dead Nomaden had as much to do with Othman's continued survival as the Wachen's vigilance and willingness to protect their Gouverneur. And even that he questioned as he glanced at the surrounding Männer. With their faces partially covered, several of the Wachen seemed unwilling to hide their disgust at their Gouverneur's words.

Soon they'll be able to do more than simply stand by while Othman speaks so casually of the Tod of other human beings.

Hoping to move the corpulent Mann away from the subject of the dead Nomaden, Kawn murmured, "You mentioned other Nomaden, mein Freund." He grimaced as he used the word and hoped it did not show in his eyes. "How many others have you captured?"

Othman hummed softly, his head tilting to the side as he thought. "Well, not sure exactly. Maybe thirty. Possibly forty. I can't be sure."

"Forty-three, Gouverneur, not including the executed."

Kawn looked sharply to the Wache who had answered and recognized the stony-faced Mann as Schönestadt's Hauptmann, Waller.

Othman blinked and turned to Hauptmann Waller. "Really?" When the Hauptmann nodded, Othman hummed and turned back to Kawn. "Well, what do you know? The Wachen are more efficient than I thought."

Kawn wasn't sure if the snort that followed the statement came from a Mann or a Pferd. Othman didn't seem to notice, and Kawn attempted to move the conversation further.

"Is that just Nomaden?"

Thankfully, Waller took up the question without waiting for Othman to try to answer it. "Ja, Mylord. We also have twelve Freunde of the Nomaden in custody. In fact," he added, directing a glance of something other than his previous stoniness at Othman, "my Männer just arrested Heiss Shmied."

Othman nodded. "Ach, a shame that. He was my favorite blacksmith." The Gouverneur shrugged. "Ach, well. He is a conspirator against the Stadt. It cannot be helped."

The Herzog finally felt anger peak within him, but he reined it in as he recognized the opening Othman had provided.

"Ach, ja, the conspirators. You mentioned in your letter about an informant who was willingly giving up these conspirators, Othman. Could you tell me about him?"

The stout Mann shrugged. "Can't tell you much, I'm afraid."

Kawn frowned. "What do you mean?"

Surely, he can't be serious.

The Mann shrugged again. "Simple, Mylord. The letters we received were anonymous and delivered by..." Othman snapped his fingers at Hauptman Waller. "What did Hunder call that verdammt Vogel?"

"I believe the phrase you're looking for is 'silent Falke', Gouverneur."

The answer was not provided by Waller but by another Mann who approached the group. None of Kawn's current companions seemed surprised by the Mann's appearance, though Othman seemed ein bisschen annoyed.

"I apologize for interrupting, Mylord," the new arrival added, turning to Kawn, "but I couldn't help overhearing and thought I might be of some assistance."

"And you—" Kawn began before Othman cut him off.

"Hunder, we hardly need your assistance."

Hunder ignored Othman and offered Kawn his hand. "Hunder Wolfmann, Tieremagier for Regierhaus, Mylord."

Kawn took the Mann's hand, surprised and impressed. He had heard of the Wolfmanns. They were a well-known Familie of Tieremagier that had run the Regierhaus's kennel since its founding.

"Can you tell me anything more about Othman's mystery informant?"

"Only that the Falke who delivered the letters was always the same and would never speak, no matter how I asked it to."

A sudden snort and nicker drew Kawn's attention to Shadow, who suddenly hovered at Kawn's back. Hunder frowned at the Pferd.

"I don't think I understand the question, Herr..."

Shadow snorted and tossed his head then pawed at the ground. His agitation was obvious, and Kawn wondered just how important this information could be. Hunder shook his head.

"Nein, it was not a Falke I recognized, but I don't see how that is significant. I can hardly be expected to know every Vogel in the Stadt."

Instead of increasing the Pferd's agitation, the words actually appeared to calm Shadow. The stallion gave Kawn a single nudge with his muzzle before backing away and lowering his head to the grass of the Hauptplatz.

"What was that about?" Othman asked, indignant.

Kawn sighed but turned his attention to placating the Gouverneur. He hoped James could make sense of whatever information he had just gained because Kawn certainly couldn't.

~~*~*

As soon as they parted ways with Kawn, James directed their small group to a nearby tavern. On the way, Sir Leal told them about the events that had unfolded in Machtstadt, especially those surrounding the city's temple.

That explains the nomads' extra bundle, at least, Ferez thought as they entered the tavern.

Now, Ferez found himself settled at a small table in a quiet corner of the tavern, cradling a pint of ale as James and Sir Leal traded stories. He listened, fascinated, as they seemed to alternate between catching up on the last seven years and reminiscing over their shared time at Cosley Estate. He would have felt forgotten, as he often had this season, if not that more than half their looks and stories were directed at him as much as each other.

So it was that Ferez learned that not only was James the childhood friend of Gemini Cosley, only child and heir of the late duke of Kensy, but that the two had been nigh inseparable until about a year after the attack. According to James, it was then that he had discovered the spy responsible for the massacre and had taken revenge. Not long after, he'd been taken in by Kephin and had not seen Gemini since.

"Can you be sure Gemini's still well, then?" Ferez had asked uncertainly. To his confusion, his two companions had smiled amusedly in response.

"I haven't seen her," James had answered, "but she's Familie, so Flame has kept tabs on her over the Jahre, you can be sure." Sir Leal had simply chuckled in response.

When Sir Leal began telling about his time in Caypan after the attack, Ferez was able to offer his own tidbits. The three were sharing anecdotes about Sir Paeter when Ferez noticed James' eyes grow distant. Pausing mid-sentence, he laid a hand gently on the boy's forearm.

"James?"

He kept his voice calm, despite his worry over his friend's sudden distraction. He idly wondered if Kawn needed their assistance but thought James might move more quickly if that were the case.

It seemed like a full minute passed before James' purple eyes grew focused once more and settled on Ferez. Immediately, the boy smiled and laid a hand on Ferez's own, squeezing.

"It's good news," he finally murmured, before quickly draining what little remained of his drink and standing. Ferez and Sir Leal followed suit, Sir Leal dropping a few gold onto the table before the younger men could.

"How so?" Ferez asked, even as he squeezed Sir Leal's shoulder in gratitude. He didn't miss James' own smile to the knight.

"I think I know who's been giving away the secrets of the Kreis."

With that, James led the two men out the door and into the streets.

~~*~*

Gemi couldn't help the smile that stretched her lips as Ferez and Sir Leal bombarded her with questions about her sudden pronouncement. She knew she should give her companions more information as she led them through the alleys of Schönestadt.

However, Flame had been the one to make the realization, and Gemi hadn't yet caught all of the Drache's reasoning. Flame might still be learning about humans, but she knew Magie and Tiere well, and Gemi trusted her judgment.

"Will you a' leas' tell us where we're goin'?" Ferez finally asked, exasperated.

Gemi chuckled and glanced over her shoulder at her Freund. "The Haus of one of the three members of the Kreis who has yet to be arrested."

Ferez rolled his eyes, a twitch of his lips indicating that he knew he'd walked right into that one. Sir Leal beat him to the next obvious question.

"Is there a name to go with this house, so we at least have an idea of who we're dealing with?"

Gemi sighed then ducked under a clothesline that was strung across the alley. "Rune Handelmann, but he's not the one responsible for this mess."

"James."

A sudden hand on her shoulder pulled Gemi up short, and she turned to find the König watching her with a steady gaze.

"Who is responsible then? We need to know wha' we're gettin' into."

Gemi nodded, knowing Ferez was right. She may not be able to explain the reasoning well enough, but she could give them this.

"Poison Clan Nomaden," she said then turned to continue down the alley.

Ferez's hand slid down her arm as she did so, and she ignored the shiver that trailed down her spine in response. Now was not the time to consider the meaning of *that*.

"We can't be sure which Clan," she added, sidestepping a drowsing Tier, which simply raised its head to eye them as they passed. "But we can be sure there's a Tieremagier, at least."

There was a moment of silence before Ferez muttered hesitantly, "Animal Mage, then."

Gemi smiled over her shoulder at her Freund and nodded. "Ja, Animal Mage."

Her smile slipped as she added, "But that's all we can be sure of. Flame hasn't seen any movement from the Haus all Tag. There's no telling how many Nomaden are hiding there, Poison Clan or otherwise."

"Which means we'll be attempting to take them by surprise, but, at the same time, we have to be careful about who we attack," Sir Leal responded, voicing the dilemma that Gemi had been considering.

She nodded. "We'll take a back entrance, similar to the one in Dame Clarimonde's Haus." She saw Ferez nod out of the corner of her eye. "We can work our way through the Haus from there. Most likely, those being held captive will be kept further inside the Haus, away from any possible exits."

"You know a general layout o' the house, aye?"

Gemi nodded, not bothering to look at Ferez. She didn't think he would mind. His voice had been thoughtful. His Geist was no doubt focused on the strategy they were forming.

"We'll follow your lead then an' watch your back. If the layout is anyt'in' like Dame Clarimonde's, we'll need to be wary of attackers from behind as much as from the front."

Gemi agreed, and they fell into silence. Now that her two companions weren't pestering her for information, Gemi was able to turn her Geist back to Flame and request a more thorough explanation.

With the nature of their bond, Flame was able to replay Shadow's conversation with Herr Wolfmann. The Drache then proceeded to point out that a 'silent Falke' meant Tieremagier, and Flame knew that none of the three remaining Kreis members employed a Tieremagier.

And, since Herr Wolfmann hadn't recognized the Vogel, it was more likely to belong to the Tieremagier that had sent it, despite Wolfmann's claim that he couldn't possibly know all of the Vogel in the Stadt.

"*Most Animal Mages do not realize that the animals they regularly use for messages and such are part of a select group. Hunder Wolfmann would probably recognize the bird if it had been called from the city rather than brought into it.*

"*As for the specific house,*" Flame added, her voice dropping to a hiss, "*once I knew that the Poison Clans were involved, I realized that there had been very limited movement around the Handelmann house, but I had noticed quite a bit around the other two.*"

Her hiss turned angry. "*I should have realized it sooner.*"

Gemi sighed and imagined smoothing her hand down Flame's neck. As she hoped, the mental touch soothed the Drache's anger somewhat.

"*You couldn't have, Flame,*" she mindspoke softly. "*You didn't know the Poison Clans were involved, so you didn't know that a lack of activity was noteworthy. Besides,*" she added with a touch of amusement, "*you haven't exactly been watching the Häuser consistently this Tag. You only knew which Haus it was through a process of elimination from pure Glück, ja?*"

Flame grumbled softly and reluctantly agreed. Leaving her bondmate
to her musings, Gemi realized that she had found the alley they needed.
Motioning for the two Männer to stop, she peered at the door that led into
the Haus of Rune Handelmann.

"Is tha' the door we wan', then?" Ferez murmured, softly enough that
his voice barely reached her ear. Gemi nodded, even as imagined the
question hovering on his tongue.

Who is guarding the door?

Through the semi-darkness of the desert Nacht, Gemi could see a figure
leaning against the alley wall beside the door. Because of the incoming
Unwetter, the darkness was growing, and she couldn't see the person very
well.

"*Flame?*" she asked, knowing the Drache had already circled lower in
anticipation of their need.

"*He is dressed in plainclothes,*" Flame rumbled. "*I do not see any
weapons, but...*"

"*But if he carries Scharfmonde, you wouldn't be able to see them,*"
Gemi finished with a sigh, thinking of her own curved blades that lay
sheathed at her lower back. If the figure was a Nomade in disguise, then,
like her, he would have his Scharfmonde hidden under his tunic.

Without taking her eyes off the sentinel, Gemi turned her head slightly
and passed the information on to her companions in a voice just as quiet
as the one Ferez had used earlier. A light pressure on her shoulder let her
know that Ferez, at least, had heard and understood.

"Then 'e may or may no' be an enemy," Ferez rejoined. "D'you think
we coul' sneak up on 'im? Knock him out afore 'e warns anyone we're
here?"

Gemi was silent as she considered their options. It was possible that
they could incapacitate him from a distance, but that would require
hurting the Mann, possibly mortally. Ferez was correct. They couldn't
yet be sure that the Mann was a Nomade, so, for now, that was out of the
question.

Gemi was considering some form of distraction so they could get close
when Flame informed her that Sir Leal was no longer behind her and
Ferez. She could do little more than glance over her shoulder and hiss a
soft "*What?*" to her bondmate before a long, low whistle pierced the air
from the other end of the alley.

Turning her eyes back to the door, she noticed movement from the
sentinel's position, but, by now, it was too dark to see what he was doing.
Thankfully, Flame's vision was unimpaired.

"*His hand is at his lower back!*"

The Drache's words were all Gemi needed to hear. Instead of reaching
for her sword or her own Scharfmonde as she had originally planned, she
dropped her hand down to her right thigh.

Quickly slipping a small blade from the leather band she wore around her thigh and depending solely on Flame's sight—a disconcerting task—Gemi threw the knife at the Nomade.

A soft grunt, followed by a heavy thump, was the only sound the Mann made when her blade hit.

Approaching the Nomade and kneeling next to him, Gemi retrieved the throwing knife from the Mann's neck, verifying Flame's claim that it had landed where Gemi had hoped it would. The soft whistle sounded again, much closer this time, and Gemi lifted her gaze to find her two Freunde standing over her.

"Impressive," Sir Leal muttered. "I see you weren't happy with just knowing standard blades, then."

Gemi shrugged and stood, though not before verifying that the Mann did carry a pair of Scharfmonde under his tunic. "I learned what those that took me in were willing to teach."

She frowned at her old tutor then. "And what was that?" she hissed, gesturing down the alley where he had surely stood when he whistled.

"A distraction," Sir Leal answered with a shrug. "I figured we would need one." Gemi gaped at her old mentor. After a moment of silence, Sir Leal chuckled. "Don't think that you're the only one with an idea of the layout of the city, James."

Gemi snapped her mouth shut and frowned.

"Who'd you learn tha' from?" Ferez whispered, finally drawing her attention away from the knight. The König had squatted next to the dead Nomad and appeared to be feeling for the wound.

Gemi sheathed the small knife before reaching for the door their fallen Feind had been guarding. Pausing, she whispered, "Not that we have time to discuss it now, but I learned it from Naldo of the Tarsurian Diebe."

She usually enjoyed answering his questions, but the beginning of a fight was not the time. Hoping Ferez would hold the rest of his curiosity in check for now, Gemi unsheathed one Scharfmond and opened the door.

~~*~*

Ferez followed James through the door, Sir Leal close behind. He paused to look around as the knight closed the door softly behind them.

Unlike Dame Clarimonde's house, this alley door opened onto a corridor. The hallway was softly lit with shaded oil lamps every few yards. Across from and underneath several of the lamps, items stood on display, and even some tapestries hung on the walls.

He stepped towards one pedestal to take a closer look at what looked like it might be a piece of tack.

"The Handelmann Familie have invested in various businesses and artisans for generations," James explained softly when Ferez asked about the displays. "Each display represents one of their interests, as I understand it."

Ferez hummed in response and turned his attention back to the corridor. Unsheathing their swords, he and Sir Leal followed James down the hallway.

Surprisingly, their journey through the corridor was unimpeded. It wasn't until they reached the end of the corridor as it came to an open doorway that spilled out both firelight and the low tone of soft voices that Ferez remembered that these nomads would have been here for almost ten days. They would be comfortable enough not to be monitoring the halls at all times.

When they reached the door, they fell to either side of it, pressing their backs against the wall. From these positions, the words of the room's occupants easily reached them.

"Verdammte Magier!" one male voice suddenly spat.

"Halt die Klappe!" a female voice hissed sharply. There was a slight pause before she hissed softly, "Those are the Häuptling's Kinder of which you speak."

The first voice snorted. "I wouldn't care if they were the Häuptling himself," he sneered. "If they had done their job correctly from the beginning, we wouldn't still be here."

"And what exactly do you think they could have done more quickly, Trennen?" a second male voice drawled.

"Wolfrik is a powerful Geistmagier," Trennen sneered. "He could have gotten the names we wanted in a single session." The man made a noise of disgust. "Instead, he has to keep going back into the Mann's Geist, and he only brings out a name or two at a time." There was another noise of disgust. "Sometimes, not even that."

There were a few moments of silence, which were broken suddenly by the dull sound of flesh hitting flesh, the sharp scrape of wood on stone, and a soft grunt.

"Dummkopf!" snarled a male voice that hadn't spoken before then. "You obviously know nothing of Magie. If Wolfrik had attempted to gain all of the names at once, he would have destroyed the Mann's Geist."

"So?" Trennen sneered, his voice sounding thicker than it had earlier. "What care should we have for our Feinde's Freunde? I still think we should kill them all."

"Of course you do," the woman huffed. "But we want the Kreis to turn on itself. They won't do so if they know that the Verräter was coerced."

"This verdammt Plan depends too much on the reactions of others. I say we—"

Trennen's words were suddenly interrupted by the sound of wood scraping against stone and muffled grunts.

For the first time since they'd taken up their positions around the door, Ferez risked a quick glance around James and into the room. Two men grappled with each other, one standing above the other, who appeared to be attempting to rise from the chair in which he was sitting.

The scuffle didn't last long. It ended with a sharp wheeze as the standing man punched the seated man in the stomach. Ferez quickly pulled himself back against the wall as the victor jerked the other man to his feet.

"You are too hitzköpfig, Trennen," someone—Ferez assumed it was the victor—growled. "It would be best if you went to your room to cool off."

James suddenly motioned sharply with one Scharfmond, though Ferez didn't need the warning. Two sets of footsteps, one strong and steady, the other stumbling, were approaching the door they were flanking. Ferez brought his sword up across his body and tightened his grip on the hilt.

The stumbling nomad was first through the door. Ferez caught a glimpse of a purpling jaw and widening eyes before James' Scharfmond sliced him across the back of his shoulder.

As the man cried out and stumbled forwards, James stepped away from the wall to follow. The movement turned James' back to the doorway and the second nomad.

Surprise flitted across the second nomad's face, but the man didn't hesitate to pull his left Scharfmond. Even as the man swung at James' back, Ferez stepped in behind the boy, raising his sword to block the attack.

To his horror, when the Scharfmond met his sword, it didn't stop. Instead, his own blade slid along the curve of the nomad's, leaving Ferez's chest vulnerable. Cursing sharply, he attempted to twist his body away from the nomad's strike. His voice dropped to a hiss as sharp steel bit into his left shoulder.

The nomad smirked as his blow landed, and he twisted the blade and pushed, knocking Ferez back against the wall and driving the blade deeper into his shoulder. The next moment, he was gone, and Ferez groaned as the pain flared brighter as the weapon was ripped from the wound.

"Frenz!" someone called urgently.

A pair of hands gripped Ferez's face, pulling his attention from the pain. He blinked open his eyes, surprised to realize he had closed them. James held him and searched his face, the worry in his eyes more powerful than Ferez had expected.

"Are you all right? Can you stand?"

The king frowned. The whispered words were concerned and urgent, but they didn't make any sense. It was just a shoulder wound, but James made it sound like he'd been incapacitated. Yet…

He pushed past the pain so he could take in his surroundings. To his surprise, he was on the floor, slumped against the wall. His sword lay nearby, and, while he couldn't remember doing so, he had the impression that he'd dropped it before he slid down the wall, rather than releasing it once on the ground.

I shouldn't have released it at all, he thought, confused. *It wasn't my sword arm that was injured.* He groaned. *And I'm usually much better at handling the pain of this kind of wound.*

The pain in his shoulder suddenly flared, and he hissed. *All right, so it's been a while since I've been injured this badly.*

Suddenly, he stiffened. "Frenz?" he heard someone whisper again, but that last thought had shocked him.

That isn't true. Images of large cats passed through his mind, and he shivered.

Maybe not, the thought slid through his mind, *but it's been a while since I've been this badly injured and remained conscious.*

Ferez might have accepted that as his own thought if it hadn't been for the previous one. Now, as his mind grew hazier with increasing pain, he remembered that the nomads had mentioned a Geistmagier: a Mindspeaker.

"James," he whispered.

He had to open his eyes once more, but he could tell they wouldn't stay open for long. James was eyeing him worriedly and nodded once Ferez was looking at him.

"The noma's...they mentioned a..." He paused and took a deep breath, trying to push past the pain, which seemed to have radiated to other parts of his body. "A Min'speaker?"

A sigh slid through his mind as his eyes once again closed against his will. This time, he had no trouble differentiating the other's words from his own.

"Es tut mir leid, Freund, but you will feel better with sleep."

A sharp burst of pain engulfed his mind, dropping him into oblivion.

Chapter 36

"Frenz?" Gemi asked sharply as Ferez's head lolled to one side. His body collapsed back against the wall. Even as she tried to get him to open his eyes and look at her again, she knew he wouldn't be able to.

"James," Sir Leal spoke as he gripped her shoulder.

She glanced at him. She knew her eyes were wide, but so much had happened recently. She couldn't stand to see Ferez like this again.

"We should bind his wound. Then we need to decide if we want to retreat or continue on."

Gemi frowned and turned back to Ferez. Pulling his tunic to the side, she grimaced as she examined the wound. It wasn't life-threatening yet, but the Nomade had managed to part the flesh more than a simple cut would have, and she could see bone. He would need to see an Arztmagier as soon as possible. Briefly wishing that she had her pack with her, she began to tear strips of fabric from Ferez's tunic.

As she worked on her Freund's shoulder, Sir Leal stood over them, keeping watch on the door they'd previously fought around and the hallway through which they'd come. They had managed to dispatch the five Nomaden fairly quickly. After taking out Trennen, which had not taken long since he had still been recovering from his scuffle with the other Nomade, Gemi had gutted the Mann who had been holding Ferez.

She hadn't been able to focus on the König until the kitchen, the room on which they'd been eavesdropping, had been emptied. However, the fact that a great swordsman like him could be injured so quickly had reminded Gemi that she hadn't had time to train him in fighting Nomaden. Using a straight blade against Scharfmonde required certain techniques that were only taught here in Zhulan. As she knelt in front of her Freund, she cursed their busy schedule and swore to find time to teach him the necessary techniques.

"*James,*" Flame hissed, and Gemi paused only briefly to let her bondmate know she was listening. "*Frenz was right. There is a Mindspeaker there. I can feel him attempting to access your mind.*"

Gemi smiled grimly, even as she finished wrapping Ferez's wound to her satisfaction. "*Any chance you can take advantage of that?*"

She knew that Drachen were capable Geistmagier, but Flame hadn't fully grown into her Magie yet. Even so, it had been a while since Flame had attempted to defeat an unknown Geistmagier on the battleground of his own Geist.

"*I do not know,*" Flame hissed. Gemi felt her grow distant then and knew that she was attempting to breach the Geistmagier's Geist.

Standing, Gemi informed Sir Leal of the situation. The knight grimaced. "You'd have a better protection against him than I would, I think."

Gemi nodded. Ever since they had first met Tante Isa, Flame had had mental barriers set up around all three of their Geister. She had set them up as a precaution against Gemi's true identity being discovered, but they doubled as protections against this kind of attack, as well.

Glancing back down at Ferez, Gemi sighed. "I would prefer to move forward since we are already here, but we can't just leave Frenz alone like this."

She turned back to her old mentor. "But if we leave now, the Poison Clans will know we're onto them, and we may not get another chance."

For the second time that evening, Gemi felt torn about what to do. *And the person on whom I've come to depend in such times of indecision is now wounded and unconscious.*

A hand on her shoulder drew Gemi's attention back to Sir Leal. The Mann looked worried but determined.

"If you think it's necessary to finish this now, you should probably continue on." He grimaced and added, "As much as I hate the idea of you going in by yourself, your skill far exceeds my own, and you're better protected from the Mindspeaker. You know the layout of this house, aye?"

Gemi nodded and knelt next to Ferez once more. Lightly brushing the impromptu bandage with her fingers, then her Freund's face, she asked idly, "And you'll stay and watch over Frenz?"

"Of course," Sir Leal answered, his voice soft, yet determined.

Gemi nodded once again, more sharply this time, and stood. With a quick wave to the knight, Gemi unsheathed her Scharfmonde and headed back down the corridor in the direction from which they'd come. She took the first side-hallway, knowing it would lead her deeper into the Haus and closer to more Poison Clan Nomaden and those they held hostage.

~~*~*

When Flame had agreed to try to do something about the Mindspeaker, she had not expected to make much progress. The last time she had attempted to enter a Mindspeaker's mind unwelcome, she had barely grazed the surface.

Of course, that had been six years ago, when she and her bondmates had first arrived in Zhulan. After that incident, Flame had decided to remain on the defensive when it came to mind magic. As a result, her defensive mental magic was more powerful than any human Mindspeaker could break.

Now, defense only was not an option. While the Mindspeaker in the Handelmann Haus could not harm Gemi with his magic, Flame's bondmate was not the only human at risk. The Mindspeaker had already incapacitated Ferez, something for which Flame would gladly repay him.

Ignoring the questions that cropped up at that thought—she still wondered at how quickly she herself had come to consider the king family—Flame felt along the barriers of Gemi's mind. The Mindspeaker was subtle, and it took the dragon a couple minutes before she found his presence.

Instead of assaulting the barrier like Flame would have expected, he lightly tested it here and there, feeling it out for any cracks or weaknesses, and he was thorough. Flame realized, with a jolt of surprise and respect, that if any Mindspeaker could break through the barriers she had set up around Gemi's mind, this man could.

Wolfrik, she thought, tasting the name that Gemi had overheard.

The other nomads had mentioned that he was the son of a Häuptling, though Flame did not know which clan since all of the nomads so far had been dressed in plainclothes. She wondered idly if he was the eldest of his siblings. Despite his current activities, Flame thought this was a man she could respect in a position of power.

A sharp hiss suddenly drew Flame's attention. *"As much as I appreciate the compliment, Dame Flammezunge,"* a voice growled lowly in her mind, *"you could have offered it a little more gently."*

Panicking, Flame struck out wildly with her mind as she searched for the Mindspeaker's presence. The more she searched for it, the more she realized that she did not recognize the mental landscape in which she was moving.

"Gratuliere, Dame Flammezunge," the Mindspeaker grunted testily. *"Somehow, you managed to bypass my barriers without even noticing."*

The thought, *And with so little effort at that,* sardonically trailed the direct words.

Flame stilled. Indeed, she had latched onto the Mindspeaker's magic where it had touched her bondmate's mind. She had hoped to follow the magic back to the man's mind since she had doubted her ability to seek out and penetrate his mind otherwise. She had not expected the process to work so well.

"I suspect that has to do with the knowledge of mental defenses that you must have if your own are anything to go by." The mind she occupied shifted uncomfortably. *"Interesting technique, I must admit,"* the voice grumbled softly.

With her mind still, Flame recognized mental pain behind the man's words and radiating from the surrounding mind, pain she had not caused in another mind since the early days of her bond with Gemi and Shadow. She hesitated when she sensed it. She did not like causing such pain to her bondmates nor, it seemed, even to her enemies.

Thoughts tumbled through the Mindspeaker's mind, surprise coloring them. *"Even though I caused such pain to your Freund?"* The voice held a note of curiosity. *"Just a moment ago, you wished to repay me for that."*

Startled, Flame realized that the voice held no trace of hostility towards her, despite the fact that she had just invaded his mind and caused him mental anguish. The thought, *I have felt worse,* slipped along her mind, and she twisted her head, curious. The thought had held more than a touch of bitterness.

"*Who are you?*"

She could not prevent incredulity from seeping into her tone. This human was nothing like what she had expected from a Poison Clan Mindspeaker.

There was a pause, the 'silence' broken only by the considering thoughts that filled the man's mind. Hesitantly, the Mindspeaker answered, "*My name is Wolfrik Giftschwanz.*" The words held a touch of subdued pride, as if the man was proud of his identity but had learned that others would not be.

"*Skorpion,*" Flame muttered, immediately recognizing the last name. The Skorpion Clan's Häuptling had born the name Giftschwanz—literally 'venom tail' in their tongue—since the Clan had first formed.

"*Of course,*" Wolfrik replied, the pride in his voice stronger.

Flame suddenly had the suspicion that it was his own clan that had taught him that others would not appreciate his true self. A mental snort echoed through the man's mind, but he otherwise ignored the thought he surely must have heard.

"*And to address one of your previous questions,*" the Mindspeaker added, drawing Flame from her contemplations, "*I am the youngest of my Brüder. Only my Schwester, Käfe, is younger than I am.*"

Wolfrik must have heard Flame's thought on his sister's name because he huffed quietly. "*Ja, her name is derived from our word that would translate into 'beetle' in your tongue.*" Flame had the sudden sense that the man was rolling his eyes as his voice turned bitter. "*It refers to her Kräftetier, but she was also given the name in derision.*"

The man's obvious bitterness increased Flame's curiosity. Distinctly aware of the pain she had caused him before, Flame attempted to lighten her presence in his mind, hoping that the techniques she used in dealing with her bondmates would translate into the minds of strangers. Once satisfied that she would cause him minimal pain, Flame began to explore the surrounding mental terrain.

A soft growl filled her mental ears as she lightly touched on various thoughts and memories, but, as it seemed to be fueled more by anger and less by pain, Flame ignored it. The deeper into the memories she went, the more resistance she met. It was not until she found herself faced with a form of resistance that mentally resembled a securely locked box guarded by a snarling animal that Flame paused in her exploration.

As Flame eyed the image of the snarling beast, she found herself oddly disappointed. She had thought the Mindspeaker was subtle, but the use of this kind of creature to guard one's most precious secrets drew the attention of an invader all too well.

She was gathering her magic to begin dissecting this piece of resistance when the irony of that thought occurred to her.

374

Releasing the gathered magic, the dragon turned from the image of the now snapping animal. Casting her mind about the nearby terrain, she sought something less obvious, something that would not draw the mental eye quite so well.

As she did so, she could feel panic rising around her. She allowed herself a small draconic smile.

She had turned her attention to a portion of the mental terrain that resembled an open field when she felt the protective beast from before lunge for her presence. However, the Mindspeaker had complimented her knowledge of mental defense earlier and rightly so. Her own defenses were still in place, so the lunging beast simply met her barriers and bounced off of them ineffectually.

"You are slipping, Wolfrik Giftschwanz," Flame hissed before immediately regretting the taunt. He may be a Skorpion, but there was no reason for her to add insult to injury.

Softening her tone, she added, *"Panic does not help your defense. It only leads your enemy where you do not want her to go."*

Then, to prove her point, the dragon snapped up the single beetle she had spotted hiding in the field.

Immediately, images tumbled through her mind, and she quickly realized the significance of the beetle guarding the Mindspeaker's most guarded secrets. As he had mentioned before, his sister's power animal was the beetle, and, while she may be female and younger than him, she was apparently the only person he trusted.

After only a minute of viewing the onslaught of memories, that singular trust was more than understandable.

When the dragon first came upon the more distressing memories, she did not want to believe what she was seeing. When Wolfrik's mind began to snarl and thrash around her presence, she knew she was interpreting the images correctly. Along with this realization came horror.

Image after image filled her mind, seeming to span many years and various instances. In all of the images, it was obvious that, out of all of their siblings, the brother and sister were inseparable.

However, this was not what shook Flame. What did was the way the two were treated by the people they should have been able to consider family.

Flame watched, disturbed, as the two children were belittled and pushed aside. She saw memories, too many for her taste, of times when they had been beaten by their older brothers. Despite these horrors, none of it compared to the treatment they received at the hands of the man who had sired them.

Never had Flame met a creature, human or magical, who was willing to use mind magic on their offspring for reasons other than communication and dire emergencies. The fact that the man who had sired them had continually torn through their minds with his magic from such a young age made Flame see red, and she pulled back from the memories roughly. She idly noted that, when she mentally dropped the beetle she had grabbed, it scurried away, shaking.

"*That is how the Skorpion Clan treats their children?*" Flame snarled, too shocked to mind the strength of her presence, and Wolfrik's mind shuddered around her.

Hesitantly, he answered, "*Nein.*"

When he seemed ready to leave it at that, Flame mentally prodded him. He winced, but grudgingly added, "*That is how our Häuptling treats his Kinder if they don't do as he says or live up to his expectations.*" His voice held no resistance now, only a tired resignation. "*He considered us weak, and, as we are the youngest and his expectations of us were therefore higher, we could never satisfy him.*"

Flame noted that Wolfrik did not call his sire 'Vater', but only referred to him as Häuptling. And the idea that this man, who had endured immeasurable mental anguish at the hands of someone whom he should have been able to trust, could be considered weak was laughable.

Considering some of the memories she had seen, she knew that Wolfrik had even learned to protect his sister from an early age and eventually build his own defenses in such a way that their sire had not even realized that his mental attacks were, by this age, ineffectual.

"*I would never consider a Mindspeaker and man of your abilities weak, Wolfrik Giftschwanz.*"

The thought-filled silence from before returned, and Flame could feel the heavy touch of his regard. Suddenly, part of his mind gave before her, and he murmured, "*Danke. You might be surprised by how gratifying it is to hear such praise from a Drache like yourself, Dame Flammezunge.*"

Flame paused as she considered his use of that name. It was a literal translation of her name into Zhulanese. She had not heard it since the first seasons she and her bondmates had lived with the nomads. It had taken several months of determined insistence on her part to get the nomads to call her Flame instead.

However, this was not the first time he had called her this, and, to her surprise, she recognized a deep respect in the man's use of the name.

For a moment, Flame considered him. Now that she had seen his most sordid secrets, he seemed to relax under her presence. The dragon wondered briefly if the man had expected her to react to the memories with disgust for him rather than respect.

Putting the thought aside for now, Flame realized with some surprise that the snarling beast from before was gone. She knew that might have been attributed to the man's relaxed state, but she doubted he could relax his defenses that much.

Turning her attention to the chest the beast had been guarding, she was startled to realize that it now resembled a simple box, unlocked and easily opened.

"You wanted me to open this?" she asked. Shock froze her briefly as she recognized that the man had used the beast to draw her attention on purpose. He had wanted her to bypass these defenses. *"But why?"*

Wolfrik did not answer. Instead, the box slid open, and memories poured over her, more quickly than any others had before. The speed did not hinder her understanding; the Mindspeaker simply seemed to be in a hurry.

"Your bondmate is getting closer."

The memories that flowed through her mind were much more recent than the others. Wolfrik's sire had assigned this task to both him and his sister, not realizing that his attempt at imposing his will on his youngest children had, once again, failed. Instead of immediately seeking out the information he was tasked to, Wolfrik had spent much of his 'sessions' with Rune Handelmann conversing with the investor and learning about him and the work he did.

Occasionally, Wolfrik would pull a name or two from the man's mind to keep his sire's men happy, but he proclaimed that the process was slow because they did not want to draw the suspicions of anyone, now nor once they had left. When Käfe was able to send these names off to the governor, she purposefully silenced the bird to hopefully draw suspicions from that side.

Throughout all of this, Wolfrik had worked his magic into the minds of his sire's men, preparing his magic to drop them into sleep the moment someone came to 'rescue' the Handelmann family.

Flame pulled herself from the memories as she recognized the significance of that last information.

"You have already dropped the other Skorpione into sleep?" At the Mindspeaker's affirmation, she narrowed her eyes and added, *"Then why did you incapacitate Frenz?"*

A tired sighed brushed against Flame's mind.

"Es tut mir leid. I had not expected to, but the wound he received was a terrible one. I did not wish for him to suffer needlessly, not when the fighting was already over."

Flame considered his words. *"And if you had not incapacitated him?"*

"If he had attempted to fight with such a wound, which I am sure he would have, it most likely would have resulted in permanent damage."

Flame winced. That was something for which Flame was sure Gemi would not have been able to forgive herself. Flame was suddenly grateful to the Mindspeaker.

"Maybe you could pass that gratitude on, Dame." Wolfrik's words were rushed, and Flame eyed him curiously as he attempted to push her from his mind. *"Your bondmate is almost upon us!"*

Startled, Flame slipped out of Wolfrik's mind. Once fully in her own, Flame turned to Gemi's and was shocked to find rage overwhelming the girl's thoughts.

Cursing, Flame plunged herself into her bondmate's mind.

~~*~*

When Gemi came across the first body, she knelt beside it and placed her fingers at its throat. The pulse she found there was strong and steady, but the Mann didn't react to her touch. Frowning, she hauled the Mann onto his back, noting, as she did so, the bulge under his plainclothes where his Scharfmonde lay.

Despite bearing no visible signs of damage, the Nomade still didn't move. Deciding that he would pose no threat to her, Gemi left his side and continued down the corridor.

Further down that hallway, she found two more unconscious bodies. One lay sprawled across the corridor, while the other sat propped up against the wall. Together, they flanked a door that was closed and barred.

This door, Gemi knew, led to a room that was most often used to house visiting Nomaden. Gemi suspected, and thought that the unconscious Wachen confirmed, that it still housed those Nomaden who had been here when the Poison Clan Nomaden arrived. It was the reason she had headed in this specific direction.

Checking the two unconscious Nomaden, Gemi found them in a similar state as the first. She eyed the sprawling Nomade—the position had to be uncomfortable—but left both as they had landed, turning her attention instead to the door.

Knowing that the Poison Clans would not guard a room for no reason, Gemi gave the door a light rap with her knuckles. Almost immediately, a stifled gasp filtered through the door, confirming that there was indeed someone trapped within.

Making short work of the bar that crossed it, Gemi quickly opened the door. As soon as it was open wide enough for her to pass through, a pair of hands roughly grabbed her shoulders and propelled her backwards.

Not to be surprised again after Raymond's assault only a few Nächte previously, Gemi planted one foot and allowed her attacker's momentum to carry him past her and into the wall opposite the door.

As footsteps sounded behind her, Gemi gripped the Mann's shoulders and forced him back against the wall as he would have done to her. She allowed herself only a few seconds to note that he still wore his Kopfabdeckung and Statusgürtel—the bright blue of which declared him a Falke—before she murmured a low, forceful, "Ruhe, Bruder!"

The words seemed to have the affect she desired. The footsteps behind her faded, and the Falke she held against the wall jerked his head to one side and eyed her warily. That wariness faded as recognition widened his eyes.

"Drache Krieger?" His voice was sharp in his confusion.

Gemi nodded and released her grip on the Mann's tunic. "Ja, I am."

She glanced away from the Falke then, taking in the faces and Statusgürtel of the surrounding Nomaden. There were seven in all: an elderly Frau, a young Kind, and the rest were young Männer.

"Are you all well?"

The seven nodded, though the Frau muttered, "As much as can be expected when we've been locked in here for Tage."

A tug on her Statusgürtel called Gemi's attention down to the Kind, a young girl who looked to be no older than Ava. "Ja?"

"Why did you take so long to open the door, Drache Krieger?" Gemi furrowed her brow in confusion, but, before she could ask for clarification, the girl pointed to the fallen Männer and added, "We heard the Skorpione drop several Minuten ago. Why did you wait so long before opening the door?"

Gemi frowned as she considered the girl's words. She hadn't considered the implications of the unconscious Nomaden before since she had been rather intent on seeking out the Nomade hostages. Now, her thoughts turned to the Geistmagier that both Ferez and Flame had mentioned.

She knew that only a Geistmagier would be able to make a person unconscious with no physical trace of the cause, but it didn't make sense. According to the Nomaden they'd overheard before, the Geistmagier was the Sohn of a Häuptling. He would have no reason to help them.

Unless this is a trap. She glanced sharply at the two fallen Nomaden. *If the Geistmagier could bring them to consciousness as quickly and easily as he knocked them unconscious...*

"Drache Krieger?" The girl's voice brought Gemi back to the situation at hand, and she shook her head.

"I'm not the one who knocked out the Skorpione, Kleine."

"You mean," a Wolf spoke up, "you have an ally here?"

Gemi shook her head again and glanced up and down the hallway.

"I'm afraid it's not that simple, Freund. It could be a trap."

"How so?" asked the old Frau.

Gemi turned to focus on the Frau. She, too, wore the blue Statusgürtel of the Falke Clan, as did the Kind, but, for the first time, Gemi noticed that their Statusgürtel were dyed at both ends. She gasped suddenly.

"You—"

The Frau smiled fiercely and repeated, "How might it be a trap, Kind?"

Gemi grimaced at the implied rebuke but understood. Whether the other Nomaden, those not from the same Clan, had recognized who the Frau and girl were, they didn't need Gemi drawing their attention to the fact.

Even so, she had recognized who the two were. She had no doubts that the Frau was Valborga, former Häuptling of the Falke Clan and Mutter of the current one. The girl had to be Lakritze, youngest Tochter of the Falke Clan's Häuptling and an Arztmagier. That last point reminded Gemi sharply of Ferez's wound.

"The Skorpione have no visible injuries," Gemi finally said, answering Valborga's question. "It's most likely the work of the Geistmagier."

"Wolfrik Giftschwanz," the Frau muttered with nod. She must have noticed Gemi's surprise because she added, "He was insistent on introducing himself to us."

"Mentally?" Gemi asked, horrified. Her horror faded as all seven shook their heads.

"Nein," the Frau answered. "It seemed he only wished to let us know who he was."

Gemi frowned and shook her head. Gesturing to the Männer on the floor, she offered, "We should probably stay wary of the unconscious Skorpione. We don't know what Giftschwanz has planned."

The others nodded, though Valborga continued to look thoughtful.

"Now, I came from the alley door and the kitchens, so we should probably head towards the main living quarters next. That's most likely where they're keeping Herr Handelmann and his Familie."

The five Männer agreed and, showing that they all still carried their Scharfmonde—and, why the Skorpione hadn't confiscated them, Gemi couldn't fathom—they quickly continued down the corridor.

When Valborga and Lakritze made to follow, Gemi gripped the Frau's arm. Valborga turned narrowed eyes on Gemi, but Gemi hurried to speak before she could follow the glare with a reprimand.

"I didn't come here alone, Dame," Gemi whispered because she didn't want the other Nomaden to overhear. "But one of my Freunde was wounded, and I was forced to leave them behind at the kitchens." Gemi glanced down at the girl then back up at her Grossmutter. "If you don't mind, I would appreciate it if the Kleine could do something for him."

Valborga harrumphed softly and laid a hand on Lakritze's shoulder, but her eyes had softened. Before she could answer, the girl nodded enthusiastically.

"Anything for a Freund of the Drache Krieger."

"Lakritze!" the Frau hissed sharply, confirming Gemi's assumptions.

The young Arztmagier turned a glare of her own up at her Grossmutter and crossed her arms over her chest.

"I want to help, Oma, and I know I can't fight. After the Drache Krieger saved us, the least I can do is Heal his Freund."

For a moment, the two glared at each other, which Gemi would have found amusing if the situation hadn't been so dire. Thankfully, Valborga seemed to remember their situation, too.

With a sigh, she directed her gaze back to Gemi. "The kitchens, you said?"

Gemi nodded and watched as the elder Frau led her charge back in the direction from which Gemi had come. As they disappeared around a corner, Gemi turned around and ran to catch up with the other Nomaden.

They passed a few more fallen Skorpione before they reached the main living quarters of the Haus. They were closer to the front of the Haus now, though there were still entertaining and business-related rooms further towards the front. Those, Gemi knew, wouldn't have seen activity since this Katastrophe began.

She led the way towards Rune Handelmann's bedroom. Most might find her intimate knowledge of the Haus uncomfortable, but she, and several others, had investigated the Haus of each member of the Kreis before they'd been allowed to use them as safe Häuser.

To her surprise, the bedroom door was open.

Gemi warily stepped through the open door and hesitated when she found six people unconscious around the room. Only two, a Frau and a Mann, still stood, and burning anger flooded Gemi as she realized that this Mann must be the Geistmagier who had incapacitated Ferez.

She growled as her vision narrowed to the single Mann and red seemed to color everything.

"You!" she snarled lowly.

She was vaguely aware of unsheathing her Scharfmonde as she rushed the Geistmagier, but no other thoughts filled her Geist beyond repaying this Mann for his treatment of her Freund. He deserved nothing less.

She was only a couple steps away from him when her vision suddenly tilted and her Geist became overfull with a presence she recognized all too well. Stumbling to a Halt, she slammed her eyes shut against the sudden oddness of her vision.

"*Flame!*" she hissed, unsure if the cry had been verbal since the Drache had forced her to suddenly focus solely on the mental.

"*He is not the enemy, James!*" Flame's hiss filled Gemi's Geist, and she winced at the mental fullness she felt.

"*How can you say that, Flame? After what he did to Frenz—*"

Flame sighed, and the fullness shifted. "*Do you not trust me?*" Gemi winced at the sadness in her bondmate's voice, and her anger eased.

"*Of course I trust you.*"

"*Then believe me when I say he is not the enemy but a potential ally.*" Gemi frowned. "*Just let him explain. Please!*"

She added the last with a force that surprised Gemi and leeched the remaining anger from her Geist.

"*All right,*" she offered softly, "*I'll listen.*"

Flame nodded and finally eased the fullness of her presence from Gemi's Geist. Gemi winced as she did and wondered idly if Flame's Magie had increased during her encounter with the Geistmagier.

Once she could see again, Gemi stared at the conscious Mann and forced herself to really see him. Unlike his fellow Skorpione, he still wore his Kopfabdeckung and Statusgürtel, which bore the double brown of a noble Skorpion. The Frau beside him wore the same.

Gemi also noted that, while she and the Nomaden who had entered with her all had their Scharfmonde unsheathed, neither Skorpione had reached for their blades. Instead, the Mann had one arm raised in surrender, the other holding his Schwester partially behind him for protection.

Gemi was sharply reminded of her own Familie and the Liebe and loyalty she held for them. With a sharp slash through the air with one Scharfmond, she silenced the shouting, of which she had only been half-aware, and brought the Mann's attention fully to her.

"You would turn against your own Familie?"

Her words might have been harsher than necessary, but she could not imagine turning her back on those she loved.

The Mann—*Wolfrik,* Flame sharply reminded her—took a small step forward, raising his second hand to show that he would not go for his Scharfmonde. He shook his head as he did so, the glance he offered her both tired and bitter.

"Käfe is the only one of them I have ever considered mein Familie, Drache Krieger," he answered, and Gemi quirked an eyebrow at the use of her title. The Poison Clans usually insisted on not using it, believing her unworthy.

"And the trust they've placed in you?"

Her words were softer than before. The Mann's willingness to consider her a Nomade despite her birth set him apart from any other Poison Clan Nomaden she had ever met.

Wolfrik snorted and shook his head again. "They do not trust us, Drache Krieger. They never have."

He met Gemi's gaze, and she was caught by the sadness that lay in the back of his eyes and seemed to have settled there permanently.

"The six Nomaden you see here were simply meant to keep us in line, not to protect us. And that was only after our Häuptling thought he had imposed his Wille over ours."

Gemi jerked back a step. She wouldn't have thought much of those last words if she hadn't remembered that Häuptling Giftschwanz was also a Geistmagier. A shudder ran through her as she considered the implications.

"Your own Vater—"

"He is *not* my Vater," Wolfrik nearly shouted, his eyes wild.

The next moment, he jerked his head back, and his eyes widened, his startled expression mirroring what Gemi herself felt.

After a moment of heavy silence, the Mann grimaced and cast his gaze to the side. "He is my Häuptling," he muttered. "That is all."

"Bruder," murmured Käfe, whom Gemi now realized was barely older than herself. The Fräulein laid a hand on Wolfrik's arm and stepped up to his side. "Don't exert yourself."

Wolfrik snorted, but he laid a hand over hers and offered her a small smile.

Gemi watched the two with interest. Wolfrik seemed to relax under Käfe's hand, and the Fräulein returned his smile with a larger one of her own. For that moment, the two seemed to forget that they weren't alone.

"All right," Gemi finally spoke, startling the pair and bringing their attention back to her. "I believe I understand."

Wolfrik's gaze turned wary, but Gemi offered him a small smile, hoping to express that he could trust her, if no one else.

After some consideration, Wolfrik nodded, and his gaze relaxed.

"You do, don't you, Drache Krieger? You, who have chosen your own Familie these past several Jahre, would understand if anyone could."

Gemi chuckled quietly. She hadn't considered that, yet she couldn't help but agree. Except....

"It's James." The Geistmagier blinked and frowned, and she chuckled again. "Call me James," she insisted. "I imagine, since you are turning your back on your Häuptling, that you will come with me to see the Erstehäuptling?" Wolfrik nodded slowly. "I'm sure we'll get to know each other ein bisschen better then, ja?"

Thinking of travel, Gemi once again remembered Ferez. "Although, I do have one more question."

"About your Freund." Wolfrik made it a statement, and Gemi frowned. The Geistmagier sighed. "I did not mean to cause him so much pain."

"So you did increase his pain levels? I mean," she added before Wolfrik could respond, "I thought you must have since Frenz recognized your presence, which he shouldn't have been able to with how subtle Flame says your Magie is."

Wolfrik chuckled, but the sound was sad and tired.

"It was a bad wound. You saw it. You must understand what I mean."

Gemi nodded. The way the attacking Nomade had managed to part Ferez's flesh looked extremely painful.

"I was only attempting to knock him unconscious so he wouldn't have to suffer through it, or, worse, force himself to fight with it."

Gemi winced. If Ferez had fought with such a wound, she knew it could have caused much worse damage than just torn flesh, damage that could have been permanent.

"But you caused him a lot of pain. I watched him suffer through that."

Wolfrik sighed. "Es tut mir leid. I had started at a surface level of his Geist only, where the senses are the easiest to manipulate. It takes more effort and some time to subtly and safely dig deeper to the level on which I can easily drop a Mann into sleep."

He shook his head. "I had hoped to overwhelm him with the pain and cause him to black out, but…"

He shrugged helplessly.

Gemi sighed in turn. "But you didn't expect Frenz to be able to fight through that level of pain."

He nodded. "It did almost work, actually, but he came back from the brink of unconsciousness, which I hadn't expected." He smiled then. "He is an amazing Mann, your Freund, truly worthy of his place."

The final words made Gemi frown. They wouldn't have made sense— and probably didn't to the other Nomaden—except Gemi caught the pointed look that Wolfrik offered her. She stiffened.

"You dug further down into his Geist." Gemi had no doubts about that, and the Skorpion's nod was simple confirmation.

"It was the only way I could make him sleep, of which he was in desperate need by then." His lips then twitched into a small smile. "But you don't need to worry about any knowledge I might have gained in doing so. I swear, on my life as a Skorpion, that I will pose no threat to your Freund."

It was Gemi's turn to eye Wolfrik warily, but the Geistmagier met her gaze steadily. After a moment, she nodded. She didn't need Flame's confirmation that he was being sincere to realize that was the truth.

"Very well," she said, finally turning away from the Skorpion. The five other Männer were ranged out behind her and still had their Scharfmonde unsheathed. She waved at them to put the blades away.

"We're safe here. Of that I believe we can be sure."

"But what about Herr Handelmann and his Familie, Drache Krieger?" a Spinne asked. "We haven't found them yet."

Gemi glanced at Wolfrik, who answered with a simple, "The Familie is in the Kinder's rooms. They are safe, I swear."

"And we still have an unknown number of unconscious Skorpione to worry about, Drache Krieger," the Falke added, even as he and the others reluctantly sheathed their blades. "Surely you don't expect them to stay unconscious for the entire time that we will be here. We still don't know when we will be allowed to leave the Stadt."

Gemi chuckled. "Soon, I imagine." Not giving the others a chance to respond, she turned back to Wolfrik. "Are there any among the unconscious who might be persuaded to become loyal to you rather than the current Häuptling?"

The Skorpion shook his head. "The Häuptling only sent those with us that would do as he said. He did not want to take any chances."

Gemi grinned. "Apparently, he's been underestimating your power for some time." She chuckled and shook her head. "Very well, I'll have no qualms, then, with turning all of the unconscious Skorpione over to the Wachen."

Gasps came from every side of her, even the Skorpione, and the Spinne who'd spoken before even gripped her arm.

"You are working with the Wachen, Drache Krieger?"

Gemi thought her grin might split her face. "Rather they are working with us, Freund. Even now—"

She was interrupted by a series of amused snorts filling her head, and she turned her attention to her Pferd bondmate.

"Shadow, what is it?"

Shadow continued to snort and even gave a loud whinny that was his version of a full-bellied laugh. Once the laughter began to calm, he finally managed to answer.

"Lord Kawn just ordered the city guards to arrest Othman. The pompous beast actually had the audacity to act confused!"

Gemi sighed as he dissolved into snickering snorts once more.

"Has Lord Kawn decided on a new Gouverneur then?"

Shadow sighed, letting the laughter dissipate finally. *"Aye, he has."* He offered Gemi an image of Lord Kawn talking seriously with Dame Clarimonde of all people.

Gemi blinked. *"Really? This is no Witz?"*

Shadow tossed his head in denial. *"Oh, it's true all right. I'm not really surprised, either. We all know how stern and political Dame Clarimonde can be. I can't think of anyone better myself."*

Gemi nodded. Although she was ein bisschen surprised that Lord Kawn would choose a Frau, she knew she shouldn't be. Here in Zhulan, Frauen had always been seen as having the potential for leadership that they hadn't been allowed in other regions.

The light touch of a hand on her arm drew her attention back to the room in which she stood. "Drache Krieger?"

Gemi turned her gaze on the Fräulein who now stood beside her. Käfe blinked up at her with large eyes, and Gemi couldn't help the smile that spread her lips.

"James," she insisted. Like Wolfrik, Käfe would be returning to Helloase with them, and Gemi didn't relish being addressed by her formal title for that length of time.

However, she was surprised when the Fräulein dropped her chin, allowing the edge of her Kopfabdeckung to droop over her eyes. When she lifted her eyes to stare up at Gemi through her lashes, Gemi groaned inwardly.

Verdammte Frauen, she cursed in her thoughts.

This wasn't the first time she had garnered such attention from other Fräulein, but she generally tried to avoid giving the impression that she was returning the attention. She thought she might have just made a mistake.

"Females," Shadow nickered, amused. *"Such tricky creatures."*

Gemi rolled her eyes and gave a mental swat to the stallion's rump, but her Freund only snorted in response.

Patting Käfe's hand and praying to the Götter that she would not make the sudden situation with the Fräulein worse, Gemi turned her attention to the other Nomaden in order to explain the new alliance with Lord Kawn and the changes he would be making in the Städte. As she did, she focused part of her Geist on Shadow once more.

"Can you ask Lord Kawn and Gouverneur Clarimonde to send us some Wachen, Shadow?" She paused a moment to consider and added, *"And an Arztmagier if one is available. I don't wish Lakritze to exhaust herself in her attempt to fully Heal Frenz."*

Shadow agreed, and Gemi turned then to Flame.

"Can you send a message to Helloase requesting that they postpone the Skorpion's interrogation? I want to give Wolfrik the chance to speak for the Mann if he wishes before Tante Isa causes any permanent damage."

385

Flame murmured her own agreement before drifting off in search of a willing Falke.

With her messages sent, Gemi turned her full attention to the Nomaden surrounding her. Their shocked questions, she knew, would require it.

Chapter 37

"Wake up, Freund."

Ferez became aware of the darkness gradually, as if it formed around him, yet he couldn't think what had been there before. He felt like he was floating, and he found the sensation disconcerting.

"The sleep accomplished its purpose, Freund. It's time to wake."

Ferez grunted. That voice sounded familiar. Before he could think why, a sharp pain filled his head, and he groaned.

"Es tut mir leid," the voice spoke again, and the pain in his head eased until it was no more than a dull ache. *"I hadn't realized I still caused you that much pain."*

Suddenly, the pain seemed to increase again, but it was no longer focused in his head. Instead, it seemed to throb sharply in his left shoulder and radiate from there. The presence in his mind seemed to shrug.

"I said that the sleep accomplished its purpose, which was to keep you from suffering through the wound and making it worse. However, your Freund insisted that I wake you sooner rather than later. But don't worry. Someone is working to Heal your shoulder."

Who...? Ferez couldn't complete the thought before the voice was chuckling quietly.

"Once you wake, I am certain your Freund will properly introduce us. But you must wake first."

Ferez suddenly became aware of voices and the press of hands on his body and people around him. Releasing a soft breath, Ferez opened his eyes slowly, blinking when he found himself face to face with a young girl.

The girl giggled when he met her gaze and turned to look over her shoulder. "He's awake!" Then, she turned back to him and smoothed her hands over his right arm, which was closest to her.

"Your shoulder's doing better, Herr Kanti, but you shouldn't move too much yet. If you're not careful, you could still wrench it and cause permanent damage."

"You are correct, Fräulein Lakritze."

The girl ducked her head as her face flushed, and Ferez turned his head to find a man to his left. His hands were pressed gently against Ferez's shoulder. When Ferez caught the man's eyes, the man smiled.

"For a Mann with your history of battle wounds, you are amazingly healthy, Herr Kanti. You seem to have been extremely lucky in your access to Arztmagier."

Before Ferez could reply to the man, whom he assumed was a Mage Healer himself, a cry of "Frenz!" reached him. He turned to find James pushing past several people. The boy dropped to his knees in the place where Fräulein Lakritze had been just moments before.

387

"How are you feeling?"

James' violet eyes were wide, and he reached a hand up to lightly touch Ferez's cheek. The king blinked at the gentle touch but offered his friend a small smile.

"Much better, I think." Suddenly loathe to break eye contact with James, Ferez nodded vaguely to his left. "I'm under the impression the Healers think it reparable as long as I don' move."

"Not much, anyway," the Mage Healer added. James' eyes darted to the other man, and Ferez sighed and reluctantly followed his gaze.

"How long before he can risk standing up?" James asked.

The Healer chuckled. "Not too long before then, but if you're hoping to get him on a Pferd any time soon, you're better off letting me Heal the shoulder completely."

James made a small sound of distress. Ferez glanced at the boy in surprise, barely catching the soft smile the Healer offered.

"Whatever your attacker did with his Scharfmond, he managed to separate the flesh from the bone. It's not a wound I would recommend attempting to recover from slowly. At least, not with your schedule as I understand it, hm?"

James nodded slowly and turned his gaze back to Ferez. The king felt his breath catch at the turmoil evident in those purple orbs.

"I swear," James whispered, "as soon as we return to Helloase, I'll show you how to protect yourself against Scharfmonde." The boy squeezed his eyes shut and shook his head. "It was dumm of me not to do it sooner."

Ferez felt his chest tighten as he took in the boy's pursed lips, clenched jaw, and the way his brow furrowed in obvious distress. Reaching up with his right hand, Ferez wrapped it around the back of James' neck. Those purple eyes flew open once more as James opened his mouth to speak. Ferez shook his head, effectively interrupting him.

"Don' blame yourself, James." He made sure to hold the boy's gaze as he spoke. "We haven' 'ad the time. Af'er all," he offered a small smirk, "when would you've taught me, hm? When we were crossin' the desert? When we wen' to see Lord Kawn?" He chuckled. "Maybe while we slep'?"

James snorted, and Ferez finally felt the boy relax under his touch. "All right, all right, I get your point. We haven't exactly had the chance to train." James finally allowed a small smile of his own to stretch his lips. "What do you think about just staying with the Clan for the rest of our time in Zhulan? I think we've both had enough of Politik for a while."

Ferez nodded and opened his mouth to agree, but another, oddly familiar, voice interrupted him.

"You still have ein bisschen of Politik to play yet, ja, Drache Krieger?"

Ferez lifted his head as James leaned to one side. He found himself staring at two nomads, a woman and a man. Despite having never met either before, Ferez instantly knew who they were.

"You," he breathed.

He thought he should feel angry—he was pretty sure the man had caused him excess pain and put him to sleep—but the words that had awakened him ran through his head.

James glanced back at him warily. When Ferez simply continued to stare, the boy seemed to relax once more.

"Frenz," he spoke softly, drawing the king's gaze. "These are Wolfrik Giftschwanz and his Schwester, Käfe." Ferez nodded and turned his gaze back to the man. "They've turned their backs on their Häuptling and agreed to meet with my Vater."

Ferez nodded again. Perhaps it should have, but the news didn't surprise him. Instead, the Mindspeaker's words continued to run through his mind.

Finally, with his eyes locked with Wolfrik's, he asked, "How long was I out?"

James startled, but Wolfrik simply smiled, seeming to understand. "About three hours."

Ferez winced. Even if the pain hadn't been as bad as he remembered it being before he'd lost consciousness, three hours straight of it would have been a nightmare. And he would have attempted to fight with it, not knowing the severity of the wound until it was too late.

Not to mention the fact that I can't even protect myself against armed nomads.

Holding the Mindspeaker's gaze, Ferez replied, "I understand you saved my shoulder."

Wolfrik dipped his head; not in agreement, Ferez realized, but in acknowledgement.

"Many in my Clan love that maneuver. I have seen many gut people suffer from such wounds. It is not a Schicksal I would wish on anyone, even if I considered them my Feind.

"Which I don't consider you," he added hastily, lifting his gaze back to Ferez's.

Ferez chuckled. "Nay, you have called me Freund too many times for me to misunderstand." He let his gaze turn serious then, despite the small curve of his lips. "Thank you."

Wolfrik actually gave a half-bow then, which his sister imitated, causing Ferez to blink. "Mit Vergnügen, mein Freund."

He placed such a heavy emphasis on the final word that Ferez wondered if he meant something more than just 'friend'. When he glanced at James curiously, the boy met his gaze and mouthed, *He knows.*

Ferez nodded, understanding. Wolfrik was recognizing him as king. Maybe that should have shocked, and even worried, him, but Ferez doubted anything could at the moment. He turned to the Mage Healer with a small frown.

"Am I in shock?"

It seemed logical. During the war, he remembered seeing so many of his men acting calmer than happy babes when they normally would have been screaming in pain or distress. He couldn't imagine any other reason that he would be taking these revelations so easily.

Wolfrik snorted and replied, "I think you underestimate your own Geist, Freund."

Meanwhile, the Healer offered a small, almost guilty smile. "I had your body release some naturally calming chemicals into your bloodstream. I didn't want you getting upset before you were fully healed."

Ferez blinked but nodded. He remembered seeing that trick, too. Some Mage Healers had been able to calm hysterical patients with a single touch, allowing them to treat them without the risk of more damage.

"*Es tut mir leid, Freund.*" Ferez glanced up at the Mindspeaker, wondering why the man had decided to keep these words between the two of them. Wolfrik offered a sad smile. "*It seems that I stirred up some nasty memories.*"

Ferez shook his head. While James glanced at him curiously, the king kept the next thought to himself and the Mindspeaker.

Not nasty, just old.

Forcing his thoughts back to the present, he asked James what else had been happening.

~~*~*

Wolfrik listened idly as the Drache Krieger described recent events to the König. His Geist, on the other hand, was focused solely on the König's. The Mann didn't know it, but the memories from the Krieg that were flitting through his Geist were simply signs of a much larger Problem; a Problem that Wolfrik was determined to fix.

Although he had told the Drache Krieger he had delved deeper into the König's Geist, the only significance the boy had recognized from that was the fact that Wolfrik now knew the Mann's true identity. The boy didn't seem to understand the force necessary for Wolfrik to reach that deeply as quickly as he had. Wolfrik had been forced to abandon the subtlety he usually depended on in order to quickly drop the Mann into sleep.

The result was that Wolfrik's Magie had torn through the König's Geist, destroying any natural mental defenses the Mann might have had. It was something that Wolfrik had immediately regretted. He had promised himself from an early age that he would never turn the full force of his Geistmagie on another human being.

Even more devastating was the realization that this Mann was not only the König of Evon, but a kind and compassionate Mann who was actively seeking to learn more about his people. It hurt the Geistmagier to know that he had hurt a Mann who would most likely forgive him with an ease Wolfrik had never known possible. With the König's Dank ringing in his ears, Wolfrik eased his Magie through the Mann's Geist. With his natural defenses torn away, the König's Geist was not only open to any Geistmagier willing to invade it, his Geist practically shouted his thoughts and would almost actively attract even the weakest Magier.

Already, Wolfrik had begun to work on rebuilding the König's defenses. He had dulled the mental pain as much as he could, but it was only hidden. It would remain until the König had recovered fully from Wolfrik's attack.

With the pain dulled, Wolfrik began to build a barrier around the Mann's Geist. In Schönestadt alone, there were tens of Geistmagier, so repelling possible intruders was of highest priority. Even so, it would take several hours to build a barrier strong and complex enough to protect the König's weakened Geist to Wolfrik's satisfaction.

He thanked me for saving his shoulder, Wolfrik mused as he worked. *The least I can do is save his Geist as well.*

~~*~*

Despite her curiosity over Ferez's thoughts, Gemi told Ferez everything that had happened since he'd fallen asleep. She even included Shadow's thoughts on Othman, knowing the König would find them amusing.

Ferez didn't disappoint as he smirked and chuckled—and looked queasy—in the appropriate places. However, only half his Geist seemed to be on the conversation, and she was less than halfway through the story before she thought she knew why. Although he'd slept, the wound, or the fact that the sleep had been Magie-induced, had kept him from properly resting.

With that thought at the front of her Geist, Gemi managed to quickly finish the story once the Arztmagier proclaimed Ferez satisfactorily healed for the Nacht.

"Mind you," the Arztmagier had conditioned, "I will be back after Mittag to make sure you're completely healed." He had let his smile soften, even as his eyes had remained stern.

"But we all need sleep, you more than the rest of us. I expect you will still be abed when I return." He'd left then, as had the remaining Wachen. On the way out, one paused to remind Gemi that Lord Kawn and Gouverneur Clarimonde would also be stopping by the next Tag.

Gemi and Sir Leal, who had insisted on remaining with them for the Nacht, helped a half-asleep Ferez to a bedroom. Rune Handelmann had offered several for those Nomaden electing to spend one more Nacht—an option most opted for with the Unwetter still drenching the Stadt.

Once they got the König into bed, Gemi insisted on taking the room's second. Sir Leal didn't argue. He simply smiled and left to find his own bed for the Nacht.

Now, Gemi fiddled with Ferez's blankets, telling herself that she was just making sure he'd be comfortable for the Nacht. She knew she was stalling, unwilling to leave his side, but she didn't care. Ferez had been badly injured this Nacht. It was the second time this Season.

Almost the third time, she thought, thinking of the incident with the Katzen.

She had panicked and almost lost herself when Ferez had lost consciousness. If it hadn't been for Sir Leal's insistence, she thought she might have broken down right then.

Even now, with Ferez alive and well and right in front of her, Gemi could feel a prickling at the back of her eyes. Closing them, she took a deep breath.

There's no reason to break down now; we're all safe.

A hand closing on hers had her opening her eyes and blinking down into sleepy silvery-blue orbs. When Ferez rubbed his thumb against the backs of her fingers, she numbly realized that she had fisted her hands in the blankets.

Relaxing her grip, she turned the hand over and gripped the Mann's hand instead. Ferez squeezed in return.

"James?" he whispered, and the word sounded half-slurred. Gemi thought he must be on the edge of sleep. "D'yeh 'member the war?"

Gemi blinked. After everything that had happened recently, the Krieg mit Fayral was the last thing on her Geist, but…

"Of course I do," she whispered back. "I probably fought in it as long as you did."

Longer, actually. But she didn't say it, not when she was two Jahre younger than Ferez.

Those silvery eyes blinked slowly, and Gemi found herself mesmerized by the colors. She'd never noticed before, but there seemed to be separate patches of blue and silver, as if the two colors mingled but refused to become one color.

It was oddly calming, the idea that one could mix with another without completely losing itself.

"Yeh shouldna had to," Ferez murmured suddenly, breaking the silence. Gemi blinked, but those blue and silver orbs were still locked on hers. "Yeh were so young…we were so young."

Gemi swallowed as a lump suddenly appeared in her throat. Leaning over the bed, she laid her other hand along Ferez's cheek. It was only slightly rough, and Gemi felt the prickling in her eyes return.

So young.

"We did what we had to, Ferez."

She knew she probably shouldn't risk using his real name, but she couldn't bring herself to speak his alias just now. It didn't feel right.

If only he knew my *real name.*

Gemi felt Flame press against her Geist then, but Gemi pushed her away. She didn't need the Drache insisting again that she should tell him who she was. Ja, the desire for him to know was there, but the Angst was still stronger.

And I don't want to jeopardize this…whatever it is.

"We shouldna had to," Ferez muttered again. His eyes fell closed, and Gemi felt her stomach clench when they didn't open immediately.

"So…much…death."

Gemi's breathing speed up. Images began to fill her head. Battlefields strewn with the dead and dying. Walking past dead Mann after dead Mann in the hopes of finding one or two who still breathed. Watching from the deck of the *Pretty Pauper* as other ships sank, hoping and praying to the Götter that their ship would not meet the same Schicksal.

Nein!

Gemi shoved the memories away. If she was good at anything, it was burying the truth in her Geist, along with whatever images accompanied it. Unfortunately, she couldn't prevent the tears that leaked from her prickling eyes as she focused on Ferez once more.

Squeezing his hand and rubbing her thumb under his eye, she murmured, "But that Tod was not in vain, Ferez. Those Männer gave their Leben for our current Frieden. Isn't that worth it, Ferez?"

"I believe *they* thought so. I *know* many of them fought in the Hoffnung that one Tag we would have Frieden; that we would have the freedom to live without fighting."

Gemi hadn't been sure if Ferez was still awake; he had certainly looked asleep. So she startled when he chuckled dryly.

"Still no' free from fightin'," he muttered lowly.

Gemi huffed a soft laugh, though amusement wasn't what drove the sound.

"Nein, not yet." She sighed. "But soon, Ferez. Remember Mama Caler's words?"

She almost choked as she said it. She remembered the Seer's words all too well, and she knew they'd overwhelm her if she thought on them too hard. But there had been Hoffnung in those words.

"It's almost over. If we can survive this Jahreszeit, this season, we can have Frieden." Uncertain that she was getting her point across in Zhulanese, she added fiercely, "We can have our peace."

"One las' obs'acle," Ferez breathed and blinked open his eyes once more. "One las' season," he muttered. "D'yeh really think…it'll be that easy?"

Gemi bit her lip. She didn't think it would be easy at all. They hadn't even reached Mitte Jahreszeit, yet so much had happened. And if Mama Caler was right—and Gemi had never known her to be wrong—then there was still so much that could go wrong.

But Gemi had been reaching for the Hoffnung in the Seer's words, and that's what she would give her Freund.

"Ja, Ferez. One last season."

Ferez closed his eyes and sighed. Then, he turned his face into her hand, and Gemi felt her breath hitch as his lips moved against her palm.

"One more season. Will I still see yeh…af'erwards, James?"

Gemi felt like her breath had frozen in her lungs. Pressure built in her throat and behind her eyes, and that desire to tell Ferez her true identity swelled until she could feel her real name burning on the tip of her tongue.

That, too, froze as Flame brushed across her Geist once more. Gemi closed her eyes against the pressure there and swallowed against that in her throat.

Nein, not yet, not yet.

"James?"

Ferez's voice was ein bisschen louder now and tinged with Panik. Startled, Gemi opened her eyes and stared back down into those blue and silver orbs that held more than ein bisschen of Angst.

"Will you leave afterwards?"

And no matter that the Angst of her true identity was still strong or that she wished, more than anything, to give it to him, she knew one thing that she wanted without a doubt. Not caring how it might seem to the half-asleep Mann, she leaned over him and placed a light kiss to his forehead.

"Nein, Ferez. I won't leave." Praying to the Götter that she was not proven wrong, she added, "No matter how this ends, I will never leave you."

~~*~*

When Ferez woke the next day, he kept his body still and his eyes shut as he took stock of himself and his surroundings. He lay on bedding that was comfortable enough to suggest a bed, yet not one belonging to an inn. It was certainly too comfortable for that. Parts of his body ached, but he was certain it had nothing to do with the bedding.

In fact, as memories from the night before slowly rose to the front of his mind, Ferez realized that the aches had more to do with the mostly healed shoulder wound and not a little bit from the way he was sure he'd been lying half against a wall for several hours.

Sighing softly, Ferez shifted under his covers and opened his eyes. The room he'd slept in was dark, but he could make out the outline of the door that he figured led to the hallway and a second bed standing in the other half of the room. Frowning at the tidy bed, the king wondered if anyone had claimed it for the night.

Suddenly, the murmur of voices from the hallway made themselves known, and Ferez became aware of other, more muffled sounds that indicated that the day had begun long ago. Ferez nodded to himself as he realized that whoever might have slept in the room as well was already awake.

A memory suddenly formed in his mind, an image of wide purple eyes. The memory, oddly, seemed to mix with scattered images from the war and the words that Ferez could remember Mama Caler speaking before he

394

and James had left Kensy. There were other words attached to the image, but they were vaguer and too indistinct to recall.

One set of words stood out in his mind against all others, words that he must have repeated to himself over and over again as he'd drifted into sleep for them to be so sharp in his mind.

No matter how this ends, I will never leave you.

It was a promise, Ferez realized, one that James had not made lightly. The thought fueled a warmth in his chest that the king suddenly knew had been building for a while.

He was drawn from his contemplation when the door to the hallway swung open and warm lamplight spilled across the floor and his bed. Squinting against the sudden brightness, Ferez noticed a figure standing in the doorway, an unknown silhouette against the bright light. Before his eyes could adjust, a familiar voice reached his ears.

"Ach, so you are awake, Herr Kanti." Ferez recognized the voice from the night before as the Mage Healer he knew it belonged to stepped closer to his bed. "Your Freund had feared you would sleep straight through the Tag."

Ferez blinked up at the Healer as a small frown tugged at his lips. "How late is it?"

"A couple hours before sunset, I'm afraid." The Healer leaned down and laid a hand on Ferez's temple. "It seems Herr Giftschwanz did ein bisschen more damage than I first suspected."

He shook his head and stood. "But it seems the sleep has helped you recover from that, at least. Now then, let me take a look at your shoulder."

It was almost an hour later when the Healer led Ferez to a parlor towards the front of the house. There, James was speaking with Kawn and a tall woman that Ferez recognized as the moneylender whose hospitality they had sampled when they'd first arrived in Schönestadt. James had his back to Ferez when he entered, but he quickly turned when Kawn nodded to him in greeting.

"Frenz!" Suddenly, James was in front of Ferez and looking him over, a hand on each of his shoulders—the grip on his left noticeably lighter than the right. "How do you feel?"

Ferez chuckled as he vaguely recalled the boy asking him the same question the night before. Reaching up and squeezing the hand on his left shoulder, he offered a smile.

"Fully healed, for the mos' part."

James frowned. "For the most part?"

Ferez shrugged and glanced uncertainly at the Healer, who still stood nearby. The man seemed to understand the look. Instead of acting insulted like Ferez had feared, he chuckled.

"It seems," the Healer said, addressing James, "your Freund has become rather verwöhnt where Arztmagier are concerned."

Ferez didn't know what 'verwöhnt' meant, but he thought he understood the gist of the man's words. He shrugged again and added, "He's not as good as Lakina."

For a moment, James simply blinked at him. Then, a grin spread across his face, and he snickered.

"Frenz, I don't think anyone is as good as Lakina." With a quick glance at the Healer, he added, "No offense, Arztmagier."

The Healer smiled warmly and shook his head. "None taken, Drache Krieger." James grimaced, and Ferez wondered if anyone else noticed or realized it was the boy's reaction to the constant use of his title.

"If this Lakina was the last Arztmagier to Heal Herr Kanti, then I can agree that her Magie far exceeds my own. She is certainly a Meister Magier."

Ferez nodded in agreement. However, the reference to his last Healing brought to mind images of large cats attacking him, images he had been attempting to avoid. His thoughts must have shown on his face as James squeezed his shoulder and turned Ferez's attention to the people with whom he had previously been conversing.

"Frenz, I want to reintroduce you to Dame Clarimonde. I know you met her several Nächte ago, but we didn't exactly spend much time in Schönestadt during our last visit."

Ferez nodded. As he made to offer the stern woman a small bow, James added, "Lord Kawn has named her the new Gouverneur of Schönestadt."

Ferez pulled himself up straight in surprise. In the next moment, he realized that he vaguely recalled hearing something similar the night before. Hoping the Dame didn't feel slighted by his startled reaction, he lowered himself into a bow once more.

"Is a pleasure to meet you 'gain, Dame Clarimonde," he greeted, using the Zhulanese title since he distinctly remembered Raymond's reaction to his previous use of 'madam'. "An' congratulations, as well. I'm sure you'll make a fine governor."

The stern-looking woman dipped her chin and offered a small smile. "Danke, Herr Kanti. I fear it is an idea to which I am still accustoming myself." She glanced at James then back to Ferez, her smile twitching into a small smirk.

"And I am glad that you are healed. Herr Caffers has been worrying himself fiercely over your Gesundheit."

James ducked his head, but not before Ferez saw red suddenly infuse his cheeks. "You were asleep for an awfully long time," the boy muttered.

Ferez's smile softened, and he laid a hand on James' shoulder. The boy lifted his gaze to Ferez's and smiled shyly.

"I told you it was only natürlich that our Freund slept so long, Drache Krieger."

Ferez blinked as the voice broke whatever had passed between him and James. Turning his gaze from the boy, Ferez realized that Wolfrik and Käfe Giftschwanz also stood nearby, though he hadn't noticed them before now.

"After all," Wolfrik added, "his Geist had to recover as much as his body. That form of exhaustion is not easily shaken."

James nodded. Turning back to Ferez, he gripped the king's shoulder once more.

"Since you're feeling better and there's less than an hour of sunlight left, we might as well leave for Helloase now." James looked to the Mage Healer but didn't release his hold on Ferez. "And you are certain he is healed enough to ride through the Nacht?"

The Healer chuckled. "Do not worry, Drache Krieger. There is no risk of the wound reopening. It might ache for ein bisschen, and he might grow tired more quickly, but riding a Pferd through the Nacht will cause no Probleme, I can assure you."

James nodded again, yet his frown told Ferez he wasn't completely satisfied with the Healer's assessment. Patting James' hand, Ferez smiled.

"I think I could use a nightlong ride after spending all day in bed."

James chuckled.

~~*~*

In the alleys of Schönestadt, not far from the Handelmann Haus, a Nomade hissed like the Schlange for which his Clan was named. Adalwolf pulled his Magie back from the Geist he had just attempted to infiltrate.

Impossible.

"Not a very accurate assessment, since he seems to have achieved it," a voice drily added.

Adalwolf scowled but didn't reply. He had first heard the voice two Siebentage ago. Although it seemed to delight in taunting him, it had also provided invaluable advice. Many in his Clan might doubt his Pläne if he told them that the ideas had come from a disembodied Geist, but this particular Geist had spoken too many truths to Adalwolf for him not to accept the voice's advice.

That advice had led to the Tod of the two Gouverneure who had been known to be freundlich with the Vereinte Clans, as well as the ten Tage of Chaos that had followed. If only the verdammt Caffers boy had kept himself out of the way, then the Vereinte Clans would have lost all of their river-dwelling allies.

"I did warn you that you needed to prepare for his interference," the voice replied, amused. *"I warned you he would strike hard and fast."*

Adalwolf hissed again, but his annoyance was directed at his own arrogance. He had believed himself prepared, despite the voice's amused warnings that Caffers would break down his Pläne.

Now, he had even lost his chance to work his way into the Geist of Caffers' new human Freund. Indeed, that chance had been lost the moment Wolfrik had worked his way into the Mann's Geist and set up a complex barrier that, after some exploring, Adalwolf knew he would be unable to bypass undetected.

It irked Adalwolf beyond measure. He *knew* Wolfrik. The other Geistmagier was weak, was Abschaum. Yet, the boy was obviously clever enough to create a barrier that Adalwolf would not be able to overcome so easily.

I knew I should have insisted on overseeing this part.

Even as he thought it, he knew he had had little choice in that matter. While he had offered the Plan originally, Häuptling Giftschwanz had claimed the idea as his own, and Adalwolf's Häuptling had forbidden him from interfering.

Dark laughter that hinted at violence filled Adalwolf's Geist.

"Are you angry because your Pläne are falling apart, or because the Giftschwanz Kinder knowingly gave up the chance to prove themselves worthy as Kinder of the Häuptling, a chance you'll never receive."

Adalwolf ignored the voice's taunts. He had learned quickly that the voice was harsh, but so were his Clan and his Leben. That was the Schicksal of an unclaimed Sohn of his Häuptling.

For Jahre, he hadn't known for certain if it was true. His Mutter had always claimed it was so, but the rest of the Clan called her Schlampe and Hexe as she seduced even the most faithful of Männer into her Zelt.

It had been the violent voice that had assured him of the truth. It had claimed that the strength of his Geistmagie, Magie that he had inherited from his Mutter, could only come from the line of the Häuptling. It was a line that Adalwolf should have been heir to since he was several Jahre older than the eldest Sohn of the Häuptling's Lebenfrau.

"So easily distracted," muttered the voice.

Adalwolf sneered. *"I am easily distracted? The Pläne fall apart before us, and you spend your efforts baiting me."*

"Be patient, Geistmagier." Amusement filled the voice more than ever. *"I have a Plan to bring down Caffers himself, a Plan I believe you will take great pleasure in carrying out."*

Chapter 38

It was about an hour after Mitternacht when their party approached Helloase. Among the Clans, Wolfrik knew that many people would still be awake at this hour. Still, he was surprised to find a group of six people waiting for them on the edge of the Lager.

One Nomade, a Mann by the tone of his voice, stepped forward to greet them as the Pferde slowed to a halt. He laid a hand on the nose of Herr Schattenrenner, the Drache Krieger's mount. The nicker that emerged from his mouth immediately marked him as a Tieremagier.

Once Herr Schattenrenner had responded, the Tieremagier turned his face up. "James, it is gut that you have returned." He hesitated a moment then added, "You are well?"

"Ja, Vater, of course" the Drache Krieger replied. There was a note of curiosity in his voice, as though he wondered why the Mann would think otherwise.

Suddenly, Wolfrik stiffened and ducked his head as the boy's words sank in. If this Mann was Vater to the Drache Krieger, then this was Häuptling Hausef Kanten, Erstehäuptling of the Vereinte Clans.

Wolfrik felt his gut twist. *What if he doesn't see me as worthy?* The thought slipped through his Geist before he could stop it. He felt himself grimace as the familiar bitterness settled through him. *It is not like he'd be the first Häuptling that doesn't.*

A hand on his arm brought him back to the present, and he glanced to his right, where Käfe rode beside him. Even in the moons-light, he could see the comforting smile she offered him. He allowed a small smile to lift his lips in return, but he knew she couldn't understand, not completely.

Though their Häuptling had started in on her Geist when she was a toddler, Wolfrik had managed to draw the Mann's Magie onto his little more than a Jahr later. Any memories she might have of that Jahr were hidden in the past and Wolfrik's Magie.

She was his little Schwester, and he wouldn't let anything happen to her if he could help it. That meant, however, that she had never felt the full extent of the pain he had, and, while he was usually happy to know that, there were times, like now, when that simply made him feel alone.

"His shoulder is fine, except for some possible soreness," a different voice brought Wolfrik's attention back to the group in front of them. He frowned, wondering if the Mann who'd spoken was an Arztmagier. "But it is not his shoulder for which I fear."

Wolfrik raised his eyebrows. The Artzmagier must be powerful if he could sense the remaining effects of his Geistmagie on the König.

"His Geist is healing," he muttered and winced when everyone turned to look at him.

He knew better than to speak so defensively when no one had even addressed him. Such action had only ever brought suspicion and anger

399

from his Häuptling, something he had learned to avoid Jahre ago. The hand on his arm tightened its grip, showing him that even Käfe seemed surprised by his outburst.

"Bruder," she whispered, but the Artzmagier spoke again, interrupting whatever words she might have thought to use.

"You think that, do you?" The Mann stepped closer. "And did you realize that there was physical damage as well as the damage to his Geist?"

Wolfrik inhaled sharply and looked to the König. Only then did he realize why they were speaking of him in the first place. The Mann was slumped in his saddle, only the Drache Krieger's hand on his shoulder keeping him at all upright.

How long has he been flagging?

He couldn't remember feeling the König's exhaustion creep up on him. Instead, it seemed to have come upon him suddenly.

"Wolfrik?" the Drache Krieger asked sharply, and the Geistmagier turned his gaze to the boy, who had turned in his saddle to look at him. Wolfrik didn't know what the Drache Krieger could see of his face, but he pursed his lips in response to whatever he saw. "You didn't tell us that there was lingering damage. Why?"

Wolfrik scrambled for a response, suddenly feeling lost. He didn't know these people, didn't know how to respond to them or how to act to get the responses he wanted. And he knew his Magie would do him no good at this point, not when he had only worked it into the Geist of one Mann and at least one of these people was a Geistmagier as well.

"James," the König sighed, stilling Wolfrik's Geist.

The Drache Krieger gripped the Mann with his second hand as he swayed, and the boy murmured an affirmation of his presence.

"Maybe we shoul' get more comfortable 'fore we 'ave this conversation."

"Right," the Drache Krieger responded without hesitation.

With the help of the Nomaden on the ground, the boy managed to get the König safely dismounted then swung off of Herr Schattenrenner. Käfe quickly dismounted as well, and, after a moment's hesitation, Wolfrik followed suit. To his surprise, as soon as he was firmly on his own feet, his Pferd followed Herr Schattenrenner and the others towards the waterhole.

"This way," said the Erstehäuptling, and the Mann led the group into a Zelt that was marked as an Arztmagier's. Once inside, the König was lowered onto a cot, and the Arztmagier turned his full attention to the Mann.

"Well, Wolfrik?" the Drache Krieger asked, crossing his arms over his chest and ignoring the flask that a Fräulein offered him. "Why didn't you tell us about the lingering damage?"

Wolfrik sighed. He was tempted to glance around at the other Nomaden but kept his gaze solely on the Drache Krieger. They knew him less than Caffers did, so he knew he would get no help from them.

"Es tut mir leid, Drache Krieger. I—"

He hesitated. He knew his reasons for not disclosing the full extent of the damage he had done to the König's Geist. How, though, was he supposed to explain his guilt and his desire to heal the damage himself? How could he tell them about his pride in his Magie and the Angst he felt when he considered the full power of it?

"James, please," the König whispered once more, startling everyone.

Wolfrik had been sure the Mann was already asleep. Focusing on his Geist, the Skorpion found the Mann's determination. He realized, with a wave of guilt and gratitude, that Ferez had spoken up not because of his own discomfort, but rather as a way to stop the Drache Krieger's impromptu interrogation.

"You need to rest, Herr Kanti," the Arztmagier scolded.

The König attempted to raise a hand, no doubt in an attempt to wave the Mann away, but the hand barely made it a few inches above the surface of the cot before he dropped it back down. He did manage to shake his head, though.

"You're bein' an idiot, James."

The muttered declaration preceded a series of gasps, though Wolfrik noted with some amusement that two Männer, who looked to be about his own age, snorted instead. The Drache Krieger stiffened.

"Wolfrik may not 'ave explicitly told us how bad the damage was, but he did mention it." The König yawned hugely then, and, when he continued, his voice seemed to drift a bit. "You may not 'ave realized it, but I knew the damage was still 'ffectin' me."

It was Wolfrik's turn to stiffen then. He wasn't sure if he had made a noise or if the König was still more aware of his surroundings than he looked, but the König's lips twitched.

"You didn' think I'd noticed, did you, Wolfrik?" Ferez shook his head slightly again. "I know my body. I've been injured an' 'Ealed too many times over the pas' few years no' to recognize my body's reactions to such things."

He paused then, and, though he didn't yawn, it seemed the exhaustion was slowly shutting him down. Wolfrik winced. He wished the Mann would let himself rest so the Arztmagier could Heal him, but that determination he had noticed in the König's Geist earlier was still strong.

"This exhaustion 'as not in' to do wi' my shoulder." Ferez's words renewed suddenly. Wolfrik frowned when he brushed the Mann's mind and found that the König didn't even realize he'd paused. "I've known tha' since the firs' time I woke."

A snort drew everyone's attention to the Zelt's entrance, where Dame Flammezunge had stuck her head through. Though she seemed to glare at the Drache Krieger, her words seemed to address anybody who could understand her.

"*Would you leave Wolfrik alone, James? Frenz obviously won't let himself sleep until you do.*"

The boy opened his mouth to protest, but Dame Flammezunge must have been reacting to his thoughts because she snapped, "*Nay, James!*"

The boy sullenly closed his mouth and pursed his lips. Drache and Drache Krieger glared silently at each other for a full minute before Caffers's expression relaxed and he looked away.

Dame Flammezunge nodded. "*Besides,*" she added, once again allowing herself to be understood by others, "*Wolfrik has been actively healing and protecting Frenz's mind almost since the damage was done.*"

Wolfrik frowned, confused. He had had the impression that the Drache wasn't old enough to be able to touch other Geister unless they could actively accept her, like he had after she'd accepted him as an ally. The Drache turned to him and hissed softly, sounding amused.

"*I may be young, but I understand what happens to a creature's mind when the natural barriers are destroyed. Even I should have been able to hear Frenz's thoughts when he woke that first time, but they were noticeably silent.*"

Silence filled the Zelt then as everyone considered the Drache's words. Only the Arztmagier, who was smoothing his hands over the König's head, and one of the two young Männer that Wolfrik had noticed earlier seemed to have missed Dame Flammezunge's words altogether. Wolfrik was surprised to note that the rest of the Zelt's occupants, then, must be either Geistmagier or Tieremagier.

One Nomade, whose scarred face spoke of tragedy, knelt beside the Arztmagier, focusing on, but not touching, the König. Wolfrik realized, with a jolt, that he knew who this Frau was.

Even among the Gift Clans, the name Isana Kanten was well-known.

Acknowledged as the strongest Geistmagier throughout the Vereinte Clans—and Wolfrik had always secretly wondered if she was the strongest in all the Clans—Isana Kanten had once been considered the most beautiful Frau, as well. As first-born, she had been in line to be Häuptling of the Katze Clan, and, even long before Unification, Männer throughout the Clans had been eager to claim her as their Lebenfrau.

But her scarred face was how Isana Kanten was now recognized, and her younger Bruder had become Häuptling instead of her. Though the right half of her face still shone strongly with the beauty for which she had once been known, the left was scarred and saggy, as though, even Jahre after the fire that had stolen her beauty and fertility, her flesh still threatened to melt right off her bones.

"Flame is right," Isana said, startling Wolfrik from his contemplations. "Frenz's Geist is well-protected now." She tilted her head and muttered, "A powerful barrier, at that."

She lifted her eyes from the König's form to Wolfrik. Those dark eyes seemed to assess him before she asked, "This is yours?"

Wolfrik ducked his head at the curiosity and awe in the Frau's voice. "Ja, Dame."

There was a soft rustling sound, like cloth moving, but the Skorpion didn't move until a pair of boots stopped in front of him. Lifting his head, he found Isana Kanten standing before him, her black eyes studying him.

"James," Isana finally said, though her eyes remained on Wolfrik, "you haven't introduced your new Freunde yet." Her tone was lightly admonishing.

"Es tut mir leid, Tante."

Though the Drache Krieger's words addressed Isana Kanten, when Wolfrik looked at the boy, he found that the boy's shy, apologetic smile was directed at him.

"Vater, Tante, these are Wolfrik and Käfe Giftschwanz."

Instead of the shock and indignation that Wolfrik thought he should expect at those words, the introduction was met simply with surprised smiles. "Giftschwanz?" the Erstehäuptling asked, curious. "As in Häuptling Giftschwanz?"

Wolfrik nodded, muttering an affirmative. Their unexpected reactions made him falter. Even Käfe's hand gripping his didn't seem as much of a comfort as it usually would.

When Isana Kanten offered her hand palm up, like she was offering a gift, Wolfrik stared at it, unsure why she would offer him, Sohn of her Feind, such a sign of Freundschaft. She seemed to understand his hesitance. Without dropping her hand, she murmured, "If you are here as you are, then you have proven yourself to my Neffe and his Drache." She offered a lopsided smile that softened her scarred face. "Neither trust easily, so their judgment is well-respected."

Wolfrik swallowed against the dryness that suddenly filled his mouth. With a small nod, he finally released Käfe's hand and took the offered one.

"Danke," he whispered.

He didn't think the one word was enough to fully express his gratitude for their acceptance, but he didn't trust his voice to carry any other words. He met her gaze and hoped she'd understand.

If she did, she didn't dwell on it. Instead, she gripped his shoulder with her free hand and offered, "Perhaps, when we are all rested, you would be interested in joining the Geisternetz of the Vereinte Clans, hm?"

Wolfrik spluttered then, shocked that Isana Kanten would offer so much so soon. To be accepted as an ally whose physical presence was trustworthy was something for which Wolfrik had thought he could only hope. But to be allowed to join the Geisternetz, which joined the Geister of all the Geistmagier throughout the Vereinte Clans, was altogether humbling.

"You would allow me to merge my Geist with the Geisternetz?"

Isana snorted, though her smile turned playful. "Don't misunderstand me, Wolfrik Giftschwanz. I am sure you understand that it is easier to keep an eye on a new ally when their Geist is easily available, ja?"

But not necessarily easily accessible.

That was the mistake his Häuptling had made again and again. Through the Geisternetz of the Skorpion Clan, the Mann had been able to prey on the Geist of any Geistmagier who opposed his will. But he had never understood that, just because he could reach a Geist, it did not mean he was able to reach inside it. That misconception had saved Wolfrik's Leben many times as his Häuptling had never realized that the pain he inflicted on his youngest two had been ineffective for Jahre.

Isana's sudden laughter startled Wolfrik from his thoughts, and he stared at the scarred Frau. Once she had calmed, she smirked.

"Your Geist may be well-protected against intrusion, Freund," and Wolfrik felt his throat tighten at her easy use of the word, "but your face is surprisingly open."

Wolfrik ducked his head again, and, this time, he could feel his embarrassment burning his cheeks. He lifted his head, though, when Käfe stepped forward.

"If you are going to insult us," she spoke fiercely, "then perhaps we shouldn't have come."

His Schwester's words surprised Wolfrik as she was usually rather mild-mannered. Her current stance, however, was anything but, and the stiffness of her shoulders suggested that she was currently glaring at Isana Kanten. Dropping the Geistmagier's hand, Wolfrik laid a hand on Käfe's shoulder, hoping to calm her.

Isana, for her part, raised her hands, her eyes turning serious.

"I meant no harm, Fräulein," she responded. "The words were meant only as a Witz in the hopes of easing your Bruder's worries." She turned her dark eyes to Wolfrik and offered a small understanding nod. "I realize now that that was not the best tactic."

That small lopsided smile returned. "You needn't be ashamed of having such an open expression, though. It speaks highly of you."

Käfe relaxed under Wolfrik's palm, but she glanced back at him, her mouth turned down in obvious confusion. Wolfrik couldn't fault her. Normally, he could keep from showing his emotions so freely, or he could at least control what emotions he did. He never would have survived Leben with his Brüder and Häuptling otherwise.

Here, he had been caught flatfooted at every turn, and hiding his tumultuous emotions was not a priority.

"James," the Erstehäuptling spoke then, pulling the attention away from Wolfrik and his Schwester. "I assume our new Freunde are the reason you asked us to postpone the Skorpion's questioning?"

Wolfrik startled and glanced sharply at the Drache Krieger. The boy had not mentioned another Skorpion.

"Ja, Vater. I wanted to give Wolfrik the chance to speak for the Mann, if he so wished."

"Speak for whom, exactly?"

The boy turned to Wolfrik and nodded. "Before we met, earlier that Tag, there was an incident in Machtstadt involving a Skorpion by the name of Jakob."

Käfe gasped, and Wolfrik grimaced. Jakob was known to them. He was disliked even by those of his own Clan. The Mann had lost his place in the Clan several Siebentage ago and had been stripped of his Statusgürtel. Whatever the Mann had done to get himself captured by the Vereinte Clans would have most likely resulted from an attempt to gain favor with their Häuptling once more.

"You know him, then?" Isana Kanten asked.

Wolfrik nodded. "What are the accusations against him?"

Käfe glanced sharply at him, no doubt thinking they should denounce the Mann without question, especially since, if he was loyal to anyone, it would be to their Häuptling.

Wolfrik, however, understood something that she might not. Not only might the Vereinte Clans see them as allies, but they might also consider Wolfrik as a potential Häuptling for a Clan they had previously considered lost. If Wolfrik was to salvage any of his Clan once the Vereinte Clans defeated his Häuptling and Brüder, then he must begin to act and think like a future Häuptling now.

These thoughts were confirmed to him when he noted the approving glances that the Erstehäuptling, his Schwester, and the Drache Krieger all sent him.

"He was found wearing the Statusgürtel of the Falke Clan, and he attempted to kill Herzog Parshen," the Drache Krieger answered.

Wolfrik nodded. "A triple transgression, then." The others made questioning sounds. Even Käfe didn't seem to understand. "The first accusation," he clarified, "would be doubly wrong on his part as he was stripped of his Statusgürtel nearly a month ago. For him to wear any Statusgürtel, even one from the Skorpion Clan, is punishable."

"Had he been exiled?" the Erstehäuptling asked warily.

Wolfrik thought he understood why. If the Mann had been exiled, then another Clan even taking him into custody as a prisoner was against the Mann's punishment. Centuries ago, when all the Clans had been vereinte under the Erstehäuptling, a Clan could be punished for doing so.

He shook his head. "Nein, he had simply been stripped of his Status within the Clan. As it is, though, he was on the verge of being denounced as a Nomade."

Shaking his head again, Wolfrik added, "I believe he deserves whatever punishment you deem just." After a short pause, he nodded to Isana. "And whatever method of questioning you deem necessary."

The Frau's lopsided smile widened, and she chuckled darkly. "Would you like to be involved in his interrogation?"

Wolfrik considered the other Geistmagier's offer. Though they seemed to have accepted him easily enough, he realized that assisting in Jakob's questioning could help him prove himself further to Isana, at the very least. Plus, if he wanted to take responsibility for the future of his Clan, then he might as well begin with this.

When he offered his assent, Isana nodded and gripped his shoulder once more.

"Ulla," the Erstehäuptling spoke after a few moments of silence, catching everyone's attention.

"Ja, Vater?" responded the Fräulein whom Wolfrik had noticed earlier.

"Now that everything has been settled, why don't you show Käfe around the Oase? And I'm sure she would appreciate it if you introduced her to your Freunde."

Wolfrik felt his Schwester stiffen, and he brushed his Geist against hers.

"We are safe here, Schwester. Already, they are treating us like guests and equals."

Käfe relaxed. It was treatment they were unused to from their own Clan, but the old ways, which Wolfrik was beginning to think the Vereinte Clans still followed, held a spirit of open heart and open Geist. It was a mindset to which Wolfrik thought he could accustom himself.

"Ulla Kanten," the Fräulein introduced herself. She had stepped forward and was offering her hand to Käfe.

Hesitantly, Käfe took Ulla's hand and muttered her own name. When the Kanten Fräulein simply beamed in response, Wolfrik could feel his Schwester's Geist stir with excitement. The sudden realization that she might find Freunde here filled her Geist as she followed Ulla from the Zelt, offering her Bruder no more than a single backward glance.

~~*~*

As the Zelt was slowly vacated, the pink Liebe took a moment to revel in the alliances and Freundschaften she had just helped begin.

In all honesty, this was her favorite part of guiding mortals through their relationships. Of course, she loved to see relationships continue and thrive, but there was nothing more enjoyable than that first blush of a relationship, whether it was a full-blown romance or a simple alliance.

Once the Zelt was mostly empty and she felt she had enjoyed the bliss of the new relationships long enough, she turned her gaze to her red twin. Idly noting that she was still affecting some Nomaden—most likely young Käfe and those Fräulein to whom she was being introduced—Liebe let her gaze settle into a glare.

"You weren't even trying."

She ignored the fact that her words sounded more pouty than angry. Even with her twin's influence, Liebe did not do anger well.

"You just let me have that one."

Hass, who had stood at the edge of the Zelt for the entire exchange, smiled at Liebe. "That's not completely true." Though his words were the denial she expected, the mild tone made Liebe frown.

"Frieda nearly turned on the Giftschwanz Geistmagier, and you let the opportunity pass."

Hass shrugged. "I tried to affect Peace in Schönestadt."

Liebe realized, with a start, that her twin wasn't attempting to affect any of the Nomaden at all. Knowing that, she stopped actively influencing the surrounding Nomaden. It wasn't fair if her Bruder wasn't trying at all.

Hate chuckled as Love pulled in her influence. "I decided that actively affecting Peace takes too much effort." Love frowned before he added, "It's difficult enough influencing her alone, but she's tempered by her bondmates, and that pretty much makes it impossible."

Love hummed. She knew her brother was right. But Love had also noticed that it seemed to be easier for one bondmate to influence the others towards a positive emotion than towards a negative one. She wondered idly if it was because Peace herself influenced a positive state.

"You've noticed it, too, haven't you?" Love glanced at her twin, wondering what he could possibly mean. "The flip side of what we discussed at the temple in Machtstadt?"

Love raised an eyebrow. It was rare that Hate offered his own thoughts on this kind of subject without her pressing him for them. He huffed and rolled his eyes as he understood her thoughts.

"I just find it unsettling, that's all."

"What exactly do you find unsettling, Brother?"

As she spoke, Love moved closer to Hate. When he automatically opened his arms to her, she snuggled against his chest. There were no relationships that they needed to fight over now, and she figured they could use as much rest as they could get. After all, Death had been right before. The season wasn't even half over.

"We all may be more susceptible to each other's influence, but actively influencing each other is more draining than ever."

Love lifted her head to look at Hate. The red demigod was staring past her, his mouth set in a frown. She reached up and smoothed her fingers over his lips in an attempt to ease the tension. Hate quirked a brow, but she simply smiled softly as her mind considered his words.

Recently, she hadn't considered the drain that actively influencing another demigod produced. They had all played with influencing each other, of course—not to mention the other immortals—when they were younger. It was part of learning the limits of their own abilities. As they did, they had all quickly learned that attempting to influence another immortal was the fastest way into the arms of their twin and a significant stint of rest.

However, Love had learned rather early on that she had a bit of an advantage over her siblings. As she influenced the emotion love, an emotion that was considered just as sacred to immortals as it was to mortals, Love had found certain pairs of immortals somewhat receptive to her influence. These, however, had mainly been limited to their parents and, surprisingly, Life and Death.

When Peace and War had been born, she'd found that Peace was just as receptive to her influence as any mortal would be. She hadn't understood why at the time since War was as resistant to love as Hate was.

It hadn't been until their mother was thrown into the Cycle of Incarnation that she'd considered the Mortal Realm as the source of Peace's receptiveness.

Love suddenly blinked as thoughts of her youngest siblings filled her mind. Focusing once more on her red brother, she found he was watching her calmly.

"Well?" he asked as she shifted in his arms.

Love shook her head. "You may be right. Not even War tries to influence Peace," she whispered.

When Hate raised an eyebrow, she rolled her eyes. "Not since that year after her parents died. And I'm not even sure he was actually attempting anything then. Her parents had just died. It's human nature that she would want revenge for that."

Hate's brow wrinkled. "But Peace is not a mortal soul, Love."

"Maybe not," Love chuckled, "but I think the only difference between us and the mortals is the strength of our spirits and our specializations. Otherwise, Peace is human." Her tone turned dry. "And if you haven't noticed, she plays human rather well."

Hate snorted and lifted his gaze. Love turned her head to see what he was looking at, and she found it easily enough. Peace was the only person still in the tent besides the unconscious king and the Mage Healer. Her expression, easily visible to both demigods, was twisted in guilt and worry.

But that wasn't what caught Love's eye.

Peace had her hands wrapped tightly around her friend's, and, while her expression spoke of sorrow for the man's wounds, the glint in her eye told of a determination to protect what was most precious to her.

"Oh, aye," Hate said with a chuckle, "Peace plays human very well."

~~*~*

Unbekanntoase, Zhulan
Several hours' ride southeast of Schönestadt

Adalwolf's lips twitched. He had just relayed the information he had learned in Schönestadt to the Gift Clan Häuptlinge. The thunderous expression on Häuptling Giftschwanz's face was enough to fill the Schlange with satisfaction, but it was the sneer that his own Häuptling aimed at the Skorpion that threatened to bring a smirk to Adalwolf's lips.

"Can't you even control your own Kinder, Giftschwanz?" Adalwolf allowed the smirk to stretch his lips when he heard the disgust that colored his Häuptling's words. "You assured me there would be no Problème."

Giftschwanz glared at Adalwolf's Häuptling. "And there shouldn't have been any." The Skorpion, a large, thickset Mann, growled. "I made sure my own Magie was thick in their Geister before I sent them to Schönestadt."

Adalwolf felt his lip rise in a sneer, unintentionally mimicking his Häuptling, who then echoed his thoughts.

"Why send someone in need of such effort? I know Wolfrik is not the only Geistmagier among your Kinder."

Giftschwanz snorted then. "And risk my heirs? Nein! I would rather lose those two than risk my eldest being imprisoned by that verdammt Gouverneur, Othman."

"And that is the very reason that he lost two Kinder." Adalwolf didn't bother glancing towards the voice. Its violence was all too recognizable. *"If he had sent his eldest Sohn, the Mann would most likely have completed the task and been back several Tage ago."*

Adalwolf nodded absently, knowing the Geist was correct. He had even mentioned it when Giftschwanz had decided to send his youngest, but Adalwolf's Häuplting had reprimanded him for interfering with a Plan that did not belong to the Schlange Clan.

"You do realize our Clans will have to migrate sooner than expected because of this." Adalwolf's Häuptling snarled and slammed his fist down on the ground beside him. "This mistake could very well cost us, Giftschwanz!"

The Skorpion Häuptling growled again. "Don't worry. I'll make Wolfrik pay for his betrayal."

"Make sure you do," Adalwolf's Häuptling snapped. "Or I'll send Adalwolf to do the job you should have done from the beginning."

Adalwolf felt the smirk slide back into place, even as warmth filled his chest. It wasn't often that his Häuptling praised him, but it was off-handed comments like that that showed exactly how highly the Mann thought of him.

Even the Geist's amused *"It's a wonder your two Clans can do anything at all"* didn't faze Adalwolf.

~~*~*

Gemi was awakened from a light doze when the flap of Mandel's Zelt dropped shut. Glancing behind her, she realized that she must have slept longer than she had thought if Wolfrik had already returned from Jakob's questioning. She nodded to the Geistmagier before turning back to watch Ferez sleep.

The König hadn't stirred, and his face was smooth and relaxed. Before Mandel had left for his living Zelt—unlike Lakina, Mandel refused to sleep in the same Zelt as his patients unless it was an emergency—the Arztmagier had assured Gemi that all of the physical wounds had healed.

The only thing left to heal fully was his Geist, but Mandel believed it wouldn't take much longer.

Then again, Mandel's expertise on weakened Geister was rather limited.

"I truly am sorry."

The words startled Gemi from her observation of her Freund, and she glanced over her shoulder once more.

"For what? You have done nichts to me, and Frenz—"

She paused and glanced around, despite knowing the three of them were the Zelt's only occupants.

"Ferez has already forgiven you," she murmured. When Wolfrik nodded slowly, she added lightly, "Besides, Flame is right. I overreacted."

The Skorpion snorted then, and Gemi frowned at him. Though she had been the one to say it, it hurt that he would agree so quickly and casually.

"You agree," she muttered.

"Nein," Wolfrik denied, taking a couples steps closer. "I wouldn't call it overreacting." Gemi raised an eyebrow, and he shrugged.

"I've seen what you two have been through together. You may not have known each other for long, but you two are rather close. And you've nearly lost him several times already." He shook his head. "I think it is only natürlich that you would be so protective of him."

Although her cheeks heated, Gemi continued to stare at him for a moment, studying his face. Finally, she nodded and glanced away. "Danke," she whispered.

Gemi turned back to watch Ferez, listening to Wolfrik's footsteps as he approached. He was nearly to the bench where she was seated when she heard him gasp and stumble. Turning sharply, she caught his arm just as his hands hit the bench and he fell to his knees.

"Scheisse!" he cursed through gritted teeth. One hand lifted and settled over his eyes, and he groaned.

"Wolfrik? What is it?" Gemi was up and beside the Geistmagier before she could think about it. Laying a hand on his back, she asked, more quietly, "What happened?"

There was a moment of silence, only broken by the Skorpion's heavy breathing. Shaking his head, he finally hissed out, "Nichts. It's nichts."

Gemi snorted. "This is hardly nichts, Wolfrik."

Even as she said it, she watched the lines of pain in his face smooth out. He chuckled dryly then, lifting his gaze to her face. "You're right." He hauled himself to his feet, and Gemi helped him onto the bench. Settling with his head in his hands, he added, "But it's nichts I can't handle."

She sighed as she sat beside him. "Are you even going to tell me what just happened?"

Wolfrik shook his head but answered anyway. "It seems my Häuptling discovered my betrayal."

Gemi inhaled sharply. "Already?" Before he could answer, another question occurred to her. "But how was he able to affect you? He can't possibly be anywhere nearby."

Wolfrik didn't look up, and Gemi thought he must still be in pain. "I'm still connected to the Skorpion Clan's Geisternetz."

Gemi frowned. The Geisternetze were practical for communication over the long distances of the desert, but...

"Is that going to be a Problem?" she asked. "Can you protect yourself from him?" She paused to consider and added, "Can you break away from the Geisternetz?"

She wasn't sure if the last would be preferable or not. While it might be useful to have an ally who was connected to the Geisternetz of one of the Poison Clans, the connection might also be a liability if Wolfrik couldn't stop another Geist from invading his own.

Wolfrik shook his head again and finally sat up. Gemi was surprised and relieved to see that he once again looked comfortable.

"No need. I'm accustomed to protecting myself against the power of my Häuptling's Geist. I am simply used to having some kind of warning and was caught off-guard."

He rubbed gently as his temple, though Gemi didn't think it was in response to pain. "I've managed to fortify my barriers, but..." He offered Gemi a wry smile. "I've had to pull some of my Magie from the barriers around our Freund's Geist."

Gemi blinked then laughed. Shaking her head, she replied, "I doubt he'll mind. Mandel's already healed all of the physical damage, and he thinks his Geist should fully recover by Morgen."

Wolfrik nodded. "I believe he is correct. Our Freund has a surprisingly resilient Geist for a Mann who bears no Magie." Gemi frowned at the Geistmagier, who shrugged. "Most non-Magier would take far longer to recover from that kind of attack, even with the kind of help he's received. Even most non-Geistmagier would suffer longer."

Gemi's frown deepened as she turned to gaze at Ferez once more. "He doesn't deserve this."

She grimaced. Her voice sounded small to her own ears. She flinched as Wolfrik laid a hand on her shoulder, though he didn't comment on it. "Few victims of such attacks ever do."

Gemi glanced sadly at Wolfrik. She remembered his words and what Flame had told her about his and Käfe's experiences.

"Nein," she whispered, "I don't suppose they do."

They fell into silence then, both watching the sleeping König. Gemi knew she should find a bed soon as Morgen would be arriving quickly, but she was loathe to leave Ferez alone after the last couple of Tage.

She was startled from her thoughts as a hand landed on her knee. She glanced sharply at Wolfrik, but the Mann still had his eyes on the König. She frowned but waited for him to speak.

"I meant what I said before, you know," he finally whispered, the words confusing her. He finally glanced at her, and his lips twitched.

"He is a gut Mann, one I am very proud to call König." He kept his voice low, for which Gemi was dankbar, even if they were alone. "To be honest, I never expected a Mann in such a position of power to be so…homely and down-to-earth."

Gemi chuckled. "I know what you mean." She shook her head. "It was a complete surprise to me when he asked me to allow him to travel the Geisterpfad with me. And when he finally managed to get it through my head that he was serious about knowing his people…"

Gemi shrugged, a small smile of admiration tugging at her lips. "He's unexpected, but I think that's what makes him such a great König."

"The others will think so, too, I believe." Gemi looked at the Mann, wide-eyed. Wolfrik shook his head. "I don't mean that I will tell them, Drache Krieger."

Gemi rolled her eyes at the use of her title but didn't say anything. She had already realized that he would continue refusing to call her by her chosen name.

"I simply meant that when they do find out that he is König, despite the deceptions, they will be happy it is he who sits on the throne. He is a gut Mann, one worthy of his title."

Gemi felt a smile slowly stretch her lips as she realized what the Mann was saying. She knew Ferez was worried about what the people he met would think when they learned that this supposed farmer who had befriended them was actually the König of Evon.

She understood quite well. After all, she had befriended them under a false name as well, and, one Tag, she would have to step forward as Herzogin of Kensy.

But Wolfrik was assuring her that the pretenses didn't matter. The name may be false, but the Freundschaft and the feelings were not.

Gemi leaned forward and picked up Ferez's hand, squeezing it as she did so. She knew Wolfrik had only been speaking about Ferez, but she felt lighter as she considered his words. If they were true for Ferez, maybe, one Tag, they would be true for her, as well.

Chapter 39

The next three days seemed to blur together for Ferez.

Oh, his mind had been fully healed; that wasn't the reason. It was simply that James managed to pack so much activity into those three days that Ferez was reminded of the first few days they had spent at Main Highwayman Camp back in Kensy.

Now, instead of introducing Ferez to every person they met, James was introducing him to life as a nomad. That included long training sessions in which the boy taught him every technique he needed to know to protect himself from the Scharfmonde of their warriors.

The comparison made Ferez chuckle lightly as James offered him a flask of water. They had just finished another training session, and the boy paused in using his Kopfabdeckung to dry his face.

"What's so funny?" James asked, a smile tilting his lips upward.

Ferez told him his thoughts, thinking he would be just as amused. He was surprised when he recognized guilt in the boy's violet eyes.

"I really am bad about that, aren't I?"

Ferez chuckled and squeezed James' shoulder. "Don' try to take all the blame. I'm the one who asked for it, 'member?"

The boy's smile returned, and Ferez felt his stomach flutter as those purple eyes brightened once more.

"James!" a female voice called.

Ferez frowned and turned towards the voice. Käfe Giftschwanz sauntered towards them, a flask, similar to the one James still held out to Ferez, in one hand. The king narrowed his eyes when he saw her pause briefly as her eyes seemed to land on James' hand. However, the bright smile on her face didn't falter, and she continued closer.

"More water?" she asked cheerfully.

She barely glanced at Ferez, her attention solely on James. The king felt the unaccountable urge to growl, and he pursed his lips to keep from making a fool of himself.

Upon waking in Helloase that first day back, Ferez had discovered an instant dislike for the Skorpion girl. He thought it was odd since he'd found himself in friendly discussions with her brother several times since then.

He had the uncomfortable feeling that the difference had something to do with the fact that Wolfrik still addressed James by his title, while Käfe had no compunction about freely using the boy's given name.

"Er, well…extra water's always a gut thing," James said hesitantly.

Ferez turned just in time to see James glance away from him.

Frowning, the king turned back to Käfe, and, wanting to save James from

413

any further awkwardness—*and, really, that's the only reason*—he took the proffered flask.

"Thank you."

He tried to keep his voice gracious, but the growl that had threatened earlier tinged the edges. The girl turned and gaped at him for a brief moment before snapping her jaw shut and pursing her lips. Ferez thought he would have smirked if that growl didn't still feel like it lingered in his throat.

"Ja, well…"

She hesitated. Then, suddenly, her confidence seemed to return, and she turned back to James, smiling brightly once more. Ferez knew his frown deepened, and he took a drink from the flask in the hopes of keeping his displeasure from becoming thoroughly obvious.

"You're such a wunderbar teacher, James!" Käfe enthused, clasping her hands behind her back. Ferez would have snorted if her words hadn't been so true.

She paused then and lowered her chin, allowing the edge of her Kopfabdeckung to sweep over her eyes. "Maybe you could teach me?" She had lowered her voice, but her tone was still bright. "I've never been very good at fighting. I received most of my training from my Vat—"

Her smile disappeared instantly, and, from what Ferez could see of her face, her skin paled dramatically. Despite the dislike that had burned in his chest a moment before, the king reached out, worried that she was about to faint.

Instead, she glanced around, her eyes wide and her face stricken. Ferez thought he knew what she was searching for even before Wolfrik appeared behind the group of young women who had, Ferez belatedly realized, accompanied Käfe.

The moment Wolfrik appeared, Käfe's expression eased some, but it wasn't until he'd wrapped an arm around her and pulled her close that she relaxed against him and the color began to return to her cheeks.

"Dummkopf," the older Skorpion muttered. His tone was affectionate, and a sad smile tugged at his lips.

Ferez suddenly felt uncomfortable. The siblings were obviously close, a result, no doubt, of their troubled upbringing. Käfe, however, suddenly seemed dependent on her brother in a way that made the confidence she'd shown since Ferez had awakened ring false.

Glancing towards James, he noticed that the boy was shifting his weight from foot to foot, a sure sign that he was just as uncomfortable.

"Shouldn' we go help the others pull down tents?" Ferez asked James.

The Clan would be leaving Helloase once the sun set, and preparations for the 'Wanderung', as they called the journey, had already begun. Ferez knew James had offered this last training session as an excuse to keep Ferez from being roped into helping with the preparations, but the king thought the preparations now provided an excellent reason to leave the siblings alone while Käfe recovered from her slip.

James seemed to agree as he nodded and, to Ferez's surprise, gripped his hand and fled.

~~*~*

Wolfrik was grateful to the König and Drache Krieger for giving them space, but, at the same time, amusement filled him as he watched the Drache Krieger's hasty retreat.

The emotion disappeared quickly when Käfe stirred against his chest. Tightening his grip on her, Wolfrik brushed his Geist against that of Ulla Kanten, who stood nearby. She responded immediately with agreement and ushered the other Fräulein away.

Cupping Käfe's cheek, Wolfrik tilted her chin up. At first, she resisted, her hands tightening in his tunic.

"Käfe," he murmured, and she relented, lifting her gaze to his with a sigh. Her face was serious, and her eyes sad, but there was no trace of the Panik he had felt in her Geist before.

"Better?" he whispered.

She closed her eyes and nodded. "Es tut mir leid," she muttered.

Wolfrik sighed and shook his head.

"Don't apologize, Schwester." He tapped her cheek with his thumb, and she opened her eyes again. "It's *his* fault, no one else's."

"Do we—do we truly not have to go back?"

The timid question startled Wolfrik, and he brushed his Geist against hers once more. He cursed himself mentally when he realized that the confidence she had shown since they arrived in Helloase had been a brittle mask, one that he was surprised had lasted the three Tage it had.

He lifted his hand from her back and laid it against her other cheek, holding her so she couldn't look away from his gaze. He didn't want her to have any reason to doubt his words.

"Never!" he breathed fiercely. "I swore when we were younger that I would protect you from him, Käfe. Now that we're away, we are never going back."

Her eyes widened, and Wolfrik nearly growled at the anxiety he could see building in them.

"But…"

She hesitated. Wolfrik listened as her breathing increased speed, but he knew there was nothing he could do about it. She had to get this out on her own. He knew he could easily pull the thought from her Geist, but, if Käfe was to find a place for herself away from their Häuptling's influence, Wolfrik had to let her do some things herself.

"What if the Vereinte Clans decide we're too much trouble?" she finally managed, her voice nearly too soft for him to hear.

"Then we'll become river-dwellers," he answered, just as fiercely as before.

He meant it, too. He didn't think the Vereinte Clans would turn them away now that they had accepted them, but, even if they did, Wolfrik would never go back to their Häuptling. He might still consider himself a

Skorpion, but, if necessary, he would give up his Leben as a Nomade if it meant protecting his little Schwester.

For a moment, Käfe simply stared at him with a brittle expression he recognized all too well. After everything they had been through, Wolfrik was really the only person his Schwester trusted, but there were still times when she seemed hesitant to believe him. She may never have felt the amount of mental pain he had, but, as the only Tochter of their Häuptling, she had been subjected to pain and humiliation of a different kind.

Finally, the tension around her eyes eased, and she offered him a tiny smile. He let his own grow in response. This was the girl he knew and loved. Although the confidence she had shown recently had made him hope that the new environment and Freunde were helping her come out of her shell, he knew the bold attitude was just not her.

He chuckled as he considered about what exactly she had been so bold.

When she frowned curiously at him, he said, "You do realize you don't have a chance with the Drache Krieger, ja?"

Käfe sighed and offered him a small smile. "I know. The other Fräulein said he'd never shown interest in anyone before." She shrugged and glanced in the direction the boy had run. "I thought that maybe…"

She trailed off, her eyes becoming distant. Wolfrik cupped her chin again, bringing her gaze back to his.

"That's not exactly what I meant." He chuckled when she frowned in response. "I believe someone's already caught his eye."

Her frown deepened. "Who? Ulla's his Schwester. Surely she would have known and said something to me." She squirmed slightly. "Then I wouldn't have made such a dummkopf of myself."

Her final words were soft and embarrassed, but Wolfrik simply kissed her forehead.

"I doubt their interest in each other is obvious to most people. I only figured it out myself because I've touched one of their Geister."

Käfe furrowed her brow, and Wolfrik chuckled again. "Do you remember Hamlin?"

Wolfrik's apparent tangent confused Käfe even more. "Ja, of course I do. But what does he have to do with…?"

Wolfrik smiled as understanding suddenly lit her face and she blinked rapidly.

Hamlin was a Skorpion whom many in the Clan had looked down on for his feminine features and ways. For Jahre, he appeared romantically apathetic, deftly ignoring the Fräulein who attempted to flirt with him.

That changed when a warrior from the Schlange Clan began to court him. The two were lifebonded a Jahr later.

Käfe finally settled her eyes on him and whispered, "You think James and…" She glanced back towards the Oase. "That might explain why he doesn't seem to like me much."

Wolfrik was suddenly glad he had decided not to tell his Schwester the true identity of the Drache Krieger's companion. The thought might have terrified her.

Käfe sighed and pouted slightly. "And here I was hoping I could attract the Sohn of the Erstehäuptling."

Wolfrik stared at her, surprised, until he noticed the amusement in her eyes. He rolled his own.

"You do realize he's not the Erstehäuptling's only Sohn, ja?" he drawled softly.

Suddenly, all amusement left Käfe's eyes as she once again lowered them, her cheeks pinking. Wolfrik blinked at the sudden change. He sighed, then, as he considered the possible reason.

"Käfe," he murmured again, hooking a finger under her chin. She didn't resist this time, but her gaze was hesitant as it met his. "Talk to me."

She took a deep breath. Letting it out, she glanced away from him. "Do you think Zuk would even be interested in someone like me?"

Ah.

"Is that who you're truly interested in, Schwester?"

Käfe pulled her lower lip between her teeth. Wolfrik nodded.

He understood that, when Käfe first showed interest in the Drache Krieger, she had been more attracted to the idea of the boy than to the boy himself. After all, while they were considered weak, they were still the Kinder of a Häuptling. They had been trained from an early age to seek partners worthy of their Status.

However, her current reaction, as well as her refusal to turn her confident attentions onto the Erstehäuptling's heir, told Wolfrik that her interest in the eldest Kanten sibling had more to do with the actual Mann than what he was.

Once again making sure she was looking at him, Wolfrik whispered, "Would you like for me to speak to him for you?"

Ja, there were some things Käfe had to do for herself, but Wolfrik knew his Schwester well enough to know that this was not one of them. When she nodded hesitantly, a faint smile touching her lips, he pulled her into a hug.

"If it will make you happy, I would be glad to."

They stayed there for a while longer, her face buried against his chest, his lips pressed against her Kopfabdeckung.

~~*~*

Gemi knew she probably shouldn't have run. She had heard the giggles issuing from the Fräulein as she pulled Ferez away, but Käfe had been making her uncomfortable for Tage. Ulla knew how Gemi felt about other Fräulein flirting with her, but her Schwester had simply watched and smirked.

So she'd been all too eager to take the excuse Ferez had offered. However, when she ran, she didn't aim for any place in particular. When

Ferez finally pulled her to a stop, she was surprised to see that they were near the spring. Flame lay nearby and lifted her head, cooing curiously.

"Are you all right?" Ferez asked.

Gemi was glad to hear only a touch of amusement in his voice. Offering him a small smile, she lifted a hand to tug at her Kopfabdeckung and nodded.

"Ja," she muttered, glancing to the side.

She could feel her cheeks heating as she debated whether she should play off her hasty retreat as a discomfort around hysterical women or simply leave it at that. Either way seemed too dishonest, and she'd found herself wanting to share more and more with the König since that conversation at the Handelmann Haus.

Hesitantly, she added, "I've never been comfortable with Fräulein's flirting."

A hand squeezing her shoulder drew her eyes back up to Ferez's face. He offered her a bright grin, while his eyes shone warmly.

"Not'in' wrong wit' that," he replied softly.

He fell silent, and Gemi stared into his eyes. Those mingling patches of blue and silver seemed to draw her in, and she found herself wanting to get lost in them.

"Oy, James!"

The voice made them both jump, and Gemi took a step back as she realized she'd only been a few inches away from Ferez. Swallowing down a sudden disappointment, she turned towards the voice.

Zuk was waving at them from a nearby Zelt that was in the process of being dismantled. "If the two of you have time to stand around, why don't you help with the preparations?"

A sharp, angry whistle had Gemi turning to gape at Flame, though Zuk only responded to the insult with a short bark of laughter and his own whistle, which Gemi couldn't understand. Whatever it was, it didn't calm Flame, who rose to all fours and began to burble angrily.

As Drache and Tieremagier continued to trade insults, Gemi felt the hand on her shoulder squeeze, and she turned back to Ferez. His grin, she noticed, had softened.

"Why don' we lend a hand, James? I'm sure they could use as much 'elp as they can get, aye?" He leaned forward and smiled conspiratorially. "'Sides, I still wanna learn as much abou' my people's lives as I can."

Gemi nodded, though mentally she snorted. She didn't think he understood exactly what he was asking to do.

But then, who am I to deny the König?

~~*~*

Ferez groaned as he settled himself into Last Chance's saddle. The pale mare twisted her neck to look back at him, the look in her dark eye one of concern. Patting her withers lightly, he offered her a small smile. He'd be all right. He was just incredibly sore.

He didn't know how the nomads managed to do this so often, but this was their way of life, according to James. They seemed to be constantly migrating. They may not move as often as James, since James said they only migrated between three different oases over one season.

But all of James' belongings fit on his person or within Shadow's saddlebags. *To pack up your entire home that often...?*

Ferez shook his head. He couldn't imagine it.

"Are you all right?"

Ferez turned to find James and Shadow sidling up next to them. To his amusement, Shadow shifted his weight so his shoulder brushed Last Chance's. Last Chance twisted her neck, in turn, and lipped his neck affectionately.

"Is it just me," Ferez asked with a nod towards the horses, "or are Last Chance an' Shadow growin' closer?"

Shadow shifted his weight away from Last Chance then and turned to eye Ferez with a snort. James laughed.

"I'd say Shadow's offended by the suggestion, but, in all honestly, that would be a lie."

Shadow twisted his neck more to give his bondmate the horse's equivalent of a glare. He relaxed with a soft nicker, though, when Last Chance lipped him once more.

Ferez chuckled. "So I'm not imaginin' it."

James shook his head with his own chuckle. Then, as he sobered, the boy reached up and squeezed Ferez's shoulder.

"How do you feel?"

The question was serious, but the tone wasn't as worried as Ferez remembered from several nights ago. The king smiled and shrugged, though he immediately winced as his left shoulder twinged.

"Jus' a little sore," he answered distractedly as he rubbed his hand over the back of his left shoulder. He had backed into the end of a tent pole at one point, and his shoulder apparently hadn't forgiven him yet. "I guess I asked for it, though," he added wryly.

Another chuckle brought his gaze back to James. He was pleasantly surprised to find a distinct lack of the guilt that had appeared earlier that day. Instead, the boy's purple eyes danced in amusement.

"You were rather insistent."

Ferez couldn't stop the grin that spread his lips then, and he chuckled in turn. Their conversation continued, only pausing briefly when Hausef gave the signal for the clan to begin the nightlong 'Wanderung' to Friedlichoase.

~~*~*

Ferez slowly opened his eyes.

For the second time, he found himself waking to the view of softly glowing, pale fabric with no memory of how he had gotten here. He could remember the journey from the night before. They'd left Helloase just before sunset. The journey had lasted so long he had apparently been

419

out of it when they finally arrived. He vaguely recalled seeing pink in the sky, being coaxed to drink something refreshing, and then being maneuvered a couple of times.

What really puzzled Ferez was the fact that he was obviously once again in a tent. How the nomads had managed to put up a tent after a full night of travel and a few hours spent dismantling the entire camp was beyond him. The very fact that he could barely remember their arrival told Ferez that he himself had certainly not been up to the task.

A sudden rustling sound caught Ferez's attention. He might have thought it was the sound of cloth moving against cloth except the sound, though soft, was too solid.

Turning his head away from the wall of fabric, he looked over the tent's interior. Unsurprisingly, the room was laid out exactly as it had been in Helloase.

It took a moment of squinting through the low lamplight before Ferez pinpointed the source of the rustling sound. As his eyes landed on the sleeping area of James' two youngest siblings, a quiet chittering joined the rustling.

He chuckled when he realized the two young mages were speaking to each other, though he doubted they actually understood what the other was saying. It seemed more likely that the two wished to let the other know that they were awake without waking anyone else.

That thought drew Ferez's attention back to the other beds, and he was shocked to find that, other than the two children, he was the first to wake. It was unprecedented. Ferez had never been one for waking early, and the schedule he and James had been pulling had found him sleeping in whenever possible.

Shaking his head in wonder, Ferez shifted his blankets to the side and carefully climbed to his feet. He tried to be quiet, but he must have made enough noise to catch the attention of the children for the tent suddenly went silent save for the even breaths and soft snores of the still sleeping nomads.

Offering a quiet chuckle to the sudden silence, Ferez stretched his arms above his head, relieved to note that his shoulder, as well as the rest of his body, seemed to have mostly recovered overnight. The rustle of cloth caught his attention as he dropped his arms, and he turned back towards Hausef's youngest.

The two had already climbed from their bedding. Ava was helping Lorenz situate his Kopfabdeckung, hers already settled atop her head. When Ava finished, she turned to Ferez with a smile and motioned him towards the tent's entrance. Grabbing his own Kopfabdeckung, he followed the children outside.

He had ducked through the entrance, his Kopfabdeckung half-settled on his head and the fabric of the entrance catching on his shoulder, when he stopped and gaped. A giggle reached his ears, and a tug on his Statusgürtel propelled him forward enough to get him out of the entrance.

"Wha'…?"

He was surrounded by tents; the very ones he'd seen around the Häuptling's tent at the other oasis. He couldn't understand how the nomads had managed to raise every tent they had before they went to sleep. It seemed impossible that they could have managed it with how exhausted they must have been.

Another giggle caught his attention, and he dropped his eyes down to Ava, who still stood next to him, grinning. In the next second, he found something else at which to gape.

The ground was green.

Grass had been sparse at Helloase, and what had been available was tough and reserved for certain food animals. While he wasn't an Animal Mage, he knew Last Chance had despaired that she had to depend on the shrub plants and the rationed grains the nomads carried for their horses.

Here, the ground was covered in greenery that spread farther than Ferez would have ever expected in a desert. There were trees, too, and not the sparse, small ones that stood about the height of a man. These trees towered in comparison to the ones at Helloase, though they couldn't compare in size to those of the northern forest.

The tugging at his Statusgürtel brought his attention back to Ava once more.

"How…?"

She twittered.

"It's part of the Wanderung for the adults to raise the Zelte once we reach a new Oasen." Her grin widened, and she pointed towards his head. "You might want to fix your Kopfabdeckung. Bruder won't be happy if you get Senf seeds in your hair."

At the mention of the desert seeds that seemed to prefer living hosts, Ferez reached up and straightened his Kopfabdeckung, which had been hanging half off his head. Once he'd settled the corded circlet around his head, securing the cloth in place, Ava took his hand and led him through the camp.

"The adults do all the work with pulling down the Zelte and putting them back up, so it's ein bisschen of a Tradition that the adults sleep late after the Wanderung. We Kinder always entertain ourselves while they sleep."

As they moved through the camp, Ferez saw more children wandering out of the surrounding tents. He noticed one adult attempting to stifle a yawn as she pushed past her tent's entrance, but the lump in the middle of her tunic told Ferez that she was a young mother who'd been awakened by her hungry infant.

"So wha' do the children do while the adults are still sleepin'?"

And is it safe?

He tried to ignore the images of giant desert cats that filled his head then. Still, he couldn't imagine allowing the clan's children such unobstructed freedom, no matter how involuntary it might be.

Ava flashed him a smile over her shoulder. "We Nomaden learn from any early age the dangers of the desert. We generally stay gathered together near the springs and play while we wait for the adults to finally wake."

Glancing around, Ferez then noticed that the other children were all making their way towards the same direction Ava was pulling him. It was also then that he noticed they were leaving behind the familiar tents.

"Where are we—"

"Ava!"

The voice that interrupted him was young and female. The owner was easy to spot as the girl was waving at them with one hand, the other gripped in the hands of a smaller child. The smaller child turned out to be Lorenz, who had left them behind when Ferez had been staring around the camp in wonder.

The girl, Ferez realized once they were closer, seemed familiar as well. "You're the young Mage Healer who helped Heal my shoulder."

The girl nodded, offering him a smile. Ava tugged her hand out of his and said, "Frenz, this is Lakritze Flügelschutz, Tochter of the Falke Clan Häuptling. Lakritze, this is Frenz Kanti, Freund of the Drache Krieger."

Lakritze gave a small bow, her smile widening. "Angenehm, Herr Kanti! Though I'm afraid I wasn't actually much help for your shoulder. I'm still in training."

Ferez offered a smile of his own. "Well, you migh' still be learnin' to control your magic, but you seem to have already perfected your bedside manner."

The girl's smile turned shy, and she ducked her head as pink tinged her cheeks. "Danke," she whispered.

"Well, this is a surprise."

The man who spoke walked up behind Lakritze and laid a hand on her shoulder. A glance at his Statusgürtel told Ferez that this man was quite possibly the Häuptling of the Falke Clan, or, at the very least, a family member.

"I wasn't expecting any Katzen adults to be awake for several hours yet."

"Vati," Lakritze replied, "this is Herr Kanti. He's the Mann whose shoulder was injured while rescuing us from the Handelmann Haus."

"Ach," the Häuptling said, lifting his gaze back to Ferez, who could feel his cheeks heating at the girl's words. "You are the Drache Krieger's companion then."

"Aye, sir," Ferez affirmed, bowing his head to the man. "An' you are the Häuptling o' the Falke Clan?"

The man grinned and offered his hand. "Meinhard Flügelschutz, Häuptling of the Falke Clan, ja." Ferez shook the offered hand. "Komme!" he continued as he dropped Ferez's hand. "I'll introduce you to the Spinne Häuptling."

Ferez hesitated. "I don' wish to be a bother."

Meinhard shook his head. "Nein, of course you're not. Ever since we learned that the Drache Krieger had taken on a human companion, we've wanted to get to know the Mann who could convince James to let someone travel with him." The Häuptling's grin softened. "The Götter know the boy needs as many Freunde as he can get."

Ferez agreed readily. The boy was certainly well-known and well-liked, but Ferez had learned that there were few he actually let close. Assenting to the man's proposal, Ferez followed him further into the oasis.

~~*~*

Gemi woke with a sigh, though she kept her eyes shut at first. The Wanderung was the only time she let herself sleep as long as she could, and, when she did finally wake, she always lingered in the dark and comfort of her bedding for several Minuten.

As the soft rustle of cloth began to fill the Zelt, Gemi finally opened her eyes. Smiling at the familiar fabric of her Familie's Zelt, she rolled over and pulled herself from her nigh irresistible bedding.

She stretched her body, happy to find a distinct lack of kinks. Her next task was to straighten her Statusgürtel and situate her Kopfabdeckung upon her head. It wasn't until her clothing was settled that she finally allowed herself to glance around the Zelt at her stirring Familie.

Ulla, who had joined the Tradition of the Wanderung at the same time Gemi had, was still sound asleep. Even Zuk, who had been a part of the Tradition for Jahre longer, was still abed, though Gemi knew he was awake as she spotted him shifting restlessly beneath his blanket. The others—Mutter, Vater, Tante Isa, and even the Giftschwanz siblings—were already out of bed, all in various stages of preparing for the Tag.

With a sense of her Familie in her Geist, Gemi glanced at Ava and Lorenz's beds. Empty, as expected. They always were when she woke from the first sleep after the Wanderung.

Nodding at the familiarity, she finally turned to Ferez's bed. She had learned over the past few Siebentage that the Mann had a tendency to sleep in whenever he could, and she figured she'd have to wake him, much like someone might have to for Ulla.

She was shocked, then, when she found Ferez's bed empty. Panik filled her throat, and she must have cried out because suddenly hands were on her arms and voices spoke to her, though she couldn't understand them. Her Geist was solely focused on Ferez's bed and the utter lack of his slumbering presence.

"*James!*" Flame's shout filled Gemi's Geist, and, still panicking, she turned her attention to the Drache.

"*Flame! Where's Ferez? Where—*"

The sudden feeling of something firm colliding with her cheek had her Panik screeching to a Halt. Gemi blinked a few times and focused on Wolfrik, who stood in front of her, one hand gripping her upper arm, the other flexing.

"Get hold of yourself, Drache Krieger!" he hissed. *"Frenz* is safe and well."

Gemi inhaled sharply as she realized what she had just done. In her Panik, she could quite easily have given away the König's true identity. As easily as Flame managed to protect their Geister from Geistmagier, the words they traded could not always be so easily protected.

Taking a deep breath in an attempt to calm the Panik that clawed at her throat, Gemi nodded to Wolfrik. Refocusing on Flame, she asked more calmly, *"Where is Frenz, Flame?"*

Flame considered her for a moment before answering, *"He is with the children."*

Nodding once more, Gemi excused herself from the Zelt, ignoring the looks her Familie was sending her. She knew they were worried about her Panik. After all, she had never been one for hysterics.

But, even after three Tage, she found she couldn't stand to let Ferez from her sight. And, no matter how much she wished to deny it, she knew that didn't come from Angst of losing the König of Evon. It was much deeper than that, much more personal.

Though she managed to keep from running further into the Oase to find Ferez, Panik still twisted her gut. When she reached the closest spring, she found the Katze Kinder playing as they usually did after the Wanderung, but there was no sign of Ferez among them. She knew Flame wouldn't lie to her, but the Panik was beginning to claw through her chest once more.

"Bruder!"

Turning wide eyes towards the voice, Gemi found Ava running towards her, a grin decorating her lips. It was the sight behind her, however, that froze the Panik in her throat.

Ferez was seated around a fire pit with several others. He offered her a small smile and a wave, but his attention was quickly drawn back to the people around him as someone addressed him.

Gemi felt herself relax as relief flooded through her. Ferez was safe. She had nothing to fear.

"Really, your trust in us is gratifying."

Shadow's words were heavy with sarcasm, and Gemi noticed for the first time that he and Last Chance were standing nearby. Last Chance tilted her head and swung it back and forth, looking between Shadow and Gemi.

When Shadow answered the mare's question a moment later, Gemi felt her cheeks heat. Suddenly, she wished the two Pferde hadn't become so close. She really didn't need any others knowing of her unreasonable Panik.

"Hardly unreasonable after everything," Flame murmured, caressing Gemi's Geist with her own.

Gemi acknowledged the words but didn't reply otherwise. Unreasonable or not, her reaction had been entirely unnecessary.

"Bruder?"

Gemi blinked and looked down. Ava was staring up at her, a small frown replacing the grin that had been on her face before.

"Are you all right?"

Gemi nodded, and a small smile tugged at her lips. "I'm well, Ava." The young Tieremagier continued to eye her for a moment before finally nodding. Gripping her hand, Ava pulled Gemi towards the fire pit.

"I see the Katzen have finally decided to rise," a Mann said as she seated herself next to Ferez. She traded a smile with the König before looking at the speaker. She was surprised to find Häuptling Meinhard Flügelschutz of the Falke Clan seated across from her.

"Ja," she answered the Häuptling, but her eyes scanned the circle of Nomaden.

It didn't take long for her to recognize everyone. Seated next to Meinhard was his Lebenfrau and his Mutter, Valborga. His Tochter, Lakritze, had been nearby as well, but she had already left with Ava and Lorenz to play with the other Kinder. On another log sat Häuptling Genevieve Seidenstrang of the Spinne Clan, her Lebenmann and her eldest Sohn seated beside her.

Once she knew who was here, she shot Ferez a smirk. "You certainly know how to make Freunde, don't you?"

Ferez raised his hands, his smile betraying the Witz of it. "They found me."

"He is right," Genevieve added, her voice melodic. Gemi glanced at the Arztmagier. "We've wanted to meet him since we learned you had taken on a human companion, James." She offered Ferez an apologetic smile. "Es tut mir leid if you have felt harassed, Herr Kanti."

"O' course not," Ferez answered with a wide smile. "Though I do wish you'd call me Frenz. Herr Kanti seems too formal."

The Spinne Häuptling's response was a ringing laugh.

Gemi glanced around the group once more and frowned as she realized why the group seemed odd.

"Where is Wüstenwolf?"

Wüstenwolf Seelenesser was Häuptling of the Wolf Clan, which was usually the first Clan to arrive at the seasonal gathering Oase. Their previous Oase was to the east of the San, farther away than any others. The Pferd Clan, whose previous Oase was also east of the San, was usually the last to arrive, so Gemi didn't actually expect them until the following Morgen.

Both Häuptlinge shook their heads. "The Wölfe have yet to arrive," Meinhard answered.

Worry filled Gemi once more, though it was nowhere near the Panik she had experienced when she had thought Ferez was missing. "Have you heard from them?"

When both Meinhard and Genevieve nodded, her worry eased. Flame made an offhand comment about how her constant state of worry could not be healthy, but Gemi pushed the thought aside and focused on the conversation with the Nomaden.

"With all of the trouble with the Städte," Genevieve elaborated, "Wüstenwolf apparently decided to stay at Schattigoase until their missing Clan members returned. I believe the last Vogel said that they'd joined the Pferd Clan at the River San." The Arztmagier glanced at Meinhard, who nodded in confirmation.

"They should arrive in the Morgen with the Pferd, then?" Gemi confirmed.

The others nodded in agreement. The group fell into silence then. For her part, Gemi was considering the Katastrophe that seemed to finally be coming to an end.

"I do have one question that I wasn't sure Frenz would be up to answering," Meinhard finally said, breaking the silence. When Gemi indicated that she was listening, he asked, "Is it true that there are those among the Skorpion Clan who are willing to join the Vereinte Clans?"

Gemi felt a grin stretch her lips then, and Ferez gave a barking laugh. When she glanced at the König, he offered a grin that she knew reflected her own, and she turned her gaze back to the other Nomaden.

"Better than that," she answered. "A Sohn and a Tochter of the Häuptling have offered their allegiances to mein Vater, and they wish to save those in their Clan who would willingly follow the Erstehäuptling."

"And you trust this?" Genevieve asked, both hopefully and warily.

Gemi knew it had saddened all five Häuptlinge of the Vereinte Clans when both the Skorpion and the Schlange Clans had not only rejected Hausef as Erstehäuptling but had actively worked against the five Clans. That a step was being taken towards total unification was exactly what the Clans had been wanting for Jahre, but nothing had moved forward for so long that this step could only be taken with caution.

Gemi nodded. "Flame and I have spoken with the Skorpione enough to know that they are sincere in their desire to join the Vereinte Clans. And…"

She trailed off and glanced at Ferez. The König seemed to understand because, when he caught her eye, his grin softened and he lifted a hand to squeeze her shoulder. Taking a deep breath, she turned back to the Häuptlinge, who were watching them with raised brows.

Ignoring the heat that filled her cheeks, Gemi added, "Wolfrik saved Frenz, both in body and in Geist. He has my Dankpflicht, if nothing else."

All six Nomaden inhaled sharply and glanced at each other. Gemi nodded. They understood the significance of her words.

Dankpflicht was more than just gratitude. It was a formal obligation born of that gratitude. Gemi had learned the importance of this Nomade Tradition early on when she earned Hausef's Dankpflicht by saving Zuk's Leben. His offer to adopt Gemi as one of his own and officially accept her as a Nomade had been his way of repaying the Dankpflicht.

Both Häuptlinge bowed their heads then. Genevieve was the one to speak the words of acceptance that Gemi hadn't expected to hear until much later.

"We would gladly accept into the Vereinte Clans him who has the Drache Krieger's Dankpflicht."

Gemi bowed her head in return. In most situations, she would be annoyed by the use of her Nomade title, but these words were formal, so the formal title was most accurate.

"Danke, Häuptling Seidenstrang, Häuptling Flügelschutz. Your acceptance is appreciated."

With the formalities completed, Gemi lifted her head and met the smiles both Meinhard and Genevieve offered with her own. However, a motion to her left quickly caught her attention, and she turned to find Ferez shaking his head.

"I still have a lo' to learn, don' I?"

Gemi laughed. Ignoring the curious looks from the others, she patted the König's knee.

"Frenz, two Siebentage is nowhere near long enough to learn everything you would want to know about the Nomaden."

Ferez chuckled, and, to Gemi's bemusement, the conversation quickly turned to educating him about Nomade Tradition.

Chapter 40

14 Mid Autumn, 224
Friedlichoase, Zhulan

Flame viewed the fire-lit area with growing exasperation. It always amazed her how long it took the nomads to begin these inter-clan meetings. It did not help, either, that two clans worth of nomads had just arrived this morning and had awoken just hours beforehand.

They really should put these meetings off an extra day, even if tomorrow they will be preparing for the Festival.

A chuckle echoed through her mind. She swung her head towards Gemi, who was currently conversing with Alys Reiter about Peppi Kluger's new position as governor of Machtstadt. When she realized that her bondmate was not even paying her any attention and had simply been amused by Flame's annoyance, the dragon felt her irritation grow.

A steadily growing rumble began to drown out the surrounding conversations. As the nomads began to quiet and look around, Flame realized the sound was coming from her. She tried to quell the growl, but she was unsuccessful, not even once all the nomads had stopped talking.

Hausef stepped up to her and laid a hand on her nose, trilling comfortingly. Gemi brushed against her mind, murmuring contritely. Flame huffed as the growling finally stopped.

"Just start the meeting already, will you?" she hissed, swinging her head out from under the Animal Mage's hand. She curled up along the edge of the surrounding crowd, the warmth of the fire lightly dancing along her scales.

~~*~*

Hausef sighed, curious as to how they had managed to irritate the Drache so thoroughly. Turning back to the gathering of Nomaden, he made sure he had everyone's attention.

"It seems we've taken ein bisschen too long in starting the meeting." He motioned towards the benches surrounding the fire. "Shall we?" There were murmurs from the others, but the benches were quickly occupied by the appropriate people.

This meeting was Tradition, one that Hausef had eagerly renewed once the Clans were vereinte once more. While held outside where anyone who wished to could attend and learn of the current events with which each Clan was dealing, the meeting was essentially a seasonal discussion between the Erstehäuptling, the Häuptlinge, and the Drache Krieger.

While the other four Häuptlinge had taken their usual places, Hausef saw Gemi hesitate near the Katze bench. When she glanced at him, he smiled and nodded, understanding her uncertainty.

There were only five benches, one for each Häuptling and any of his, or her, Familie who wished to take part in the discussion. While the two of them were often joined by Isa and Mina, the bench was not nearly long enough for all four of them plus the two Skorpione.

And Frenz, he realized with a start when his Tochter continued to hesitate, casting her eyes towards the farmer. He frowned. *She wishes him to be involved in the discussion?*

Hausef knew they were close—very close if the looks they'd been exchanging for the past few Tage were any indication. That she would want to involve him in the Politik of the Nomaden though…

That spoke of a position of importance that Hausef had not yet considered.

But why does a farmer register such importance to Gemi?

They had hesitated long enough for everyone else to notice, and the standing Nomaden began to mutter curiously.

"Erstehäuptling?"

Genevieve of the Spinne Clan was the Häuptling who finally spoke up, breaking him from his thoughts. He nodded in acknowledgement of her question and turned back to his Tochter.

"James," he said, motioning to their bench. He simply raised an eyebrow when she opened her mouth, and she snapped it shut, her cheeks darkening. He had called her by name, not by title, and he knew she had recognized it for the order it was.

Apparently, she'd also fully understood his message as she beckoned Frenz and the Giftschwanz Kinder to sit beside her, her companion to her left and the Geistmagier to her right. She glanced at Hausef for confirmation, which he gave with a small nod.

To his surprise, the rest of his Familie settled into guarded stances behind the four, even young Ava and Lorenz looking serious.

Hausef checked a sigh as he realized how the other Häuptlinge might take this. It had been Jahre since his Familie had felt the need to stand together like this when facing the other Clans.

The rest of the Nomaden seemed to recognize this as well.

"What is going on, Hausef?"

He did sigh then. He wasn't surprised that Roswalt Reiter, Häuptling of the Pferd Clan, was the first to speak up. Hausef walked around his Familie, approaching the fire, as Roswalt continued.

"Who are these…?"

A sharp inhale seemed to echo through the crowd. Hausef pursed his lips, knowing that Roswalt wasn't the only one to have suddenly noticed the brown of the newcomers' Statusgürtel. He wondered briefly if Chaos would interrupt this meeting in a way it hadn't since that first Jahr. Genevieve and Meinhard might have formally accepted the Skorpione, but neither had met them either.

"Skorpione!" Roswalt hissed; the sound was closer to wind rushing over a blade of grass than a snake's hiss. "What are these Köter doing here?"

Hausef stiffened at the use of the slur. Before he could answer, Meinhard leaned forward.

"Ruhe, Roswalt! Is this how you would treat those who would willingly join the Vereinte Clans?"

"Do not scold me, Meinhard!" Roswalt snapped. "How can we possibly trust any Skorpione when they were behind this Katastrophe?"

Meinhard opened his mouth to respond, but a quiet voice interrupted him.

"I can promise you, Häuptling Reiter, that we have no intention of betraying your Clans, or hurting them in any way."

All eyes turned to Wolfrik, who sat up straight and held his head high. "Already, we have turned our backs on our Häuptling. Would you judge us by the color of our Statusgürtel as the river-dwellers judge us by our dress?"

Roswalt opened his mouth then hesitated. Hausef knew the comparison would have caught the Mann off-guard. His eldest Tochter, Alys, who sat to his right, laid a hand on his knee.

"Vater," she said sternly, making Roswalt look at her. "Even the river-dwellers are learning to hold their judgment. Shall we do any less?"

Roswalt didn't look like he wanted to drop the issue, but he seemed to realize quickly that he was the only one. Even Wüstenwolf of the Wolf Clean, which, like the Pferd Clan, had arrived just that Morgen, seemed to accept the Skorpione's presence. However, as a Geistmagier, Hausef thought it possible the Wolf had at least had the benefit of a mental introduction.

Roswalt finally huffed and turned a glare on Wolfrik. "What possible reason could you have for joining the Vereinte Clans and turning your backs on your own Clan?"

Silence followed, long enough that Hausef began to doubt that the Geistmagier would even answer.

"Wolfrik," Gemi murmured.

As she spoke, she and Käfe each touched one of his knees, while Frenz laid a hand on his shoulder. Hausef thought the show of support might be more convincing than whatever words the Skorpion might use.

"You misunderstand me, Häuptling Reiter," Wolfrik finally whispered.

"How so?" Roswalt sneered. Beside him, Alys rolled her eyes

"We have not betrayed our Clan, simply our Häuptling."

Murmurs ran through the crowd then, and Roswalt's sneer changed to a confused frown. "How are those not the same thing?"

Hausef cleared his throat, thinking now was the best time to introduce the Skorpione. The four Häuptlinge turned their attention to him. Roswalt was still frowning, but the other three offered him attentive, if slightly knowing, smiles.

"Häuptlinge, may I present Wolfrik and Käfe Giftschwanz, youngest Kinder of the Häuptling of the Skorpion Clan."

Even as he spoke, he knew the final words were unnecessary. The name Giftschwanz was as old and as well-known as any of the Häuptlinge's names. Indeed, gasps and whispers broke out among the crowd the moment he spoke the name. Roswalt looked like the Pferd he had been riding had come to a sudden Halt.

"You are…" he began, but he seemed at a loss for words. Instead, it was Wüstenwolf who hummed and nodded, then spoke up.

"You would take up the mantle of Häuptling once those in your Familie who follow your V—er, the current Häuptling are defeated?"

Hausef raised an eyebrow. Now he was certain Wüstenwolf had spoken mentally with Wolfrik. It seemed he'd already had a taste of the Skorpion's temper when it came to referring to his Vater as such.

Curious how the two Geistmagier had received the mental introduction long enough ago for such conversation, Hausef glanced towards his own Familie and caught Isa's eye. He felt the familiar brush of her Geist against his as she gleaned the question he wanted to ask.

"*Remember, Bruder,*" she answered with a touch of amusement, "*I had invited him to join the Geisternetz.*"

Hausef nodded and turned back to the discussion.

"I would," Wolfrik answered, sounding more confident, "as long as the Erstehäuptling agrees."

"And I already have," Hausef answered. "Although it could be a while," he added with an apologetic smile. "We haven't been able to find the Gift Clans in Jahre."

Surprisingly, Wolfrik smirked. "It doesn't have to be."

Hausef frowned at the Skorpion, confused.

"You had said that your Häuptling already knew of your betrayal." When Wolfrik nodded, Hausef frowned. "He would not have allowed the Clan to remain at the same Oase, would he?"

Wolfrik shook his head. "Nein, he wouldn't have, but that matters little."

He paused, and Hausef wondered if the Mann would explain. Only Gemi, Frenz, and Käfe seemed to understand to what he was referring, though the twist of Isa's lips proved she might already be privy to the knowledge as well.

"As I said," the Skorpion finally continued, "our Häuptling knows of our betrayal. I know this because my Geist is still merged with our Clan's Geisternetz."

Shocked murmurs broke out among the Nomaden, and Wolfrik quickly added, "I have protected and hidden my Geist from others in the Geisternetz."

Hausef sighed, even as the crowd quieted. Despite the young Mann's assurances, he questioned the wisdom of Wolfrik's Geist being connected to both their Geisternetz and the Skorpion Clan's.

"Our Häuptling doesn't even know I still live, let alone that I've salvaged the connection."

"But you can learn of the Clan's location through it."

This was Wüstenwolf, and other Geistmagier in the crowd nodded in agreement. Hausef knew, then, that their own Geisternetz had been opened and that the matter was being discussed on another level.

"Enough!" Isa spoke sharply, silencing the group. Several in the crowd grumbled softly. "We can hold a Kriegrat later, after the Fest. Now is not the time to consider Krieg."

"I agree," Hausef spoke.

Letting his eyes skim over the crowd, he added, "The next few Tage are for celebration and the Adlerfest. Only afterwards should we let ourselves consider Krieg."

Reluctant murmurs of agreement spread through the crowd.

"Well then, Erstehäuptling," Genevieve said, drawing the attention back to herself, "shall we return to the topic at hand?"

Hausef nodded to the Arztmagier. While she was the gentlest of the Häuptlinge, she was also the most formal in this type of setting.

Hausef watched her trade looks with Meinhard before she spoke again. "The Spinne and Falke Clans have already accepted these Skorpione into the Vereinte Clans."

After a short pause, she nodded towards the Katzen. "If the Drache Krieger will be our witness?"

"I will," Gemi answered with a bright smile.

"Very well, then," Wüstenwolf muttered.

Hausef frowned at the Wolf. He had sounded more serious than usual. At the age of 26, Wüstenwolf was the youngest of the Häuptlinge. His Vater had died unexpectedly only a Jahre after Unification, and the young Geistmagier had become Häuptling at the age Zuk was now, the same age Hausef had been when he had taken up the mantle. While Hausef had found the sudden responsibility difficult and heavy, Wüstenwolf had managed to keep a boyish, yet mischievous, charm that endeared him to his people.

Hausef watched as the Wolf sat up straighter, his eyes and lips firm as he met each of the Häuptlinge's gazes. "As the Häuptling of the Wolf Clan, I, Wüstenwolf Seelenesser, accept Wolfrik and Käfe Giftschwanz as representatives of the Skorpion Clan within the Vereinte Clans."

The moment he finished citing the acceptance, Wüstenwolf broke into a grin, and added, "Now I'll have another Häuptling my age with whom I can Mindspeak."

Hausef snorted, as did several others, and even Genevieve rolled her eyes and shook her head.

"You would accept him so easily because of that, Wüstenwolf?" Roswalt snapped.

The Wolf shrugged. "My personal reasons have nothing to do with my acceptance of them as Häuptling. I've heard enough to deem them acceptable for the Vereinte Clans. That he will be a Geistmagier Häuptling is simply an extra prize."

Roswalt made a series of rustling sounds that Hausef suspected were curses in the Pflanze language, especially when Lorenz made a shushing sound and buried his head against Ava's arm. Hausef glared at the Pferd, but it was Alys who elbowed and scolded the Pflanzenmagier.

"Vater! There are Kinder present who can understand you."

Roswalt quieted and pursed his lips, still looking upset. Alys huffed and shifted away from him.

"Very well. If you are going to be like that, then I, as the future Häuptling, will speak for the Pferd Clan and accept them."

Roswalt looked shocked, and Hausef raised his brows in surprise. Alys was proud enough to take such decisions from her Vater, but that she would accept the Skorpione when her Vater would not was unexpected.

"Why...?" Roswalt asked.

Alys glared at Roswalt. "They have proven themselves to the Drache Krieger and his Drache." When the words appeared to have no effect on her Vater, she added, "And if that is not enough for you, then know that the Drache Krieger owes them Dankpflicht."

Roswalt's face contorted. Hausef could see the conflict in his eyes and nodded. A Dankpflicht was important enough to outweigh whatever personal vendetta he might hold against the Skorpion Clan.

Eventually, Roswalt sighed, and his shoulders slumped.

"Very well," he muttered. "The Pferd Clan will accept those who hold the Drache Krieger's Dankpflicht."

"Such enthusiasm."

The soft hiss came from behind Hausef, and he turned to Flame. The Drache hadn't moved, but she seemed more relaxed now. He wondered if this was the reason she'd been so anxious before the meeting began. She was the one who had originally spoken for the Skorpione. She must have understood that there might be some who would be reluctant to accept them.

Hausef caught the Drache's eye and offered her a small smile. She lifted her head from the ground and nodded, crooning softly. As reluctant as the acceptance was, they both knew it was the best they could hope for at this point.

After all, Roswalt was a Pflanzenmagier. Considering some of the Pflanze that managed to survived Zhulan's harsh desert climate, it only made sense that he would be the most stubborn of the Häuptlinge.

The meeting turned to other topics then. Each Häuptling shared their Clan's experience during the ten Tage of Chaos. Gemi spoke about the renewed alliance with the river-dwellers, including the Herzog's apparent long-time interest in the Nomaden and the newly chosen Gouverneure.

To the surprise of most of the Nomaden, Wolfrik even spoke of the tentative agreement between the two Gift Clans.

"They do not get along?" Genevieve asked, surprise coloring her tone. When Wolfrik shook his head, she added, "Then how did they manage to agree to an alliance?"

"Why did they even want an alliance?" Roswalt put in.

Wolfrik eyed the Pferd. "You underestimate the incentive of a common Feind, Häuptling Reiter. Both our Häuptling and that of the Schlange Clan see the Drache Krieger as a powerful enough threat to our Clans to necessitate an alliance."

Gemi jerked and turned to stare at the Skorpion. "Me?" She shook her head. "I may be Drache Krieger, but I'm just a Kind. Surely, they can't feel that threatened by me."

Hausef snorted. His Tochter often underestimated the importance of her position.

"You forget, James, that, to the Gift Clans, you are the one who instigated the Unification. They would feel more threatened by the idea of you, at the very least, than they would be by anyone else, even me."

"The Erstehäuptling's correct, Drache Krieger," Wolfrik confirmed. "According to our Häuptlinge, you are the greatest threat to our Clans' ways of Leben. Whether or not it is true, there are those in our Clans who believe that if you were removed, the Vereinte Clans would fall apart."

All of a sudden, Frenz Kanti straightened. Hausef heard the farmer mutter, "Speaking of...", and he frowned at the Mann.

He had remained quiet so far, and the Erstehäuptling had begun to think that Gemi had simply wished to keep the Mann by her side rather than having any intention of getting him involved in the meeting.

Now, the farmer turned purposefully towards Hausef, and, after a brief pause, he asked, "May I speak?"

Complete silence fell over the crowd then. Most likely, those Nomaden who had not already met the Mann had thought him a companion of the Skorpione. His accent, however, would have made it clear that he was not even a Zhulanbürger, let alone a Nomade.

As quickly as the silence fell, it was broken just as quickly by murmurs spreading through the crowd. Hausef could hear confusion, and even anger, in many of the voices, and he stifled a groan. He realized, then, that he might have made a mistake in allowing Kanti a seat at the Katze bench.

No matter how important the Mann might be to Gemi, the Tradition of this meeting was a trading of information between those of highest rank within the Clans. As such, even the Giftschwanz siblings had the right to speak at this meeting, since they were the Kinder of a Häuptling and one was to be the future Häuptling of his Clan.

Kanti, on the other hand, was a simple farmer and, worse, an Ausländer. That Hausef had let him have a place in this meeting meant that he acknowledged that the stranger held a rank higher than most Nomaden.

Even considering his Freundschaft with Gemi, Hausef did not believe the farmer had earned such a rank. He also knew that many would resent such a position being held by an Ausländer, whether the position was real or not.

Despite his sudden misgivings about letting the farmer sit at the Katze bench, Hausef knew he would have to acknowledge him and let him speak. If he denied him a chance to speak when he had allowed him a place at the meeting, then the trouble Hausef faced would only worsen.

"You may," he finally answered, ignoring several cries of outrage from the surrounding crowd. They might wish to protest, but they weren't allowed to speak formally in the meeting unless called to by someone seated at a bench.

Kanti dipped his head in acceptance of the acknowledgment. Hausef glanced briefly at Gemi, and saw that she, too, watched Kanti curiously. He decided then that his previous thought had been correct. His Tochter had not expected her companion to speak, and she was just as clueless as he was about what the farmer wished to discuss.

When Kanti turned to face the fire, Hausef twitched his gaze back to him and stared. The Mann had shifted his posture so that he now sat straight and tall and...proud?

Hausef blinked and shook his head.

The farmer suddenly seemed to radiate an aura of power that Hausef hadn't sensed before. It wasn't the power he associated with a Magier, either, but that of a leader who respected his people.

And his words, as he began to speak, were much clearer than Hausef had become accustomed to hearing from the Mann.

Hausef abruptly remembered his earlier question of the Mann's importance in Gemi's eyes. Was it possible that Gemi had actually been mindful of the meeting's Tradition? Whoever Frenz Kanti was, Hausef was now certain he was not just a simple farmer.

He was also certain that Gemi knew the Mann's true identity. It would explain why she had insisted from the beginning that he be involved in everything she did.

An intense curiosity burned through Hausef, but he quickly squashed it. He knew his Tochter well enough to know that she would not have kept this secret from him without good reason. Keeping that in his Geist, he turned his attention to the Mann's words.

Kanti offered an introduction of himself to the Clans first, something Hausef hadn't expected but which only solidified his suspicions of the Mann's true position, whatever it was. He called himself a farmer, and Hausef doubted a real farmer would have made the distinction.

A glance at the four Häuptlinge revealed looks of surprise and, possibly, suspicion.

As Kanti paused to scan the crowds, Hausef noticed Wüstenwolf glance sharply at Wolfrik. The Skorpion jerked his head to one side, as unobtrusive a denial as one could give in this setting.

Hausef knew that Wolfrik had invaded Kanti's Geist and had even protected it afterwards. He must still be doing so, especially if he wished to protect the Mann's true identity. If even a Mann born to the Clans, even a Skorpion, thought the secret safe and important enough to keep, Hausef thought they had little reason to attempt to uncover it.

"I would place before the Erstehäuptling," Kanti began, and Hausef snapped his gaze back to the Mann, "the Häuptlinge, and all the Nomaden of the Clans,"—Hausef raised a brow at that address—"a request for information. Not just for myself, but for the Drache Krieger, as well."

"Frenz!" Gemi muttered sharply.

By then, silence had fallen over the crowd, and her complaint was loud enough for everyone to hear. Kanti simply turned towards her and caught the wrist of the hand she'd raised in protest.

"You are not alone, James, remember? You can depend on others. You don't have to do everything alone."

Gemi's mouth opened, and Hausef knew she would argue. If the Drache Krieger was known for one thing throughout the Clans, it was his insistence that others depend on him, not the other way around.

Instead, Gemi slowly closed her mouth, a thoughtful frown marring her features. Finally, to Hausef's surprise, she nodded and offered Kanti a small smile.

"You're right."

That was it. No further protest, no arguments, just a soft, simple agreement.

Hausef knew he was staring as Kanti turned back to the fire, but he found himself too shocked to care.

He had known Gemini Cosley for five and a half Jahre. During that time, he had learned that getting her to accept help from others was a battle. She simply couldn't allow herself to depend on others. He knew that even her bondmates struggled with it.

Yet, this Mann, Kanti, had known her for less than half a Jahreszeit, and he had managed to get her to accept help with three sentences.

With a shake of his head, Hausef acknowledged that, whoever he was, Frenz Kanti was important to Gemi in a way that had nothing to do with his mysterious position.

~~*~*

Gemi knew she'd surprised many Nomaden with her seemingly easy acquiescence, but it had been far from easy. Flame and Shadow both had had to remind her of the conversation she'd shared with Ferez as they traveled along the San just a Siebentag ago.

Even then, it had taken a lot to overcome the pride and Angst that the thought of asking for help evoked.

Through it all, Ferez had held her gaze, and the look in his eyes, or possibly the way he held himself, told her that, while he respected her and her opinion, he would not back down from this.

Is that how I need to be handled, then, she thought snidely, *with a firm grip and unyielding stubbornness?*

"*It is not that simple,*" Flame answered.

Gemi knew she was right. She was simply mocking her own responses. Gemi trusted Ferez in a way that she trusted so few, and there were times, like now, when that scared her.

"*Settle, James,*" Flame soothed. "*Listen.*"

Gemi acknowledged the Drache and focused on Ferez's words. She realized, with a start, that he was describing the situation they'd discovered at Parshen Gut with young Gretchen Parshen and Der Geist. She had forgotten about his recommendation that they ask others for information. Bringing it up now, in front of a large representation of the Vereinte Clans, was, she realized, a smart move.

She was shocked, however, when she realized that his description, and in fact his entire speech, was littered with Zhulanese words. Despite his accent, he spoke like a Zhulanbürger, mingling the Fayralese and Zhulanese in a way that had been perfected by the Zhulanese over the Jahre.

Gemi shook her head. Once again, she found she had underestimated the König, who seemed to recognize the formality of this setting through his words just as much as through his speech and his actions.

"My request," Ferez finished, after telling of the message that Gretchen had passed on, "is for any information that might reveal to whom the names Markos and Eirene refer."

Whispers passed through the crowd, their tone different from those that had preceded Ferez's speech. Gemi felt her lips twitch as she realized that the Nomaden were taking the König seriously despite whatever anger or resentment they might feel towards him as an Ausländer.

That is a gut Omen.

The more they could accept him now, the more likely she thought it would be that they would accept him as König when the revelation occurred.

"Häuptling."

The voice was soft, but it carried, and the crowd fell silent once more. Gemi turned towards the Spinnen. Genevieve was waving forward the Mann who had appeared behind her, turning to Hausef as she did so.

"May my Mann speak, Erstehäuptling?"

"He may."

As the Mann stepped closer to the fire, Gemi realized he was old. Although she couldn't see his hair for his Kopfabdeckung, his face was thick with wrinkles and his eyebrows were bushy and white.

"May I present Altmann Seeleweber, Heilig of the Spinne Clan."

Gemi startled. She hadn't realized that the Spinne Clan had its own Heilig. How she hadn't after five Jahre with the Clans, she didn't know.

Then again, since her parents' Tode, she had avoided as much mention of religion as she could. She briefly recalled the strange tapestries she had seen in Tearmann before forcing her attention to the present.

"Markos and Eirene are ancient names," the Heilig began. "They come from the ancient culture and ancient language that ruled this land before Zhulanese and Fayralese replaced it.

"Even so, they are relatively young names. They were not used for long before they were replaced with the names we use today, so I doubt many would recognize them."

"And the names we use today?" Gemi asked.

She twitched as Ferez's hand landed on her knee and squeezed, but she couldn't remove her gaze from the Heilig. He claimed to recognize the two names, and it seemed she and Ferez were on the verge of learning exactly who it was that stood against them.

She wasn't sure if the sudden churning in her stomach came from anticipation or dread.

Heilig Altmann gave a small shake of his head. "Markos is known to us as Krieg, and Eirene as Frieda."

~~*~*

Ferez cursed softly and grabbed James' shoulder as the boy suddenly slumped. On his other side, Wolfrik did the same, his own face pale in the firelight.

Ignoring the gasps that rang through the crowd, Ferez murmured lowly to James, hoping to rouse him from his sudden shock. Even as he did, he considered the holy man's words; words he'd understood well enough despite the language barrier.

War and Peace.

Despite the frightening implication of those words, Ferez thought he could understand the use of the latter, at least. James had been working for peace for about six years now. After that long, it only made sense that he be called Peace.

Forcing aside the revelation, Ferez cupped James' cheek and turned his face towards him. The boy's breathing was quick and shallow, his eyes stared sightlessly, and his skin held a pallor Ferez had never seen on him.

"James," he murmured lowly, ignoring Wolfrik and Käfe and the Kantens who stood over them. "Snap out of it. You can't let him have this power over you. It's what he wants."

A hand on his shoulder drew Ferez's attention up to Mandel, but he shook his head and turned back to James, focusing on those dark purple eyes. He didn't think a Healer was what James really needed right now.

"Focus on me," he murmured. The crowd seemed to go silent then, and even the crackling of the fire and the whisper of the wind seemed to quiet.

"Listen to my voice and focus on me. You are safe here. You are among friends. You have your clan. You have your family. You have your bondmates." He paused and let his voice soften. "You have me."

As Ferez murmured rhythmically, James' breathing began to slow and deepen. When Ferez paused, James began to blink again, those amethyst orbs shifting to focus on Ferez.

When Ferez whispered the last, James' lips twitched. He lifted a hand and wrapped it around the wrist of the hand Ferez had at his cheek and squeezed firmly.

"Danke," he breathed.

Ferez nodded and squeezed his shoulder in turn but didn't remove his hand from James' face. He didn't think he could if he'd wanted to with the tight grip the boy now had on his wrist.

When James' gaze finally darted from Ferez's face, red bloomed across his cheeks. Ferez glanced around and found that everyone around them was watching them with various looks of concern, awe, and surprise.

James pulled Ferez's hand from his face but didn't let go, instead lowering it to his lap, locking the fingers of one hand with Ferez's, and squeezing the other around Ferez's wrist. Ferez rubbed his other hand across the boy's back, offering as much comfort as he could.

"Do you really think the very essence of Krieg is against us?"

James' voice, when he finally spoke, was soft and hesitant, but, with everyone still silent, the words were easily heard.

"Ach, I doubt the actual Halbgott Krieg is the one responsible for Fräulein Parshen's distress."

Ferez glanced up at the holy man, surprised. He sounded very confident in that.

"Even if that is the third time we've heard that name this season?"

The holy man shook his head. "The Halbgötter simply do not involve themselves so personally with specific humans. Nein, it is most likely some vengeful Geist who is trying to scare you with such references."

Ferez pursed his lips at the old man's unconcerned tone and glanced at James. The boy had relaxed with the holy man's words, his eyes wide and desperately hopeful.

The king felt his heart clench. It hadn't passed his notice that, since the incident at the Handelmann home in Schönestadt, James had been a bit desperate to keep Ferez with him at all times. He thought the boy was teetering on the edge of a full breakdown, of which the panic attack from which Ferez had just pulled him was just a glimpse.

Unwilling to let that happen, Ferez nodded to James when the boy turned to him. He would agree with the holy man's words for now.

No matter that I don't believe them.

Seyan had told him it was a young man that had called himself Markos in Cautzel. Charlen, the Animal Mage in Kensy, had called Markos 'more than man' and 'more powerful than any mage'.

Ferez doubted either of those descriptions could match a simple ghost or spirit, even a vengeful one. But the demigods...

With the little he knew of them, he wouldn't be surprised to learn they had the ability to take physical form or to express their power and desires to a human.

He didn't necessarily disbelieve the holy man, either, when he said that the demigods didn't involve themselves personally with specific humans.

439

That Markos had addressed James as Eirene, as Peace, made Ferez wonder if it was more than a simple reference.

If Markos really is the demigod War, could James actually be his counterpart, Peace?

"Strange, but not wholly impossible, I think."

The familiar voice whispered through Ferez's mind, and he glanced at Wolfrik. Still pale, the Mindspeaker switched his concerned gaze from James to the king.

"But, whether or not the Drache Krieger is actually a Halbgott, I do agree with you about Krieg."

Ferez blinked. Wolfrik must have heard his questioning thought because he quickly continued.

"I do. I did not wish to alarm the others, but there is a voice that has been encouraging the recent violence of the Gift Clans. The voice has been speaking to one Geistmagier in particular, but I have heard him myself on occasion. I would not be surprised if that voice belonged to Krieg."

Ferez shuddered, but James didn't seem to notice. *Thank you,* he thought, hoping Wolfrik would hear. *I don't think James would have been able to handle that information right now.*

"I believe you are right."

Ferez soon felt the mage's presence in his mind lessen, but he didn't think it left completely. It seemed the Mindspeaker was still protecting his mind, even after he'd been declared fully healed.

Someone has to make sure your secret is safe.

The lingering thought was barely noticeable, and Ferez smiled.

~~*~*

War cursed and kicked the ground, growling loudly when the surface didn't provide the resistance he desired. He had provided Peace a perfectly simple message, one that had been relatively easy to decipher if they could just find someone who knew the ancient names.

Even that had been ruined. The holy man had deciphered the message in one moment and given a perfect reason why it couldn't be accurate in the next.

He cursed again.

"It didn't go as planned, did it?"

War snarled at the soft words and lashed out at the speaker, but Love was farther away than he'd thought. She shook her head.

"I'd ask you to control your temper, but I think you lost your control Jahre ago."

War snarled again and turned away from his pink sister. He knew she was right. He had lost control of himself, and he felt like he was quickly losing his sanity, as well.

Sometimes, he wanted to simply scream at Peace, beg her to remember who she was. There were times when he wanted her to feel the torture he did, to know what it felt like to lose the one person that understood you better than anyone else.

And there were times, more recently, when he simply wanted to watch her die.

That, more than anything, scared him. He had already been without her for two centuries. Logically, to watch her die would only bring him more pain, but that urge to have her killed was only growing stronger.

War released a frustrated scream and swiped at the air again, but there was nothing here on which he could take out his sudden rage. Nothing except…

He swung around and stalked towards Love. He barely noticed the sigh she gave and didn't care that she just stood there, waiting for him. Once he was close enough, he raised his fist, intent on taking out his anger on something, anything.

A hand grabbed his fist, stilling him mid-swing. Red filled his vision, and he snarled at the brother who had stopped him.

"Release me!" he spat.

"Nein," Hate said. His voice was calm and low, but it only served to make War angrier. He brought his other fist around, and Hate caught that one, too. "We're not the ones with which you're angry, Bruder."

War snarled and stepped back, attempting to pull his hands from Hate's, but his older brother wouldn't let go. Shaking his head and giving a short yell, he lifted a leg and aimed it at his brother.

He fell backwards then, his hands no longer clamped in Hate's grip. The moment he hit the ground, War snapped his eyes shut and Transported himself elsewhere.

He couldn't stand the looks he knew his siblings would give him. He couldn't stand the Chaos that filled him.

He couldn't stand it; he just couldn't.

I have to do something, he thought savagely, snapping his eyes open on the camp of the Poison Clans.

The plan that had been forming in his head lately, the one he'd mentioned to Adalwolf, swiftly filled his mind. It calmed the rage and Chaos and all the other unwelcome emotions that had plagued him a moment ago.

Aye, I have to do something.

Chapter 41

16 Mid Autumn, 224
Friedlichoase, Zhulan

On the afternoon of Mid-Season, Ferez was rousted from his bed, not by any humans—Ferez was rather amused to find that, once again, he was one of the first awake in the Kanten tent—but by the thick scent of roasting meat. With a smile spreading his lips and his Kopfabdeckung in hand, Ferez eagerly pushed his way through the tent's entrance.

Mid-Season was Ferez's favorite day of the season. Every season without fail, Ferez made time to celebrate the holy days.

Most seasons, he managed to celebrate them in Caypan; the one day each season when he could wander the streets as king without worrying about the usual reverence and fear from the citizens. Those seasons during the war when he couldn't return to the capital, he would convince Fayral to agree to a ceasefire so their men and his could all celebrate in peace.

His father, Eden Katani, was the one who had instilled in him an appreciation for the importance of the holy days, but the anticipation he felt every Mid-Season was all his own. Every Mid-Season, since he could remember, he would wake at the earliest possible time, eager to enjoy the festivities of the day.

This season was no different. In fact, Ferez thought the idea of enjoying the holy day through the perspective of another culture made this day even more exciting.

Once outside the Kanten tent, Ferez spun in a circle as he secured his Kopfabdeckung. He knew he was grinning like a fool, but he just couldn't wait to experience this Adlerfest, as the nomads called the Festival.

Already, the camp was decked out in all its glory. Lamps, yet unlit, were hung in every spot imaginable, and brightly colored cloth hung over all the tents and trees in a brilliant spray of color.

What intrigued Ferez most were the small statuettes of eagles that now perched at the top of every tent. The day before, when all of the preparations had been made, Ferez had learned that Adlerfest actually meant 'Eagle Festival' in Zhulanese.

To his amusement, James hadn't actually known why. The Skorpion siblings, who had accompanied them in their work, had teased James for not knowing after being a nomad for five years, and they had told Ferez that he would learn the reason during the Festival if he really wanted.

Putting the thought from his mind, Ferez turned his attention back to the scents that had originally drawn him from his slumber. He followed his nose to one of the cooking fires that he knew were burning throughout the oasis.

As he approached, he felt the sweltering heat of the fire combine with that of the desert sun and grimaced, stopping several feet away. He didn't know how the nomads managed to tend these cooking fires for so many hours during the hottest part of the desert day, but the food was to be ready a couple of hours before sunset, so the tortuous task was apparently considered necessary.

Ferez's mouth began to water from the tantalizing scents of roasting meat, underscored with a spiced scent that he imagined came from a mulled cider or ale. As he glanced around the fire, the king found that not only were various meats roasting over the fire, but bowls of berries and roots and other foods that he couldn't even name lay around, tempting him with their plumpness and bright colors.

A sharp sting on the back of his hand suddenly had Ferez wincing. Pulling the hand back to his chest from where he'd unconsciously reached for the nearest bowl of berries, he glanced up at the woman who'd slapped his hand. She glared at him, her arms akimbo and her lips pressed together sternly.

"Nein! Not until the Fest begins, young Mann."

The woman sounded as stern as she looked. Ferez was sharply reminded of the head cook at the palace, who had always been quick to scold him whenever she caught him attempting to sneak snacks between meals.

He smiled apologetically and murmured, "Sorry, Ma'am. I wasn' tryin' to cause trouble."

To his surprise, the woman's expression softened, and she offered a small smile. "Ach, Herr Kanti." She shook her head. "As bad as a Kind you are."

Ferez raised his brows at her teasing tone, but she made a shooing motion with her hands. "Away with you now. I'm sure the Drache Krieger will make sure you get a little of everything later, but no food until the Fest begins."

Ferez chuckled as he left the cooking fire behind. He hadn't actually meant to reach for the berries. Even in Caypan, people really didn't eat much before the Festival began. The food had just looked so tempting that he apparently hadn't been able to resist.

He stopped by the spring that bordered the Katze Clan's camp, one of three large springs that made up the lush oasis. Once he'd drunk his fill, he wandered around the spring's edge towards the open field between the three.

When he'd first noticed the large open area, which had been unoccupied at the time, he'd asked James why none of the clans set up camp there. Ferez thought it might be large enough to fit nearly an entire clan.

James had answered that the middle ground of the oasis was an inter-clan area. It was reserved for those activities in which all the clans participated. Indeed, the meeting that had taken place two nights before had been held within the central area.

Now, it was solely dedicated to the Festival.

The night before, the middle ground had seemed to be filled with chaos, but, as Ferez surveyed it now, he found his anticipation steadily climbing.

There were still several open areas, including one especially large area nearby where Flame currently lounged, her long tail sweeping idly across the grass. On the other side of the field, another open area stood adjacent to one of the openings between two of the springs.

There, outside the ring of water, no clan had camped. Instead, herds of horses, goats, and other animals that the clans kept stood or lay about, lazing in the heat of the desert sun.

Turning his gaze back to the middle space, Ferez eyed the stages that ranged throughout it. One, which stood furthest to his right, past the open area where Flame lounged, was crowded with objects. He couldn't see what they were from this distance, but he made a note to find out later.

Meanwhile, he was more interested in one of the other stages, around which several people were crowded.

The stage stood at waist height. As he approached, he realized it held two people. They appeared to be sparring, their Scharfmonde flashing in the bright sunlight as they swung at each other. The murmurs of the watching nomads rose and fell as the two fighters lunged back and forth, seeming to dance around each other even as they engaged in a fight.

Just as Ferez joined the group, a sharp whistle split the air, and the two fighters immediately broke apart and sheathed their weapons. Slapping each other on the back, they jumped down from the stage and joined the others, who quickly congratulated them on a good practice.

"Oi, Katze!"

Ferez blinked when he realized that the speaker was addressing him. The man who'd spoken nodded his head up at the stage.

"Are you participating in the Boxkämpfe, then?"

"Don't be dumm," said another man, who bore the purple Statusgürtel of a Katze. "That's the Drache Krieger's companion, Herr Kanti. He doesn't know how to use the Scharfmonde."

"That doesn't mean he can't boxen," said the first man, a Pferd. He was wiping his face with his Kopfabdeckung, and Ferez realized he was one of the two who had been sparring previously. "What say you, farmer? Can you boxen?"

"You think an Ausländer would know how to boxen?" sneered a Spinne, the Pferd's sparring partner.

The Pferd shrugged, his eyes not leaving Ferez. "Well, farmer? Can you?"

Ferez glanced around at the surrounding young men. He was surprised by the nearly hostile looks with which many of them regarded him. Only the Pferd and the Katze seemed open to his presence, despite the anxious glances the Katze was shooting him and the Pferd.

Unsure if he should attempt to spar with people that didn't want him around, he turned his gaze back to the Pferd.

"I've never participated in the sport."

Another young man, one of two Falken in the group, snorted.

"Of course you haven't, Ausländer."

Several of the others chuckled, but the Pferd continued to hold Ferez's gaze.

"Even if you haven't participated in a Boxkampf before, surely you have fought with your fists, ja?"

The others quieted and frowned as Ferez considered the Pferd's words.

It was true that he had been in fistfights before. It was not uncommon for noble children to ignore their parents' preferences for the fine art of dueling with swords and simply attack each other with flying fists when they were in disagreement.

He had also learned during the war that, when necessary, one's fists were just as powerful a weapon as one's blade. He'd learned that lesson rather well from one particular Fayralman. The swordsman had disarmed Ferez, but then he fell to Ferez's fists because he couldn't adapt to the close range that Ferez had then demanded.

Shaking his head to rid himself of the war memories, the king eyed the Pferd once more.

"Aye, but surely boxin' is not as simple as that?"

Several of the nomads sneered, but the Pferd simply smirked. "There is nothing simple about depending solely on your fists, Freund." He jerked his head towards the stage once more. "Care to give it a try?"

Protests erupted from each of the surrounding nomads. The Pferd mostly ignored them, pausing only when the Katze grabbed his arm.

"Are you sure you want to do that, Eloy? The Drache Krieger's rather fond of him. If you hurt him too much, you'll have to deal with both the Drache Krieger and the Erstehäuptling."

Eloy offered a small shrug. "I am hardly going to use my full power against a beginner, Reiner. And I have heard that the Drache Krieger has involved Herr Kanti in every Aspekt of Clan Leben possible, ja?"

The Pferd glanced inquiringly at Ferez, who nodded.

"Then he should get a chance to experience a Boxkampf since he cannot handle the Scharfmonde."

The explanation only seemed to upset most of the others, even as Reiner nodded reluctantly and released Eloy's arm. The Pferd waved Ferez towards the stage.

Once they stood next to the platform, Eloy paused and unsheathed his Scharfmonde. Ferez frowned, but the Pferd simply chuckled as he passed the blades off to one of the other young men.

"It is customary to remove all weapons from your person before beginning a bladeless Boxkampf. Pulling blades can be instinctual, especially for those who are not accustomed to depending solely on themselves."

Ferez nodded and bent down to retrieve the knives he kept in his boots. When he straightened and offered them to the nomad who had taken Eloy's Scharfmonde, he was met with surprised stares.

"What?"

Eloy hesitated before shaking his head. "I had not even noticed you were armed, Freund. I never expected a farmer to carry hidden blades."

Ferez shrugged. "When you've spent years fightin' a war, even we farmers learn to never be unarmed."

The others hesitated, and Reiner attempted to catch Eloy's arm again, but the Pferd shook him off and waved for someone to take Ferez's blades. Once Ferez had been disarmed, the sport's few rules were explained: fists only, no blows below the Statusgürtel, and crossing the bound line resulted in an automatic loss.

Ferez frowned at the last one and glanced at the stage. There, a couple feet from the edge of the platform, was a chalk line he hadn't noticed before.

He remembered the one match he had seen with his father several years before in Wildestadt. Then, they had had rope surrounding the platform to keep the boxers from falling off. Apparently, the nomads hadn't adapted that little variation.

Ferez's hands were wrapped in what looked like un-dyed Statusgürtel before he was helped onto the stage. As they faced each other several feet apart, Eloy nodded to one of the nearby young men.

"Two minutes since he's a beginner." Then he turned back to Ferez, and a sharp whistle pierced the air.

To Ferez, the following bout seemed to last much longer than the two minutes for which the Pferd called. Even so, Ferez wasn't exactly sure just what they had done.

He remembered ducking and sidestepping to avoid blows, as well as a particularly strong blow that connected with his left shoulder, reminding him it was freshly healed only a sevenday beforehand. He didn't remember landing any blows himself, despite being assured later that he had landed several good ones, including a spectacular uppercut to the Pferd's midsection.

What Ferez did remember clearly about the fight was how it ended. James' voice seemed to cut through the fight-induced fog in his mind. He pivoted, both to avoid the coming blow from Eloy and to glimpse James, whose voice had come from behind him beyond the growing crowd.

The next moment, Eloy stumbled past Ferez and nearly slipped right off the edge of the platform.

~~*~*

Gemi paused at the edge of the crowd as Eloy barely managed to keep from stumbling off the platform. The surrounding crowd seemed to press against him to keep him upright, but an uneasy silence fell over the Nomaden as it became obvious that the Pferd had lost the match.

Certainly, no one had expected Eloy, one of the best Boxer in the Vereinte Clans, to lose to a stranger.

What none of them seemed to realize was the very reason Gemi had broken into a run when both Flame and Wolfrik told her that Ferez was being coaxed into a Boxkampf.

She pushed through the crowd until she reached the Pferd, who was now seated on the edge of the platform. He was hunched over with one arm wrapped around his midsection.

Once close enough, she cuffed his ear. He cried out and covered his ear, but Gemi doubted it was as much from pain as from surprise. When he met her glare, he gaped.

"Drache Krieger?"

Gemi huffed. "Dummkopf."

Looking past the Boxer, she beckoned Ferez down from the platform. He winced as he lowered himself to the ground, and she frowned worriedly. He shook his head.

"He gave me a good knock to my lef' shoulder, I think."

Nodding, Gemi murmured, "We'll have Mandel look at it later." Certain that her Freund would be all right, Gemi turned back to the still seated Pferd.

"Dummkopf," she repeated, louder this time so most of the crowd could hear her. "What did you think you were doing?"

Eloy hunched his shoulders more. "It was just a freundlich Boxkampf, Drache Krieger. There was no harm meant."

Gemi snorted. "Maybe not, but you could have gotten yourself killed."

That caught everyone's attention. While the Pferd and his Freunde frowned at her, Ferez touched her shoulder.

"James?"

His voice reflected the confusion on the Nomaden's faces, and Gemi offered Ferez a sad smile.

"Es tut mir leid, Frenz, but Boxen has certain customs and rules for a reason, some of which these Boxer have blatantly ignored."

She eyed the young Männer distastefully. When she saw that they still didn't understand, she changed tactics and focused on the Pferd.

"Would you have challenged me to a bladeless Boxkampf, Eloy?"

The Boxer paled and shook his head rather vigorously.

"And why not?"

Eloy glanced around at the surrounding Nomaden, but even his Freunde had backed away from him. Gemi sighed. She hadn't meant to be mean, especially since Flame had said he'd only attempted to include Ferez as Gemi had done.

But the Mann was a dedicated Boxer and knew all the rules and customs surrounding Boxen. He had risked his life because he underestimated Ferez, something that everybody seemed to be doing lately, even Gemi.

And, for once, Ferez himself didn't realize the danger surrounding him. Gemi had to make sure everyone was aware of this so it wouldn't happen again.

When nobody seemed willing to help Eloy, he met Gemi's gaze once more. "I wouldn't challenge you because your instincts are attuned to Krieg, not to Boxen."

Gemi nodded. "Exactly."

The Pferd frowned. "But he's a farmer. I should have been able to treat him as a beginner."

Gemi sighed. "Ja, he's a farmer, but he's also from Kensy, the center of the Krieg mit Fayral. He's been fighting for..."

She paused and glanced at the König, who still frowned at her. "How old were you when you first fought in the Krieg?"

She asked to prove her point, but she was also curious about the answer. She didn't remember hearing anything about Ferez before he was crowned König, despite knowing he had fought before then.

Ferez tilted his head to the side then said, "Jus' pas' my fourteenth year." He paused, met Gemi's gaze, and then added, "'Bou' four an' a half years ago."

Murmurs spread through the crowd then, and all of the Boxer paled at the implication.

"Fourteen," muttered Eloy. He shook his head then stared at Ferez with a look of Respekt that Gemi hadn't expected. "So young?"

Ferez shifted uncomfortably and shrugged. "The land is our livelihood. We couldn' le' the Fayralese take it from us."

Gemi smiled bemusedly. The König had become very dedicated to the story of Frenz Kanti.

The Pferd bowed his head. "Es tut mir leid, my Freund, for endangering both of us."

Ferez shifted again. "It turned out all right; no real harm done." After a brief pause, he quickly added, "I didn' hurt you too badly, did I?"

The worry in his voice made Gemi smile, and the Pferd shook his head, chuckling.

"Nein, Freund, no more than I can handle. Besides, I've had much worse. I will admit, though, that I was surprised and impressed by your power." He chuckled again, "I guess that's what I get for inviting a raw warrior to boxen."

Gemi nodded, satisfied that she had gotten her point across. Turning back to Ferez, she laid a hand on his right shoulder. "Shall we find Mandel, then, and have him take a look at your shoulder?"

"No need to go looking for him, Drache Krieger."

Gemi startled when Häuptling Seidenstrang suddenly spoke up behind her. She turned to find the Frau eying Ferez with a small frown, which morphed into a soft smile after a moment.

"If you'll let me Heal your Freund, that is."

Gemi nodded and dropped her hand from Ferez's shoulder. She took a small, hopefully inconspicuous, step away from the König as Genevieve approached.

The Frau was considered the most powerful Arztmagier in the Vereinte Clans and, while she had never indicated that she knew Gemi's true gender, Gemi was reluctant to give her the chance. Lakina had discovered Gemi's secret through her Magie, and Genevieve was quite possibly more powerful than the Kensian Arztmagier.

As the Spinne laid her hands on Ferez's shoulder, she continued talking.

"I agree with you, Drache Krieger, that Eloy should not have challenged Herr Kanti to a Boxkampf, but I now find myself curious about his skill and power."

Gemi frowned. "What do you mean?"

Genevieve flashed Gemi a smile.

"I wonder if the two of you might provide us with a demonstration to start off the Boxkämpfe. After all, I'm sure I'm not the only one curious to see the two of you cross swords after that."

Many in the crowd, which had grown much larger during Ferez's bout, raised their voices in agreement.

Gemi hesitated. It wouldn't have been the first time she had participated in such a demonstration, especially for Mitte Jahreszeit, but it had been Jahre since she had done so with a sword. Not that she doubted her ability to do so, but…

She glanced at Ferez, unsure how to respond to the Häuptling's request. To her surprise, Ferez was grinning, an obvious excitement shining in his eyes. When she met his gaze, his grin widened.

"Can we, James?" Gemi blinked at the Kind-like tone his voice had taken. "We haven' exactly had a chance to spar wit' swords since we met."

Despite her uncertainty, a smile spread her lips as she realized he was right. She hadn't unsheathed her sword since they crossed into the desert, and, when they had practiced in Kensy, it was always with other people who needed the extra training.

Then, she had believed there was no reason for them to practice together, not when she had seen his skill first-hand in that first battle on the highway and again in Puretha.

Now, Ferez's excitement hinted that there was a reason for them to spar that had less to do with practicing and more to do with the simple enjoyment of the challenge. When Gemi nodded her agreement, Ferez let out a soft whoop, much to the amusement of the surrounding Nomaden.

"We'll need to get our swords," Gemi added.

"No need," a voice called from the edge of the crowd.

The crowd parted, and the Kanten Familie filed through the gap, Hausef in front, two swords in his hands.

"I believe these are yours."

Gemi gaped at her Vater as he offered her the swords. "How…?"

He chuckled and nodded to the Skorpione, who had accompanied them. "Wolfrik said you might want them. It seems he was right."

Gemi shook her head as she took the offered swords. "Danke," she murmured then offered Ferez his as Genevieve proclaimed him fit to spar.

Despite being ready then, they waited until Adlerfest officially began a half hour later to spar. Hausef climbed up onto the platform, as he did every Fest, to introduce Gemi and Ferez to the crowd as the first demonstration. This was how each Fest began, and Gemi smiled at the continuation of Tradition.

She and Ferez took the stage to the cheering of the crowd. As they settled across from each other, their swords unsheathed, Gemi took in Ferez's stance.

He held himself lightly on his feet, the heels of his boots just touching the platform. He stood with his right foot forward, the stance wider than necessary. Gemi frowned until she noticed that he also held his sword more vertically than would be practical for a normal swordfight.

Gemi blinked as she recognized the stance. It was one Sir Paeter had taught her when she was much younger, the offensive beginning stance for the Sword Dance of Carith.

She lifted her gaze to Ferez's and found him eying her with raised brows and a wide grin. She chuckled softly. Well, it had been a while, but Gemi was sure she remembered the Sword Dance well enough.

She answered his challenge by shifting her weight to her back leg and lifting and turning her sword so that she held it parallel to the ground in front of her.

When the sharp whistle sounded, there was a beat of stillness before Ferez moved. He flowed forward, in a rhythm faster than she had expected, but she easily matched the speed and met his first blow. She quickly responded with her own blow, which he easily deflected.

They moved through the first steps of the Sword Dance in that way, faster than Gemi remembered from her childhood, but at a speed that Gemi knew matched their abilities.

And that was the true purpose behind the Sword Dance: to demonstrate the participants' abilities to their fullest. In the beginning, the abilities were displayed in the speed of the well-rehearsed motions. Later, the Dance became unscripted, allowing the participants to battle for dominance.

As the swordsman who began in the offensive position, Ferez began with a slight advantage, but Gemi didn't think it would make a difference. She hadn't lost a one-on-one swordfight since her days under Sir Paeter and Sir Leal.

When they reached the more creative part of the Dance, however, she found herself still on the defensive.

Her grin widened, and she laughed, even as she scrambled to block Ferez's next blow. She had known Ferez was a powerful swordsman, had learned recently that he too was trained by the same mentors, but, until now, she hadn't considered that he might actually be her equal.

Gemi finally managed to counter one of Ferez's blows, knocking him back several steps. Taking advantage of his momentary stumble, she aimed a blow towards his neck and shoulder.

As expected, he lifted his sword to catch the blow, but he lifted it higher than she thought warranted. For that split second before the blow landed, she feared she would catch his wrist instead of his blade, and she attempted to lighten the blow.

Metal clashed against metal as her blade struck the shoulder of Ferez's, just above the guard, and Ferez slid his blade down hers and twisted it.

Before Gemi could process what he had done, she found herself facing the crowd, her back to Ferez, and he had both of their swords crossed in front of her chest. Stunned, she idly mused that the move seemed to be an adaptation of a maneuver she'd taught him to disarm Nomaden.

Cheering quickly petered out into silence as shock followed the news of just who had won. Grinning breathlessly, Gemi tapped Ferez's arm to offer her surrender, and he quickly released her.

Once she'd turned around, he offered a half-bow and her sword. She grasped the outstretched hand with both of hers and laughed.

As if that had been their cue, the crowd of Nomaden surrounding the stage broke into cheers and whooping calls, and Ferez lifted his head and grinned widely at her. Taking her sword back, Gemi gripped his hand and led him off the stage as a pair of Boxer prepared for the next spar.

As they moved through the crowd, they received hearty claps on the back and shouts of compliments and congratulations. They were met at the edge of the crowd, which had begun to disperse for the various other activities of the Fest, by Zuk, Ulla, Wolfrik, and Käfe. The four complimented them on their bout then insisted on helping Gemi introduce Ferez to a Nomade Fest.

~~*~*

Wolfrik might have known the König's Geist, but not even that had prepared him for the duel that the König and Drache Krieger shared. It wasn't just their obvious skill that made the duel an amazing spectacle, but their obvious enjoyment, as well. Wolfrik thought that their laughter, when they'd had breath for it, had been heard even at the edges of the crowd.

When they joined Wolfrik and the others, they were both grinning and unarmed, their hands clasped tight. Wolfrik knew they would have left their blades by the platform—there was no chance of them being stolen and no point to carrying them around during the Fest.

Everyone insisted on food first—Wolfrik was sure most Nomaden did—and they made their way to one of the cooking fires that were distributed around the Oase. To everyone's amusement, Ferez tried ein bisschen of everything, even a couple of fire-cracked insects, which Wolfrik hadn't expected from someone unused to their culture.

With their appetites settled for the moment, they returned to the central area to continue watching the spars and other displays that the various stages offered. When Ferez asked again about the reason for the Fest's name, Zuk answered with a chuckle.

"Patience, Frenz. That doesn't come until sunset."

The words didn't settle any of the König's confusion, but he didn't ask again.

Less than an hour into the festivities, they were joined by Zuk's Freund, Raymond, who greeted them all gruffly before leaning in and whispering something to Zuk. Almost immediately, Zuk shoved the other Mann away and shook his head.

"Who do you think I am, Raymond?" He jerked his head towards the rest of them and added, "Ask her yourself."

Raymond's face burned red as he turned to Ulla. Wolfrik raised his brows. The few times he had seen the two interact, they hadn't seemed to get along, so he couldn't imagine what the Mann wanted to ask his Freund's Schwester.

There was a Minute of silence as everyone waited for Raymond to speak, but the Mann suddenly seemed rather unwilling to open his mouth. Finally, Ulla huffed and grabbed Raymond by the arm.

"Dummkopf," she muttered before dragging him away from their group.

Zuk started laughing as soon as the two disappeared, and even the Drache Krieger chuckled some. Wolfrik eyed them curiously, uncertain he would be welcomed in asking about what had just happened. Ferez apparently didn't have any such misgivings.

"Wha' was that about?" the König asked, his wide grin milder than it had been.

The Drache Krieger simply settled with a smile as Zuk answered the question.

"Raymond was asking for my permission to court Ulla, which is ridiculous because you just don't tell Kanten Frauen what to do." He shook his head. "Especially when they're Geistmagier."

Wolfrik frowned. "I didn't think they got along that well."

The Drache Krieger chuckled. "Oh, they get along well enough. They've just danced around each other for a while, is all."

The next moment, he frowned towards the large open space where Wolfrik knew Dame Flammezunge still lounged.

"Well," Zuk added, turning towards Käfe and offering his hand, "since this is a Nacht for pairing off, would you do me the honor of accompanying me around the Clans to admire the decorations, Fräulein Käfe?"

Wolfrik stifled the chuckle that wanted to make itself known. He'd spoken to Zuk not long after their arrival in Friedlichoase, and the Kanten

Tieremagier had appeared both surprised and curious at Wolfrik's request. He'd agreed to at least get to know Käfe better, but this was the first time Wolfrik had seen the Mann request his Schwester's presence alone.

Käfe dropped her chin as her cheeks tinted, but Wolfrik didn't miss the small smile that played on her lips. She twittered softly, something she did when she was nervous.

To their surprise, Zuk made a chittering sound in response, and Käfe's head shot up, her eyes wide and her mouth slightly ajar as she met his gaze.

When she finally gained control of herself, she swallowed and darted a glance to Wolfrik. He smiled and nodded, waving for her to accept the Tieremagier's invitation. He knew it was what she wanted, and he wasn't about to interfere.

Käfe turned back to Zuk, that small smile once again playing at her lips. She took his hand and practically whistled her response.

Wolfrik did chuckle then as Zuk led her away. *"Viel Glück, Schwester,"* he murmured against her Geist, and happiness flooded through her.

Wolfrik accompanied the Drache Krieger and the König for a while longer, his thoughts distant. He was glad that Käfe had found someone among the Vereinte Clans so easily, but he doubted he'd find anyone for himself. To most of these people, he was just a Skorpion, a Mann whose trustworthiness was still uncertain.

As the sun began to set, Wolfrik directed his two companions towards the stage closest to Dame Flammezunge, which hadn't been used yet. Zuk had told him that was where they held the Geisterstücke, which would answer the König's questions about the reason behind the name 'Adlerfest'.

As soon as they were settled near the stage, Wolfrik excused himself. He wasn't keen to watch the Geisterstücke himself as he knew the stories well. Every Nomaden grew up learning about the Immortals, including the four Guardians of the Cycle of Incarnation: Adler, the Royal Eagle; Wolf, the Hungry Wolf; Schlange, the Great Serpent; and Phönix, the Splendid Phoenix.

Adlerfest recognized Adler's role in the Cycle of Incarnation. It celebrated his great flights between Carith's Realm or the Mortal Realm and the Cycle of Incarnation as he transported newly created, or newly dead, Seelen.

And it was the same for every Fest. Wölfefest in Winter celebrated Wolf's eternal hunger for the memories of the newly dead. Schlangenfest in Spring celebrated Schlange's fierce protection of the Seelen within the Cycle. Phönixfest in Summer celebrated the Seelen's rebirth as Phönix placed Seelen from the Cycle in fertile wombs.

Wolfrik was jarred from his contemplations as he heard someone call his name. Turning, he found Wüstenwolf Seelenesser, Häuptling of the Wolf Clan, approaching him, a Fräulein striding along beside him.

Smiling, Wolfrik offered his hand in greeting.

"Wüstenwolf, it is gut to see you again."

"Ja, and you," the Häuptling answered, clasping his hand. "I had hoped to speak to you sooner, but we haven't had much chance since the inter-Clan meeting."

Wolfrik resisted the urge to roll his eyes. That wasn't completely true since they had spoken several times since Wolfrik joined the Vereinte Clans' Geisternetz. However, he understood that the words might be more for Wüstenwolf's companion than Wolfrik, so he nodded.

"What did you wish to speak about?"

Wüstenwolf offered a sly smile, more than worthy of the name Wolf, and indicated the Fräulein.

"I wished to introduce you to mein Schwester, Eule Seelenesser."

Wolfrik raised his brows. "You are a Tieremagier?" Eulen, for which the Fräulein had been named, were Vögel of the Nacht, fierce predators, and often considered wise.

The Fräulein nodded and smiled softly. Her silence and soft expression might have reminded Wolfrik of his own Schwester, but the way she held herself was more reminiscent of Zuk's Schwester, Ulla.

"Eule was curious about your Pläne for your Clan once you become Häuptling."

Wolfrik glanced at the other Geistmagier in surprise, and Wüstenwolf shrugged.

"I thought it might be easier for you to tell her yourself. Besides," he added with a grin, "Eule was a great help for me when I first became Häuptling. I thought you might enjoy some proven assistance."

He clapped Wolfrik on the shoulder then and bid the two of them a "Gute Nacht".

After watching the other Geistmagier walk away, Wolfrik shook his head and turned back to Eule. She was a very pretty Fräulein, and he was sharply reminded that the Feste represented fertility, among other things.

He quickly pushed the thought aside. He doubted she was interested in more than discussing his Pläne for his Clan.

"Did you have anything in particular that you wished to discuss, or did you just wish to hear what I was considering for my Clan at the moment?"

Eule's smile sharpened, and she stepped closer. To Wolfrik's surprise, he realized that she was nearly the same height as he was, and the edges of her Kopfabdeckung just brushed the edges of his.

"Well," she said, her voice dark and low, "there is that."

Her eyes shifted down then back to his face, and Wolfrik felt his breath catch. Her eyes had sharpened, as well, giving her the look of the Vogel for which she was named or even the Wolf that her Clan represented.

"But there are other things we could...discuss, as well."

Wolfrik hesitated. He was not used to bold Frauen. Such an attitude would not have been tolerated by his Häuptling and the Männer who supported him. Since he'd joined the Vereinte Clans, he'd met Frauen who were rather strong-willed, like Ulla and Isana, but he hadn't actually believed that any of them would be interested in a Skorpion.

When Wolfrik didn't answer, amusement softened the angle of Eule's smile.

"If you're not comfortable with anything else, we could just stick to your Pläne. I helped my Bruder learn to sharpen his Zähne and Klauen," she added, referring to the main weapons of a Wolf. "I'm sure I can help you sharpen your Stachel and strengthen your Scheren, as well."

She laid a firm hand against his elbow then and stroked her thumb once along the inside of his arm. He jerked and swallowed.

"I...think I would appreciate that," he finally managed to say.

The sharpness returned to her smile, and Wolfrik felt his own lips curving in response. His Häuptling might have disparaged him for falling to the Klauen of such a bold Frau, but Wolfrik could imagine the truth of her words.

Perhaps I can match her predator for predator instead of falling as her prey.

Chapter 42

The Geisterstücke, as Wolfrik had called them, ended just as the last traces of light disappeared from the sky. Ferez turned to James to ask what they should do next, when a loud explosion behind them made him jump.

Another explosion sounded above them, and Ferez spun around, dropped into a crouch, and looked up, wondering if they were being attacked.

The thought was abandoned at the sight that met him. Ferez straightened and stared in amazement at the brilliant red splashed across the sky.

He was accustomed to watching the sky fires during the Mid-Season Festivals in Caypan, so he had thought he'd known how beautiful they could be. However, as more explosions sounded and more colors painted the sky, he thought they looked brighter and more vibrant than any he had ever seen.

The yellows shone more like the sun, the reds as deep as the richest rubies, and the greens looked so alive that the sky seemed to become an entire living world of its own. Whether it was because they were in the desert, where there was little other light, or because the nomads had a skill with the sky fires that surpassed even that of the Royal Fire Masters, Ferez was stunned.

"Is it always like this?" he asked James in awe.

The boy chuckled. "Why do you think I'm so insistent on staying with the Nomaden during Mitte Jahreszeit?"

He tilted his head back as Flame suddenly took wing, steadily burning sky fires hanging off her body and dangling from her tail, talons, and wingtips.

"Nomaden hold the best Feste," James whispered, "and Flame always enjoys taking part when she can."

Ferez watched as the dragon flew among the sky fires the nomads sent up. She seemed to dance in the fires, reveling in the Festival as much as any of the humans. The sky fires that hung from her body reflected off her red and purple scales, outlining her in the dark night.

When one of the more temporary sky fires exploded against her side, Ferez leaned closer to James and whispered, "Aren't the sky fires dangerous at such a close range?"

James laughed. Ferez snapped his gaze down to the boy's, and his breath caught at how his face shone. A light that seemed to rival the sky fires above them danced in his purple eyes, and Ferez was suddenly struck by just how beautiful he was.

The king blinked and pulled back then, both physically and mentally. He'd never looked at another man that way before.

Then again, he reckoned, as the protest seemed to unveil deeper thoughts, *I've never seriously considered anyone else before, have I?*

"Flame Tongue is a Feuerdrache, a fire dragon," James answered, oblivious to Ferez's thoughts. "She was literally born to bathe in fire. At least," he added with a softer chuckle, "that's what Flame tells me."

Ferez nodded and looked back up at the sky. He hoped there was little enough light that the blush he could now feel heating his cheeks wouldn't be noticed. He tried to convince himself that it was the beauty of the lights and the joyous atmosphere of the Festival that formed such thoughts in his head.

But memories of James' grace in battle and his kindness, patience, and fairness in his dealings with different peoples rose in his mind, and Ferez knew that he had noticed the boy's beauty. He just hadn't let himself acknowledge it before now.

But my throne and duty demand I court a woman, he thought, his lips pursing in his anxiety. *Am I willing to abandon both because I find a man beautiful?*

A sudden strain of drifting notes cut through Ferez's increasingly disturbing thoughts. Turning his gaze towards the sound, he sought the source.

He briefly noted the soft whistle of bone flutes and the deep vibration of hide drums, but it was in recognition of the bright strumming of the strings of the Saitens that his heart leapt and his fingers twitched.

Abandoning his previous distress, Ferez crowed joyously and grabbed James' hand, pulling him towards the sounds.

~~*~*

Gemi laughed as Ferez began pulling her towards the open area the Musiker occupied, adjacent to where the Tiere were kept. The König was acting like a Kind at his first Fest.

He had been so excited during the Boxkämpfe, and he seemed to have utterly enjoyed tasting the different foods the Nomaden had to offer. Even the Himmelfeuer, the sky fires, which Gemi knew he had seen before, had left him gaping in awe.

Now, he led her through the crowds, his excitement showing through in his grin and the way he clutched at her hand. She felt a pang in her heart that this side of him had to be buried beneath the kingly façade. Everyone deserved a Nacht like this, when they could simply enjoy themselves without worrying about consequences, especially Ferez.

"*And you,*" Flame added softly, but Gemi pushed the thought aside. *This is not a Nacht for introspection.*

She was startled from her thoughts when one of the Musiker, with whom Ferez had bent to speak, suddenly grinned and handed him his instrument. Gemi watched, open-mouthed, as the König seated himself on the ground, cross-legged, and cradled the instrument, a Saiten, against his chest.

He ran one hand lovingly over the edge of the Saiten's wooden belly and the other over the long neck. Then, he curled his fingers in against the Spinnenseide strings and plucked some chords, drawing an appreciative murmur from the Saiten's owner.

"Do you know any Fest songs?" the Musiker asked.

Ferez grinned up at the Mann then and began to play in earnest. The Musiker gave a loud whoop as the tune was easily recognizable as one of the more traditional Fest dance songs. The other Musiker quickly took up the song as well, adding the beats and tunes of their own instruments to Ferez's song.

As many of the Nomaden around her began to dance to the Musik filling the air, Gemi found she could only stare at her Freund, stunned. Never once, in all the time they'd traveled together, had she considered that the König might play an instrument. It just hadn't crossed her Geist.

For that matter, it didn't really make sense except for the passion that Gemi could see shining in Ferez's eyes. The nobles didn't encourage their Söhne to take up Musik. To them, it was a skill for their Töchter and Lebenfrauen. Gemi knew that she herself would have been encouraged to take up Musik in some form if her 'lady training' had ever actually begun.

"*Stop thinking so hard,*" Shadow nickered sharply, drawing Gemi's attention away from Ferez. She glanced out to the adjacent area outside the Ring of water, where only a large herd of Pferde now milled. "*You're ruining the mood for the rest of us.*" He nudged Last Chance and nickered calmingly.

Gemi grinned at the sight of the Pferde gathering. Turning back to the Musiker as the first song wound down, she laid a hand on Ferez's shoulder. When he looked up at her, his body relaxed and his smile still firmly in place, she whispered, "I don't suppose you know the *Pferdetanz?*"

Ferez's smile grew to a grin. "Aye, I know the *Pferdetanz*: the Horse Dance." And he launched himself into the song, the other Musiker quickly joining him.

Gemi knew, as she had learned from the first time she'd heard it, that the *Pferdetanz* was not a song meant for dancing. Not human dancing, at any rate. According to Shadow, the song actually had the power to make a Pferd move. Some even said that the song had been created by Tieremagier.

Now, as Gemi wondered at the König's skill, a sharp whinny filled the air. Turning back to the Pferde, Gemi watched, awed as she always was, as the largest stallion, a chestnut beauty that stood at 18 hands at the withers, dropped back down to all fours.

Then, as the Musik filled the Nomaden with a sense of the wild, the entire herd began to move.

~~*~*

458

When Ferez had first learned the *Pferdetanz*, he had believed the name came from the wildness of the music. Now, as he drove his fingers into the silk strings, he found himself learning the truth of the song, and it left him breathless.

He'd been so startled by that first whinny, as the large stallion raised himself up on his hind legs and pawed at the air, that he'd nearly stopped playing. The shouts of the nomads and the screams of the horses were all that drove his fingers through his shock.

His fingers moved over the strings automatically as he played a song he'd learned as a boy—at his own insistence. His mind, on the other hand, was completely focused on the horses flowing together, their movements distinct to each horse, but the overall effect striking.

The horses moved together: running, kicking up their heels, rising up on their hind legs, bowing, leaping, and some moves that Ferez thought must have been trained into them. The sounds that rose up from the herd—nickers, whinnies, outright screams of excitement—filled the air and mingled with the music, complementing it in a way that made Ferez marvel.

About a minute into the song, Ferez finally spotted Last Chance and Shadow. His mare seemed to be following Shadow, her movements only slightly off-beat from the stallion's.

The king smiled sadly as he watched her dance. He knew this was as new to her as it was to him. Although she mimicked the black stallion's movements, Ferez could tell by the arch of her neck that she wasn't as relaxed as he might wish she would be.

~~*~*

Shadow could still remember his first Mid-Season Festival with the nomads, when he had unsuspectingly succumbed to the magic of the *Pferdetanz*. He'd been so upset by the loss of control that he'd run off into the desert the moment the music ended. Flame and Gemi had flown after him to comfort him, effectively ruining the Festival for all three of them.

It had been Gemi who helped him recognize the pleasure he'd felt beneath the panic at losing control. He'd eventually found himself looking forward to the next Mid-Season and its *Pferdetanz*, to which he gave himself up completely.

Ever since, he always looked forward to giving himself up to the wildness of the *Tanz*, a feeling that was unavailable in the day-to-day life of a domesticated horse.

When he and Last Chance began their friendship anew on their way from Schönestadt, Shadow had begun to anticipate introducing the mare to the magic of the *Pferdetanz*. As the herd gathered for the *Tanz*, he tried to explain that the *Tanz* was a dance that encouraged the horses to let themselves go to the wild nature of their ancestors. When Last Chance hadn't relax, Shadow had nickered soothingly.

Now, even a minute into the *Tanz*, Shadow could tell Last Chance wasn't letting herself go. He could sense her edginess radiating from her in waves. That edginess increased the wildness of the other horses, which only seemed to increase her panic.

Giving a mental sigh that pricked his bondmates' attention, Shadow suddenly stopped, directing the wildness of the music into the perfect stillness of his body.

It took Last Chance a bare moment to follow his lead, though, instead of stopping beside him, the mare surprised him by executing a perfect about turn maneuver. For a couple beats, they simply stared at each other. Once he was sure she wouldn't move either, he dropped into a half-bow, so he could still watch her as he spoke.

"You're not relaxing," he snorted.

He didn't mean to make it sound like an accusation, but he was frustrated that she wasn't simply letting the music take over.

"It's Animal Magic!" she whinnied sharply, as though that should have been enough of an explanation.

Shadow tilted his head, his ears flicking forward in curiosity. *"Aye, and?"*

Last Chance snorted and pawed at the ground nervously. *"I was trained to resist Animal Magic."*

Shadow suddenly felt like an idiot. He knew that; quite distinctly remembered Ferez sharing that information along with Last Chance's history. He should have realized how that would affect the mare in this.

It also saddened him, that he wouldn't be able to see her enjoy the wildness of the *Tanz*. And not for his own sake, as might have been the case for any other mare. He may be a flirt, but he had never felt the respect for other mares that he felt for Last Chance.

A thought occurred to Shadow then and he shifted his ears forward. *"Just because you can resist, doesn't mean you have to, does it?"*

The way Last Chance shifted her weight from one side to the other was answer enough.

Dropping into a full bow—the music demanded Shadow move in some way, and he wasn't sure he should look at the mare as he said this next part—he nickered gently.

"This isn't Animal Magic that's trying to harm you or use you to harm others. How can it, when your own master is leading the song?"

Shadow could practically feel Last Chance's surprise as she no doubt turned her gaze towards the musicians.

"The only thing standing between you and enjoying the wildness of the Tanz *is your pride. Believe me; I know how hard it can be to get over that."*

He briefly considered the numerous instances he had had to face his own pride then pushed the memories away. Gemi was right, tonight was not a night for introspection, but for enjoyment.

"Just relax for tonight. Drop your training. You can always regain it tomorrow."

Shadow let silence fall between them then. Not that there was actual silence, with the music of the *Tanz* filling the air and the hoof beats and the screams of the herd flowing around them. Shadow gave a single thought to what they must look like, two still horses, one bowing, one standing, surrounded by the constant flow of the herd as their bodies responded to the pure wildness of the *Pferdetanz*.

Just as Shadow knew he would have to move—the instincts inspired by the *Tanz* were screaming that the courtship of this one mare was not as important as the wildness of the dance—he felt a sharp nip at his ear. He jerked up to all fours in shock, his eyes wide as he stared at Last Chance.

Last Chance, whose muscles had stopped twitching and who now eyed him with amusement.

"I'll give myself over to the Tanz," she nickered, *"as long as we're agreed that we're both equals in this relationship; that neither of us will submit to the other."*

Shadow would have flushed if he had been human. Aye, the bow had been a sign of submission, that he would follow her decision, no matter what it was. But Shadow knew, and it seemed Last Chance might, as well, that there was a meaning behind the bow that had nothing to do with Shadow attempting to persuade the mare to dance with him. It had a more primal meaning, one that Shadow didn't wish to contemplate right now.

"Agreed," he answered, hoping the gray mare would leave it at that.

And she did. As though his response had been her cue, Last Chance raised herself onto her hind legs and released a scream of pleasure so pure Shadow found himself responding in kind.

As both horses landed on all fours once more, they turned as one and began to dance with the rest of the herd, lending themselves to a dance as old as horsekind. But even as they danced with the herd, both knew that they might as well have been dancing alone, just the two of them.

\~*\~*\~*

Ferez handed the Saiten back to its owner after several more songs. Even then, he continued to contemplate the scene he'd watched play out between Last Chance and Shadow. He didn't know what Shadow had done, but Ferez had never seen his mare as relaxed as she was afterwards. He promised himself that he would thank the stallion later.

As the Saiten player thumbed a few chords, Ferez took the hand that James offered and climbed to his feet. When he found himself nearly nose-to-nose with the boy, his breath caught, and his earlier thoughts returned with renewed force.

"That was amazing," James breathed, his eyes bright and his grin wide. "How long have you been playing?"

Ferez blinked and took a step back to gain some distance and clear his head. "Since I was seven. I asked a travelling musician to show me how to play."

James chuckled and shook his head. "Did your Vater know you were taking up the Saiten?" His grin had turned playful.

Ferez stared at James in wonder. He didn't get to see this side of James very often, not with how much time they seemed to spend working on political issues and training with weapons. He wondered briefly if James was like Last Chance: that he had to force himself to relax.

"Actually," Ferez said, returning to James' question with a smile. "My father was shocked to learn that afternoon when he found me learning the chords."

He joined James in chuckling. Leaning forward and lowering his voice, he added, "But he was the one who offered to have a Saiten made for me and to hire a Zhulanese musician to teach me when he found out how much I wanted to play."

As soon as he finished speaking, Ferez wondered if James would understand the significance of his father's support. After all, Ferez didn't think that most people realized how much the noble class disapproved of boys learning music when they could be learning something of more importance.

The soft smile James offered and the gentle look in his eyes told Ferez he understood exactly how much the old king's acceptance had meant to him.

More than his beauty, it was that understanding that had the king leaning closer to the purple-eyed young man. Despite his earlier conflict, Ferez didn't hesitate to lightly grip his shoulder in one hand and lay his lips gently against James'.

~~*~*

Gemi stilled when Ferez kissed her. It wasn't so much from surprise—*"I should hope not,"* Flame rumbled; *"you two have been dancing around each other for most of the season,"*—as much as from wariness.

"Relax," Shadow nickered calmly. *"Enjoy yourself."*

"Easy for you to say," Gemi replied as she slowly pulled back from the kiss. *"You're not hiding your true identity from a potential lover."*

"Not that he could," Flame added dryly.

Blithely ignoring Flame, Shadow nickered, *"Well, it's not like you'll be doing much more than kissing tonight. Let's face it; you two are not the types to begin mating on the first night."*

Gemi gave a short bark of laughter. Immediately, she threw a hand over her mouth, and her eyes shot up to Ferez's.

"Es tut mir leid," she whispered quickly as she attempted to shove her bondmates' presences away. "Unrelated comment from Shadow." She reached for Ferez's hand and gripped it.

"*Not entirely,*" Shadow muttered before Gemi managed to shove her awareness of her Freunde to the back of her Geist. It settled there as a quiet buzz.

Gemi watched, relieved, as Ferez, who had stiffened when she laughed, began to relax again. She noted, though, that, despite the red decorating his cheek bones, there was a determined set to his jaw, as if he had decided how he felt and he wasn't changing his Geist no matter how she reacted.

Gut, she thought, and, leaning forwards, she proceeded to kiss him right back.

She was able to enjoy the kiss for all of two seconds—long enough for Ferez's grip on her to tighten approvingly—before whistling and clapping had her pulling back and looking around her in surprise.

Big grins decorated the faces of the surrounding Nomaden. Even the Musiker, who hadn't played anything since Ferez gave up the Saiten, were clapping and otherwise showing their approval.

Gemi felt her face burn. She had lived through a lot in the seven Jahre since her parents' Tode, but this had to be one of the most embarrassing. Glancing at Ferez, she noticed that, while his face was also flushed, his mouth still curved in a small smile, and his eyes were focused solely on her.

That warmed her and brought her own smile back.

"Come on; give it a rest," a voice shouted.

Pulling her gaze from Ferez, Gemi was surprised to see Zuk and Käfe making their way towards them.

"Leave them be, you Köter!" Zuk shouted at the crowd as he reached Gemi. Laughter answered his insult. Turning to the Musiker, Zuk added, "This is a Fest, isn't it? Musik!"

As the Musiker picked up their instruments once more and struck up a lively dance tune, the laughter subsided, and the dancing began again. Once the other Nomaden were sufficiently distracted, Zuk turned back to Gemi and slapped her on the back.

"That should get you some Frieden for now. But, you know," he added with a smirk, "everyone's going to want to congratulate you on your first kiss."

Gemi ducked her head as the fire in her cheeks reignited. When Zuk laughed, she reached out and shoved him. If he was going to tease her, she saw no reason not to be childish, too.

"Excuse me for being too busy to care," she growled.

Zuk's laughter subsided, and his grin softened. "You know I'm just teasing, Bruder." He squeezed Gemi's shoulder. "Everyone's just happy you've finally found someone you find interesting enough to kiss.

"And Frenz?" he added, turning to the König.

Ferez tore his gaze from Gemi. "Aye?"

Zuk leaned forwards menacingly. "If you hurt my little Bruder...." He let the threat hang in the air between them.

Ferez nodded solemnly. "I wouldn' dream of it."

Zuk and Ferez continued to stare at each other, until Zuk finally nodded, satisfied. Grinning once more, he clapped them both on the shoulders. "Enjoy the rest of the Fest, you two."

Gemi grimaced as she watched her Bruder grip Käfe's hand and walk away. "Es tut mir leid about that," she said to Ferez. "Unfortunately, you'll probably be getting a lot of…that…."

She trailed off as Ferez gripped her arm, and she looked up to see him staring at her, his eyes still solemn.

"I mean it, James," he murmured, his voice just loud enough for her to hear over the Musik. "I won' hurt you. I promise."

Gemi swallowed as she stared into his silver and blue eyes. Thoughts of the secret she still kept from him surfaced in her Geist.

I have to tell him.

"*Not tonight,*" Flame breathed against her Geist, startling Gemi. "*Just enjoy tonight. You can worry about the secret tomorrow.*"

"*You want me to put it off?*" Flame had been pestering her to tell Ferez the truth almost since she first accepted him as a companion.

The Drache sighed. "*You deserve the chance to enjoy this night without worrying about consequences.*"

Gemi relaxed and smiled sofly. Flame was right. She could worry about it tomorrow. She wanted to enjoy this Nacht with Ferez. She wanted to just be herself with him before the pressures and expectations that the truth would bring clouded their relationship.

"I know," Gemi answered Ferez's proclamation, smiling. "Danke."

Turning to glance at the dancing Nomaden, Gemi added jovially, "Now, I've been waiting to dance since you started playing." She grinned at Ferez and held out a hand. "Care to join me?"

Ferez's smile returned full force, and he grasped her hand. "Of course."

Together, they joined the other Nomaden in dance.

The remainder of the evening sped by in a blur for Gemi. There was dancing and laughter, food and conversation. At one point, Ulla and Raymond found them and congratulated them on the new dimension of their relationship.

While Raymond shook Ferez's hand and pounded him on the shoulder, Ulla leaned into Gemi and whispered, "You couldn't have found a better one, Gemi. I'm so proud of you."

Gemi's grin widened at her Schwester's words, which Gemi would have thought impossible. She knew she was grinning like a dummkopf the entire evening, but she couldn't bring herself to care. Somehow, being with Ferez made the whole Fest, something she had always found enjoyable, more wonderful.

Once Gemi and Ferez decided they'd had enough dancing, Gemi led Ferez further out into the desert, away from the Oase. She had not had a reason to leave the Lager during the Fest since her first Jahreszeit with the

Nomaden, though she knew many took advantage of the privacy the desert provided. She felt an extra thrill run through her, among all the other emotions she felt, that, for once, she was doing something others her age normally would.

As they settled on the ground, nothing but their Kopfabdeckungen and each other to keep them warm in the chill desert Nacht, they spoke softly and watched Flame's continued flight, trading kisses occasionally. As Gemi drifted into sleep, curled happily against Ferez, she realized that, for the first time in Jahre, she was truly happy.

For how long? she wondered idly as sleep claimed her.

~~*~*

Adalwolf watched the bright colors of the Himmelfeuer light up the sky, a sneer pulling at his lips. Ja, the Himmelfeuer were beautiful, but the Vereinte Clans didn't seem to care that they also gave away their position to any who cared to look.

"Yet I sense you wish you could celebrate Adlerfest with such carelessness," taunted the voice that had guided him these past few Siebentage.

Adalwolf sneered. *"To drop one's guard so completely is more than dumm. It's insane."*

The voice chuckled darkly. *"Then there is a great deal of insanity at that Oase."*

"Oi, Schlange!"

The Geistmagier growled as a hand landed on his arm. He turned and shook it off, glaring at the Skorpion who had dared to touch him.

"What?"

The Skorpion sneered. "You were muttering to yourself, Schlange. I thought you Geistmagier were supposed to keep everything in your head."

"Stein," muttered the other Skorpion, who didn't move from the edge of the tiny spring by which they'd stopped. "Stop baiting him."

Stein frowned at his fellow Skorpion, and Adalwolf felt his lip twitch. He turned back towards Friedlichoase so neither Skorpion could see the smirk that wanted to form. He was not freundlich with Skorpion as a principle, but he was always amused when his Feinde were chastised by their fellows.

Not long, he thought, eyeing the eastern sky. Soon, the sky would begin to lighten, and the Drache, whom he could see outlined against the sky with the Himmelfeuer hanging from her body, would return to the Lager and find her rest.

Then, we can destroy Caffers.

"I thought you might enjoy this task," the voice returned.

Adalwolf only nodded. The Geist had mentioned the Plan when he was still in Schönestadt, but he hadn't actually detailed it until two Tage ago. Adalwolf knew the only reason that had been enough time to put the Plan in motion was because both Häuptlinge had agreed that it was a very gut idea. Thankfully, Häuptling Giftschwanz still refused to risk his heirs, so Adalwolf hadn't had to argue to be in charge of the task.

The three Nomaden silently watched as the sky turned predawn gray and continued to lighten, the only sounds surrounding them the soft nickers of their Pferde. As predicted, the Drache soon returned to the ground, but they continued to wait until the sun had pulled itself fully over the Tarsur Mountains in the east. By then, they were sure the Drache would be asleep, along with the rest of the Lager

Knowing they had to move quickly lest they risk being caught, the three Gift Clan Nomaden walked towards Friedlichoase, leaving their Pferde at the small spring. The two Skorpione carried a litter between them; Adalwolf led them, his eyes half-closed as he sought the Geist of the Caffers boy.

Adalwolf smirked when he found the boy. They had expected the possibility of having to move through the Lager and risk exposure that way. However, the Schicksale seemed to be on their side; the Caffers boy and his human companion had decided to leave the safety of the Lager for the supposed privacy of the desert.

The two were sleeping on the ground, the long black hair of the Caffers boy spread out underneath them. Their heads were tilted together, as though they shared secrets only they knew. Sneering in disgust at the display, he kicked the brown-haired Mann away from their prey.

"Oi!" Stein hissed, grabbing Adalwolf's arm once more. "Careful, Schlange! You could wake them."

The Geistmagier turned a glare on the Skorpion and shrugged his hand off once again. The Mann was really beginning to annoy him. Before he could spit out the insult that sat on his tongue, the second Skorpion pulled Stein back.

"Easy, Stein," he murmured, though his eyes met and held Adalwolf's. "Don't you know how easily Geistmagier can suppress your Geist?"

Stein stiffened then, and Adalwolf allowed his glare to ease into a smirk as he turned his attention to the second Skorpion. He, at least, spoke sense, more than most Skopione with whom Adalwolf was acquainted.

It's a shame, really, he thought, as he dropped his gaze down to the Mann's Statusgürtel. *He would make a good Schlange, and his Tieremagie would be useful, as well.*

"So how are we doing this, Stach?"

Adalwolf gave a mental snort as Stein turned fully to the Tieremagier, apparently having decided to ignore Adalwolf.

"We," muttered Stach, indicating Stein and himself, "are doing nothing more than transporting the Ausländisch Krieger." He motioned to the black-haired boy.

A soft snort sounded behind Adalwolf. *"You Gift Clan Nomaden are amusing, aren't you?"* Adalwolf fought to keep his expression neutral despite the sudden annoyance that thrummed through him. *"Ausländisch*

Krieger, indeed. You deny him the ancient title, yet you still acknowledge him as a warrior in his own right." The dark chuckle that followed seemed to echo through the Geistmagier's bones. *"You allow him a Respekt that you do not even allow each other."*

Adalwolf turned back to his prey then, though he knew he was turning towards the taunting Geist. He couldn't prevent his mouth from opening in a silent snarl, and he was unwilling to let the Skorpione see it. Allies they might be, but he refused to show them such weakness.

Dropping into a crouch beside his prey, Adalwolf examined the Caffers boy. His face was relaxed in sleep, a smile curving his lips slightly. Despite this, the lines of his face spoke of stress and hardship.

Gut! Adalwolf thought, letting his snarl relax into a smirk. *If he has found a happiness to which he is unaccustomed, it will be that much more satisfying to bring him down from it.*

Adalwolf laid a hand on the boy's forehead. Though physical contact was unnecessary for his Magie to work, it would speed up the process and increase his hold on his prey's Geist. Diving past the first layer, which he had already claimed in order to keep the boy from waking, he found the barrier the Drache had placed around his Geist.

Under normal circumstances, this barrier would have been successful at keeping Adalwolf from his goal. Even among the Gift Clans, the defensive Geistmagie of the Drache was legendary. Even now, with the Drache's concentration weakened by her Nacht-long flight and her current deep sleep, bypassing the barrier was no small challenge.

Once past the barrier, Adalwolf was assaulted by the secrets of his prey, secrets that made him still and nearly remove himself from the Geist in disgust. Anger suddenly thrummed through his veins.

This is the Drache Krieger? This is the...creature which we all fear: a verdammt girl?

He had thought it preposterous that they considered a mere boy such a threat to their Clans' ways of Leben, but that it was a mere girl...

Adalwolf snarled silently as the bodiless Geist chuckled darkly. More determined than ever for this Plan to succeed, he worked his Magie through the Band that connected the verdammt girl to her Drache and stallion.

Once satisfied with his work on the two Tiere, he pulled back into his prey's Geist. With another silent snarl, he built up a barrier between her and her bondmates so thick, nichts would leak through and no one but he would be able to break it.

Certain that neither Pferd nor Drache would prove a threat to them, Adalwolf secured the prey's unconsciousness for the next few hours, pulled out of the prey's Geist, and nodded stiffly to the Skorpione. The two Männer moved forward and lifted their prey onto the litter.

"What about him?" Stein asked, nodding to their prey's companion. "We can't just leave him here alive."

Adalwolf frowned down at the sleeping stranger. "*Kill him!*" hissed the Geist, but Adalwolf didn't think it was worth the blood on his Scharfmond to kill the Ausländer.

"He is of little consequence," he answered the Skorpion.

"*You must kill him,*" the voice hissed again, and Adalwolf's frown deepened.

It was true that the Geist had yet to lead him wrong, but Adalwolf saw no reason to shed this Mann's blood when they had completed their task and could return to their Lager triumphantly.

"*He is dangerous,*" the Geist hissed. "*He will lead an army to hunt you down if you leave him alive.*"

An image filled Adalwolf's head then, not of an army, but of this seemingly unremarkable Mann seated upon a throne, a simple gold Krone decorated with a handful of gems resting upon his brow.

Adalwolf smiled grimly when he realized that that knowledge had been available in the...girl's Geist, but he simply hadn't made the connection.

The smile disappeared with a sharp hiss as he focused on the newly revealed König once more. A small, brown Skorpion, all the more deadly for its dull color and small size, was crawling steadily across the König's tunic towards his bare throat.

With the speed and precision of a Schlange, Adalwolf drew his right Scharfmond and struck the Skorpion, knocking it off the Mann's chest. It landed on the ground several feet away and skittered a few steps before Stein snatched it by the tail and dropped it in a bag at his hip.

"Why did you do that?" Stein asked indignantly. "You said he didn't matter."

Adalwolf glared at Stein. "I meant to leave him be," he growled. "Even if we were to kill him, I would not let you use your Skorpion. Such a Tod would lead the Vereinte Clans straight to yours. While I may not care about your Clan, my own Clan is allied to yours in this, and I will not have you creating such a risk."

Stein narrowed his eyes and opened his mouth, but Stach laid a hand on his shoulder, effectively quieting him. Adalwolf turned his glare to the Tieremagier, wondering why the Mann had let his fellow Clansmann place the Skorpion on the still sleeping König.

"Your argument makes no sense, Adalwolf," Stach murmured, his gaze steady as he met the Schlange's glare. Adalwolf frowned, unaccustomed to others returning his looks with such a calm, steady gaze. "The Vereinte Clans will suspect our Clans either way. They would still have to find our Lager in order to save the Ausländisch Krieger and exact revenge. That is something they haven't managed to do in the five Jahre since they unified."

Adalwolf growled. He knew Stach had a point. After all, if they had not felt that their Clans' location was safe, they would simply have killed their prey rather than attempt to kidnap her as they were.

Still, Adalwolf did not wish to kill the brown-haired Mann, especially now that he knew who he was. There was something he could do to the Mann that was much worse than Tod.

"This discussion is moot. We will not kill him." When Stach raised an eyebrow, Adalwolf added, "I have my own Pläne for his Geist."

The Tieremagier continued to gaze at him steadily for a moment before eventually nodding. Gripping Stein's shoulder, he turned back to their prey. "Stein and I will head back to the Pferde then," he murmured over his shoulder. "We'll wait for you there."

Adalwolf nodded and turned back to his new prey, not bothering to watch the Skorpione leave with their first. Kneeling beside the young König, he held one hand above the Mann's head and paused, listening.

The Geist remained surprisingly quiet. It hadn't left—he could still sense it—but it seemed unwilling to speak, even to taunt him as it often did.

Adalwolf shrugged and laid his hand on the König's forehead. Smiling grimly, he began to work his Magie into the König's Geist, easing past barriers that were similar to, yet nowhere near as strong as, those he'd found in his first prey's Geist.

"I am afraid you will not be returning to Caypan, Eure Majestät," he murmured as he dug deeper and deeper. "No need to worry, though. You will not remember enough to care."

To be continued in
Peace of Evon:
Lost King

Language
Glossaries

Pecalini Glossary

el/la amigo/a (*ah-MEE-ghoh/ghah*) – friend
el Animal Poder (*ah-nee-MAHL poh-DEHR*) – Power Animal
la arma (*AHR-mah*) [-s] – weapon
el barco (*BAHR-koh*) [-s] – ship
el caballero (*kah-bah-YEHR-oh*) – knight
el caballo (*kah-BYE-yoh*) – horse
¡Cállate! (*KYE-yah-tay*) – Be quiet!
el camino (*kah-MEE-noh*) – path, road
el capitán (*kah-pee-TAHN*) – captain
la casa (*KAH-sah*) – house
el cercado (*sehr-KAH-doh*) – paddock
cercano (*sehr-KAH-noh*) – close
el chico/a (*CHEE-koh/kah*) – boy/girl
La Ciudad Ocultada (*see-yoo-DAHD oh-kool-TAH-dah*) – Hidden City;
  home of the hidden ones
el/la cobarde (*koh-BAHR-day*) [-s] – coward
correcto (*kohr-RAYK-toh*) – correct
la cresta (*KRAY-stah*) – crest
el crimen (*KREE-mehn*) [crímenes (*KREE-meh-nehs*)] – crime
El Curandero Mágico (*kure-ahn-DAYR-oh MAH-hee-koh*) – Mage Healer
demasiado (*day-mah-see-AH-doh*) – too, too much, too many
el día (*DEE-ah*) – day
el/la dueño/a (*DWAYN-yoh*) – master/mistress (owner)
la duquesa (*doo-KAY-sah*) – duchess
el enemigo (*eh-neh-MEE-goh*) (-s) – enemy
la estación (*eh-stah-see-OHN*) – season
el fuego (*FWAY-goh*) – fire
El Fuego de Mauro (*FWAY-goh de MOWR-oh*) – Maurus's Fire
la gente (*HEHN-tay*) – people
el grupo (*GROO-poh*) – group
la guerra (*GHEHR-ah*) – war
el/la hijo/a (*EE-hoh/hah*) – son/daughter
la historia (*ee-STOHR-ee-ah*) – history
el hombre (*OHM-bray*) – man
la hora (*ORE-ah*) – hour
el huérfano (*WEHR-fah-noh*) – orphan
el humano (*oo-MAH-noh*) – human
la idea (*ee-DAY-ah*) – idea
la inteligencia (*een-tehl-ee-HEHN-see-ah*) – intelligence
inteligente (*een-tehl-ee-HEHN-tay*) – intelligent
interesante (*een-tehr-eh-SAHN-tay*) – interesting
el ladrón (*lah-DROHN*) [ladrones (*lah-DROH-nehs*)] – thief
loco/a (*LOH-koh/kah*) – crazy

el/la loro/a (*LOHR-oh/ah*) – large multi-colored bird that can mimic
  human languages; native to Pecali's rainforests; similar to a parrot, but
  Fayralese has no name for the bird other than loro/a
la luz (*looz*) – light
la madre (*MAH-dray*) – mother
el Mago Animal (*MAH-goh ah-nee-MAHL*) – Animal Mage
el Mago Botánico (*MAH-goh boh-TAH-nee-koh*) – Plant Mage
el Mago Mental (*MAH-goh mehn-TAHL*) – Mindspeaker
Majestad (*mah-hay-STAHD*) – Your Majesty; *Su Majestad* – His Majesty
maldito (*mahl-dee-toh*) – damn; evil
más (*moss*) – more
Mauro (*MOWR-oh*) – Maurus
la mente (*mehn-tay*) – mind
la montaña (*n*) (*mohn-TAHN-yah*) – mountain
montañés (*adj*) (*mohn-tahn-YEHS*) – mountain
muy (*mwee*) – very
nada (*NAH-dah*) – nothing
nadie (*NAH-dee-ay*) – no one; *Nadie* – James Caffers' title in Tarsur
no (*noh*) – nay
la noche (*NOH-chay*) – night; por la noche – at night
el/la nómada (*NOH-mah-dah*) [-s] – nomad
el nombre (*NOHM-bray*) [-s] – name
nuestro/a (*NWEHS-troh/trah*) – our
los Ocultados (*oh-kool-TAH-dohs*) – Hidden Ones; preferred name of the
  unified thieves in Tarsur
ocupado (*oh-koo-PAH-doh*) – busy
otro (*OH-troh*) – other
la pelea (*peh-LAY-ah*) – fight
la persona (*pehr-SOH-nah*) – person
el pirata (*peer-AH-tah*) [-s] – pirate
por favor (*pohr fah-VOHR*) – please
el problema (*proh-BLAY-mah*) [-s] – trouble, problem
la provincia (*proh-VEEN-see-ah*) – province
el pueblo (*PWAY-bloh*) – village
el puñal (*poon-YAHL*) [-es] – throwing knife
querido/a (*kay-REE-doh/dah*) – dear
el rebaño (*ray-BAHN-yoh*) – flock (of sheep); Pastora Ovillana uses the
  term to refer to the children she's taken in
el/la rebelde (*reh-BEHL-day*) [-s] – rebel
el rey (*RAY-ee*) – king
ridículo (*ree-DEE-kew-loh*) – ridiculous
risueño/a (*ree-SWAYN-yoh/yah*) – smiling
salvaje (*sahl-VAH-hay*) – wild; savage
la semana (*say-MAH-nah*) – sevenday
Señor (*sehn-YOHR*) – mister
Señora (*sehn-YOHR-ah*) – madam

sí (*see*) – yes
sin (*seen*) – without
la situación (*see-too-ah-see-OHN*) – situation
el sol (*sohl*) – sun
el soldado (*sohl-DAH-doh*) [-s] – soldier
surcando/a (*sir-KAHN-doh/dah*) – sailing
tarde (*TAHR-day*) – late
tarsuro (*tahr-SIR-oh*) – Tarsurian
todo (*TOH-doh*) – all
tonto (*TOHN-toh*) – stupid, foolish
único (*OO-nee-koh*) – only
El Valle Ocultado (*VYE-yay oh-kool-TAH-doh*) – Hidden Valley
la verdad (*vehr-DAHD*) – truth
¡Ven! (*vehn*) – Come!
la vida (*VEE-dah*) – life
El/La Vidente (*vee-DEHN-tay*) – Seer
la vista (*VEE-stah*) – sight; vision
la voz (*vohz*) – voice

Zhulanese Glossary

aber (*ah-behr*) – but

Abschaum (*ahb-showm*) – scum

Adlerfest (*ahd-lehr-fehst*) – Mid-Autumn Festival; literally, "Eagle Festival"; represents the Royal Eagle, first guardian of the Cycle of Incarnation

Adlige (*ahd-lee-ghuh*) – noblewoman, lady; old term; generally used more for nomad ruling families, while Mylady is used for nobles recognized by the Evonese monarchy

Adliger (*ahd-lee-ghehr*) – nobleman, lord; old term; generally used more for nomad ruling families, while Mylord is used for nobles recognized by the Evonese monarchy

Altar (*all-tar*) [Altäre (*all-tair-uh*)] – altar

Angenehm! (*ahn-gheh-nem*) – old, formal greeting used more among nomads than river-dwellers

Angst (*ahngst*) – fear; the demigod, Fear

Arzt (*ahrzt*) [-e (*ahrz-tuh*)] – non-magical healer

Ärztin (*airz-teen*) [-nen (*airz-teen-ehn*)] – female non-magical healer

Arztmagie (*arzt-mah-ghee*) – Healing Magic

Arztmagier (*arzt-mah-gheer*) [-] – Mage Healer

Aspekt (*ah-spect*) [-e (*ah-spec-tuh*)] – aspect

Ausländer (*ouse-land-uh*) [-] – foreigner

Ausländisch Krieger (*ouse-land-ish kree-ghehr*) – Foreign Warrior; one of the names the Poison Clans use for James Caffers

Band (*bahnd*) [-e (*bahn-duh*)] – bond

bitte (*biht-uh*) – please

boxen (*v*) (*bohk-sin*) – to box

Boxen (*n*) (*bohk-sin*) – sport of boxing

Boxer (*bohk-sehr*) [-] – boxer

Boxkampf (*bohks-kahmpf*) [-kämpfe (*bohks-kaym-fuh*)] – boxing match

Bruder (*broo-dehr*) [Brüder (*brew-dehr*)] – brother

Bürger (*bewr-ghehr*) [-] – citizen

Caypanbürger (*kay-pahn-bewr-ghehr*) [-] – citizen of Caypan

Chaos (*kay-ohs*) – chaos

Clan (*klahn*) [-s (*klahns*)] – clan

Clansmann (*klahns-mahn*) [-männer (*klahns-may-nehr*)] – clansman

Dame (*dah-muh*) [-n (*dah-min*)] – madam

Dank (*dahnk*) – thanks

dankbar (*dahnk-bahr*) – thankful

danke (*dahn-kuh*) – thank you

Dankpflicht (*dahnk-flickt*) – formal thanks; obligation born of gratitude; held in high regard by the nomads

Dieb (*deeb*) [-e (*dee-buh*)] – thief

Drache (*drah-kuh*) [-n (*drah-kin*)] – dragon

Drache Krieger (*drah-kuh kree-ghehr*) – James Caffers' title in Zhulan;
  literally means "dragon warrior"; title originally belonged to first
  Erstehäuptling of the Clans
Dracheband (*drah-kuh-bahnd*) [-e (*drah-kuh-bahn-duh*)] – dragonbond
dumm (*doom*) – stupid; dumb
Dummkopf (*doom-kohpf*) [-köpfe (*doom-kehrp-fuh*)] – idiot
ein bisschen (*ine bees-shin*) – a bit
Erstehäuptling (*ehr-stuh-hoypt-ling*) [-e (*ehr-stuh-hoypt-lin-guh*)] – leader
  of unified clans
es tut mir leid (*ehs toot meer lyde*) – I'm sorry; literally "it gives me
  sorrow"
Eule (*oy-luh*) [-n (*oy-lin*)] – owl
Exempel (*ehk-sehm-pehl*) – example
Falke (*fahl-kuh*) [-n (*fahl-kin*)] – falcon
Familie (*fah-mih-lee*) [-n (*fah-mih-leen*)] – family
Feind (*find*) [-e (*fine-duh*)] – enemy
Fest (*fehst*) [-e (*feh-stuh*)] – festival
Feuer (*fewr*) [-] – fire
Feuerdrache (*fewr-drah-kuh*) [-n (*fewr-drah-kin*)] – fire dragon
Flammezunge (*flah-muh-zoon-guh*) – Flame Tongue's Zhulanese name
Frau (*frow*) [-en (*frow-in*)] – woman
Fräulein (*froy-line*) [-] – young woman; Miss
Freund (*froynd*) [-e (*froyn-duh*)] – friend
freundlich (*froynd-leesh*) – friendly
Freundschaft (*froynd-shahft*) [-en (*froynd-shahf-tin*)] – friendship
Frieda (*free-dah*) – the demigoddess Peace
Frieden (*free-din*) – peace
Gang (*gahng*) [-s (*gahngs*)] – gang
Gast (*gahst*) [Gäste (*gay-stuh*)] – guest
Gasthaus (*gahst-house*) [-häuser (*gahst-hoy-sehr*) – inn
Gefängnis (*guh-fayng-nees*) [-se (*guh-fayng-nees-suh*)] – prison
Geist (*ghyste*) [-er (*guy-stehr*)] – non-physical part of a creature: mind,
  spirit, soul, ghost; *Der Geist (dehr ghyste)* – The Ghost
Geisterpfad (*guy-stehr-fahd*) – Ghost Trail
Geisternetz (*guy-stehr-nehtz*) [-e (*guy-stehr-neht-zuh*)] – mental net; web
  of Mindspeakers
Geisterstück (*guy-stehr-stewk*) [-e (*guy-stehr-stew-kuh*)] – Spirit play
Geistmagie (*ghyste-mah-ghee*) [-] – mental magic
Geistmagier (*ghyste-mah-gheer*) [-] – Mindspeaker
General (*gheh-neh-rahl*) [Generäle (*gheh-neh-ray-luh*)] – war general
Gesundheit (*gheh-zoond-hyte*) – health
Gift (*ghift*) [-e (*ghif-tuh*)] – poison
Glück (*glewk*) – luck; *viel Glück (veel glewk)* – good luck
Gör (*ghehr*) [-en (*ghehr-in*)] – brat
Gott (*ghoht*) [Götter (*ghehr-tehr*)] – god
Gouverneur (*goo-vehr-newr*) [-e (*goo-vehr-newr-uh*)] – governor

Gratuliere (*grah-too-leer-uh*) – congratulations
Grossmutter (*grohs-moo-tehr*) [-mütter (*grohs-mew-tehr*)] – grandmother
gut (*a*) (*goot*) – good; Gute Nacht *(goo-tuh nahkt)* – good night; *Guten Morgen (goo-tehn moor-ghehn)* – good morning; *Guten Tag (goo-tehn tahgh)* – good day
Gut (*n*) (*goot*) [Güter (*ghew-tehr*)] – estate
Gutes (*n*) (*goo-tehs*) – good
Halbgott (*hahlb-ghoht*) [-götter (*hahlb-ghehr-tehr*)] – demigod
hallo (*hah-loh*) – hello
Halt (*n*) (*hahlt*) – halt
Halt die Klappe (*hahlt dee klah-puh*) – shut up; harsh form of "be quiet"
Hass (*hahs*) – hate; hatred; the demigod Hate
Häuptling (*hoypt-ling*) [-e (*hoypt-lin-guh*)] – clan leader
Hauptmann (*howpt-mahn*) [-männer (*howpt-may-nehr*)] – title of military leaders in Zhulan's cities
Hauptplatz (*howpt-plahtz*) [-plätze (*howpt-plate-zuh*)] – main square; city's central plaza
Haus (*house*) [Häuser (*hoy-sehr*)] – house
Heilig (*high-lihgh*) – holy man
Heiligesicht (*high-lihgh-uh-sihkt*) – Sight; literally means "Holy Sight"
Heiligetier (*high-lihg-uh-teer*) [-e (*high-lıhg-uh-teer-uh*)] – sacred animal
Herr (*hehr*) [-en (*hehr-rihn*)] – Sir, Mister
Herzog (*hehr-zohgh*) [Herzöge (*hehr-zehr-guh*)] – duke
Herzogin (*hehr-zoh-ghihn*) [-nen (*hehr-zoh-ghih-nihn*)] – duchess
Hexe (*hehk-suh*) [-n (*hehk-sin*)] – derogatory word for a female
Himmelfeuer (*hihm-mehl-fewr*) [-] – sky fire
hitzköpfig (*heetz-kehrp-feegh*) – hot-headed
Hoffnung (*hohf-noong*) – hope; the demigoddess, Hope
Hund (*hoond*) [-e (*hoon-duh*)] – dog
ja (*yah*) – aye
Jahr (*yahr*) [-e (*yahr-uh*)] – year
Jahreszeit (*yahr-uh-zite*) [-en (*yahr-uh-zye-tin*)] – season
Kandidat (*kahn-dee-daht*) [-en (*kahn-dee-dah-tin*)] – candidate
Katastrophe (*kah-tah-stroh-fuh*) [-n (*kah-tah-stroh-fin*)] – catastrophe
Katze (*kaht-zuh*) [-n (*kaht-zihn*)] – desert cat
Katzenauge (*kaht-zihn-ow-guh*) – cat eye (gemstone)
kein (*kine*) – no (number)
Kind (*kihnd*) [-er (*kihn-dehr*)] – child
Klaue (*klow-uh*) [-n (*klow-inn*)] – claw (as of a bird or mammal)
Kleine (*klye-nuh*) – little one
Koch (*kohk*) – cook
komm (*kohm*) [-e (*koh-muh*)] [-t (*kohmt*)] – Come!
König (*kehr-neegh*) [-e (*kehr-nee-ghuh*)] – king
Kopfabdeckung (*kohp-fahb-deh-koong*) [-en (*kohp-fahb-deh-koong-inn*)] – head covering; square of spider silk worn over the head to protect wearer from the sun and hair from Senf seeds

Köter (*kehr-tehr*) [-] – cur
Kräftetier (*krayf-tuh-teer*) [-e (*krayf-tuh-teer-uh*)] – Power Animal; the
    animal with which an Animal Mage's magic connects most powerfully
Kreis (*kryse*) – those river-dwellers who are friendly to nomads
Krieg (*kreegh*) [-e (*kree-ghuh*)] – war; the demigod, War
Krieg mit Fayral (*kreegh meet fay-rahl*) – war with Fayral
Kriegrat (*kreegh-raht*) [-räte (*kreegh-ray-tuh*)] – war council
Kriegschrift (*kreegh-shrihft*) – war script
Krone (*kroh-nuh*) [-n (*kroh-nihn*)] – crown
Lager (*lah-ghehr*) [-] – camp
Leben (*leh-bin*) [-] – life; the demigoddess, Life
Lebenfrau (*leh-bin-frow*) [-en (*leh-bin-frow-inn*)] – female lifemate
Lebenmann (*leh-bin-mahn*) [-männer (*leh-bin-may-nehr*)] – male lifemate
Letztechance (*lets-tuh-chahn-tsuh*) – Last Chance's Zhulanese name
Liebe (*lee-buh*) – love; the demigoddess, Love
Liebling (*leeb-ling*) – darling
Luftmagie (*looft-mah-ghee*) – Air Magic
Lügner (*lewgh-nehr*) [-] – liar
Lügnerin (*lewgh-nehr-inn*) [-] – female liar
Magie (*mah-ghee*) [-] – magic
Magier (*mah-gheer*) [-] – mage
Majestät, Eure/Seine (*mah-jheh-state, oy-ruh/sigh-nuh*) – Your/His
    Majesty
Mann (*mahn*) [Männer (*may-nehr*)] – man
Marktplatz (*mahrkt-plahts*) – Market Place
mehr (*mehr*) – more
mein (*mine*) – my
Meister (*mye-stehr*) [-] – master
Minute (*mih-noo-tuh*) [-n (*mih-noo-tehn*)] – minute
mit (*miht*) – with
mit Vergnügen (*miht vehrgh-new-ghehn*) – with pleasure
Mittag (*miht-tahgh*) – midday
Mitte Jahreszeit (*miht-tuh yahr-eh-zite*) – Mid-Season
Mitternacht (*miht-tehr-nahkt*) – midnight
Mörder (*mehr-dehr*) [-] – murderer
Morgen (*mohr-ghehn*) [-] – morning
Musik (*moo-sihk*) [-en (*moo-sih-kehn*)] – music
Musiker (*moo-sih-kehr*) [-] – musician
Mutter (*muh-tehr*) [Mütter (*mew-tehr*)] – mother
Mylady (*mye-lah-dee*) – Milady
Mylord (*mye-lohrd*) – Milord
Nacht (*nahkt*) [Nächte (*nayk-tuh*)] – night
natürlich (*nah-tewr-leesh*) – natural
Neffe (*neh-fuh*) [-n (*neh-fehn*)] – nephew
nein (*nine*) – nay
nichts (*nikshts*) – nothing

noch nicht (*nohk niksht*) – not yet
Nomade (*noh-mah-duh*) [-n (*noh-mah-dehn*)] – nomad
nomadisch (*noh-mah-deesh*) – nomadic
Oase (*oh-ah-suh*) [-n (*oh-ah-sehn*)] – oasis
Offizier (*oh-fih-zeer*) [-e (*oh-fih-zeer-uh*)] – officer
Oma (*oh-mah*) – Grandma
Omen (*oh-mehn*) [-] – omen
Ordnung (*ohrd-noong*) – order; opposite of Chaos
Panik (*pah-nihk*) – panic
Pazifistin (*pah-zih-fihs-tin*) – female pacifist
Perle (*pehr-luh*) [-n (*pehr-lehn*)] – pearl
Pferd (*ferd*) [-e (*fer-duh*)] – horse
Pferdetanz (*fer-duh-tahnz*) – the Horse Dance; a song created by Animal
  Mages that bears magic powerful enough to make a horse dance
Pflanze (*flahn-zuh*) [-n (*flahn-zihn*)] – plant
Pflanzenmagier (*flahn-zihn-mah-gheer*) [-] – Plant Mage
Phönixfest (*fehr-nihks-fehst*) – Mid-Summer Festival; literally "Phoenix
  Festival"
Plan (*plahn*) [Pläne (*play-nuh*)] – plan
Politik (*poh-lih-tik*) – politics
Problem (*proh-blehm*) [-e (*proh-bleh-muh*)] – problem
Rat (*raht*) [Räte (*ray-tuh*)] – council
Recht (*rehkt*) [-e (*rehk-tuh*)] – right
Regierhaus (*reh-gheer-house*) [-häuser (*reh-gheer-hoy-sehr*)] – home of
  the city's governor
Reisende (*rye-zehn-duh*) [-n (*rye-zehn-dehn*)] – traveler
Respekt (*reh-spehkt*) – respect
Ring (*ring*) [-e (*ring-uh*)] – ring
Rotvogel (*roht-voh-ghehl*) – red bird; name of Berg's inn in Machtstadt
Ruhe! (*roo-huh*) – Silence!; Quiet!
Saiten (*sigh-tehn*) [-s (*sigh-tehns*)] – stringed instrument similar to a
  guitar
Scharfmond (*sharf-mohnd*) [-e (*sharf-mohn-duh*)] – Twin Moon Blade;
  literally means "sharp moon"
Schattenrenner (*shah-tehn-rehn-nehr*) – Shadow Racer's Zhulanese name
scheisse (*shice-uh*) – curse word
Schere (*shehr-uh*) [-n (*shehr-ehn*)] – claw (as of a scorpion)
Schicksal (*shihk-sahl*) [-e (*shihk-sah-luh*)] – fate; the Fates
Schlampe (*shlahm-puh*) [-n (*shlahm-pehn*)] – immoral woman
Schlange (*shlahng-uh*) [-n (*shlahng-ehn*)] – snake
Schlangenfest (*shlahng-ehn-fehst*) – Mid-Spring Festival; literally
  "Serpent Festival"
Schlingel (*shling-ehl*) [-] – street runners; children, often thieves, who
  roam the streets of cities in Zhulan
Schützling (*shewts-ling*) [-e (*shewts-ling-uh*)] – protégé
Schutzmagie (*shoots-mah-ghee*) – Protection Magic

Peace of Evon

Schutzmagier (*shoots-mah-gheer*) [-] – Protection Mage
Schwester (*shwehs-tehr*) [-n (*shwehs-tehrn*)] – sister
Seele (*see-luh*) [-n (*see-lehn*)] – soul
Seide (*sigh-duh*) [-n (*sigh-dehn*)] – silk
Senf (*sehnf*) – desert plant whose seeds do not need earth or water to
    grow; these seeds will latch onto anything, including living creatures,
    and grow; travelers must be wary of these, and often require
    'deseeding' after a long journey
Siebentag (*zee-behn-tahgh*) [-e (*zee-behn-tah-ghuh*)] – sevenday
Skorpion (*skohr-pee-ohn*) [-e (*skohr-pee-oh-nuh*)] – scorpion
Sohn (*sohn*) [Söhne (*sehr-nuh*)] – son
Soldat (*sohl-daht*) [-en (*sohl-dah-tehn*)] – soldier
Spinne (*spin-nuh*) [-n (*spin-nehn*)] – spider
Spinnenseide (*spin-nehn-sigh-duh*) [-n (*spin-nehn-sigh-dehn*)] – spider
    silk
Stachel (*shtah-kehl*) [-n (*shtah-kehln*)] – stinger
Stadt (*shtahdt*) [Städte (*shtayd-tuh*)] – city
Status (*stah-toos*) [-] – status
Statusgürtel (*stah-toos-gewr-tehl*) [-] – status belt; thick spider silk belt
    dyed at one or both ends, it declares a nomad's clan and status
Tag (*tahgh*) [-e (*tah-ghuh*)] – day
Tante (*tahn-tuh*) [-n (*tahn-tehn*)] – aunt
Tanz (*tahnz*) [Tänze (*tayn-zuh*)] – dance
Tempel (*tehm-pehl*) [-] – temple
Tier (*teer*) [-e (*teer-uh*)] – animal
Tieremagie (*teer-uh-mah-ghee*) – Animal Magic
Tieremagier (*teer-uh-mah-gheer*) [-] – Animal Mage
Tochter (*tohk-tehr*) [Töchter (*tehrk-tehr*)] – daughter
Tod (*tohd*) [-e (*toh-duh*)] – death; the demigod, Death
Tradition (*trah-diht-see-ohn*) [-en (*trah-diht-see-oh-nehn*)] – tradition
Trick (*trik*) [-s (*triks*)] – trick
Unwetter (*oon-veh-tehr*) – desert rainstorm
Vater (*fah-tehr*) [Väter (*fay-tehr*)] – father
verdammt (*fehr-dahmt*) [-e (*fehr-dahm-tuh*)] – damn
vereinte (*fehr-ine-tuh*) – unified
verliebt (*fehr-leebt*) – in love
Verräter (*fehr-ay-tehr*) [-] – traitor
verwöhnt (*fehr-vehrnt*) – spoilt
Violettauge Nomade (*fee-oh-leht-ow-guh noh-mah-duh*) – Purple-Eyed
    Nomad; a rare title used for James Caffers
Vogel (*foh-ghehl*) [Vögel (*fehr-ghehl*)] – bird
Wache (*vah-kuh*) [-n (*vah-kehn*)] – guard
Wanderung (*vahn-dehr-oong*) – migration; a clan's journey across the
    desert from one oasis to another
Wasser (*vahs-sehr*) – water

Wasserdrache (*vahs-sehr-drah-kuh*) [-n (*vahs-sehr-drah-kehn*)] – water
 drake
Wille (*vih-luh*) – will
Witz (*vihtz*) – joke
Wohl (*vohl*) – well-being
Wolf (*vohlf*) [Wölfe (*vehrl-fuh*)] – wolf
Wölfefest (*vehrl-fuh-fehst*) – Mid-Winter Festival; literally "Wolf
 Festival"
wunderbar (*voon-dehr-bahr*) – wonderful
Zahn (*zahn*) [Zähne (*zay-nuh*)] – tooth
Zelt (*zehlt*) [-e (*zehl-tuh*)] – tent
Zhulan (*jhoo-lahn*) – middle province of Evon
Zhulanbürger (*jhoo-lahn-bewr-gehr*) [-] – citizen of Zhulan
Zofe (*zoh-fuh*) [-n (*zoh-fehn*)] – lady's maid

Excerpt from Peace of Evon: Lost King

Chapter 1

Frenz Kanti woke with a groan. He hated mornings, and this one seemed to be particularly hot and bright.

Wrinkling his nose, the farmer squinted open one eye and quickly closed it when all that met his gaze was overwhelming sunlight.

Too bright for bed. I must have camped outside last night.

It wouldn't be the first time he'd decided to sleep out in the fields. With the war now two years gone, Frenz was the only person available to tend the crops, and it was often simpler to spend the nights outside, especially during harvest.

Determined to enjoy a few minutes of quiet before he had to begin his day, Frenz sighed and let his head loll to one side.

All too soon, he realized that something just wasn't quite right. Despite the sunlight beating down on his body, there was a distinct lack of birdsong, which was a constant around his home in the forest of Kensy.

"Odd," he muttered, opening his eyes and blinking against the incessant light. Once he'd sat up and could see past the brightness, he continued blinking as he took in his current surroundings.

"Where…?"

Gone were the trees he had grown up knowing. Instead, Frenz was surrounded by a flat, barren landscape, broken only by a large camp nearby that appeared to contain a modicum of greenery.

Nothing compared to Kensy's old forest though.

"'Ow in Maurus' fire did I end up in Zhulan?"

The desert province may have been no more than two day's ride south of his farm, but Frenz had never passed Kensy's borders, not even to escape the constant violence of the war. Both he and his father had fought in the war against Fayral, and his father had even died to protect their land. As far as Frenz was concerned, he had no reason to leave Kensy.

Yet I apparently did.

Climbing to his feet, Frenz scanned the mostly empty horizon, noting what looked like a mountain range in the distance on the other side of the camp. He'd made a full turn before he finally realized that, not only did he not remember how he came to be in Zhulan, he was also completely alone.

Uttering a curse, he spun around again and shouted, "Last Chance! Last Chance!"

Please let her be nearby.

He could handle being in such a strange place as long as he had his Last Chance for Hope and Freedom with him. If not, he knew panic wouldn't be far off.

Made in the USA
San Bernardino, CA
01 February 2014